Also by Ben Kane

The Forgotten Legion
The Silver Eagle
The Road to Rome

Hannibal: Enemy of Rome

BEN KANE

preface

Published by Preface Publishing 2011

10 9 8 7 6 5 4 3 2

First published in Great Britain in 2011 by Preface Publishing

20 Vauxhall Bridge Road
London SW1V 2SA

An imprint of The Random House Group Limited

www.randomhouse.co.uk

Addresses for companies within The Random House Group Limited
can be found at www.randomhouse.co.uk

The Random House Group Limited Reg. No. 954009

A CIP catalogue record for this book is available from
the British Library

Hardback ISBN 978 1 84809 227 3
Trade paperback ISBN 978 1 84809 228 0

The Random House Group Limited supports The Forest Stewardship Council (FSC),
the leading international forest certification organisation. All our titles that are printed
on Greenpeace approved FSC certified paper carry the FSC logo. Our paper procurement
policy can be found at www.randomhouse.co.uk/environment

Typeset in Fournier MT by Palimpsest Book Production Limited
Falkirk, Stirlingshire

Printed and bound in Great Britain by Clays Ltd, St Ives plc

For Ferdia and Pippa, my wonderful children.

GAUL

Alps

Rhodanus

Pyrenees

Taurasia • Placentia • **CISALPINE**
Padu **GAUL**
Genua •

IBERIA

Iberus

Massilia •

Pisae •

ITALIA

Tagus

CORSICA

Rome •

Saguntum •

Balearic Islands

SARDINIA

Gades •

New Carthage •

M A R E

NUMIDIA

Carthage • SICILY

CARTHAGE

N

0   100   200   300   400   500

Miles

The Mediterranean World in 219 BC

ILLYRICUM

Mare Adriaticum

THRACE

Danuvius

PONTUS EUXINU

GREECE

ASIA MINOR

SELEUCID EMPIRE

Syracuse

I N T E R N U M

CYPRUS

CRETE

Tyre

Alexandria

EGYPT

LIBYA

Nilus

Rubrum Mare

Chapter I: Hanno

Carthage, spring

'Hanno!' His father's voice echoed off the painted stucco walls. 'It's time to go.'

Stepping carefully over the gutter that carried liquid waste out to the soakaway in the street, Hanno looked back. He was torn between his duty and the urgent gestures of his friend, Suniaton. The political meetings his father had recently insisted he attend bored him to tears. Each one he'd been to followed exactly the same path. A group of self-important, bearded elders, clearly fond of the sound of their own voices, made interminable speeches about how Hannibal Barca's actions in Iberia were exceeding the remit granted to him. Malchus – his father – and his closest allies, who supported Hannibal, said little or nothing until the greybeards had fallen silent, when they would stand forth one by one. Invariably, Malchus spoke last of all. His words seldom varied. Hannibal, who had been commander in Iberia for just three years, was doing an outstanding job in cementing Carthage's hold over the wild native tribes, forming a disciplined army and, most importantly, filling the city's coffers with the silver from his mines. Who else was pursuing such heroic and worthy endeavours while simultaneously enriching Carthage? In defending the tribes who had been attacked by Saguntum, a city allied to Rome, he was merely reinforcing their people's sovereignty in Iberia. On these grounds, the young Barca should be left to his own devices.

Hanno knew that what motivated the politicians was fear, partly assuaged by the thought of Hannibal's forces, and greed, partly satisfied by the shiploads of precious metal from Iberia. Malchus' carefully chosen words therefore normally swayed the Senate in Hannibal's favour, but only after endless hours of debate. The interminable politicking made Hanno want to scream, and to tell the old fools what he really thought of them. Of course he would never shame his father in that manner, but nor could he face yet another day stuck indoors. The idea of a fishing trip held too much appeal.

One of Hannibal's messengers regularly came to bring his father news from Iberia, and had visited not a week since. The night-time rendezvous were supposed to be a secret, but Hanno had soon come to recognise the cloaked, sallow-skinned officer. Sapho and Bostar, his older brothers, had been allowed to stand in on the meetings for some time. Swearing Hanno to secrecy, Bostar had filled him in afterwards. Now, if he was able, Hanno simply eavesdropped. In a nutshell, Hannibal had charged Malchus and his allies with the task of ensuring that the politicians continued to back his actions. A showdown with the city of Saguntum was imminent, but conflict with Rome, Carthage's old enemy, was some way off yet.

The deep, gravelly voice called out again, echoing down the corridor that led to the central courtyard. There was a hint of annoyance in it now. 'Hanno? We'll be late.'

Hanno froze. He wasn't afraid of the dressing down his father would deliver later, more of the disappointed look in his eyes. A scion of one of Carthage's oldest families, Malchus led by example, and expected his three sons to do the same. At seventeen, Hanno was the youngest. He was also the one who most often failed to meet these exacting standards. For some reason, Malchus expected more of him than he did of Sapho and Bostar. At least that's how it seemed to Hanno. Yet farming, the traditional source of their wealth, interested him little. Warfare, his father's preferred vocation, and Hanno's great fascination, was barred to him still, thanks to his youth. His brothers would be sailing for Iberia any day. There, no doubt, they would cover themselves in glory in the taking of Saguntum. Frustration and resentment filled Hanno. All he could do was practise his riding and weapons skills. Life as ordained by his father was so boring, he thought, choosing to ignore Malchus' oft-repeated statement: 'Be patient. All good things come to those who wait.'

'Come on!' urged Suniaton, thumping Hanno on the arm. His gold earrings jingled as he jerked his head in the direction of the harbour. 'The fishermen found huge shoals of tunny in the bay at dawn. With Melqart's blessing, the fish won't have moved far. We'll catch dozens. Think of the money to be made!' His voice dropped to a whisper. 'I've taken an amphora of wine from Father's cellar. We can share it on the boat.'

Unable to resist his friend's offer, Hanno blocked his ears to Malchus' voice, which was coming closer. Tunny was one of the most prized fish in the Mediterranean. If the shoals were close to shore, this was an opportunity too good to miss. Stepping into the rutted street, he glanced once more at the symbol etched into the stone slab before the flat-roofed house's entrance. An inverted triangle topped by a flat line and then a circle, it represented his people's pre-eminent deity. Few dwellings were without it. Hanno asked Tanit's forgiveness for disobeying his father's wishes, but his excitement was such that he forgot to ask for the mother goddess's protection.

'Hanno!' His father's voice was very near now.

Without further ado, the two young men darted off into the crowd. Both their families dwelled near the top of Byrsa Hill. At the summit, reached by a monumental staircase of sixty steps, was an immense temple dedicated to Eshmoun, the god of fertility, health and well-being. Suniaton lived with his family in the sprawling complex behind the shrine, where his father served as a priest. Named in honour of the deity, Eshmuniaton – abbreviated to Suniaton or simply Suni – was Hanno's oldest and closest friend. The pair had scarcely spent a day out of each other's company since they were old enough to walk.

The rest of the neighbourhood was primarily residential. Byrsa was one of the richer quarters, as its wide, straight thoroughfares and right-angled intersections proved. The majority of the city's winding streets were no more than ten paces across, but here they averaged more than twice this width. In addition to wealthy merchants and senior army officers, the suffetes –judges – and many elders also called the area home. For this reason, Hanno ran with his gaze directed at the packed earth and the regular soak-away holes beneath his feet. Plenty of people knew who he was. The last thing he wanted was to be stopped and challenged by one of Malchus' numerous political opponents. To be dragged back home by the ear would be embarrassing and bring dishonour to his family.

As long as they didn't catch anyone's eye, he and his friend would pass unnoticed. Bare-headed and wearing tight-fitting red woollen singlets, with a central white stripe and a distinctive wide neckband, and breeches that reached to the knee, the pair looked no different to other well-to-do youths. Their garb was far more practical than the long straight wool tunics and conical felt hats favoured by most adult men, and more comfortable than the ornate jacket and pleated apron worn by those of Cypriot extraction. Sheathed daggers hung from simple leather straps thrown over their shoulders. Suniaton carried a bulging pack on his back.

Although people said that they could pass for brothers, Hanno couldn't see it most of the time. While he was tall and athletic, Suniaton was short and squat. Naturally, they both had tightly curled black hair and a dark complexion, but there the resemblance ended. Hanno's face was thin, with a straight nose and high cheekbones, while his friend's round visage and snub nose were complemented by a jutting chin. They did both have green eyes, Hanno conceded. That feature, unusual among the brown-eyed Carthaginians, was probably why they were thought to be siblings.

A step ahead of him, Suniaton nearly collided with a carpenter carrying several long cypress planks. Rather than apologise, he thumbed his nose and sprinted towards the citadel walls, now only a hundred paces away. Stifling his desire to finish the job by tipping over the angry tradesman, Hanno dodged past too, a grin splitting his face. Another similarity he and Suniaton shared was an impudent nature, quite at odds with the serious manner of most of their countrymen. It frequently got both of them in trouble, and was a constant source of irritation to their fathers.

A moment later, they passed under the immense ramparts, which were thirty paces deep and nearly the same in height. Like the outer defences, the wall was constructed from great quadrilateral blocks of sandstone. Frequent coats of whitewash ensured that the sunlight bounced off the stone, magnifying its size. Topped by a wide walkway and with regular towers, the fortifications were truly awe-inspiring. Yet the citadel was only a small part of the whole. Hanno never tired of looking down on the expanse of the sea wall that came into view as he emerged from under the gateway's shadow. Running down from the north along the city's perimeter, it swept southeast to the twin harbours, curling protectively around them before heading west. On the steep northern and eastern sides, and to the south, where the sea gave its added protection, one wall was deemed sufficient, but on the western, landward side of the peninsula, three defences had been constructed: a wide trench backed by an earthen bank, and then a huge rampart. The walls, which were in total over 180 stades in length, also contained sections with two-tiered living quarters. These could hold many thousands of troops, cavalry and their mounts, and hundreds of war elephants.

Home to nearly a quarter of a million people, the city also demanded attention. Directly below lay the Agora, the large open space bordered by government buildings and countless shops. It was the area where residents gathered to do business, demonstrate, take the evening air, and vote. Beyond it lay the unique ports: the huge outer, rectangular merchant harbour, and the inner, circular naval docks with its small, central island. The first contained hundreds of berths for trading ships, while the second could hold more than ten-score triremes and quinqueremes in specially constructed covered sheds. To the west of the ports was the old shrine of Baal Hammon, no longer as important as it had previously been, but still venerated by many. To the east lay the Choma, the huge man-made landing stage where fishing smacks and small vessels tied up. It was also their destination.

Hanno was immensely proud of his home. He had no idea what Rome, Carthage's old enemy, looked like, but he doubted it matched his city's grandeur. He had no desire to compare Carthage with the Republic's capital, though. The only view he ever wanted of Rome was when it fell – to a victorious Carthaginian army – before seeing it burned to the ground. As Hamilcar Barca, Hannibal's father, had inculcated a hatred of all things Roman in his sons, so had Malchus in Hanno and his brothers. Like Hamilcar, Malchus had served in the first war against the Republic, fighting in Sicily for ten long, thankless years.

Unsurprisingly, Hanno and his siblings knew the details of every land skirmish and naval battle in the conflict, which had actually lasted for more than a generation. The cost to Carthage in loss of life, territory and wealth had been huge, but the city's wounds ran far deeper. Her pride had been trampled in the mud by the defeat, and this ignominy was repeated just three years after the war's conclusion. Carthage had been unilaterally forced by Rome to give up Sardinia, as well as paying more indemnities. The shabby act proved beyond doubt, Malchus would regularly rant, that all Romans were treacherous dogs, without honour. Hanno agreed, and looked forward to the day hostilities were reopened once more. Given the depth of anger still present in Carthage towards Rome, conflict was inevitable, and it would originate in Iberia. Soon.

Suniaton turned. 'Have you eaten?'

Hanno shrugged. 'Some bread and honey when I got up.'

'Me too. That was hours ago, though.' Suniaton grinned and patted his belly. 'Best get a few supplies.'

'Good idea,' Hanno replied. They kept clay gourds of water in their little boat with their fishing gear, but no food. Sunset, when they would return, was a long way off.

The streets descending Byrsa Hill did not follow the regular layout of the summit, instead radiating out like so many tributaries of a meandering river. There were far more shops and businesses visible now: bakers, butchers and stalls selling freshly caught fish, fruit and vegetables stood beside silver- and coppersmiths, perfume merchants and glass blowers. Women sat outside their doors, working at their looms, or gossiping over their purchases. Slaves carried rich men past in litters or swept the ground in front of shops. Dye-makers' premises were everywhere, their abundance due to the Carthaginian skill in harvesting the local *Murex* shellfish and pounding its flesh to yield a purple dye that commanded premium prices all over the Mediterranean. Children ran hither and thither, playing catch and chasing each other up and down the regular sets of stairs that broke the street's steep descent. Deep in conversation, a trio of well-dressed men strolled past. Recognising them as elders, who were probably on their way to the very meeting he was supposed to be attending, Hanno took a sudden interest in the array of terracotta outside a potter's workshop.

Dozens of figures – large and small – were ranked on low tables. Hanno recognised every deity in the Carthaginian pantheon. There sat a regal, crowned Baal Hammon, the protector of Carthage, on his throne; beside him Tanit was depicted in the Egyptian manner: a shapely woman's body in a well-cut dress, but with the head of a lioness. A smiling Astarte clutched a tambourine. Her consort, Melqart, known as the 'King of the City', was, among other things, the god of the sea. Various brightly coloured figures depicted him emerging from crashing waves riding a fearful-looking monster and clutching a trident in one fist. Baal Saphon, the god of storm and war, sat astride a fine charger, wearing a helmet with a long, flowing crest. Also on display was a selection of hideous, grinning painted masks – tattooed, bejewelled demons and spirits of the underworld – tomb offerings designed to ward off evil.

Hanno shivered, remembering his mother's funeral three years before. Since her death of a fever his father, never the most warm of men, had become a grim and forbidding presence who lived only to gain his revenge on Rome. For all his youth, Hanno knew that Malchus was portraying a controlled mask to the world. He must still be grieving, as surely as he and his brothers were. Arishat, Hanno's mother, had been the light to Malchus' dark, the laughter to his gravitas, the softness to his strength. The centre of the family, she had been taken from them in two horrific days and nights. Harangued by an inconsolable Malchus, the best surgeons in Carthage had toiled over her to no avail. Every last detail of her final hours was engraved in Hanno's memory. The cups of blood drained from her in a vain attempt to cool her raging temperature. Her gaunt, fevered face. The sweat-soaked sheets. His brothers trying not to cry, and failing. And lastly, her still form on the bed, tinier than she had ever been in life. Malchus kneeling alongside, great sobs racking his muscular frame. That was the only time Hanno had ever seen his father weep. The incident had never been mentioned since, nor had his mother. He swallowed hard and, checking that the elders had passed by, moved on. It hurt too much to think about such things.

Suniaton, who had not noticed Hanno's distress, paused to buy some bread, almonds and figs. Keen to lift his sombre mood, Hanno eyed the blacksmith's forge off to one side. Wisps of smoke rose from its roughly built chimney, and the air was rich with the smells of charcoal, burning wood and oil. Harsh metallic sounds reached his ears. In the recesses of the open-fronted establishment, he glimpsed a figure in a leather apron using a pair of tongs to carefully lift a piece of glowing metal from the anvil. There was a loud hiss as the sword blade was plunged into a vat of cold water. Hanno felt his feet begin to move.

Suniaton blocked his path. 'We've got better things to do. Like making money,' he cried, shoving forward a bulging bag of almonds. 'Carry that.'

'No! You'll eat them all anyway.' Hanno pushed his friend out of the way with a grin. It was a standing joke between them that his favourite pastime was getting covered in ash and grime while Suniaton would rather plan his next meal. He was so busy laughing that he didn't see the approaching group of soldiers – a dozen Libyan spearmen – until it was too late. With a thump, Hanno collided with the first man's large, round shield.

This was no street urchin, and the spearman bit back an instinctive curse. 'Mind your step,' he cried.

Catching sight of two Carthaginian officers in the soldiers' midst, Hanno cursed. It was Sapho and Bostar. Both were dressed in their finest uniforms. Bell-shaped helmets with thick rims and yellow-feathered crests covered their heads. Layered linen *pteryges* hung below their polished bronze cuirasses to cover the groin, and contoured greaves protected their lower legs. No doubt they too were on their way to the meeting. Muttering an apology to the spearman, Hanno backed away, looking at the ground in an attempt not to be recognised.

Oblivious to Sapho and Bostar's presence, Suniaton was snorting with amusement at Hanno's collision. 'Come on,' he urged. 'We don't want to get there too late.'

'Hanno!' Bostar's voice was genial.

He pretended not to hear.

'Hanno! Come back!' barked a deeper, more commanding voice, that of Sapho.

Unwillingly, Hanno turned.

Suniaton tried to sidle away, but he had also been spotted.

'Eshmuniaton! Get over here,' Sapho ordered.

With a miserable expression, Suniaton shuffled to his friend's side.

Hanno's brothers shouldered their way forward to stand before them.

'Sapho. Bostar,' Hanno said with a false smile. 'What a surprise.'

'Is it?' Sapho demanded, his thick eyebrows meeting in a frown. A short, compact man with a serious manner like Malchus, he was twenty-two. Young to be a mid-ranking officer, but like Bostar, his ability had shone through during his training. 'We're all supposed to be heading to listen to the elders. Why aren't you with Father?'

Flushing, Hanno looked down. Damn it, he thought. In Sapho's eyes, duty to Carthage was all-important. In a single moment, their chances of a day on the boat had vanished.

Sapho gave Suniaton a hard stare, taking in his pack and the provisions in his hands. 'Because the pair of you were skiving off, that's why! Fishing, no doubt?'

Suniaton scuffed a toe in the dirt.

'Cat got your tongue?' Sapho asked acidly.

Hanno moved in front of his friend. 'We were going to catch some tunny, yes,' he admitted.

Sapho's scowl grew deeper. 'And that's more important than listening to the Council of Elders?'

As usual, his brother's high-handed attitude rankled with Hanno. This type of lecture was all too common. Most often, it felt as if Sapho was trying to be their father. Unsurprisingly, Hanno resented this. 'It's not as if the greybeards will say anything that hasn't been said a thousand times before,' he retorted. 'Just about every one is full of hot air.'

Suniaton sniggered. 'Like someone else not too far away.' He saw Hanno's warning look and fell silent.

Sapho's jaw clenched. 'You pair of impudent—' he began.

Bostar's lips twitched, and he lifted a hand to Sapho's shoulder. 'Peace,' he said. 'Hanno has a point. The elders *are* rather fond of the sound of their own voices.'

Hanno and Suniaton tried to hide their smiles.

Sapho missed Bostar's amusement, but he lapsed into a glowering silence. He was acutely aware, and resentful, that he was not the senior officer present. Although Sapho was a year older, Bostar had been promoted before him.

'It's not as if this meeting will be a matter of life and death,' Bostar continued reasonably. His wink – unseen by Sapho – told Hanno that all hope was not lost. He slyly returned the gesture. Like Hanno, Bostar resembled their mother, Arishat, with a thin face and piercing green eyes. Where Sapho's nose was broad, his was long and narrow. Rangy and athletic, his long black hair was tied in a ponytail, which emerged from under his helmet. Hanno had far more in common with the gentle Bostar than he did with Sapho. Currently, his feelings for his eldest brother often verged on dislike. 'Does our father know where you are?'

'No,' admitted Hanno.

Bostar turned to Suniaton. 'I would assume, therefore, that Bodesmun is also in the dark?'

'Of course he is,' Sapho butted in, eager to regain control. 'As usual where these two are concerned.'

Bostar ignored his brother's outburst. 'Well?'

'Father thinks I'm at home, studying,' Suniaton revealed.

Sapho's expression grew a shade more self-righteous. 'Let's see what Bodesmun and Father have to say when they discover what you were both really up to. We have enough time to do that before the Council meets.' He jerked a thumb at the spearmen. 'Get in amongst them.'

Hanno scowled, but there was little point arguing. Sapho was in a particularly zealous mood. 'Come on,' he muttered to Suniaton. 'The shoals will be there another day.'

Before they could move a step, Bostar spoke. 'I don't see why they shouldn't go fishing.'

Hanno and Suniaton stared at each other, amazed.

Sapho's brows rose. 'What do you mean?'

'Such activities will shortly be impossible for both of us, and we'll miss them.' Bostar made a face. 'That same day will come for Hanno soon enough. Let him have his fun while he can.'

Hanno's heart leaped; the gravity of Bostar's words was lost on him.

Sapho's face grew thoughtful. After a moment, though, his sanctimonious frown returned. 'Duty is duty,' he declared.

'Lighten up, Sapho. You're twenty-two, not fifty-two!' Bostar threw a glance at the spearmen, who were uniformly grinning. 'Who would notice Hanno's absence apart from us and Father? And you're not Suni's keeper any more than I am.'

Sapho's lips thinned at the teasing, but he relented. The idea of Bostar pulling rank on him was too much to bear. 'Father won't be happy,' he said gruffly, 'but I suppose you're right.'

Hanno could hardly believe what he was hearing. 'Thank you!' His cry was echoed by Suniaton.

'Go on, before I change my mind,' Sapho warned.

The friends didn't need any further prompting. With a grateful look at Bostar, who threw them another wink, the pair disappeared into the crowd. Broad grins creased both their faces. They would still be held to account, thought Hanno, but not until that evening. Visions of a boat full of tunny filled his mind once more.

'Sapho's a serious one, isn't he?' Suniaton commented.

'You know how he is,' Hanno replied. 'In his eyes, things like fishing are a waste of time.'

Suniaton nudged him. 'Just as well I didn't tell him what I was thinking, then.' He grinned at Hanno's enquiring look. 'That it would do him good to relax more – perhaps by going fishing!'

Hanno's mouth opened with shock, before he laughed. 'Thank the gods you didn't say that! There's no way he would have let us go.'

Smiling with relief, the friends continued their journey. Soon they had reached the Agora. Its four sides, each a stade in length, were made up of grand porticoes and covered walkways. The beating heart of the city, it was home to the building where the Council of Elders met, as well as government offices, a library, numerous temples and shops. It was also where, on summer evenings, the better-off young men and women would gather in groups, a safe distance apart, to eye each other up. Socialising with the opposite sex was frowned upon, and chaperones for the girls were never far away. Despite this, inventive methods to approach the object of one's desire were constantly being invented. Of recent months, this had become one of the friends' favourite pastimes. Fishing beat it still, but not by much, thought Hanno wistfully, scanning the crowds for any sign of attractive female flesh.

Instead of gaggles of coy young beauties, though, the Agora was full of serious-looking politicians, merchants and high-ranking soldiers. They were heading for one place. The central edifice, within the hallowed walls of which more than three hundred elders met on a regular basis as, for nearly half a millennium, their predecessors had done. Overseen by the two suffetes – the rulers elected every year – they, the most important men in Carthage, decided everything from trading policy to negotiations with foreign states. Their range of powers did not end there. The Council of Elders also had the power to declare war and peace, even though it no longer appointed the army's generals. Since the war with Rome, that had been left to the people. The only prerequisites for candidature of the council were citizenship, wealth, an age of thirty or more, and the demonstration of ability, whether in the agricultural, mercantile, or military fields.

Ordinary citizens could participate in politics via the Assembly of the People, which congregated once a year, by the order of the suffetes, in the Agora. During times of great crisis, it was permitted to gather spontaneously and debate the issues of the day. While its powers were limited, they included electing the suffetes and the generals. Hanno was looking forward to the next meeting, which would be the first he'd attend as an adult, entitled to vote. Although Hannibal's enormous public popularity guaranteed his reappointment as the commander-in-chief of Carthage's forces in Iberia, Hanno wanted to show his support for the Barca clan. It was the only way he could at the moment. Despite his requests, Malchus would not let him join Hannibal's army, as Sapho and Bostar had done after their mother's death. Instead, he had to finish his education. There was no point fighting his father on this. Once Malchus had spoken, he never went back on a decision.

Following Carthaginian tradition, Hanno had largely fended for himself from the age of fourteen, although he continued to sleep at home. He'd worked in a forge, among other places, and thus earned enough to live on without committing any crimes or shameful acts. This was similar to, but not as harsh, as the Spartan way. He had also taken classes in Greek, Iberian and Latin. Hanno did not especially enjoy languages, but he had come to accept that such a skill would prove useful among the polyglot of nationalities that formed the Carthaginian army. His people did not take naturally to war, so they hired mercenaries, or enlisted their subjects, to fight on their behalf. Libyans, Iberians, Gauls and Balearic tribesmen were among those who brought their differing qualities to Carthage's forces.

Hanno's favourite subject was military matters. Malchus himself taught him the history of war, from the battles of Xenophon and Thermopylae to the victories won by Alexander of Macedon. Central to his father's lessons were the intricate details of tactics and planning. Particular attention was paid to Carthaginian defeats in the war with Rome, and the reasons for them. 'We lost because of our leaders' lack of determination. All they thought about was how to contain the conflict, not win it. How to minimise cost, not disregard it in the total pursuit of victory,' Malchus had thundered during one memorable lesson. 'The Romans are motherless curs, but by all the gods, they possess strength of purpose. Whenever they lost a battle, they recruited more men, and rebuilt their ships. They did not give up. When the public purse was empty, their leaders willingly spent their own wealth. Their damn Republic means everything to them. Yet who in Carthage offered to send us the supplies and soldiers we needed so badly in Sicily? My father, the Barcas, and a handful of others. No one else.' He'd barked a short, angry laugh. 'Why should I be surprised? Our ancestors were traders, not soldiers. To gain our rightful revenge, we must follow Hannibal. He's a natural soldier and a born leader – as his father was. Carthage never gave Hamilcar the chance to beat Rome, but we can offer it to his son. When the time is right.'

A red-faced, portly senator shoved past with a curse. Startled, Hanno recognised Hostus, one of his father's most implacable enemies. The self-important politician was in such a hurry that he didn't even notice whom he'd collided with. Hanno hawked and spat, although he was careful not to do it in Hostus' direction. He and his windbag friends complained endlessly about Hannibal, yet were content to accept the shiploads of silver sent from his mines in Iberia. Lining their own pockets with a proportion of this wealth, they had no desire to confront Rome again. Hanno, on the other hand, was more than prepared to lay down his life fighting their old enemy, but the fruit of revenge wasn't ripe. Hannibal was preparing himself in Iberia, and that was good enough. For now, they had to wait.

The pair skirted the edge of the Agora, avoiding the worst of the crowds. Around the back of the Senate, the buildings soon became a great deal less grand, looking as shabby as one would expect close to a port. Nonetheless, the slum stood in stark contrast to the splendour just a short walk away. There were few businesses, and the single- or twin-roomed houses were miserable affairs made of mud bricks, all apparently on the point of collapse. The iron-hard ruts in the street were more than a handspan deep, threatening to break their ankles if they tripped. No work parties to fill in the holes with sand here, thought Hanno, thinking of Byrsa Hill. He felt even more grateful for his elevated position in life.

Snot-nosed, scrawny children wearing little more than rags swarmed in, clamouring for a coin or a crust, while their lank-haired, pregnant mothers gazed at them with eyes deadened by a life of misery. Half-dressed girls posed provocatively in some doorways, their rouged cheeks and lips unable to conceal the fact that they were barely out of childhood. Unshaven, ill-clad men lounged around, rolling sheep tail bones in the dirt for a few worn coins. They stared suspiciously, but none dared hinder the friends' progress. At night it might be a different matter, but already they were under the shadow of the great wall, with its smartly turned-out sentries marching to and fro along the battlements. Although common, lawlessness was punished where possible by the authorities, and a shout of distress would bring help clattering down one of the many sets of stairs.

The tang of salt grew strong in the air. Gulls keened overhead, and the shouts of sailors could be heard from the ports. Feeling his excitement grow, Hanno charged down a narrow alleyway, and up the stone steps at the end of it. Suniaton was right behind him. It was a steep climb, but they were both fit, and reached the top without breaking sweat. A red concrete walkway extended the entire width of the wall – thirty paces – just as it did for the entire length of the defensive perimeter. Strongly built towers were positioned every fifty steps or so. The soldiers visible were garrisoned in the barracks, which were built at intervals below the ramparts.

The nearest sentries, a quartet of Libyan spearmen, glanced idly at the pair but, seeing nothing of concern, looked away. In peacetime, citizens were allowed on the wall during the hours of daylight. Perfunctorily checking the turquoise sea below their section, the junior officer fell back to gossiping with his men. Hanno trotted past, admiring the soldiers' massive round shields, which were even larger than those used by the Greeks. Although fashioned from wood, they were covered in goatskin, and rimmed with bronze. The same demonic face was painted on each, and denoted their unit.

Trumpets blared one after another from the naval port, and Suniaton jostled past. 'Quick,' he shouted. 'They might be launching a quinquereme!'

Hanno chased eagerly after his friend. The view from the walkway into the circular harbour was second to none. In a masterful feat of engineering, the Carthaginian warships were invisible from all other positions. Protected from unfriendly eyes on the seaward side by the city wall, they were concealed from the moored merchant vessels by the naval port's slender entrance, which was only just wider than a quinquereme, the largest type of warship.

Hanno scowled as they reached a good vantage point. Instead of the imposing sight of a warship sliding backwards into the water, he saw a purple-cloaked admiral strutting along the jetty that led from the periphery of the circular docks to the central island, where the navy's headquarters were. Another fanfare of trumpets sounded, making sure that every man in the place knew who was arriving. 'What has he got to swagger about?' Hanno muttered. Malchus reserved much of his anger for the incompetent

Carthaginian fleet, so he had learned to feel the same way. Carthage's days as a superpower of the sea were long gone, their fleet smashed into so much driftwood by Rome during the two nations' bitter struggle over Sicily. Remarkably, the Romans had been a non-seafaring race before the conflict. Undeterred by this major disadvantage, they had learned the skills of naval warfare, adding a few tricks of their own in the process. Since her defeat, Carthage had done little to reclaim the waves.

Hanno sighed. Truly, all their hopes lay on the land, with Hannibal.

Some time later, Hanno had forgotten all his worries. Half a mile offshore, their little boat was positioned directly over a mass of tunny. The shoal's location had not been hard to determine, thanks to the roiling water created by the large silver fish as they hunted sardines. Small boats dotted the location and clouds of seabirds swooped and dived overhead, attracted by the prospect of food. Suniaton's source had been telling the truth, and neither youth had been able to stop grinning since their arrival. Their task was simple: one rowed, the other lowered their net into the sea. Although they had seen better days, the plaited strands were still capable of landing a catch. Pieces of wood along the top of the net helped it to float, while tiny lumps of lead pulled its lower edge down into the water. Their first throw had netted nearly a dozen tunny, each one longer than a man's forearm. Subsequent attempts were just as successful, and now the bottom of the boat was calf-deep in fish. Any more, and they would risk overloading their craft.

'A good morning's work,' pronounced Suniaton.

'Morning?' challenged Hanno, squinting at the sun. 'We've been here less than an hour. It couldn't have been easier, eh?'

Suniaton regarded him solemnly. 'Don't put yourself down. I think our efforts deserve a toast.' With a flourish, he produced a small amphora from his pack.

Hannibal laughed; Suniaton was incorrigible.

Encouraged, Suniaton went on talking as if he were serving guests at an important banquet. 'Not the most expensive wine in Father's collection, I recall, but a palatable one nonetheless.' Using his knife, he prised off the wax seal and removed the lid. Raising the amphora to his lips, he gulped a large mouthful. 'Acceptable,' he declared, handing over the clay vessel.

'Philistine. Sip it slowly.' Hanno took a small swig and rolled it around his mouth as Malchus had taught him. The red wine had a light and fruity flavour, but little undertone. 'It needs a few more years, I think.'

'Now who's being pompous?' Suniaton kicked a tunny at him. 'Shut up and drink!'

Grinning, Hanno obeyed, taking more this time.

'Don't finish it,' cried Suniaton.

Despite his protest, the amphora was quickly drained. At once the ravenous pair launched into the bread, nuts and fruit that Suniaton had bought. With their bellies full, and their work done, it was the most natural thing in the world to lie back and close their eyes. Unaccustomed to consuming much wine, before long they were both snoring.

It was the cold wind on his face that woke Hanno. Why was the boat moving so much? he wondered vaguely. He shivered, feeling quite chilled. Opening gummy eyes, he took in a prone Suniaton opposite, still clutching the empty amphora. At his feet, the heaps of blank-eyed fish, their bodies already rigid. Looking up, Hanno felt a pang of fear. Instead of the usual clear sky, all he could see were towering banks of blue-black clouds. They were pouring in from the northwest. He blinked, refusing to believe what he was seeing. How could the weather have changed so fast? Mockingly, the first spatters of rain hit Hanno's upturned cheeks an instant later. Scanning the choppy waters, he could see no sign of the fishing craft that had surrounded theirs earlier. Nor could he see the land. Real alarm seized him.

He leaned over and shook Suniaton. 'Wake up!'

The only response was an irritated grunt.

'Suni!' This time, Hanno slapped his friend across the face.

'Hey!' Suniaton cried, sitting up. 'What's that for?'

Hanno didn't answer. 'Where in the name of the gods are we?' he shouted.

All semblance of drunkenness fell away as Suniaton turned his head from side to side. 'Sacred Tanit above,' he breathed. 'How long were we asleep?'

'I don't know,' Hanno growled. 'A long time.' He pointed to the west, where the sun's light was just visible behind the storm clouds. Its position told them that it was late in the afternoon. He stood, taking great care not to capsize the boat. Focusing on the horizon, where the sky met the threatening sea, he spent long moments trying to make out the familiar walls of Carthage, or the craggy promontory that lay to the north of the city.

'Well?' Suniaton could not keep the fear from his voice.

Hanno sat down heavily. 'I can't see a thing. We're fifteen or twenty stades from shore. Maybe more.'

What little colour there had been in Suniaton's face drained away. Instinctively, he clutched at the hollow gold tube that hung from a thong around his neck. Decorated with a lion's head at one end, it contained tiny parchments covered with protective spells and prayers to the gods. Hanno wore a similar one. With great effort, he refrained from copying his friend. 'We'll row back,' he announced.

'In these seas?' screeched Suniaton. 'Are you mad?'

Hanno glared back. 'What other choice have we? To jump in?'

His friend looked down. Both were more confident in the water than most, but they had never swum long distances, especially in conditions as bad as these.

Seizing the oars from the floor, Hanno placed them in the iron rowlocks. He turned the boat's rounded bow towards the west and began to row. Instantly, he knew that his attempt was doomed to fail. The power surging at him was more potent than anything he'd ever felt in his life. It felt like a raging, out-of-control beast, with the howling wind providing its terrifying voice. Ignoring his gut feeling, Hanno concentrated on each stroke with fierce intensity. Lean back. Drag the oars through the water. Lift them free. Bend forward, pushing the handles between his knees. Over and over he repeated the process, ignoring his pounding head and dry mouth, and cursing their foolishness in drinking all of the wine. If I had listened to my father, I'd still be at home, he thought bitterly. Safe on dry land.

Finally, when the muscles in his arms were trembling with exhaustion, Hanno stopped. Without looking up, he knew that their position would have changed little. For every three strokes' progress, the current carried them at least two further out to sea. 'Well?' he shouted. 'Can you see anything?'

'No,' Suniaton replied grimly. 'Move over. It's my turn, and this is our best chance.'

Our last chance, Hanno thought, gazing at the darkening sky.

Gingerly, they exchanged places on the little wooden thwarts that were the boat's only fittings. Thanks to the mass of slippery fish underfoot, it was even more difficult than usual. While his friend laboured at the oars, Hanno strained for a glimpse of land over the waves. Neither spoke. There was no point. The rain was now drumming down on their backs, combining with the wind's noise to form a shrieking cacophony that made normal speech impossible. Only the sturdy construction of their boat had prevented them from capsizing thus far.

At length, his energy spent, Suniaton shipped the oars. He looked at Hanno. There was a glimmer of hope in his eyes.

Hanno shook his head once.

'It's supposed to be the summer!' Suniaton cried. 'Gales like this shouldn't happen without warning.'

'There would have been signs,' Hanno snapped back. 'Why do you think there are no other boats out here? They must have headed for the shore when the wind began to get up.'

Suniaton flushed and hung his head. 'I'm sorry,' he muttered. 'It's my fault. I should never have taken Father's wine.'

Hanno gripped his friend's knee. 'Don't blame yourself. You didn't force me to drink it. That was my choice.'

Suniaton managed a half-smile. That was, until he looked down. 'No!'

Hanno followed his gaze and saw the tunny floating around his feet. They were shipping water, and enough of it to warrant immediate action. Trying not to panic, he began throwing the precious fish overboard. Survival was far more important than money. With the floor clear, he soon found a loose nail in one of the planks. Removing one of his sandals, he used the iron-studded sole to hammer the nail partially home, thereby reducing the influx of seawater. Fortunately, there was a small bucket on board, containing spare pieces of lead for the net. Grabbing it, Hanno began bailing hard. To his immense relief, it didn't take long before he'd reduced the water to an acceptable level.

A loud rumble of thunder overhead nearly deafened him.

Suniaton moaned with fear, and Hanno jerked upright.

The sky overhead was now a menacing black colour, and in the depths of the clouds a flickering yellow-white colour presaged lightning. The waves were being whipped into a frenzy by the wind, which was growing stronger by the moment. The storm was approaching its peak. More water slopped into the boat, and Hanno redoubled his efforts with the bucket. Any chance of rowing back to Carthage was long gone. They were going one direction. East. Into the middle of the Mediterranean. He tried not to let his panic show.

'What's going to happen to us?' Suniaton asked plaintively.

Realising that his friend was seeking reassurance, Hanno tried to think of an optimistic answer, but couldn't. The only outcome possible was an early meeting for them both with Melqart, the marine god.

In his palace at the bottom of the sea.

Chapter II: Quintus

Near Capua, Campania

Quintus woke soon after dawn, when the first rays of sunlight crept through the window. Never one to linger in bed, the sixteen-year-old threw off his blanket. Wearing only a *licium*, or linen undergarment, he padded to the small shrine in the far corner of his room. Excitement coursed through him. Today he would lead a bear hunt for the first time. It was not long until his birthday, and Fabricius, his father, wanted him to mark his transition to manhood in fitting fashion. 'Assuming the toga is all well and good,' he'd said the night before, 'but you have Oscan blood in your veins too. What better way to prove one's courage than by killing the biggest predator in Italy?'

Quintus knelt before the altar. Closing his eyes, he sent up his usual prayers requesting that he and his family remain healthy and prosperous. Then he added several more. That he would be able to find a bear's trail, and not lose it. That his courage would not fail him when it came to confronting the beast. That his spear thrust would be swift and true.

'Don't worry, brother,' came a voice from behind him. 'Today will go well.'

Surprised, Quintus turned to regard his sister, who was peering around the half-open door. Aurelia was almost three years younger than he, and loved her sleep. 'You're up early,' he said with an indulgent smile.

She yawned, running a hand through her dense black hair, a longer version of his own. Sharing straight noses, slightly pointed chins and grey eyes, they were clearly siblings. 'I couldn't sleep, thinking about your hunt.'

'Are you worried for me?' he teased, glad to be distracted from his own concerns.

Aurelia came a little further into the room. 'Of course not. Well, a little. I've prayed to Diana, though. She will guide you,' she declared solemnly.

'I know,' Quintus replied, expressing a confidence that he did not entirely feel. Bowing to the figures on the altar, he rose. Ducking his head into the bronze ewer that stood by the bed, he rubbed the water from his face and shoulders with a piece of linen. 'I'll tell you all about it this evening.' He shrugged on a short-sleeved tunic, and then sat to lace up his sandals.

She frowned. 'I want to see it for myself.'

'Women don't go hunting.'

'It's so unfair,' she protested.

'Many things are unfair,' Quintus answered. 'You have to accept that.'

'But you taught me how to use a sling.'

'Maybe that wasn't such a good idea,' Quintus muttered. Much to his surprise, Aurelia had proved to be a deadly shot, which had naturally re-doubled her desire to partake of forbidden activities. 'We've managed to keep our secrets safe so far, but imagine Mother's reaction if she found out.'

'You're on the brink of womanhood,' said Aurelia, mimicking Atia, their mother. 'Such behaviour does not befit a young lady. It must come to an immediate end.'

'Precisely,' Quintus replied, ignoring her scowl. 'Never mind what she'd say if she knew you were riding a horse.' He didn't want to lose his favourite companion, but this matter was beyond his control. 'That's how life is for women.'

'Cooking. Weaving. Taking care of the garden. Supervising the slaves. It's so boring,' Aurelia retorted hotly. 'Not like hunting or learning to use a sword.'

'It's not as if you're strong enough to wield something like a spear anyway.'

'Isn't it?' Aurelia rolled up one sleeve of her nightdress and flexed her biceps. She smiled at his surprise. 'I've been lifting stones like you do.'

'Eh?' Quintus' jaw dropped further. Keen to get as fit as possible, he'd been doing extra training in the woods above the villa. He'd clearly failed to conceal his tracks. 'You've been spying on me? And copying me?'

She grinned with delight. 'Of course. Once my lessons and duties are over, it's easy enough to slip away without being noticed.'

Quintus shook his head. 'Determined, aren't you?' Persuading her to give it all up would be harder than he had thought. He was glad that the duty wouldn't fall to him. Guiltily, Quintus remembered hearing his parents talking about how it would soon be time to find her a husband. He knew how Aurelia would take that announcement. Badly.

'I know that it can't go on for ever,' she declared gloomily. 'They'll be looking to marry me off shortly, no doubt.'

Quintus hid his shock. Even if Aurelia hadn't heard that particular conversation, it wasn't surprising that she was aware of what would happen. Maybe he could help, then, rather than pretending it would never come to pass? 'There's a lot to be said for arranged marriages,' he ventured. It was true. Most nobles arranged unions for their children that were mutually beneficial to both parties. It was how the country ran. 'They can be very happy.'

Aurelia gave him a scornful look. 'Do you expect me to believe that? Anyway, our parents married for love. Why shouldn't I?'

'Their situation was unusual. It's not likely to happen to you,' he countered. 'Besides, Father would keep your interests at heart, not just those of the family.'

'Will I be happy, though?'

'With the help of the gods, yes. Which is more than might happen to me,' he added, trying to lighten the mood. 'I could end up with an old hag who makes my life a misery!' Quintus was glad, though, to be male. No doubt he would eventually wed, but there would be no unseemly rush to marry him off. Meanwhile, his adolescent libido was being satisfied by Elira, a striking slave girl from Illyricum. She was part of the household, and slept on the floor of the atrium, which facilitated sneaking her into his room at night. Quintus had been bedding her for two months, ever since he'd realised that her sultry looks were being directed at him. As far as he was aware, no one else had any idea of their relationship.

Finally, she smiled. 'You're far too handsome for that to happen.'

He laughed off her compliment. 'Time for breakfast,' he announced, continuing to move away from the awkward subject of marriage.

To his relief, Aurelia nodded. 'You'll need a decent meal to give you energy for the hunt.'

A knot of tension formed in Quintus' belly, and what appetite he'd had vanished. He would have to eat something, though, even if it was only for appearance's sake.

Leaving Aurelia chatting to Julius, the avuncular slave who ran the kitchen, Quintus sloped out of the door. He had barely eaten, and he hoped that Aurelia hadn't noticed. A few steps into the peristyle, or courtyard, he met Elira. She was carrying a basket of vegetables and herbs from the villa's garden. As usual, she gave him a look full of desire. It was wasted on Quintus this morning. He gave her a reflex smile and brushed past.

'Quintus!'

He jumped. The voice was one of the most recognisable on the estate. Atia, his mother. Quintus could see no one, which meant that she was probably in the atrium, the family's primary living space. He hurried past the pattering fountain in the centre of the colonnaded courtyard, and into the cool of the *tablinum*, the reception room that led to the atrium, and thence the hallway.

'She's a good-looking girl.'

Quintus spun to find his mother standing in the shadows by the doors, a good vantage point to look into the peristyle. 'W-what?' he stammered.

'Nothing wrong with bedding a slave, of course,' she said, approaching. As always, Quintus was struck by her immense poise and beauty. Oscan nobility through and through, Atia was short and slim and took great care with her appearance. A dusting of ochre reddened her high cheekbones. Her eyebrows and the rims of her eyelids had been finely marked out with ash. A dark red *stola*, or long tunic, belted at the waist, was complemented by a cream shawl. Her long raven-black hair was pinned back by ivory pins, and topped by a diadem. 'But don't make it so frequent. It gives them ideas above their station.'

Quintus' face coloured. He'd never discussed sex with his mother, let alone had his activities commented upon. Somehow, he wasn't surprised that it was she who had brought it up, though, rather than his father. Fabricius was a soldier, but as he often liked to say, his wife had only been prevented from being one by virtue of her sex. Much of the time, Atia was sterner than he was. 'How did you know?'

Her grey eyes fixed him to the spot. 'I've heard you at night. One would have to be deaf not to.'

'Oh,' Quintus whispered. He didn't know where to look. Mortified, he studied the richly patterned mosaic beneath his feet, wishing it would open up and swallow him. He'd thought they'd been so discreet.

'Get over it. You're not the first noble's son to plough the furrow with a pretty slave girl.'

'No, Mother.'

She waved her hands dismissively. 'Your father did the same when he was younger. Everyone does.'

Quintus was stunned by his mother's sudden openness. It must be part of becoming a man, he thought. 'I see.'

'You should be safe enough with Elira. She is clean,' Atia announced briskly. 'But choose new bed companions carefully. When visiting a brothel, make it an expensive one. It's very easy to pick up disease.'

Quintus' mouth opened and closed. He didn't ask how his mother knew that Elira was clean. As Atia's *ornatrix*, the Illyrian had to help dress her each morning. No doubt she'd been grilled as soon as Atia had become aware of her involvement with him. 'Yes, Mother.'

'Ready for the hunt?'

He twisted beneath her penetrating scrutiny, wondering if she could see his fear. 'I think so.'

To his relief, his mother made no comment. 'Have you prayed to the gods?' she asked.

'Yes.'

'Let us do it again.'

They made their way into the atrium, which was lit by a rectangular hole in the ceiling. A downward-sloping roof allowed rainwater to fall into the centre of the room, where it landed in a specially built pool. The walls were painted in rich colours, depicting rows of columns that led on to other, imaginary chambers. The effect made the space seem even bigger. This was the central living area of the large villa, and off it were their bedrooms, Fabricius' office, and a quartet of storerooms. A shrine was situated in one of the corners nearest to the garden.

There a small stone altar was decorated with statues of Jupiter, Mars, or Mamers as the Oscans called him, and Diana. Guttering flames issued from the flat, circular oil lamps sitting before each. Effigies of the family's ancestors hung on the wall above. Most were Fabricius' ancestors: Romans, the warlike people who had conquered Campania just over a century before, but, in a real testament to his father's respect for his wife, some were Atia's forebears: Oscan nobility who had lived in the area for many generations. Naturally, Quintus was fiercely proud of both heritages.

They knelt side by side in the dim light, each making their silent requests of the deities.

Quintus repeated the prayers he'd made in his room. They eased his fear somewhat, but could not dispel it. By the time he had finished, his embarrassment about Elira had subsided. He was still discomfited, however, to find his mother's eyes upon him as he rose.

'Your ancestors will be watching over you,' she murmured. 'To help with the hunt. To guide your spear. Do not forget that.'

She *had* seen his fear. Ashamed, Quintus nodded jerkily.

'There you are! I've been looking for you.' Fabricius came into the room from the hall. Short and compact, his close-cut hair was more grey now than brown. Clean-shaven, he had a ruddier complexion than Quintus, but possessed the same straight nose and strong jawline. He was already wearing his hunting clothes – an old tunic, a belt with an ivory-handled dagger, and heavy-duty leather sandals. Even in civilian dress, he managed to look soldier-like. 'Made your devotions?'

Quintus nodded.

'We had best get ready.'

'Yes, Father.' Quintus glanced at his mother.

'Go on,' Atia urged. 'I will see you later.'

Quintus took heart. She must think I'll succeed, he thought.

'It's time to choose your spear.' Fabricius led the way to one of the storerooms, where his weapons and armour were stored. Quintus had only entered the chamber a handful of times, but it was his favourite place in the house. A ripple of excitement flowed through him as his father produced a small key and slipped it into the padlock. It opened with a quiet click. Undoing the latch, Fabricius pulled wide the door, allowing the daylight in.

A dim twilight still dominated the little room, but Quintus' eyes were immediately drawn to a wooden stand upon which was perched a distinctively shaped, broad-brimmed Boeotian helmet. What made it stand out was its flowing red horsehair crest. Now faded by time, its effect was dramatic nonetheless. Quintus grinned, remembering the day his father had left the door ajar, and he'd illicitly tried the helmet on, imagining himself as a grown man, a cavalryman in one of Rome's legions. He longed for the day when he'd possess one himself.

A pair of simple bronze greaves made from the same material lay on the floor beneath the helmet. A round cavalry shield, made from ox-hide, was propped up nearby. Leaning against it was a long, bone-handled sword in a leather scabbard bound with bronze fastenings: a *gladius hispaniensis*. According to his father, the weapon had been adopted by Rome after they had encountered it in the hands of Iberian mercenaries fighting for Carthage. Although it was unusual still for a cavalryman to bear one, virtually every legionary was now armed with a similar sword. Possessing a straight, double-edged blade nearly as long as a man's arm, the gladius was lethal in the right hands.

Quintus watched in awe as Fabricius traced his fingers affectionately over the helmet, and touched the hilt of the sword. This evidence of his father's former life fascinated him; he also yearned to learn the same martial skills. While Quintus was proficient at hunting, he had undergone little in the way of weapons training. Romans received this when they joined the army, and that couldn't happen until he was seventeen. His lessons, which included military history and tactics, and hunting boar, would have to do. For now.

Finally, Fabricius moved to a weapons rack. 'Take your pick.'

Quintus admired the various types of javelin and hoplite thrusting spears before him, but his needs that day were quite specific. Bringing down a charging bear was very different to taking on an enemy soldier. He needed far more stopping power. Instinctively, his fingers closed on the broad ash shaft of a spear that he had used before. It had a large, double-edged, leaf-shaped blade attached to the rest of the weapon by a long hollow shank. A thick iron spike projected from each side of the base of this. They were designed to prevent the quarry from reaching the person holding the spear. Him, in other words. 'This one,' he said, trying to keep his mind clear of such thoughts.

'A wise choice,' his father said, sounding relieved. He clapped Quintus on the shoulder. 'What next?'

He was being given complete control of the hunt, Quintus realised with a thrill. The days and weeks he'd spent learning to track over the previous two years were over. He thought for a moment. 'Six dogs should be enough. A slave to control each pair. Agesandros can come too: he's a good hunter, and he can keep an eye on the slaves.'

'Anything else?'

Quintus laughed. 'Some food and water would be a good idea, I suppose.'

'Very good,' agreed his father. 'I'll go to the kitchen and organise those supplies. Why don't you select the slaves and dogs you want?'

Still astonished by their role reversal, Quintus headed outside. For the first time he felt the full weight of responsibility on his shoulders. It was critical that he make the correct decisions. Bear hunting was extremely dangerous, and men's lives would depend on him.

Not long after, the little party set off. In the lead was Quintus, with his father walking alongside. Both were unencumbered except for their spears and a water bag each. Next came Agesandros, a Sicilian Greek who had belonged to Fabricius for many years. Trusted by his master, he also carried a hunting spear. A pack hung from his back, containing bread, cheese, onions and a hunk of dried meat.

Through sheer hard work, Agesandros had worked his way up to become the *vilicus*, the most important slave on the farm. He had not been born into captivity, though. Like many of his people, Agesandros had fought alongside the Romans in the war against Carthage. Captured after a skirmish, he had been sold into slavery by the Carthaginians. It was ironic, thought Hanno, that the Sicilian had become the slave of a Roman. Yet Fabricius and Agesandros got on well. In fact, the overseer had a good relationship with the entire family. His genial manner and willingness to answer questions meant that he had been a favourite with Quintus and Aurelia since they were tiny children. Although he was now aged forty or more, the bandy-legged vilicus was in excellent physical shape, and ruled over the slaves with an iron grip.

Last came three sturdy Gauls, chosen by Quintus because of their affinity with the hunting dogs. One in particular, a squat, tattooed man with a broken nose, spent all his free time with the pack, teaching them new commands. Like the other slaves, the trio had been toiling in the fields under Agesandros' supervision that morning. It was sowing time, when they had to work from dawn till dusk under the hot sun. The diversion of a bear hunt was therefore most welcome, and they chatted animatedly to each other in their own tongue as they walked. In front of each man ran a pair of large brindle dogs, straining at the leather leashes tied around their throats. With broad heads and heavily muscled bodies, they were the opposite of Fabricius' smaller dogs, which had tufted ears and feathered flanks. The former were scent hounds, while the latter relied on sight.

The sun beat down from a cloudless sky as they left behind the fields of wheat that surrounded the villa. The sundial in the courtyard had told Quintus it was only just gone *hora secunda*. The characteristic whirring sound of cicadas was starting up, but the heat haze that hung in the air daily had not yet formed. He led the way along a narrow track that twisted and wound through the olive trees dotting the slopes above the farm.

Having traversed an area of cleared earth, they entered the mixed beech and oak woods that covered most of the surrounding countryside. Although the hills were much lower than the Apennines, which ran down Italy's spine, they were home to an occasional bear. It was unlikely that he would find traces this near the farm, however. Solitary by nature, the large creatures avoided humans if at all possible. Quintus scanned the ground anyway, but seeing nothing, he picked up speed.

Like every other large town, Capua held its own *ludi*, or games, affording Quintus the opportunity to see a bear fight once before. It had not been a pretty sight. Terrified by the alien environment and baying crowds, the beast had had little chance against two trained hunters armed with spears. He had vivid memories, though, of the tremendous power in its strong jaws and slashing claws. Facing a bear in its own territory, alone, would be an entirely different prospect to the one-sided spectacle he'd witnessed in Capua. Quintus' stomach clenched into a knot, but his pace did not slacken. Fabricius, like all Roman fathers, held the power of life and death over his son, and he had chosen the task. Quintus could not let down his mother either. It was his duty to succeed. By sunset, I'll be a man, he thought proudly. Quintus couldn't help imagining, however, that he might end his days bleeding to death on the forest floor.

They climbed steadily, leaving the deciduous woods behind. Now they were surrounded by pines, junipers and cypress trees. The air grew cooler and Quintus began to worry. He'd seen piles of dung, and treetrunks with distinctive claw marks scratched into the bark, in this area before. Today, he saw nothing that wasn't weeks, even months, old. He kept going, praying to Diana, the goddess of the hunt, for a sign, but his request was in vain. Not a single bird called; no deer broke from cover. Finally, not knowing what else to do, he stopped, forcing everyone else to do the same. Acutely aware of his father at his back, Agesandros staring, and the Gauls giving each other knowing looks, Quintus racked his brains. He knew this ground like the back of his hand. Where was the best place to find a bear on such a warm day?

Quintus glanced at his father, who simply stared back at him. He would get no help.

Attempting to conceal his laughter, one of the Gauls coughed loudly. Quintus flushed with anger, but Fabricius did nothing. Nor did Agesandros. He looked at his father again, but Fabricius' gaze was set. He would get no sympathy, and the Gaul no reprimand. Today of all days he had to earn the vilicus' and the slaves' respect. Again Quintus pondered. At last an idea popped into his mind.

'Blackberries,' he blurted. 'They love blackberries.' Higher up, in the clearings on the south-facing slopes, were sprawling bramble bushes, which fruited far earlier than those growing on slopes with a different orientation. Bears spent much of their life in search of food. It was as good a place to look as any.

Right on cue, the staccato sound of a woodpecker broke the silence. A moment later, the noise was repeated from a different location. His pulse racing, Quintus searched the trees, finally seeing not one, but two black woodpeckers. The elusive birds were sacred to Mars, the warrior god. Good omens. Turning on his heel, Quintus headed in an entirely different direction.

His smiling father was close behind, followed by Agesandros and the Gauls.

None was laughing now.

Not long after, Quintus' prayers were answered in royal style. He'd checked several glades, with no luck. Finally, though, in the shade of a tall pine tree, he found a lump of fresh dung. Its shape, size and distinctive scent was unmistakable, and Quintus could have cheered at the sight. He stuck a finger into the dark brown mass. The centre had not grown completely cold, which meant that a bear had passed by in the recent past. There were also plenty of brambles nearby. Jerking his head at the tattooed man, Quintus pointed at the ground. The Gaul trotted up, and his two dogs instantly converged on the pile of evidence. Both began whining frantically, alternately sniffing the dung and the air. Quintus' pulse quickened, and the Gaul gave him an enquiring look.

'Let them loose,' ordered Quintus. He glanced at the other slaves. 'Those too.'

Aurelia's foul mood crept up on her after Quintus and their father had left. The reason for her ill humour was simple. While her brother went hunting for a bear, she had to help her mother, who was supervising the slaves in the garden outside the villa. This was one of the busiest times of the year, when the plants were shooting up out of the ground. Lovage sat alongside mustard greens, coriander, sorrel, rue and parsley. The vegetables were even more numerous, and provided the family with food for most of the year. There were cucumbers, leeks, cabbages, root vegetables, as well as fennel and brassicas. Onions, a staple of any good recipe, were grown in huge numbers. Garlic, favoured for both its strong flavour and its medicinal properties, was also heavily cultivated.

Aurelia knew that she was being childish. A few weeks earlier, she had enjoyed setting the lines where the herbs and vegetables would grow, showing the slaves where to dig the holes and ensuring that they watered each with just the right amount of water. As usual, she had reserved the job of dropping the tiny seeds into place for herself. It was something she'd done since she was little. Today, with the plants growing well, the main tasks consisted of watering them and pulling any weeds that had sprouted up nearby. Aurelia couldn't have cared less. As far as she was concerned, the whole garden could fall into rack and ruin. She stood sulkily off to one side, watching her mother direct operations. Even Elira, with whom she got on well, could not persuade her to join in.

Atia ignored her for a while, but eventually she had had enough. 'Aurelia!' she called. 'Come over here.'

With dragging feet, she made her way to her mother's side.

'I thought you liked gardening,' Atia said brightly.

'I do,' muttered Aurelia.

'Why aren't you helping?'

'I don't feel like it.' She was acutely aware that every slave present was craning their neck to hear, and hated it.

Atia didn't care who heard her. 'Are you ill?' she demanded.

'No.'

'What is it then?'

'You wouldn't understand,' Aurelia mumbled.

Atia's eyebrows rose. 'Really? Try me.'

'It's . . .' Aurelia caught the nearest slave staring at her. Her furious glare succeeded in making him look away, but she got little satisfaction from this. Her mother was still waiting expectantly. 'It's Quintus,' she admitted.

'Have you had an argument?'

'No.' Aurelia shook her head. 'Nothing like that.'

Tapping a foot, Atia waited for further clarification. A moment later, it was clear that it would not be forthcoming. Her nostrils flared. 'Well?'

Aurelia could see that her mother's patience would not last much longer. In that moment, however, she caught sight of a buzzard hanging overhead on the thermals. It was hunting. Like Quintus. Aurelia's anger resurged and she forgot about their captive audience. 'It's not fair,' she cried. 'I'm stuck here, in the *garden*, while he gets to track down a bear.'

Atia did not look surprised. 'I wondered if that was what this is about. So you would also hunt?'

Glowering, Aurelia nodded. 'Like Diana, the huntress.'

Her mother frowned. 'You're not a goddess.'

'I know, but . . .' Aurelia half turned, so the slaves could not see the tears in her eyes.

Atia's face softened. 'Come now. You're a young woman, or will be soon. A beautiful one too. Consequently, your path will be very different to that of your brother.' She held up a finger to quell Aurelia's protest. 'That doesn't mean your destiny is without value. Do you think I am worthless?'

Aurelia was aghast. 'Of course not, Mother.'

Atia's smile was broad, and reassuring. 'Precisely. I may not fight or go to war, but my position is powerful nonetheless. Your father relies on me for a multitude of things – as your husband will one day. Maintaining the household is but one small part of it.'

'But you and Father chose to marry each other,' Aurelia protested. 'For love!'

'We were lucky in that respect,' her mother acknowledged. 'Yet we did so without the approval of either of our families. Because we refused to follow their wishes not to wed, they cut us off.' Atia's face grew sad. 'It made life quite difficult for many years. I never saw my parents again, for example. They never met you or Quintus.'

Aurelia was flattered. She'd never heard any of this before. 'Surely it was worth it?' she pleaded.

There was a slow nod. 'It may have been, but I would not want the same hard path for you.'

Aurelia bridled. 'Better that, surely, than being married to some fat old man?'

'That won't happen to you. Your father and I are not monsters.' Atia lowered her voice. 'But realise this, young lady: we *will* arrange your betrothal to someone of our choice. Is that clear?'

Seeing the steel in her mother's eyes, Aurelia gave in. 'Yes.'

Atia sighed, glad that her misgivings had gone unnoticed. 'We under-stand each other then.' Seeing Aurelia's apprehension, she paused. 'Do not fear. You will have love in your marriage. It can develop over time. Ask Martialis, Father's old friend. He and his wife were betrothed to each other by their families, and ended up devoted to one another.' She held out her hand. 'Now, it's time to get stuck in. Life goes on regardless of how we feel, and our family relies on this garden.'

With a faint smile, Aurelia reached out to grasp her mother's fingers. Maybe things weren't as bad as she'd thought.

All the same, she couldn't help glancing up at the buzzard, and thinking of Quintus.

Quintus had followed the pack for perhaps a quarter of an hour before there was any hint that the quarry had been found. Then a loud yelping bark rang out from the trees ahead. It quickly died away to a shrill, repeti-tive whine. With a racing heart, Quintus came to a halt. The dogs' role was merely to bring the bear to bay, but there was always one more eager than its fellows. Its fate was unfortunate, but unavoidable. What mattered was that the bear had been found. In confirmation, a renewed succession of growls was met by a deep, threatening rumble.

The terrifying sound made a hot tide of acid surge up Quintus' throat. Another piercing yelp told him that a second dog had been hurt, or killed. Ashamed of his fear, Quintus willed away his nausea. This was no time for holding back. The dogs were doing their job, and he must do his. Muttering more prayers to Diana, he pounded towards the din.

As he burst into a large clearing, Quintus frowned in recognition. He had often picked berries here with Aurelia. A sprawl of thorny brambles, taller than a man, ran across the floor of the glade, which was bathed in dappled sunlight. A stream pattered down the slope towards the valley below. Fallen boughs lay here and there amidst a profusion of wildflowers, but what drew Quintus' eyes was the struggle going on in the shadow cast by a nearby lofty cypress. Four dogs had a bear cornered against the tree's trunk. Growling with fury, the creature made frequent lunges at its tormentors, but the hounds dodged warily to and fro, just beyond reach. Each time the bear moved away from the tree, the dogs ran in to bite at its haunches or back legs. It was a stalemate – if the bear left the tree's protection, the dogs swarmed in from all sides, but if the beast remained where it was, they could not overcome it.

Two motionless shapes lay outside the semicircle, the casualties Quintus had heard. A cursory glance told him that one dog might survive. It was bleeding badly from deep claw wounds on its ribcage, but he could see no other injuries. The second, on the other hand, would definitely not make it. Shallow movements of its chest told him it still lived, but half its face had been torn off, and shiny, jagged ends of freshly broken bone protruded from a terrible injury to its left foreleg, the result of a bite from the bear's powerful jaws.

Quintus approached with care. Rushing in would carry a real risk of being knocked over, and the Gauls would soon be here. Once they called off the hounds, his task would begin in earnest. He studied the bear, eager for any clue that might help him kill it. Preoccupied with the snapping dogs, it paid him little notice. Its sheer size meant that it had to be a male. The creature's dense fur was yellowish-brown, and it had a typical large, rounded head and small ears. Massive shoulders and a squat body at least three times bigger than his own reinforced Quintus' awareness of just how dangerous his prey was. He could feel his pulse hammering in the hollow at the base of his throat, its speed reminding him that he was not in total control. Calm down, he thought. Breathe deeply. Concentrate.

'Thinking of the berries was a good idea,' said Fabricius from behind him. 'You've found a big bear too. A worthy foe.'

Startled, Quintus turned his head. The others had arrived. All eyes were on him. 'Yes,' he replied, hoping that the growling and snarling a dozen steps away would hide the fear in his voice.

Fabricius moved closer. 'Are you ready?'

Quintus quailed mentally. His father had seen his anxiety, and was prepared to step in. A fleeting look at Agesandros and the slaves was enough to see that they also understood the question's double meaning. A trace of disappointment flashed across the Sicilian's visage, and the Gauls slyly eyed each other. Damn them all, Quintus thought, his guts churning. Have they never been scared? 'Of course,' he replied loudly.

Fabricius gave him a measured stare. 'Very well,' he said, coming to a halt.

Quintus wasn't sure that his worried father would obey. There was more at stake than his life now, though. Killing the bear would prove nothing if the Sicilian and the slaves thought he was a coward, who relied on Fabricius for back-up. 'Do not interfere,' he shouted. 'This is my fight. I must do this on my own, whatever the outcome.' He glanced at his father, who did not immediately respond.

'Swear it!'

'I swear,' Fabricius said reluctantly, stepping back.

Quintus was satisfied to see the first signs of respect return to the others' faces.

A dog howled as the bear caught it with a sweeping arm. It was thrown through the air by the powerful blow, landing with an ominous thud by Quintus' feet. He squared his shoulders and prepared himself. Three hounds weren't enough to contain the quarry. If he didn't act at once, it had a chance of escaping. 'Call them back,' he shouted.

With shrill whistles, the Gauls obeyed. When the enraged dogs did not comply, the tattooed man ran in. Ignoring the bear, and using a leash as a whip, he beat them backwards, out of the way. His actions worked for two of the hounds, but the largest, its lips and teeth reddened with the bear's blood, did not want to withdraw. Cursing, the Gaul half turned, trying to kick it out of the way. He missed, and it darted past him, intent on rejoining the fray.

Aghast, Quintus watched as the dog jumped, sinking its teeth into the side of the bear's face. Rearing up in pain, the bear lifted it right into the air. At once this allowed it to use its front legs, raking the dog's body repeatedly with its claws. Far from releasing its grip, the hound clamped its jaws tighter than ever. It had been bred to endure pain, to hold on no matter what. Quintus had heard of such dogs having to be knocked unconscious before their mouths could be prised open. Yet this stubborn courage would not be enough: it needed help from its companions, which were now restrained. Or from him. The Gaul was in the way, though, screaming his anger and distress. He swung the useless leash across the bear's head, once, twice, three times. It harmed the beast not at all, but would hopefully distract it from killing his favourite dog. That was the theory, anyway.

The Gaul's plan failed. With the skin and hair on both sides of the hound's abdomen ripped away, the bear eviscerated it with several powerful rakes of its claws. Slippery loops of pink bowel tumbled out into the air, only to be sheared off like so many fat sausages. Sensing the dog's grip on its face weaken, the bear redoubled its efforts. Quintus felt his gorge rise as purple lumps of liver tissue cascaded to the ground. Finally a claw connected with a major blood vessel, tearing it asunder. Gouts of dark red blood sprayed from the ruin of the dog's belly, and its jaws loosened.

A moment later, it dropped lifelessly away from the bear.

'Get back!' Quintus screamed, but the Gaul ignored him.

Instead, the wild-eyed slave launched another attack. The loss of his canine friend had driven him into battle rage, which Quintus had often heard of, but never seen. The Romans and Gauls were enemies of old and had fought numerous times. More than a hundred and seventy years before, Rome itself had been sacked by the fierce tribesmen. Just six years previously, more than seventy thousand of them had invaded northern Italy again. They had been defeated, but stories still abounded of berserker warriors who, fighting naked, threw themselves at oncoming legionaries with complete disregard for their own safety.

This man was no such enemy, however. He might be a slave, but his life was still worth saving. Quintus jumped forward, shoving his spear at the bear. To his horror, the animal moved at the last moment, and his blade ran deep into its side rather than its chest, as he had intended. His blow was not mortal, nor was it enough to stop the beast reaching up to seize the Gaul by the neck. A short choking cry left the man's lips, and the bear shook him as a dog would a rat.

Not knowing what else to do, Quintus thrust his spear even deeper. The only reaction was an annoyed growl. In his haste, he'd stabbed into the creature's abdomen. It was potentially a mortal wound, but not one that would stop it quickly. Satisfied that the Gaul was dead, the bear flung him to one side. Naturally, its gaze next fell upon Quintus, who panicked. Although his spear was buried in its flesh, the creature's deep-set eyes showed no fear, just a searing anger. Bears normally avoided conflict with humans, but when aroused they became extremely aggressive. This individual was irate. It snapped at his spear shaft and splinters flew into the air.

There was nothing for it. Quintus took a deep breath and pulled his spear free. Roaring with pain, the bear revealed a genuinely fearsome set of teeth, the largest of which were as long as Quintus' middle fingers. Its red, gaping mouth was big enough to fit his entire head inside, and was well capable of crushing his skull. Quintus wanted to move away, but his muscles were paralysed by terror.

The bear took a step towards him. Gripping his spear in both hands, Quintus aimed the point at its chest. Advance, he told himself. Go on the attack. Before he could move, the animal lunged at him. Catching the end of the spear, it swept the shaft to one side as though it were a twig. With nothing between them, they stared at each other for a breathless moment. In slow motion, Quintus saw its muscles tense in preparation to jump. He nearly lost control of his bladder. Hades was a whisker away, and he could do nothing about it.

For whatever reason, however, the bear did not leap at once, and Quintus was able to bring down his spear again.

His relief was momentary.

As Quintus moved to the attack, he slipped on a piece of intestine. Both of his feet went from under him, and he landed flat on his back. With a rush, all the air left his lungs, winding him. Quintus was vaguely aware of the butt of his spear catching in the dirt and wrenching itself free of his grasp. Frantically, he lifted his head. To his utter horror, he could see the bear not five paces away, just beyond his sandals. It roared again, and this time Quintus received the full force of its fetid breath. He blinked, knowing that death was at hand.

He had failed.

Chapter III: Capture

The Mediterranean Sea

Hours passed in a blur of driving rain and pounding waves. Darkness fell, which increased the magnitude of the friends' terror manyfold. The small boat was tossed up and down, back and forth, helpless before the sea's immense power. It took all of Hanno's energy just to stay on board. Both of them were sick multiple times, vomiting a mixture of food and wine over themselves and the vessel's floor. Eventually there was nothing left but bile to come up. Flashes of lightning regularly illuminated the pathetic scene. Hanno wasn't sure which was worse: not being able to see his hand in front of his face, or looking at Suniaton's wan, terrified features and puke-spattered clothes.

Slumped on the bench opposite, his friend alternated between hysterical bouts of weeping, and praying to every god he could think of. Somehow Suniaton's distress helped Hanno to remain in control of his own terror. He was even able to take some solace from their situation. If Melqart had wanted to drown them, they would already be dead. The storm had not reached the heights it would have done in winter, nor had their boat capsized. Besides these minor miracles, there had been no further leaks. Sturdily built from cypress planks, its seams were sealed with lengths of tightly packed linen fibre as well as a layer of beeswax. They had not lost the oars, which meant that they could row to land, should the opportunity arise. Moreover, every stretch of coastline had its Carthaginian trading post. There they could make themselves known, promising rich reward for a passage home.

Hanno pinched himself out of the fantasy. Don't get your hopes up, he thought bitterly. The bad weather showed no signs of letting up. Any one of the waves rolling in their direction was capable of flipping the boat.

Melqart hadn't drowned them yet, but deities were capricious by nature, and the sea god was no different. All it would take was a tiny extra surge in the water for their craft to overturn. Hanno struggled to hold back his own tears. What real chance had they? Even if they survived until sunrise and their families worked out where they had gone, the likelihood of being found on the open sea was slim to none. Adrift with no food or water, they would both die, painfully, within a few days. At this stark realisation Hanno closed his eyes and asked for a quick death instead.

Despite the heavy rain which had soaked him to the skin, Malchus had returned from the meeting with the Council of Elders in excellent humour. He stood now, a cup of wine in hand, under the sloping portico that ran around the house's main courtyard, watching the raindrops splashing off the white marble mosaic half a dozen steps away. His impassioned speech had gone down as he'd wished, which relieved him greatly. Since Hannibal's messenger had given him the weighty task a week before of announcing to the elders and suffetes that the general planned to attack Saguntum, Malchus had been consumed by worry. What if the council did not back the Barca? The stakes were higher than he'd ever known.

Saguntine reprisals against the tribes allied to Carthage were purportedly the reason for Hannibal's assault, but, as everyone knew, its intent was to provoke Rome into a response. Yet, thanks to the general's perfect timing, that response would not be militaristic. Severe unrest in Illyricum meant that the Republic had already committed both consuls and their armies to conflict in the East. For the upcoming campaign season, Rome would only be able to issue empty threats. After that, however, retribution would undoubtedly follow. Hannibal was not worried. He was convinced that the time for war with their old enemy was ripe, and Malchus agreed with him. Nonetheless, bringing those who led Carthage round to the same opinion had been a daunting prospect.

It was a pity, thought Malchus, that Hanno had not been there to witness his finest oratory yet. By the end, he'd had the entire council on their feet, cheering at the idea of renewed conflict with Rome. Meanwhile Hanno had most likely been *fishing*. News of the huge shoals of tunny offshore that day had swept the city. Now Hanno was probably spending the proceeds of his catch on wine and whores. Malchus sighed. A moment later, hearing

39

Sapho and Bostar's voices in the corridor that led to the street, his mood lifted. At least two of his sons had been there. They soon emerged into view, wringing out their sodden cloaks.

'A wonderful speech, Father,' said Sapho in a hearty tone.

'It was excellent,' agreed Bostar. 'You had them in the palm of your hand. They could only respond in one way.'

Malchus made a modest gesture, but inside he was delighted. 'Finally, Carthage is ready for the war that we have been preparing for these years past.' He moved to the table behind him, upon which sat a glazed red jug and several beakers. 'Let us raise a toast to Hannibal Barca.'

'Shame Hanno didn't hear your speech too,' said Sapho, throwing a meaningful glance at Bostar. Busily pouring wine, their father didn't see it.

'Indeed,' Malchus replied, handing each a full cup. 'Such occasions do not come often. For the rest of his life, the boy will regret that he was playing truant while history was made.' He swallowed a mouthful of wine. 'Have you seen him?'

There was a short, awkward silence.

He looked from one to the other. 'Well?'

'We ran into him this morning,' Sapho admitted. 'On our way to the Agora. He was with Suniaton.'

Malchus swore. 'That must have been just after he'd scarpered out of the house. The little ruffian ignored my shouts! Did the pair of them give you the slip?'

'Not exactly,' Sapho replied awkwardly, giving Bostar another pointed stare.

Malchus caught the tension between his sons. 'What's going on?'

Bostar cleared his throat. 'We talked, and then let them go.' He rephrased his words. '*I* let them go.'

'Why?' Malchus cried angrily. 'You knew how important my speech was.'

Bostar flushed. 'I'm sorry, Father. Perhaps I acted wrongly, but I couldn't help thinking that, like us, Hanno will soon be at war. For the moment, though, he's still a boy. Let him enjoy himself while he can.'

Tapping a finger against his teeth, Malchus turned to Sapho. 'What did you say?'

'Initially, I thought that we should force Hanno to come with us, Father, but Bostar had a point. As he was the senior officer present, I gave way to his judgement.' Bostar tried to interrupt, but Sapho continued talking. 'In hindsight, it was possibly the wrong decision. I should have argued with him.'

'How dare you!' Bostar cried. 'I made no mention of rank! We made the decision together.'

Sapho's lip curled. 'Did we?'

Malchus held up his hands. 'Enough!'

Throwing each other angry looks, the brothers fell silent.

Malchus thought for a moment. 'I am sorely disappointed in you, Sapho, for not protesting more at your brother's desire to let Hanno do as he wished.' He regarded Bostar next. 'Shame on you, as a senior officer, for forgetting that our primary purpose is to gain revenge on Rome. In comparison, frivolities such as fishing are irrelevant!' Ignoring their muttered apologies, Malchus raised his cup. 'Let us forget Hanno and his wastrel friend, and drink a toast to Hannibal Barca, and to our victory in the coming war with Rome!'

They followed his lead, but neither brother clinked his beaker off the other's.

Hanno's wish for an easy death was not granted. Eventually the storm passed, and the ferocious waves died down. Dawn arrived, bringing with it calm seas and a clear sky. The wind changed direction; it was now coming from the northeast. Hanno's hopes rose briefly, before falling again. The breeze was not strong enough to carry them back home, and the current continued to carry their small vessel eastwards. Silence reigned; all the seabirds had been driven off by the inclement weather. Suniaton's exhaustion had finally got the better of him, and he lay slumped on the boat's sole, snoring.

Hanno grimaced at the irony of it. The peaceful scene could not have been more at odds with what they had endured overnight. His sodden clothes were drying fast in the warm sunshine. The boat rocked gently from side to side, wavelets slapping off the hull. A pod of dolphins broke the surface nearby, but the sight did not bring the usual smile to Hanno's face. Now, their graceful shapes and gliding motion were an acute reminder that he belonged on the land, which was nowhere to be seen. Apart from the dolphins, they were utterly alone.

Regret, and an unfamiliar feeling, that of humility, filled Hanno. I should have done my duty, he thought. Gone to that meeting with Father. The idea of listening to dirtbags like Hostus and his cronies was now most appealing. Hanno stared bleakly at the western horizon, knowing that he would never see his home, or his family, again. Suddenly, his sorrow became overwhelming. Hanno's eyes filled with tears, and he was grateful that Suniaton was asleep. Their friendship ran deep, but he had no wish to be seen crying like a child. He did not despise Suni for his extreme reaction during the storm, though. Thinking that a calm mien might help his friend was all that had prevented him from acting similarly.

A short time later, Suniaton awoke. Hanno, who was still feeling fragile, was surprised and irritated to see that his spirits had risen somewhat.

'I'm hungry,' Suniaton declared, glancing around with greedy eyes.

'Well, there's nothing to eat. Or drink,' Hanno replied sourly. 'Get used to it.'

Hanno's foul mood was obvious and Suniaton had the wisdom not to reply. Instead he busied himself by bailing out the handsbreadth of water in the bottom of the boat. His housekeeping complete, he lifted the oars and placed them in their rowlocks. Squinting at the horizon and then the sun, he began rowing due south. After a moment, he started whistling a ditty that was currently popular in Carthage.

Hanno scowled. The tune reminded him of the good times they had spent carousing in the rough taverns near the city's twin ports. The pleasurable hours he had spent with plump Egyptian whores in the room above the bar. 'Isis', as she called herself, had been his favourite. He pictured her kohl-rimmed eyes, her carmine lips framing encouraging words, and his groin throbbed. It was too much to bear. 'Shut up,' he snapped.

Hurt, Suniaton obeyed.

Hanno was spoiling for a fight now. 'What are you doing?' he demanded, pointing at the oars.

'Rowing,' Suniaton replied sharply. 'What does it look like?'

'What's the point?' Hanno cried. 'We could be fifty miles out to sea.'

'Or five.'

Hanno blinked, and then chose to ignore his friend's sensible answer.

He was so angry he could hardly think. 'Why choose south? Why not north, or east?'

Suniaton gave him a withering glance. 'Numidia is the nearest coastline, in case you hadn't realised.'

Hanno flushed and fell silent. Of course he knew that the southern shore of the Mediterranean was closer than Sicily or Italy. In the circumstances, Suniaton's plan was a good one. Nonetheless, Hanno felt unwilling to back down, so he sat and stared sulkily at the distant horizon.

Stubbornly, Suniaton continued to paddle southwards.

Time passed, and the sun climbed high in the sky.

After a while, Hanno found his voice. 'Let me take a turn,' he muttered.

'Eh?' Suniaton barked.

'You've been rowing for ages,' said Hanno. 'It's only fair that you have a break.'

'"What's the point?"' Suniaton angrily repeated his friend's words.

Hanno swallowed his pride. 'Look,' he said. 'I'm sorry, all right? Heading south is as good a plan as any.'

Suniaton's nod was grudging. 'Fair enough.'

They changed position, and Hanno took control of the oars. A more comfortable atmosphere fell, and Suniaton's good humour returned. 'At least we're still alive, and still together,' he said. 'How much worse would it have been if one of us had been washed overboard? There'd be no one to throw insults at!'

Hanno grimaced in agreement. He lifted his gaze to the burning disc that was the sun. It had to be nearly midday. It was baking hot now, and his tongue was stuck to the roof of his dry mouth. What I'd give for a cup of water, he thought longingly. His spirits reached a new low, and a moment later, he shipped the oars, unable to work up the enthusiasm to continue rowing.

'My turn,' said Suniaton dutifully.

Hanno saw the resignation he was feeling reflected in his friend's eyes. 'Let's just rest for a while,' he murmured. 'It looks set to remain calm. What does it matter where we make landfall?'

'True enough.' Despite the lie, Suniaton managed to smile. He didn't vocalise what they were both thinking: if, by some miracle, they did manage to reach the Numidian coastline, would they find water before succumbing to their thirst?

43

Some time later, they both took another turn at the oars, applying themselves to the task with a vigour born of desperation. Their exertions produced no discernible result: all around, the horizon was empty. They were totally alone. Lost. Abandoned by the gods. At length, exhausted by thirst and the extreme heat, the friends gave up and lay down in the bottom of the boat to rest. Sleep soon followed.

Hanno dreamed that he was on one side of a door while his father was on the other, hammering on the timbers with a balled fist and demanding he open it at once. Hanno was desperate to obey, but could find no handle or keyhole on the door's featureless surface. Malchus' blows grew heavier and heavier, until finally Hanno became aware that he was dreaming. Waking to a pounding headache and a feeling of distinct disorientation, he opened his eyes. Above, the limitless expanse of the blue sky. Beside him, Suniaton's slumbering form. To Hanno's amazement, the thumping in his head was replaced by a regular, and familiar, cadence: that of men singing. There was another voice too, shouting indistinct commands. It was a sailor, calling the tune for the oarsmen, thought Hanno disbelievingly. A ship!

All weariness fell away, and he sat bolt upright. Turning his head, Hanno searched for the source of the noise. Then he spotted it: a low, predatory shape not three hundred paces distant, its decks lined with men. It had a single mast with a square sail supported by a complex set of rigging, and two banks of oars. The red-coloured stern was curved like a scorpion's tail, and there was a small forecastle at the prow. Amidst his exultation, Hanno felt the first tickle of unease. This didn't look like a merchant vessel; it was clearly no fishing smack either. However, it was not large enough to be a Carthaginian, or even a Roman, warship. These days, Carthage had very few biremes or triremes, relying instead on the bigger, more powerful quinqueremes and, to a lesser extent, quadriremes. Rome possessed some smaller ships, but he could see none of their standards. Yet the craft had a distinctly military air.

He nudged Suniaton. 'Wake up!'

His friend groaned. 'What is it?'

'A ship.'

Suniaton shot into a sitting position. 'Where?' he demanded.

Hanno pointed. The bireme was beating a northward course, which would bring it to within a hundred paces of their little boat. It was in a hurry to be using both its sail and the power of its oars, and it seemed no one had seen them. Hanno's stomach lurched. If he didn't act, it might pass them by.

He stood up. 'Here! Over here,' he began shouting in Carthaginian. Suniaton joined in, waving his arms like a man possessed. Hanno repeated his cry in Greek. For a few heart-stopping moments, nothing happened. Finally, a man's head turned. With the sea almost flat calm, it was impossible not to see them. Guttural shouts rang out, and the chanting voices halted abruptly. The oars on the port side, which was facing them, slowed and stopped, reducing the bireme's speed at once. Another set of bellowed commands, and the sail was reefed, allowing the ship to bear away from the wind. The nearest banks of oars began to back water, turning the bireme towards them. Soon they could see the base of the bronze ram that was attached to the bow. Carved in the shape of a creature's head, it was only possible to make out the top of the skull and the eyes. Now pointing straight at them, the vessel gave off a most threatening air.

The two friends looked at each other, suddenly unsure.

'Who are they?' whispered Suniaton.

Hanno shook his head. 'I don't know.'

'Maybe we should have kept quiet,' said Suniaton. He began muttering a prayer.

Hanno's certainty weakened, but it was far too late now.

The sailor who led the oarsmen's chant began a slower rhythm than before. In unison, the oars on both sides lifted and swept gracefully through the air before arcing down to split the sea's surface with a loud, splashing sound. Encouraged by the shouts of their overseer, the oarsmen sang and heaved together, dragging their oars, carved lengths of polished spruce, through the water.

Before long, the bireme had drawn alongside. Its superstructure was decorated red like the stern, but around each oar hole a swirling blue design had been painted. It was still bright and fresh, showing the work had been done recently. Hanno's heart sank as he studied the grinning men – a mixture of nationalities from Greek and Libyan to Iberian – lining the rails and forecastle. Most were clad in little more than a loincloth, but all were armed to the teeth. He could see catapults on the deck as well. He and Suniaton had only their daggers.

'They're fucking pirates,' Suniaton muttered. 'We're dead meat. Slaves, if we're lucky.'

'Would you rather die of thirst? Or exposure?' Hanno retorted, furious at himself for not seeing the bireme for what it was. For not keeping silent.

'Maybe,' Suniaton snapped back. 'We'll never know now, though.'

They were hailed by a thin figure near the prow. With black hair and a paler complexion than most of his dark-skinned comrades, he could have been Egyptian. Nonetheless, he spoke in Greek, the dominant language of the sea. 'Well met. Where are you bound?'

His companions snorted with laughter.

Hanno decided to be bold. 'Carthage,' he declared loudly. 'But, as you can see, we have no sail. Can we take passage with you?'

'What are you doing so far out to sea in just a rowing boat?' the Egyptian asked.

There were more hoots of amusement from the crew.

'We were carried away by a storm,' Hanno replied. 'The gods were smiling, however, and we survived.'

'You were lucky indeed,' agreed the other. 'Yet I wouldn't give much for your chances if you stay out here. By my reckoning, it is at least sixty miles to the nearest landfall.'

Suniaton gestured towards the south. 'Numidia?'

The Egyptian threw back his head and laughed. It was an unpleasant, mocking sound. 'Have you no sense of direction, fool? I talk of Sicily!'

Hanno and Suniaton gaped at one another. The storm had carried them much further than they could have imagined. They had been mistakenly rowing out into the Mediterranean. 'We have even more reason to thank you,' said Hanno boldly. 'As our fathers will, when you return us safely to Carthage.'

The Egyptian's lips pulled up, revealing a sharp set of teeth. 'Come aboard. We can talk more comfortably in the shade,' he said, indicating the awning in the forecastle.

The friends exchanged a loaded glance. This hospitality was at odds with what their eyes were telling them. Every man in sight looked capable of slitting their throats without even blinking. 'Thank you,' said Hanno with a broad smile. He rowed around to the back of the bireme. There they found a jolly boat about the same size as theirs tied to an iron ring. A knotted rope had already been lowered to their level from above. A pair of grinning sailors waited to haul them up.

'Trust in Melqart,' Hanno said quietly, tying their boat fast.

'We didn't drown, which means he has a purpose for us,' Suniaton replied, desperate for something to believe in. Yet his fear was palpable.

Struggling not to lose his own self-control, Hanno studied the planks before him. This close, he could see the black tar that covered the hull below the waterline. Telling himself that Suniaton was right, Hanno took hold of the rope. How else could they have survived that storm? It *must* have been Melqart. Helped by the sailors, he ascended, using his feet to grip on the warm wood.

'Welcome,' said the Egyptian as Hanno reached the deck. He raised a hand, palm outwards, in the Carthaginian manner.

Pleased by this, Hanno did the same.

Suniaton arrived a moment later, and the Egyptian greeted him similarly. Leather water bags were then proffered, and the two drank greedily, slaking their fierce thirst. Hanno began to wonder if his gut instinct had been wrong.

'You're from Carthage?' The question was innocent enough.

'Yes,' replied Hanno.

'Do you sail there?' asked Suniaton.

'Not often,' the Egyptian replied.

His men sniggered, and Hanno noticed many were lustfully eyeing the gold charms that hung from their necks. 'Can you take us there?' he asked boldly. 'Our families are wealthy, and will reward you well for our safe return.'

The Egyptian rubbed his chin. 'Will they indeed?'

'Of course,' Suniaton asserted.

A prolonged silence fell, and Hanno grew more uneasy.

At last the Egyptian spoke. 'What do you think, boys?' he asked, scanning the assembled men. 'Shall we sail to Carthage and collect a handsome prize for our efforts?'

'No bloody way,' snarled a voice. 'Just kill them and have done.'

'Reward? We'd all be crucified, more like,' shouted another.

Suniaton gasped, and Hanno felt sick to the pit of his stomach. Crucifixion was one of the punishments reserved for lawbreakers of the worst kind. Pirates, in other words.

Raising his eyebrows mockingly, the Egyptian lifted a hand, and his companions relaxed. 'Unfortunately, people like us aren't welcome in Carthage,' he explained.

'It doesn't have to be Carthage itself,' Hanno said nonchalantly. Beside him, Suniaton nodded in nervous agreement. 'Any town on the Numidian coast will do.'

Raucous laughter met his request, and now Hanno struggled not to despair. He glanced at Suniaton, but he had no inspiration to offer.

'Supposing we agreed to that,' said the grinning Egyptian, 'how would we get paid?'

'I would meet you afterwards with the money, at a place of your choosing,' Hanno replied, flushing. The pirate captain was playing with him.

'And you'd swear that on your mother's life, I suppose?' the Egyptian sneered. 'If you had one.'

Hanno swallowed his anger. 'I did, and I would.'

Catching him off guard, the Egyptian swung forward and delivered a solid punch to his solar plexus. The air shot from Hanno's lungs, and he folded over in complete agony. 'Enough of this shit,' the Egyptian announced abruptly. 'Take their weapons. Tie them up.'

'No!' Hanno mumbled. He tried to stand upright, but strong hands grabbed his arms from behind, pinioning them to his sides. He felt his dagger being removed, and a moment later the gold charm around his neck was torn away. Weaponless and without the talisman he had worn since infancy, Hanno felt utterly naked. Alongside, the same was happening to Suniaton, who screamed as his earrings were ripped out. Greedy hands pulled and tugged at their valuables as the pirates fought for a share of the spoils. Hanno glared at the Egyptian. 'What are you going to do with us?'

'You're both young and strong. Should fetch a good price on the slave block.'

'Please,' begged Suniaton, but the pirate captain had already turned away.

Hanno hawked and spat after him, and received a heavy blow across the head for his pains. They then had their arms tied tightly behind their backs and were bundled unceremoniously below decks, into the cramped space where the slaves sat on two tiers of benches. Slumped over their oars, and with barely enough room to sit erect, they sat twenty-five to each row, fifty on each side of the bireme. At the base of the steps, on a central walkway, stood a lone slave, the man whose chant had woken Hanno. Near the stern, a narrow iron cage contained a dozen or so prisoners. Hanno and Suniaton glanced at each other. They weren't alone.

It was hot outside, but here the presence of more than a hundred sweating men increased the temperature to that of an oven. Countless pairs of deadened eyes stared at the newcomers, but not a single slave spoke. The reason soon became apparent. Bare feet slapped off the timbers as a short barrel of a man approached. The friends stood head and shoulders over him, but the crop-haired newcomer's muscles were enormous, reminding Hanno of Greek wrestlers he'd seen. His only garment was a leather skirt, but he exuded authority, not least because of the knotted whip dangling from his right fist. His scarred features were roughly hewn, as if from granite, his lips a mere slit in the stone.

Still winded, Hanno couldn't stop himself from meeting the overseer's cold, calculating eyes.

'Fresh meat, eh?' His voice was nasal and irritating.

'Two more for the slave market, Varsaco,' answered one of the men holding Hanno.

'Consider yourself lucky. Most prisoners end up on the benches, but we have a full complement at the moment.' Varsaco gestured at the long-haired wretches all around them. 'So you get to stay in our select accommodation.' He jerked a thumb at the cage and laughed.

Hanno felt a thrill of dread. Their fate would be no better than that of the oarsmen. They would be totally at the mercy of whoever bought them.

Suniaton's eyes were pools of terror. 'We could end up anywhere,' he whispered.

His friend was right, thought Hanno. The Carthaginians' weakened navy no longer had the power to keep the western Mediterranean free of pirates, and thus far the Romans had not bothered to police the high seas. The bireme could roam wherever it wanted. There were few ports indeed where the security inspection was more than cursory. Sicily, Numidia or Iberia were possibilities. As was Italy. Every decent-sized town had a slave market. Hanno felt as if he was drowning in an ocean of despair.

The Egyptian's voice carried from the deck above. 'Varsaco!'

The overseer answered straightaway. 'Captain?'

'Resume former course and speed.'

'Yes, sir.'

Hanno and Suniaton were ignored as Varsaco bellowed orders at the oarsmen on the starboard side. Leaning into the task, the slaves used their oars to back water until the overseer gestured at them to stop. At once the figure on the walkway began singing a chant that set the oarsmen into a steady rhythm.

His duties in hand, Varsaco returned. There was a predatory look in his eyes that had not been there before. 'You're a handsome boy,' he said, running his stubby fingers down Hanno's arm. He slipped a hand under Hanno's tunic and tweaked a nipple. Hanno shuddered and tried to pull away, but with a man either side of him, he could not go far. 'I prefer those with a bit more meat on their bones, though,' Varsaco confided. He moved to Suniaton's side and roughly squeezed his buttocks. Suniaton twisted away, but the pirates holding him tightened their grip. 'But look, you're hurt.' Varsaco touched one of Suniaton's still oozing earlobes, then, to Hanno's horror, licked the blood off his fingertip.

Suniaton wailed with fear.

'Leave him alone, you whoreson,' Hanno roared, struggling uselessly to free himself.

'Or what?' teased Varsaco. Abruptly, his voice hardened. 'I am the master below decks. I do as I please. Take him over there!'

Tears of rage streamed down Hanno's face as he watched his friend being dragged to a large block of wood nailed down near the bow. Its surface, approximately the length of a man's torso, was covered in irregular, dark patches, and heavy iron fetters were in place at each corner at floor level. Releasing Suniaton from his bonds, the pirates slammed him face down on to the wood. He kicked and struggled, but his captors were too many. An instant later, the manacles clicked shut around his wrists and ankles.

Varsaco moved to stand behind him and, realising what was about to happen, Suniaton began to scream. His protests intensified as the overseer was handed a knife and used it to slit his breeches from waistband to crotch. Varsaco did the same to Suniaton's undergarment, laughing as the tip of the blade snagged in his flesh, causing him to moan with pain. Finally, the overseer pulled apart the cut fabric, and his face twisted with lust. 'Very nice,' he muttered.

'No!' cried Suniaton.

It was too much for Hanno to bear. Summoning every reserve of his strength, he twisted and bucked like a wild horse. Engrossed by the spectacle, the two men holding him were caught unawares, and he slipped their grasp. Sprinting forward, he reached Varsaco in a dozen steps. The overseer's broad back was towards him, and he was busily unbuckling the belt that held up his leather skirt. It dropped to the floor and he sighed with satisfaction, shuffling forward to complete the outrage.

Panting with fury, Hanno steadied himself and did the only thing he could think of. Drawing back his right leg, he swung it through the air and between Varsaco's thighs. With a meaty thump, the front of his sandal connected with the soft mass of the overseer's dangling scrotum. Letting out a high-pitched scream, Varsaco collapsed to the deck in a heap. Hanno snarled with delight. 'How do you like that?' he screamed, stamping his iron-studded sole on the side of Varsaco's head for good measure. He managed to deliver several more kicks before the men who had been holding him came barrelling in. Hanno saw one raising the butt of his sword. He half turned, awkward because of the ropes binding his arms, but was unable to avoid the blow. Stars exploded across Hanno's vision as the hilt connected with the back of his head. His knees buckled and he toppled forward to land on the semi-conscious Varsaco. A rain of blows followed and he slipped into the darkness.

'Wake up!'

Hanno felt someone nudge him in the back. Slowly, he came to. He was lying on his side, still trussed up like a hen for the pot. Every part of his body hurt. His head, belly and groin had obviously received special attention, however. It was agony to breathe in, and Hanno suspected that two or three of his ribs were cracked. He could taste blood, and warily he used his tongue to check that all his teeth were still in place. They were, thankfully, although two felt loose, and his top lip was bruised and swollen.

He was prodded again.

'Hanno! It's me, Suniaton.'

Finally, Hanno focused on his friend, who was lying only a few steps away. To his surprise, they were on the forecastle deck, under the cloth awning he had spied earlier. As far as he could tell, they were alone.

'You've been unconscious for hours.' Suniaton's voice was concerned.

The temperature had dropped significantly, Hanno realised. In the gap between the gunwale and the awning, he could see an orange tinge to the sky. It was nearly sunset. 'I'll live,' he croaked. His last memories came flooding back. 'What about you? Did Varsaco . . .?' He couldn't finish the question.

Suniaton screwed up his face. 'I'm fine,' he muttered. Amazingly, he grinned. 'Varsaco couldn't stand for a long time, you know.'

'Good! The fucking bastard.' Hanno frowned. 'Why didn't his men kill me?'

'They were going to,' whispered Suniaton. 'But—'

Hearing the stairs that led to the main deck creak, he fell silent. Someone was approaching. A moment later, the Egyptian stooped over Hanno. 'You've come back to us,' he said. 'Good. A man who sleeps too long after a beating like that often doesn't wake.'

Hanno glared.

'Don't give me that look,' said the Egyptian reproachfully. 'If it wasn't for me, you'd be dead by now. Raped before you died, like as not.'

Suniaton flinched, but Hanno's fury knew no bounds. 'Am I supposed to be grateful?'

The Egyptian squatted down alongside him. 'Spirited, aren't you? A different prospect to your friend.' He nodded in approval. 'I hope to sell you as a gladiator. You'd be wasted as an agricultural or household slave. Are you able to get up?'

Hanno let the other help him to a sitting position. A stabbing pain from his chest made him grimace in pain.

'What is it?'

Hanno was disconcerted by the Egyptian's concern. 'It's nothing. Just a couple of broken ribs.'

'That's all?'

'I think so.'

The Egyptian smiled. 'Good. I thought I'd come too late. It wouldn't be the first time that one of Varsaco's little games got out of hand.'

'"Little games"?' Suniaton asked faintly.

The Egyptian made an offhand gesture. 'Usually, he's content to screw whichever poor bastard takes his fancy. Several times a day, normally. As long as that's it, I don't mind. It doesn't affect their sale value. After what you did, though, he would have killed you both. I don't mind him having his fun, but there's no point destroying valuable merchandise. That's why you're up here, where I sleep. Varsaco has a key to the cage, and I wouldn't trust him not to slip a knife between your ribs one night.'

Hanno longed to wrap his fingers around the captain's throat, choking the life out of him, ridding his face of its perpetual smug expression. It stung that their lives had been saved for purely financial reasons. Deep down, though, Hanno was unsurprised by the Egyptian's action. He'd once seen his father stop a slave from beating a mule for much the same reason.

'This is the best place on the ship. You're out of the sun here, and it catches the evening breeze as well.' The Egyptian got to his feet. 'Make the most of it. We're on course for Sicily, and then Italy,' he said, disappearing from view.

'At least in Iberia or Numidia, we might have had a chance of getting word to Carthage,' muttered Suniaton despairingly.

Hanno's nod was bitter. Instead, they were to be sold to their people's worst enemies, as gladiators. 'Melqart can't be solely responsible for this ill fortune. There's more to it.' He cast his mind about, wondering why they should suffer such a terrible fate. All at once, the memory of how he had left home came crashing back. Hanno cursed. 'I'm a fool.'

Suniaton threw him a confused look. 'What is it?'

'I didn't ask for Tanit's blessing as I walked out of the front door.'

Suniaton's face paled. Although she was a virginal mother figure, Tanit was the most important Carthaginian deity. She was also the goddess of war. Angering her carried the risk of severe punishment. 'It's not a crime to forget,' he said, before quickly adding, 'but you could ask pardon of her anyway.'

In a cold sweat, Hanno did as his friend advised.

Great Mother, he pleaded. Forgive me. Do not forget us, please.

* * *

The next morning, Hanno had not returned home. In itself, that was not particularly unusual. But the hours passed, and still there was no sign of him. At midday, Bostar began to look worried. He paced up and down the corridor from the courtyard, checking the street for his youngest brother. By the early afternoon, he could take it no more. 'Where is Hanno?'

'Nursing a hangover somewhere, probably,' Sapho growled.

Bostar pursed his lips. 'He's never been this late before.'

'Maybe he heard about Father's speech, and got even drunker than normal.' Sapho looked at their father for approval. Surprisingly, he got none.

Malchus' face now also registered concern. 'You're right, Bostar. Hanno always comes back in time for his lessons. I'd forgotten, but this afternoon, at his request, we were to discuss the battle of Ecnomus again.'

Sapho frowned. 'He wouldn't miss it then.'

'Precisely.'

Suddenly, the situation felt very different.

A familiar voice cut through their dismay. 'Malchus? Are you at home?'

All three turned to see a stout, bearded man appearing in the courtyard's entrance. A long cream linen robe reached almost to his feet, and a headcloth concealed his hair.

Bowing, Malchus hurried forward. 'Bodesmun. I am honoured by your presence.'

Behind him, Sapho and Bostar were also making obeisance. Eshmoun was not their family's favoured god, but he was an important deity. His temple at the top of Byrsa Hill was the largest in Carthage, and Bodesmun was one of the senior priests there.

'Can I offer you refreshment?' asked Malchus. 'Some wine or pomegranate juice? Bread and honey?'

Bodesmun waved a podgy hand in dismissal. His round, gentle face was worried. 'Thank you, but no.'

Malchus was nonplussed. He had little in common with a peace-loving priest. 'How can I help you?' he enquired awkwardly.

'It's about Suniaton.'

Malchus' response was instant. 'What's Hanno made him do?'

Bodesmun managed a weak grin. 'It's nothing like that. Have you seen Suni today?'

Malchus' heart gave an involuntary leap. 'No. I could ask you the same about Hanno.'

The smile left Bodesmun's face. 'He hasn't returned yet either?'

'No. Apparently, the tunny were running in their thousands yesterday. Any fool with a net could catch a boatload, and I'm sure they did the same. When Hanno didn't return, I presumed they had gone out to celebrate,' Malchus replied heavily, his imagination already running riot. 'It's odd that you should arrive when you did. I was just starting to get worried. Hanno has never skipped a lesson on tactics before.'

'Suni has never missed the devotions in the temple at midday either.'

Bostar's face fell. Even Sapho frowned.

The two older men stared at each other in disbelief. All at once, they had a great deal in common. Bodesmun was close to tears. 'What should we do?' he asked in a quavering voice.

Malchus refused to let the panic that had flared in his breast grow. He was a soldier. 'There'll be some easy explanation to this,' he declared. 'We might have to check every inn and whorehouse in Carthage, but we'll find them.'

Bodesmun's normal commanding demeanour had disappeared. He nodded meekly.

'Sapho! Bostar!'

'Yes, Father,' they replied in unison, eager to be given something to do. By now, Bostar was distraught. Sapho didn't look happy either.

'Rouse as many soldiers as you can from the barracks,' Malchus ordered. 'I want the city combed from top to bottom. Concentrate on their favourite haunts around the ports. You know the ones.'

They nodded.

Despite his best efforts, Malchus' temper frayed. 'Go on, then! When you're done, find me here, or in the Agora.'

Bostar turned at the entrance to the corridor. 'What are you going to do?'

'Talk to the fishermen at the Choma,' Malchus answered grimly. His mind was full of the storm that had battered the city the previous night. 'I want to know if anyone saw them yesterday.' He glanced at Bodesmun. 'Coming?'

The priest pulled himself together. 'Of course.'

With a sinking feeling in their bellies, they left the house.

On the Choma, Malchus and Bodesmun found scores of the fishermen who plied the waters off the city. Their day's work was long done. With their boats tied up nearby, they lounged about, gossiping and repairing holes in their nets. Unsurprisingly, the appearance of a noble and a high-ranking priest filled them with awe. Most went their entire lives without ever being in the presence of someone so far up the social scale. Their guttural argot was also quite hard to understand. Consequently, it was hard to get a word of sense out of them.

'We're wasting our time. They're all idiots,' Malchus muttered in frustration. He forced himself not to scream and lash out with rage. Losing his temper would be completely counterproductive. The best chance of discovering anything about their sons' disappearance was surely to be found here.

'Not all, perhaps.' Bodesmun indicated a wiry figure sitting on an upturned boat, whose silver hair marked him out as older than his companions. 'Let's ask him.'

They strolled over. 'Well met,' Bodesmun said politely. 'The blessings of the gods be upon you.'

'The same to you and your friend,' replied the old man respectfully.

'We come in search of answers to some questions,' Malchus announced.

The other nodded, unsurprised. 'I was thinking that you were after more than fresh fish.'

'Were you out on the water yesterday?'

There was a faint smile. 'With the tunny running like they were? Of course I was. It's just a shame that the weather changed so early, or it would have been the best day's catch in the last five years.'

'Did you see a small skiff, perhaps?' Malchus asked. 'With two crew. Young men, well dressed.'

His urgent tone and Bodesmun's anxious stance would have been obvious to all but an imbecile. Nonetheless, the old man did not answer immediately. Instead, he closed his eyes.

Each instant that went by felt like an eternity to Malchus. He clenched his fists to stop himself from grabbing the other by the throat.

It was Bodesmun who cracked first. 'Well?'

The old man's eyes opened. 'I did spot them, yes. A tall lad and a shorter, stockier one. Well dressed, as you say. They're out here regularly. A friendly pair.'

Malchus and Bodesmun gave each other a look full of hope, and fear.

'When did you last see them?'

The old man's expression became wary. 'I'm not sure.'

Malchus knew when he was being lied to. A tidal wave of dread swamped him. There was only one reason for the other to withhold the truth. 'Tell us,' he commanded. 'You will come to no harm. I swear it.'

The old man studied Malchus' face for a moment. 'I believe you.' Taking a deep breath, he began. 'When the wind rose sharply, I saw that a storm was coming. I quickly pulled my net on board and headed for the Choma. Everyone else was doing the same. Or so I thought. When I was safe on dry land, I saw one skiff still over the tunny. I knew it for the young men's craft by its shape. At first I imagined that they had been consumed by greed and were trying to catch even more fish, but as it was carried out of sight, I realised I was mistaken.'

'Why?' Bodesmun's voice was strangled.

'The boat appeared to be empty. I wondered if they'd fallen overboard and drowned. That seemed improbable, for the sea was still not that rough yet.' The old man frowned. 'I came to the assumption that they were asleep. Oblivious to the weather.'

'What do you take us for?' cried Malchus. 'One dozing, maybe, but both of them?'

The old man quailed before Malchus' wrath, but Bodesmun laid a restraining hand on his arm. 'That is a possibility.'

Wild-eyed, Malchus turned on Bodesmun. 'Eh?'

'A flask of good wine is missing from my cellar.'

Malchus gave him a blank look. 'I don't understand.'

'Suniaton is the likely culprit,' Bodesmun revealed sadly. 'They must have drunk the wine and then fallen asleep.'

'When the wind began to rise, they didn't even notice,' Malchus whispered in horror.

Tears formed in Bodesmun's eyes.

'So they were just washed out to sea?' Malchus muttered in disbelief.

'You are old. I can understand why you might have held back, but those?' Furiously, he indicated the younger fishermen. 'Why did none of them help?'

The old man found his voice once more. 'They were your sons, I take it?'

Anguish overtook Malchus' fury, and he nodded.

The other's eyes filled with an unhealed sorrow. 'I lost my only child to the sea ten years hence. A son. It is the gods' way.' There was a short pause. 'The rules of survival are simple. When a storm strikes, it is every craft for itself. Even then, death is quite likely. Why would those men risk their own lives for two youths they barely knew? Otherwise Melqart would likely have had more corpses entering his kingdom.' He fell silent.

Part of Malchus wanted to have every person in sight crucified, but he knew that it would be a pointless gesture. Glancing back at the old man, he was struck by his calm manner. All his deference had vanished. Looking once more into the other's eyes, Malchus understood why. What difference would threats make here? The man's only son was dead. He felt strangely humbled. At least he still had Sapho and Bostar.

Beside him, silent sobs racked Bodesmun's shoulders.

'Two deaths is enough,' Malchus acknowledged with a heavy sigh. 'I'm grateful for your time.' He began fumbling in his purse.

'I need no payment,' the old man intoned. 'Such terrible news is beyond a price.'

Mumbling his thanks, Malchus walked away. He was barely aware of a weeping Bodesmun following him. While he retained his composure, Malchus too was riven by grief. He had expected to lose one son – perhaps more – in the impending war with Rome, but not beforehand, and so easily. Had Arishat's death not been enough unexpected tragedy for one lifetime? At least he'd been able to say goodbye to her. With Hanno, there hadn't even been that chance.

It all seemed so cruel, and so utterly pointless.

Several days went by. The friends were kept on the forecastle and given just enough food to keep them alive: crusts of stale bread, a few mouthfuls of cold millet porridge and the last, brackish drops from a clay water gourd. Their bonds were untied twice a day for a short period, allowing them to stretch the cramped muscles in their arms and upper backs. They

soon learned to answer calls of nature at these times, because at others
their guards would laugh at any request for help. On one occasion, desperate,
Hanno had been forced to soil himself.

Fortunately, Varsaco was not allowed near them, although he sent
frequent murderous glances in their direction. Hanno was pleased to note
that the overseer walked with a decided limp for days. Other than making
sure Hanno was recovering from his injuries, the Egyptian ignored them,
even moving his blankets to the base of the mast. Strangely, Hanno felt
some pride at this clear indication of their value. Their solitude also meant
that the pair had plenty of occasions to confer with each other. They spent
all their time plotting ways to escape. Of course both knew that their
fantasies were merely an attempt to keep their spirits up.

The bireme reached the rugged coastline of Sicily, travelling past the
walled towns of Heraclea, Acragas and Camarina. Keeping a reasonable
distance out to sea meant that any Roman or Sicilian triremes could be
avoided. The Egyptian made sure that the friends saw Mount Ecnomus,
the peak off which the Carthaginians had suffered one of their greatest
defeats to the Romans. Naturally, Hanno had heard the story many times.
Sailing over the very water where so many of his countrymen had lost
their lives nearly forty years before filled him with a burning rage: partly
against the Egyptian for his lascivious telling of the tale, but mainly against
the Romans, for what they had done to Carthage. The *corvus*, a spiked
boarding bridge suspended from a pole on every enemy trireme, had been
an ingenious invention. Once dropped on to the Carthaginian ships' decks,
it had allowed the legionaries to storm across, fighting just as they would
on land. In one savage day, Carthage had lost nearly a hundred ships, and
her navy had never recovered from the blow.

A day or so after rounding Cape Pachynus, the southernmost point of
Sicily, the bireme neared the magnificent stronghold of Syracuse.
Originally built by the Corinthians more than five hundred years before,
its immense fortifications sprawled from the triangular-shaped plateau
of Epipolae on the rocky outcrop above the sea, right down to the island of
Ortygia at the waterline. Syracuse was the capital of a powerful city-state,
which controlled the eastern half of Sicily and was ruled by the aged
tyrant Hiero, a long-term ally of the Republic, and enemy of Carthage.
The Egyptian took his ship to within half a mile of the port before deciding

not to enter it. Large numbers of Roman triremes were visible, the captains
of which would relish crucifying any pirates who fell into their hands.

It mattered little to Hanno and Suniaton where they landed. In fact, the
longer their journey continued, the better. It delayed the reality of their
fate.

Rather than make for the towns located on the toe or heel of Italy, the
Egyptian guided the bireme into the narrow strait between Sicily and the
mainland. Only a mile wide, it afforded a good view of both coasts.

'It's easy to see why the Romans began the war with Carthage, isn't it?'
Hanno muttered to Suniaton. Sicily dominated the centre of the Mediterranean, and, historically, whoever controlled it, ruled the waves. 'It's so
close to Italy. Our troops' presence must have been perceived as a threat.'

'Imagine if our people hadn't lost the war,' Suniaton replied sadly. 'We
would have stood a chance of being rescued by one of our ships now.'

It was another reason for Hanno to hate Rome.

In the port of Rhegium, on the Italian mainland, the pirate captain
prepared to sell his captives. The street gossip soon changed his mind. The
forthcoming games at Capua, further up the coast, had produced an unprece-
dented demand for slaves. It was enough to make the Egyptian set sail for
Neapolis, the nearest shore town to the Campanian capital.

As the end of their voyage drew near, Hanno found that his increasing
familiarity with the pirates was, oddly, more comforting than the unknown
fate that awaited him. But then he remembered Varsaco: remaining on the
bireme was an impossibility for it would only be a matter of time before
the brutal overseer took his revenge. It was with a sense of relief, therefore, that two days later Hanno clambered on to the dock at Neapolis. The
walled city, formerly a Greek settlement, had been one of the *socii*, allies
of the Republic, for over a hundred years. It possessed one of the largest
ports south of Rome, a deep-water harbour filled with warships, fishing
boats and merchant vessels from all over the Mediterranean. The place was
jammed, and it had taken the Egyptian an age to find a suitable mooring
spot.

With Hanno were Suniaton and the other captives, a mixture of young
Numidians and Libyans. The Egyptian and six of his burliest men accompanied the party. To prevent any attempt at escape, the iron ring around
each captive's neck was connected to the next by a length of chain. Enjoying

the solidity of the quayside's broad stone slabs beneath his feet, Hanno found himself beside a heap of roughly cut cedar planks from Tyre. Alongside those lay golden mounds of Sicilian grain and bulging bags of almonds from Africa. Beyond, stacked higher than a man, were wax-sealed amphorae full of wine and olive oil. Fishermen bantered with each other as they hauled their catch of tunny, mullet and bream ashore. Off-duty sailors in their striking blue tunics swaggered along the dock in search of the town's fleshpots. Laden down by their equipment, a squad of marines prepared to embark on a nearby trireme. Spotting them, the sailors filled the air with jibes. Bristling, the marines began shouting back. The groups were only stopped from coming to blows by the intervention of a pug-nosed *optio*.

Hanno couldn't help himself from drinking the hectic scene in. It was so reminiscent of home, and his heart ached with the pain of it. Then, amidst the shouts in Latin, Greek and Numidian, Hanno heard someone speaking Carthaginian, and being answered in turn. Complete shock, then joy, filled him. At least two of his countrymen were here! If he could speak with them, word might be carried to his father. He glanced at Suniaton. 'Did you hear that?'

Stricken, his friend nodded.

Hanno frantically stood on tiptoe, but the press on the quay was too great.

With a brutal yank, the Egyptian pulled on the chain, forcing his captives to follow. 'It's only a short walk to the slave market,' he announced with a cruel smile.

Hanno dragged his feet, but the pull around his neck was inexorable. To his immense distress, within a dozen paces he could no longer discern his mother tongue from the plethora of other languages being spoken. It was as if the last window of opportunity had been shut in their faces. It felt a crueller blow than anything that had befallen them thus far.

A tear rolled down Suniaton's cheek.

'Courage,' Hanno whispered. 'Somehow we will survive.'

How? his mind screamed. *How?*

Chapter IV: Manhood

T he bear lunged at his feet, and Quintus lashed out, delivering a flurry of kicks in its direction. He had to bite his tongue not to scream in terror. At this rate, the animal would seize him by the thigh, or groin. The pain would be unbelievable, and his death lingering, rather than the swift end suffered by the Gaul. Quintus could think of no way out. Desperately, he continued flailing out with his *caligae*. Confused, the animal growled, and it batted at him with a giant paw. It half ripped off one of Quintus' sandals.

A moan of fear ripped free of his lips at last.

Footsteps pounded towards Quintus, and relief poured through his veins. His life might not be over. He was simultaneously consumed by shame. He did not want to live the rest of his days known as the coward who had had to be rescued from a bear.

'HOLD!' shouted his father.

'But Quintus—' Agesandros protested.

'Must do this on his own. He said so himself,' Fabricius muttered. 'Stand back!'

Waves of terror washed over Quintus. In obeying his wishes, his father was consigning him to certain death. He closed his eyes. Let it be quick, please. A moment later, he realised that the bear had not pressed home its attack. Quintus peered at the animal, which was still only a few steps away. Was it Agesandros' charge, or his father's voice that had caused it to hesitate? He wasn't sure, but it gave him an idea. Taking a deep breath, Quintus let out a piercing cry. The animal's small ears flattened, which encouraged him to repeat the shrill sound. This time, he waved his arms as well.

To Quintus' immense relief, the bear backed off a pace. He was able to climb to his feet, still shrieking his head off. Unfortunately, his spear was beyond his reach. It lay right beneath the animal's front paws. Quintus knew that without it, he had no chance of success. Nor would there be any pride to be had in driving off the bear with noise. He had to regain his weapon and kill it. Swinging his arms like a madman, he took a step towards it. The animal's head swung suspiciously from side to side, but it gave way. Remembering Agesandros' advice about what to do if confronted by a bear in the forest, Quintus redoubled his efforts. His damaged sandal was still attached to his calf by its straps, and he had to take great care how he placed his feet. Despite this hindrance, it wasn't long before he regained his spear.

Quintus could have cheered. The animal was now looking all around it, searching for a way to escape, but there was no easy way. Fabricius had directed the others to spread out. They formed a loose circle around the pair. The remaining dogs filled the air with an eager clamour. His courage renewed, Quintus went on the offensive. After all, the bear was wounded. It had to be within his ability to kill it now.

He was mistaken.

Every time he stabbed his spear at the animal, it either snapped at the blade, or swept it out of the way with its massive arms. Quintus' heart thumped off his ribs. He would have to go a lot closer. How, though, could he deliver a death stroke without coming within range of its deadly claws? The bear's reach was prodigious. He could think of only one way. He'd seen pigs slaughtered many times in the farmyard, had even wielded the knife himself on occasion. With their tough skin and thick layer of subcutaneous fat, they were difficult animals to kill, quite unlike sheep or oxen. The best way was to run the blade into their flesh directly under the chin, cutting the major vessels that exited the heart. Quintus prayed that bears' anatomy was similar, and that the gods granted him a chance to finish the matter like this.

Before he could carry out his plan, the animal lunged forward on all fours, catching Quintus off guard. He backed away hastily, forgetting his damaged sandal. Within a few steps, the studded sole snagged on a protruding root. They pulled the straps attached to his calf taut, in the process unbalancing him. Quintus fell heavily, landing this time on his backside. Somehow, he hung on to his spear, which landed flat on the glade floor beside him. That didn't stop his heart from shrivelling with fear. The bear's attention focused in on him and, moving incredibly fast, it swarmed in his direction.

Quintus' eyes flickered to one side. The shocked expression on his father's face said it all. He was about to die.

Despite his horror, Fabricius kept his oath. He did not budge from his position.

Quintus' gaze returned to the bear. Its gaping mouth was no more than a handsbreadth from his feet. He had but the briefest instant to react before it ripped one of his legs off. Fortunately, the end of his spear protruded beyond his sandals. Gripping the shaft, he raised it off the ground. Sunlight flashed off the polished iron tip, and bounced into the bear's eyes, distracting it, and causing it to snap irritably at the blade. Swiftly, Quintus pulled his legs to one side. At the same time, he jammed the weapon's butt into the earth by his elbow and gripped it fiercely with both hands.

When the bear closed in, he aimed the sharp point at the flesh below its wide-open jaws. Intent on seizing him, it paid no attention. Lowering its head, it lunged at his legs. Desperately, Quintus slid them away as fast as he could. The movement brought the animal right on to his spear, and its momentum was great enough for the razor-sharp iron to slice through the skin. There was a grating feeling as it pushed over the larynx before running onwards into the deeper, softer tissues. Fully capable of tearing him apart yet, the bear bucked and reared, its immense strength threatening to rip Quintus' weapon from his hands. He hung on for dear life as, half suspended above him, the animal clawed furiously at the thick wooden shaft. It was so close that his nostrils were filled with its pungent odour. He could almost touch the fangs that had torn apart the Gaul and three of the dogs.

It was utterly terrifying.

The animal's immense weight eventually worked against it, forcing the deadly blade further into its flesh. Quintus was far from happy, however. The bear was very much alive, and it was drawing ever nearer. It filled his entire range of vision – a great angry mass of teeth and claws. Any closer and it would rip him to shreds. Could the protruding spikes at the base of the iron shank take the strain? Quintus' mouth was bone dry with fear. *Die, you whoreson. Just die.*

It lurched a further handsbreadth down the spear shaft.

He thought his heart would stop.

Abruptly, the bear gagged, and a bright red tide of blood sprayed from its mouth, covering the ground beyond Quintus. He had sliced through a large artery! Jupiter, let its heart be next, he prayed. Before it reaches me. The shaft juddered as the iron spikes slammed against the creature's neck, and it came to an abrupt stop. It snarled in Quintus' face, and he closed his eyes. There was no more he could do.

To his immense relief, the bear stopped struggling. Another torrent of blood poured from its gaping jaws, covering Quintus' face and shoulders. Disbelieving, he looked up, stunned to see the light in its amber eyes weaken, and then go out. All at once, the bear was a dead weight on the end of his spear. Quintus' exhausted muscles could take the pressure no longer, and he let go.

The animal landed on top of him.

To Quintus' immense relief, it did not move. And although he could barely breathe, he was alive.

An instant later, he felt the bear's body being hauled off.

'You're unhurt,' his father cried. 'Praise be!'

Agesandros growled his agreement.

Quintus sat up gingerly. 'Someone was watching over me,' he muttered, wiping some of the bear's blood away from his eyes.

'They were indeed, but that doesn't take away from what you've done,' said Fabricius. There was tangible relief in his voice. 'I was sure you were going to be killed. But you held your nerve! Few men can do that when faced with certain death. You should be proud. Not only have you proved your courage, but you've honoured our ancestors in the finest way possible.'

Quintus glanced at Agesandros and the two slaves, who were regarding him with new respect. His chin lifted. He had succeeded! Thank you, Diana and Mars, he thought. I will make a generous offering to you both. Inevitably, though, Quintus' eyes were drawn to the tattooed slave's body. Guilt seized him. 'I should have saved him too,' he muttered.

'Come now!' Fabricius replied. 'You are not Hercules. The fool should have known better than to risk his life for a dog. Your achievement is worthy of any Roman.' He drew Quintus to his feet and embraced him warmly.

Quintus' emotions suddenly became overwhelming: sadness at the Gaul's death mixed with relief that he had triumphed over his fear. He struggled not to cry. During the fight, he'd forgotten about becoming a man. Somehow, he had achieved the task set out by his father.

At last they drew apart.

'How does it feel?' Fabricius asked.

'No different,' Quintus replied with a grin.

'Are you sure?'

Quintus stared at the bear and realised that things *had* changed. Before, he'd been unsure of his ability to kill such a magnificent creature. Indeed, he'd nearly failed because of his terror. Staring death in the face was a lot worse than he'd imagined. Yet wanting to survive had been a gut instinct. He looked back to find Fabricius studying him intently.

'I saw that you were afraid,' his father said. 'I would have intervened, but you had made me promise not to.'

Quintus flushed, and opened his mouth to speak.

Fabricius raised a hand. 'Your reaction was normal, despite what some might say. But your determination to succeed, even if you died in the attempt, was stronger than your fear. You were right to make me swear not to step in.' He clapped Quintus on the arm. 'The gods have favoured you.'

Quintus remembered the two woodpeckers he'd seen, and smiled.

'As you are to be a soldier, we shall have to visit the temple of Mars as well as that of Diana.' Fabricius winked. 'There's also the small matter of buying a toga.'

Quintus beamed. Visits to Capua were always to be looked forward to. Living in the countryside afforded few opportunities for socialising or pleasure. They could visit the public baths and his father's old comrade, Flavius Martialis. Flavius' son, Gaius, was the same age as he was, and the two got along famously. Gaius would love to hear the story of the bear hunt.

First, though, he had to tell Aurelia and his mother. They would be waiting eagerly for news.

While Agesandros and the slaves stayed to bury the tattooed Gaul and to fashion carrying poles for the bear, Quintus and his father headed for home.

It didn't take the Egyptian long to sell the friends. Thanks to the impending games at Capua, sales at the Neapolis slave market were brisk. There were few specimens on sale to compare with the two Carthaginians' muscular build, or the Numidians' wiry frames, and buyers crowded round the naked men, squeezing their arms and staring into their eyes for signs of fear. Although Hanno's miserable demeanour was not that of a combatant, he impressed nonetheless. Cleverly, the Egyptian refused to sell them except as a pair. Several dealers bid against each other to purchase the two friends, and the eventual victor was a dour Latin by the name of Solinus. He also bought four of the Egyptian's other captives.

Hanno took little notice of what was going on in the noisy market place. Suniaton's efforts to revive his spirits with whispers of encouragement were futile. Hanno felt more hopeless than he ever had in his life. Since surviving the storm, every possible chance of redemption had turned to dust. Unknowingly, they had rowed out to sea rather than towards the land. Instead of a merchant vessel, fate had brought them the bireme. In a heaven-sent opportunity, Carthaginians had been present at Neapolis, but he hadn't been able to speak to them. Lastly, they were to be sold as gladiators rather than the more common classes of slaves, which guaranteed their death. What more proof did he need that the gods had forgotten them completely? Hanno's misery coated him like a heavy, wet blanket.

Along with an assortment of Gauls, Greeks and Iberians, the six captives were marched out of the town and on to the dusty road to Capua. It was twenty miles from Neapolis to the Campanian capital, a long day's walk at most, but Solinus broke the journey with an overnight stop at a roadside inn. As the prisoners watched miserably, the Latin and his guards sat down to enjoy a meal of wine, roast pork and freshly baked bread. All the captives got was a bucket of water from the well, which afforded each man no more than half a dozen mouthfuls. At length, however, a servant delivered several stale loaves and a platter of cheese rinds. However paltry the portions, the waste food tasted divine, and revived the captives greatly. As Suniaton bitterly told Hanno, they would be worth far less if they arrived in Capua at death's door. It was therefore worth spending a few coppers on provisions, however poor.

Hanno didn't respond. Suniaton soon gave up trying to raise his spirits, and they sat in silence. Deep in their own misery, and strangers to each other, none of the other slaves spoke either. As it grew dark, they lay down side by side, staring at the glittering vista of stars illuminating the night sky. It was a beautiful sight, reminding Hanno again of Carthage, the home he would never see again. His emotions quickly got the better of him, and, grateful for the darkness, he sobbed silently into the crook of an elbow.

Their current suffering was nothing. What was to come would be far worse.

In the morning, Quintus had his first hangover. During the celebratory dinner the previous night, Fabricius had plied him with wine. Although he had often taken surreptitious tastes from amphorae in the kitchen, it had been the first time Quintus was officially permitted to drink. He had not held back. His approving mother had not protested. With Aurelia hanging on his every word, Elira casting smouldering glances each time she delivered food and his father throwing him frequent compliments, he'd felt like a conquering hero. Agesandros too had been full of praise when, after dinner, he had brought the freshly skinned bear pelt to the table. Flushed with success, Quintus rapidly lost count of how many glasses he'd downed. While the wine was watered down in the traditional manner, he was not used to handling its effects. By the time the plates were cleared away, Quintus had been vaguely aware that he was slurring his words. Atia had swiftly moved the jug out of his reach and, soon after, Fabricius had helped him to bed. When a naked Elira had slipped under the covers a short time later, Quintus had barely stirred; he hadn't noticed her leave either.

Now, with the early morning sun beating down on his throbbing head, he felt like a piece of metal being hammered on a smith's anvil. It was little more than an hour since his father had woken him, and even less since they had set off from the farm. Nauseous, Quintus had refused the breakfast proffered him by a sympathetic Aurelia. Encouraged by a grinning Agesandros, he'd drunk several cups of water, and mutely accepted a full clay gourd for the journey. There was still a foul taste in Quintus' mouth, though, and every movement of the horse between his knees threatened to make him vomit yet again. So far, he'd done so four times. The only things keeping him on the saddle blanket were his vice-like hold on the reins, and his knees, which were tightly gripping the horse's sides. Fortunately, his mount had a placid nature. Eyeing the uneven track that stretched off into the distance, Quintus muttered a curse. Capua was a long distance away yet.

They travelled in single file, with his father at the front. Dressed in his finest tunic, Fabricius sat astride his grey stallion. His gladius hung from a gilded baldric, necessary protection against bandits. Also armed, Quintus came next. The tightly rolled bear pelt was tied up behind his saddle blanket. It needed to dry out, but he was determined to show it to Gaius. His mother and his sister were next, sitting in a litter carried by six slaves. Aurelia would have ridden, but Atia's presence precluded that. Despite the tradition that women did not ride, Quintus had given in to his sister's demands years before. She had turned out to be a natural horsewoman. Their father had happened to see them practising one day, and had been amazed. Because of her ability, Fabricius had chosen to indulge her in this, but Atia had been kept in the dark. There was no way that she would have agreed to it. Knowing this, Aurelia had not protested as they'd left.

Taking up the rear was Agesandros, his feet dangling either side of a sturdy mule. He was to visit the slave market and find a replacement for the dead Gaul. A metal-tipped staff was slung over his back, and his whip, the badge of his office, was jammed into his belt. The Sicilian had left his deputy, a grinning Iberian with little brain but plenty of brawn, to supervise the taking in of the harvest. Last of all came a pair of prize lambs, bleating indignantly as Agesandros dragged them along by their head ropes.

Time passed and gradually Quintus felt more human. He drained the water gourd twice, refilling it from a noisy stream that ran parallel to the road. The pain in his head was lessening, allowing him to take more of an interest in his surroundings. The hills where they had hunted the bear were now just a hazy line on the horizon behind them. On either side sprawled fields of ripe wheat, ground which belonged to their neighbours. Campania possessed some of the most fertile land in Italy, and the proof lay all around. Groups of slaves were at work everywhere, wielding their scythes, gathering armfuls of the cut stalks, stacking sheaves. Their activities were of scant interest to Quintus, who was beginning to feel excited about wearing his first adult toga.

Aurelia drew the curtain as the litter came alongside. 'You look better,' she said brightly.

'A little, I suppose,' he admitted.

'You shouldn't have drunk so much,' Atia scolded.

'It's not every day a man kills a bear,' Quintus mumbled.

Fabricius turned his head. 'That's right.'

Aurelia's lips thinned, but she didn't pursue the issue.

'A day like yesterday comes along only a few times in a lifetime. It is right to celebrate it,' Fabricius declared. 'A sore head is a small price to pay afterwards.'

'True enough,' Atia admitted from the depths of the litter. 'You have honoured your Oscan, as well as your Roman, heritage. I'm proud to have you as my son.'

Shortly after midday, they reached Capua's impressive walls. Surrounded by a deep ditch, the stone fortifications ran around the city's entire circumference. Watchtowers had been built at regular intervals, and six gates, manned by sentries, controlled the access. Quintus, who had never seen Rome, loved it dearly. Originally built by the Etruscans more than four hundred years before, Capua had been the head of a league of twelve cities. Two centuries previously, however, marauding Oscans had swept in, seizing the area for their people. My mother's race, thought Quintus proudly. Under Oscan rule, Capua had grown into one of the most powerful cities in Italy, but was eventually forced to seek aid from Rome when successive waves of Samnite invaders threatened its independence.

Quintus' father was descended from a member of the Roman relief force, which meant that his children were citizens. Campania's association with the Republic meant that its people were also citizens, but only the nobility were allowed to vote. This distinction was still the cause of resentment among many Campanian plebeians, who had to present themselves for military service alongside the legions, despite their lack of suffrage. The loudest among them claimed that they were remaining true to their Oscan ancestors. There was even some talk of Capua regaining its independence, which Fabricius decried as treason. Quintus felt torn if he thought about their protests, not least because his mother conspicuously remained silent at such times. It seemed hypocritical that local men who might fight and die for Rome were not permitted to have a say in who ran the Republic. It also brought Quintus to the thorny question of whether he was denying his mother's heritage in favour of his father's? It was a point that Gaius, Flavius Martialis' son, loved to tease him about. Although they had Roman citizenship and could vote, Martialis and Gaius were Oscan nobility through and through.

Their first stop was the temple of Mars, which was located in a side street a short distance from the forum. While the family watched, one lamb was offered up for sacrifice. Quintus was relieved when the priest pronounced good omens. The same assertion was made at Diana's shrine, delighting him further.

'No surprise there,' Fabricius murmured as they left.

'What do you mean?' asked Quintus.

'After hearing what happened on the hunt, the priest was hardly going to give us an unfavourable reading.' Fabricius smiled at Quintus' shock. 'Come now! I believe in the gods too, but we didn't need to be told that they were pleased with us yesterday. It was obvious. What was important today was to pay our respects, and that we have done.' He clapped his hands. 'It's time to clean up at the baths, and then buy you a new toga.'

An hour later, they were all standing in a tailor's shop. Thanks to its proximity to the fullers' workshops, the premises reeked of stale urine, increasing Quintus' desire to get on with the matter in hand. Workers were busy in the background, raising the nap on rolls of cloth with small spiked boards, trimming it with cropping shears to give a soft finish, and folding the finished fabric before pressing it. The proprietor, an obsequious figure with greasy hair, laid out different qualities of wool for them to choose from, but Atia quickly motioned at the best. Soon Quintus had been fitted in his toga *virilis*. He shifted awkwardly from foot to foot while a delighted Atia fussed and bothered, adjusting the voluminous folds until they met with her approval. Fabricius stood in the background, a proud smile on his lips while Aurelia bobbed up and down excitedly alongside.

'The young master looks very distinguished,' gushed the shopkeeper.

Atia gave an approving nod. 'He does.'

Feeling proud but self-conscious, Quintus gave her a tight smile.

'A fine sight,' Fabricius added. Counting out the relevant coinage, he handed it over. 'Time to visit Flavius Martialis. Gaius will want to see you in all your glory.'

Leaving the proprietor bowing and scraping in their wake, they walked outside. There Agesandros, who had taken their mounts to a stables, was waiting. He bowed deeply to Quintus. 'You are truly a man now, sir.'

Pleased by the gesture, Quintus grinned. 'Thank you.'

Fabricius looked at his overseer. 'Why don't you go to the market now?

You know where Martialis' house is. Just come along when you've bought the new slave.' He handed over a purse. 'There's a hundred *didrachms*.'

'Of course,' Agesandros replied. He turned to go.

'Wait,' Quintus cried on impulse. 'I'll tag along. I need to start learning about things like this.'

Agesandros' dark eyes regarded him steadily. '"Things like this"?' he repeated.

'Buying slaves, I mean.' Quintus had never really given much thought to the process before, which, for obvious reasons, still impacted on Agesandros. 'You can teach me.'

The Sicilian glanced at Fabricius, who gave an approving nod.

'Why not?' Atia declared. 'It would be good experience for you.'

Agesandros' lips curved upwards. 'Very well.'

Aurelia rushed to Quintus' side. 'I'm coming too,' she declared.

Agesandros arched an eyebrow. 'I'm not sure . . .' he began.

'It's out of the question,' said Fabricius.

'There are things in the slave market which are not fitting for a girl to see,' Atia added.

'I'm almost a woman, as you keep telling me,' Aurelia retorted. 'When I've been married off, and I'm mistress of my own house, I will be able to visit such places whenever I choose. Why not now?'

'Aurelia!' Atia snapped.

'You do what I say!' interrupted Fabricius. 'I am your father. Remember that. Your husband, whoever he may be, will also expect you to be obedient.'

Aurelia dropped her eyes. 'I'm sorry,' she whispered. 'I just wanted to accompany Quintus as he walked through the town, looking so fine in his new toga.'

Disarmed, Fabricius cleared his throat. 'Come now,' he said. He glanced at Atia, who frowned.

'Please?' Aurelia pleaded.

There was a long pause, before Atia gave an almost imperceptible nod.

Fabricius smiled. 'Very well. You may go with your brother.'

'Thank you, Father. Thank you, Mother.' Aurelia avoided Atia's hard stare, which promised all kinds of dressing-down later.

'Go on, then.' Fabricius made a benevolent gesture of dismissal.

As Agesandros silently led them down the busy street, Quintus gave

Aurelia a reproving look. 'It's not only my exercises that you've been spying on, eh? You're quite the conspirator.'

'You're surprised? I have every right to listen in to your little conversations with Father.' Her blue eyes flashed. 'Why should I just play with my toys while you two discuss possible husbands? I may be able to do nothing about it, but it's my right to know.'

'You're right. I should have told you before,' Quintus admitted. 'I'm sorry.'

Suddenly, her eyes were full of tears. 'I don't want an arranged marriage,' she whispered. 'Mother says that it won't be that bad, but how would she know?'

Quintus felt stricken. Such a bargain might help them climb to the upper level of society. If so, their family's fate would be changed for ever. The price required made him feel very uncomfortable, however. It didn't help that Aurelia was right beside him, waiting for his response. Quintus didn't want to tell an outright lie, so, ducking his head, he increased his pace. 'Hurry,' he urged. 'Agesandros is leaving us behind.'

She saw through his pretence at once. 'See? You think the same.'

Stung, he stopped.

'Father and Mother married for love. Why shouldn't I?'

'It is our duty to obey their orders. You know that,' said Quintus, feeling awful. 'They know best, and we must accept that.'

Agesandros turned to address them, abruptly ending their conversation. Quintus was relieved to see that they had reached the slave market, which was situated in an open area by the town's south gate. Already it was becoming hard to make oneself heard above the din. Aurelia could do little but fall into an angry silence.

'Here we are,' the Sicilian directed. 'Take it all in.'

Mutely, the siblings obeyed. Although they had seen the market countless times, neither had paid it much heed before. It was part of everyday life, just like the stalls hawking fruit and vegetables, and the butchers selling freshly slaughtered lambs, goats and pigs. Yet, Quintus realised, it *was* different here. These were people on sale. Prisoners of war or criminals for the most part, but people nonetheless.

Hundreds of naked men, women and children were on display, chained or bound together with rope. Chalk coated everyone's feet. Black-, brown- and white-skinned, they were every nationality under the sun. Tall, muscular Gauls with blond hair stood beside short, slender Greeks. Broad-nosed, powerfully built Nubians towered over the wiry figures of Numidians and Egyptians. Full-breasted Gaulish women clustered together beside rangy, narrow-hipped Judaeans and Illyrians. Many were sobbing; some were even wailing with distress. Babies and young children added their cries to that of their mothers. Others, catatonic from their trauma, stared into space. Dealers stalked up and down, loudly extolling the qualities of their merchandise to the plentiful buyers who were wandering between the lines of slaves. On the fringes of the throng, groups of hard-faced, armed men lounged about, a mixture of guards and *fugitivarii*, or slave-catchers.

'The choice is enormous, so you have to know what you want in advance. Otherwise, it would take all day,' said Agesandros. He looked enquiringly at Quintus.

Quintus thought of the tattooed Gaul, whose primary duty had been working in the fields. His skill with the hunting dogs had merely been an added bonus. 'He needs to be young and physically fit. Good teeth are important too.' He paused, thinking.

'Anything else?' Agesandros barked.

Quintus was surprised by the change in the Sicilian, whose usual genial manner had disappeared. 'There should be no obvious infirmities or signs of disease. Hernias, poorly healed fractures, dirty wounds and so on.'

Aurelia screwed up her face in distaste.

'Is that it?'

Irritated, Quintus shook his head. 'Yes, I think so.'

Agesandros pulled out his dagger, and Aurelia gasped. 'You're forgetting the most important thing,' the Sicilian said, raising the blade. 'Look in his eyes, and decide how much spirit he has. Ask yourself: will this whoreson ever try to cut my throat? If you think he might, walk away and choose another. Otherwise you might regret it one dark night.'

'Wise words,' Quintus said, levelly. Now, put him on the back foot, he thought. 'What did my father think when he looked in your eyes?'

It was Agesandros' turn to be surprised. His eyes flickered, and he lowered the dagger. 'I believe he saw another soldier,' he answered curtly. Turning on his heel, he plunged into the crowd. 'Follow me.'

'He's just playing games, that's all. Trying to impress me,' Quintus lied

74

to Aurelia. He actually reckoned that Agesandros had been trying to scare him. It had partially worked too. The only reply he got, though, was a scowl. His sister was still angry with him for not telling her what he thought of her chances of happiness in an arranged marriage. Quintus walked off. *I'll sort it out later.*

The Sicilian ignored the first slaves on offer, and then stopped by a line of Nubians, poking and prodding several, and even opening the mouth of one. Their owner, a scrawny Phoenician with gold earrings, instantly scuttled to Agesandros' side, and began waxing lyrical about their quality. Quintus joined them, leaving Aurelia to simmer in the background. After a moment, Agesandros moved on, ignoring the Phoenician's offers. 'Every tooth in that Nubian's head was rotten,' he muttered to Quintus. 'He wouldn't last more than a few years.'

They wandered up and down for some time. The Sicilian said less and less, allowing Quintus to decide which individuals fitted the bill. He found several, but with each Agesandros found a reason not to buy. Quintus decided to stand his ground when he found the next suitable slave. A moment later, two dark-skinned young men with tightly curled black hair caught his eye. He hadn't noticed them before. Neither was especially tall, but both were well muscled. One kept his gaze firmly directed at the ground, while the other, who had a snub nose and green eyes, glanced at Quintus, before looking away. He paused to assess the pair. There was enough spare chain for the slaves to step out of line. Beckoning the first forward, Quintus began his examination, watched closely by the Sicilian.

The youth was about his age, in excellent physical condition, with a good set of teeth. Nothing he did made the slave look at him, which increased his interest. Agesandros' warning was still fresh in his mind, so Quintus grabbed the other's chin and lifted it. Startlingly, the slave's eyes were a vivid green colour, like those of his companion. Quintus saw no defiance there, just an inconsolable sadness. He's perfect, he thought. 'I'll take this one,' he said to Agesandros. 'He meets your requirements.'

The Sicilian glanced the youth up and down. 'Where are you from?' he demanded in Latin.

The slave blinked, but did not answer.

He understood that question, thought Quintus with surprise.

Agesandros appeared not to have noticed, though. He repeated his question in Greek.

Again no reply.

Sensing their interest, the dealer, a dour Latin, moved in. 'He's Carthaginian. His friend too. Strong as oxen.'

'Guggas, eh?' Agesandros spat on the ground. 'They'll be no damn use.'

Quintus and Aurelia were both shocked at the change in his demeanour. The abusive term meant 'little rat'. Immediately, Agesandros' past came to Quintus' mind. It was Carthaginians who had sold the Sicilian into slavery. That wasn't a reason not to buy the slave, however.

'There's been a lot of interest in them this morning,' said the dealer persuasively. 'Good gladiator material, they are.'

'You haven't managed to sell them, though,' replied Quintus sarcastically; beside him, Agesandros snorted in agreement. 'How much are you asking?'

'Solinus is an honest man. 150 didrachms each, or 300 for the pair.'

Quintus laughed. 'Nearly twice the price of a farm slave.' He made to leave. His face a cold mask, Agesandros did too. Then Quintus paused. He was growing tired of the Sicilian's negative attitude. The Carthaginian *was* as good as any of the others he'd seen. If he could barter the Solinus down, why not buy him? He turned. 'We only need one,' he barked. The slaves glanced fearfully at each other, confirming Quintus' hunch that they spoke Latin.

The Solinus grinned, revealing an array of rotten teeth. 'Which?'

Ignoring Agesandros' frown, Quintus pointed at the slave he'd examined.

The Latin leered. 'How does 140 didrachms sound?'

Quintus made a dismissive gesture. 'One hundred.'

Solinus' face turned hard. 'I have to make a living,' he growled. '130. That's my best price.'

'I could go ten didrachms more, but that's it,' said Quintus.

Solinus shook his head vehemently.

Quintus was incensed by Agesandros' delighted look. 'I'll give you 125,' he snapped.

Agesandros leaned in close. 'I haven't got that much,' he muttered sourly.

'I'll sell the bear pelt, then. That's worth at least twenty-five didrachms,'

Quintus retorted. He'd planned on using it as a bed cover, but winning this situation came first.

Suddenly keen, Solinus stepped forward. 'It's a fair price,' he said.

Agesandros' fists closed over the purse.

'Give it to him,' ordered Quintus. When the Sicilian did not react, his anger boiled over. 'I am the master here. Do as I say!'

Reluctantly, Agesandros obeyed.

The small victory pleased Quintus no end. 'That's a hundred. My man here will bring the rest later,' he said.

Even as he pocketed the money, Solinus' mouth opened in protest.

'My father is Gaius Fabricius, an equestrian,' Quintus growled. 'The balance will be paid before nightfall.'

Solinus backed off at once. 'Of course, of course.' Pulling a bunch of keys from his belt, he selected one. He reached up to the iron ring around the Carthaginian's neck. There was a soft click, and the slave stumbled forward, freed.

For the first time, Aurelia looked at him. I have never seen anyone so handsome, she thought, her heart pounding at the sight of his naked flesh.

The Carthaginian's dazed expression told Quintus that he hadn't quite taken in what was happening. It was only when his companion muttered something urgent in Carthaginian that the realisation sank in. Tears welled in his eyes, and he turned to Quintus.

'Buy my friend as well, please,' he said in fluent Latin.

I was right, thought Quintus triumphantly. 'You speak my language.'

'Yes.'

Agesandros glowered, but the siblings ignored him.

'How come?' Aurelia asked.

'My father insisted I learn it. Greek too.'

Aurelia was fascinated, while Quintus was delighted. He had made a good choice. 'What's your name?'

'Hanno,' the Carthaginian answered. He indicated his comrade. 'That's Suniaton. He's my best friend.'

'Why didn't you answer the overseer's question?'

For the first time, Hanno met his gaze. 'Would you?'

Quintus was thrown by his directness. 'No . . . I suppose not.'

Encouraged, Hanno turned to Aurelia. 'Buy us both – I beg you. Otherwise my friend could be sold as a gladiator.'

Quintus and Aurelia glanced at each other in surprise. This was no peasant from a faraway land. Hanno was well educated, and from a good family. So was his friend. It was a bizarre, and uncomfortable, feeling.

'We require one slave. Not two.' Agesandros' clarion voice was a harsh call back to reality.

'We could come to some arrangement, I'm sure,' said Solinus ingratiatingly.

'No, we couldn't,' the Sicilian snarled, cowing him into submission. He addressed Quintus. 'The last thing the farm needs is an extra mouth to feed. Your father will already want to know why we spent so much. Best not blow any more of his money, eh?'

Quintus wanted to argue, but Agesandros was right. They only needed one slave. He gave Aurelia a helpless look. Her tiny, anguished shrug told him she felt the same way. 'There's nothing I can do,' he said to Hanno.

The smirk of satisfaction that flickered across Agesandros' lips went unnoticed by all except Hanno.

The two slaves exchanged a long glance, laden with feeling. 'May the gods guide your path,' Hanno said in Carthaginian. 'Stay strong. I will pray for you every day.'

Suniaton's chin trembled. 'If you ever get home, tell my father that I am sorry,' he said in an undertone. 'Ask him for his forgiveness.'

'I swear it,' vowed Hanno, his voice choking. 'And he will grant it, you may be sure of that.'

Quintus and Aurelia could not speak Carthaginian but it was impossible to misunderstand the overwhelming emotion passing between the two slaves. Quintus took his sister's arm. 'Come on,' he said. 'We can't buy every slave in the market.' He led her away, without looking at Suniaton again.

Agesandros waited until they were out of earshot, then he whispered venomously in Hanno's ear, in Carthaginian. 'It wasn't my choice to buy a gugga. But now you and I are going to have a pleasant time on the farm. Don't think you can run away either. See those types over there?'

Hanno studied the gang of unshaven, roughly dressed men some distance away. Every one was heavily armed, and they were watching the proceedings like hawks.

'They are fugitivarii,' Agesandros explained. 'For the right price, they'll track down any man. Bring him back alive, or dead. With his balls, or without. Even in little pieces. Is that clear?'

'Yes.' A leaden feeling of dread filled Hanno's belly.

'Good. We understand each other.' The Sicilian grinned. 'Follow me.' He strode off after Quintus and Aurelia.

Hanno turned to look at Suniaton one last time. His heart felt as if it was going to rip apart. It hurt even to breathe. Whatever his fate, Suni's would undoubtedly be worse.

'You can't help me,' Suniaton mouthed. Remarkably, his face was calm. 'Go.'

Hot tears blinded Hanno at last. He turned and stumbled away.

Chapter V: Malchus

Carthage

In what had become his daily routine, Malchus finished his breakfast and left the house. Although Bostar had already shipped for Iberia, Sapho was still at home. However, he mostly stayed at his rooms in the garrison's quarters. When Sapho did call by, it was rare for him even to mention Hanno, which Malchus found slightly odd. It was his eldest son's way of dealing with bereavement, he supposed. His was to shun all human contact. It meant that apart from the rare occasions when he had visitors, Malchus' only companions were the domestic slaves. It had been thus since Hanno's disappearance a few weeks before. Scared of Malchus' fierce temper and obvious sorrow, the slaves tiptoed around, trying not to attract his attention. In consequence, Malchus was even more aware of – and annoyed by them. While he longed to lash out, the slaves were not to blame, so he bit down on his anger, bottling it up. Yet he could not bear to stay indoors, staring at the four walls, obsessed with thoughts of Hanno, his beloved youngest son – his favourite son – whom he would never see again.

Malchus headed towards the city's twin harbours. Alone. The adage that one's grief eased with time was utter nonsense, he thought bitterly. In fact, it grew by the day. Sometimes he wondered if his sorrow would overcome him. Render him unable to carry on. A moment later, Malchus caught sight of Bodesmun. He cursed under his breath. He found it increasingly hard even to look at Suniaton's father. The opposite seemed true of the priest, who sought him out at every opportunity.

Bodesmun raised a solemn hand in greeting. 'Malchus. How are you today?'

Malchus scowled. 'The same. And you?'

Bodesmun's face crumpled with anguish. 'Not good.'

Malchus sighed. The same thing happened every time they met. Priests were supposed to lead by example, not crack under pressure. He had enough problems of his own without having to deal with Bodesmun's too. Was he not carrying the weight of two losses on his shoulders? Malchus' rational side knew that he was not responsible for the death of either Arishat, his wife, or Hanno, but the rest of him did not. During the frequent nights when he lay awake, Malchus had become painfully aware that his self-righteousness was partly to blame for Hanno's bad behaviour. After Arishat's death, he had become somewhat of a fanatic, interested in nothing except Hannibal Barca's plans for the future. There had been no brightness or light in the house, no laughter or fun. Sapho and Bostar, already adult men, had not been so affected by his melancholy, but it had hit Hanno hard. Since that realisation, guilt had clawed at Malchus constantly. I should have spent more time with him, he thought. Even gone fishing, instead of droning on about ancient battles. 'It's hard,' he said, doing his best to be sympathetic. He ushered the priest out of the way of a passing cart. 'Very hard.'

'The pain,' Bodesmun whispered miserably. 'It just gets worse.'

'I know,' Malchus agreed. 'There are only two things I know of that make it ease somewhat.'

A spark of interest lit in Bodesmun's sorrowful brown eyes. 'Tell me, please.'

'The first is my loathing of Rome and everything it stands for,' Malchus spat. 'For years, it seemed that the opportunity for revenge would never come. Hannibal has changed all this. At last, Carthage has a chance at settling the score!'

'It's more than two decades since the war in Sicily ended,' Bodesmun protested. 'More than a generation.'

'That's right.' Malchus could remember how weakened the flames of his hatred had been before Hannibal's emergence on to the scene. Now, they had been fanned white-hot by his grief for Hanno. 'Even greater reason not to forget.'

'That can be of no help to me. Begetting violence is not Eshmoun's way,' Bodesmun murmured. 'What's your other means of coping?'

'I scour the streets near the merchant port, listening to conversations and studying faces,' Malchus answered. Seeing the confusion on the other's face, he explained. 'Looking for a clue, the smallest snippet of information, anything that might help to ascertain what happened to Hanno and Suni.'

Bodesmun looked baffled. 'But we know what took place. The old man told us.'

'I know,' Malchus muttered, embarrassed at having to reveal his innermost secret. He had spent a fortune on sacrifices to Melqart, the 'King of the City', his sole request being that the god had somehow seen a way to prevent the boys' boat from sinking. Of course, he'd had no answer, but he wouldn't give up. 'It's just possible that they might be alive. That someone found them.'

Bodesmun's eyes widened. 'That's a dangerous thing to go on believing,' he said. 'Be careful.'

Malchus' nod was brittle. 'How do you go on?'

Bodesmun looked up at the sky. 'I pray to my god. I ask him to look after them both in paradise.'

That was too much for Malchus. Too final. 'I have to go,' he muttered. He strode off, leaving a forlorn Bodesmun in his wake.

A short while later, Malchus reached the Agora. Seeing large numbers of senators and politicians, he cursed. He'd forgotten that there was an important debate on this morning. He considered changing his plans and attending, but decided against it. The majority in the Senate now backed Hannibal solidly, and this was unlikely to change in the foreseeable future. As well as restoring Carthaginian pride with his conquests of Iberian tribes and intimidation of Saguntum, a Roman ally, Hannibal had helped to restore the city's wealth. Although his long-term plans weren't common knowledge, there could be few elders who didn't suspect the truth.

Catching sight of Hostus, Malchus' lip curled. He for one thought war against Rome was coming, and was forever speaking out against it. The fool, thought Malchus. As Carthage's prosperity and pride returned, so conflict with Rome was inevitable. The annexation of Sardinia was a primary reason, and just one example of the wrongs visited upon his people by the Republic. In recent years it had continued to treat them in a disrespectful manner. Constantly sending snooping embassies to Iberia, where it had no jurisdiction, Rome had forged an alliance with Saguntum, a Greek city many hundreds of miles from Italy. It had then had the effrontery to impose a unilateral treaty on Carthage, forcing it not to expand its territories northwards towards Gaul.

Deep in thought, Malchus did not see Hostus recognise him. By the time the fat man had waddled self-importantly to his side, it was too late to get away. Cursing his decision to take the shorter route to the harbours, Malchus gave Hostus a curt nod.

Hostus flashed a greasy smile. 'Not coming to the debate this morning?'

'No.' Malchus tried to brush past.

Moving adroitly for his size, Hostus blocked the way. 'We have noted your absence in the chamber of late. Missed your valuable insights.'

Malchus stopped in his tracks. Hostus wouldn't care if he died, let alone wasn't present at council meetings. He fixed the other with a flinty stare. 'What do you want?'

'I know that of late you have had more important things than Carthage on your mind.' Hostus leered. 'Family matters.'

Malchus wanted to choke Hostus until his eyeballs popped out, but he knew that would be rising to the bait. 'Of course you always act for the good of Carthage,' he snapped. 'Never for the silver from the Iberian mines.'

A tinge of colour reddened Hostus' round cheeks. 'The city has no more loyal servant than I,' he blustered.

Malchus had had enough. He elbowed past without another word.

Hostus wasn't finished. 'If you tire of visiting Melqart's temple, there is always the Tophet of Baal Hammon.'

Malchus spun around. 'What did you say?'

'You heard me.' Hostus' smile was more of a grimace. 'You may have only livestock to offer, but there are plenty in the slums who will sell a newborn or young child for a handful of coins.' Seeing Malchus' temper rising, Hostus gave him a reproving look. 'Such sacrifices have saved Carthage before. Who is to say a suitable offering would not please Baal Hammon and bring your son back?'

Hostus' barbed taunt sank deep, but Malchus knew that the best form of defence was attack. Give the dog no satisfaction. 'Hanno is dead,' he hissed. 'Any fool knows that.'

Hostus flinched.

Malchus poked a finger in his chest. 'Unlike you, I would not murder another's child to make a request of a god. Nor would I have ever offered my own, unlike some around here. To do so is the mark of a savage. Not of someone who truly loves Carthage and would lay down his own life for it.' Leaving Hostus gaping in his wake, Malchus stalked off.

His patrol of the port area that morning yielded nothing. It was little more than Malchus had come to expect. He had overheard talk of the weather conditions between Carthage and Sicily, the most auspicious place to make an offering to the Scylla, and an argument over which of the city's whorehouses was best. He'd seen merchant captains holding guarded conversations, trying to glean information from each other without giving away any of their own, and drunken sailors singing as they weaved back to their ships. Housewives sat in the open doorways of their houses, working their spinning wheels, but the whores had gone to bed. Trickles of smoke rose from the chimneys of the pottery kilns a short distance away. The open-fronted taverns that dotted the streets weren't busy at this time of day, but the stalls selling fresh bread were a different story. Stopping to buy a loaf, Malchus ran into an acquaintance, a crippled veteran of the war in Sicily whom he paid to listen out for any interesting news. So far, the man had provided him with nothing.

Nonetheless, Malchus paid for the other's bread. It didn't cost much to retain the goodwill of the poor, something Hostus would never understand. Together they walked down the street, ignoring the urchins who pestered them for a crust. Malchus watched as the cripple devoured his food before silently handing over his own. This too disappeared rapidly. Studying the man's lined, weary face, Malchus wondered if he had ever had a wife and family. Been faced with an offer from a creature like Hostus for one of his children. It didn't bear thinking about, and Malchus was grateful that the dark practices that went on in the Tophet were no longer practised by many.

'Thank you, sir,' mumbled the veteran, wiping crumbs from his lips.

Malchus inclined his head. He waited, out of habit rather than any expectation, for any information.

The veteran coughed uneasily, and scratched at the shiny red stump that was the only remnant of his lower right leg. 'I saw something last night,' he said. 'It was probably nothing.'

Malchus stiffened. 'Tell me.'

'Down on the docks, I noticed a bireme I've never seen before.' The veteran paused. 'That in itself is nothing unusual, but I thought the crew were a bit sharp-looking for ordinary traders. Seemed like they were trying too hard, if you know what I mean, sir? Talking loudly about their goods, and the prices they hoped to get for them.'

Malchus felt his heart begin to beat faster. 'Could you point the ship out?'

'Better than that, sir. I happened to spot the captain and some of his crew this morning. They were in a tavern, maybe four streets away. Much the worse for wear too.' The veteran hesitated, looking awkward.

Even the poorest can have pride, thought Malchus. 'You will be well rewarded.'

Clutching his homemade crutch with renewed vigour, the smiling veteran hobbled off.

Malchus was one step behind him.

A short time later, they had arrived at the hostelry, a miserable low-roofed brick structure with crudely hewn benches and tables arrayed outside. Although it was early, this tavern was packed. Sailors, merchants and lowlifes of every nationality under the sun sat cheek by jowl with each other, swigging from clay cups or singing out of tune. Prostitutes with painted faces were sitting on men's laps, whispering in their ears in an attempt to win some business. Amidst the pieces of broken pottery littering the sawdust-covered ground, scrawny mongrels fought over half-gnawed bones. Malchus' stomach turned at the stench of cheap wine and urine, but he followed the veteran to an empty table. They both took a seat. Neither looked at the other customers. Instead they occupied themselves by trying to attract the attention of the tavern keeper or his assistant, a rough-looking woman in a low-cut dress.

Finally, they succeeded. A glazed red jug and two beakers arrived at the table soon after, borne by the owner. He cast an idle glance at the mismatched pair, but was called away before he could decide what to make of them. The veteran poured the wine, and handed a cup to Malchus.

He took a sip, and wrinkled his face with disgust. 'This is worse than horse piss.'

The veteran took a deep swallow. He gave an apologetic shrug. 'Tastes fine to me, sir.'

There was silence then, and the customers' din washed over them.

'They're right behind me,' whispered the veteran at length. 'Four men. One looks like an Egyptian. Another is the ugliest man you've ever seen, with scars all over his mug. The others could be Greek. Do you see them?'

Casually, Malchus glanced over the other's shoulder. At the next table, he saw a thin, pale-skinned figure with black hair sitting beside a barrel of a man whose scarred features could have been carved from granite. Their two companions had their backs towards Malchus, but he could see from their dark skin and raven hair that the veteran's guess at their nationality was probably correct. Dressed in ochre and grey woollen tunics, with daggers at their belts, the quartet were similar to many of the other customers. And yet they weren't. Malchus studied them carefully from the corner of his eye. Their faces were cruel, almost hatchet-like. Not the faces of merchants.

Gradually, Malchus began to discern their voices from the others around them. They were speaking in Greek, which was not unusual when individuals of more than one nationality crewed together. It was, after all, the predominant language used at sea. 'It's good to visit a big city at last,' mumbled one of the men with his back to Malchus. 'Not like where we usually berth. At least here there's more than one tavern to visit.'

'Plenty of whorehouses too, with decent-looking women,' growled the figure beside him.

'And boys,' added the scarred man with a leer.

The Egyptian laughed unpleasantly. 'Never change, do you, Varsaco?'

Varsaco smirked. He lowered his voice slightly. 'I just want a piece of Carthaginian arse.'

The Egyptian wagged a reproachful finger.

One of their companions sniggered, and Varsaco scowled.

'You've got a long memory,' said the last man. 'Is this revenge for the one that got away?'

'Watch your mouth,' the Egyptian snarled, confirming Malchus' suspicion that he was the leader of the group. A subdued silence fell for a moment before Varsaco and the Egyptian began whispering to each other. They cast frequent glances at the other tables.

At once, Malchus looked down. Carefully, he considered what he'd heard and seen. The men did not visit cities often. They looked a lot tougher

than merchants should do. The veteran thought the same of their ship-
mates. Tellingly, they had had a Carthaginian crewmember in the recent
past. Or had he been a prisoner? Alarm bells were now ringing in Malchus'
mind. Not once since Hanno's disappearance had he had anything to go
on like this. It wasn't much, but Malchus didn't care. Sliding a coin across
the table with a fingertip, he watched the veteran's eyes widen. 'Stay here,'
he whispered. 'If I haven't returned by the time they leave, follow them.
Use a street urchin to bring me news of their location.'

'Where are you going?'

Malchus' smile was mirthless. 'To get some help.'

Malchus went straight to Sapho's commanding officer. His status was such
that the captain fell over himself to be of assistance. At once, a dozen
Libyan spearmen were put at Malchus' disposal. Although they had little
idea of their mission, the men liked the sound of escaping weapons drill.

Sapho had been asleep when Malchus arrived, but the mention of possible
news about Hanno sent him leaping from his bed. While Bostar had the
guilt of knowing he should have made Hanno and Suniaton stay in the
city, Sapho was saddled with the fact that he should not have given way.
His darkest secret was that part of him was glad that Hanno was gone.
Hanno had never done what Malchus wanted, while he, Sapho, did everything according to the book. Yet it was Hanno who had made their father's
eyes light up. Of course Bostar knew nothing of Sapho's feelings.
Unsurprisingly, the two brothers had fallen out over the matter anyway,
and it hadn't been long before they were barely speaking. The issue had
only subsided with Bostar's recent departure for Iberia. Hearing Malchus'
news scraped raw Sapho's guilt. As he threw on his long tunic and bronze
muscled cuirass, and donned his Thracian helmet and greaves, he
bombarded his father with questions. Malchus had the answers to almost
none of them.

'The sooner we get down there, the sooner we'll find out something,'
he growled.

Half an hour after he'd left the tavern, Malchus returned with Sapho
and the spearmen in tow. The Libyans wore simple conical bronze helmets,
and each was clad in a beltless, knee-length red tunic. They were armed
with short thrusting spears.

Malchus was mightily relieved to see that the veteran and the four men he'd been watching over were still at their respective tables. The Greeks were dozing; Varsaco was talking to the Egyptian. As Malchus and his companions came to a halt outside the tavern, the two sailors looked around. Their faces twisted briefly with concern, but they did not move a muscle.

'Where are they?' demanded Sapho.

There was no need for concealment any longer. Malchus pointed. He was delighted when the Egyptian and Varsaco jumped to their feet and tried to escape. 'Seize them,' he shouted.

The soldiers swarmed forward and surrounded the pair with a circle of threatening spear points. The two sleeping men were kicked awake and heaved into the ring with their companions. All four were forced to throw down their daggers. Ignoring the bleary stares of the other customers, Malchus stalked forward and into view.

'What's this about?' asked the Egyptian in fluent Carthaginian. 'We've done nothing wrong.'

'I'll be the one to decide on that,' replied Malchus. He jerked his head.

'Back to the barracks,' Sapho ordered. 'Quickly!'

The veteran looked on in amazement as the captives were escorted away. A metallic clunk drew his attention back to the table surface. On it lay four gold coins, their faces decorated with the image of Hannibal Barca.

'One for each of the whoresons,' said Malchus. 'If they turn out to be the right men, I'll give you the same again.' Leaving the veteran stuttering his thanks, he followed Sapho and the soldiers.

There was urgent business to attend to.

It didn't take long to reach the Libyans' quarters, which were located east of the Agora, in the wall that faced on to the sea. Whole series of rooms, on two tiers, stretched for hundreds of paces in either direction. Dormitories led to eating and bathing areas. Officers' quarters were situated beside armouries, administrative and quartermasters' offices. Like any military base, there were also cells. It was to these last that Sapho guided the spearmen. Nodding in a friendly manner at the gaolers, he directed the party into a large room with a plain concrete floor. It was empty apart from the sets of manacles that hung from rings on the wall, a glowing brazier and a table covered in a variety of lethal-looking metal instruments and tools.

As the last man entered, Sapho slammed the door shut and locked it.

'Chain them up,' ordered Malchus.

As one, the soldiers placed their spears aside, and turned on the prisoners. Struggling uselessly, the four were restrained side by side. Terror filled the two Greeks' eyes, and they began to wail. Varsaco and the Egyptian tried to maintain their composure, filling the air with questions and pleas. Studying the implements on the table, Malchus ignored them until silence fell.

'What are you doing in Carthage?'

'We're traders,' muttered the Egyptian. 'Honest men.'

'Really?' Malchus' tone was light and friendly.

The Egyptian looked confused. 'Yes.'

Malchus stared at the faces of the Egyptian's companions. He turned to Sapho. 'Well?'

'I think he's lying.'

'So do I.' Malchus' intuition was screaming at him now. These were definitely no merchants. The idea that they might know something about Hanno became all-consuming. Malchus wanted information. Fast. How they obtained it was immaterial. He indicated one of the Greeks. 'Break his arms and legs.'

Clenching his jaw, Sapho picked up a lump hammer. He moved to stand in front of the man Malchus had indicated, who was now moaning in fear. Silently, Sapho delivered a flurry of blows, smashing first the Greek's arms, and then his lower legs, against the wall. His victim's screams made a thin, cracked sound that reverberated throughout the room.

It took a long time, but Malchus waited until the man's cries had died to a low moaning. 'A different question this time,' he said coldly. 'Who was the Carthaginian you were talking about earlier?'

The Egyptian shot a venomous glance at Varsaco.

A surge of adrenaline surged through Malchus. He waited, but there was no response. 'Well?'

'He was nobody, just one of the crew,' muttered Varsaco fearfully. 'He didn't like my attentions, so he deserted at some shithole settlement on the Numidian coast.'

Again Malchus looked at his son.

'Still lying,' growled Sapho.

'It's the truth,' Varsaco protested. He glanced at the Egyptian. 'Tell him.'

'It is as he says,' the Egyptian agreed with a nervous laugh. 'The boy ran away.'

'What kind of fool do you take me for? There's far more to it than that,' snapped Malchus. He pointed at Varsaco. 'Cut his balls off.'

Sapho laid down his hammer and picked up a long, curved dagger.

'No,' pleaded Varsaco. 'Please.'

Stone-faced, Sapho unbuckled Varsaco's belt and threw it to the floor. Next, he cut away the bottom of his tunic, exposing his linen undergarment. Sliding the blade underneath the fabric on each side of Varsaco's groin, Sapho slit it from top to bottom. The garment dropped to the floor, leaving Varsaco naked from the waist down, and gibbering with fear. 'There were two of them,' he babbled, squirming this way and that. 'They were adrift off the coast of Sicily.'

The Egyptian's visage twisted with fury. 'Shut up, you fool! You'll only make things worse.'

Varsaco ignored him. Tears were running down his scarred cheeks. 'I'll tell you everything,' he whispered.

Sapho began to feel very guilty indeed. Taking in a shuddering breath, he looked over his shoulder.

Malchus motioned his son to stand back. Volcanic emotions swept through him. The walls came pressing in, and he could feel the blood rushing in his ears. 'Speak,' he commanded.

Varsaco nodded eagerly. 'There was a bad storm a few weeks back. We were caught in it, and our bireme nearly sank. We didn't, thank the gods. The next day, we came across an open boat, with two young men in it.'

Sapho leaped up and placed his dagger across Varsaco's throat. 'Where were they from?' he screamed. 'What were their names?'

'They came from Carthage.' Varsaco's eyes flickered like those of a cornered rat. 'I don't remember what they were called.'

Malchus grew very calm. 'What did they look like?' he asked quietly.

'One was tall, and had an athletic build. The other was shorter. Both had black hair.' Varsaco thought for a moment. 'And green eyes.'

'Hanno and Suniaton!' Sapho's face twisted with anguish. Despite his relief at Hanno's disappearance, he couldn't bear that this might be the dreadful truth.

Malchus felt physically sick. 'What did you do with them?'

Varsaco turned a pasty shade of grey. 'Naturally, we were going to return them to Carthage,' he stammered. 'But the ship had sprung a leak during the storm. We had to make for the nearest land, which was Sicily. They disembarked there, in Heraclea, I think it was.' He looked to the Egyptian and received a nod of confirmation. 'Yes, Heraclea.'

'I see.' An icy calm blanketed Malchus. 'If that's the case, why have they not returned? Finding a ship to Carthage from the south coast of Sicily should pose a problem to no man.'

'Who knows? Young lads who have just left home are all the same. Only interested in wine and women.' Varsaco shrugged as nonchalantly as he could.

'"Just left home"?' Malchus shouted. 'You make it sound as if they had chosen to be washed out to sea. That it was a matter of no consequence. If you let them off in Heraclea, then my name is Alexander of Macedon.' He glanced at Sapho. 'Castrate him.'

Sapho lowered his knife.

'Not that, please, not that,' Varsaco shrieked. 'I'll tell the truth!'

Malchus raised his hand, and Sapho paused. 'You've probably guessed by now that you and these other sewer rats are dead men. You have condemned yourself with your own words.' Malchus paused to let his sentence sink in. 'Tell me honestly what you did with my son and his friend, and you'll keep your manhood. Receive a quick death too.'

Varsaco nodded dully in acceptance of his fate. 'We sold them as slaves,' he whispered. 'In Neapolis. We got an excellent price for both, according to the captain. That's why we came to Carthage. To abduct more.'

Malchus took a deep breath. It was much as he had suspected. 'Whom did you sell them to?'

'I don't know,' Varsaco stuttered. 'I wasn't there. The captain did it.' His gaze turned to the Egyptian, who spat contemptuously on the floor.

'So you are the one who is responsible for this outrage?' Cold fury bathed Malchus once more. 'Cut *his* balls off instead,' he roared.

At once Sapho stripped the Egyptian of his clothing. Grabbing hold of the moaning pirate captain's scrotum, he tugged down to draw it taut. Sapho threw a quick glance at Malchus, and received a nod. 'This is for my brother,' he muttered, lining his blade up, praying that the act would assuage his guilt.

'Varsaco was the one who would have raped them,' shouted the Egyptian. 'I stopped him.'

'How good of you,' Malchus snarled. 'You had no problem selling them, though, did you? Who bought them?'

'A Latin. I didn't get his name. He was going to take both to Capua. Sell them as gladiators. I don't know any more.' The Egyptian looked down at Sapho, and then towards Malchus. All he saw from both was an implacable hatred. 'Give me a quick death, like Varsaco,' he pleaded.

'You expect me to keep my word after what you have done to two innocent boys? Those who engage in piracy merit the most terrible fate possible.' Malchus' voice dripped with contempt. He turned to the soldiers. 'You've heard what these scum have done to my boy and his friend.'

An angry growl left the Libyans' throats, and one stood forth. 'What shall we do with them, sir?'

Malchus let his gaze linger on the four pirates, one by one. 'Castrate them all, but cauterise the wounds so they do not bleed to death. Break their arms and legs, and then crucify them. When you're done, find the rest of their crew and do the same to every last one.'

To a background of terrified protests, the spearman snapped off a salute. 'Yes, sir.'

Malchus and Sapho watched impassively as the soldiers set about their task. Dividing into teams of three, they stripped the prisoners with grim purpose. Light flashed off knife blades as they rose and fell. The screaming soon grew so loud that it was impossible to talk, but the soldiers did not pause for breath. Blood ran down the pirates' legs in great streams to congeal in sticky pools on the floor. Next, the stench of burning flesh filled the air as red-hot pokers were used to stem the flow from the prisoners' gaping wounds. The pain of the castration and cautery was so severe that all the pirates passed out. Their respite was brief. A moment later, they were woken by the agony of their bones breaking beneath the blows of hammers. Low repetitive thuds mingled with their shrieks in a new, dreadful cacophony.

Malchus pressed his lips to Sapho's ear. 'I've seen enough. Let's go.'

Even in the corridor outside, with the door closed, the din was incredible. Although it was now possible to talk, father and son looked at each other in silence for long moments.

Malchus spoke first. 'He could still be alive. They both could.' Rare tears glinted in his eyes.

Sapho felt bad for Hanno. Drowning was one thing, but fighting as a gladiator? He hardened his heart. 'They won't be for long. It's a mercy in a way.'

Unaware of Sapho's motivations, Malchus clenched his jaw. 'You're right. We can do no more than to hope that they died well. Let us join Hannibal Barca's army in Iberia, and wage war on Rome. One day, we will bring ruination, fire and death to Capua. Then, vengeance will be ours.'

Sapho looked stunned. 'Hannibal would invade Italy?'

'Yes,' replied Malchus. 'That is his long-term plan. To defeat the enemy on their own soil. I am one of only a handful of men who know this. Now you are another.'

'The secret is safe with me,' whispered Sapho. Obviously, he and Bostar had not been party to all of the information carried by Hannibal's messenger. Finally, he understood his father's threat to raze Capua. 'Our revenge will come one day,' he muttered, thinking of the golden opportunities to prove his worth that would arise.

'Speak after me,' ordered Malchus. 'Before Melqart, Baal Saphon and Baal Hammon, I make this vow. With all my might, I will support Hannibal Barca on his quest. I will find Hanno, or die avenging him.'

Slowly, Sapho repeated the words.

Satisfied, Malchus led the way outside.

The screaming continued unabated behind them.

Chapter VI: Servitude

Near Capua, Campania

Hanno trudged despondently behind Agesandros' mule, swallowing the clouds of dust sent up by those in front. Ahead of the Sicilian was the litter containing Atia and Aurelia, and beyond that, in the lead, were Fabricius and Quintus. It was the morning following his purchase by Quintus, and, after spending the night at Martialis' house, the family was returning to their farm. During their short stay, Hanno had been left in the kitchen with the resident household slaves. Dazed, still unable to believe that he had been separated from Suniaton, he had simply slumped in a corner and wept. Other than placing a loincloth, a beaker of water and a plate of food beside him, no one had offered him any comfort. Hanno would remember their curious stares afterwards, however. No doubt it was something they had all seen countless times before: the new slave, who realises that his life will never be the same again. It had probably happened to most of them. Mercifully, sleep had finally found Hanno. His rest had been fitful, but it had provided him with an escape of sorts: the possibility of denying reality.

Now, in the cold light of day, he had to face up to it.

He belonged to Quintus' father, Fabricius. Like his family, Suni was gone for ever.

Hanno still didn't know what to make of his master. Since a cursory examination when they had first returned to Martialis' house, Fabricius had paid him little heed. He had accepted his son's explanation that, because of his literacy and skill with languages, the Carthaginian was worth his high purchase price, the balance of which Quintus was paying anyway. 'It's your business the way you spend your money,' he'd said. He seemed decent enough, thought Hanno, as did Quintus. Aurelia was but a child. Atia, Fabricius' wife, was an unknown quantity. So far, she'd barely even looked at him, but Hanno hoped that she would prove a fair mistress.

It was strange to be considering people whom he'd always considered evil as normal, yet it was Agesandros whom Hanno was most concerned about. The Sicilian had taken a set against him from the beginning. For all his concerns, at least his own situation had a positive side to it, for which he felt immensely guilty. Suniaton's fate still hung by a thread, and Hanno could only ask every god he knew to intercede on his friend's behalf. At the worst, to let him die bravely.

Hearing the word 'Saguntum' mentioned, he pricked his ears. A Greek city in Iberia, allied to the Republic, it had been the focus of Hannibal's attention for months. Indeed, it was where the war on Rome would start.

'I thought that the Senate had decided there was no real threat to Saguntum?' asked Quintus. 'After the Saguntines had demanded recompense for the attacks on their lands, all Hannibal did was to send them a rudely worded reply.'

Hanno hid his smirk. He'd heard that insult several weeks before, at home. 'Scabby, flea-bitten savages,' Hannibal had called the city's residents. As everyone in Carthage knew, the rebuttal presaged his real plan: an attack on Saguntum.

'Politicians sometimes underestimate generals,' said Fabricius heavily. 'Hannibal has done far more than issue threats now. According to the latest news, Saguntum is surrounded by his army. They've started building fortifications. It's going to be a siege. Carthage has finally regained its bite.'

Quintus threw an angry glance at Hanno, who looked down at once. 'Can nothing be done?'

'Not this campaigning season,' Fabricius replied crossly. 'Hannibal couldn't have picked a better moment. Both the consular armies are committed to the East, and the threat there.'

'You mean Demetrius of Pharos?' asked Quintus.

'Yes.'

'Wasn't he an ally of ours until recently?'

'He was. Then the miserable dog decided that piracy is more profitable. Our entire eastern seaboard has been affected. He's been threatening Illyrian cities under the Republic's protection too. But the trouble should be over by the autumn. Demetrius' forces have no chance against four legions and double that number of socii.'

Quintus couldn't hide his disappointment. 'I'll miss it all.'

'Never fear. There'll always be another war,' said his father with an amused smile. 'You'll get your turn soon enough.'

Quintus was partly mollified. 'Meanwhile, Saguntum just gets left to hang in the wind?'

'It's not right, I know,' his father replied. 'But the main faction in the Senate has decided that this is the course we shall follow. The rest of us have to obey.'

So much for Roman *fides*, thought Hanno contemptuously.

Father and son rode in silence for a few moments.

'What will the Senate do if Saguntum falls?' probed Quintus.

'Demand that the Carthaginians withdraw, I imagine. As well as hand over Hannibal.'

Quintus' eyebrows rose. 'Would they do that?'

Never, thought Hanno furiously.

'I don't think so,' Fabricius replied. 'Even the Carthaginians have their pride. Besides, their Council of Elders will have known about Hannibal's plan to besiege Saguntum. They're hardly going to offer their support on that only to withdraw it immediately afterwards.'

Unseen, Hanno spat on to the road. 'Damn right they're not,' he whispered.

'Then war is unavoidable,' Quintus cried. 'The Senate won't take an insult like that lying down.'

Fabricius sighed. 'No, it won't, even though it's partly to blame for the whole situation. The indemnities forced on Carthage at the end of the last war were ruinous, but the seizure of Sardinia soon after was even worse. There was no excuse for it.'

Hanno could scarcely believe what he was hearing: a Roman express regret for what had been done to his people. Perhaps they weren't all monsters? he wondered for the second time. His gut reaction weighed in at once. *They are still the enemy.*

'That conflict was a generation ago,' said Quintus, bridling. 'This is now. Even if it comes late, Rome has to defend one of her allies who has been attacked without due cause.'

Fabricius inclined his head. 'She does.'

'So war with Carthage is coming, one way or another,' said Quintus. He threw a further look at Hanno, who affected not to notice.

'Probably,' Fabricius replied. 'Not this year perhaps, but next.'

'I could be part of that!' Quintus cried eagerly. 'But I want to know how to use a sword properly first.'

'You're proficient with both bow and spear,' admitted Fabricius. He paused, aware that Quintus was hanging on his every word. 'Strictly speaking, of course, it's not necessary for the cavalry, but I suppose a little instruction in the use of the gladius wouldn't go amiss.'

Quintus' grin stretched from ear to ear. 'Thank you, Father.' He raised a hand to his mouth. 'Mother! Aurelia! Did you hear that? I am to become a swordsman.'

'That's good news indeed.' Coming from the depths of the litter, Atia's voice was muffled, but Quintus thought he detected a tinge of sadness in it.

Aurelia lifted the cloth and stuck her head outside. 'How wonderful,' she said, forcing a smile. Inside, she was consumed by jealousy.

'We'll start tomorrow,' said Fabricius.

'Excellent!' Instantly, Quintus forgot both his mother and Aurelia's reactions. His head was full of images of him and Gaius serving in the cavalry, winning glory for themselves and Rome.

Despite his guilt over Suniaton, Hanno's spirits had also risen. While he had Agesandros to contend with, he was not destined to die as a gladiator. And, although he might not be able to take part, his people were about to take on Rome again, with Hannibal Barca to lead them. A man whom his father reckoned to be the finest leader Carthage had ever seen.

For the first time in days, a spark of hope lit in Hanno's heart.

One summer morning, word came from the port that Malchus and Sapho had landed. Bostar shouted with delight at the news. As he hurried through the streets of New Carthage, the city founded by Hasdrubal nine years before, he couldn't stop grinning. Catching a glimpse of the temple of Aesculapius, which stood on the large hill to the east of the walls, Bostar offered up a prayer of thanks to the god of medicine and his followers. If it hadn't been for the injury to his sword arm, sustained in overexcited training with naked blades, he would have already set out for Saguntum with the rest of the army. Instead, on the orders of Alete, his commanding officer, Bostar had had to stay behind. 'I've seen too many wounds like that turn bad,' Alete had muttered. 'Remain here, in the care of the priests, and join us when you've recovered. Saguntum isn't going to fall in a day, or a month.' At the time, Bostar had not been happy. Now, he was overjoyed.

It wasn't long until he'd reached the port, which looked out over the calm gulf beyond New Carthage. The city's location was second to none. Situated at the point of a natural, enclosed bay which was furthest from the Mediterranean, it was surrounded on all sides by water. To the east and south lay the sea, while to the north and west was a large, saltwater lagoon. The only connection with the mainland was a narrow, heavily fortified causeway, which made the city almost impregnable. It was no surprise that New Carthage had replaced Gades as the capital of Carthaginian Iberia.

Bostar sped past the ships nearest the quay. New arrivals would have to moor further away. As always, the place was extremely busy. The vast majority of the army might have left with Hannibal, but troops and supplies were still coming in daily. Javelins clattered off each other as they were laid in piles, and stacks of freshly made helmets glinted in the sun. There were wax-sealed amphorae of olive oil and wine, rolls of cloth and bags of nails. Wooden crates of glazed crockery stood beside bulging bags of nuts. Gossiping sailors coiled ropes and swept the decks of their unloaded vessels. Fishermen who had been out since before dawn sweated as they hauled their catch on to the dock.

'Bostar!'

He craned his head, searching for his family among the dense forest of masts and rigging. Finally, Bostar spotted his father and Sapho on the deck of a trireme that was tied up two vessels from the quay. He vaulted on to the first craft's deck and made his way to meet them. 'Welcome!'

A moment later, they had been reunited. Bostar was shocked by the change in both. They were different men since he'd last seen them. Cold. Hard-faced. Ruthless. He bowed to Malchus, trying not to let his surprise show. 'Father. It is wonderful to see you at last.'

Malchus' severe expression softened briefly. 'Bostar. What happened to your arm?'

'It's a scratch, nothing more. A stupid mistake during training,' he replied. 'Lucky it happened, though, because it's the only reason I'm still here. I receive treatment daily at Aesculapius' temple.' He turned to Sapho, and was surprised to see that his brother looked downright angry. Bostar's hopes for a reconciliation vanished. The rift caused by their argument over releasing Hanno and Suniaton was clearly still present. As if he didn't feel guilty enough, thought Bostar sadly. Instead of an embrace, he saluted. 'Brother.'

Stiffly, Sapho returned the gesture.

'How was your journey?'

'Pleasant enough,' Malchus answered. 'We saw no Roman triremes, which is a blessing.' His face twisted with an unreadable emotion. 'Enough of that. We have discovered what happened to Hanno.'

Bostar blinked with shock. 'What?'

'You heard,' snapped Sapho. 'He and Suni didn't drown.'

Bostar's mouth opened. 'How do you know?'

Malchus took over. 'Because I never lost faith in Melqart, and because I had eyes and ears in the port, who looked and listened out day and night for any clues.' He smiled sourly at Bostar's bafflement. 'A couple of months ago, one of my spies struck gold. He overheard a conversation he thought might interest me. We took the men in for questioning.'

Bostar was riveted by his father's story. Hearing that Hanno and Suniaton had been captured by pirates, he began to weep. Neither of the others did, which only increased his grief. His anguish grew deeper with the revelation of the pair's sale into slavery. *I thought it was a kind gesture to let them go fishing. How wrong I was!* 'That's a worse fate than drowning. They could have been taken anywhere. Bought by anyone.'

'I know,' Sapho snarled. 'They were sold in Italy. Probably as gladiators.'

Bostar's eyes filled with horror. 'No!'

'Yes,' Sapho shot back venomously, 'and it's all your fault. If you had stopped them, Hanno would be standing here beside us today.'

Bostar swelled with indignation. 'That's rich coming from you!'

'Stop it!' Malchus' voice cut in like a whiplash. 'Sapho, you and Bostar came to the decision together, did you not?'

Sapho glowered. 'Yes, Father.'

99

'So you are both responsible, just as I am for not being easier on him.' Malchus ignored his sons' surprise at his admission of complicity. 'Hanno is gone now, and fighting over his memory will serve none of us. I want no more of this. Our task now is to follow Hannibal, and take Saguntum. If we are lucky, the gods will grant us vengeance for Hanno afterwards, in the fight against Rome. We must put everything else from our minds. Clear?'

'Yes, Father,' the brothers mumbled, but neither looked at the other.

Bostar had to ask. 'What did you do to the pirates?'

'They were castrated, and then their limbs were broken. Lastly, the scum were crucified,' Malchus replied in a flat tone. Without another word, he climbed up on to the dock and headed for the city's centre.

Sapho held back until they were alone. 'It was too good for them. We should have gouged out their eyes too,' he added viciously. Despite his apparent enthusiasm, the horror of what he'd seen still lingered in his eyes. Sapho had thought that the punishments would stop him feeling relief at Hanno's disappearance, but he'd been wrong. Seeing his younger brother again rammed that home. I will be the favourite! he thought savagely. 'Just as well that you weren't there. You wouldn't have been up to any of it.'

Despite the implication about his courage, Bostar retained his composure. He wasn't about to pull rank here, now. He was also uncertain what his own reaction might have been if he'd been placed in the same situation, handed the opportunity for revenge on those who had consigned Hanno to a certain death. Deep down, Bostar was glad that he had not been there. He doubted that either his father or Sapho would understand. Melqart, he prayed, I ask that my brother had a good death, and that you allow our family to put aside its differences. Bostar gained small consolation from the prayer, but it was all he had at that moment.

That, and a war to look forward to.

Checking that Agesandros was nowhere in sight, Hanno pulled the mules to a halt. The sweating beasts did not protest. It was nearly midday, and the temperature in the farmyard was scorching. Hanno jerked his head at one of the others who was threshing the wheat with him. 'Water.'

The Gaul made a reflex check for the Sicilian before putting down his pitchfork, and fetching the leather skin which lay by the storage shed. After drinking deeply, he replaced the stopper and tossed it through the air.

Hanno nodded his thanks. He swallowed a dozen mouthfuls, but was careful to leave plenty of the warm liquid for the others. He threw the bag to Cingetorix, another Gaul.

When he was done, Cingetorix wiped his lips with the back of his hand. 'Gods, but it's hot.' He spoke in Latin, which was the only language he and his countrymen had to communicate with Hanno. 'Does it never rain in this cursed place? At home . . .' He wasn't allowed to finish.

'We know,' growled Galba, a short man whose sunburnt torso was covered with swirling tattoos. 'It rains much more. Don't remind us.'

'Not in Carthage,' said Hanno. 'It's as dry there as it is here.'

Cingetorix scowled. 'You must feel right at home then.'

Despite himself, Hanno grinned. For perhaps two months after his arrival, the Gauls, with whom he shared sleeping quarters, had ignored him completely, speaking their own rapid-fire, guttural tongue at all times. He'd done his best to win them over, but it had made no difference. When it came, the change had been gradual. Hanno wasn't sure whether the extra, unwanted attention he received from Agesandros was what had prompted the tribesmen to extend the hand of friendship to him, but he no longer cared. The camaraderie they now shared was what made his existence bearable. That, and the news that Hannibal's iron grip on Saguntum had tightened. Apparently, the city would fall before the end of the year. Hanno prayed for the Carthaginian army's success every night. He also asked that one day he be granted an opportunity to kill Agesandros.

There were five of them in the yard altogether, continuing the work which had begun weeks previously with the harvest. It was late summer, and Hanno had grown used to life on the farm, and the immense labour expected of him every day. Things were made much harder by the heavy iron fetters that had been attached to his ankles, preventing him moving at any speed faster than a shuffle. Hanno had thought he was fit beforehand, but soon realised otherwise. Working twelve or more hours a day in summer heat, wearing manacles and fed barely enough, he was a taut, wiry shadow of his former self. His hair fell in long, shaggy tresses either side of his bearded face. The muscles on his torso and limbs now stood out like whipcord, and every part of exposed skin had darkened to a deep brown colour. The Gauls looked no different. We're like wild beasts, Hanno thought. It was no wonder that they rarely saw Fabricius or his family.

Catching sight of Agesandros in the distance, he whistled the agreed signal to alert his companions. Swiftly, the skin was hurled back to its original position. Hanno dragged his mules into action again, pulling a heavy sledge over the harvested wheat, which had been laid right across the hard-packed dirt of the large farmyard. The Gauls began winnowing the threshed crop, tossing it into the air with their pitchforks so that the breeze could carry away the unwanted chaff. Their tasks were time-consuming and mind-numbing, but they had to be done before the wheat could be shovelled into the back of a wagon and deposited in the nearby storage sheds, which were built on brick stilts to prevent rodent access.

When Agesandros arrived a few moments later, he stood in the shade cast by the buildings and watched them silently. Uneasy, the five slaves worked hard, trying not to look in the Sicilian's direction. Soon a fresh coat of sweat coated their bodies.

Every time he turned the sledge, Hanno caught a glimpse of Agesandros, who was staring relentlessly at him. He was unsurprised when the overseer stalked in his direction.

'You're walking the mules too fast! Slow down, or half the wheat won't come off the stalks.'

Hanno tugged on the nearest animal's lead rope. 'Yes, sir,' he mumbled.

'What's that? I didn't hear you,' Agesandros snarled.

'At once, sir,' Hanno repeated loudly.

'Stinking gugga. You're all the damn same. Useless!' Agesandros drew his whip.

Hanno steeled himself. It didn't seem to matter what he did. The mules' speed was just the latest example. His technique with the scythe and pitchfork, and how long he took to fetch water from the well had also recently been called into question. Everything he did was wrong, and the Sicilian's response was the same every time.

'You're all idle bastards.' Lazily, Agesandros drew the long rawhide lash along the ground. 'Motherless curs. Cowards. Vermin.'

Hanno clicked his tongue at the mules, trying to block out the insults.

'Maybe you did have a mother,' Agesandros admitted. He paused. 'She must have been the most diseased whore in Carthage, though, to spawn something that looks like you.'

Hanno's knuckles tightened with fury on the lead rope, and his shoulders bunched. From the corner of his eye, he saw Galba, who was behind the Sicilian, shaking his head in a gesture that said 'No'. Hanno forced himself to relax, but Agesandros had already seen his barb's effect.

'Didn't like that?' The Sicilian laughed, and raised his right arm. A heartbeat later, the whip came singing in to wrap itself across Hanno's back and under his right armpit. *Crack* went the tip as it opened the skin under his right nipple. The pain was intense. Hanno stiffened, and his pace decreased a fraction. It was all Agesandros needed. 'Did I tell you to slow down?' he screamed. The whip was withdrawn, only to return. Hanno counted three, six, a dozen lashes. Although he did his utmost not to make a sound, eventually he couldn't help but moan.

The overseer smiled at this proof of Hanno's weakness, and ceased. His skill with the lash was such that Hanno was always left in extreme pain, but still able to work. 'That should keep you moving at the right speed,' he said.

'Yes, sir,' Hanno muttered.

Satisfied, Agesandros gave the Gauls a hard stare and made as if to go.

Hanno did not relax. There was always more.

Sure enough, Agesandros turned. 'You'll find your bed softer tonight,' he confided.

Slowly, Hanno raised his gaze to meet that of the Sicilian.

'I've pissed in it for you.'

Hanno did not speak. This was even worse than Agesandros spitting in his food, or halving his water ration. His anger, which had been reduced to a tiny glow in the centre of his soul, was suddenly fanned to a white-hot blaze of outrage and indignation. With supreme effort, he kept his face blank. Now is not the time, he told himself. Wait.

Agesandros sneered. 'Nothing to say?'

I won't give the bastard what he wants, thought Hanno furiously. 'Thank you, sir.'

Cheated, Agesandros snorted and walked away.

'Dirty fucker,' whispered Galba when he was out of earshot. There was a rumble of agreement from the others. 'You can have some of our bedding. We'll replace the wet stuff in the morning in case he checks up on you.'

'Thanks,' muttered Hanno absently. He was imagining running after the overseer and killing him. Thanks to Agesandros' expert needling, his warrior spirit had just reawakened. If he was to meet Suniaton in the next world, he wanted to be able to hold his head up high. Things would come to a head soon, Hanno realised. But it didn't matter. Death would be better than this daily indignity.

Unusually, Quintus found himself at a loose end one fine morning. It had rained overnight, and the temperature was cooler than it had been for many months. Invigorated by the crisp, fresh air, he decided to make amends with Aurelia. Over the previous few months, much to her displeasure, Aurelia had been put in the care of a strict tutor, a sour-faced Greek slave loaned to Atia by Martialis. Rather than roaming the farm as she pleased, nowadays Aurelia had to sit demurely and learn Greek and mathematics. Atia continued to teach her how to weave and sew, and how to comport herself in polite company. Aurelia's protests fell on deaf ears. 'It's time you learned to be a lady, and that's an end to it,' Atia had snapped a number of times. 'If you keep protesting, I'll give you a good whipping.' Aurelia dutifully obeyed, but her stony silences at the dinner table since revealed her true opinion.

Fabricius knew better than to intervene in his wife's business, which left Quintus as Aurelia's only possible ally. However, he felt caught in the middle. While he felt guilty at his sister's plight, he also knew that an arranged marriage was the best thing for the family. All his attempts to lighten her mood failed, and so Quintus began to avoid her company when his day's work was done. Hurt, Aurelia spent more and more time in her room. It was a vicious circle from which there seemed no way out.

Meanwhile Quintus had been fully occupied with the work his father set him: paperwork, errands to Capua and regular lessons in the use of the gladius. Despite the time that had passed, Quintus still missed his sister keenly. He made a snap decision. It was time to make her an apology and move on. They did not have for ever. Although Fabricius had found no suitable husband for Aurelia yet, he had begun the search during his visits to Rome.

Throwing some food into a pack, Quintus headed for the chamber off the courtyard where Aurelia took her lessons. Barely pausing to knock, he entered. The tutor glanced up, a small frown of disapproval creasing his brow. 'Master Quintus. To what do we owe the pleasure?'

Quintus drew himself up to his full height. He was now three fingers width taller than his father, which meant that he towered over most people. 'I am taking Aurelia on a tour of the farm,' he announced grandly.

The tutor looked taken aback. 'Who sanctioned this?'

'I did,' Quintus replied.

The tutor blew out his cheeks with displeasure. 'Your parents—'

'Would approve wholeheartedly. I will explain everything to them later.' Quintus made an airy gesture. 'Come on,' he said to Aurelia.

Her attempt to look angry faded away, and she jumped to her feet. Her writing tablet and stylus clattered unnoticed to the floor, drawing reproving clucks from the tutor. Yet the elderly Greek did not challenge Quintus further, and the siblings made their way outside unhindered.

Since killing the bear, Quintus' confidence had grown leaps and bounds. It felt good. He grinned at Aurelia.

Abruptly, she remembered their feud. 'What's going on?' she cried. 'I haven't seen you for weeks, and then suddenly you barge into my lessons unannounced.'

He took Aurelia's hand. 'I'm sorry for deserting you.' To his horror, tears formed in her eyes, and Quintus realised how hurt she had been. 'Nothing I said seemed to make any difference,' he muttered. 'I couldn't think of a way to help you. Forgive me.'

She smiled through her grief. 'I was at fault too, staying in a mood for days. But come, you're here now.' A mischievous look stole across her face. 'A tour of the farm? What have I not seen a thousand times before?'

'It was all I could think of,' he replied, embarrassed. 'Something to get you out of there.'

Grinning, she nudged him. 'It was enough to shut up the old fool. Thank you. I don't care where we go.'

Arm in arm, they strolled along the path that led to the olive groves.

Hanno could see that Agesandros was in a bad mood. Any slave who so much as missed a step was getting a tongue-lashing. Ten of them were walking ahead of the Sicilian, carrying wicker baskets. Fortunately, Hanno was near the front, which meant that Agesandros was paying him little attention. Their destination was the terraces containing plum trees, the fruit of which had lately, and urgently, become ripe. Picking the juicy crop would be an easy task compared to the work of the previous weeks, and Hanno was looking forward to it. Agesandros could only be so vigilant. Before the day was over, plenty of plums would have ended up in his grumbling belly.

A moment later, he cursed his optimism.

Galba, the man behind him, missed his footing and fell heavily to the ground. There was a grunt of pain, and Hanno turned to see a nasty gash on his comrade's right shin. It had been caused by a sharp piece of rock protruding from the earth. Blood welled in the wound, running down Galba's muscular calf and on to the dry soil, where it was soaked up at once.

'That's your day over,' Hanno said in a low voice.

'I doubt Agesandros would agree,' Galba replied, grimacing. 'Help me up.'

Hanno bent to obey, but it was too late.

Shoving past the other slaves, the Sicilian had reached them in a dozen strides. 'What in the name of Hades is going on?'

'He fell and hurt his leg,' Hanno began to explain.

Agesandros spun around, his eyes like chips of flint. 'Let the piece of shit explain for himself,' he hissed before turning back to Galba. 'Well?'

'It's as he said, sir,' said the Gaul carefully. 'I tripped and landed on this rock.'

'You did it deliberately, to get out of work for a few days,' Agesandros snarled.

'No, sir.'

'Liar!' The Sicilian tugged free his whip and began belabouring Galba.

Hanno's fury overflowed at last. 'Leave him alone,' he shouted. 'He didn't do anything.'

Agesandros delivered several more strokes and a hefty kick before he paused. Nostrils flaring, he glared at Hanno. 'What did you say?'

'Picking plums is an easy job. Why would he try and get out of it?' he growled. 'The man tripped. That's it.'

The Sicilian's eyes opened wide with disbelief and rage. 'You dare to tell me what to do? You piece of maggot-blown filth!'

Hanno would have given anything for a sword in that instant. He had nothing, though, but his anger. In the rush of adrenaline, it felt enough. 'Is that what I am?' he spat back. 'Well, you're nothing but low-born Sicilian scum! Even if my feet were covered in shit, I wouldn't wipe them on you.'

Something inside Agesandros snapped. Raising his whip, he smashed the metal-tipped butt into Hanno's face.

There was a loud crunch and Hanno felt the cartilage in his nose break. Half blinded by the intense pain, he reeled backwards, raising his hands protectively against the blow he knew would follow. He had no opportunity to pick up a rock, anything to defend himself. Agesandros was on him like a lion on its prey. Down came the whip across Hanno's shoulders, its tip licking around to snap into the flesh of his back. It whirled away but came singing back a heartbeat later, lacing cut after cut across his bare torso. He backed away, but the laughing Sicilian followed. When Hanno stumbled on a tree root, Agesandros shoved him in the chest, sending him sprawling. Winded, he could do nothing as the other loomed over him, his face twisted in triumph. A mighty kick in the chest followed, and the ribs broken by Varsaco cracked for the second time. The pain was unbearable and, hating himself, Hanno screamed. Worse was to follow. The beating went on until he was barely conscious. Finally, Agesandros rolled him on to his back. 'Look at me,' he ordered. Prompted by more kicks, Hanno managed to open his eyes. The moment he did, the Sicilian lifted his right leg high, revealing the hobnailed sole of his sandal. 'This is for all my comrades,' he muttered. 'And my family.'

Hanno had no idea what Agesandros was talking about. The bastard is going to kill me, he thought dazedly. Strangely, he didn't really care. At least his suffering would be over. He felt a numbing sense of sorrow that he would never see his family again. There would be no opportunity to apologise to his father either. Let it be so. Resigned, Hanno closed his eyes and waited for Agesandros to end it.

The blow never fell.

Instead, a commanding voice shouted, 'Agesandros! Stop!'

Initially, Hanno didn't grasp what was going on, but when the order was repeated, and he sensed the Sicilian back away, the realisation sank in. Someone had intervened. Who? He lay back on the hard ground, unable to do anything more than draw shallow breaths. Each movement of his ribcage stabbed knives of pain through every part of his being. It was the only thing that kept him from lapsing into unconsciousness. He was aware of Agesandros throwing hate-filled glances in his direction, but the Sicilian did nothing further to him.

A heartbeat later, Quintus and Aurelia, Fabricius' children, appeared at the edge of Hanno's vision. Outrage filled both their faces.

'What have you done?' Aurelia cried, dropping to her knees by Hanno's side. Although the bloodied Carthaginian was almost unrecognisable, her stomach still fluttered at the sight of him.

Hanno tried to smile at her. After Agesandros' cruel features, she resembled a nymph or other suchlike creature.

'Well?' Quintus' voice was stony. 'Explain yourself.'

'Your father leaves the running of the farm, and the care of the slaves, to me,' Agesandros blustered. 'That's the way it has been since before you were born.'

'And if you killed a slave? What would he say then?' Aurelia challenged.

Agesandros was taken aback. 'Come now,' he said in a placating manner. 'I was administering a beating, nothing more.'

Quintus' laugh was derisory. 'You were about to stamp on his head. On this rocky ground, a blow like that could stave a man's skull in.'

Agesandros did not reply.

'Couldn't it?' Quintus demanded. His fury at the Sicilian, who had looked intent on murder, had doubled when he realised the victim's identity. Any residual awe he felt towards Agesandros had evaporated. 'Answer me, by all the gods.'

'I suppose so,' Agesandros admitted sullenly.

'Was that your intention?' Aurelia demanded.

The Sicilian glanced at Hanno. 'No,' he said, folding his arms across his chest. 'My temper got the better of me, that's all.'

Liar, thought Hanno. Above him, Aurelia's face twisted with disbelief, reinforcing his conviction.

Quintus could also see that Agesandros was lying, but to accuse him further would bring the situation into completely uncharted waters. He didn't feel quite that confident. 'How did it happen?'

Agesandros indicated Galba. 'That slave fell deliberately and injured his leg. He was trying to get off work. It's an old trick, and I saw through it at once. I laid a few blows into the dog to teach him a lesson, and the gugga told me to stop, that it had been a genuine accident.' He snorted. 'Such defiance cannot be tolerated. He needed to be taught the error of his ways on the spot.'

Quintus looked down at Hanno. 'I think you succeeded,' he said sarcastically. 'He's halfway to Hades.'

One corner of Agesandros' mouth tugged upwards.

The only one to see it was Hanno. *Agesandros wants me dead. Why?*

It was the last coherent thought he had.

Quintus' confidence was bolstered by his success over Agesandros. Rather than let the injured Hanno be carried back to the villa like a sack of grain as the Sicilian wanted, he insisted that a litter be fetched. Galba could limp alongside. Scowling, Agesandros could do little but obey his command, sending a slave off at the run. The overseer watched with a surly expression as, using a strip of cloth, Aurelia cleaned the worst of the blood from Hanno's face. Tears poured down her cheeks, but she did not make a sound. She would not give Agesandros the satisfaction.

A short time later, when Hanno had been carefully transferred into the litter, she finally stood. A mixture of blood and dust covered the lower half of her dress, from where she had knelt in the dirt. Though reddened, her eyes were full of anger, and her face was set. 'If he dies, I will see that Father makes you pay,' she said. 'I swear it.'

Agesandros tried to laugh it off. 'It takes more than that to kill a gugga,' he declared.

Aurelia glared at him, afraid and yet unafraid.

'Come,' said Quintus, gently leading her away. Agesandros made to follow, but Quintus had had enough. 'Go about your business,' he barked. 'We will care for the two slaves.'

They installed Hanno on blankets and a straw mattress in an empty stable off the farmyard, where he lay as still as a corpse. Quintus was concerned by his pale face. If the Carthaginian died, his father would be severely out of pocket, so he ordered hot water to be fetched from the kitchen, along with strips of linen and a flask of *acetum*, or vinegar. When they arrived, he was surprised by Aurelia's reaction. She would suffer no other to clean the Carthaginian's wounds. Meanwhile Elira treated Galba, with Quintus watching appreciatively. The Illyrian's medical knowledge was good, courtesy of her upbringing. As she'd told Quintus, her mother had been the woman to whom everyone in the tribe came with their ailments. First she washed the wound with plenty of hot water. Then, ignoring Galba's hisses of discomfort, she sluiced the area with *acetum* before patting it dry and applying a dressing. 'Two days' rest, and light duties for a week,' Quintus said when she was done. 'I'll make sure Agesandros knows.'

Muttering his gratitude, the Gaul shuffled off.

There was a moan from behind him, and Quintus turned. Hanno's face twisted briefly at whatever Aurelia was doing, before relaxing again. 'He's alive,' he said with relief.

'No thanks to Agesandros,' Aurelia shot back vehemently. 'Imagine if we hadn't come along! He might still die.' Her voice tailed off as she bit back a sob.

Quintus patted her shoulder, wondering why she was so upset. Hanno was only a slave, after all.

Elira moved to the bed. 'Let me take a look at him,' she said.

To Quintus' surprise, Aurelia moved aside. They watched in silence as the Illyrian ran expert hands over Hanno's battered body, gently probing here and there. 'I can find no head injury apart from his broken nose,' she said eventually. 'He has three cracked ribs, and all these flesh wounds from the whip.' She pointed to his prominent ribcage and concave belly. 'Someone hasn't been feeding him enough either. He's strong, though. Some good nursing and decent food, and he could be up and about inside a week.'

'Jupiter be thanked,' Aurelia cried.

Quintus smiled his own relief and went in search of Fabricius. Agesandros' cruelty must be reported at once. He suspected that his father would not seriously punish the Sicilian, who, no doubt, would deny everything if challenged. He could hear Fabricius' voice already. Discipline was part of the overseer's remit, and no slave had the right to question his authority as Hanno had. This was the first time that Agesandros had gone overboard. In Fabricius' eyes, it would be a one-off occurrence. Quintus knew what he had seen, however. His jaw hardened.

Agesandros would have to be watched from now on.

Hanno was woken by the pain radiating from his ribs each time he took a breath. The dull throbbing from his face reminded him of his broken nose. He lifted his hands, feeling the heavy strapping that circled his chest. The manacles around his ankles had been removed. This could hardly be Agesandros' work. Quintus must have insisted I be treated, Hanno thought. His surprise grew when he opened his eyes. Instead of the damp straw in his miserable cell, he was lying on blankets in an empty stable. Occasional whinnies told him that there were horses nearby. He eyed the stool alongside him. Someone had been keeping vigil.

A shadow fell across the threshold and Hanno looked up to see Elira carrying a clay jug and two beakers.

Her face lit up. 'You're awake!'

He nodded slowly, drinking her beauty in.

She rushed to his side. 'How do you feel?'

'Sore all over.'

She reached down and lifted a gourd from the floor. 'Drink some of this.'

'What is it?' he asked suspiciously.

Elira smiled. 'A dilute solution of *papaverum*.' Seeing his confusion, she explained. 'It will dull the pain.'

He was too weak to argue. Taking the gourd, Hanno took a deep swallow of the painkilling draught, screwing up his face at the bitter taste of the liquid within.

'It won't take long to work,' Elira murmured reassuringly. 'Then you can sleep some more.'

Abruptly, the Sicilian came to mind, and he tried to sit up. The small effort felt exhausting. 'What about Agesandros?'

'Don't worry. Fabricius has seen your injuries, and warned him to leave you alone. The gods must have been in good humour, because he also agreed to let me care for you. It took a bit of persuasion, but Aurelia won him over,' Elira said. She raised a hand to his sweating face. 'Look, you are as weak as a kitten,' she scolded. 'Lie down.'

Hanno obeyed. Why would Aurelia care what happened to him? he wondered. Feeling the papaverum begin to take effect, he closed his eyes. It was a huge relief to know that one of his owner's children was on his side, but Hanno doubted that Aurelia could shield him from Agesandros' ill will. She was only a girl. Still, he thought wearily, his situation was better now than it had been. Perhaps the gods were showing him favour once more? Keeping that idea uppermost, Hanno relaxed and let sleep take him.

Chapter VII: A Gradual Shift

anno did little more than sleep and eat for the next three days. Under Elira's approving eyes, he devoured plate after plate of food from the kitchen. His strength returned, and the pain of his injuries subsided. Soon he insisted that the strapping around his chest be removed, complaining that it was restricting his breathing. By the fourth day, he felt alert enough to venture outside. Fear stopped him, however. 'Where's Agesandros?'

Elira's full lips flattened. 'The whoreson is in Capua, thankfully.'

Relieved, Hanno shuffled outside. The yard was empty. All the slaves were at work in the fields. They sat down together in the sunshine and rested their backs against the cool stone of the stable walls. Hanno didn't mind that there was no one around. It meant he could be alone with Elira, whose physical attractions were daily becoming more obvious. As the ache in his groin constantly told him, he hadn't had a woman for many months. Yet merely to entertain such thoughts was dangerous. Even if Elira was willing, slaves were forbidden from having sexual relations with each other. What's more, Hanno had seen the way she and Quintus looked at one another. Stay well away, he told himself sternly. Screwing the master's son's favourite slave would not be clever. There was a simpler way of satisfying himself. Less enjoyable, but far safer.

He needed something to take his mind off sex. 'How did you come to be a slave?'

Elira's surprise was instantly replaced by sadness. 'That's the first time anyone has asked me such a question.'

'I guess it's because we all have the same miserable story,' said Hanno gently. He raised his eyebrows in an indication that she should continue.

Elira's eyes took on a distant look. 'I grew up in a little village by the sea in Illyricum. Most people were fishermen or farmers. It was a peaceful place. Until the day that the pirates came. I was nine years old.' Her face darkened with anger, and sorrow. 'The men fought hard, but they weren't warriors. My father and my older brother, they . . .' Her voice wobbled for a moment. 'They were killed. But what happened to Mother was just as bad.' Tears formed in her eyes.

Horrified, Hanno reached out to squeeze Elira's hand. 'I'm sorry,' he whispered.

She nodded, and the movement made the tears spill down her cheeks. 'We were taken to their ships. They sailed to Italy and sold us there. I haven't seen Mother or my sisters since.'

As Elira wept, Hanno cursed himself for opening his mouth. Yet the Illyrian's sorrow made her even more attractive. It was hard not to imagine wrapping her in his arms to comfort her. He was therefore relieved to see Aurelia approaching from the direction of the villa. Nudging Elira, he scrambled to his feet. The Illyrian had barely enough time to pull her hair down around her face and wipe away her tears.

Aurelia felt a tinge of jealousy at seeing Elira so close to Hanno. 'You're up and about!' she said tartly.

He bobbed his head. 'Yes.'

'How do you feel?'

Hanno touched his ribs. 'Much better than I did a few days ago, thank you.'

Aurelia's sympathy surged back at the sight of Hanno wincing. 'It's Elira you should be grateful to. She's a marvel.'

'She is,' agreed Hanno, giving Elira a slanted grin.

The Illyrian blushed. 'Julius will be wondering where I am,' she muttered, before hurrying off.

Aurelia's annoyance returned, but, irritated with herself for even feeling it, she dismissed it at once. 'You're Carthaginian, aren't you?'

'Yes,' Hanno replied warily. He'd never yet had a proper conversation with Fabricius or any of his family. In his mind, they were still very much the enemy.

'What's Carthage like?'

He couldn't help himself. 'It's huge. Perhaps a quarter of a million people live there.'

Despite herself, Aurelia's eyes widened. 'But that's far bigger than Rome!'

Hanno had the sense not to utter the sarcastic response that rose to his lips. 'Indeed.' Aurelia seemed interested, so he launched into a description of his city, picturing it in his mind's eye as he did. Realising eventually that he had lost the run of himself, Hanno fell silent.

'It sounds beautiful,' Aurelia admitted. 'And you looked so happy while you were talking.'

Feeling utterly homesick, Hanno stared at the ground.

'It's not surprising, I suppose,' said Aurelia kindly. Looking curious, she tipped her head to one side. 'I remember that you speak Greek as well as Latin. In Italy, only nobles learn that tongue. It must be much the same in Carthage. How did someone so well educated end up as a slave?'

Balefully, Hanno lifted his gaze to hers. 'I forgot to ask a blessing of our most powerful goddess before I went on a fishing trip with my friend.' He saw her enquiring expression. 'Suni, the one you saw in Capua. After catching plenty of tunny, we drank some wine and fell asleep. A sudden storm took us far out to sea. Somehow, we survived the night, but the next day a pirate ship found us. We were sold in Neapolis, and taken to Capua to be sold as gladiators. Instead I was bought by your brother.' Hanno hardened his voice. 'Who knows what happened to my friend, though?' He was pleased to see her flinch.

Annoyed, Aurelia recovered quickly. Handsome or not, he's still a slave, she thought. 'Everyone at the slave market has a sad story. That doesn't mean that we can buy them all. Consider yourself lucky,' she snapped.

Hanno bowed his head. *She might be young, but she's got spirit.*

An awkward silence fell.

It was broken by Atia's voice. 'Aurelia!'

Aurelia's face took on a hunted look. 'I'm in the yard, Mother.'

Atia appeared a moment later. She was wearing a simple linen stola and elegant leather sandals. 'What are you doing here? We were supposed to be practising the lyre.' Her gaze passed over Hanno. 'Isn't this the slave whom Agesandros beat? The Carthaginian?'

'Yes, Mother.' A touch of colour appeared in Aurelia's cheeks. 'I was checking with Elira that his recovery was satisfactory.'

'I see. It's good that you are taking an interest in things like that. It's all part of running the household.' Atia eyed Hanno with more interest. 'That broken nose isn't healed, but otherwise he looks fine.'

Hanno shifted from foot to foot, uncomfortable with being talked about as if he weren't present.

Aurelia became a little flustered. 'I suppose . . . Elira didn't say when he'd be ready to return to work.'

'Well?' Atia demanded. 'Are you sufficiently recovered?'

Hanno couldn't exactly refuse. 'Yes, mistress,' he murmured.

'He's got three cracked ribs,' Aurelia protested.

'That's no reason to stop him working in the kitchen,' Atia replied. She stared at Hanno. 'Is it?'

It would be far less effort than toiling in the fields, thought Hanno. He bowed his head. 'No, mistress.'

Atia nodded. 'Good. Follow us back to the house. Julius will have plenty for you to do.'

Secretly delighted, Aurelia followed her mother. She would no longer need an excuse to come and see Hanno.

'Quintus wants us to watch him sparring with your father,' said Atia in a proud yet wistful tone.

'Oh.' Aurelia managed to convey all of her disapproval and jealousy in one word.

Atia turned. 'Enough of that attitude! Would you rather spend the time playing the lyre or talking Greek with your tutor?'

'No, Mother,' Aurelia muttered furiously.

'Fine.' Atia's frown eased. 'Come on then.'

Hanno was fascinated. All the girls he'd ever met were perfectly happy to stick with womanly pursuits. Aurelia was made from a different mould.

They entered the house via a small postern gate. It was incorporated into one of the two large timber doors that formed the entrance. Hanno looked around keenly. It was the first time he had been in the villa proper. The simple elegance of its design did not fail to impress him. Carthaginian homes were typically built for functionality, rather than beauty. Elegant mosaics and colourful wall paintings were the exception, not the rule.

In the courtyard, they found Fabricius and Quintus moving carefully around each other. Both were clad in simple belted tunics, and carrying wooden swords and round cavalry shields.

Seeing Atia and Aurelia, they paused.

Fabricius raised his weapon in salute to Atia, who smiled.

'Finally,' said Quintus drolly to his sister.

Aurelia did her best to look enthusiastic. This *is* better than music lessons, she told herself. 'I'm here now.'

Quintus looked to his father. 'Ready?'

'When you are.'

The two stepped closer, raising their swords. The points met with a dull clunk. Both remained still for a moment, trying to gauge when the other would move.

Atia clapped her hands. 'Fetch some fruit juice,' she ordered Hanno. She pointed. 'The kitchen is over there.'

He tore his eyes away from the contest. 'Yes, mistress.' Adopting the preferred slave walk, slow and measured, Hanno did as he was told. Happily, he was able to continue observing.

Quintus was first to act. He swept his gladius down, carrying his father's blade towards the ground. In the same movement, he drew back his right arm and thrust forward, straight at the other's chest. Fabricius quickly met the attack with his shield. With a great heave, he lifted it in the air. Quintus' sword was also carried up by the move, which exposed his right armpit. Knowing that his father would strike at his weak point, Quintus desperately twisted to the left and retreated several steps. Fabricius was on him like a striking snake. Despite his father's ferocity, Quintus managed to hold off the assault. 'Not bad,' Fabricius said at length, pulling back. They paused to catch their breath before renewing the engagement.

To Quintus' delight, he drew first blood. His success came thanks to an unexpected shoulder charge at his father that enabled him to thrust his gladius around their shields. The point snagged in the left side of Fabricius' tunic. Despite the fact that the blade was wooden, it tore a great hole in the fabric, raked along his ribs and broke the skin. He bellowed in pain, and staggered backwards. Knowing that his father would now find it agonising to lift his sword, Quintus prepared to follow through and win the bout.

'Are you all right?' Aurelia cried.

Fabricius did not answer. 'Come on,' he growled at Quintus. 'Think you can finish me?'

Stung, Quintus lifted his gladius and ran forward. When he was only a step away, he feinted to the right and then to the left. A backward slash at Fabricius' head followed, and his father's response was barely enough to prevent the blow from landing. Quintus crowed with triumph and pushed on, keen to press home his advantage. Surprising him utterly, Fabricius backed away so fast that Quintus overbalanced and fell. As he landed, Fabricius spun round and placed his sword tip at the base of Quintus' neck. 'Dead meat,' he said calmly.

Furious and embarrassed, Quintus got to his feet. Catching sight of Hanno, he scowled. 'What are you looking at?' he yelled. 'Get about your business!'

Ducking his head to conceal his own anger, Hanno headed for the kitchen.

'Don't take it out on a slave,' cried Aurelia. 'It's not his fault.'

Quintus glared at his sister.

'Calm down,' said Fabricius. 'You were undone because you were over-confident.'

Now Quintus' face went beetroot.

'You did well until then,' reassured his father. In the background, Atia was nodding in agreement. 'If you'd just taken your time, I would have had no chance.' He lifted his left arm and showed Quintus the long bloody graze along the side of his chest. 'Even a scratch like this slows a man right down. Remember that.'

Pleased, Quintus smiled. 'I will, Father.'

At that moment, Hanno emerged with a polished bronze tray. Perched upon it were a fine glass jug and four cups of the same style. Seeing him, Quintus beckoned peremptorily. 'Get over here! I'm thirsty.'

Arrogant little shit, thought Hanno as he hurried to obey.

Fabricius waited until the whole family had a drink before raising his cup. 'A toast! To Mars, the god of war. That his shield always remains over us both.'

Hanno blocked out the words as best he could and prayed silently to his own martial god. Baal Saphon, guide Hannibal's army to victory over Saguntum. And Rome.

Gulping down his juice, Fabricius indicated that Hanno should pour him a refill. He frowned in recognition. 'Fully recovered?'

'Very nearly, master,' Hanno replied.

'Good.'

'I was impressed to find Aurelia checking up on his progress,' Atia added. 'He's not up to field work yet, but I didn't see any reason why Julius couldn't put him to use in the kitchen.'

'Fair enough. He's ready to go back to his cell then.' Aurelia's mouth opened in protest, and Fabricius raised a hand. 'He's not a horse,' he said sternly. 'That stable is needed. His manacles should be replaced too.' Seeing the apprehension in Hanno's face, Fabricius' face softened. 'Obey orders, and Agesandros will not lay a hand on you. You have my word on that.'

Hanno muttered his thanks, but his mind was racing. Despite Fabricius' reassurance, his troubles were far from over. Agesandros would undoubtedly be holding a grudge against him. He would constantly have to be on his guard. Without thinking, Hanno remained where he was, close to the family.

An instant later, Quintus turned and their eyes met. I'd love to take you on in a swordfight, thought Hanno. Teach you a lesson. Almost as if he understood, Quintus' top lip curled. 'What are you still doing here? Get back to the kitchen.'

Hanno quickly retreated. He was grateful for the smile Aurelia threw in his direction.

The conversation resumed behind him.

'Can we practise again tomorrow, Father?' Quintus' voice was eager.

'The enthusiasm of youth!' Touching his side, Fabricius grimaced. 'I doubt that my ribs would permit it. But I can't anyway.'

'Why not?' Quintus cried.

'I must travel to Rome. The Senate is meeting to consider how it will respond when Saguntum falls. I want to hear for myself what they plan.'

War, thought Hanno fervently. I hope they decide on war. Because that's what they're going to get in any case.

Quintus was crestfallen, but he didn't argue further. 'How long will you be gone?'

'At least ten days. Maybe more. It depends on the success of my other mission,' Fabricius replied. He fixed Aurelia with his grey eyes. 'To find a suitable husband for you.'

Aurelia paled, but she did not look away. 'I see. I'm not to be allowed to fall in love as you and Mother did, then?'

'You'll do as you're damn well told!' Fabricius snapped.

Atia flushed and looked down.

'Never mind, children,' intervened Atia in a brisk tone. 'It will be an opportunity for both of you to catch up on your studies. Quintus, the tutor reports that your grasp of geometry is not what it should be.'

Quintus groaned.

Atia turned to Aurelia. 'Don't think that you're going to escape either.'

Even as she scowled, Aurelia was struck by an idea. Her heart leaped at its brilliance. If she could pull it off, neither of them would care about extra lessons. And it would help her not to think about her father's quest.

Like all the best plans, Aurelia's was simple. She wasn't sure if Quintus would go along with it, however, so she said nothing until their father had been gone for several days. By then, her brother's frustration at not being able to do any weapons training was reaching new highs. Aurelia picked her moment carefully, waiting until her mother was occupied with the household accounts. Quintus' morning lessons had ended a short time before, and she found him pacing around the fountain in the centre of the courtyard, angrily scuffing his sandals along the mosaic.

'What's wrong?'

He glanced at her, scowling. 'Nothing, apart from the fact that I've had to spend two hours trying to calculate the volume of a cylinder. It's impossible! And it's not as if I'll ever use the method again. Typical bloody Greeks for discovering how to work out something so stupid in the first place.'

Aurelia made a sympathetic noise. She wasn't fond of the subject either. 'I was wondering . . .' she began. Deliberately, she did not continue.

'What?' Quintus demanded.

'Oh, it's nothing,' she replied. 'Just a silly idea.'

The first trace of interest crossed Quintus' face. 'Tell me.'

'You've been complaining a lot about Father being away.'

He gave an irritable nod. 'Yes, because I can't practise my sword play.'

Aurelia smiled impishly. 'There might be a way around that.'

Quintus' look was pitying. 'Riding to Capua and back to train with Gaius each day isn't an option. It would take far too long.'

'That's not what I've got in mind.' Aurelia found herself hesitating. Say it! she thought. You've got nothing to lose. 'I could be your sparring partner.'

'Eh?' His eyebrows rose in shock. 'But you've never used a sword before.'

'I learn fast,' Aurelia shot back. 'You said so yourself when you taught me to use a sling.' She held her breath, praying that he would agree.

A slow grin spread across Quintus' face. 'We could go "for a walk" up to the woods, to the place where I train.'

'That's exactly what I was thinking,' cried Aurelia delightedly. 'Mother doesn't mind what we do as long as all of our homework is done, and our duties are completed.'

A frown creased his brow. 'What's in it for you? You'll never be able to do it again once you're . . .' He gave her a guilty look.

'That's precisely why,' Aurelia said fervently. 'I'll be married off within the year, most likely. Then I'll have to resign myself to childminding and running a household for the rest of my life. What an opportunity to forget that fate!'

'Mother will kill you if she finds out,' Quintus warned.

Aurelia's eyes flashed. 'I'll face that day if, or when, it comes.'

Quintus saw his sister's resolve, and nodded. In truth, he felt glad to be able to help her, even if it would only be a temporary affair. He wouldn't want the future she'd painted. 'Very well.'

Aurelia stepped in to kiss his cheek. 'Thank you. It means a lot to me.'

The moment that their tasks were done the following day, they met up in the atrium. Quintus slung an old sack over his shoulder; within were two of the wooden gladii, as well as a few snares. The latter could be pulled out in the event of any awkward questions from their mother. 'Ready?' Aurelia whispered excitedly.

He nodded.

They had gone a dozen steps when Atia appeared from the tablinum, a roll of parchment in one hand. She threw them a curious glance. 'Where are you two going?'

'For a walk,' Aurelia replied lightly. She lifted the wicker basket in her right hand. 'I thought you might like some mushrooms.'

'I need to set some traps as well,' Quintus added. He tapped his bow. 'This is in case I see a deer.'

'Make sure you're back well before dark.' Atia had taken a few steps when she turned. 'Actually, why don't you take the new slave with you? Hanno, I think he's called. While he's working in the kitchen, he might as well learn about foraging and catching game.'

'That's a good idea,' said Aurelia, her face lighting up. Despite the fact that Hanno now worked in the house, she had found there was still hardly ever a chance to speak to him.

'Is it?' asked Quintus, looking irritated. 'He might run away.'

Atia laughed. 'With the manacles he's wearing? I don't think so. Besides, you can both practise your Greek with him. You'll all be learning something.'

'Yes, Mother,' Quintus muttered unenthusiastically.

With an absent smile, Atia left them to it.

Aurelia poked Quintus. 'She didn't suspect a thing!'

Quintus grimaced. 'No, but we've got to take the Carthaginian with us.'

'So what? He can carry the sack.'

'I suppose,' Quintus admitted. 'Go and get him then. Let's not hang around.'

A short time later, they were following one of the narrow tracks that led through the fields to the edge of the farm. Shuffling because of his manacles, a bemused Hanno took up the rear. Aurelia's offer of a trip into the woods had come as a welcome surprise. Although his job in the kitchen kept him safe from Agesandros, Hanno had begun to miss being in the open air. He longed for the companionship of Galba, Cingetorix and the other Gauls too. Julius and the rest of the domestic slaves were pleasant, but they were soft, and did little but gossip with each other. He wouldn't see the Gauls today, but Hanno liked the sound of picking mushrooms, an activity that was unknown in Carthage, and of hunting, something he enjoyed greatly. Today he would have no time to brood.

It was when the two young Romans stopped in a large clearing that Hanno started to feel suspicious. The mushrooms that Aurelia had shown him on the way up had grown in shady areas under fallen trees, and only a fool would lay a snare or try waiting for a deer in the middle of an open space.

Quintus stalked over. 'Give me the sack,' he ordered.

Hanno obeyed. A moment later, he was most surprised to see two wooden swords clattering on to the soft earth. Gods, but how long it had been since he'd held a weapon! He still hadn't fully realised what was going on when Quintus tossed one of the gladii to Aurelia.

'These hurt like Hades if you land a blow, but they're not likely to spill your guts on the ground.'

Aurelia moved the blade to and fro once or twice. 'It feels very unwieldy.'

'It's double the weight of a real sword, to build up your fitness.' Quintus saw her frown. 'We don't have to do this.'

'Yes, we do,' she retorted. 'Show me how to hold the damn thing properly.'

Smiling, Quintus obeyed, gripping her wrist to move it slowly through the air. 'As you know, it was made to cut and thrust. But it can slash too, which is how we use it in the cavalry.'

'Shouldn't we have shields too?'

He laughed. 'Of course. But I think Mother might have realised what we were up to. Give me a few days. I'll take them up here on my own one evening, when she's taking her bath.'

Quintus began to teach Aurelia how to thrust the gladius forward. 'Keep your feet close together as you move. It's important not to over-extend yourself.'

After a while, Hanno began to grow bored. He would have loved to take Aurelia's place, but that wasn't going to happen. He glanced at his nearly empty basket, and coughed to get the young Romans' attention.

Quintus turned, a frown creasing his brow. 'What?'

'We didn't find many mushrooms on the way here. Should I go and pick some more?'

Quintus nodded in surprise. 'Very well. You're not to go far. And don't get any ideas about running away.'

Aurelia looked more grateful. 'Thank you.'

Hanno left them to it. He cast about the edge of the clearing, but found no mushrooms. Unnoticed by Quintus and Aurelia, he moved off into the undergrowth. The sounds of their voices became muffled and then were lost. Sunlight pierced the dense canopy above, lighting up irregular patches of the forest floor. Nonetheless, the air felt heavy. Hanno's presence made birds flit from branch to branch, sounding their alarm calls. Soon he felt as if he was the only person in the world. He felt free. Right on cue, the manacles around his ankles clanked, and reality struck. Hanno cursed. Even if he tried to run, he wouldn't get far. The moment Agesandros was alerted, he'd get out the hunting dogs. They'd track him down in no time. And of course there was the debt he owed Quintus. Sighing, Hanno got back to his task.

His luck was in. A quarter of an hour later, he returned to the clearing with a full basket.

Aurelia saw him first. 'Well done!' she cried, rushing over. 'Those slender mushrooms with the flat caps are delicious when fried. You'll have to try some later.'

Hanno's lips turned up. 'Thank you.'

Quintus glanced at the basket, but didn't comment. 'Race you to the stream,' he said to Aurelia. 'We can cool off before going back.'

With a giggle, she took off towards the far side of the clearing, from where the babble of running water could be heard.

'Hey!' Quintus shouted. 'That's cheating!' Aurelia didn't reply, and he sprinted after her.

Hanno looked after them wistfully, remembering similar good times with Suniaton. An instant later, though, his gaze fell on the two wooden swords, which had been left on the ground nearby. Quintus' bow and quiver lay alongside. Without thinking, Hanno walked over and picked up a gladius. As Aurelia had said, it was awkward to hold, but Hanno didn't care. Gripping the hilt tightly, he thrust it to and fro. It was the most natural thing to imagine sticking it in Agesandros' belly.

'What are you doing?'

Hanno almost jumped out of his skin. He turned to find a dripping wet Quintus regarding him with extreme suspicion. 'Nothing,' he muttered.

'Slaves aren't allowed to use bladed weapons. Drop it!'

With great reluctance, Hanno let the gladius fall.

Quintus picked it up. 'No doubt you were thinking about murdering us all in our beds,' he said in a hard voice.

'I'd never do that,' Hanno protested. Agesandros is a different matter of course, he thought. 'I owe you my life twice over. That's something I will never forget.'

Quintus was nonplussed. 'I only bought you in the first place because Agesandros didn't want me to. As for when he was beating you, well, injuring a slave badly is a waste of money.'

'That's as maybe,' Hanno muttered. 'But if it weren't for you, I'd surely be dead by now.'

Quintus shrugged. 'Don't pin your hopes on paying me back. There aren't too many dangers around here!' He pointed at his sack. 'Pick that up. I've spotted a good place on the bank to set a snare.'

Stooping so that Quintus didn't see his scowl, Hanno obeyed. Curse him and his arrogance, he thought. I should just run away. But his pride wouldn't let him. A debt was a debt.

Quintus and Aurelia managed to fit in three more trips to the clearing before Fabricius' return a week later. Atia had been so pleased by the basket of mushrooms that Quintus insisted Hanno accompany him and his sister each time. Hanno was glad to obey. Aurelia was friendly, and Quintus' manner towards him had changed fractionally. He wasn't exactly warm, but his high-handed manner, which Hanno despised, was no longer so evident. Whether it was because he had revealed the debt that he owed to Quintus, Hanno could not tell.

Although Fabricius' homecoming meant that the secret trips stopped, Hanno was pleased to learn that his master was soon to return to Rome. Eavesdropping as he served food to the family, Hanno heard how the debates in the Senate about Hannibal were constant now, with some factions favouring negotiations with Carthage and others demanding an immediate declaration of war. 'There's far more interest in that than the eligible daughter of a country noble,' Fabricius revealed to Atia.

Aurelia was barely able to conceal her delight, but her mother pursed her lips. 'Have you found no one suitable?'

'I've found plenty,' Fabricius replied reassuringly. 'I just need more time, that's all.'

'I want to know the best candidates,' said Atia. 'I can write to those of their mothers who are living. Arrange a meeting.'

Fabricius nodded. 'Good idea.'

Let it take for ever, Aurelia prayed. In the meantime, I can practise with Quintus. It had been a joy to discover that handling a sword came naturally to her. She burned to train further, while she still could.

Her brother's reaction, however, was the opposite to hers. 'How long will you be gone?' he asked glumly.

'I'm not sure. It could be weeks. I'll definitely be back for Saturnalia.'

Quintus looked horrified. 'That's months away!'

'It's not the end of the world,' said Fabricius, clapping him on the shoulder. 'You'll be starting your military training next spring anyway.'

Quintus was about to protest further but Atia intervened. 'Your father's business is far more important than your desire to train with a gladius. Be content that he is here now.'

Reluctantly, Quintus held his silence.

Bending their heads together, their parents fell into a private conversation.

It was probably about her prospective husbands, thought Aurelia furiously. She kicked Quintus under the table and framed the words 'We can go to the clearing more often' at him. When he raised his eyebrows, she repeated them and thrust an imaginary sword at him.

At last Quintus understood, and a happier expression replaced the sullen one.

Hanno hoped that Quintus and Aurelia would take him along too. Agesandros could not do a thing to him while he was with them. Moreover, he had come to enjoy the outings.

'Do you still think this is a good idea?' asked Atia when the children were gone.

Fabricius grimaced. 'What do you mean?'

'You said yourself that no one suitable is interested in finding a bride at the moment.'

'So?'

'Maybe we should leave it for six months or a year?'

His frown deepened. 'Where's the benefit in that? Don't tell me that you're having second thoughts?'

'I—'

'You are!'

'Do you remember our reason for getting married, Fabricius?' she asked gently.

A guilty look stole on to his face. 'Of course I do.'

'Is it so surprising, then, that it's hard for me to think of forcing Aurelia into an arrangement against her will?'

'It's difficult for me too,' he objected. 'But you know why I'm doing it.'

Atia sighed.

'I'm trying to better our family. I can't do that with a huge debt hanging over my head.'

'You could always ask Martialis for help.'

'I might owe thousands of didrachms to a moneylender in Capua, but I've still got my pride!' he retorted.

'Martialis wouldn't think any less of you.'

'I don't care! I wouldn't ever be able to look him in the eye again.'

'It's not as if you gambled the money away on chariot racing! You needed the money because of the terrible drought two years ago. There's no shame in telling him that we had no crops to sell.'

'Martialis isn't a farmer,' said Fabricius heavily. 'He might understand if my problems were about property, but this . . .'

'You could try,' Atia murmured. 'He's your oldest comrade, after all.'

'A friend is the worst possible person to borrow from. I'm not doing it.' He fixed her with his stare. 'If we don't want the farm to be repossessed in the next few years, the only way forward is to marry Aurelia into a wealthy family. That knowledge alone will keep the moneylender off our backs indefinitely.'

'Maybe so, but it won't make the money appear from thin air.'

'No, but with the gods' favour, I will win more recognition in this war than I did in the last. After it's over, I'll secure a local magistrate's job.'

'And if you don't?'

Fabricius blinked. 'It'll be down to Quintus. With the right patronage, he could easily reach the rank of tribune. The yearly pay that position brings in will make our debts seem like a drop in the ocean.' He leaned in and kissed her confidently. 'You see? I have it all worked out.'

Atia didn't have the heart to protest any further. She couldn't make Fabricius go to Martialis, nor could she think of another strategy. She smiled bravely, trying not to think of an alternative, but entirely possible scenario.

What if Fabricius didn't come home from the war? What if Quintus never achieved the tribuneship?

Over the following weeks, it became the siblings' daily norm to go to the clearing. Pleased by the constant stream of mushrooms, hazelnuts, and the occasional deer brought down by Quintus' arrows, Atia did not protest. Because Aurelia had given Hanno the credit for their haul, he was allowed to accompany them. To Hanno's surprise, Aurelia's skill with the gladius was slowly improving, and Quintus had begun teaching her to use a shield. Not long after that, he brought two genuine swords with him. 'These are just to give you an idea of what using the real thing feels like,' he said, as he handed one to Aurelia. 'I want no funny stuff.'

Hanno eyed the long, waisted blade in Aurelia's hand with unabashed pleasure. It wasn't that different to the weapon he'd owned in Carthage.

Quintus saw his interest and frowned. 'You know how to use one of these?'

Hanno jerked back to the present. 'Yes,' he muttered unwillingly.

'How?'

'My father used to train me.' Hanno deliberately made no mention of his brothers.

'Is he a soldier?'

'He was,' lied Hanno. The less Quintus knew, the better.

'Did he fight in Sicily?'

Hanno nodded reluctantly.

Quintus looked surprised. 'So did mine. He spent years in the cavalry there. Father says that your people were worthy enemies, who only lacked a decent leader.'

No longer, thought Hanno triumphantly. Hannibal Barca will change all that. With an effort, he shrugged at Quintus. 'Maybe.'

Quintus' mouth opened to ask another question.

'Let's practise!' interjected Aurelia.

To Hanno's relief, the moment passed. Quintus responded to his sister's demand, and the two began sparring gently with the gladii.

Hanno headed off to check their snares. Shortly afterwards, and some distance from the clearing, he found the trail of a wild boar. He hurried back with the news as fast as his manacles would let him. Because of its rich flavour, boar meat was highly prized. The creatures were secretive too, and hard to find. An opportunity to kill one should not be passed up. Hanno's news immediately stopped Quintus practising with Aurelia. Sheathing the gladii, he rolled them up in a blanket and stuffed them into his pack. 'Come on!' he cried, sweeping up his bow.

Aurelia rushed after him. She was as keen as any to bring a boar back to the house.

Within a hundred paces, Hanno had fallen well behind. 'I can't go any faster,' he explained when the young Romans turned impatiently.

'We might as well give up now, then,' said Quintus with a scowl. 'Or you can just stay here.' He had the grace to flush.

Despite this, Hanno clenched his fists. I found the damn trail, he thought. Not you.

There was a short, uncomfortable pause.

'I can help,' Aurelia announced suddenly. From inside her dress she produced a small bunch of keys. Kneeling by Hanno's side, she tried several on one of his anklets before it fell apart.

'What do you think you're doing?' demanded Quintus.

Aurelia ignored him. Smiling broadly at Hanno, she opened the other. She couldn't help thinking how like the statue of a Greek athlete he looked.

Incredulous, Hanno lifted his feet one after another. 'Baal Hammon's beard, that feels good.'

Quintus stepped forward. 'How in Hades did you get those keys?'

Aurelia swelled with pride. 'You know how Agesandros likes to drink in the evenings. He's often snoring before *Vespera*. All I had to do was creep in and take an impression of each in wax, and get the smith to make them for me. I told him that they were for Father's chests, and gave him a few coins to make sure he told no one.'

Quintus' eyes widened at his sister's daring, but he still wasn't happy. 'Why did you do it?'

Aurelia wasn't going to admit the real reason, which was that she had come to abhor Hanno's fetters. Most slaves didn't have theirs removed until they'd been around for years and were no longer deemed a flight risk, but a small number were never trusted. Naturally, Agesandros had persuaded

Fabricius that Hanno fell into this category. 'For a day like this,' she challenged, lifting her chin. 'So we could hunt properly.'

'He'll run away!' Quintus cried.

'No, he won't,' Aurelia retorted hotly. She turned to Hanno. 'Will you?'

Caught off guard by the bizarre situation, and stunned by Aurelia's action, Hanno stuttered to find an answer. 'N-no, of course not.'

'There!' Aurelia gestured in triumph at her brother.

'You believe that? He's a slave!'

Aurelia's eyes blazed. 'Hanno is trustworthy, Quintus, and you know it!'

Quintus matched her gaze for a moment. 'Very well.' He looked at Hanno. 'Do you give your word not to run away?'

'I swear it. May Tanit and Baal Hammon, Melqart and Baal Saphon be my witnesses,' said Hanno in a steady voice.

'If you're lying,' muttered Quintus, 'I'll hunt you down myself.'

Hanno stared stolidly back at him. 'Fine.'

Quintus gave him a curt nod. 'Lead on, then.'

Relishing the freedom of being able to run for the first time in months, Hanno bounded off towards the spot where he'd seen the boar's spoor. Of course he thought of escape, but there was no way Hanno would break the vow he'd just made.

Frustratingly, the boar proved elusive to the point of exasperation.

An hour later, they had still not laid eyes on it. The animal's trail had led them to a point where the forest thinned as it climbed the mountain slope above, and there it had disappeared. A large area of bare rock meant that their chances of finding it again were very slim.

Quintus looked at the darkening sky and cursed. 'We'll have to give up soon. I don't fancy spending the night here. Let's spread right out. That's probably our best option.'

While Aurelia walked off to Quintus' left, Hanno moved slowly to the right. He kept his eyes fixed on the ground, but saw nothing at all for a good two hundred paces. His gaze wandered to the slopes above them. Much of the ground was covered in short scrubby grass, and fit only for sheep or goats.

Hanno frowned. Some distance above them, and partially obscured by a scattering of juniper and pine trees, he could see a small wooden structure. Smoke rose lazily from a hole in the apex of its roof. Latticed fencing around it revealed the presence of sheep pens. It didn't surprise him. Like most landowners, Fabricius' flocks wandered the hills during the spring and summer, accompanied by solitary shepherds and their dogs. Makeshift huts, and enclosures for the animals, were situated regularly across the landscape, shelter in case of bad weather and protection against predators such as wolves. To his astonishment, however, Hanno heard the sound of bleating. He looked up at the sky. It was early for the animals to be back from pasture. He glanced at Quintus, who was still casting about for signs of the boar. Aurelia was visible beyond. She too appeared oblivious.

Hanno was about to give a low whistle, when something stopped him. Instead, he trotted back towards the two Romans.

Quintus grew excited as he saw Hanno approach. 'Seen something?'

'The sheep up there are penned in,' said Hanno. 'A bit soon, isn't it?'

Quintus raised a hand to his eyes. 'By Jupiter, you're right,' he admitted, annoyed that he hadn't noticed first. 'Libo is the shepherd around here. He's a good man, not one to avoid work.'

Hanno's stomach clenched.

'I'm not happy.' Quintus took off his pack and emptied it on the ground. He unrolled the cloak. Carefully shoving one gladius into his belt, he handed the other to Aurelia, who had caught up with them. 'You probably won't need it,' he said with a falsely confident smile. Bending the stave with his knee, Quintus slipped his bowstring into place. There were ten arrows in his quiver. Plenty, he thought.

'What's wrong?' Aurelia demanded.

'Probably nothing,' replied Quintus reassuringly. 'I'm just going to take Hanno and check out that hut.'

Fear flared in Aurelia's eyes, but when she spoke, her voice was steady. 'What shall I do?'

'Remain here,' Quintus ordered. 'Stay hidden. Under no circumstances are you to follow us. Is that clear?'

She nodded. 'How long should I wait?'

'A quarter of an hour, no more. If we haven't reappeared by then, return to the farm as fast as you can. Find Agesandros, and tell him to bring plenty of men. Well armed.'

At this, Aurelia's composure cracked. 'Don't go up there,' she whispered. 'Let's just fetch Agesandros together.'

Quintus thought for a moment. 'Libo could be in danger. I have to check,' he declared. He patted Aurelia's arm. 'Everything will be fine, you'll see.'

Aurelia saw that her brother was not to be swayed. She took a step towards Hanno, but stopped herself. 'Mars protect you both,' she whispered, hating the way her voice trembled.

And Baal Saphon, thought Hanno, invoking the Carthaginian god of war.

Leaving Aurelia peering from behind a large pine, the two young men began to ascend. Quintus was surprised by the imperceptible change that had already taken place in their relationship. Although they could see no human activity above, both were instinctively using the few bushes present for cover. As soldiers would. *Don't be stupid. He's a slave.* 'It's bandits,' Quintus muttered to himself. 'What else can it be?'

'That's what it would be in the countryside around Carthage,' replied Hanno.

Quintus cursed. 'I wonder how many there are?'

Hanno shrugged uneasily, wishing he had a weapon. It wasn't surprising that Quintus had given the other gladius to Aurelia, but it grated on him nonetheless. 'Your guess is as good as mine.'

Quintus' lips had gone very dry. 'What if there are too many for me to take on?'

'We try not to shit ourselves, and then crawl out of there on our bellies,' Hanno answered dryly. 'Before going to get help.'

'That sounds like a good plan.' Despite himself, Quintus grinned.

The rest of the climb was made in silence. The last point of cover before the shepherd's hut was a stunted cypress tree, and they reached it without difficulty. Recovering their breath, each took turns to peer at the pens and the miserable structure alongside, which was little more than a leanto. His lips moving silently, Quintus counted the sheep. 'I make it more than fifty,' he whispered. 'That's Libo's entire flock.'

Be logical, thought Hanno. 'Maybe he's ill?'

'I doubt it,' Quintus replied. 'Libo is as hard as nails. He's lived in the mountains all his life.'

'Let's wait a moment then,' Hanno advised. 'No point rushing into a situation without assessing it first.'

Hanno's observation made Quintus bridle. Slaves do not advise their masters, he told himself angrily. Yet the Carthaginian's words were wise. Biting his lip, he drew a goose-feathered arrow from his quiver. It was his favourite, and he'd killed with it many times. Never a man, he thought with a rush of fear. Taking a deep breath, Quintus exhaled slowly. It might not come to that. Nonetheless, he picked out three more shafts and stabbed them into the earth by his feet. Suddenly, an awful thought struck him. If there were bandits about, and he was outnumbered, his bow was the only advantage he had. That might not be enough. Quintus was prepared for the potential danger he'd placed himself in, but he hadn't really considered his sister. He turned to Hanno. 'If anything happens to me, you're to run down and get Aurelia the hell out of here. Do you understand?'

It was too late to say that Quintus should have given him a sword, thought Hanno angrily. It would have been two of them against however many bandits might be in the hut. He nodded. 'Of course.'

It wasn't long before there was movement inside the building, which was perhaps twenty paces away. A man coughed, and cleared his throat in the manner of someone who has just woken. Quintus stiffened, listening hard. Hanno did likewise. Then they heard the rickety door on the far side of the hut being thrown open. A short figure wearing a sheepskin waist-coat over a homespun tunic stepped into view. Stretching and yawning, he pulled down his breeches and began to relieve himself. Glancing sunlight lit up the yellow arc of his urine.

Quintus cursed under his breath.

Despite the other's reaction, Hanno had to ask. 'Is that the shepherd?' he whispered.

Quintus' lips framed the word 'No.' Carefully, he fitted his favourite arrow to his bowstring and drew a bead on the stranger.

'Could it be another shepherd?'

'I don't recognise him.' Quintus drew back until the goose feathers at the base of the arrow nearly touched his ear.

'Wait!' Hanno hissed. 'You have to be sure.'

Quintus was again angered by Hanno's tone. Nonetheless, he did not release: he too had no desire to kill an innocent man.

'Caecilius? Where are you?' demanded a voice from inside the hut.

The pair froze.

With a final shake, the man pulled up his trousers. 'Out here,' he replied lazily. 'Taking a piss on the shepherd. Making sure he's still dead.'

There was a loud guffaw. 'Not much chance of the whoreson being anything else after what you did to him.'

'You can't talk, Balbus,' added a third voice. 'He screamed the most when you were using the red hot poker.'

Quintus threw Hanno a horrified glance.

Balbus laughed, a deep, unpleasant sound. 'What do you think, Pollio?' There was no immediate answer, and they heard Balbus kicking someone. 'Wake up, you drunken sot.'

'The point of my boot up his arse should do the trick,' Caecilius bellowed, heading for the door.

Desperately, Hanno turned his head to tell Quintus to loose before it was too late. He barely had time to register the arrow as it flashed past his eyes and shot through the air to plant itself in the middle of Caecilius' chest. With a stunned look, the bandit dropped to his knees before toppling sideways to the dirt. He made a few soft choking sounds and lay still.

'Well done,' whispered Hanno. 'Three left.'

'At least.' Quintus did not think about what he had done. He notched another shaft and waited. The layout of the hut was such that if the remaining bandits merely looked out of the doorway, they would see Caecilius' body without exposing themselves to his arrows. Jupiter, Greatest and Best, he begged silently, let the next scumbag come right outside.

Hanno clenched his teeth. He too could see the danger.

'Caecilius? Fallen over your own prick?' demanded Balbus.

There was no answer. A moment later, a bulky-framed man with long greasy hair emerged partially into view. It took the blink of an eye for him to notice his companion's body, to take in the arrow protruding from his chest. A strangled cry left Balbus' throat. Frantic to regain the safety of the hut, he spun on his heel.

Quintus released. His shaft flew straight and true, driving deep into Balbus' right side with a meaty thump. The bandit cursed in pain, but managed to get through the doorway. 'Help me,' he cried. 'I'm hit.'

Shouts of confusion and anger rang out from within. Hanno heard Balbus growl, 'Caecilius is dead. An arrow to the chest. No, Sejanus, I don't fucking know who did it.' Then, apart from low muttering, everything went silent.

'They know that I'm just outside,' Quintus whispered, suddenly wondering if he'd bitten off more than he could chew. 'But they have no idea that I'm on my own. How will they react?'

Hanno scowled. *You're not on your own, you arrogant fool.* 'What would you do?'

'Try to get away,' Quintus said, fumbling for an arrow.

In the same instant, loud cracking sounds filled the air and the back wall of the hut disintegrated in a cloud of dust. Three bandits burst into the open air, hurtling straight towards them. In the lead was a skinny man in a wine-stained tunic. He grasped a hunting spear in both hands. This had to be Pollio, thought Hanno. Beside him ran a massive figure carrying a club. Hanno blinked in surprise. It was not Balbus, because he was two steps behind, clutching the arrow in his side with one hand and a rusty sword with the other. Despite being twice Balbus' size, the big man was his spitting image. The pair had to be brothers.

The two sides goggled at each other for a heartbeat.

Pollio was the first to react. 'They're only children. And one isn't even armed,' he screamed. 'Kill them!' His companions needed no encouragement. Bellowing with rage, the trio charged forward.

Perhaps fifteen paces now divided them. 'Quick,' Hanno shouted. 'Take one of the bastards down.'

Quintus' heart hammered in his chest, and he struggled to notch his arrow correctly. Finally it slipped on to the string, but, desperate to even the odds, he loosed too soon. His shaft flashed over Pollio's shoulder and into the wreckage of the hut. He had no time to reach for another. The bandits were virtually upon them. Dropping his bow, he pulled the gladius from his belt. 'Get out of here!' he shouted. 'You know what to do!'

Facing certain death if he stayed without a weapon, Hanno turned and fled.

'Let him go!' shouted Pollio. 'The shitbag looks as if he can run like the wind.'

Quintus had just enough time to throw up a prayer of thanks to Jupiter before Pollio, leaping over a fallen log, reached him.

'So you're the one who would murder a man while he takes a piss,' the bandit snarled, lunging forward with his spear.

Quintus dodged sideways. 'He got what was coming to him.'

Leering, Pollio stabbed at him again. 'It was a quicker death than the shepherd had.'

Quintus tried not to think of Libo, or of the fact that he was outnumbered three to one. Holding his gladius with both hands, he swept the spear shaft away. Sejanus, the big man, was still a few steps away, but already there was no sign of Balbus. *Where is the son of a whore?* Quintus wondered frantically. He might be wounded, but he's still armed. The realisation made him want to vomit. *The bastard's coming to stab me in the back.* All Quintus could think of doing was to place himself against a tree. Driving Pollio off with a flurry of blows, he sprinted towards the nearest one he could see, a cypress with a thick trunk. He could make a stand there.

To Quintus' exhilaration, he made it.

The only trouble was that, a heartbeat later, he had the grinning bandits ringed around him in a semicircle.

'Surrender now, and we'll give you an easy death,' said Pollio. 'Not like the poor shepherd had.'

Even the wounded Balbus laughed.

What have I done? Somehow, Quintus swallowed down his fear. 'You're fucking scum! I'll kill you all,' he shouted.

'You think?' sneered Pollio. 'It's your choice.' Without warning, he thrust his spear at Quintus' midriff.

Quintus threw himself sideways. Too late, he realised that Sejanus had aimed his club at the very spot he was heading for. In utter desperation, he deliberately fell to the ground. With an almighty *crack*, the club smacked into the treetrunk. The knowledge that the blow would have brained him if it had landed drove Quintus to his feet. Seizing his opportunity, he slashed out at Sejanus' arm and was delighted when his blade connected with the big man's right arm. The flesh wound it cut was enough for Sejanus to bellow in pain and stagger backwards, out of the way. Quintus' relief lasted no more than an instant. The injury wouldn't be enough to stop the brute from rejoining the fight. To survive, he immediately had to disable or kill one of the other two.

With that, a sword hilt smashed into the side of his head. Stars burst across Quintus' vision, and his knees buckled. Half-conscious, he dropped to the ground.

* * *

Hanno had probably run fifty paces before he glanced over his shoulder. Delighted that no one was pursuing him, he sprinted on for another fifty before looking back again. He was on his own. In the clear. Safe. So too, therefore, was Aurelia.

What of Quintus? he wondered with a thrill of dread.

You ran. Coward! Hanno's conscience screamed.

Quintus told me to, he thought defensively. The idiot couldn't bring himself to trust me with a gladius.

Does that mean you should leave him to die? his conscience shot back. What chance has he against three grown men?

Hanno screeched to a halt. Turning, he ran uphill as fast as his legs could take him. He took care to count his steps. At eighty, he slowed to a trot. Peering through the trees, he saw the three bandits standing over a motionless figure. Claws of fear savaged Hanno's guts as he took refuge behind a bush. *No! He can't be dead!* When Pollio's kick made Quintus moan, Hanno was nearly sick with relief. Quintus was alive still. Clearly, he wouldn't be for long. Hanno clenched his empty fists. *What in the name of Baal Saphon can I do?*

'Let's take him back to the hut,' Pollio declared.

'Why?' complained Balbus. 'We can just kill the fucker here.'

'That's where the fire is, stupid! It won't have gone out yet,' replied Pollio with a laugh. 'I know you're injured, but Sejanus and I can carry him between us.'

A cruel smile spread across Balbus' face. 'Fair enough. There'll be more sport with some heat, I suppose.' He watched each of his comrades take one of Quintus' arms and begin dragging him towards the hut. There was little resistance, but they retained their weapons nonetheless.

This is my chance. All three men had their backs to him, and half a dozen steps separated Balbus from the others. Hanno's mouth felt very dry. His prospects of success were tiny. Like as not, he'd end up dead, or being tortured alongside Quintus. He could still run. A wave of self-loathing swept over him. *He saved you from Agesandros, remember?*

Clenching his teeth, Hanno emerged from his hiding place. Grateful for the damp vegetation, which muffled the sound of his feet, he stole forward as fast as he could. Balbus was limping after his comrades, who were alternately grumbling about how much Quintus weighed and waxing lyrical about what they'd do to him. Hanno fixed his gaze on the rusty sword that dangled from Balbus' right hand. First, he *had* to arm himself. After that, he had to kill one of the bandits. After that . . . Hanno didn't know. He'd have to trust in the gods.

To Hanno's relief, his first target didn't hear him coming. Taking careful aim, he thumped Balbus near the point where Quintus' arrow had entered his flesh, before neatly catching the sword as it dropped from the screaming bandit's fingers. Switching it to his right hand, Hanno sprinted for the other two. 'Hey!' he shouted.

Their faces twisted with alarm, but Hanno's delight turned to fear as they dropped Quintus like a sack of grain. Do not let him be hurt, Hanno prayed. Please.

'You must be a slave,' Pollio growled. 'You were unarmed before. Why don't you join us?'

'We'll let you kill your master,' offered Sejanus. 'Any way you want.'

Hanno did not dignify the proposal with a reply. Sejanus was nearest, so he went for him first. The big man might have been injured, but he was still deadly with his club. Hanno ducked under one almighty swing, and dodged out of the way of another before seeing Pollio's spear come thrusting in at him. Desperate, Hanno retreated a few paces. Sejanus lumbered in immediate pursuit, blocking his comrade's view of Hanno. There was a loud curse from Pollio, and Sejanus' attention lapsed a fraction.

Hanno darted forward. As the other's eyes widened in disbelief, Hanno slid his sword deep into his belly. The blade made a horrible, sucking sound as it came out. Blood spurted on to the ground. Sejanus roared with agony; his club fell from his nerveless fingers and both his hands came up to clutch at his abdomen.

Hanno was already spinning to meet Pollio's attack. The little bandit's spear stabbed in, narrowly missing his right arm. His heart pounding, Hanno shuffled backwards. His eyes flickered to the side. Despite being in obvious pain, Balbus was about to join the fray. He'd picked up a thick branch. It wouldn't kill, thought Hanno, but if Balbus landed a blow, he'd easily knock him from his feet. Panic bubbled in his throat, and his sword arm began to tremble.

Get a grip of yourself! Quintus needs you.

Hanno's breathing steadied. He fixed Balbus with a hard stare. 'Want a blade in the guts as well as that arrow?'

Balbus flinched, and Hanno went for the kill. 'Creating fear in an enemy's heart wins half the battle,' his father had been fond of saying. 'Carthage!' he bellowed, and charged forward. Even if Pollio took him down from behind, Hanno was determined that Balbus would die.

Balbus saw the suicidal look in Hanno's eyes. He dropped his length of wood and raised both his hands in the air. 'Don't kill me,' he begged.

Hanno didn't trust the bandit as far as he could throw him; he didn't know what Pollio was doing either. Dropping his right shoulder, he crashed into Balbus' chest, sending him flying.

When he turned to face Pollio, the skinny bandit was gone. Pumping his arms and legs as if Cerberus himself were after him, he tore up the slope and was soon lost to view among the trees. Let the bastard go, Hanno thought wearily. He won't come back. A few steps away, Balbus was in the foetal position, moaning. Further off, Sejanus was already semi-conscious from the blood he'd lost.

The fight was over.

Elation filled Hanno for a moment – before he remembered Quintus.

He rushed to the Roman's side. To his immense relief, Quintus smiled up at him. 'Are you all right?' Hanno asked.

Wincing, Quintus lifted a hand to the side of his head. 'There's an apple-sized lump here, and it feels as if Jupiter is letting off thunderbolts inside my skull. Apart from that, I'll be fine, I think.'

'Thank the gods,' said Hanno fervently.

'No,' replied Quintus. 'Thank you – for coming back. For disobeying my orders.'

Hanno coloured. 'I'd never have been able to live with myself if I hadn't.'

'But you didn't have to do it. Even when you did, you could have taken up the bandits' offer. Turned on me.' A trace of wonder entered Quintus' voice. 'Instead, you took on the three of them, and won.'

'I—' Hanno faltered.

'I'm only alive because of you,' interrupted Quintus. 'You have my thanks.'

Seeing Quintus' sincerity, Hanno inclined his head. 'You're welcome.'

As the realisation sank in that they had survived the most desperate of situations, the two grinned at each other like maniacs. These were strange circumstances for both. Master saved by his slave. Roman allied with Carthaginian. Yet both were very aware of a new bond: that of comradeship forged in combat.

It was a good feeling.

Chapter VIII: The Siege

Outside the walls of Saguntum, Iberia

M alchus regarded the immense fortifications with a baleful eye and spat on the ground. 'They're determined, you have to give them that,' he growled. 'They must know now that there's no help coming from Rome. But the pig-headed Greek bastards still won't give up.'

'Neither will we,' Sapho responded fiercely. His breath plumed in the cool, autumn air. 'And when we get inside, the defenders will regret the day they slammed the gates in our faces. The whoresons won't know what hit them. Eh, Bostar?' He elbowed his brother in the ribs.

'The sooner the city falls, the better. Hannibal will find a way,' Bostar replied confidently, sidestepping Sapho's needling. In the months since their argument in New Carthage, their relationship had improved somewhat, but Sapho never missed an opportunity to undermine him, or to call into question his loyalty to their cause. Just because I don't enjoy torturing enemy prisoners, thought Bostar sadly. What has he become?

In a way, though, it was unsurprising that Sapho resorted to violence in his attempts to garner intelligence that might gain them entry. Nearly six months had elapsed since Hannibal's immense army had begun the siege, and they were not much nearer to taking Saguntum. A mile from the sea, it sat on a long, naked piece of rock that towered three to four hundred paces above the plain below. The position was one of confident dominance, and made it a fearsome prospect to besiege. The only way of approaching the city, which was encircled by strongly built fortifications, was from the west, where the slope was least steep. Naturally, it was here that the defences were strongest. Surrounded by thick walls, a mighty tower sat astride the tallest part of the rock. Hannibal had encamped the majority of his forces below this point. He had also ordered the erection of a wall that ran all the way around the base of the rock. The circumvallation was dotted with towers whose function was merely to ensure that no enemy messengers escaped.

'The gods willing, *we* are that way,' Malchus added.

Both his sons nodded. Hannibal had shown their family considerable honour by picking their units to lead the impending attack. The rest of those who would take part, thousands of Libyans and Iberians, waited on the slopes below.

Sapho's face twitched, and he gestured at the massed ranks of their spearmen, who were arrayed around the massive shapes of four *vineae*, or 'covered ways', attacking towers with a massive battering ram at their base. These would form the basis for their assault. 'The men are nervous. It's no surprise either. We've been waiting for an hour. Where is he?'

Bostar could see that Sapho was right. Some soldiers were chatting loudly with each other, their voices a tone higher than normal. Others remained silent, but their lips moved in constant prayer. A nervous air hung over every phalanx. Hannibal will come soon, he told himself.

'Patience,' advised Malchus.

Reluctantly, Sapho obeyed, but he burned to prove himself once and for all. Show his father that he was the bravest of his sons.

Moments later, their attention was drawn by murmurs of anticipation, which began spreading forward from the rear of the throng.

'Listen!' said Malchus in triumph. 'Hannibal is talking to them as he passes by. There are many things that make a good general, and this is one of them. It's not just about leading from the front. You have to engage with your soldiers as well.' He gave Bostar an approving nod, which made Sapho mutter something under his breath.

Bostar's temper frayed. This was an area he paid a lot of attention to. 'What?' he demanded. 'If you tried that instead of punishing every tiny infraction of the rules, your troops might respect you more.'

Sapho's face darkened, but before he could reply, loud cheering broke out. Men began stamping their feet on the ground in a repetitive, infectious rhythm. The other officers did nothing to intervene. This was what they had all been waiting for. The noise grew and grew, until gradually a single word became audible. 'HANN-I-BAL! HANN-I-BAL! HANN-I-BAL!'

Bostar grinned. One could not help but be infected by the soldiers' enthusiasm. Even Sapho was craning his neck to see.

Eventually, a small party emerged from the midst of the spearmen. It was a hollow square, formed by perhaps two dozen *scutarii*. These Iberian infantry were some of Hannibal's best troops. As always, the scutarii were wearing their characteristic black cloaks over simple tunics and small breast-plates. Their fearsome array of weapons included various types of heavy throwing spear, most notably the all-iron *saunion*, as well as long, straight swords, and daggers. Within their formation walked a lone figure, partially obscured from view. This was who everyone wanted to see. Finally, nearing Malchus and his sons, the scutarii fanned out in two lines. The man within was revealed.

Hannibal Barca.

Bostar gazed at his general with frank admiration. Like most senior Carthaginian officers, Hannibal wore a simple Hellenistic gilded bronze helmet. Sunlight flashed off its surface, reflecting into the soldiers' eyes. The blinding light concealed Hannibal's face apart from his beard. A dark purple cloak hung from his broad shoulders. Under it, he wore a tunic of the same colour, and an ornate muscled bronze cuirass, its details picked out in silver. Layered strips of linen guarded the general's groin, and polished bronze greaves covered his lower legs. His feet were encased in sturdy leather sandals. A hide baldric swept down from his right shoulder to his left hip, suspending a falcata sword in a well-worn scabbard. He moved forward, limping slightly.

The commander of the scutarii barked an order, and in unison his soldiers slammed their brightly painted shields on to the rock. The crashing sound instantly silenced the assembled troops. 'Your general, the lion of Carthage, Hannibal Barca!' screamed the officer.

Everyone stiffened to attention and saluted.

'General!' cried Malchus. 'You honour us with your presence.'

The corners of Hannibal's mouth tugged up. 'At ease, gentlemen.' He made his way to Malchus' side. 'Are you ready?'

'Yes, sir. We have checked over the siege engines twice. Every man knows his task.'

Malchus' sons muttered in agreement.

Hannibal glanced at each of them in turn before giving a satisfied nod. 'You will do well.'

'May Baal Saphon strike us down if we do not,' said Sapho fervently.

Hannibal looked a little surprised. 'I hope not. The city will fall eventually, but we haven't succeeded so far. Who's to say that today will be any different? And valuable officers are hard to come by.' Ignoring Sapho's obvious discomfort, he smiled at Malchus. 'Understand that you're only being granted this chance because I can't run.' He touched the heavy strapping on his right thigh.

'Your injury was most unfortunate, sir,' said Malchus, 'but we are grateful for the opportunity that it has granted us today.'

Hannibal smiled. 'Your eagerness is commendable.'

Bostar could still picture the heart-stopping moment several weeks previously, during an assault similar to the one they were about to lead. As was his nature, Hannibal had been at the front. Bostar wished it had been he who had taken the arrow through the thigh. 'How's it healing, sir?'

'Slowly enough.' Hannibal grimaced. 'I should be thankful, I suppose, that the defenders aren't better archers.'

Father and sons laughed nervously. That eventuality was something no one wanted to entertain.

'Well, don't let me stand in your way. The Saguntines await you.' Hannibal indicated the walls, which were thickly manned. He pointed back down the steep slope at the other companies of troops: reinforcements should the attack break through. 'So do they.'

'Yes, sir.' Malchus lifted his sword.

His men, who had been watching closely, stiffened.

'Gods, but I wish Hanno were here,' muttered Bostar.

Sapho's face hardened. 'Eh? Why?'

'He spent his time dreaming about things like this.'

'Well, he's dead,' Sapho whispered back savagely. 'So you're wasting your time.'

Bostar gave him a furious stare. 'Don't you miss him?'

Sapho had no chance to reply.

'What are you waiting for?' Malchus demanded, who had missed the exchange. 'Get into position!'

With a quick salute to Hannibal, Bostar and Sapho sprinted off to join their respective phalanxes. Each was in charge of one of the vineae, and their increasingly bitter rivalry meant that both burned to command the siege engine which smashed the decisive hole in the walls, and allowed their comrades a way into Saguntum. Of course it might not be they who succeeded, thought Bostar. Their father commanded the third vinea, and Alete, a doughty veteran whom both brothers admired, had the last.

Malchus waited until they were in place before he chopped his arm downward. 'Forward!' he shouted.

Using whistles, the officers encouraged the Libyans towards the walls. Dozens of men who had been selected earlier handed their spears to comrades and ran to place their shoulders against the backs of the vineae, or to stand alongside the wheels. Scores of others used their large shields to form protective screens around those who were now unprotected. More commands rang out, and the soldiers around the siege engines began to push. With loud creaks, the vineae rumbled forward, past Hannibal. When the machines were perhaps fifty paces up the slope, the remaining Libyans began to follow in tight phalanxes.

As they drew nearer, Bostar's stomach clenched. He could clearly see the faces of those above, the defenders who were waiting to rain death down upon him and his men. Upon his father and brother. Baal Saphon, let us smash the enemy's walls asunder, he prayed. Keep your shield over all of us. As the first missiles came pattering down, Bostar couldn't help wondering if Sapho was asking for similar protection for him.

He doubted it.

Taking great care, Bostar peered out at the ramparts above him. Perhaps an hour had passed, and the assault was going well. The battering rams suspended in the bottoms of the vineae were smashing great holes in the base of the wall. Thanks to the siege engines' wooden and leather roofs, which had been pre-soaked in water, the defenders' clouds of fire arrows, stones and spears were having limited effect. Bostar had lost fifteen men, which was perfectly acceptable. The phalanxes on either side, those of Sapho and Alete, looked to have suffered much the same.

Soon after, a large section of the wall collapsed. A wry grin split Bostar's face at the sight. The area lay directly between his and Sapho's positions, so neither could claim the credit. That wasn't the point now, of course. Hannibal was watching them. Bostar roared at his men to redouble their efforts. He fancied he heard Sapho's voice above the din, enjoining his soldiers to do the same. Their efforts were not in vain. Before long, two, and then three, towers had fallen outwards, crushing dozens of the garrison, and spearmen, to death. But a sizeable breach had now been forced, large enough to gain entry. Bostar did not wait until the dust had settled. This opportunity had to be seized by the throat, before the bewildered defenders had a chance to react. Screaming at his men to pick up their weapons and follow him, he climbed on to the mounds of broken masonry that stood before the siege engines. He was pleased to note that Sapho's soldiers were also spilling into view. Catching sight of his brother twenty paces away, Bostar raised his spear in salute. 'I'll see you inside!'

'Not if I get there before you,' Sapho snarled back. He turned to his soldiers, who were straining like hunting dogs on the leash. 'Five gold pieces to the first man to get within the walls. Forward!'

Bostar sighed. Even this had to be a contest. So be it, he thought angrily. The race was on.

Pursued by their men, the two brothers scrambled up towards the breach. They risked their lives with every step, not just from the continuing rain of missiles from the ramparts to either side, but from the treacherous footing beneath. Carrying a spear in one hand and a shield in the other made it even more difficult to balance. Bostar kept his gaze fixed firmly on the ground. The enemy missiles were beyond his control, but he could make sure that he didn't break an ankle in the ascent. He'd seen it happen before, consigning the unfortunates affected to being trampled by their comrades, or killed by the torrent of death being thrown by the Saguntines.

Bostar was first to reach the highest point of the smashed wall. The clouds of dust sent up by the towers' collapse formed a choking cloud that hid any defenders from sight. Perhaps there were none? wondered Bostar. His heart leaped, but then he glanced around and cursed. In his haste, he'd outstripped his soldiers. The nearest were twenty paces down the slope. 'Get a move on,' he roared. 'This isn't a walking party!'

An instant later, Sapho arrived from the gloom. He had a dozen or more Libyans in tow; more were hauling themselves up nearby. A happy smile spread across his face when he saw that Bostar was alone. 'On your own still? It's not surprising, really. Nothing like the promise of gold to speed things along.'

Bostar bit back his instinctive response. 'This is not the time for such bullshit,' he snarled. 'Let's seize the damn breach. We can argue later.'

Sapho gave a nonchalant shrug. 'As you wish.' He levelled his spear. 'Third Phalanx! On me! Form a line!'

Only four of Bostar's men had arrived. He watched in frustration as his brother led his spearmen forward. Of course he would be following in the blink of an eye, but it still rankled. A moment later, Bostar was glad that he hadn't been first into the gap. Like avenging ghosts, scores of screaming Saguntines emerged from the dust cloud. Every one of them carried a *falarica*, a long javelin with a burning ball of pitch-soaked tow wrapped around the middle of the shaft.

'Look out!' Bostar screamed, knowing that his warning was already too late.

Responding to an officer's command, the Saguntines drew back and released. They aimed short. Clouds of flaming missiles scudded through the air. Horror-struck, Sapho and his soldiers slowed down. And then the falaricae landed. Driving through shields. Maiming, killing and setting men alight.

Cursing, Bostar counted his spearmen. There were about twenty of them now. It wasn't enough, but he couldn't just stand by. If he did, Sapho would be killed, and his soldiers would run away. Their chance would be lost. 'Forward!' Raising his shield, Bostar ran at the enemy. He did not look back. To his immense relief, he felt his men's presence at each shoulder. Death might take them all, thought Bostar, but at least they followed him through loyalty, not lust for gold.

He aimed for the spot where it looked as if Sapho's soldiers might be overwhelmed. Seeing him, the nearest Saguntines took aim and released their falaricae. Hunching his shoulders, Bostar ran on. Streaming flames, the javelins hummed right past him. There was a strangled scream, and he looked around. He wished he hadn't. A falarica had struck the man to his rear in the shoulder, driving deep into his flesh. In turn, the burning section had set alight the soldier's tunic. Gobbets of white-hot tow were dropping on to his face and neck. His screams were ear-splitting. Bostar's nostrils filled with the stench of cooking flesh. 'Leave him!' he roared at the men who instinctively went to help. 'Keep moving!' Grateful it wasn't him, and hoping the soldier died quickly, he spun back to the front.

If there was one small advantage to be gained from the enemy's secret weapon, it was that after launching them, the defenders were momentarily defenceless. In addition, many weren't even wearing armour. Snarling with fury, Bostar charged at a skinny Saguntine who was frantically trying to tug free his sword. He didn't succeed. Bostar's spear took him through the chest, punching through his ribcage with ease. The man's eyes nearly popped out of their sockets with the force of the impact. He was dead before Bostar pulled free his weapon, showering the ground in gouts of blood.

Panting, Bostar rounded on the next soldier within reach, a youth who couldn't have been more than sixteen. Despite his rusty sword and blood-curdling cries, he looked petrified.

Bostar parried his clumsy blows with little difficulty before sliding his spear into the youngster's belly. He killed two more defenders before an opportunity presented itself to assess the situation.

Perhaps a hundred of his own men were present; more were still arriving. A similar number of Sapho's soldiers were battling steadily around them. No doubt their father and Alete's phalanxes were trying to reach them too. Remarkably, however, they were being held back by the Saguntines, who were performing acts of heroism and suicidal bravery. No ground had been gained at all. Bostar realised why as he took in hundreds of civilians, who, just a few steps from the periphery of the fighting, were frantically repairing the breach with their bare hands. He could see old men, women and even children heaving rocks into place. Grudging respect filled him. Knowing that their loved ones were so close would make any man, soldier or not, fight like a demon. Bostar was not dismayed. Even now, thousands more troops would be climbing the slope to join them. Against such overwhelming numbers, even the gallant Saguntines could not hold for much longer. All they needed to do was to press home the attack.

Abruptly, his attention was drawn back to the present. Through the dust, he could make out a line of flickering flame approaching from the enemy citadel. Bostar's stomach clenched as the vision came into full focus. It was two further waves of warriors, carrying scores more burning falar-icae. 'Shields up!' he yelled. 'Incoming javelins!'

His men hurried to obey.

Responding to a shouted order, the enemy lines came to a halt perhaps fifty paces away. Drawing back, the Saguntines threw their falaricae up in a steep arc, far over their own men. Over Bostar and Sapho's soldiers.

'Clever bastards,' Bostar muttered. 'They don't want to hit us.' He watched in total dread as the flaming javelins turned to point downwards. Like deadly shooting stars, they returned to earth to land amidst the still ascending Carthaginian troops. Thanks to the clouds of dust, these densely packed men had no idea what was about to hit them until the very last moment. Understandably, the falaricae caused utter chaos. Practically every one found a home in human flesh, running through shields and mail shirts with impunity. Yet their effect was far more profound. It was why the Saguntines had aimed at the unsuspecting soldiers to the rear, thought Bostar as the screams and wails of the injured filled his ears. The falaricae struck fear into the heart of every man who stood in their path. He knew exactly why. Who could bear to watch his comrades being turned into pillars of flame, or having the flesh blistered from their bones? No amount of training could prepare soldiers for that.

The entire advance below him had already come to a halt. As Bostar watched, the second wave of enemy javelins came rocketing down. An instant later, the Carthaginian attack became a rout. Despite the shouts of their officers, hundreds of men turned and fled. They hurled themselves down the slope with such abandon that many fell and were trampled by those following. The soldiers to either side, who had not been struck by the enemy volley, took one look at their retreating comrades and stopped dead. Then, as one, they turned on the spot and began running too.

Bostar cursed. The moment was lost. No one, even Hannibal, could turn this situation around. He caught the arm of the nearest spearman. 'Pull back! Our reinforcements are withdrawing. We have to save ourselves. Spread the word.' Repeating his command to every soldier he passed, Bostar fought his way through the press to Sapho's side. Oblivious to the volley's effect, his brother was urging a quartet of spearmen forward at a bunch of poorly armed defenders.

'Sapho!' Bostar yelled. 'Sapho!'

Eventually his brother heard him. 'What?' he snarled over his shoulder.

'We must pull back!'

Sapho's face contorted with anger. 'You're crazy! Any moment, the whoresons will break, and then we'll have them. Victory is at hand!'

'No, it isn't!' Bostar bellowed. 'We have to retreat. NOW.'

Some of Sapho's soldiers began to look uneasy.

Sapho glared furiously at Bostar, but realised that he was serious. Shouting encouragement to his men, Sapho elbowed his way out of the front rank. With his arms and face covered in blood, he was like some creature from the underworld. 'Have you entirely lost your wits?' he hissed. 'The enemy is giving ground at last. Another big push, and they'll break.'

'It's too late,' Bostar replied in a flat tone. 'Have you not seen what those fucking falaricae have done to the troops behind us?'

Sapho's rejoinder was instantaneous. 'No. I keep my eyes to the front, not the back.'

Bostar's fists clenched at the imputation. 'Well,' he muttered, 'let me tell you, our entire attack has come to a halt.'

Sapho bared his teeth. 'So? Those motherless curs will turn and run any moment. Then we'll get a foothold inside the walls.'

'Where we will be cut off and annihilated.' Bostar jabbed a finger into Sapho's chest for emphasis. 'Don't you understand? We're on our own up here!'

'Coward!' Sapho screamed. 'You're scared of dying, that's all.'

Bostar's anger surged out of control. 'When the time comes, I will fight and die for Hannibal,' he shouted. 'What's more, I will do it proudly. But there's a difference between dying well, and like a fool. There's nothing to be gained from sacrificing your life, or those of your men, here.'

Spitting on the ground, Sapho made to return to the fight.

'Stop!' Bostar's order was like the crack of a whip.

Stiff-backed, Sapho came to a halt, but he did not turn to face Bostar.

'As your superior officer, I command you to withdraw your men at once,' Bostar cried, making sure that every soldier within earshot heard him.

Defeated, Sapho spun around. 'Yes, *sir*,' he snarled. He raised his voice. 'You heard the order! Fall back!'

It didn't take long for Sapho's men to get the idea. Re-energised by the effect that their volleys had had on the ascending Carthaginian troops, the defenders were beginning to advance again. Behind them, freshly lit falaricae were being carried forward. Encouraged by this, even the civilians who were repairing the breach joined in, hurling stones and fist-sized pieces of masonry at the spearmen.

This increased the ignominy and fuelled Sapho's anger to new levels, all the more because he could now see that Bostar had been right to sound the recall. 'Fool,' he told himself nonetheless. 'It was there for the taking.'

Hannibal was waiting with Malchus and Alete at the bottom of the slope. The general greeted the brothers warmly. 'We were getting worried about you,' he declared.

Malchus rumbled in agreement.

'Sapho here didn't want to leave the fight,' said Bostar generously.

'Last on the field?' Hannibal clapped Sapho on the shoulder. 'But still with the sense to withdraw. Good man! Once the whoresons had panicked your reinforcements, there was no point staying there, eh?'

Sapho flushed and hung his head. 'No, sir.'

'It was a good effort from both of you,' said Malchus encouragingly. 'But it wasn't to be.'

Hannibal took Sapho's reaction to be disappointment. 'Never mind, man. My spies tell me that their food is fast running out. We'll take the place soon! Now, see to your injured.' He waved a hand in dismissal.

'Come on,' said Bostar, leading Sapho away.

'Let go!' Sapho whispered after a few steps. 'I'm not a child!'

'Stop acting like one then!' said Bostar, releasing his grip. 'The least you could do is thank me. I didn't have to cover up for you there.'

Sapho's lip curled. 'I'm damned if I'll do that.'

Bostar threw his eyes to heaven. 'Of course not! Why would you recognise that I just saved your arse from a severe reprimand?'

'Fuck you, Bostar,' Sapho snapped. He felt completely backed into a corner. 'You're always right, aren't you? Everyone loves you, the perfect fucking officer!' Turning on his heel, he stalked off.

Bostar watched him go. Why couldn't he have gone fishing instead of Hanno? he thought. His remorse for even thinking such a thing was instant, but the feeling lingered as he began organising rescue parties for the injured.

For the next two months, the siege went on in much the same fashion. Every full frontal assault made by the Carthaginians was met with dogged, undying determination by the defenders. The vineae regularly smashed more holes in the outer wall, but the attackers could not press home their advantage fully, despite their overwhelming superiority of numbers. Relations between Bostar and Sapho did not improve, and the constant activity meant that it was easy to avoid each other. When they weren't fighting, they were sleeping or looking after their wounded. Malchus, who had not only his own phalanx to deal with, but the extra duties given him by Hannibal, remained unaware of the feud.

Incensed by the manner in which the siege was dragging on, Hannibal eventually ordered the construction of more siege engines: vineae, which protected the men within, and an immense multi-storey tower on wheels. This last, holding catapults and hundreds of soldiers on its various levels, could be moved to whichever point was weakest on a particular day. Its firepower was so great that the battlements could be cleared of defenders within a short time, allowing the wooden terraces which would protect the attacking infantry to be carried forward without hindrance. Fortunately for the Carthaginians, the ramparts had been built on a base of clay, not cement. Using pickaxes, the troops in the terraces set to work, undermining the base of the walls. In this way, a further breach was made, and the attackers' spirits were briefly lifted. Yet all was not as it seemed. Beyond the gaping hole, the Carthaginians found that a crescent-shaped fortification of earth had been thrown up in preparation for this exact eventuality. From behind its protection came repeated volleys of the terrifying falaricae.

At this point, despite the showers of burning javelins, the Carthaginians' relentless determination and superior numbers began to tell. The Saguntines did not have time to rebuild the new damage to their defences properly, and repeated waves of attack finally smashed a passage behind the walls. Despite the defenders' heroism, the position was held. Further successes followed in the subsequent days, but then, with winter approaching, Hannibal was called away by a major rebellion of the fierce tribes that lived near the River Tagus. Maharbal, the officer he left in command, proceeded vigorously with the assault. He gained further ground, driving the weakened defenders into the citadel. The attackers' situation was strengthened by the fact that cholera and other illnesses were now causing heavy casualties among the Saguntines; their food and supplies were also running dangerously low.

By the time Hannibal had put down the uprising and returned, the end was near. The Carthaginian general offered terms to the Saguntine leaders. Incredibly, they were rejected out of hand. With the end of the year nigh, preparations were made for a final, decisive assault. Thanks to their repeated valour, Malchus, his sons and their spearmen had been chosen to be part of the last attack. Typically, Hannibal and his corps of scutarii were also present.

Long before the winter sun had tinted the eastern horizon, they assembled some fifty paces from the walls. Behind them, reaching all the way to the bottom of the slope, were units from every section of the army except the cavalry. Apart from the occasional jingle of mail or muted cough, the soldiers made little noise. The breath of thousands plumed the chill, damp air, the only manifestation of the excitement every man felt. As reward for their long struggle and because of the Saguntines' refusal to parley, Hannibal had told his troops that they had free rein when the city fell. Carthage would take some of the spoils, but the rest was theirs, including the inhabitants: men, women and children.

In serried ranks, they waited as the wooden terraces were pushed forward by torchlight. There was no longer any need for the huge tower with its slingers, spearmen and catapults. Either from lack of men, or missiles, the defenders had recently given up trying to destroy the Carthaginian siege engines. This good fortune meant that the work to undermine the fortifications had been able to proceed much faster than before. According to the engineer in charge, the citadel itself would fall by mid-morning at the latest.

His prediction was accurate. As the first orange fingers of sunlight crept into the sky, ominous rumbles began to fill the air. Within moments, great clouds of smoke began to rise from the centre of the citadel. The crackle of burning wood could also be heard. The Carthaginians paid it no heed. They no longer cared what the Saguntines were doing. With all possible speed, the majority of the soldiers at work in the terraces were pulled back. The danger of being crushed had grown too great. Yet, despite the extreme danger, some remained to finish the task.

They did not have to wait long. With frightening speed, a large piece of the citadel wall suddenly tumbled to the ground. In a chain reaction, it precipitated the thunderous collapse of other, bigger sections. With loud cracks, brickwork and carved stones, which had been in place for decades, even centuries, crumbled and gave way. The noise as they fell more than five storeys was deafening. Inevitably, some of those in the wooden terraces failed to escape in time. A short chorus of strangled screams announced their horrifying demise. Bostar clenched his jaw at the sound. It was what he had expected. As his father had said, ordinary soldiers were expendable. The loss of a certain number meant nothing. And yet to Bostar it did, like the widespread rape, torture and killing of civilians that would shortly take place. Malchus' grim nature and Sapho's even darker personality appeared not to be affected by such things, but Bostar felt it damage his soul. He did not let his determination weaken, however. There were too many things at stake. The defeat of Rome. Revenge for his beloved younger brother, Hanno. The building of a new relationship with Sapho. Whether he would ever achieve any of them, Bostar had no idea. Somehow the last seemed the most unlikely.

Immense clouds of dust clogged the air, but as they finally began to clear, the waiting Carthaginians could see an indefensible breach had been created. A swelling cheer rippled down the slope. At last, victory was at hand.

Bostar felt his spirits rise. He threw Sapho a tight smile, but all he got in return was a scowl.

Drawing his falcata sword, Hannibal led the advance.

It was at this precise moment, because of a warning from the surviving defenders on the battlements perhaps, that the screams began. Ululating, despairing, yet still with shreds of dignity, they filled the air. The Carthaginians' heads shot up. No one could ignore such terrible sounds.

'It's the nobility burning themselves to death.' Malchus' voice revealed an unusual respect. 'They're too proud to become slaves. May it never fall to that in Carthage.'

'Ha! That day will never come,' Sapho replied.

Bostar's instinctive reaction, however, was to utter a prayer to Baal Hammon. Watch over our city for ever, he prayed. Keep it safe from savages such as the Romans.

Hannibal wasn't listening to the noise. He was keen to end the matter. 'Charge!' he screamed in Iberian, and then, for the benefit of the Libyans, he repeated it in his own tongue. Followed by his faithful scutarii, he trotted towards the gaping hole in the citadel. Bellowing the same command,

Malchus, Sapho and Bostar sprang forward with their men. Behind them, the order rang out in half a dozen languages, and, like so many thousand ants, the host of soldiers followed.

Sapho and Bostar's rivalry resurfaced with a vengeance. Whoever reached the top of the breach first would win praise from Hannibal and the respect of the entire army. Outstripping their men, they clambered neck and neck across the uneven and treacherous piles of rubble and broken masonry. With their spears in one hand, and their shields in the other, they had no way of breaking a fall. It was lunacy, but there was no going back now. Hannibal was leading, and they must follow. Soon, the brothers had drawn alongside their leader, who was two steps in front of his scutarii. Hannibal gave them an encouraging grin, which they reciprocated, before glaring at each other.

Glancing over his shoulder an instant later, Bostar's eyes widened. The downward angle of the gradient afforded him a perfect view of the Carthaginian attack. It was a magnificent and terrible sight, guaranteed to drive terror into the hearts of the defenders who remained on the walls. Bostar doubted that any would dare. With the leaders immolating themselves rather than surrender, the ordinary soldiers would be cowering in their homes with their families, or also committing suicide.

He was wrong. Not all the Saguntines had given up the struggle.

As his gaze returned to the slope before him, his attention was drawn by movement up and to the right, on a section of the battlements that was still complete. There Bostar saw six men crouched around an enormous block of stone. Working together, they were pushing it towards the broken end of the walkway that ran along the top of the wall. Bostar followed the trajectory the block would take when it fell, and his heart leaped into his mouth. While the Saguntines' purpose was to cause as many casualties as possible, the potential cost to the Carthaginians was far greater. Bostar could see that within a few heartbeats, Hannibal would be standing full square in the stone's path. A glance at Sapho, and at Hannibal himself, told Bostar that he was the only one to have seen the danger.

When he looked up again, the irregularly shaped block was already teetering on the edge. As Bostar opened his mouth in a warning shout, it tipped forward and fell. Gathering speed unbelievably fast, the stone tumbled and bounced down the slope. Its passage sent showers of brick and masonry into the air, each piece of which was capable of smashing a man's skull. Screaming with delight, the defenders turned and fled, secure in the knowledge that their final effort would kill dozens of Carthaginians.

Bostar did not think. He simply reacted. Dropping his spear, he charged sideways at Hannibal. The air filled with a sudden thunder. Bostar did not look up, for fear of soiling himself. Several scutarii, whose advance his action was checking, mouthed confused curses. Bostar paid no heed. He just prayed that none of the Iberians would think he was trying to harm Hannibal and get in his way. Now he had covered six steps. A dozen. Sensing Bostar's approach, Hannibal turned his head. Confused, he frowned. 'What in the name of Baal Hammon are you doing?' he demanded.

Bostar didn't answer. Leaping forward, he swept his right arm around Hannibal's body and drove them both to the ground, with the general trapped beneath. With his left arm, Bostar raised his shield to cover both their heads. There was a heartbeat's delay, and then the earth shook. Their ears were filled with a reverberation of sound that threatened to deafen them. Thankfully it did not last, but diminished as the block crashed down the slope.

Bostar's first concern was not for himself. 'Are you hurt, sir?'

Hannibal's voice was muffled. 'I don't think so.'

Thank the gods, thought Bostar. Gingerly, he moved his arms and legs. To his delight, they all seemed to work. Discarding his shield, he sat up, helping Hannibal to do the same.

The general swore softly. Perhaps three steps from their position, lay a scutarius. Or at least, what had once been a scutarius. The man had not so much been broken apart as smeared across the uneven ground. His bronze helmet had provided little protection. Chunks of brain matter were spread like white paste on the rocks, providing a sharp contrast to the bright red blood that oozed from the tangled mess of tissue that had been his body. Jagged pieces of brick protruded from the scutarius' back, poking holes in his tunic. His limbs were bent at unnatural, terrible angles, exposing in multiple places the gleaming white ends of broken bones.

He was just the first casualty. Below the corpse stretched a swathe of destruction as far as the eye could see. Bostar had never witnessed anything like it. Dozens of soldiers, perhaps more, had been killed. No. Pulverised,

Bostar thought. A wave of nausea washed over him, and he struggled not to be sick.

Hannibal's voice startled him. 'It appears that I owe you my life.'

Numbly, Bostar nodded.

'My thanks. You are a fine soldier,' said Hannibal, clambering to his feet. He helped Bostar to do the same.

In the same instant, those of Hannibal's scutarii who had not been harmed came swarming in, their faces twisted with alarm. Naturally, the attack had been stalled by the Saguntines' daring action. Anxious questions filled the air as the Iberians established that their beloved commander had not been hurt. Hannibal quickly brushed them off. Picking up his falcata sword, which had fallen to the ground, he looked at Bostar. 'Are you ready to finish what we started?' he asked.

Bostar was stunned by the speed at which Hannibal's composure had returned. He himself was still in shock. He managed to nod his head. 'Of course, sir.'

'Excellent,' replied Hannibal with a brief smile. He indicated that Bostar should advance beside him.

Retrieving his spear, Bostar obeyed. He barely took in the pleased grin that Malchus gave him, and the equally poisonous expression on Sapho's face. Elation had replaced his terror, and he could try to patch things up with his brother later.

For now, it was all about following Hannibal.

A true leader of men.

Chapter IX: Minucius Flaccus

Near Capua, Campania

Hanno leaned against the wall of the kitchen, admiring the view as Elira bent over a table laden down with food. Her dress rode up, exposing her shapely calves and tightening over the swell of her buttocks. Hanno's groin throbbed, and he shifted position to avoid his excitement being obvious. Elira and Quintus were still lovers, but that didn't mean Hanno couldn't admire her from a distance. Alarmingly, Elira had noticed his glances, and returned them with smouldering ones of her own, but Hanno had not risked taking things any further. His newly born – and potentially valuable – friendship with Quintus was too fragile to survive a revelation like that.

Since the fight at the hut, his circumstances had become much easier. Fabricius had been impressed by Quintus' account of the fight and the physical evidence of two live, if wounded, prisoners. Hanno's reward was to be made a household slave. His manacles were removed and he was allowed to sleep in the house. Initially, Hanno was delighted. At one stroke, he had been removed from Agesandros' grasp. Weeks later, he was not so sure. The harsh reality of his situation seemed starker than ever before.

Three times a day, Hanno had to attend the family at their meals. Naturally, he was not allowed to eat with them. He saw Aurelia and Quintus daily from morning to night, but could not talk to them unless no one else was about. Even then, conversations were hurried. It was all so different from the time they had spent together in the woods. Despite the enforced distance between them, Hanno was relieved that the palpable air of comradeship – which had so recently sprung up – had not vanished. Quintus' occasional winks and

Aurelia's shy smiles now lit up his days. Lastly, there was Elira, whose bedroll was not twenty paces from his, on the floor of the atrium, and whom he dared not approach. Hanno knew that he should be grateful for his lot. On the occasions that he and Agesandros came face to face, it was patently clear that the Sicilian still wished him harm.

'Father!' Aurelia's delighted voice echoed from the courtyard. 'You're back!'

As curious as any, Hanno followed the other kitchen slaves to the door. Fabricius hadn't been expected home for at least two weeks.

Dressed in a belted tunic and sandals, Fabricius stood by the main fountain. A broad smile creased his face as Aurelia raced up to him. 'I'm filthy,' he warned. 'Covered in dust from the journey.'

'I don't care!' She wrapped her arms around him. 'It's so good to see you.'

He gave her an affectionate hug. 'I have missed you too.'

A pang of sadness at his own plight plucked at Hanno's heart, but he did not allow himself to dwell on it.

'Husband. Thank the gods for your safe return.' With a sedate smile, Atia joined her husband and daughter. Aurelia pulled away, allowing Fabricius to kiss his wife on the cheek. They gave each other a pleased look, which spoke volumes. 'You must be thirsty.'

'My throat's as dry as a desert riverbed,' Fabricius replied.

Atia's eyes swivelled to the kitchen doorway, and the gaggle of watching slaves. She caught Hanno's gaze first. 'Bring wine! The rest of you, back to work.'

The doorway emptied in a flash. Every slave knew not to cross Atia, who ruled the household with a silken yet iron-hard grip. Quickly, Hanno reached down four of the best glasses from the shelf and placed them on a tray. Julius, the friendly slave who ran the kitchen, was already reaching for an amphora. Hanno watched as he diluted the wine in the Roman fashion with four times the amount of water. 'There you go,' Julius muttered, placing a full jug on the tray. 'Get out there before she calls again.'

Hanno hurried to obey. He was keen to know what had brought about Fabricius' early return. With pricked ears, he carried the tray towards the family, who had just been joined by Quintus.

Quintus grinned broadly, before he remembered that he was now a man. 'Father,' he said solemnly. 'It is good to see you.'

Fabricius pinched his son's cheek. 'You've grown even more.'

Quintus blushed. To cover his embarrassment, he turned expectantly to Hanno. 'Come on, then. Fill them up.'

Hanno stiffened at the order, but did as he was told. His hand paused over the fourth glass, and he looked to Atia.

'Yes, yes, pour one for Aurelia too. She's practically a woman.'

Aurelia's happy expression slipped away. 'Have you found me a husband?' she asked accusingly. 'Is that why you've come back?'

Atia frowned. 'Do not be so presumptuous!'

Aurelia's cheeks flamed red and she hung her head.

'I wish it were that simple, daughter,' Fabricius answered. 'While I have made some progress in that regard, there are far greater events occurring on the world stage.' He clicked his fingers at Hanno, whose heart raced as he moved from person to person, distributing the wine.

'What has happened?' asked Atia.

Instead of answering, Fabricius raised his glass. 'A toast,' he said. 'That the gods, and our ancestors, continue to smile on our family.'

Atia's face tightened a fraction, but she joined in the salutation.

Quintus was less ruled by decorum than his mother, and jumped in the moment his father had swallowed. 'Tell us why you've returned!'

'Saguntum has fallen,' Fabricius replied flatly.

Blood rushed through Hanno's ears, and he was acutely aware of Quintus spinning to regard him. Carefully, he wiped a drop of wine from the jug's lip with a cloth. Inside, every fibre of his being was rejoicing. Hannibal! his mind shouted. Hannibal!

Quintus' gaze shot back to his father. 'When?'

'A week ago. Apparently, they spared virtually no one. Men, women, children. The few who survived were taken as slaves.'

Atia's lips tightened. 'Absolute savages.'

Hanno found Aurelia staring at him with wide, horrified eyes. It's not as if your people don't do exactly the same thing when they sack a city, he thought furiously. Of course he could say nothing, so he turned his face away.

In contrast to his sister, Quintus looked angry. 'It was bad enough that the Senate did nothing to help one of our allies for the last eight months. Surely they'll act now?'

'They will,' Fabricius replied. 'In fact, they already have.'

The following silence echoed louder than a trumpet call.

'An embassy has been sent to Carthage, its mission to demand that Hannibal and his senior officers be handed over immediately to face justice for their heinous actions.'

Hanno squeezed the cloth so hard that it dripped wine on to the mosaic between his feet.

No one noticed. Not that Hanno would have cared. How dare they? his mind screamed. Bastard Romans!

'They will hardly do that,' said Atia.

'Of course not,' Fabricius answered, unaware of Hanno's silent but fervent agreement. 'No doubt Hannibal has his enemies, but the Carthaginians are a proud race. They will want redress for the humiliations we subjected them to after the war in Sicily. This grants them that opportunity.'

Quintus hesitated for a moment. 'You're talking about war?'

Fabricius nodded. 'I think that's what it will come to, yes. There are those in the Senate who disagree with me, but I think they underestimate Hannibal. A man who has achieved what he has in a few short years would not have embarked on the siege of Saguntum without it being part of a larger plan. Hannibal wanted a war with Rome all along.'

How right you are, thought Hanno exultantly.

Quintus was also jubilant. 'Gaius and I can join the cavalry!'

Fabricius' obvious pride was tempered by Atia's reticence. Even she could not hide the sadness that flashed across her eyes. Her composure returned quickly. 'You will make a fine soldier.'

Quintus blew out his chest with satisfaction. 'I must tell Gaius. Can I go to Capua?'

Fabricius gave an approving nod. 'Go on. You'll need to hurry. It's not long until dark.'

'I'll come back tomorrow.' With a grateful smile, Quintus was gone.

Looking after him, Atia sighed. 'And the other matter?'

'There is some good news.' Seeing Aurelia's instant interest, Fabricius clammed up. 'I'll tell you later.'

Aurelia's face fell. 'Everything is so unfair,' she cried, and hurried off to her room.

Atia touched Fabricius' arm to still his rebuke. 'Let her go. It must be hard for her.'

Hanno was oblivious to the family drama. Suddenly, his desire to escape, to reach Iberia and join his countrymen in their conflict, was overwhelming. It was what he had dreamed of for so long! Yet his debt to Quintus loomed large in his mind too. Had it been repaid by what he'd done at the shepherd's hut or not? Hanno wasn't sure. Then there was Suniaton. How could he even entertain leaving without trying to find his best friend? Hanno was grateful when he heard Julius' voice calling him. The conflicting emotions in his head were threatening to tear him apart.

Time went by, and Hanno was still working in the kitchen. Although an answer regarding his obligation to Quintus evaded him yet, he could not bring himself to abandon the farm without some attempt to find Suniaton. How the quest would be achieved, Hanno had no idea. Apart from him, who knew, or even cared, where Suniaton was now? The unanswerable dilemma kept him awake at night, and even distracted him from his usual lustful thoughts about Elira. Tired and irritable, he paid little attention one day when Julius announced an exhaustive menu that Atia had ordered for the following evening. 'Apparently, she and the master are expecting an important visitor,' said Julius pompously. 'Caius Minucius Flaccus.'

'Who in the name of Hades is that?' asked one of the cooks.

Julius gave him a disapproving look. 'He's a senior figure in the Minucii clan, and the brother of a former consul.'

'He'll be an arrogant prick then,' muttered the cook.

Julius ignored the titters this produced. 'He's also a member of the embassy that has just returned from Carthage,' he declared as if the matter were of some importance to him.

Hanno's stomach turned over. 'Really? Are you sure?'

Julius' lips pursed. 'That's what I heard the mistress saying,' he snapped. 'Now get on with your work.'

Hanno's heart was thudding off his ribs like that of a caged bird as he went out to the storage sheds. Would Fabricius' visitor speak of what he'd seen? Hanno begged the gods that he would. Passing the entrance to the heated bathroom, he saw Quintus stripping off. Well for him, thought Hanno sourly. He hadn't had a hot bath since leaving Carthage.

Blithely unaware of Hanno's feelings, Quintus' excitement was rising by the moment. Wanting to look his best that evening, he bathed, before enjoying a massage by a slave. Sleepily imagining how Flaccus might recount everything that had gone on in Carthage, he was barely aware of Fabricius entering the room.

'This visit is very important, you know.'

Quintus opened his eyes. 'Yes, Father. And we will play our part in the war, if it comes.'

Fabricius half smiled. 'That goes without saying. When Rome calls, we answer.' Clasping his hands behind his back, he walked up and down in silence.

The feel of the strigil on his skin began to irritate Quintus, and he gestured at the slave to stop. 'What is it?'

'It's about Aurelia,' Fabricius answered.

'You've arranged to marry her off, then,' he said, shooting his father a bitter glance.

'It's not definite yet,' said Fabricius. 'But Flaccus liked what he heard of Aurelia when I visited him in the capital some time ago. Now he wants to see her beauty for himself.'

Quintus scowled at his naïveté. Why else would a high-ranking politician pay a social visit to equestrians as lowly as they?

'Come now,' said Fabricius sternly. 'You knew this would happen one day. It's for the good of the family. Flaccus is not that old, and his clan is powerful and well connected. With the support of the Minucii, the Fabricii could go far.' He stared at Quintus. 'In Rome, I mean. You understand what I'm saying?'

Quintus sighed. 'Does Aurelia know yet?'

'No.' It was Fabricius' turn to look troubled. 'I thought I would speak to you first.'

'Make me part of it?'

'Don't take that line with me. You would also benefit,' snapped his father.

Excitement flared in Quintus' breast, and he hated himself for it. He'd seen Aurelia mooning over Hanno. An impossible infatuation for her, but one he'd done nothing to end. And now this. 'What made you decide on Flaccus?'

'I've been trying to organise something for the last two years,' Fabricius replied. 'Searching for the right man for our family, and for Aurelia. It's a tricky business, but I think Flaccus could be the one. He was going to be passing close to here anyway upon his return from Carthage. All I did was to make sure that an invitation was waiting for him when he landed.'

Quintus was surprised by his father's cunning. No doubt his mother had had a hand in it, he thought. 'How old is he?'

'Thirty-five or so,' said Fabricius. 'That's a lot better than some of the old goats who wanted to meet her. I hope she appreciates that.' He paused. 'One last thing.'

Quintus looked up.

'Don't ask any questions about what happened in Carthage,' his father warned. 'It is still a matter of state secrecy. If Flaccus chooses to fill us in on some of the details, so be it. If he does not, it's none of our business to ask.' With that, he was gone.

Quintus lay back on the warm stone slab, but all his enjoyment was gone. He would go to Aurelia the moment his father had finished speaking with her. What he would say, Quintus had no idea. His mood dark, he got dressed. The best place to watch Aurelia's doorway unobtrusively was from a corner of the tablinum. Quintus made his way to the large reception room. He hadn't been there long when Hanno entered, carrying a tray of crockery.

Seeing Quintus, Hanno smiled. 'Looking forward to this evening?' I am, he thought with glee.

'Not really,' Quintus replied dourly.

Hanno raised his eyebrows. 'Why not? You don't receive many visitors.'

Quintus was surprised to find that his excitement about what Flaccus might say was muted by his friendship with Hanno. 'It's hard to explain,' he replied awkwardly.

At that moment, Fabricius strode from Aurelia's room, banging the door behind him. His jaw was set with anger.

Their conversation instantly came to an end. Hanno could only watch as Quintus entered his sister's chamber in turn. Hanno was genuinely fond of Aurelia. Part of him wondered what was going on, but part of him didn't care. Finally, Carthage was at war with Rome once more.

Somehow, he would be involved in it.

Quintus found Aurelia lying on her bed, huge sobs racking her body. He rushed to kneel by her side. 'It will be all right,' he whispered, reaching out to stroke her hair. 'Flaccus sounds like a good man.'

Her crying redoubled, and Quintus muttered a curse. Mentioning the man's name was the worst possible thing he could have done. Not knowing what to do, he rubbed Aurelia's shoulders comfortingly. They stayed in that position without talking for a long time. Finally, Aurelia rolled over. Her cheeks were red and blotchy, and her eyes swollen from weeping. 'I must look terrible,' she said.

Quintus gave her a crooked smile. 'You're still beautiful,' he replied.

She stuck out her tongue. 'Liar.'

'A bath will help,' advised Quintus. He put on a jovial face. 'Won't it?'

Aurelia could not keep up the pretence. 'What am I going to do?' she whispered miserably.

'It was going to happen sometime,' said Quintus. 'Why don't you give him the benefit of the doubt? If you really hate him, Father would not make you go ahead with the marriage.'

'I suppose not,' Aurelia replied dubiously. She thought for a moment. 'I know I have to do what Father says. It's so hard, though, especially when . . .' Her voice died away, and new tears filled her eyes.

Quintus raised a finger to her lips. 'Don't say it,' he whispered. 'You can't.' He didn't want to hear it spoken out loud.

With great effort, Aurelia regained control of her emotions. She nodded resolutely. 'Better get ready, then. I have to look my best tonight.'

Quintus drew her into a warm embrace. 'That's the spirit,' he whispered. Possessing courage was not an exclusively male quality, he realised. Nor was it confined to the battlefield or the hunt. Aurelia had just shown that she had plenty of it too.

Flaccus arrived mid-afternoon, accompanied by a large party of slaves and soldiers, and was immediately ushered to the best guest room to freshen up. Apart from his personal slaves, most of Flaccus' retinue stayed outside, where they were quartered in the farmyard. Hanno was busy in the kitchen and saw little of the proceedings for some time. An hour later, loud voices announced the appearance of Martialis and Gaius. They were greeted jovially by Fabricius, and guided to the banqueting hall off the courtyard where, following tradition, they were first served *mulsum*, a mixture of wine and honey. Elira performed this task, leaving Hanno to wait impatiently in the kitchen. As darkness fell, he walked around the courtyard, lighting the bronze oil lamps that hung from every pillar. At the corner furthest from the tablinum, Hanno sensed movement behind him. He turned, gaining an impression of a handsome man in a toga with thick black hair and a big nose before Flaccus disappeared into the banqueting hall. Quintus and his sister arrived soon after, wearing their best clothes. Hanno had never seen Aurelia wearing make-up before. To his surprise, he liked what he saw.

Finally, the meal was ready, and Hanno could enter the room with the other slaves. He was to remain there for the duration of the meal, serving food, clearing away plates and, most importantly of all, listening to the conversation. He waited attentively behind the left-hand couch, where Fabricius reclined with Martialis and Gaius. As an important guest, Flaccus had been given the central couch, while Atia, Quintus and an impassive Aurelia occupied the right-hand one. In customary fashion, the fourth side of the table had been left open.

Flaccus spent much of his time complimenting Aurelia on her looks and trying to engage her in conversation. His attempts met with little initial success. Finally, when Atia began to glare at her openly, she started to respond. To Hanno, it was obvious that she was being insincere, merely doing what her mother wished. Flaccus did not seem to notice this, or that apart from Fabricius, the others present did not dare to address him. Quintus and Gaius alone cast frequent glances at Flaccus, hoping in vain for news of Carthage. Quaffing large amounts of mulsum and wine, the black-haired politician seemed more and more taken by Aurelia as the night went on.

Over the sweet platters, Flaccus turned to Fabricius. 'My compliments on your daughter. She is as beautiful as you said. More so, perhaps.'

Fabricius inclined his head gravely. 'Thank you.'

'I think we should talk further on this matter in the morning,' boomed Flaccus. 'Come to a mutually satisfactory arrangement.'

Fabricius allowed himself a small smile. 'That would be a great honour.'

Atia murmured her agreement.

'Excellent.' Flaccus looked at Hanno. 'More wine.'

Hanno hurried forward, his face a neutral mask. He wasn't sure how he felt about what had just been said. Not that it mattered, he reflected bitterly. Here I am a slave. His resentment over his status surged back, stronger than ever, and he dismissed his concern about Aurelia's possible betrothal. The bonds that tied him to the farm were weakening. If Aurelia married Flaccus, she would go to live in Rome. Quintus was always talking about joining the army. When he left, Hanno would be left friendless and alone. On the spot, he resolved to begin planning his escape.

Quintus had decided that Flaccus seemed quite personable and glanced sidelong at Aurelia. He was delighted to see no sign of distress in her face, and marvelled at her equanimity. Then he noted the slight flush to her cheeks, and her empty glass. Was she drunk? It wouldn't take much. Aurelia rarely consumed wine. In spite of this, Quintus found his head full of the possibilities that an alliance between the Fabricii and Minucii would create. Aurelia and Flaccus would get used to each other, he told himself. That's the way most marriages worked. He reached out to touch Aurelia's hand. She smiled, and he was reassured.

The conversation flitted about for some time, with talk of the weather, the crops and the quality of the games in Capua compared to Rome. No one mentioned the one topic that everyone wanted to know about: what had happened in Carthage?

It was Martialis who eventually broached the subject. As was his wont, he had been drinking large amounts. Draining his cup yet again, he saluted Flaccus. 'They say that the Carthaginian wines are very drinkable.'

'They are agreeable enough,' accepted Flaccus. He pursed his lips. 'Unlike the people who produce them.'

Martialis was oblivious to Fabricius' frowns. 'Will we be seeing such vintages in Italy more often?' he asked with a wink.

Flaccus dragged his eyes away from Aurelia. 'Eh?'

'Tell us what happened in Carthage,' begged Martialis. 'We are all dying to know.'

Hanno held his breath, and he could see Quintus doing the same.

Slowly, Flaccus took in the rapt faces around him. His features took on a self-important expression, and he smiled, pompously. 'Nothing I say is to travel beyond these walls.'

'Of course not,' Martialis murmured. 'You can be assured of our discretion.'

Even Fabricius joined in with the buzz of agreement.

Satisfied, Flaccus began. 'I was but a minor member of the party, although I like to think my contribution was noted. We were led by the two consuls, Lucius Aemilius Paullus and Marcus Livius Salinator. Our spokesman was the former censor Marcus Fabius Buteo.' He let the important names sink in. 'From the start, it seemed that our mission would be successful. The omens were good, and the crossing from Lilybaeum uneventful. We reached Carthage three weeks ago to the day.'

Hanno closed his eyes and imagined the scene. The massive fortifications gleaming in the winter sun. The magnificent temple of Eshmoun dominating the top of Byrsa Hill. The twin harbours full of ships. Home, he thought with a jolt of longing. Will I ever see it again?

Flaccus' next words brought him back to earth with a jolt. 'Arrogant sons of whores,' he growled. He glanced at Atia. 'My apologies. But the most significant men in Rome had arrived, and who had they sent to meet us? A junior officer of the city guard.'

Martialis' face went purple with rage, and he nearly choked on a mouthful of wine.

Fabricius was of a calmer disposition. 'It must have been a mistake, surely,' he said.

Flaccus scowled. 'On the contrary. The gesture was quite deliberate. They had made up their minds before we even disembarked from our ships. Instead of being allowed time to wash and recover from the journey, we were escorted straight to the Senate.'

Martialis snorted. 'Typical bloody guggas. No sense of decorum.'

Aurelia cast Hanno a quick, sympathetic glance.

The Carthaginian was so angry that he dared not look back at her. He longed to smash the clay jug in his hands over Martialis' head, but of course he did nothing. Punishment aside, what Flaccus had to say next was of far more importance.

'And when you got there?' asked Quintus eagerly.

'Fabius announced who we were. No one responded. They just stood there looking at us. Waiting, like so many jackals around a corpse. And so Fabius demanded to know if Hannibal's attack on Saguntum had been carried out with their approval.' Flaccus paused, breathing heavily. 'Do you know what they did then?' A vein pulsed in his forehead. 'They laughed at us.'

Martialis slammed his beaker on the table. Fabricius spat a curse, while Quintus and Gaius gaped at each other, stunned that anyone would treat the Republic's most prominent statesmen in such a manner. Atia took the opportunity to mutter something in Aurelia's ear. Hanno, meanwhile, had to bite the inside of his cheek to stop himself from laughing out loud. Carthage had not lost all of its pride when it lost Sicily and Sardinia to Rome, he reflected proudly.

'There were some who spoke out against Hannibal,' Flaccus conceded. 'The loudest among them was a fat man called Hostus.'

Treacherous bastard! thought Hanno. What I'd give to stick a knife in his belly.

'But they were shouted down by the vast majority, who disputed the treaty signed by Hasdrubal six years ago and rejected any need to acknowledge Saguntum's links with Rome. They were shouting and hurling abuse at us,' growled Flaccus. 'We took counsel with each other, and decided we had only one option.'

Quintus glanced at Hanno. He had had no idea that the Carthaginians would react with such force. Stunned by what he saw, he looked again. Quintus knew Hanno's body language well enough to realise that he *had* known. Flaccus' voice stopped him from dwelling on the matter further.

'Fabius walked into the middle of the chamber. That shut the guggas up,' said Flaccus fiercely. 'Gripping the folds of his toga, he told them that within he held both peace and war. They could have whichever they pleased. At his words, the place descended into chaos. It was impossible even to hear yourself speak.'

'Did they opt for war?' demanded Fabricius.

'No,' revealed Flaccus. 'Instead, the presiding suffete told Fabius that he should choose.'

By now everyone in the room, even Elira, was hanging on his every word.

'Fabius looked at us to confirm that we were of one mind, and then he told the guggas that he let fall war.' Flaccus barked a short, angry laugh. 'They've got balls, I'll grant them that. Fabius had hardly finished speaking when practically every single man in the chamber stood up and yelled, "We accept it!"'

Hanno found he could no longer conceal his delight. Picking up two handfuls of dirty plates, he headed for the kitchen. No one except Aurelia noticed him leave. But once outside the door, Hanno's desire to hear more was so great that he lingered on, eavesdropping.

'I always hoped that another war with Carthage could be avoided,' said Fabricius heavily. His jaw hardened. 'But they leave us no choice. Insulting you and your colleagues, and especially the consuls, in that manner is unforgivable.'

'Absolutely right,' thundered Martialis. 'The curs must be taught an even better lesson than last time.'

Flaccus was pleased by their reactions. 'Good,' he muttered. 'Why don't you both come with me to Rome? Much needs to be arranged, and we will need men who have fought Carthage before.'

'It would be my honour,' replied Fabricius.

'And mine,' added Martialis. An embarrassed look crossed his florid face, and he tapped his right leg. 'Except for this. It's an old injury, from Sicily. Nowadays, I can barely walk more than a quarter of a mile without stopping for a rest.'

'You have more than done your duty for Rome,' said Flaccus reassuringly. 'I shall just take Fabricius.'

Quintus was on his feet before he knew it. 'I want to fight too.'

Gaius echoed his cry a heartbeat later.

Flaccus' smile was patronising. 'Both quite the dogs of war, aren't you? But I'm afraid that you're still too young. This struggle needs to be won fast, and the best men to do that are veterans.'

'I'm seventeen,' protested Quintus. 'So is Gaius.'

Flaccus' face darkened. 'Remember whom you are speaking to,' he snapped.

'Quintus! Sit down,' Fabricius ordered. 'You too, Gaius.' As the two reluctantly obeyed, he turned to Flaccus. 'My apologies. They're eager, that's all.'

'It's of no matter. Their time will come,' Flaccus replied smoothly, shooting Quintus a look of venom. It was gone so fast that no one else noticed. Quintus wondered if he'd been mistaken, but a moment later he saw something else. Aurelia made her excuses and retired for the night. Flaccus watched her retreating back as a serpent might look at a mouse. Quintus blinked, trying to clear his head, which was fuzzy from wine. When he looked again, Flaccus' expression was benevolent. I must have been imagining it, he concluded. Quintus was then disappointed to see the three older men gather in a huddle and begin muttering in low voices. Atia jerked her head at him in a clear sign of dismissal. Frustrated, Quintus beckoned Gaius outside to the courtyard.

Their appearance startled Hanno. Having hidden from Aurelia, he was only just emerging from behind an ornamental statue. Looking guilty, he scuttled off to the kitchen.

Gaius frowned. 'What in Hades is he up to?'

Later, Quintus was not sure whether it was because of the wine he'd drunk or his anger at the treatment of the Roman embassy. Either way, he wanted to lash out at someone. 'Who cares?' he snapped. 'He's a gugga. Let him go.' Quintus regretted the words the instant they left his mouth. He made to walk after Hanno, but Gaius, who was laughing, dragged him over to a stone bench by the fountain. 'Let's talk,' his friend muttered drunkenly.

Quintus dared not pull away. The darkness concealed his stricken face.

His shoulders stiff with repressed fury, Hanno did not look back. It was ten more steps to the kitchen, where he clattered the dishes angrily into the sink. So much for friendship with a Roman, he thought, bitterness coursing through his veins. He knew that Aurelia was sympathetic towards him, but he could not be sure of anyone else. Especially Quintus. The anger he'd heard in all the nobles' voices at Flaccus' revelation was natural, yet it changed Hanno's situation completely. In principle, he was now an enemy. His own delight at the matter would have to be buried so deeply that no one could see it. In the close confines of the house, Hanno knew how difficult this would prove. He exhaled slowly. An important decision had just been made for him. He should run away. Soon. But to Carthage or Iberia? And was there any chance of finding Suniaton before he left?

Chapter X: Betrayal

T he next morning Quintus had another hangover, and his memories of Flaccus' facial expressions were hazy. Enough disquiet
remained in his mind, however, for him to seek out his father.
He found Fabricius closeted in his office with Flaccus. The pair were
busily drawing up Aurelia's betrothal papers, and looked irritated by the
distraction. Fabricius brushed off Quintus' muttered request for a word.
Seeing his son's disappointment, he relented slightly. 'Tell me later,' he
said.

Glumly, Quintus shut the door. He had other things on his mind too.
He had insulted Hanno cruelly and he was ashamed. The Carthaginian's
status meant that Quintus could treat him in any way he chose, but of
course that was not the point. *He saved my life. We are friends now,*
thought Quintus. *I owe him an apology.* Yet his quest to resolve this
problem proved as frustrating as his attempt to speak with his father. He
found Hanno easily enough, but the Carthaginian pretended not to hear
Quintus' voice when he called, and avoided all attempts to make eye contact.
Quintus didn't want to make a scene, and there was so much going on
that he could not even find a quiet corner to explain. Fabricius' decision
to accompany Flaccus to Rome and thence to war meant that the place
was a flurry of activity. Every household slave was occupied in one way
or another. Clothes, furniture and blankets had to be packed, armour
polished and weapons sharpened.

Quintus went miserably in search of Aurelia. He wasn't sure whether
he should mention anything about Flaccus. All he had to go on were two
fleeting glimpses, observed while under the influence of too much wine.
He decided to see what frame of mind Aurelia was in before saying a word.
If she was still feeling positive about the marriage, he would say nothing.

The last thing Quintus wanted to do was upset his sister's fragile acceptance of her lot.

To his surprise, Aurelia was in excellent humour. 'He is so handsome,'
she gushed. 'And not that old either. I think we will be very happy.'

Burying his doubts, Quintus nodded and smiled.

'He strikes me as being quite arrogant, but what man of his position
isn't? His loyalty to Rome is beyond doubt, and that is all that matters.'
Aurelia's face grew troubled. 'I felt so sorry for Hanno last night. The
horrible names they were calling his people were so unnecessary. Have you
spoken with him?'

Quintus looked away. 'No.'

Aurelia reacted with typical female intuition. 'What's wrong?' she
demanded.

'Nothing,' Quintus replied. 'I have a hangover, that's all.'

She bent to catch his eye. 'Did you argue with Hanno?'

'No,' he answered. 'Yes. I don't know.'

Aurelia raised her eyebrows, and Quintus knew that she would not leave
it alone until he told her. 'When I left with Gaius, it looked like Hanno
had been eavesdropping outside the door,' he said.

'Is that surprising? We were talking about a war between his people and
ours,' Aurelia observed tartly. 'What does it matter anyway? He was there
in the room when Flaccus told us the most important part of his story.'

'I know,' Quintus muttered. 'It seemed suspicious, though. Gaius wanted
to challenge him, but I told him not to bother. That Hanno was just a
gugga.'

Aurelia's hand rose to her mouth. 'Quintus! How could you?'

Quintus hung his head. 'I wanted to say sorry straightaway . . . but
Gaius wanted to talk,' he finished lamely. 'I couldn't walk off and leave
him.'

'I hope you've apologised this morning,' Aurelia said sternly.

Quintus could not get over Aurelia's level of self-assurance. It was as
if her betrothal had added five years to her age. 'I've tried,' he answered.
'But there's too much going on to get a quiet moment alone with him.'

Aurelia pursed her lips. 'Father is leaving in a few hours. There will be
plenty of time after that.'

Finally, Quintus met her gaze. 'Don't worry,' he said. 'I'll do it.'

He had cause to rethink his opinion of Flaccus later that morning. With the betrothal agreement signed, the black-haired politician suddenly started to make much of his new brother-in-law-to-be. 'No doubt this war with Carthage will be over quickly – maybe even before you've completed your military training,' he declared, throwing an arm around Quintus' shoulders. 'Never fear. There will be other conflicts for you to win glory in. The Gauls on our northern borders are forever causing trouble. So too are the Illyrians. Philip of Macedon cannot be trusted either. A brave young officer like you could go far indeed. Perhaps even make tribune.'

Quintus grinned from ear to ear. While the Fabricii were of equestrian rank, their status was not so high that it was likely he'd reach the tribuneship. Under the patronage of someone really powerful, however, the process would be much more straightforward. Flaccus' words did much to soothe Quintus' disappointment at not accompanying his father. 'I look forward to serving Rome,' he said proudly. 'Wherever it may send me.'

Flaccus clapped him on the back. 'That's the attitude.' Seeing Aurelia, he pushed Quintus away. 'Let me talk with my betrothed before I go. It's a long time until June.'

Delighted by the prospect of a glittering military career, Quintus put down Flaccus' powerful shove as nothing more than the excitement of a prospective bridegroom. Aurelia was turning into a beautiful young woman. Who wouldn't want to marry her? Leaving Flaccus alone, Quintus went in search of his father.

'Aurelia!' called Flaccus, entering the courtyard.

Aurelia, who had been wondering what married life would be like, jumped. She made a stiff little bow. 'Flaccus.'

'Walk with me.' He made an inviting gesture.

Twin points of colour rose in Aurelia's cheeks. 'I'm not sure Mother would approve . . .'

'What do you take me for?' Flaccus' tone was mildly shocked. 'I would never presume to take you outside the villa without a chaperone. I meant a stroll here in the courtyard, where everyone can see us.'

'Naturally,' Aurelia replied, flustered. 'I'm sorry.'

'The fault is all mine for not explaining,' he said with a reassuring smile. 'I merely thought that, with us to be wed, it would be good for us to spend a little time together. War is coming, and soon occasions such as this will be impossible.'

'Yes, of course.' She hurried to his side.

Flaccus drank her in. 'Bacchus can make the most crab-faced crone look appealing, and the gods know I drank enough of his juice to think that last night. But your beauty is even more evident in the light of the sun,' he said. 'That *is* a rare quality.'

Unused to such compliments, Aurelia blushed to the roots of her hair. 'Thank you,' she whispered.

They strolled around the perimeter of the courtyard. Awkward with the silence, Aurelia began pointing out the plants and trees that occupied much of the space. There were lemon, almond and fig trees, and vines snaking across a wooden latticework that formed an artificial shaded corridor. 'This is such a bad time of year to see it,' she said. 'During the summer, the place is so beautiful. By the Vinalia Rustica, you can barely move for the fruit.'

'I'm sure it's spectacular, but I didn't come here to talk about grapes.' Seeing her embarrassment increase, Flaccus continued, 'Tell me about yourself. What do you like to do?'

Anxious, Aurelia wondered what he'd want to hear. 'I enjoy speaking Greek. And I'm better at algebra and geometry than Quintus.'

The corners of his mouth twitched. 'Are you indeed? That's wonderful. An educated girl, then.'

She flushed again. 'I suppose.'

'You'd probably give me a run for my money. Mathematics was never my favourite subject.'

Aurelia's confidence grew a little. 'What about philosophy?'

He looked down his long nose at her. 'The concepts of *pietas* and *officium* were being taught to me before I'd even been weaned. My father made sure that serving Rome means everything to me and my brother. We had to be schooled too, of course. Before we had any military experience, he sent us to study at the Stoic school in Athens. I didn't enjoy my time there much, however. All they did was sit around and talk in stuffy debating chambers. It reminds me a little of the Senate.' Flaccus' face brightened.

'Soon, though, I might be granted a senior position in one of the legions. I'm sure that will be more to my style.'

Aurelia found his enthusiasm endearing. It reminded her of Quintus, which made her think of what he might achieve once she had married into such an important family. 'Your brother has already served as consul, hasn't he?'

'Yes,' Flaccus replied proudly. 'He crushed the Boii four years ago.'

Aurelia had never heard of the Boii, but she wasn't going to admit it. 'I've heard Father mention that campaign,' she said knowledgeably. 'It was a fine victory.'

'May the gods grant that I achieve the same level of success one day,' Flaccus said fervently. His gaze went distant for a moment before returning to Aurelia. 'Not to say I don't like ordinary pleasures like watching chariot races, or going riding, and hunting.'

'So do I,' Aurelia said without thinking.

He smiled indulgently. 'The racing in Rome is the best in Italy. I'll take you to see it as often as you wish.'

Aurelia felt slightly annoyed. 'That's not what I meant.'

There was a small frown. 'I don't understand.'

Her courage wavered for a moment. Then she thought naïvely, If he's to be my husband, we should tell each other everything. 'I love riding too.'

Flaccus' frown grew. 'You mean watching your father or Quintus as they train their horses?'

'No. I can ride.' She was delighted by his astonishment.

It was Flaccus' turn to be irritated. 'How? Who taught you?' he demanded.

'Quintus. He says I'm a natural.'

'Your brother taught you how to ride?'

Pinned by his direct stare, Aurelia's confidence began to seep away. 'Yes,' she muttered. 'I made him.'

Flaccus barked a short laugh. 'You *made* him? Fabricius mentioned none of this when he was singing your praises.'

Aurelia looked down. I should have kept my mouth shut, she thought. Lifting her head, she found Flaccus scrutinising her. She shifted uneasily beneath his gaze.

'Do you fight also?'

Aurelia's mouth opened at his unexpected tack.

He thrust his right arm forward, mimicking a sword thrust. 'Can you wield a gladius?'

Worried by what she'd already revealed, Aurelia kept her lips sealed.

'I asked you a question.' Flaccus' voice was soft, but his eyes were granite hard.

What I've done isn't a crime, thought Aurelia angrily. 'Yes, I can,' she retorted. 'I'm far better with a sling, though.'

Flaccus threw his hands in the air. 'I'm to be married to an Amazon!' he cried. 'Do your parents know of this?'

'Of course not.'

'No, I don't suppose Fabricius would be too pleased. I can only imagine what Atia's reaction might be.'

'Please don't tell them,' Aurelia begged. 'Quintus would be in so much trouble.'

He watched her for a moment, before a wolfish smile crossed his lips. 'Why would I say a word?'

Aurelia couldn't believe her ears. 'You don't mind?'

'No! It shows your Roman spirit, and it means that our sons will be warriors.' Flaccus held up a warning finger. 'Don't expect that you can carry on using weapons when we're married, however. Such behaviour is not acceptable in Rome.'

'And riding?' Aurelia whispered.

'We'll see,' he said. He saw her face fall, and a strange look entered his eyes. 'My estate outside the capital is very large. Unless I tell them, no one knows what goes on there.'

Overwhelmed by Flaccus' reaction, Aurelia missed the silky emphasis he laid on the last seven words. Perhaps marriage would not be as bad as she'd thought. She took his arm. 'It's your turn to tell me about yourself now,' she murmured.

He gave her a pleased look, and began.

Quintus found his father outside, supervising the loading of his baggage on to a train of mules.

Fabricius smiled as he emerged. 'What was it that you wanted to tell me earlier?'

'It was nothing important,' Quintus demurred. He had decided to give Flaccus the benefit of the doubt. He cast a dubious eye over the pack animals, which were laden down with every piece of his father's military equipment. 'How long do you think this war will last? Flaccus seems certain that it will be over in a few months.'

Fabricius checked that no one was in earshot. 'I think he's a little over-confident. You know what politicians can be like.'

'But Flaccus is talking about getting married in June.'

Fabricius winked. 'He wanted to settle on a date. I obliged. What could be better than the most popular month of the year? And if it can't take place because we're still on campaign, the betrothal agreement ensures that it will happen at some stage.'

Quintus grinned at Fabricius' guile. He thought for a moment, deciding that his father was more likely to be correct than Flaccus about the war's duration. 'I'm already old enough to enlist.'

Fabricius' face turned serious. 'I know,' he said. 'As well as keeping an eye on you, I have asked Martialis to enrol you in the local cavalry unit, alongside Gaius. In my absence, your mother is obviously responsible for Aurelia and the care of the farm, but you will have to help her in every way possible. Yet I see no reason why you should not also begin your training.'

Quintus' eyes glittered with delight.

'Don't get any madcap ideas,' his father warned. 'There is no question of being called up in the immediate future. The horsemen supplied by Rome and its surrounding area will be more than enough for the moment.'

Quintus did his best not to look disappointed.

Fabricius took him by the shoulders. 'Listen to me. War is not all valour and glory: far from it. It's about blood, filth and fighting until you can barely grip a sword. You'll see terrible things. Men bleeding to death for lack of a tourniquet. Comrades and friends dying in front of you, crying for their mothers.'

It was becoming more difficult to hold his father's gaze.

'You are a fine young man,' said Fabricius proudly. 'Your time to fight in the front line will come. Until then, gain every bit of experience you can. If that means you miss the war with Carthage, so be it. Those initial weeks of training are vital if you want to survive more than the first few moments of a battle.'

'Yes, Father.'

'Good,' said Fabricius, looking satisfied. 'May the gods keep you safe and well.'

'And you also.' Despite his best effort, Quintus' voice wobbled.

Atia waited until Quintus had gone inside before emerging. 'He's almost a man,' she said wistfully. 'It only seems the blink of an eye since he was playing with his wooden toys.'

'I know.' Fabricius smiled. 'The years fly by, don't they? I can remember saying goodbye to you before leaving for Sicily as if it were yesterday. And here we are again, in much the same situation.'

Atia reached up to touch his face. 'You have to come back to me, do you hear?'

'I will do my best. Make sure that the altar is well stocked with offerings,' he warned. 'The lares have to be kept happy.'

She pretended to look shocked. 'You know I'll do that every day.'

Fabricius chuckled. 'I do. Just as you know that I'll pray daily to Mars and Jupiter for their protection.'

Atia's face became solemn. 'Are you still sure that Flaccus is a good choice for Aurelia?'

His brows lowered. 'Eh?'

'Is he the right man?'

'I thought he came across well last night,' said Fabricius with a surprised look. 'Arrogant, of course, but one expects that from someone of his rank. He was plainly taken with Aurelia too, which was good. He's ambitious, presentable and wealthy.' He eyed Atia. 'Isn't that enough?'

She pursed her lips.

'Atia?'

'I can't put my finger on it,' she said eventually. 'I don't trust him.'

'You need more than a vague idea, surely, for me to break off a betrothal with this potential?' asked Fabricius, looking irritated. 'Remember how much money we owe!'

'I'm not saying that you should call off the arrangement,' she said in a conciliatory tone.

'What then?'

'Just keep an eye on Flaccus when you're in Rome. You'll be spending plenty of time with him. That will give you a far better measure of the man than we could ever gain in one night.' She caressed his arm. 'That's not too much to ask, is it?'

'No,' he murmured. A relenting smile twitched across his lips, and he bent to kiss her. 'You do have a knack of sniffing out the rotten apple in the barrel. I'll trust you one more time.'

'Stop teasing me,' she cried. 'I'm serious.'

'I know you are, my love. And I'll do what you say.' He tapped the side of his nose. 'Flaccus won't have a clue, but I'll be watching his every move.'

Atia's expression lightened. 'Thank you.'

Fabricius gave her backside an affectionate squeeze. 'Now, why don't we say goodbye properly?'

Atia's look grew kittenish. 'That sounds like an excellent idea.' Taking his hand, she led him into the house.

An hour later, and a deathly quiet hung over the house. Promising a quick victory over the Carthaginians, Fabricius and Flaccus had departed for Rome. Feeling thoroughly depressed, Quintus sought out Hanno. There was little left to do in the way of household chores, and the Carthaginian could not refuse when Quintus asked him out into the courtyard.

An awkward silence fell the instant they were alone.

I'm not going to speak first, thought Hanno. He was still furious.

Quintus scuffed the toe of one sandal along the mosaic. 'About last night,' he began.

'Yes?' snapped Hanno. His voice, his manner was not that of a slave. At that moment, he didn't care.

Quintus bit back his reflex, angry response. 'I'm sorry,' he said sharply. 'I was drunk, and I didn't mean what I said.'

Hanno looked in Quintus' eyes and saw that, despite his tone, the apology was genuine. Immediately, he was on the defensive. This wasn't what he had expected, and he wasn't yet willing to back down himself. 'I am a slave,' he growled. 'You can address me in whatever way you please.'

Quintus' face grew pained. 'First and foremost, you are my friend,' he said. 'And I shouldn't have spoken to you the way I did last night.'

Hanno considered Quintus' words in silence. Before being enslaved, any foreigner with the presumption to call him 'gugga' would have received a bloody nose, or worse. Here, he had to smile and accept it. Not for much longer, Hanno told himself furiously. Just keep up the pretence for now. He nodded in apparent acceptance. 'Very well. I acknowledge your apology.'

Quintus grinned. 'Thank you.'

Neither knew quite what to say next. Despite Quintus' attempt to make amends, a distance now yawned between them. As a patriotic Roman citizen, Quintus would back his government's decision to enter into conflict with Carthage to the hilt. Hanno, while unable to join Hannibal's army, would do the same for his people. It drove a wedge deep into their friendship, and neither knew how to remove it.

Long moments dragged by, and still neither spoke. Quintus didn't want to mention the impending war because both had such strong feelings about it. He wanted to suggest some weapons practice, but that also seemed like a bad idea: for all that he now trusted Hanno, it seemed too much like the impending combat between Roman and Carthaginian. Irritated, he waited for Hanno to speak first. Angry yet, and fearful of giving away something of his escape plan, Hanno kept his lips firmly shut.

Both wished that Aurelia were present. She would have laughed and dissipated the tension in a heartbeat. There was no sign of her, however.

This is pointless, thought Hanno at last. He took a step towards the kitchen. 'I'd best get back to work.'

Irritated, Quintus moved out of his way. 'Yes,' he said stiffly.

As he walked away, Hanno was surprised to feel sadness rising in his chest. For all of his current resentment, he and Quintus shared a strong bond, forged by the incredible, random manner of his purchase, followed by the fight at the shepherd's hut. Another thought struck Hanno. It must have taken a lot for Quintus to come and apologise, particularly because of their difference in status. Yet here *he* was, haughtily walking off as if he were the master, and not the slave. Hanno turned, an apology rising to his lips, but it was too late.

Quintus was gone.

Several weeks passed, and the weather grew warm and sunny. Encouraged by the officers, widespread rumours of Hannibal's intentions had spread throughout the huge tented encampment outside the walls of New Carthage.

It was all part of the general's plan. Because of the vastness of his host, it was impossible to inform every soldier directly about what was going to happen. This way, the message could be put across rapidly. By the time Hannibal called for a meeting of his commanders, everyone knew that they would be heading for Italy.

The entire army assembled in formations before a wooden platform not far from the gates. The soldiers covered an enormous area of ground. There were thousands of Libyans and Numidians, and even greater numbers of Iberians from dozens of tribes. Roughly dressed men from the Balearic Islands waited alongside rows of proud, imperious Celtiberians. Hundreds of Ligurians and Gauls were also present, men who had left their lands and homes weeks before so that they could join the general who would wage war on Rome. A small proportion of the soldiers would be able to see and hear whoever stood before them, but interpreters had been positioned at regular intervals to relay the news to the rest. There would only be a short delay before everyone present heard Hannibal's words.

Malchus, Sapho and Bostar stood proudly at the front of their Libyan spearmen, whose bronze helmets and shield bosses glittered in the morning sun. The trio knew exactly what was going to happen, but the same nervous excitement controlled them all. Since returning from their mission weeks before, Bostar and Sapho had put their differences aside to prepare for this moment. Now history was about to be made, in much the same fashion as when Alexander of Macedon had set forth on his extraordinary journey more than a hundred years previously. The greatest adventure of their lives was just beginning. With it, as their father said, came the chance of further revenge for Hanno. Although he didn't voice it, Malchus treasured a tiny, deeply buried hope that he might actually be alive. So too did Bostar, but Sapho had given up trying to feel anything similar. He was still glad that Hanno was gone. Malchus gave Sapho more attention and praise now than he could ever remember receiving before. And Hannibal knew his name!

The army did not have to wait long. Followed by his brothers Hasdrubal and Mago, the cavalry commander Maharbal, and the senior infantry officer Hanno, Hannibal approached the platform and climbed into view. A group of trumpeters came last, and filed around in front of the general's position, where they waited for their orders. Their leaders' appearance caused spontaneous cheering to break out among the assembled troops. Even the officers joined in. The men whistled and shouted, stamped their feet on the ground and clashed their weapons off their shields. As those who could not see joined in, the clamour swelled immeasurably. On and on it went, louder and louder, in a dozen tongues. And, as he had done on similar occasions, Hannibal did nothing to stop it. Raising both his arms, he let his soldiers' acclaim wash over him. This was his hour, which he had spent years preparing for, and moments like this boosted morale infinitely more than a host of minor victories.

Finally, Hannibal signalled to the musicians. Raising their instruments to their lips, the men blew a short set of notes. It was the call to arms, the same sound that alerted soldiers to the nearby presence of enemy forces. Immediately, the crescendo of sound died away, leaving in its place an expectant hush. Bostar excitedly nudged Sapho in the ribs, and received a similar dig in return. An admonitory look from Malchus had them both standing to attention as if on parade. This was no time for childish behaviour.

'Soldiers of Carthage,' Hannibal began. 'We stand on the brink of a great adventure. But there are those in Rome who would stop us from the outset.' He held up a hand to quell his men's angry response. 'Would you hear the words of the latest Roman embassy to visit Carthage?'

A few moments went by as the interpreters did their work, and then an enormous cry of affirmation went up.

'"The heinous and unwarranted attack on Saguntum cannot go unanswered. Deliver to us, in chains, the man they call Hannibal Barca, and all of his senior officers, and Rome will consider the matter closed. If Carthage does not comply with this request, it should consider itself at war with the Republic."' Hannibal paused, letting the translations sink in, and his soldiers' fury build. He gestured dramatically at those behind him on the platform. 'Should these men and I hand ourselves in to the nearest Roman ally so that justice can be done?'

Again, a short delay. But the roar of 'NO!' that followed exceeded the combined volume of all the cries that had gone before.

Hannibal smiled briefly. 'I thank you for your loyalty,' he said, sweeping his right arm from left to right, encompassing the entire host.

Another immense cheer shredded the air.

'Instead of accepting Rome's offer then, I would lead most of you to Italy. To carry the war to our enemies,' Hannibal announced to more deafening acclaim. 'Some must remain here, under the command of my brother Hasdrubal; your mission is to protect our Iberian territory. The rest will march with me. Because the Romans control the sea, we will travel overland and take them by surprise. You might imagine that we would be alone in Italy, and surrounded by hostile forces. But do not fear! Theirs is a fertile region, and ripe for the plunder. We will also have many allies. Rome controls less of the peninsula than you might think. The tribes in Cisalpine Gaul have promised to join us, and I have no doubt that the situation will be the same in the central and southern parts. It will not be an easy struggle, and I ask only those men who would freely accompany me to engage in this enterprise.' Hannibal let his gaze wander from formation to formation, catching the eye of individual soldiers. 'With all of your help,' he continued, 'the Republic will be torn asunder. Destroyed, so that it can no longer threaten Carthage!' Calmly, he waited for his message to spread.

It did not take long.

The noise of over a hundred thousand men expressing their agreement resembled a rumbling, threatening thunder. Malchus, Sapho and Bostar trembled to hear it.

Hannibal raised a clenched fist in the air. 'Will you follow me to Italy?'

There was but one answer to his question. And, as every man in his army gave voice to the loudest cry of all, Hannibal Barca stood back and smiled.

In the weeks following their argument, Hanno and Quintus both made half-hearted attempts at reconciliation. None succeeded. Hurt by the other's attitude, and full of youthful self-importance, neither would give way. Soon they had virtually stopped talking to one another. It was a vicious circle from which there was no escape. Aurelia did her best to mediate, but her efforts were in vain. Yet for all of his resentment, Hanno had realised that he could not now run away. Despite his feud with Quintus, he owed him and Aurelia too much. And so, growing increasingly morose, he remained, wary always of Agesandros' menacing presence in the background. Quintus, meanwhile, threw himself into his cavalry training with the socii. He was often absent from the house for days at a time, which suited him fine. It meant that he didn't even have to see Hanno, let alone speak to him.

Spring was well underway when a note from Fabricius arrived. Followed by an eager Aurelia, Atia took it to the courtyard, which was filled with watery sunshine. Quintus, who was outside with Agesandros, would have to hear the news later.

Aurelia watched excitedly as her mother opened the missive and began to read. 'What does it say?' she demanded after a moment.

Atia looked up. The disappointment on her face was clear. 'It's a typical man's letter. Full of information about politics and what's going on in Rome. There's even a bit about some chariot race he went to the other day, but almost nothing about how he's feeling.' She traced a finger down the page. 'He asks after me, obviously, and you and Quintus. He hopes that there are no problems on the farm.' At last Atia smiled. 'Flaccus has asked him to send you his warmest regards, and says that although your marriage will have to be postponed because of the war, he cannot wait until the day it comes to pass. Your father has given him permission to write to you directly, so you may receive a letter from him soon.'

Aurelia was pleased by news of the postponement, but the thought of her wedding day – and night – still made her turn scarlet. Catching sight of Hanno in the kitchen doorway, she went an even brighter shade of red. His being a slave did not stop her from thinking – yet again – that, despite his newly crooked nose, he was extremely good-looking. For an instant, Flaccus was replaced by Hanno in her mind's eye. Aurelia stifled a gasp and shoved the shocking image away. 'That's nice. What else has Father to say?'

Hanno was oblivious to Aurelia's emotions. He was pleased because Julius had just told him to sweep the courtyard, which in turn allowed him to listen in on the conversation. With his ears pricked, he poked the broom into the crevices gaping between some of the tesserae on the mosaic floor, carefully hooking out as much dirt as possible.

Atia read on, sounding more interested. 'The majority of what he writes about is the Republic's response to Hannibal. The Minucii and their allies are working tirelessly to help the preparations for war. Flaccus hopes to be made tribune of one of the new legions. Most importantly of all, Tiberius Sempronius Longus and Publius Cornelius Scipio, the two new consuls, have been granted the provinces of Sicily and Africa, and Iberia, respectively. The mission of the former is to attack Carthage while that of the latter is to confront, and defeat, Hannibal. Father is pleased that he and Flaccus will serve with Publius.'

'That's because all the glory will fall on the army that defeats Hannibal,' mused Aurelia. Sometimes she wished she were a man, so that she too could go to war.

'Men are all the same. We women have to stay behind and worry,' said her mother with a sigh. 'Let's just ask the gods to bring both of them back safely.'

Hanno didn't like what he had heard. Hated it, in fact. Stinking bloody Romans, he thought bitterly. There were no generals of any ability in Carthage, which meant that the Senate would recall Hannibal to defend the city, thus ending his plans to attack Italy. His departure would leave Iberia, Carthage's richest colony, at the mercy of an invading Roman army. Hanno's fingers clenched furiously on his broom handle. The war seemed over before it had begun.

Aurelia frowned. 'Didn't an assault on Carthage come close to succeeding in the previous war?'

'Yes. And Father says that whatever Hannibal's qualities, Rome will be victorious. We have no reason to believe that the Carthaginians' resolve is any stronger than it was twenty years ago.'

Hanno's black mood grew even worse. Fabricius was right. His city's record in the face of direct attacks was not exactly glorious. Of course Hannibal's return would make a huge difference, but would it be enough? His army wouldn't be with him: even without the Romans' control of the seas, the general simply didn't possess enough ships to transport tens of thousands of troops back to Africa.

It was then that Quintus arrived. Instantly, he took in Aurelia standing over his mother with the letter in her hand. 'Is that from Father?'

'Yes,' Atia replied.

'What news does he send?' he asked eagerly. 'Has the Senate decided on a course of action?'

'To attack Carthage and Iberia at the same time,' answered Aurelia.

'What a fantastic idea! They won't know what hit them,' Quintus cried. 'Where is Father to be sent?'

'Iberia. So too is Flaccus,' said Atia.

'What else?'

Atia handed the parchment to Quintus. 'Read it for yourself. Life goes on here, and I have to talk to Julius about the provisions that need buying in Capua.' She brushed past Hanno without as much as a second glance.

Hanno's anger crystallised. Whatever debt he might owe, it was time to run away. Carthage would now need every sword she could get. Nothing and no one else mattered. *What about Suni?* asked his conscience. *I have no idea where he is,* thought Hanno desperately. *What chance is there of finding him?*

Quintus scanned the letter at top speed. 'Father and Flaccus are going to Iberia,' he muttered excitedly. 'And I am nearly finished my training.'

'What are you talking about?' Aurelia demanded.

He gave her a startled look. 'Nothing, nothing.'

Aurelia knew her brother well. 'Don't go getting any crazy ideas,' she warned. 'Father said you were to remain here until called for.'

'I know.' Quintus scowled. 'From the sound of it, though, the war *will* actually be over in a few months. I don't want to miss it.' His gaze flickered across the courtyard and made contact with Hanno. Instantly, Quintus glanced away, but it was too late.

Hanno's fury overflowed at last. 'Are you happy now?' he hissed.

'What do you mean?' Quintus replied defensively.

'The guggas will be defeated, again. Put in their rightful place. I expect you're delighted.'

Quintus' face grew red. 'No, that's not how it is.'

'Isn't it?' Hanno shot back. Clearing his throat, he spat on the mosaic floor.

'How dare you?' Quintus roared, taking a step towards Hanno. 'You're nothing but a—'

'Quintus!' cried Aurelia, aghast.

With great effort, her brother stopped himself from saying any more.

Contempt twisted Hanno's face. 'A slave. Or a gugga! Is that what you were going to say?'

Quintus' visage turned a deeper shade of crimson. Bunching his fists with anger, he turned away.

'I've had enough of this.' Hanno grabbed his broom.

Aurelia could take no more. 'Stop it, both of you! You're acting like children.'

Her words made no difference. Quintus stormed out of the house, and Aurelia followed him. Hanno retreated to the kitchen, where misery settled over him as it never had before. The news he'd heard a few months before, of Hannibal's successful siege of Saguntum, and the challenge it had issued, had bolstered his flagging spirits. Given him a reason to go on. Fabricius' letter had destroyed this utterly. Rome's plan seemed unbeatable. Even if he reached Hannibal's army, what difference could he make?

Aurelia came looking for Hanno upon her return. She found him slumped on a stool in the kitchen. Ignoring the other slaves' curious stares, she dragged Hanno outside. 'I've spoken to Quintus,' she muttered the moment they were alone. 'He didn't mean to offend you. It was just a spontaneous reaction to you spitting.' She gave Hanno a reproachful look. 'That was so rude.'

Hanno flushed, but he didn't apologise. 'He was gloating at me.'

'I know it seemed like that,' said Aurelia. 'But I don't think that's what he was doing.'

'Wasn't it?' Hanno shot back.

'No,' she replied softly. 'Quintus isn't like that.'

'Why did he call me a gugga originally, then?'

'People say things that they don't mean when they're drunk. I suppose that you haven't called him any names in your head since?' Aurelia asked archly.

Stung, Hanno did not answer.

Aurelia glanced around carefully, before reaching out to touch his face.

Startled by the intimacy this created, Hanno felt his anger dissipate. He looked into her eyes.

Alarmed by her suddenly pounding heart, Aurelia lowered her hand. 'On the surface, this argument looks quite simple,' she began. 'If it weren't for your misfortune, you would be a free man and, in all probability, enlisting in the Carthaginian army. Like Quintus will do in the legions. There would be nothing wrong with either of those actions. Yet Quintus is free to do as he chooses, while you are a slave.'

That's it in a nutshell, thought Hanno angrily.

Aurelia wasn't finished. 'The real reason, however, is that first you, and then Quintus, were hurt by what the other said. Both of you are too damn proud to make a sincere apology and put it behind you.' She glared at him. 'I'm sick of it.'

Amazed by Aurelia's insight and sincerity, Hanno gave in. The quarrel had been going on long enough. 'You're right,' he said. 'I'm sorry.'

'It's not me you should be saying that to.'

'I know.' Hanno considered his next words with care. 'I will apologise to him. But Quintus has to know that, whatever the law of this land, I am no slave. I never will be.'

'Deep down, I'm sure he knows that. That's why he stopped himself from calling you one earlier,' Aurelia replied. Her face grew sad. 'Obviously, I don't think of you like that. But to everyone else, you *are* a slave.'

Hanno was about to tell Aurelia of his plans, when, out of the corner of his eye, he sensed movement. Through the open doors of the tablinum, he could see into part of the atrium. Outside the square of floor illumin-ated by the hole in its roof, everything lay in shadow. There Hanno could discern a tall figure, watching them. Instinctively, he pulled away from Aurelia. When Agesandros walked into the light, Hanno's stomach constricted with fear. What had he seen or heard? What would he do?

Aurelia saw the Sicilian in the same moment. She drew herself up proudly, ready for any confrontation.

To their surprise, Agesandros came no nearer. A tiny smile flickered across his face, and then he disappeared whence he had come.

Hanno and Aurelia turned back to each other, but Elira and another domestic slave emerged from the kitchen. The brief moment of magic they had shared was gone. 'I will talk to Quintus,' said Aurelia reassuringly. 'Whatever happens, you must hold on to your friendship. As we two will.'

Keen to make things as they were before he left the farm for ever, Hanno nodded. 'Thank you.'

Unfortunately, Aurelia was unable to remonstrate with her brother that day. As she told Hanno later, Quintus had taken off for Capua without a word to anyone but the bowlegged slave who worked in the stable. The afternoon passed and night fell, and it became apparent that he would not be returning. Hanno didn't know whether to feel angry or worried by this development. 'Don't be concerned,' Aurelia said before retiring. 'Quintus does this sometimes, when he needs time to think. He stays at Gaius' house, and returns in a few days.'

There was nothing Hanno could do. He lay back on his bedroll and dreamed of escape.

Sleep was a long time coming.

Chapter XI: The Quest for Safe Passage

After the fall of Saguntum, Bostar took to visiting his wounded men every morning, talking to those who were conscious and passing his hand over those who were still asleep, or who would never wake. There were more than thirty soldiers in the large tent, of whom half would probably never fight again. Despite the horror of his soldiers' injuries, Bostar had begun to feel grateful for his losses. All things considered, they had been slight. Far more Saguntines had died when Hannibal's troops had entered the city, howling like packs of rabid wolves. For an entire day, the predominant sound throughout Saguntum had been that of screams. Men's. Women's. Children's. Bostar squeezed his eyes shut and tried to forget, but he couldn't. Butchering unarmed civilians and engaging in widespread rape was not how he made war. While he hadn't tried to stop his men – had Hannibal not promised them a free rein? – Bostar had not taken part in the slaughter. Commanded by their general to guard the chests of gold and silver that had been found in the citadel, Malchus had not either. Bostar sighed. Inevitably, Sapho had.

A moment later, Malchus' touch on his shoulder made him jump. 'It's good that you're up so early checking on them.' Malchus indicated the injured men in their blankets.

'It's my job,' Bostar replied modestly, knowing that his father would have already visited his own casualties.

'It is.' Malchus fixed him with a solemn stare. 'And I think Hannibal has another one for you. Us.'

Bostar's heart thudded off his ribs. 'Why?'

'We've all been summoned to the general's tent. I wasn't told why.'

Excitement filled Bostar. 'Does Sapho know?'

'No. I thought you could tell him.'

'Really?' Bostar tried to keep his tone light. 'If you wish.'

Malchus gave him a knowing look. 'Do you think I haven't noticed how you two have been with each other recently?'

'It's nothing serious,' lied Bostar.

'Then why are you avoiding my gaze?' demanded Malchus. 'It's about Hanno, isn't it?'

'That's how it started,' Bostar replied. He began to explain, but his father forestalled him.

'There are only two of you now,' said Malchus sadly. 'Life is short. Resolve your differences, or one of you might find that it's too late.'

'You're right,' replied Bostar firmly. 'I'll do my best.'

'As you always do.' Malchus' voice was proud.

A pang of sadness tore at Bostar's heart. Did I do my best by letting Hanno go? he wondered.

'I'll see you both outside the headquarters in half an hour.' Malchus left him to it.

After telling his orderly to polish his armour, Bostar headed straight for Sapho's tent. There wasn't much time for getting ready, never mind a reconciliation. But their father had asked, so he would try.

Recognising the tent lines of Sapho's phalanx by their standard, Bostar quickly located the largest tent, which, like his, was pitched on the unit's right. The main flap was closed, which meant that his brother was either still in bed, or busy with his duties. Given his brother's recent habits, Bostar suspected the former. 'Sapho?' he called.

There was no answer.

Bostar tried again, louder.

Nothing.

Bostar took a step away. 'He must be with his men,' he said to himself in surprise.

'Who is it?' demanded an annoyed voice.

'Of course he's not,' Bostar muttered, turning back. He untied the thong that kept the tent flap closed. 'Sapho! It's me.' A moment later, he threw wide the leather. Sunlight flooded inside, and Bostar lifted a hand to his nose. The reek of stale sweat and spilt wine was overpowering. Stepping over the threshold, he picked his way over discarded pieces of clothing and equipment. Bostar was shocked to see that every item was filthy. Sapho's shield, spear and sword were the only things that had been cleaned. They leaned against a wooden stand to the side. He came to a halt before Sapho's bed, a jumble of blankets and animal skins. His brother's bleary eyes regarded him from its depths. 'Good morning,' said Bostar, trying to ignore the smell. He hasn't even washed, he thought with disgust.

'To what do I owe the pleasure?' Sapho's voice was acid.

'We've been summoned to a meeting with Hannibal.'

Sapho's lips thinned. 'The general told you that over breakfast, did he?'

Bostar sighed. 'Despite what you may think, I didn't save Hannibal's life to curry favour, or to make you jealous. You know I'm not like that.' He was pleased when Sapho's eyes dropped away. He waited, but there was no further response. Bostar pressed on. 'Father sent me. We need to be there in less than half an hour.'

Finally, Sapho sat up. He winced. 'Gods, my head hurts. And it tastes like something died in my mouth.'

Bostar kicked the amphora at his feet. 'Drank too much of this?'

Sapho gave him a rueful grin. 'Not half! Some of my men broke into a wine merchant's when the city fell. We've kept it under guard since. You should see the place. There's vintage stuff from all over the Mediterranean!' His expression grew hawkish. 'Shame his three daughters aren't still alive. We had some fun with them, I can tell you.'

Bostar wanted to punch Sapho in the face, but instead he proffered a hand. 'Get up. We don't want to be late. Father thinks Hannibal has a task for us.'

Sapho looked at Bostar's outstretched arm for a moment before he accepted it. Swaying gently, he looked around at the chaos of his tent floor. 'I suppose I'd better start cleaning my breastplate and helmet. Can't appear in front of Hannibal with filthy gear, can I?'

'Can't your orderly do it?'

Sapho made a face. 'No. He's down with the flux.'

Bostar frowned. Sapho was in no state to wash himself, prepare his uniform and present himself to their general in the time remaining. Part of him wanted to leave his brother to it. That's what he deserves, Bostar thought. The rest of him felt that their feud had been going on too long.

He made a snap judgement. His own servant would have everything ready by now. It would only take him a few moments to get ready. 'Go and stick your head in a barrel of water. I'll clean your armour and helmet.'

Sapho's eyebrows rose. 'That's kind of you,' he muttered.

'Don't think I'm going to do it for you every day,' Bostar warned. He gave Sapho a shove. 'Get a move on. We don't want to be late. Hannibal must have something special lined up for us.'

At this, Sapho's pace picked up. 'True,' he replied. He stopped by the tent's entrance.

Bostar, who was already following with Sapho's filthy breastplate, paused. 'What?'

'Thank you,' said Sapho.

Bostar nodded. 'That's all right.'

The air between them grew a shade lighter, and for the first time in months, they smiled at each other.

Bostar and Sapho found their father waiting for them near Hannibal's tent. Malchus eyed their gleaming armour and helmets and gave an approving nod.

'What's this about, Father?' asked Sapho.

'Let's go and find out,' Malchus answered. He led the way to the entrance, where two dozen smartly turned-out scutarii stood. 'The general is expecting us.'

Recognising Malchus, the lead scutarius saluted. 'If you'll follow me, sir.'

As they were led inside, Bostar winked at Sapho, who returned the gesture. Excitement gripped them both. Although they had met Hannibal before, this was the first time they'd been invited into his headquarters.

In the tent's main section, they found Hannibal, his brothers Hasdrubal and Mago, and two other senior officers grouped around a table upon which a large map was unrolled. The scutarius came to a halt and announced them.

Hannibal turned. 'Malchus. Bostar and Sapho. Welcome!'

Father and sons saluted crisply.

'You will know my brother Hasdrubal,' said Hannibal, nodding at the corpulent, brooding man with a florid complexion and full lips beside him.

'And Mago.' He indicated the tall, thin figure whose eager, hawk-like face and eyes threatened to fix one to the spot. 'This is Maharbal, my cavalry commander, and Hanno, one of my top infantry officers.' The first man had a mop of unruly black hair and a ready smile, and the other a stolid but dependable look.

The trio saluted again.

'For many years, Malchus acted as my eyes and ears in Carthage,' Hannibal explained. 'Yet when the time came for first his sons, and then he himself, to join me here in Iberia, no one was better pleased than I. They are good men all, and they proved their worth more than once during the siege, most recently when Bostar saved my life.'

The officers murmured in loud appreciation.

Malchus inclined his head, while Bostar flushed at the attention. Beside him, he was aware of Sapho glowering. Bostar cursed inwardly, praying that the fragile peace between him and his brother had not just been broken.

Hannibal clapped his hands together. 'To business! Come and join us.'

They eagerly crossed to the table, where the others made room.

At once Bostar's eyes drank in the undulating coast of Africa, and Carthage, their city. The island of Sicily, almost joining their homeland to its arch-enemy, Italy.

'Obviously, we are here, at Saguntum.' Hannibal tapped his right forefinger halfway up the east coast of the Iberian peninsula. 'And our destination is here.' He thumped the boot-like shape of Italy. 'How best to strike at it?'

Silence reigned. It was an affront to every Carthaginian's pride that Rome enjoyed supremacy over the western Mediterranean, an historical preserve of Carthage. Transporting the army by ship would be foolish in the extreme. Yet no one dared to suggest the only alternative.

Hannibal took the initiative. 'There will be no assault by sea. Even if we took the short route to Genua, our entire enterprise could be undone in a single battle.' He moved his finger northeast, across the River Iberus, to the narrow 'waist' that joined Iberia to Gaul. 'This is the route we shall take.' Hannibal continued to the Alps, where he paused for a moment before moving into Cisalpine Gaul, and thence into northern Italy.

Bostar's heart quickened. Although Malchus had told him of Hannibal's plan, the general's daring still took his breath away. A glance at Sapho told him that his brother shared his feeling. Their father's face, however, remained expressionless. How much does he know? Bostar wondered. He himself had no idea how the immense task Hannibal had just mentioned would be achieved.

Hannibal saw Sapho straining forward eagerly. He raised an eyebrow. 'When do we march, sir?'

'In the spring. Until then, our Iberian allies have permission to return to their families, and the rest of the army can rest at New Carthage.' He saw Sapho's disappointed look and chuckled. 'Come now! Winter is no time to wage war, and things will be hard enough for us as it is.'

'Of course, sir,' Sapho muttered awkwardly.

'There are some things in our favour, however. Earlier in the year, my messengers journeyed to Cisalpine Gaul. They were received favourably by nearly all the tribes that they encountered,' Hannibal said. 'In fact, the Boii and the Insubres promised immediate aid when we arrive.'

Malchus and his two sons exchanged pleased glances. This was new information for all of them. Hannibal's companions did not react, however, instead studying the trio intently.

Hannibal held up a warning finger. 'There are many hurdles to cross before we reach these possible allies. Traversing the Alps will be the greatest by far, but another will be the fierce natives north of the Iberus, who will undoubtedly give violent resistance. We already have plans in train for our journey through these regions. However, there is an area about which we know very little.' Hannibal's forefinger returned to the mountains between Iberia and Gaul. He tapped the map meaningfully.

Bostar's mouth went dry.

Hannibal stared at Malchus. 'I need someone to sound out the tribes' possible reactions to a massive army entering their land. To discover how many might fight us. I must have this information by the onset of spring. Can you do it?'

Malchus' eyes glittered. 'Of course, sir.'

'Good.' Hannibal regarded Bostar and Sapho next. 'The old lion might lead the pack, but he still needs young males to hunt successfully. Will you accompany your father?'

'Yes, sir!' the brothers cried in unison. 'You show our family great honour by entrusting this mission to us, sir,' Sapho added.

The general smiled. 'I am sure that you will repay my trust amply.'

Delighted by this recognition of Sapho, Bostar gave his brother a small, pleased look. He was rewarded with a fierce nod.

'What are your thoughts, Malchus?'

'We'll need to set out at once, sir. It's a long way to the Iberus.'

'Nearly three thousand stades,' agreed Hannibal. 'As you know, it is generally peaceful as far as the river. After that, up to the border with Gaul, may be a different matter. The place is a jumble of mountains, valleys and passes, and the tribes there are rumoured to be fiercely independent.' He paused. 'How many men will you require?'

'Winning our passage by force of arms is simply not an option. Nor is it our purpose. We are to be an embassy, not an army,' said Malchus. 'What's important are the abilities to move fast and to see off possible attacks by bandits.' He looked at his sons, who nodded in agreement. 'Two dozen of my spearmen and the same number of scutarii should be sufficient, sir.'

'You shall have the pick of any unit you wish. And now, a toast to your success!' Hannibal clicked his fingers and a slave appeared from the rear of the tent. 'Wine!' As the man scurried off, the general looked solemnly at each of those around the table. 'Let us ask Melqart and Baal Saphon, Tanit and Baal Hammon to guide and protect these valiant officers on their mission.'

As the room filled with muttered agreement, Bostar added a request of his own. *Let Sapho and I put aside our differences once and for all.*

Braving frost, mud and bitter winter wind, the embassy slogged its way to the Iberus. Thereafter, the inhabitants inland could not be trusted, and so Malchus led them along the more secure coastal route, a densely inhabited area full of towns used to traders from overseas. The party passed by Adeba and Tarraco, before safely reaching the city of Barcino, which was located at the mouth of the River Ubricatus.

There were several routes through the mountains that led to Gaul, and Hannibal had advised that he would probably divide his army between them. This necessitated visiting the tribe that controlled each of the passes. A period of unseasonably calm, dry weather prompted Malchus to head north into the mountainous terrain first, rather than starting with the easiest way into Gaul, that which hogged the coastline via the towns of Gerunda and Emporiae. That could be left until last. Hiring locals as guides, the embassy spent many days on narrow paths that wound and twisted into the hills and valleys. Inevitably, the weather worsened, and a journey that might have taken several weeks stretched into two months. Pleasingly, their ordeals were not all in vain. The chieftains who received the Carthaginians seemed impressed with the tales of Hannibal's military victories throughout Iberia, and the descriptions of his enormous army. Most importantly, though, they welcomed the gifts Malchus offered: the bags of silver coinage, the finely made *kopides* and Celtiberian short swords.

Eventually, the only people left to contact were the Ausetani, who controlled the coastal route into Gaul. Having returned to the town of Emporiae to reshoe their horses and stock up on supplies, Malchus retired to the one inn which was large enough to quarter all of his men. He immediately demanded a meeting with their guides, three swarthy hunters. Soon after sunset, they convened around a table in his room. Small oval oil lamps cast a warm amber glow on to the grubby plaster on the wall. Malchus' sons sat opposite each other. Their relationship remained civil, even fairly cordial, but Bostar had stopped trying to be Sapho's friend. Each time he'd tried, his brother had remained indifferent to his advances. So be it, Bostar decided. It's better than fighting all the time. Such thoughts always brought Hanno, and his guilty wish that it had been Sapho who had been lost at sea, to mind. Disquieted, Bostar shoved away the idea.

Malchus himself served the guides with wine. 'Tell me about this tribe,' he commanded in rough Iberian.

The three glanced at one another. The oldest, a wiry man with a nut-brown, weather-beaten face, leaned forward on his chair. 'Their main village is in the foothills above the town, sir. It's a straightforward journey.'

'Not like the paths that we had to take before, then?'

'No, sir, nothing like that.'

Bostar and Sapho were both relieved. Neither had enjoyed the days spent on winding, treacherous tracks, where a single slip meant a precipitous fall.

'How far?'

'It's not quite a day's ride, sir.'

'Excellent! We'll set out at dawn,' Malchus declared. He eyed his sons. 'A night's rest upon our return, and we'll head south. Spring is around the corner, and we mustn't keep Hannibal waiting any longer.'

The lead guide cleared his throat. 'The thing is, sir, we were wondering if . . .' His nerve failed him and he stopped.

Keen to get in before Bostar, Sapho jumped in. 'What?'

The man rallied his courage. 'We wondered if you could pay us and make your own way there,' he said falteringly. 'We've spent so long away from our wives and families, you see?'

Malchus' brows lowered.

'The directions are simple. There's no way that you could get lost.' He looked at his two companions, who shook their heads in vigorous agreement.

Malchus did not answer. Instead, he glanced at Bostar and Sapho. 'What do you think?' he asked in Carthaginian.

Sapho bared his teeth. 'He's lying,' he snarled in Iberian. 'I say we tie the double-crossing dog down on the table and see what he says after I've cut a few strips of skin off him.' He calmly placed a dagger before him. 'This will make the shitbag sing like a caged bird.'

'Bostar?' asked Malchus.

Bostar studied the three guides, who seemed absolutely terrified. Then he looked at his brother, who was tapping his blade off the table's surface. He didn't want to upset Sapho, but nor was he prepared to see innocent individuals suffer for no reason. 'I don't think there's any need for torture,' Bostar said in Iberian, ignoring Sapho's scowl. 'These men have been with us day and night for weeks. They've had no chance to commit treachery. I think they're probably scared of the Ausetani. But I see no reason why they shouldn't fulfil their oath, which was to guide us until we discharged them.'

Malchus considered their answers in silence. At length, he turned to the lead guide. 'Has my son the right of it? Are you frightened of the Ausetani?'

'Yes, sir. They're prone to banditry.' There was a brief pause. 'Or worse.'

Alarm filled Bostar. Before he could react, Sapho butted in again. 'When, precisely, were you going to tell us this?' he demanded.

He got no answer.

Sapho threw a triumphant look at Bostar. 'Why don't we just get the directions, and then kill them?'

Perhaps his brother was correct, thought Bostar resentfully. He didn't want to admit that he'd made a bad judgement by trusting the guides.

His father's challenge surprised him. 'And if they had warned us? What would we have done?'

A flush spread slowly up Sapho's face and neck. 'Gone to the village anyway,' he muttered.

'Precisely,' replied Malchus evenly. He glared at the guides. 'It's not that I wouldn't end your miserable lives for withholding vital information, but I see no point in killing you when we would have followed the same course of action anyway.'

The three stammered their thanks. 'We will be honoured to guide you to the Ausetani settlement tomorrow, sir,' said the lead guide.

'That's right. You will.' Malchus' tone was silky soft, but there was no mistaking the threat in it. 'Myrcan! Get in here.'

A broad-chested spearman entered from the corridor. 'Sir?'

'Take these men's weapons and escort them to their quarters. Set guards at the windows and door.'

'Yes, sir.' Myrcan held out a meaty hand and the guides meekly handed over their knives before following him from the room.

'It appears you both still have something to learn about judging men's characters,' Malchus admonished. 'Not everyone is as honourable as you, Bostar. Nor do they all require torturing, Sapho.'

Both of his sons took a sudden interest in the tabletop before them.

'Get some rest,' Malchus said in a more kindly voice. 'Tomorrow will be a long day.'

'Yes, Father.' As one, the brothers shoved back their chairs and headed for the door.

Neither spoke on the way to their bedchambers.

The guide's estimate of the distance to the Ausetani village was accurate. After nearly a day's ride, the fortified settlement finally came into view at the end of a long, narrow valley. Perhaps half a mile away, it occupied a high, easily defensible point. Like many such in Iberia, it was ringed by a wooden palisade. The tiny figures of sentries could be seen patrolling the ramparts. Flocks of sheep and goats grazed the slopes to either side. It was a peaceful scene, but the guides looked most unhappy.

Malchus gave them a long, contemptuous stare. 'Go!'

The three men goggled at him.

'You heard me,' Malchus growled. 'Unless you'd like to spend some time with Sapho here.'

They needed no further encouragement and had the sense not to mention payment. Turning their mules' heads, the trio fled.

'It appears that we are about to enter a den of hungry wolves.' Malchus regarded each of his sons in turn. 'What's our best option?'

'Go straight in there and demand to see the headman,' Sapho declared boldly. 'As we did in every other village.'

'We can't go back to Hannibal without some information,' Bostar admitted. 'But nor should we foolishly place our heads on the executioner's block.'

Sapho's top lip curled. 'Are you afraid even to enter that excuse for a settlement?'

'No,' retorted Bostar hotly. 'I'm just saying that we know nothing about these whoresons. If they're as untrustworthy as the guide said, charging in there like raging bulls will get their backs up from the very outset.'

Sapho shot him a disbelieving look. 'So what? We're emissaries of Hannibal Barca, not some pisspot Iberian chieftain.'

They glared at each other.

'Peace,' said Malchus after a moment. 'As usual, both your opinions have some merit. If we had the time, I would perhaps advise waylaying one of their hunting parties. A few hostages would make a powerful bargaining tool before we made an entry. That might take days, however, and we must act now.' He glanced at Sapho. 'Not in quite the way you advised. We will take a more peaceable approach. Remember, the stroked cat is less likely to scratch or bite. Yet we must be confident or, like a cat, they will turn on us anyway.'

Turning to their escorts, Malchus laid out the situation in Carthaginian and basic Iberian. There was little reaction. The Libyans and scutarii had been chosen for their loyalty and bravery. They would fight and, if necessary, die, for Hannibal. Wherever, and whenever, they were ordered to.

'Which of you two speaks the best Iberian?' Malchus asked his sons. While rusty, his command of the language sufficed most of the time. In a dangerous situation, however, it was best to minimise the chance of miscommunication.

'I do,' replied Bostar at once. Although he and Sapho had spent roughly

the same amount of time in Iberia, it was he who had shown more apti-
tude for the rapid-fire, musical tribal tongues.

Sapho concurred with a reluctant nod.

'You act as interpreter, then,' Malchus directed.

Bostar didn't try to hide his smirk.

Without further ado, they set off. Malchus took the lead, with Bostar
and a glowering Sapho following. Their escorts marched to their rear,
first the spearmen, and last the scutarii. The party had not gone far when
a horn blared out from the nearest hillside. It was quickly echoed by
another nearer the village. Shouts rang out on the ramparts. When they
were about four hundred paces from the settlement, the front gates
creaked open, and a tide of warriors poured out. Forming up in an unruly
mass that blocked the entrance, they waited for the Carthaginians to
approach.

Bostar felt his stomach clench. He glanced sidelong at Sapho, who was
half pulling his sword from its sheath before slamming it home again. He's
worried too, thought Bostar. In front, the only sign of tension in their
father was his rigid back. Bostar took heart from Malchus' self-assurance.
Show no fear, he told himself. They will smell it the way a wolf scents its
prey. Taking a deep breath, he fixed his features into a stony expression.
Coming to the same realisation, Sapho let go of his sword hilt. Their escorts
marched solidly behind them, reassurance that if there was trouble, plenty
of men would die before they did.

Malchus rode his horse straight up to the mob of Ausetani. Taken aback
by his confidence and the size of his mount, some of the warriors retreated
a little. The advantage did not last long. Prompted by their companions'
angry mutters, the men stepped forward once more, raising their weapons
threateningly. Shouted challenges rang out, but Malchus did not move a
muscle.

Like most Iberian tribesmen, few of the Ausetani were dressed identi-
cally. Most were bareheaded. Those who wore headgear sported sinew,
bronze bowl or triple-crested helmets. The majority carried a shield,
although these also varied in size and shape: tall and straight-sided with
rounded ends, oval, or round with a conical iron boss. All were brightly
painted with swirling serpents, diamonds, or alternating thick bands of
colour. The Ausetani were also heavily armed. Every man carried at least

one saunion, but many had two. In addition, each warrior had a dagger and either a *kopis* or a typical Celtiberian straight-edged sword.

Malchus turned his head. 'Tell them who we are, and why we're here.'

'We are Carthaginians,' said Bostar loudly. 'We come in peace.' He ignored the sniggers that met this remark. 'With a message for your chieftain, from our leader, Hannibal Barca.'

'Never heard of the prick,' bellowed a hulking figure with a black beard. Hoots of amusement from his comrades followed. Encouraged by this, the warrior shoved his way out of the throng. Long raven tresses spilled out from under his bronze helmet. His black quilted linen tunic could not conceal the massive muscles of his chest and upper arms, and his sinew greaves barely fitted around his trunk-like calves. He was so big that the shield and saunion clutched in his ham fists looked like child's toys. The warrior gave the Libyans and scutarii a contemptuous glance, before returning his cold gaze to Bostar. 'Give me one good reason why we shouldn't just kill you all,' he snarled.

Snarls of agreement followed his challenge, and the Ausetani moved forward a step.

Bostar tensed, but managed to keep his hands in his lap, on his reins. He watched Sapho sidelong and was relieved when his brother didn't reach for his sword either.

'The guide was telling the truth,' Malchus remarked dryly under his breath. He raised his voice. 'Tell him that we bring a message, and gifts, for his leader from our general. His chieftain will not be pleased if he does not hear these words for himself.'

Carefully, Bostar repeated his father's words in Iberian. It was exactly the right thing to say. Confusion and anger mixed on the big man's face for a moment, but a moment later, he stood back. When one of his companions queried his action, the warrior simply shoved him aside with an irritated grunt. Relief flooded through Bostar. The first hurdle had been crossed. It was like watching a landslide beginning. First one man moved out of the way, then a second and a third, followed by several more, until the process took on a life of its own. Soon the group of Ausetani had split apart, leaving the track that led to the village's front gate clear apart from the warrior with the black beard. He trotted ahead to carry the news of their arrival.

Without looking to left or right, Malchus urged his horse up the slope. The rest of the party followed, shadowed closely by the mass of warriors.

Inside, the settlement was like a hundred others Bostar had seen before. A central open area was ringed by dozens of single-storey wooden and brick huts, the outermost of which had been built right up against the palisade. Plumes of smoke rose from the roofs of many. Small children and dogs played in the dirt, oblivious to the drama about to unfold. Hens and pigs scuffled about, searching for food. Women and old people stood in the doorways of their houses, watching impassively. The acrid smell of urine and faeces, both animal and human, laced the air. At the far side of the open space stood a high-backed wooden chair, which was occupied by a man in late middle age, and flanked by ten warriors in mail shirts and crimson-crested helmets. The bearded hulk was there too, busily muttering to the chieftain.

Without hesitation, Malchus headed for this group. Reaching it, he dismounted, indicating that his sons should do the same. At once three Libyan spearmen darted forward to take the horses' reins. Malchus made a deep bow towards the chief. Bostar quickly copied him. It was prudent to treat the Ausetani leader with respect, he thought. The man was head of a tribe, after all. Yet he looked an untrustworthy ruffian. The chieftain's red linen tunic might be woven from quality fabric, and the sword and dagger on his belt well made, but the tresses of lank, greasy hair that dangled on to his pockmarked cheeks told a different story. So did his flat, dead eyes, which reminded Bostar of a lizard. Sapho was last of all to bend from the waist. His gesture was shallower than the others had been. His insolence did not go unnoticed; several of the nearby warriors snarled with anger. Bostar glared at his brother, but the harm had been done.

The trio of Carthaginians and the Ausetani leader stared at each other in silence for a moment, each trying to gauge the other. The chieftain spoke first. He aimed his words at Malchus, the embassy's obvious leader.

'He says that our message must indeed be important to keep his men from their sport,' muttered Bostar.

'He's playing with us. Trying to put fear in our hearts,' Malchus murmured contemptuously. 'He's not about to kill us out of hand, or his warriors would have done so already. The news of our presence in the area must have reached him before now, and he wants to hear what we have to say for himself. Tell him what we told the other leaders. Lay it on thick about the size of our army.'

Bostar did as he was told, politely explaining how Hannibal and his host would arrive in the next few months, seeking only safe passage to Gaul. There would be well-paid jobs for Ausetani warriors who wished to serve as guides. Any supplies required by the Carthaginians would be purchased. Looting and theft of the locals' property or livestock would be forbidden, on pain of death. As he spoke, Bostar studied the chief intently but was frustrated in his attempt to gauge what the man was thinking. All he could do was to continue in a confident, self-assured vein. Hope for the best.

Bostar began to wax lyrical about the different groups that made up Hannibal's immense force, describing the thousands of spearmen and scutarii like those who stood behind him; the slingers and skirmishers who softened up an enemy before the real fighting began; the peerless Numidian cavalry, whose stinging attacks no soldiers in the world could withstand; and the elephants, which were capable of smashing apart troop formations like so much firewood. Bostar was still in mid-flow when the chieftain peremptorily held up his hand, stopping him. 'And you say this army is how big?' he demanded.

'A hundred thousand men. At the very least.' The instant the words had left his lips, Bostar could see that the Ausetani leader did not believe him. His spirits fell. It was an enormous figure to take in, yet the other tribes visited by the embassy had done so. Perhaps, thought Bostar, it was because they were a lot smaller than the Ausetani. In those villages, the fifty Carthaginian soldiers had seemed altogether more intimidating than they did here. This tribe was a different proposition; reportedly, there were numerous other villages like this one. Combined, the Ausetani might be able to field a force of two or even three thousand warriors, which for Iberia was a considerable achievement. Imagining a host thirty to fifty times larger than that number called for a good imagination.

Sure enough, the chief and his bodyguards exchanged a series of disbelieving looks.

'Scum,' Sapho whispered furiously in Carthaginian. 'They'll shit themselves when they actually see the army.'

Not knowing what else to do, Bostar ploughed on. 'Some evidence of our good faith.' He clicked his fingers and a quartet of scutarii trotted forward, carrying heavy, clinking bags and armfuls of tightly rolled leather. Placing the items in front of the chieftain, they returned to their positions.

The gifts were opened and examined with unseemly speed. Avarice glittered in the faces of every Ausetani watching as mounds of silver coins showered on to the ground. There were loud mutters of appreciation too for the shining weaponry that emerged into view as the leather bundles were unrolled.

Malchus' attitude was still confident, or appeared to be so. 'Ask the chief what answer he would have us take back to Hannibal,' he directed Bostar.

Bostar obeyed.

The Ausetani leader's face grew thoughtful. For the space of twenty heartbeats, he sat regarding the riches laid out before him. Finally, he asked a short question.

'He wants to know how much more they can expect when Hannibal arrives,' Bostar relayed unhappily.

'Greedy bastard,' Sapho hissed.

Malchus' eyebrows drew together in disapproval, yet he did not look surprised. 'I can promise him the same again, and the dog will probably let us go,' he said. 'But I have no idea if Hannibal will agree with my decision. We've already handed over a fortune.' He glanced at his sons. 'What do you think?'

'Hannibal will think we are fools, pure and simple,' muttered Sapho, his nostrils flaring. 'All the other tribes have accepted our gifts, yet this one got twice as much?'

'We can't offer him more or the son of a whore will think we're a walkover,' Bostar conceded. He scowled. 'Hannibal's goodwill should be more than enough for him!'

'But I don't think it will be,' said Malchus grimly. 'If that amount of silver and weaponry hasn't done it, then a vague promise certainly won't.'

Bostar could see no way out that didn't involve major loss of face. Although he and his companions were few in number, *they* were the representatives of a major power, not these cut-throats around them. To accede to the chieftain's demand would show fear on their part, and by implication, weakness on the part of their general. His eyes narrowed as an idea struck. 'You could promise him a private meeting with Hannibal,' he suggested. 'Suggest that an alliance between his people and Carthage would be beneficial to both parties.'

'We don't have the authority to grant that,' growled Sapho.

'Of course we don't,' Bostar replied witheringly. 'But it's not a climb-down either.'

'I like it,' breathed Malchus. He glanced at Sapho, who gave a sulky shrug. 'I think it's our best shot. Tell him.'

Calmly, Bostar delivered their answer.

A ferocious scowl spread across the chieftain's face straightaway, and he spat out an irate, lengthy response. It was delivered so fast that Malchus and Sapho struggled to understand much of it. Bostar did not bother trans-lating before he replied. At once the leader's bodyguards and the huge warrior moved forward in unison. Simultaneously, the men who had followed the Carthaginians inside fanned out on either side of the party, surrounding it.

'What in the name of all the gods did he say?' Malchus demanded.

Bostar's lips thinned. 'That the Ausetani have no need of an alliance with the louse-ridden son of a Phoenician whore.'

Sapho clenched his fists. 'How did you answer?'

'I told him that an immediate sincere apology *might* mean Hannibal's clemency when the army arrives. Otherwise, he and his entire tribe could expect to be annihilated.'

Malchus clapped him on the arm. 'Well said!'

Even Sapho gave Bostar a look of grudging admiration.

Malchus eyed the circle of warriors around them. 'It appears that our road ends here then,' he said in a hard voice. 'We will never have the opportunity to avenge Hanno. Yet we can die well. Like men!' He turned towards their escorts, and repeated his words. He was pleased when, as one, they laid hands to their weapons.

'On your command, sir,' muttered the officers in charge.

'Wait,' interrupted Sapho. 'I have an idea.' Without asking for Malchus' approval, he drew his sword and moved to stand in front of the hulk who had laughed at them when they arrived. The warrior leered unpleas-antly. 'Can this freak actually fight?' Sapho demanded in reasonable Iberian.

The Ausetani leader couldn't believe his ears. Sapho barely reached up to the warrior's shoulder. 'That's my eldest son. He's never been beaten in single combat.'

'What's he doing?' Bostar whispered to Malchus.

For once, Malchus looked worried. 'I don't know, but I hope the gods are smiling on him.'

Sapho raised his voice. 'If I defeat him, then you will apologise, accept Hannibal's gifts and allow us to leave unharmed. When our army arrives, you will offer it safe passage.'

The chieftain laughed. So did everyone within earshot. 'Of course. If you fail, though, he will take your head, and those of all your companions, as trophies.'

'I would expect no less,' Sapho replied disdainfully.

The chieftain gave a callous shrug. At his command, the mass of warriors formed a large, hollow circle. Malchus seized the initiative and used his soldiers to force a passage through so that they could form part of what was to be the combat area. He and Bostar stood at the very front. Many of the Ausetani did not like this move, and began pushing and shoving at the Carthaginian troops, until an angry shout from their leader stopped them. Surrounded by his bodyguards, the chief took up a position directly opposite Malchus.

Gripping his drawn sword, Sapho stalked through a narrow corridor of leering, unfriendly faces. A few paces behind him, the huge warrior received a rapturous welcome. When they were both in the centre of the circle, the crowd of Ausetani closed ranks. From a distance of perhaps a dozen paces, the two faced each other. Sapho was armed with a sword and a dagger. In contemptuous concession, his opponent had laid aside his shield and saunion, leaving him with a long, straight, double-edged blade. It still looked like a totally uneven match.

Bostar's gorge rose. Sapho was a skilled swordsman, but he'd never faced a prospect like this. Judging by his father's clenched jaw and fixed expression, he was thinking similar thoughts. Whatever he had been thinking about Sapho recently, Bostar didn't want him to die losing to this giant. Closing his eyes, he prayed to Baal Saphon, the god of war, to help his brother. To help them all.

Sapho rolled his shoulders, loosening his muscles and wondering what was his best course of action. Why had he thrown down such a stupid challenge? The explanation was simple. Since Bostar had saved Hannibal's life, Sapho's jealousy had soared to new heights. There had always been a keen rivalry between them, but this was a step too far. In the months since they'd left Saguntum, Sapho had appeared to go along with Bostar's wish to lay the matter to rest, but the feeling gnawed constantly at his guts like a malignant growth. Perhaps now some of his wounded pride could be reclaimed. Sapho studied his opponent's bulging muscles and tried not to despair. What chance had he of succeeding? He had only one, Sapho realised with a thrill. His speed.

The chieftain raised his right arm, and a hushed silence fell. Glancing at both men to ensure they were ready, he made a downward chopping gesture.

With an almighty roar, the warrior launched himself forward, his sword raised high. For him, the contest was to be ended quickly. Brutally. Closing in on Sapho, he hammered down an immense blow. Instead of cleaving flesh, the blade whistled through the air to clash off the pebble-strewn ground, sending up a shower of sparks. Sapho was gone, dancing nimbly around to his opponent's rear. The warrior bellowed with rage and spun to face him. Again he swung at Sapho, to no avail. He didn't seem to care. With greater strength and reach, and a longer weapon, he had all the advantage.

Speed isn't enough, thought Sapho. Desperately, he twisted away from a thrust that would have driven through both his bronze breastplate and his ribcage had it connected. So far, the warrior's quilted linen tunic had turned away the glancing blows he had managed to land. Without getting dangerously close, it was impossible to do any more. Backing away from his sneering opponent, Sapho did not see one of the Ausetani stretch out his foot. An instant later, he tripped over it and fell backwards on to the hard packed dirt. Fortunately, he retained hold of his sword.

The warrior stepped closer and Sapho saw death looking him in the eyes. He waited until his enemy had begun to swing downwards, and then, with all his might, he rolled away into the centre of the circle. Behind him, Sapho heard his opponent's sword slam into the ground with a bone-jarring thump. Knowing that speed was of the essence, he turned over and over before trying to get up. Mocking laughs from the watching Ausetani filled the air, and the huge warrior raised his arms in anticipation of victory.

Rage filled Sapho at their treachery. He knew too that this fight couldn't be won by ordinary means. It was time to cast the dice. Take his chance. He drew his dagger with his left hand, ignoring the jeers this provoked.

Breathing deeply, Sapho waited. What he needed the warrior to do was take a great sideways slash at him. The only way he could think of drawing the hulk in was to stay put – without defending himself. It was a complete gamble. If the other didn't take the bait and respond exactly as he wished, he'd be dead, but Sapho couldn't think of anything else to do. Weariness threatened to overcome him, and his shoulders slumped.

The huge warrior shuffled in, grinning.

With a thrill, Sapho realised that his opponent thought he'd given up. He didn't move a muscle.

'Prepare to die,' the warrior growled. Lifting his right arm, he swung his sword around in a curving arc, aiming for the junction between Sapho's neck and shoulders. The blow was delivered with unstoppable force, at a target that was standing stock still. To those watching, it looked as if the duel was over.

At the last moment, Sapho dropped to his knees, letting the other's blade split the air over his head. Throwing himself forward, he stretched out his arm and plunged his dagger into the warrior's left thigh. It wasn't a fatal wound, but nor was it meant to be. As he landed helplessly on his chest, Sapho heard a loud scream of pain. A grimace of satisfaction twisted his lips as he scrambled to his feet, still clutching his sword. A few steps away, the bleeding warrior was listing to one side like a ship in a storm. All his attention was focused on pulling the knife from his leg. Stabbing him in the back would be simple.

A quick glance at the snarling faces surrounding them helped Sapho to make a snap decision. Mercy would be far more useful here than ruthlessness. Swiftly, he swept in and completed the task. Drawing his blade across the back of his enemy's left leg, he hamstrung him. As the bellowing warrior collapsed, Sapho stamped on his right hand, forcing him to drop his weapon. Touching the point of his blade to the other's chest, he growled, 'Yield.'

Moaning with pain, the warrior extended both his hands upwards, palms extended.

Sapho lifted his gaze to the chieftain, whose face registered stunned disbelief. 'Well?' he asked simply.

Eventually, the chief managed to compose himself. 'I apologise for insulting Hannibal, your leader. The Ausetani accept these generous gifts, with thanks,' he muttered with bad grace. 'You and your companions are free to go.'

'Excellent,' replied Sapho with a broad smile. 'Your son will be coming with us.'

The chief jumped to his feet. 'He needs medical attention.'

'Which he will receive in plenty. We will leave him in the care of the best surgeon in Emporiae. You have my word on that.' Sapho leaned on his sword slightly, eliciting a loud moan from the huge warrior. 'Or I can end it right here. It's your choice.'

The chieftain's lips peeled back with fury, but he was powerless in the face of Sapho's resolve. 'Very well,' he replied.

Only then did Sapho glance at his father and Bostar. Both gave him fierce nods of encouragement. Sapho found himself grinning like an idiot. Against all the odds, he had redeemed the situation, won his father's approval and his brother's admiration. Inside, though, he knew that the Ausetani would have to be defeated before this particular passage to Gaul was safe.

Chapter XII: Plans

A boot in the ribs woke Hanno the next morning. Grunting in pain, he opened his eyes. Agesandros was standing over him, flanked by two of the largest slaves on the farm. Hanno knew them for dumb brutes who did whatever they were told. Sets of manacles hung from their ham-like fists. Confusion and dread filled Hanno. Quintus' and Fabricius' absence hit home like hammer blows. This had to be more than coincidence. 'What was that for?' he croaked.

Instead of answering, the Sicilian kicked him again. Several times.

Protecting his head with his hands, Hanno rolled into the foetal position and prayed that Aurelia would hear.

At length, Agesandros ceased. He'd made no effort to remain quiet. 'Gugga son of a whore,' he snarled.

Through squinted eyes, Hanno looked up. He was alarmed to see the Sicilian clutching a dagger in one hand and a small purse in the other.

'I found these under your pathetic pile of possessions. So you would steal money and weapons from your owner?' Agesandros thundered. 'Probably cut all our throats in the middle of the night too, before running away to join your scumbag countrymen in their war against Rome.'

'I've never seen those things before in my life,' Hanno cried. Immediately, an image of Agesandros lurking in the atrium came to mind. That's what the Sicilian had been doing! 'You bastard,' Hanno muttered, trying to sit up. He received a kick in the face for his troubles. Sprawling back on his bedroll, waves of agony washed over him. Blood filled his mouth, and a moment later he spat out two teeth.

Agesandros laughed cruelly. 'Fit him with manacles,' he ordered. 'Neck as well as ankles.'

Dazed, Hanno watched as the slaves stepped forward and fastened the heavy iron rings around his flesh. Three loud clicks, and he was back to where he'd been in the slave market. As before, a long chain extended from the metal band around his neck. With a brutal tug, Hanno was jerked to his feet and towards the door.

'Stop!'

All eyes turned.

Still in her nightdress, Aurelia stood framed in the doorway to her room. 'Just what do you think you are doing?' she screeched. 'Hanno is a household slave, not one of the farm workers, to do with as you please.'

The Sicilian bowed extravagantly. Mockingly. 'Forgive me, my lady, for waking you so early. After hearing of the news in your father's letter, I became concerned about how this slave would react. I worried that he was planning to do you and your family harm, before escaping. Unfortunately, I was correct.' He held up the evidence. 'These clearly aren't his.'

Horrified, Aurelia's gaze shot to Hanno. She flinched at the sight of his bloodied face.

'*Someone* planted them among my things,' Hanno muttered, throwing Agesandros a poisonous look.

Understanding at once, Aurelia started forward. 'You see?'

The Sicilian chuckled. 'He would say that, wouldn't he? Every gugga's a liar, though.' He jerked his head at the two hulks. 'Come on. We have a long journey ahead of us.'

'I forbid you,' Aurelia shouted. 'Do not move another step.'

The slaves holding Hanno froze, and Agesandros turned. 'Forgive me, my lady, but in this instance I am going to override your authority.'

Atia's voice cut in like a whiplash. 'What about mine?' she demanded. 'In Fabricius' absence, I am in charge, not you.'

Agesandros blinked. 'Of course you are, mistress,' he replied smoothly.

'Explain yourself.'

Agesandros held up the knife and purse once more and repeated his allegations.

Atia looked suitably horrified.

'What would Fabricius say if he found out that I had left such a dangerous slave on the premises, mistress?' the Sicilian asked. 'He would have me crucified, and rightly so.'

You clever bastard, thought Hanno. Make your move when you only have two women to intimidate. Fabricius was far away, and who knew when Quintus would return?

Atia nodded in acceptance. 'Where are you taking him?'

'To Capua, mistress. Clearly, the dog is too dangerous to sell as an ordinary slave, but I've heard of a local government official who died there recently. The funeral is in two days, and the man's son wants to honour his father's passing with a gladiator fight. A pair of prisoners are to fight each other to the death, and then the survivor is to be executed.'

Atia's lips thinned. 'I see. Will my husband be out of pocket?'

'No, mistress. For an event like this, I'll get far more than we paid for him.'

Tears of impotent rage ran down Aurelia's cheeks. Frantically, she racked her brains. What could she do?

Atia crossed to give Aurelia a hug. 'Don't fret. He's a slave, dear,' she said. 'A murderous one too.'

'No,' Aurelia whispered. 'Hanno wouldn't do something like that.'

Atia frowned. 'You've seen the evidence for yourself. The only way we can confirm the Carthaginian's guilt is have him tortured and see what he says. Is that what you want?'

Defeated, Aurelia shook her head. 'No.'

'Fine. The matter's closed,' her mother said firmly. 'Now, I'm going for a bath. Why don't you join me?'

'I couldn't,' whispered Aurelia.

'Suit yourself,' said Atia. She turned to Agesandros. 'Better get going, hadn't you? It's a long way to Capua.'

The Sicilian flashed an oily smile. 'Yes, mistress.'

With a satisfied nod, Atia disappeared from sight.

Hanno, meanwhile, was in a daze. Agesandros must have been planning this ever since Quintus and Aurelia rescued me, he realised. Waiting for the right time.

His horror was only to grow.

'I forgot to say.' Revelling in the moment, the Sicilian looked from Hanno to Aurelia and back. 'The other fighter is also a gugga. A friend of this shitbag, I believe.'

Hanno's stomach lurched. It seemed too much of a coincidence to be true. 'Suniaton?'

Agesandros revealed his teeth. 'That's his name, yes.'

'No,' cried Aurelia. 'That is so cruel.'

'Quite apt, I thought,' said Agesandros.

Hanno's relief that Suni was alive vanished. Blinding fury consumed him, and he lunged forward, desperate to close with Agesandros. Within three steps, he was pulled up short. The slave holding the chain attached to his neck had simply tightened his grip. Hanno ground his teeth in rage. 'You will pay for this,' he growled. 'I curse you for ever. May the gods of the underworld act as my witness.'

There were few who were not afraid of such powerful oaths, and Agesandros flinched. But he regained control quickly. 'It's you who will be visiting Hades, along with your friend. Not me.' Clicking his fingers at the slaves, he stalked to the front door.

Hanno could not bear to look at Aurelia as he was dragged away. It hurt too much. The last thing he heard was the patter of her feet on the mosaic, and her voice calling for Elira. Then he was outside, in bright spring sunshine. Walking to Capua, where he would fight Suniaton to the death. Hanno stared at Agesandros' broad back, begging all the gods for a lightning bolt to strike him down on the spot. Of course, nothing happened.

The last remnants of Hanno's hope disappeared.

It returned within a matter of moments. They had not even reached the end of the lane before shouts and cries rang out behind them. Agesandros spun around, and his eyes widened. Without even looking at Hanno, he sprinted back towards the farm buildings. In slow motion, Hanno turned to see what was happening. To his amazement, tendrils of smoke were rising from one of the granaries. Aurelia, he thought, exultantly. She must have started a fire.

There was no way under the sun that Agesandros could have done anything but return. Aurelia had bought him some time. How would that be enough? Hanno wondered, desperation tearing at his soul.

It was several hours before the blaze was brought under control. Roaring like a demon, Agesandros supervised as every slave on the farm ferried water to the grain stores. Even Hanno had his manacles unfastened for the task. Hurling the contents of their buckets on to the flames, the slaves ran to the well and back, over and over again. Aurelia and Atia watched from a distance. Horrified expressions adorned both their faces. There was no sign of Elira.

The Sicilian let no one rest until he was happy that the fire was dying down. Despite himself, Hanno felt a grudging admiration for Agesandros. Covered in soot from head to toe like everyone else, he looked exhausted. The granaries' stone construction had helped, but the supreme effort the overseer had exacted from everyone was the main reason that the blaze had not spread to more of the farm buildings.

By the time the last of the flames had been extinguished, the afternoon was over. There was no question of walking to Capua that day. To Hanno's relief, the Sicilian didn't bother beating him further. His manacles were replaced, and he was locked into a small cell that adjoined Agesandros' quarters. In pitch darkness, Hanno slumped to the floor and closed his eyes. He was absolutely parched with thirst, and his belly was growling like a wild beast, but Hanno doubted that any food or drink would be forthcoming. He could only try to rest, and hope that Aurelia had another trick up her sleeve.

Hours passed. Hanno dozed fitfully, but the cold and his manacles prevented him from sleeping properly. Nonetheless, he dreamed of many things. The streets of Carthage. His two brothers, Sapho and Bostar, training with swords. Hannibal's messenger visiting by night. Fishing with Suniaton. The storm. Slavery and his unlikely friendship with Quintus and Aurelia. Bloody war between Carthage and Rome. Two gladiators fighting before a baying crowd. The last images were horrifyingly violent. Covered in sweat, Hanno jerked upright.

Desolation swamped him. After all his requests to be reunited with Suniaton, this is what it would come to. They would die together to commemorate the death of a crusty Roman official. Frustration and rage filled Hanno by turns. Alone in the darkness, he prayed that Agesandros stayed to watch the fight. When he and Suniaton were handed their weapons, they could make a suicidal attack on the Sicilian. Gain some retribution before they died. His plan was implausible, but Hanno hung on to it for dear life.

Some time later, he was startled by the sound of a key entering the lock. Surely dawn had not come yet? Hanno backed fearfully away from the door, raising his hands against the arc of light that spread into the room.

To his utter surprise, the person who entered was none other than Quintus, clad in a heavy cloak. He was clutching a bunch of keys in one hand and a small bronze lamp in the other. A sheathed gladius hung from a baldric over his right shoulder.

Hanno was stunned. 'What are you doing here?'

'Helping a friend,' replied Quintus simply. Placing the lamp on the floor, he tried a key on Hanno's fetters. It didn't work, but the second one did. A moment later, he had also unlocked the iron ring around his neck. Quintus grinned. 'Let's go.'

Hanno could scarcely contain his joy. 'How did you know to come back?'

A wry smile tugged Quintus' lips upwards. 'You can thank Aurelia. The instant you had left, she sent Elira to find me. Next she set a fire in the granary.'

Hanno was still confused. 'But the keys,' he said. 'There was no time to make an impression of them.'

'These are the originals,' replied Quintus. He saw Hanno's bewilderment, and explained. 'I commended Agesandros on his excellent work by giving him a jug of Father's best wine. The fool was delighted. What he didn't know was that I had laced it with enough papaverum to knock out an elephant. I simply waited until he had drunk it and fallen asleep. Then I took his keys.'

'You're a genius. So is Aurelia.' He grabbed Quintus' arm. 'Thank you. I owe you both my life for the second time.'

Quintus nodded. 'I knew that Agesandros was lying about you planning to kill us. If you wanted me dead, you wouldn't have come back to save me at the hut. Besides, I know you would help me in a similar situation.' He moved towards the door. 'Now, come on. Dawn is not far off. Aurelia is at the pens, feeding the dogs scraps to keep them from barking, but she can't stay there for ever. She said to say that you would be in her prayers.' He didn't mention his sister's tears. What was the point? Hers was an impossible fantasy.

Sad that he would not see Aurelia, and unaware of Quintus' emotions, Hanno followed him outside. The farmyard was deserted, and the only audible sounds were Agesandros' loud snores. Within a hundred paces, they had left the buildings behind. Along the lane, the cypress trees stood tall and threatening, their branches creaking in the slight breeze. A crescent moon hung low in the sky, reminding Hanno of Tanit and home. And Suniaton. Suddenly, the immense relief he had felt at Quintus' appearance began to ebb away. He might be free, but his friend was not.

Quintus stopped when they reached the shadow of the trees. He lifted the baldric over his shoulder and handed the gladius to Hanno. 'You'll need this.' Next, he proffered his thick woollen cloak and a leather satchel.

Hanno muttered his thanks.

'The bag contains food for several days, and twenty-five didrachms. Make your way to the coast and take passage to Syracuse. You should be able to find a merchant ship there which can take you to Carthage.'

'I'm going nowhere without Suniaton,' said Hanno.

Quintus' face changed. 'Have you gone mad?' he hissed. 'You don't even know where he is being held.'

'I'll find him,' Hanno answered stolidly.

'And get yourself killed into the bargain.'

'Would you leave Gaius behind if you were in my shoes?' Hanno demanded.

'Of course not,' Quintus retorted.

'Well, then.'

'Stubborn bloody Carthaginian. There's no telling you.' Quintus scowled. 'Going to Capua on your own is tantamount to committing suicide. I can't let you do that. Not after all the trouble I've gone to. Can you find the shepherd's hut where we fought the bandits?'

Hanno stared at Quintus, not understanding. 'I think so, yes.'

'Head up there and wait for me. I'll see about finding Suniaton later.'

The immensity of Quintus' offer sank in. 'You don't have to do this.'

'I know.' Quintus regarded him solemnly. 'But you are my friend.'

A lump rose in Hanno's throat. 'Thank you. If I can ever repay this debt, I will. You have my word.'

'Let us pray that I never have need to call on you.' Quintus pushed him towards the hills. 'Go.'

With a lightness in his heart that he had not felt since leaving Carthage, Hanno ran off into the darkness.

Hanno made his way to the hut without difficulty, reaching it less than two hours after sunrise. He spent the climb marvelling at how he'd escaped

Agesandros' clutches for the second time. Of course it was solely thanks to Quintus and Aurelia. Yet again, Hanno was forced to admit that Romans were capable of great kindness. They were not all the deceitful monsters described by his father. His charitable feelings did not last long. Hanno only had to think of Flaccus and his tale to remember the incredibly harsh conditions imposed on Carthage at the end of the last war, and the arrogant manner with which Rome had treated her over Saguntum. Even the genial Martialis didn't like the Carthaginians. 'Typical guggas,' he'd said.

He calmed himself with thoughts of how a Roman – Quintus – was at this very moment trying to free Suniaton, a Carthaginian condemned to die. His ploy didn't last long. As the hours dragged by, Hanno found it ever harder not to head for Capua. His promise to Quintus was what made him stay. He busied himself by repairing the hut, which had been left damaged after the fight. First Hanno collected every piece of fallen wood he could find. Then, using some old but serviceable tools he found lying inside, he sawed and chopped the timber into suitable lengths. He was no carpenter, but the construction was straightforward. All he had to do was study the undamaged sides, and copy them. It was undemanding yet rewarding labour and, as the sun set, Hanno stood back and admired his handiwork.

Worry was niggling away at him, however. He could no longer ignore the fact that Quintus would not return that day. Did this mean that his attempt had failed? Hanno had no idea. He pondered his options for some time, concluding that it was too dangerous to return to the farm. Agesandros would be on the lookout for trouble. Nor was there any point in making for Capua. Hanno knew no one there, and if he didn't manage to find Quintus, he would have no idea what had transpired since the morning. His only choice was to stay put. Slightly more at ease, Hanno lit a fire in the hut's stone-ring fireplace, and wolfed down some of the olives, cheese and bread he found in the satchel.

Wrapped in Quintus' cloak, Hanno sat watching the yellow-orange flames and thinking of the people he held most dear in the world. His father. Sapho and Bostar. Suniaton. Hanno paused before adding two more individuals to the list. Quintus. Aurelia. How many of them would he ever see again? Sadness, his constant companion since the storm, washed over Hanno in great waves. In all likelihood, he would never be reunited with his family. They were probably with Hannibal's army in Iberia by now, with every chance of being killed. Although it was his greatest desire to find them, doing so in the midst of a war would be virtually impossible. Finding Suniaton was perhaps his best hope, Hanno realised. If, by some stroke of luck, this came to pass, he would leave, never to see Quintus or Aurelia again. That conclusion brought even more pain. All he could wish for was a reunion with his loved ones in the next world. This bleak insight was the last thing Hanno remembered as sleep drew him into its embrace.

Dawn found Hanno in a better frame of mind. There was much to be grateful for. Despite what he had been through, he was no longer a captive. Moreover, Quintus had a greater chance of freeing Suniaton than he did. If the attempt was successful, he and his friend had a reasonable chance of making it to the coast, and finding a ship bound for Carthage. Never give up hope, Hanno thought. Without it, life is pointless.

He spent the morning practising with his gladius and scanning the slopes below for movement. It was nearly midday when Hanno spotted a lone figure on horseback. His heart leaped in his chest at the sight. There was no way of knowing who it was, so he withdrew into the cover granted by a clump of juniper trees some fifty paces from the hut. With bated breath, Hanno waited as the rider drew nearer. From its broad shoulders, he judged it to be male. There was no sign of any dogs, which pleased him. It increased the likelihood that this was not someone sent to track him down.

Finally, he recognised Quintus' features. Disappointment flooded Hanno that Suniaton was not with him. As the other drew close enough to speak, Hanno emerged from his hiding place.

Quintus raised a hand in apologetic salute.

'What happened? Did you discover anything about Suniaton?'

Quintus' lips twisted in a grimace. 'He's still alive, but he was injured during training two days ago. The good news is that he won't be able to take part in the *munus*.' He saw Hanno's alarm. 'It's just a flesh wound. Apparently, he'll be fine in a month or so.'

Hanno closed his eyes to relish the wave of relief. Suni wasn't dead! 'The official's son wouldn't sell him, then?'

Quintus shook his head. 'He didn't seem to care that you and Suniaton wouldn't be fighting each other,' he said. 'But he didn't want to sell Suni either. Stupidly, I let the mangy dog see how much I wanted to buy him. The prick told me to come back when Suniaton is fully recovered and I can see a demonstration of his full abilities. "That will show you his true worth," he said. I wouldn't hold your breath, though. The man fancies himself as a gladiator trainer. There must have been a dozen slaves with weapons training in his yard. I'm sorry.'

Hanno felt the last of his reborn hope slipping away.

Quintus glanced uneasily down the slope. 'You'd be wise to get moving.'

Hanno gave him a questioning look.

'Agesandros was furious when he discovered that you were gone,' Quintus said. 'The arrogant bastard wouldn't take it from me that I had freed you. He said only my father had the power to do that. Naturally, my mother agreed with him. She's furious with me,' he added glumly.

'But your father won't be back for months.'

Quintus gave him a grim nod. 'Precisely. Which makes you a runaway, and hunting *them* down is something Agesandros is rather good at. I told him that you headed towards Capua, and I think he believed me. He started looking in that direction.' He winked. 'Fortunately, Aurelia made Elira drag an old tunic of yours all the way to the river, and then swim downstream to a ford where her tracks would be mixed up with plenty of others. She left the garment in the water, which should trick the hounds.'

'Your sister is incredible,' said Hanno in amazement.

Quintus grinned briefly. 'It would still be best to get a head start now. Skirt around the farm to arrive at Capua tomorrow morning. Agesandros should have returned home by that stage, and you can catch a boat down-river to the coast.'

A knot formed in Hanno's stomach. 'I can't desert Suniaton,' he muttered. 'He's so near.'

'And so far,' Quintus replied harshly. 'He might as well be in Hades for all you can do.'

'That's as maybe,' Hanno retorted. 'But you said the official's son would talk again in a few weeks.'

Unsurprised, Quintus sighed. 'Stay, then,' he said. 'I'll bring you food every two or three days. I will try to keep an eye on Suniaton. We'll work out some way of getting him out.'

Hanno could have cried with relief. 'Thank you.'

Quintus pulled around his horse's head. 'Be vigilant. You never know when Agesandros might appear.'

Bostar's phalanx was marching behind those of Sapho and his father, so the messenger reached him first. 'Is there a Captain Bostar here?' he cried.

'Yes. What do you want?'

'Hannibal wants to talk to you, sir. Now,' he said, matching the Libyans' pace easily.

Bostar stared at the strapping scutarius, who was one of the general's bodyguard. 'Do you know what it's about?'

'No, sir.'

'Did he want to see my father or brother?'

'Just you, sir,' replied the Iberian stolidly. 'What shall I say to the general? He's pulled out of the column about a mile back.'

'Tell him I will be there at once.' Bostar thought for a moment. 'Wait! I'll come with you.'

The scutarius looked pleased. 'Very good, sir.'

Bostar muttered instructions to his second-in-command, who was riding beside him, before turning his horse's head and directing it out of his soldiers' way. Few of the men looked up as he trotted by, but those who did grinned. Bostar nodded in acknowledgement, glad that his efforts in winning their trust had paid off. The Libyans' large round shields knocked off their backs as they walked, and their short spears looked skywards in a forest of points. A junior officer was situated every fifty paces, and beside each marched a standard-bearer. Their wooden poles were decorated with sun discs, lunar crescents and red decorative ribbons.

Bostar eyed the long, winding column approaching from the southwest. 'Feast your eyes on that,' he said to the scutarius, who was trotting along-side. 'It's some spectacle.'

'I suppose so, sir.' The man cleared his throat and spat. 'It would look a damn sight better with forty thousand more of my countrymen, though.'

'Not all are as loyal as you and your comrades,' replied Bostar. In his heart, he too was sorry that the host had shrunk by more than a third in little over three months. Much of the decrease could be accounted for by the casualties suffered thus far, and those who made up the garrisons along the route back to Iberia. In addition, plenty of men, perhaps ten thousand more, had been discharged by Hannibal before they could desert. To discuss the matter with an ordinary soldier was bad for morale, so Bostar kept his lips sealed. His spirits soon lifted, however. It was impossible not to be exhilarated by the sight of such a massive Carthaginian army, the first such to go on the offensive against Rome in more than a generation.

After the last of the spearmen had passed, there was a short delay until the next units reached them. These were massed ranks of fierce-looking, tattooed Libyan skirmishers in bare feet and red goatskin tunics. They were armed with small round shields and handfuls of javelins. Hundreds of Balearic slingers followed, wild half-dressed men from the Mediterranean islands, whose skill with their slings was legendary. Bostar wouldn't have trusted a single man among them, but they were a supreme asset to Hannibal's army.

After came the light Iberian infantry, the *caetrati*, with their round leather bucklers, javelins and falcata swords. Further down the track, Bostar made out Hannibal and his officers, surrounded by the mounted part of his body-guard, local cavalry in crested bronze helmets and red cloaks. Behind the general marched the heavy Celtiberian foot, the scutarii.

Bostar could not see the final units of the army, which trailed behind the baggage train, thousands of laden-down mules led by Iberian peasants. Protecting the rear were thirty-seven elephants, and more Celtiberians. Bostar thought that their uniform was probably the most striking in the entire force: black cloaks, bronze helmets with crimson crests and greaves made of sinew. Their shields were either round like those of the caetrati, or flat, elongated ovals, and they carried short straight swords and all-iron spears. Last of all, mobile and fast moving, were the many protective squadrons of Iberian and Numidian cavalry. These – the finest horsemen in the world – were Hannibal's secret weapon.

They reached the general's position not long after. The scutarius gave the password to the cavalryman who challenged them, which saw the protective cordon open up. Bostar dismounted quickly and threw his reins to the Iberian. As he approached, he felt Hannibal's eyes upon him. Bostar moved even faster. He snapped off a salute. 'You wished to see me, sir?'

Hannibal smiled. 'Yes. I wasn't expecting you so soon.'

Bostar couldn't help but grin. 'I wanted to find out what you had in mind for me, sir.'

Hannibal glanced at the officers to either side. 'Eager, this lion cub, isn't he?'

There was a ripple of laughter, and Bostar flushed, not least because the general and his brothers – the sons of Hamilcar Barca – were known as the 'lion's brood'.

Hannibal noticed at once. 'Do not take offence, for I meant none. It's soldiers like you who are the backbone of this army. Not like the thousands of men I had to let go after our recent campaign. Faint hearts.'

Bostar nodded gratefully. 'Thank you, sir.'

Hannibal turned his eyes to the southwest, whence they had come. 'It's hard to believe that we only crossed into Gaul a few weeks ago, isn't it? Seems like we haven't fought a battle in an age.'

'I won't forget the journey in a hurry, sir.' After the hostile, sun-scorched lands north of the Iberus, Bostar appreciated the fertile land of southern Gaul, with its tilled fields, large villages and friendly natives.

Hannibal's nod was rueful. 'Nor will I. Losing ten thousand men in under three months was most unfortunate. But it couldn't be helped. Speed was of the essence, and our tactics worked.'

Mago shot his brother a disgruntled look. 'Don't forget the same number of troops, plus cavalry, that you had to leave to keep the bastards pacified.'

'Soldiers who will also protect the area against Roman invasion,' retorted Hannibal. 'After defeating the troublesome natives, they should be able to take on a legion or two.' He scratched his beard and eyed Bostar. 'The worst of the lot were that tribe you had trouble with. The whoresons who would have slaughtered you but for the duel your mad brother fought.'

Bostar hid his amusement at Hannibal's description of Sapho. 'The Ausetani, sir.'

'The same ones who wouldn't allow the army to march through their lands unhindered. They were fools. But brave all the same,' Hannibal acknowledged. 'At the end, hardly any of them had wounds in their backs.'

'They fought well, sir,' agreed Bostar. 'Especially the champion whom Sapho defeated. I counted ten of our soldiers lying around his corpse. His wound from the duel hadn't even healed either.'

'Malchus pointed him out to me afterwards,' said Hannibal. 'It's incredible that your brother managed to beat him in single combat. The man was as big as Herakles.'

'He was, sir,' agreed Bostar fervently. His memories of the fight were still vivid. 'Sapho had the gods on his side that day.'

'He did. For all his bravery, though, your brother has a tendency to be rash. To act first, and think later.'

'If you say so, sir.' While Bostar agreed with his general's assessment, it felt wrong to openly say so.

Hannibal gave him a shrewd look. 'Your loyalty is commendable, but don't think I didn't hear about his refusal to pull back during that attack on Saguntum. If it hadn't been for you, hundreds of men would have lost their lives unnecessarily. Eh?'

Bostar met his general's gaze with reluctance. 'Maybe so, sir.'

'That's why you're here. Because you think before you take action.' Hannibal waved at the rolling countryside, much of which was full of ripe wheat and barley. 'Things are easy now. We can buy as much grain as we need from the locals, and live off the land the rest of the time. But the journey won't all be like this. The weather will get worse and, sooner or later, we'll come across someone who wants to fight us.'

'Indeed, sir,' said Bostar soberly.

'We can only pray that it's not the Romans at any stage before we reach Cisalpine Gaul. Hopefully, those bastards still have no idea of our plans. The good news is that my scouts, who have just returned from the River Rhodanus, saw no sign of them.'

Mago's smile was like that of a wolf. 'And the trail a legion leaves can't be missed, so we have one less thing to worry about. For now.'

'Have you heard of the Rhodanus?' asked Hannibal.

'Vaguely, sir,' said Bostar. 'It's a big river quite near the Alps.'

'That's right. By all accounts, most of the tribes in the area are well disposed towards us. Naturally, there's one that is not. The Volcae, they're called, and they live on both sides of the water.'

'Will they try to deny us the passage, sir?'

'It would appear so,' Hannibal answered grimly.

'That could be very costly, sir, especially when it comes to taking the horses and elephants across.'

Hannibal scowled. 'That's right. Which is why, while the army prepares to cross, you're going to lead a force upriver of the Volcae camp. You'll swim over at night, and find a hidden position nearby. Your dawn signal will tell me to order the boats launched.' He smacked a fist into his palm. 'We'll squash them like a man stamps on a beetle. How does that sound?'

Bostar's heart thumped in his chest. 'It sounds good, sir.'

'That's what I like to hear.' Hannibal gripped his shoulder. 'You'll get further instructions nearer the time. Now, you'll be wanting to get back to your men.'

Bostar knew when he was being dismissed. 'Yes, sir. Thank you, sir.'

Hannibal called out when Bostar was ten steps away. 'Not a word about this to anyone.'

'Of course, sir,' Bostar replied. The order was a relief, for it meant that Sapho would have no chance to be jealous because he had not been selected for the duty. Yet Bostar was already worrying how his brother would react when he did find out.

Chapter XIII: Departure

Hanno soon grew used to living in the hut, which had lain vacant since the shepherd's murder. According to Quintus, Fabricius' sheep were being grazed elsewhere and there was little likelihood of anyone passing by. Nonetheless, Hanno stayed alert. While Agesandros was his main concern, he had no wish to be seen at all. Hanno's luck held out; the only visitors he had were Quintus, and occasionally Aurelia.

There was little news of Suniaton. Quintus did not want to appear too eager by visiting the official's son earlier than had been arranged. Finally, though, Quintus reported that Suniaton had made an uneventful recovery. Hanno's spirits soared upon hearing this, but his hopes were immediately dashed. 'The whoreson still won't sell. He says Suniaton is too promising a fighter. He wanted 250 didrachms for him.' Quintus gave Hanno an apologetic look. 'I haven't got that type of money. Father does, of course, but I'm not sure he'd give it to me, even if I managed to find him.'

'We can't give up now. There must be another way,' said Hanno fiercely.

'Unless we can bribe someone to let Suniaton escape . . . I just don't know who to approach.' Quintus' frown disappeared. 'I could ask Gaius.' He held up a reassuring hand as Hanno jerked forward in alarm. 'Gaius and I have been friends since we could walk. He doesn't necessarily approve of my helping you escape, but he won't tell a soul. Who knows? He might be prepared to help.'

Hanno forced himself to sit down. Gaius' trustworthiness had already been proved by the fact that nobody had come looking for him at the shepherd's hut. It also seemed as if he was Suniaton's only hope. 'Let us pray to the gods that he agrees, then.'

'Leave it to me,' said Quintus, hoping that his confidence in Gaius was not misplaced. In an effort to protect Hanno, he had concealed the fact that Suniaton was already fighting as a gladiator once more.

Time was not on their side.

When Quintus finally brought word that Gaius' efforts had come to fruition, Hanno's relief was overwhelming. Autumn had arrived, and the woods were a riot of colour. The temperature had dropped noticeably too. Hanno was growing used to being woken by the cold at night. Quintus' direction to pack all his gear was most welcome. Hopefully, he'd be leaving the hut for ever. 'What are we going to do?' he asked as they headed towards Capua.

'Gaius didn't want me to say,' Quintus replied, avoiding Hanno's gaze.

Worry clawed at Hanno's insides. 'Why?'

Quintus shrugged. 'I'm not sure. I think he wants to tell you himself.' He saw Hanno's disappointment. 'It's only a few hours longer.'

'I know,' Hanno replied, forcing a smile. 'And I owe you both so much for what you've done.'

'It's not about debts,' said Quintus generously. 'A man tries to help his friends if he can. Let's just hope that Gaius' idea works.'

Hanno nodded grimly. If it didn't, there was a hard choice to be made. He couldn't hang around for ever.

It was nearly dark by the time they reached Capua. Their journey had been uneventful, but Hanno still faltered as the massive walls loomed into view. Even though he was coming to help free Suniaton, entering the city now meant real danger. There would be guards at the gate, who could ask awkward questions. Descriptions of him pinned to the walls of houses. Hanno knew how fugitive slaves were hunted in Carthage. It wouldn't be much different here. His feet dragged to a halt.

Quintus turned. 'What is it?'

'I'm not just an escaped slave. What if someone recognises me as a Carthaginian?'

Quintus' chuckle died away as he saw Hanno's real distress. 'You don't have to worry,' he said reassuringly. 'There are plenty of dark-skinned slaves in Capua. Greeks, Libyans, Judaeans. No one knows the difference. And apart from Gaius, no one knows what you've done. Nor do they care. You're a slave, remember? Most people won't even notice you, let alone challenge you.' He dismounted. 'Follow me. Look miserable and don't catch anyone's eye.'

'Very well,' said Hanno, wishing that he had the comfort of a weapon to defend himself.

To his relief, things went smoothly. The sentries didn't even look up as he shuffled after Quintus. It was the same on the streets, which, thanks to the fast-approaching sunset, were emptying fast. People were more interested in getting home safely than studying a young noble and his slave. Housewives with baskets full of food muttered a few words with each other rather than having a full-blown gossip. Stallholders were boxing up their unsold produce and loading it on to mules. Many of the shops were already boarded up for the night.

Before long, they had reached Martialis' house. Quintus' loud knock was answered at once by Gaius himself, who grinned at his friend as he pulled open the gate. 'I've been waiting for you.' He gave Hanno a hard glance, but did not speak.

All of Hanno's doubts returned. He ducked his head awkwardly, telling himself that Gaius must be prepared to help. Why else were they here?

With several domestic slaves looking on, however, there was no chance of asking. One of them scurried past to take the horse's reins, and Gaius threw an arm around Quintus' shoulders. 'Let's go inside. Father can't wait to see you. He ordered a piglet roasted in your honour.' Gaius eyed the stable boy. 'Make sure my friend's slave gets fed. Find him a bed too.'

'Yes, sir.'

Hanno's unease abated a little when Quintus turned and gave him a wink. Hanno forced himself to relax as the gate shut, leaving him on the street. He followed the boy around the corner of the house to the stables, which were in a separate walled courtyard. The young slave proved to be as taciturn as he was ugly. They rubbed down, fed and watered Quintus' mount in complete silence, which suited Hanno down to the ground. Next they entered Martialis' kitchen through a door in the adjoining wall. Similar to Julius' jurisdiction, it was a hot, busy place, filled with the clatter of pans and shouted orders. The rich smell of cooking pork filled Hanno's nostrils and set his stomach rumbling. Keen to avoid attention, he found a quiet spot in the corridor that led to the pantry, where he sat down.

A few moments later, the stable boy appeared bearing two plates heaped high with bread, roast meat and vegetables. He shoved one at Hanno. 'You're in luck tonight. The piglet could feed twenty people, so the master won't notice if his slaves also have a share.'

'Thank you.' Hanno seized the platter. This was a better feed than he'd had in months.

When they'd finished, the stable boy squinted at Hanno. 'Do you play dice?'

Hanno did, but he felt as tense as the arm on a cocked catapult. So much was at stake tonight. 'No.'

Looking vaguely disappointed, the slave shuffled off. 'Come on. I'll show you a place to sleep.'

Hanno was taken back to the stables, and shown a quiet corner near the door. 'No lights can be left in here. Too great a risk of fire.' The stable boy indicated his small oil light. 'I'll be taking this with me.'

'Fine,' replied Hanno.

With a shrug, the slave left him to it. As the flickering glow of the other's lamp receded, Hanno was left in complete darkness. He didn't mind about that. It was more the fact that, with Suniaton's escape so close, he was about to spend several hours alone. After a while, he began to look forward to the occasional stamp of a hoof or a gentle whinny. The frequent noise of rats scurrying to and fro was less welcome, but it was a minor inconvenience compared to his reason for being there.

To Hanno's annoyance, the evening dragged by more slowly than an entire week. He spent an age praying to the gods, asking for their aid in ensuring that Gaius helped to free Suniaton. Growing frustrated with the overwhelming silence that met each of his requests, Hanno tried to sleep. He had no luck at all. His spirits rose when the stable boy and two other slaves entered the building. Despite his frustration, time *was* passing. Pretending to be asleep, Hanno heard them clamber up the rickety ladder to the hay store over the horses' stalls. Their incoherent mumbling led him to assume that they'd been drinking. Their oil light was extinguished almost immediately, and it wasn't long before a cadence of snores from above filled Hanno's ears. After what seemed an age, he felt his way over to the kitchen door, where Quintus had told him to wait.

When the door opened smoothly inwards, it caught Hanno unawares. 'Who is it?' he whispered nervously.

'Pluto himself, come to carry you away,' Quintus muttered. 'Who do you think?'

Hanno shivered. Even mentioning the Roman god of the underworld felt like bad luck. He offered up another prayer to Eshmoun, asking for his protection.

Quintus was followed by Gaius, who was carrying a small, shuttered lantern. Both were wearing dark cloaks.

Hanno could take it no more. 'What are we going to do?'

'Outside.' Gaius led them to the stable door, where he lifted the locking bar and gently laid it on the floor. A waft of cool air hit their faces as he tugged the door open. Gaius padded out and checked the street. 'All clear!' he hissed an instant later.

Quintus shoved Hanno out first, and pulled the portal to behind them.

'Come on, Gaius. Are you finally going to tell us what you've planned?' asked Quintus.

Hanno's stomach clenched into a knot.

'I will,' muttered Gaius, 'but your slave should know something first.'

'He's not a slave any more,' Quintus hissed. 'I freed him.'

'You and I know that that holds about as much water as a leaky bucket.'

Quintus did not reply.

Hanno's breath caught in his chest. Gaius was clearly cut from different cloth to Quintus. He wanted to leave, but that would mean extinguishing whatever hope there was of freeing his friend. Gritting his teeth, he waited.

'I was stunned when you first told me what you'd done, Quintus,' Gaius whispered. 'I said nothing of course. You're my oldest friend. But you took a step too far when you asked me to help free another slave. That I could not do.'

'Gaius, I—' Quintus began. The poor light could not conceal the embarrassment in his voice.

'I changed my mind, however, when I found out who owned the slave you were interested in.' Gaius paused. 'The official who died was none other than the biggest persecutor of Oscan nobility that this city has ever seen. His shitbag of a son is little better. Stealing . . . freeing . . . one of his slaves is the least I would do to the bastard.'

Hanno let out a long sigh.

'Thank you, Gaius,' whispered Quintus. He wasn't going to question his friend's motives at a moment such as this.

At once Gaius brought them into a little huddle. 'I started off by spending days hanging around in the street where the official's son lives. I found out little, but I did get to know the faces of everyone who lived in his house. Then my luck changed. About a week ago, I saw the major-domo coming out of a brothel in a different part of town.'

'So what?' demanded Quintus. 'That's hardly unusual.'

Gaius' teeth flashed white in the darkness. 'Except when I went inside and asked who he'd been fucking, the madam went all coy. I slipped her a few coins, and she soon changed her tune. It seems that the major-domo has a taste for young boys.'

'Filthy bastard,' muttered Quintus.

An image of Hostus popped into Hanno's mind. His father's enemy was known for a similar taste in flesh. 'It's disgusting, but is it a crime?' he asked. 'It's not in Carthage, unfortunately.'

'The practice is frowned upon by many, but it isn't against the law for citizens, like us,' Gaius replied. 'Slaves are a different matter, however. I doubt that the official's son would be too pleased to find out about his major-domo's habits. The madam said that he tends to get overexcited. Violent. She's had to intervene a number of times to stop her boys from being badly injured.'

'Fucking animal,' said Quintus, looking revolted.

Hanno was just grateful that he and Suniaton hadn't been sold to a similar fate. 'So you're blackmailing him?'

'Basically, yes,' Gaius answered. 'He's agreed to drug the slave who guards the door, which will give him a chance to let Suniaton out. Of course the poor bastard doorman will probably end up on a cross for letting another slave escape, but the major-domo doesn't care about that. He's only thinking of his own skin.'

'And if he doesn't play along?' enquired Quintus. His words made Hanno's stomach clench.

'His owner will receive an anonymous letter detailing his sordid activities to the letter, and giving the brothel's address should he wish to corroborate the details.'

'Excellent,' murmured Quintus.

For a moment, Hanno's delight at Gaius' plan was soured by the know-ledge that an innocent slave would suffer, or even die, so that Suni might be free. He quelled the thought without remorse. He would kill to save his friend. How was this any different? 'It sounds foolproof,' he said. 'Thank you.'

'I'm not doing it for you,' Gaius replied curtly. 'I'm doing it because it gives me an opportunity to get back at the official's son.' He chuckled at the others' confusion. 'By sunset tomorrow, everyone in the town will have heard the rumour that he likes to screw young boys. Not the best way to start a political career, is it?' He looked at Gaius, who gave a resigned shrug. 'Best get moving now, though. Stay close.'

Telling himself that it didn't matter what Gaius' reasons for helping were, Hanno followed the two Romans through the darkened streets. The only living thing that they encountered was a scrawny dog, which raised its hackles and growled at the interlopers to its territory. It darted, yelping, out of the way when Gaius aimed a hefty kick at it, and it wasn't long before they were crouched by the front door of a nondescript house, three shadows that could barely be seen. Apart from the chinks of light that escaped the wooden shutters of a flat on the opposite side of the lane, it was pitch black.

Checking the street yet again, Gaius rapped lightly on the door with his knuckles. There was no response from within, and Hanno began to panic. He glanced at the myriad of stars that lit the night sky. Eshmoun, he begged, do not forget Suniaton, your devoted follower, and son of your priest in Carthage. Great Tanit, have mercy.

His prayers were answered a moment later when, with a faint creak, the door opened inwards. 'Who is it?'

'Gaius.'

A short man emerged cautiously on to the street. Seeing Quintus and Hanno, he stiffened. Gaius was quick to jump in with the reassurance that they were friends, and the figure relaxed a fraction. His receding hair, long nose, and darting eyes made him resemble a rat, thought Hanno distaste-fully. It was no surprise that he fucked little boys. Yet this was the major-domo of the house, who was also about to set Suniaton free.

'Well, where's the Carthaginian?' demanded Gaius.

'Just inside. I'll get him,' the major-domo replied, bobbing his head. 'And you'll say nothing to my master?'

'I give you my word,' Gaius answered dryly.

The other nodded uneasily, knowing that this was all he'd get. 'Very well.'

He scuttled from view, and Hanno felt a tinge of suspicion at his speed. There was a short delay before he heard the sound of shuffling feet. Then Hanno saw a stooped figure framed in the doorway, and he leaped forward. 'Suniaton?'

'Hanno?' croaked the other.

Throwing his arms around Suniaton, Hanno clung to his friend like a drowning man. He was dimly aware of the door shutting and a bolt sliding across to lock it. Hanno didn't care. Hot tears of joy scalded his cheeks; he felt moisture soak into his tunic as Suniaton wept too. For a moment, they just stood there, each revelling in the fact that the other was still alive. Abruptly, Suniaton's knees gave way beneath him. Hanno had to stop him from falling. He studied Suniaton's face. Gone was the round-faced young man he was familiar with. In his place stood a gaunt-cheeked, unshaven wretch with long hair. 'You're half starved,' Hanno cried.

'It's not that,' replied Suniaton. His eyes were deep pools of pain. 'I'm hurt.'

Suddenly, Hanno understood the reason for Suniaton's hunched posture. 'How badly?'

'I'll live.' Despite his brave words, Suniaton grimaced. 'I got beaten in a fight two days ago. I've got several wounds, but the worst is a slash across the top of my right thigh.'

Gaius thumped on the door. 'Treacherous bastard! You said nothing about this.'

To his surprise, the major-domo replied. 'I was told only to bring him out at the appointed hour. No one said anything about whether he was well or not.'

'You whoreson!' hissed Hanno. 'I should cut your balls off.' He leaned his shoulder against the timbers and heaved.

Quintus intervened. 'It's not safe here.' He moved to stand by Suniaton. 'You take one arm, and I'll take the other,' he said to Hanno.

Hanno nodded. There was no point wasting time. The major-domo could take his own chances now. Only the gods knew whether the drugging of the doorman would fool his master. It mattered not at all. They had to get Suniaton back to Gaius' house, where they could examine his wounds.

Fortunately, Suniaton was proved to be right about his injuries. Although he was in considerable pain, the clean sword cuts were not life-threatening. As far as Hanno could tell, they had been stitched reasonably well. Yet the worst wound concerned him greatly. The biggest muscle in Suniaton's right thigh had nearly been severed. There was nothing they could do about it, and so they prepared to leave. They had to get to safety before dawn. Bidding farewell to Gaius, the pair heaved Suniaton up on to Quintus' mount. Having bribed a sentry, they passed out of the town with relative ease. The horse's movement caused Suniaton so much pain, however, that he soon passed out. Hanno could do nothing but support his friend as he walked alongside. He would ask Quintus to get some papaverum from Elira later. For now, he thanked Tanit and Eshmoun, and asked for their continued blessing. Hopefully, Suniaton just needed time. Hanno was desperate to head for Iberia, but he would not leave his friend behind now.

The war would have to wait.

Bostar eyed the figures on the other side of the Rhodanus. Although the deep, fast-flowing water was more than five hundred paces across at this point, the Volcae camp was easy to make out between the trees that dotted the far bank. There were scores of tents and lines of tethered horses, denoting the presence of hundreds of warriors. Sentries patrolled the water-line day and night. Given that the tribesmen normally lived on both sides of the river, their intent could not be more plain. They would pay dearly for their combative stance, thought Bostar. Hannibal had given him his orders not an hour since. Once he'd made an offering to the gods, it was time to go. His phalanx and the three hundred scutarii the general had insisted he also take were already assembled beyond the Libyans' tent lines. Their destination, an island at a narrow point in the river, was a day's march to the north.

Sapho's voice made him jump. 'Why couldn't the stupid bastards be like the other tribes around here?'

'Sell us boats and supplies, you mean?' Bostar asked, trying to look pleased to see his brother. What was Sapho, who still had no idea of his mission, doing here at this early hour? Why did I mention it to Father? thought Bostar, panicking. He took a deep breath. Calm down. I asked him not to mention it to a soul. He won't have.

'Yes. Instead, they'll kill a tiny fraction of our troops before being annihilated themselves. Even simple savages such as they must know that our army can't be stopped from crossing the Rhodanus.'

Bostar shrugged. 'I suppose they're like the Ausetani. Defending their territory is a matter of pride. It doesn't matter how badly they're outnumbered. Death in battle is not something to be ashamed of.'

'Sheep-shagging inbreds,' said Sapho with a derisive snort. 'Why can't they understand that all we want to do is cross this poxy river and be on our way?'

Bostar refrained from asking the obvious question: wasn't the response of the Volcae how Sapho, or he, might act in a similar situation? 'Never mind. Hannibal gave them their chance. Now, what was it that you wanted? I was about to take my phalanx out on a march,' he lied bluffly, unable to think of what else to say.

'Gods, your men must *love* you. Haven't we done enough of that recently? That explains why you're in full uniform at this hour.' Sapho made a dismissive gesture. 'It was nothing that can't wait. Just that I noticed plenty of game trails leading down to the water's edge. I thought I'd follow them beyond the camp. Would you like to come along?'

Bostar was completely taken aback by this. 'What, and go looking for boar?' he faltered.

'Or deer.' Sapho threw him a crooked, awkward grin. 'Anything to vary our current diet.'

'A bit of fresh meat wouldn't go amiss,' Bostar admitted ruefully. He felt torn. The proposal was clearly a bridge-building effort on Sapho's part, but he couldn't disobey Hannibal's orders; nor could he reveal them. They were still top secret. What to say? 'I'd love to, but not today,' he managed eventually. 'Who knows what time I'll get back?'

Sapho wasn't to be put off. 'How about tomorrow?' he asked cheerfully.

Bostar's anguish grew. Great Melqart, he thought, what have I done to deserve this? He and his men would only be getting into position by the following evening. On the far bank. 'I'm not sure . . .' he began.

Sapho's good humour fell away. 'So you'd rather spend time with your men than your own brother?'

'It's not that,' Bostar protested. 'Going hunting with you sounds wonderful.'

'What is it then?' Sapho snarled.

Bostar's mind was empty of ideas. 'I can't say,' he muttered.

Sapho's lip curled even further. 'Admit it. I'm not good enough for you, am I? Never have been!'

'That's not true. How can you say such a thing?' Bostar cried, horrified.

'Bostar!' Their father's cheerful voice cut across the argument like a knife. Startled, both brothers glanced around. Malchus was approaching from the direction of his tent lines. 'I thought you'd be gone by now,' he said as he drew nearer.

'I was just leaving,' replied Bostar uneasily. Let me get away without any more problems, Baal Saphon, he prayed. 'I'll see you later.'

Bostar's plea was not answered; Malchus gave him a broad wink. 'Good luck.'

'Eh?' said Sapho with a puzzled frown. 'Why would he need that on a training march?'

Malchus looked uncomfortable. 'You never know, he might break an ankle. The trails around here are very uneven.'

'That's a lie if I ever heard one. Besides, when have you ever wished us luck for so trivial a matter?' Sapho scoffed. He turned on Bostar. 'Something else is going on, isn't it? That's why you won't come hunting!'

Bostar felt his face grow red. 'I've got to go,' he muttered, picking up his shield.

Furious, Sapho blocked his path. 'Where are you going?'

'Get out of my way,' said Bostar.

'Is that an order, *sir*?' Contempt dripped from the last word.

'Move, Sapho!' snapped Malchus. 'Your brother's orders come from Hannibal himself.'

'It's like that, is it?' Sapho stepped aside, his eyes filled with jealousy. 'You could have said. Just a hint.'

Bostar looked at him, and knew he'd made a mistake. 'I'm sorry.'

'No, you're not,' Sapho hissed. He lowered his voice even further. 'Lick-arse. Perfect fucking officer.'

A towering fury took hold of Bostar. Somehow, he managed to keep it in check. 'Actually, I said nothing because I didn't want you to feel that you'd been overlooked.'

'You're so fucking kind,' Sapho shouted, the veins in his neck bulging. 'I hope you get killed wherever you're going.'

Malchus' mouth opened in rebuke, but Bostar held his hand up. Oddly, his anger had been replaced by sorrow. 'I trust that you wish the mission to be successful at least?'

Shame filled Sapho's face, but he had no chance to reply.

Bostar turned to Malchus. 'Farewell, Father.'

Malchus' eyes were dark pools of sorrow. 'May the gods watch over you and your men.'

Bostar nodded and walked away.

'Bostar!'

He ignored Sapho's cry.

It felt as if he'd just lost another brother.

Two days later, Bostar and his men were in position. Theirs had been a hard journey. After a long march on the first day, their guides had brought them to a fork in the Rhodanus. The island in the centre of the river had made their crossing much easier. Not knowing if there were any Volcae on the opposite bank, they had waited until nightfall. Then, using rafts constructed from a combination of chopped-down trees and inflated animal skins, Bostar and ten handpicked men had swum to the other side. To their immense relief, the woods had been empty of all but owls and foxes. Soon after, the remaining soldiers had safely joined him. Bostar had not forgotten to give thanks to the gods for this good fortune. Hannibal and the entire army were relying on them. If they failed, hundreds, or even thousands, of men would die at the hands of the Volcae when the Carthaginian forces began to cross.

At sunrise, they had marched south, halting only when the enemy encampment had been identified. Leaving his party to rest in the dense thickets that occupied the high ground overlooking the river, Bostar and a few sentries had spent the night on their bellies, watching the Volcae sitting around their fires. The tribesmen seemed oblivious to any danger, which pleased him. Somehow that made his anguish over the argument with Sapho easier to bear. Bostar had no wish to be enemies with his brother. Let us both survive the struggle to come, he prayed, and make our peace afterwards.

As dawn arrived, it became possible to make out the enormous Carthaginian camp on the far bank. With growing tension, Bostar waited until he could see troops near the water's edge, cavalrymen climbing into the larger craft, and infantry scrambling into the canoes. He even spied Hannibal in his burnished cuirass, directing operations. Still Bostar held on. Picking the right moment to charge was vital. Too soon, and he and his men risked being slaughtered; too late, and innumerable soldiers in the boats would die.

It wasn't long before the Volcae sentinels noticed the activity opposite their position and raised the alarm. Clutching their weapons, hundreds of warriors emerged from their tents and ran down to the bank. There they paced threateningly up and down, screaming abuse at the Carthaginians and bragging of their exploits. Bostar was thrilled. The enemy's camp had been abandoned, and every man's gaze was fixed on the flotilla of vessels opposite. It was time to move. 'Light the fires!' he hissed. 'Quickly!'

A trio of kneeling spearmen, who had been regarding him nervously, struck their flints together. *Clack, clack, clack,* went the stones. Sparks dropped on to the little mounds of dry tinder before each man. Bostar sighed with relief as a tiny flame licked first up the side of one pile, and then another. The third heap took flame a moment later. The soldiers encouraged the fires by blowing on them vigorously.

Fretfully chewing a fingernail, Bostar waited until each blaze was strong enough. 'Add the green leaves,' he ordered. He watched intently as thick eddies of smoke from the damp foliage curled up into the air and climbed above the tops of the trees. The instant it had, Bostar's gaze shot to the opposite bank. 'Come on,' he muttered. 'You have to be able to see it now.'

His prayers were answered as Hannibal and his soldiers sprang into action. Boat after boat was pushed out into the water. The larger craft, carrying the cavalrymen, who were each leading six or seven horses, stayed upstream. Their size and number helped to reduce the impact of the powerful current on the smaller vessels containing the infantry. The Volcae responded at once. Every man with a bow or spear pushed forward to the water's edge and waited for his chance.

'Come on,' muttered Bostar to his three spearmen. 'It's time to give those shitbags a surprise they'll never forget.'

Moments later, he and most of his force were trotting down the slope towards the riverbank. The remainder, a hundred scutarii, were heading for the Volcae camp. They ran in silence, hard and fast. Rivulets of sweat ran from under Bostar's bronze helmet to coat his face. He did his best to ignore it, counting his steps instead. During the long wait, he had made repeated estimates of the distance from where they had lain hidden to the water's edge. Five hundred paces, Bostar told himself. To the enemy tents, it was only 350. It seemed an eternity, but the Volcae were so busy shouting at the approaching boats that they had soon covered a hundred paces without being challenged. Then it was 150; 175. Hannibal's boats had reached the midpoint of the river. As Bostar counted two hundred, he saw a figure turn to address one of his companions. An expression of stunned disbelief crossed the man's face as he took in the mass of soldiers running towards him. Bostar had covered another ten steps before the warrior's warning cry ripped through the air. It came far too late, he thought triumphantly.

Bostar threw back his head and roared, 'Charge! For Hannibal and Carthage!'

There was an inarticulate roar of agreement from his men as they closed in on the bewildered Volcae, who were already wailing in fright at the prospect of being attacked from the front and rear. Suddenly, their enemies' distress grew even greater and Bostar glanced over his shoulder. To his delight, the Volcae tents were going up in flames. The scutarii were following their orders perfectly.

The warriors' disarray helped greatly to reduce the Carthaginian casualties. The tribesmen were far more concerned with protecting their own backs than aiming missiles at the helpless troops in their boats. However, their poor discipline and general panic meant that the Volcae had little success with Bostar's soldiers either. They loosed their spears and arrows in ragged, early volleys that had barely enough power to reach the spearmen's front ranks. Fewer than two dozen men had been downed before they had come within what Bostar considered proper range.

Calmly, he ordered his soldiers to throw their spears. This massed effort stood in stark comparison to the tribesmen's pathetic efforts. Hundreds of shafts curved up into the air, to fall in dense shoals among the unprepared Volcae, most of whom were not wearing armour. The volley caused heavy casualties. The screams of the injured and dying served to increase the warriors' fear and confusion. Bostar laughed at the magnificence of Hannibal's plan. One moment, the Volcae had been waiting for an easy slaughter, and the next, they were being attacked from behind while their tents went up in flames.

It was then that the lead Carthaginian boats pulled into the riverbank. Led by their general, scores of scutarii and caetrati threw themselves into the shallows. Their fierce battle cries were the final straw for the terrified Volcae, who could take no more. Faces twisted in fear, they broke and ran. 'Draw swords!' Bostar shouted delightedly, leading his men to complete the rout. The crossing of the river was theirs, which proved that the gods were still smiling on Hannibal and his army.

Within a quarter of an hour, it was all over. Hundreds of Volcae lay dead or dying on the grass, while the broken survivors ran for their lives into the nearby woods. Squadrons of whooping Numidians were already in pursuit. Few of the fugitives would live to tell the tale of the ambush, thought Bostar. But some would, and the legend of Hannibal's passing would spread. Bloody lessons such as this were like the siege of Saguntum. They sent a clear message to the surrounding tribes that to resist the Carthaginian army resulted in just one thing. Total defeat. Bostar wished vainly that it proved to be this simple with the Romans.

His task completed, he stood his men down and went in search of Hannibal. By now, the bank was thronged with infantry, slingers and cavalrymen leading their horses away from the river. Officers shouted in frustration, trying to assemble their scattered units. The river was dotted with dozens of boats travelling in each direction. The mammoth task of ferrying tens of thousands of men and vast quantities of supplies over the Rhodanus was under way.

Bostar threaded his way through the soldiers, scanning the faces for his family. When he saw Malchus, his heart leaped with joy. Sapho was by his side. Bostar hesitated, before recognising that he felt relief at the sight of his brother. He was grateful for this gut instinct. Whatever the circumstances of their parting, blood was thicker than water.

Telling himself that all would be well, Bostar raised a hand. 'Father!' Sapho!' he shouted.

It rapidly became clear that Suniaton would take months to recover; that was, if his wounds ever healed fully. Hanno was not at all sure they would. Certainly, his friend would never be fit to fight again. There was little doubt now that Suniaton's heavy limp would be lifelong. But, as he repeatedly told Hanno, at least he was alive.

Hanno nodded and smiled, trying to ignore the resentment that clawed at his happiness over Suniaton's rescue. He failed, because his friend was not fit to journey on his own, and might never be. Hanno grew irritable and withdrawn, and took to spending his time outside the hut, away from Suniaton. This made him feel even worse, but when he returned, determined to make amends, and saw his friend hobbling about on his home-made crutch, Hanno's anger always returned.

On the fourth day, the pair had an unexpected visit from Quintus and Aurelia. 'It's all right, there's been no news from Capua,' Quintus said as he dismounted.

Hanno relaxed a fraction. 'What brings you here then?'

'I thought you'd want to know. Father and Flaccus are about to leave. Finally, Publius Cornelius Scipio and his legions are ready.'

Hanno's heart stopped for a moment. 'Are they headed for Iberia?'

'Yes. The northeast coast. That's where they think that Hannibal is,' replied Quintus in a neutral tone.

'I see,' said Hanno, fighting to remain calm. Inside, his desire to leave had resurfaced. 'And the army that's bound for Carthage?'

'It will be leaving soon too.' Quintus looked awkward. 'I'm sorry.'

'There's nothing to be sorry for,' Hanno muttered gruffly. 'It's not your doing.'

Quintus was still uncomfortable, because he moved off to check Suniaton's injured thigh without answering. Hanno thought guiltily, I should be doing that. For all the good it would do, his mind retorted. He'll never walk properly again.

Aurelia's voice cut into his reverie. 'We won't see Father for months,' she said sadly. 'And Quintus never stops talking about going to join him. Before long, Mother and I may be left alone.'

Hanno made a sympathetic gesture, but he wasn't concentrating; all he could think of was following Publius' army to Iberia.

Aurelia mistook his silence for sorrow. 'How could I be so thoughtless? Who knows when you will see your family?'

Hanno scowled, but not because of what she'd said. Hannibal and his host would shortly face a Roman consular army. Meanwhile, he was stuck here with Suniaton.

'Hanno? What is it?'

'Eh?' he answered. 'Nothing.'

Aurelia followed his gaze to Suniaton, who was gingerly following Quintus' instructions. The realisation hit her at once. Like a cat, she pounced. 'You want to go to war too,' she whispered. 'But you can't, because of your loyalty to Suni.'

Stricken, Hanno stared at the ground.

Aurelia touched his arm. 'There is no greater love you could show a friend than standing by him in his time of need. It requires true courage.'

Hanno swallowed hard. 'I should be happy to stay with him, though, not angry.'

'You can't help it.' Aurelia sighed. 'You're a soldier, like my father and brother.'

Almost on cue, Quintus came striding over. 'What's that?'

Neither Aurelia nor Hanno answered.

Quintus grinned. 'What's the big secret? Have you guessed that I'm going to go and find Father?'

Aurelia's mouth opened in horror. Hanno was similarly shocked, but before either could respond, Suniaton joined them, obviously intent on speaking. Surprised by the Carthaginian's interruption, Quintus deferred to him. Suni's words struck everyone dumb. 'I know how hard it is for you, Hanno. Waiting for me to recover, when all you want to do is join Hannibal's army.'

Hanno's guilt swelled immeasurably. 'I will stay with you as long as necessary. That's all there is to it,' he declared. Quickly, he turned to Quintus. 'What made you decide to leave now?'

'I have to tell Father about the way Agesandros has been carrying on. Power has gone to his head.'

Aurelia butted in angrily. 'That's not your reason. It would be crazy to get rid of an experienced overseer at a time like this, and you know it. Besides, Agesandros hasn't done enough to warrant being replaced. We'll have to live with him.'

Quintus set his jaw. 'Well, I'm going anyway. My training is finished. The war could be over in a few months. I'll miss it if I just wait to be called up.'

You underestimate Hannibal, thought Hanno darkly.

'You're crazy,' accused Aurelia. 'How will you find Father in the middle of a war?'

A flicker of fear flashed across Quintus' face. 'I'll reach him before that,' he declared, full of apparent bravado. 'All I need to do is take passage to the Iberian port that Publius made for. I'll buy a horse there, and follow the legions. By the time I find Father, it will be far too late to send me back.' He glared, daring Hanno and his sister to challenge him.

'It's madness to talk about travelling so far on your own,' Aurelia cried. 'You've never been further than Capua before.'

'I'll manage,' Quintus muttered, glowering.

'Really?' demanded Aurelia sarcastically. She was surprised by how angry she felt when she'd known this was going to happen sooner or later.

'Why wouldn't I?' Quintus shot back.

An awkward silence fell.

Suniaton cleared his throat. 'Why don't you go with Quintus?' he asked, astonishing Hanno. 'Two swords on the road will be better than one.'

Suddenly, Aurelia's heart started pounding. Shocked by her emotions, she had to bite her lip not to protest aloud.

Hanno saw the flash of hope in Quintus' eyes. To his surprise and shame, he felt the same emotion in his heart. 'I'm not leaving you, Suni,' he protested.

'You've done more than enough for me, especially when it's my fault that we're here in the first place,' insisted Suniaton. 'You have been waiting your whole life for this war. I have not. You know that I'd rather be a priest than a soldier. So, with Quintus' and Aurelia's permission, I will remain here.' Quintus nodded his acquiescence, and Suniaton continued, 'When I'm fully recovered, I will travel to Carthage, alone.'

'I don't know what to say,' Hanno stuttered, his feelings fluctuating between sadness and excitement.

Suniaton held up a hand, stalling his protest. 'I will have it no other way.'

Hanno's protest died in his throat. 'I'm still in your debt, Quintus,' he said. 'Accompanying you might repay part of that obligation. What do you say?'

'I'd be honoured to have you as a companion,' said Quintus, bowing his head to conceal his relief.

Now, Aurelia's grief knew no bounds. She was going to lose not only her brother, but also Hanno, and there was nothing she could do about it. A tiny sob escaped her lips. Quintus put an arm around her, and Aurelia managed to rally herself. 'Come back safely.'

'Of course I will,' he murmured. 'Father will also.'

Nervously, Aurelia fixed her eyes on Hanno. 'You too,' she whispered.

Quintus' mouth opened as the two words hung in the air.

Hanno was stunned. Aurelia was promised to another, and a high-ranking Roman at that. Did she really mean what he thought? He studied her face for a moment.

'I will,' he said finally. 'One day.'

Chapter XIV: Confrontation

Massilia, on the southern coast of Gaul

Fabricius stared at the Greek columns on the temples opposite the quay and smiled. 'Very different to those at home,' he said. 'It feels good to be in a foreign land at last.'

Five days before, the Roman fleet and its commander, the consul Publius Cornelius Scipio, had finally set sail. Fabricius and Flaccus had been on board one of the sixty quinqueremes that had left from Pisae, on the west coast of Italy. Hugging the Ligurian shoreline all the way to the Greek city of Massilia, a long-term Roman ally on the south coast of Gaul, the flotilla had arrived not two hours previously.

'Too many months were spent talking,' Flaccus agreed. 'It's time now to carry war to the Carthaginians, and settle the matter swiftly.' He eyed Fabricius, who was nodding in vigorous agreement. 'You don't like sitting on your hands, eh?'

'No.' His recent spell in Rome had brought home to Fabricius the fact that he was no politician. He'd stayed in the capital because he was eager to fight. His desire for action, however, had vanished beneath a wave of debates in the Senate, just one of which could take more than a week. 'I know that the politicians' original reasons for delaying were simple,' he admitted. 'With most of the army disbanded, it was logical to wait for the new consuls to be appointed before making any far-reaching decisions. But to take so long after that?'

'Don't forget the other matters of foreign policy which had to be discussed.' Flaccus' tone was reproving. 'Rome has many concerns other than what goes on in Iberia.'

'Of course.' Fabricius sighed. That had been one of the hardest lessons for him to learn.

'Philip V of Macedon has never been the greatest friend of Rome,' said Flaccus. 'But giving refuge to Demetrius of Pharos showed that he really wishes us ill.'

'True.' Demetrius, the deposed King of Illyricum, had himself been the cause of much recent trouble to the Republic. 'Is a month of debates about the two of them really necessary, though?'

Flaccus' face took on a pompous expression. 'Such is the Senate's way, as it has been for nearly three hundred years. Who are we to question such a hallowed process?'

Fabricius bit back his pithy response. In his mind, the Senate would work far more efficiently if only the debates were better controlled. He smiled diplomatically. 'To be fair, it reacted fast when word came of the unrest among the Gaulish tribes.'

Flaccus looked pleased. 'And as soon as it became clear that the proposed new Latin colonies at Placentia and Cremona would not be enough, it requisitioned one of the legions from our expeditionary force. While I was stuck in Rome, raising and training the new units that were required, at least you got a taste of action!' He wagged a finger at Fabricius. 'Three months of it.'

Fabricius had grown used to the other's patronising manner, but still found it irritating. 'You weren't there. The Boii and Insubres are no pushover,' he growled. 'Don't you remember Telamon? We did well to end it so swiftly. Hundreds of our soldiers were slain, and many more were injured.'

Flaccus flushed. 'I apologise. I did not mean to belittle your efforts, or those of the men who died.'

'Good,' Fabricius replied, placated. 'It doesn't take away from the fact that we should have been in Iberia three months ago!'

Flaccus made a conciliatory gesture. 'At least we're in Massilia now. Soon the Saguntines will be avenged.'

'A bit late, isn't it?' demanded Fabricius sourly. The Senate's refusal to act had meant leaving the Saguntines to their fate, which had not sat well with his conscience. It still didn't.

'Come now,' entreated Flaccus. 'We've just been through all that.'

'I know,' Fabricius replied heatedly. 'But an ally of Rome should never be treated as Saguntum was.'

Flaccus' voice grew soft. 'You know that I agree with you. Did I not speak repeatedly in the Senate about the dishonour of abandoning the city?'

'You did.' Yet you probably knew that your words would make little difference, thought Fabricius. It had sounded good, however, and showed a pleasingly combative side to his prospective son-in-law's character.

'Thank all the gods that we're serving under Publius rather than Tiberius Sempronius Longus,' said Flaccus. 'We shall see action far sooner than they will. Last I heard, Longus' fleet wasn't going to be ready for another month.'

'How frustrating.'

'Whereas we can set sail the moment that the fleet's supplies of food and water have been renewed.' Flaccus rattled the hilt of his ornamental sword.

'Let's not forget to hear what information the local intelligence has gathered,' warned Fabricius. 'Nothing has been heard of Hannibal for several months.'

'That's because he's sitting on his hairy gugga arse in Iberia, drinking local wine and waiting for us to arrive!' Flaccus sneered.

'Maybe he is,' said Fabricius with a smile, 'but being forewarned is to be forearmed.'

He had no idea that, within the next few hours, his words would be proven true.

Hannibal was no longer in Iberia.

According to the exhausted Massiliote messengers who rode in on lathered mounts, he was probably no more than a day's march away.

Flaccus and the other senior officers received an immediate summons to attend Publius in his headquarters, a sprawling tent at the centre of one of the legions' temporary forts. Fabricius was pleased and surprised to receive a similar order less than an hour later. As he arrived, Fabricius saw Flaccus standing outside with the other high-ranking officers, including Gnaeus, Publius' elder brother, a former consul who was also his *legatus*, or second-in-command. Fabricius saluted, and nodded at Flaccus. To his surprise, his future son-in-law barely acknowledged the gesture. Indeed, his face wore such a thunderous expression that Fabricius wondered what had gone on in the moments prior. He had no time to find out. Recognising Fabricius, the officer in charge of the sentries ushered him inside at once.

They found Publius talking animatedly with a young Massiliote soldier over a table on which a crudely drawn map had been laid out. Both men were wearing Hellenistic bronze cuirasses, layered pteryges, which protected the groin and the tops of the thighs, and bronze greaves. Yet there was no question, even to the untrained eye, who was in charge. The Massiliote's armour was well made, but, with its magnificent depiction of Hercules' face, Publius' positively exuded quality and wealth. The same could be said of his ornate plumed Attic helmet, which sat on a nearby stool. Although the Massiliote towered over the grey-haired consul, Publius' confidence more than made up for the difference in height. Fabricius had come to know his commander a little, and liked him. Publius' calm presence and direct manner were popular with everyone, from the rank and file to the military tribunes. Gnaeus, his brother, was no different.

Publius looked up. 'Ah, Fabricius! Thank you for coming.'

Fabricius saluted. 'How can I be of service, sir?'

'First meet the commander of the unit that brought us the dramatic news. Fabricius, this is Clearchus. Clearchus, meet Fabricius, of whom I have spoken.'

The two exchanged courteous nods.

'Obviously, you have heard about Hannibal's whereabouts,' Publius enquired archly. 'You'd have to be deaf not to.'

Fabricius grinned. The news *had* been shouted from the rooftops. 'They say that he and his army have crossed the Rhodanus, sir, and are camped on the eastern shore.'

'Indeed.' Publius regarded the Massiliote. 'Clearchus?'

'Since word came that Hannibal had crossed into Gaul, we have been patrolling deep inland, using small, highly mobile cavalry units. One such sighted the Carthaginians about two weeks ago, and shadowed them to the river's western bank. It's a long day's ride from here.'

Fabricius' heart thumped in his chest. The rumour *was* true. 'And their number?'

'Perhaps fifty thousand men all told. Not quite a quarter of that is made up of cavalry.'

Fabricius' eyebrows rose. This was a larger army than he'd ever faced in Sicily.

Publius saw his reaction. 'I was surprised too. Hannibal means to attack Italy. Fortuna had been generous indeed to alert us to his purpose before he arrived. Go on, Clearchus.'

'They camped by the river for several days, constructing rafts and boats, and no doubt planning their tactics against the Volcae, the hostile natives on the eastern side. The result was extraordinary, sir. Hannibal sent a strong force upriver, which crossed undetected and fell on the tribesmen's rear.' Clearchus made a circle of his thumb and forefinger. 'They crushed them with ease. Nearly the whole army has traversed safely since then. Only the elephants remain on the far bank.'

'Imagine if we had landed a week earlier, and been there to contest the passage of the river. The war might already be over!' Publius cried in frustration. His face turned cunning. 'We still might have a chance, though, Clearchus?'

'That's right, sir. Getting the elephants across will take at least two to three days. Perhaps more. Several attempts have already failed.'

'Excellent. Now, I need someone to take a look at the Carthaginian army. A Roman officer.' Publius glanced at Clearchus. 'Not to belittle our Massiliote allies in any way.'

'No insult taken, sir,' said Clearchus, raising his hands.

'Naturally, others wanted this job, but I felt that the task was suited to a veteran. A man who knows how to keep his cool. I thought of you.' Publius fixed his eyes on Fabricius. 'Well?'

Fabricius felt his breath quicken. Had Flaccus asked for the duty, and been turned down? That might explain his sour expression. 'Of course I'll do it, sir.'

Publius gave a small smile of approval. 'Speed is of the essence. If you leave at once, you could be back by tomorrow night. The next day, at the latest. I will want good estimates of their numbers, and a breakdown of the troop types.'

Fabricius wasn't going to back down from a challenge like this. 'I will do my best, sir.'

'How many men have you?'

'About two hundred and fifty, sir.'

'Take all of them. Clearchus will guide you.' Publius looked at the Massiliote. 'How strong is your force?'

'Two hundred riders, sir, all experienced.'

'It should be enough.' Publius turned back to Fabricius. 'You're in charge. Avoid contact with the enemy unless it cannot be helped. Return quickly. I'll have the army ready to march the moment you return.'

'Yes, sir.' Fabricius saluted crisply; Clearchus did the same.

They left the consul poring over his map.

Fabricius wasted no time. Less than an hour later, he led the ten *turmae* – cavalry units – under his command out of the camp and towards Massilia's north gate. It was a pity that he hadn't had time to replace his losses from the recent campaign, thought Fabricius. Still, he was reasonably happy with the rest of his cavalrymen, who had fought well during the summer. As citizen cavalry, his men were equestrians, and most dressed in a Hellenistic style similar to his own. They wore Boeotian helmets and bleached white tunics, which had a purple stripe running from each shoulder to the hem. Sturdy leather boots that completely enclosed the feet were ubiquitous. All carried thrusting spears, and round cavalry shields, made of ox hide. Few carried swords. The heavy cavalry cloak, or *sagum*, owned by each man and used in bad weather, was tied up in a roll behind the saddlecloth.

They met Clearchus and his riders just outside the city walls. The Massiliote cavalry were irregulars, and no two were dressed alike. With their helmets, spears and small shields, however, they were similar in appearance to the Roman cavalrymen. Fabricius was reassured by Clearchus' calm manner, and the way his men responded to his orders. If it came to a fight, they'd probably do all right.

With the Massiliotes in the lead, they rode north, stopping only when it grew too dark to continue. Clearchus knew the countryside well, but, as he confided to Fabricius, it was possible that Carthaginian patrols could be operating in the area too. There was no point exposing themselves to unnecessary danger, and riding at night fell into that category. Fabricius did not argue. Clearchus' judiciousness made perfect sense. Ordering no fires to be lit, he had the men set up camp. Double the normal number of sentries were stationed around the perimeter. Long after the soldiers had retired, Fabricius walked from picket to picket, his ears pricked. This was a mission of the utmost importance. If that meant hardly any sleep, then so be it. Nothing could go wrong. Thankfully, he heard nothing other than the occasional screech of an owl.

He and Clearchus had their men up long before dawn. Tension among both sets of riders was immediately palpable. Contact with the enemy was likely before the day was out. After a brief chat with Clearchus, Fabricius sent ten Massiliote riders to scout the trail a mile in advance of the main party. One turma, under the command of his best decurion, accompanied them. Their orders were to return at the slightest hint of anything untoward.

Fabricius' hunch turned out to be the best decision he had ever made.

They had ridden for an hour or so when an outrider returned at the gallop. He dragged his horse to a stop beside Fabricius and Clearchus, who were riding together, and saluted.

Fabricius took a deep breath. 'What news?'

'We've spotted a group of Numidians, sir. Perhaps two miles away.'

Fabricius went very still. His memories of fighting against the lightly armed African horsemen were exclusively bad. 'Did they see you?'

The cavalryman grinned. 'No, sir. We were able to get behind a stand of trees.'

Fabricius hissed in relief. Their mission had escaped discovery – for the moment. 'How many of them were there?'

'Perhaps three hundred in total, sir.'

'Anything else?'

'Yes, sir. The decurion said to tell you that there's a copse about a mile from here that would make a perfect place for an ambush. If you move fast, you could get in place before the Numidians reach it.'

Fabricius' mouth went dry. Publius had ordered him to avoid confrontation at all costs. How was that possible in this situation, however? To let the enemy cavalry pass while continuing with their own mission would leave his patrol at risk of attack from behind. Aware that everyone's eyes were on him, Fabricius closed his eyes. 'Three hundred men, you say?' he demanded.

'Yes, sir.'

Fabricius made up his mind. They were 450 strong. Easily enough.

Opening his eyes, he laid a hand to his sword and was pleased by Clearchus' fierce nod of agreement. 'Swiftly, then,' he said. 'Take us to the copse.'

A short time later, Fabricius found himself in an excellent position overlooking the narrow track they had been following. Thanks to Clearchus' quick-witted suggestion, the entire patrol had ridden up and out of view well before the far entrance to the stand of trees. The trap would be sprung long before the Numidians saw their incriminating tracks – he hoped. Fabricius also wished that they could have concealed themselves better, and effected some method of preventing the Numidians from retreating. With time running out, that had not been possible. Instead, they had to place their trust in the gods. He glanced to either side, seeing the same tense expression on his riders' faces that he felt twisting his own.

The reasons were simple.

Soon, they would set eyes upon the first Carthaginian troops to act in aggression against Rome for more than twenty years. The enemy were not on Sicily either, their historical hunting grounds. The unthinkable had happened, and Fabricius still couldn't quite take it in. Hannibal was in Gaul, and heading for Italy! Calm down, he thought. Of more relevance right now was the fact that if he and his men weren't very lucky, the approaching Numidians would spot them and flee before the ambush began.

The following quarter of an hour felt like eternity to Fabricius. Focusing his gaze on the point where the track entered the copse, he ignored the faint jingle of harness around him, and bird song from the branches above. He couldn't block out all sound, however. A horse stamped a hoof as it grew restless. Someone coughed, drawing a muttered rebuke from the nearest officer. Fabricius glared at the rider responsible before returning his attention to the path. Spotting movement, he blinked. Then his arm shot out, pointing. 'Pssst!' he hissed to the man on either side. A judder of anticipation rippled through the line of waiting cavalrymen.

Amazingly, the pair of enemy scouts who emerged into view were only a short distance in front of the main body of their countrymen. The Numidians appeared no different to the men Fabricius had fought in Sicily. Dark-skinned, lithe, athletic, they rode small horses without saddles, bridles or bits. Their loose tunics had large armholes and were pinned at the shoulder and belted at the waist. The Numidians carried javelins and light, round shields without bosses. Instead of looking around for danger, they were busy talking to each other. Given the empty countryside, thought Fabricius delightedly, it wasn't that surprising. He'd made similar mistakes himself before, and been lucky enough to get away with it.

In they rode, without so much as a glance up the gentle slopes where the Romans and Massiliotes lay hidden. Fabricius held his breath, counting the distance. Eighty, then fifty paces. The front ranks of Numidians entered the copse, and Fabricius' mind flashed back to the war in Sicily. They did not look like much, but these were some of the finest cavalry in the world. Sublime horsemen, they were best at skirmishing, and frustrating the enemy with their stinging attacks. He knew from personal experience that the Numidians' pursuit of a vanquished foe was even more deadly.

It was too soon to sound the charge. As many riders as possible had to come into the copse where the trees would ensnare them. With every passing moment, though, the risk of being discovered grew. Fabricius' stomach clenched painfully, but he did not stir. By the time two-thirds of the horsemen had ridden in, he saw that his men were on the verge of breaking ranks. He could no longer take the pressure either. 'Charge!' he shouted, urging his horse down the slope. 'For Rome!' Bellowing with excitement, 250 cavalry followed. An instant later, Clearchus and his Massiliotes emerged from the other side of the track, screaming at the top of their lungs.

Fabricius revelled in the look of stunned disbelief on the Numidians' faces. It was their job to ambush and fall on an unsuspecting enemy, not the other way around. Surprised, outnumbered and with the advantage of height against them, they instantly wheeled their mounts' heads and tried to flee. Within the space of a dozen heartbeats, total confusion reigned. Although some of those at the rear were already riding away, the vast majority were trapped by the trees. Horses reared in panic; men shouted contradictory orders at each other. Only an occasional rider prepared to fight. All the rest wanted to do was escape. Fabricius bared his teeth exultantly. They had ridden within thirty paces of the enemy without suffering a single casualty, and things were about to get even better. For all their horsemanship and skirmishing skill, the tribesmen were poor at close combat. 'Ready spears,' Fabricius yelled. 'Kill as many as you can!'

With an inarticulate roar, his men obeyed.

* * *

Casting fearful looks over their shoulders, the surviving Numidians fled for their lives. Eyeing the bodies littering the ground, Fabricius estimated that more than a hundred of their number had been slain or injured in the initial ambush. The Roman and Massiliote casualties were perhaps half that number. Given the circumstances, this was more than satisfactory. Catching sight of Clearchus, Fabricius beckoned him urgently. 'We've got to follow them,' he said. 'Stick tight to their tails, or there'll be no chance to assess Hannibal's forces.'

Clearchus nodded. 'The wounded, sir?'

'They can fend for themselves. We'll pick them up on the way back.'

'Very good, sir.' The Massiliote turned to relay the order.

'Clearchus?'

'Sir?'

'I want no further engagement with the enemy. A running battle could easily lead to disaster, especially if we encounter more Carthaginian forces. Our mission is more important now than killing a few more Numidians. Understood?'

Clearchus' teeth flashed in the sunshine. 'Of course, sir. Publius is waiting for us.'

Soon all the able-bodied men had formed up and were ready to ride. Without a backward glance, Fabricius and Clearchus led them after the Numidians. This time, there was no advance party. They rode at top speed, four abreast, knowing that the chance of an attack from the panicked enemy riders was slim to none. It wasn't long before they glimpsed the last of the tribesmen, who screamed in dismay. At once Fabricius ordered his men to slow down. He was relieved when his command was obeyed without question. Poor discipline was too often the reason for battles being lost.

They followed the Numidians along the winding track for perhaps five miles. The flat terrain and the well-beaten track made the pursuit easy. Fabricius had no idea how far the Rhodanus was, but Clearchus reached him as they neared a low, stone-topped hill that stood alone, dominating the surrounding wooded area.

'The river is on the other side of that, sir.'

Immediately, Fabricius held up his hand. 'Halt!' As his order was obeyed, he fixed the Massiliote with his stare. 'Let's go up. Just you and me.'

Clearchus looked startled. 'Are you sure, sir? There could be enemy pickets at its crest.'

'They'll be running after the Numidians!' Fabricius replied confidently. 'And when we come leathering back down here, I want everyone ready to ride, not bunched up on a narrow path.'

Clearchus blinked; then a mischievous smile twitched across his lips. 'I suppose two men against an entire host are as good as a few hundred.'

With a fierce grin, Fabricius slapped his thigh. 'That's the attitude.' He turned to the nearest of his decurions. 'Rest the men. We're going to take a look at what's on the other side of the hill. I want you ready to leave at a moment's notice.'

'Yes, sir!'

Fabricius led the way up the path. He was surprised to find himself feeling more nervous than he had in years. He would never have expected to be the first Roman to set eyes on Hannibal's army. Yet here he was.

Nearing the crest, they found evidence of a sentry post: a stone fireplace full of smoking ash, and bedding rolls, which still bore the imprint of those who'd been sitting on them. They dismounted and tethered their horses before clambering to the peak. Instinctively, Fabricius went down on his belly. The first thing that caught his attention as he peered over the edge was the mob of yelling Numidians driving their horses down the slope. Behind them were a dozen or more running figures: the sentries from the abandoned picket. Fabricius' lips peeled up in a snarl of satisfaction, but as he took in the scene beyond, his mouth fell open in wonder.

In the middle distance glittered the wide band that was the River Rhodanus. Perhaps a hundred paces from the water's edge, the enemy tent lines began. They stretched as far as the eye could see. Fabricius was used to legionary camps that could hold 5,000 men, or even 10,000. What lay before him was much less organised, but far larger. It was more than twice as large as a consular army, which was made up of approximately 20,000 men. 'You weren't exaggerating. This host is immense!' he muttered to Clearchus. 'Publius should have moved on your intelligence. We'd have caught the bastards napping.'

The Massiliote looked pleased.

Fabricius scanned the encampment, mentally noting everything he saw. Hannibal had superior numbers of horsemen compared to an equivalent

Roman force, which worried him. Few things were more important than the quantity of horse at one's disposal. There were the usual Carthaginian stalwarts: Libyan spearmen and skirmishers, Balearic slingers and Numidian and Iberian cavalry. Most plentiful of all were the infantry, the majority of which were scutarii and caetrati. And last but not least, there were the elephants: the battering rams that had so terrified Roman armies in the past. Perhaps twenty of the massive beasts were already on the near bank. 'Gods,' Fabricius whispered in amazement. 'How in the name of Jupiter did they get them over the river?'

Clearchus touched his arm and pointed. 'On those.'

Fabricius peered at the two massive wooden rafts being pulled back to the far side by rowing boats. There, he could see a dozen or more elephants waiting to be ferried across. Before them, an enormous jetty formed by a double line of square platforms projected some sixty paces out into the fast-flowing water. Dozens of ropes and cables secured the makeshift affair to trees upriver from the pier. He shook his head at the scale of the engineering that had gone into the pier's construction. 'I've heard that elephants are intelligent creatures. Surely they wouldn't just walk on to a floating square of wood?'

Clearchus squinted into the bright light. 'I can see a layer of earth all along the walkway. Maybe it's meant to look like dry land?'

'Clever bastards. So they lead their charges to the end of the jetty, and on to the rafts. Then they cut them free and row across the river.' Rapt, Fabricius watched as, encouraged by its mahout, an elephant was slowly led down the walkway. Even from a distance, it was clear that the creature was not happy. Bugles of distress blared out again and again. It had only walked a third of the jetty's length before it stopped dead in its tracks. In an effort to make the elephant continue, a group of men behind it began shouting and playing drums and cymbals. However, instead of continuing to the raft, which was now tethered to the end of the pier, the creature jumped into the water. There was a wail from its unfortunate mahout as he disappeared from sight, and Fabricius closed his eyes. What a way to die, he thought. When he looked up, the elephant was swimming strongly across the river. Fabricius was engrossed. He had never seen such an incredible sight before.

Suddenly, Clearchus tugged at his arm. 'The Numidians have raised the alarm, sir.'

At the edge of the camp, Fabricius could see the tribesmen milling around. Many were pointing at the hill and beyond. Faint shouts of anger carried through the air, and he smiled mirthlessly. 'Time to go. Publius will want to hear the news. Good, and bad.'

Fabricius was delighted by Publius' instantaneous response to his dramatic news. The consul was not afraid of confrontation. Ordering the heavy baggage to be loaded on to the quinqueremes for safety, Publius led the army north as soon as was humanly possible. Nonetheless, it was three full days before the legions and their allies arrived at the point where the Carthaginians had crossed the river. It was a huge disappointment to find the vast encampment abandoned. As the Roman officers picked their way across the remnants of thousands of campfires, the only life to be seen were the skulking forms of jackals looking for scraps, and the countless birds of prey that hovered overhead for similar reasons.

Hannibal had gone. North, to avoid a battle.

Publius had difficulty concealing his amazement. 'Who would have thought it?' he muttered. 'He is heading for the Alps, and thence to Cisalpine Gaul.'

Fabricius was still astonished too. He knew no one who had even contemplated that Hannibal would pursue such a plan. Stunning in its simplicity, it had taken them all completely unawares. It was lucky chance that had them standing here today. Now Publius faced a hard choice. What was the best thing to do?

The consul immediately convened a meeting of his senior officers on the riverbank. As well as Gnaeus, his legatus, there were twelve tribunes present, six for each regular legion. Following tradition, alternate legions had three senior tribunes, men who had served for more than ten years, while the others had two. The junior tribunes needed only to have seen five years' service. It was a mark of the times, and of the influence of the Minucii, that Flaccus, who had no military experience, should be accorded even the lower rank of junior tribune. As the patrol leader, Fabricius was also present. He felt distinctly nervous in the presence of so many senior officers.

'We are faced with four choices, all of them difficult,' Publius began. 'To pursue Hannibal and force him to fight, or to withdraw to the coast and return with the whole army to Cisalpine Gaul. The third option would be merely to send word to the Senate of Hannibal's intentions, before continuing as charged to Iberia. Or . . . I could bring the news to Rome myself while Gnaeus takes the legions west.' He scanned his officers' faces, waiting for a response.

Fabricius thought that either the second or fourth options were the best, but he certainly wasn't going to say anything before any of his superiors did. As the silence lengthened, it appeared that none of them were prepared to speak up either. Fabricius fumed. This was one of the most pivotal moments in Roman history, and no one wanted to say the wrong thing. That is, he realised, apart from one. Flaccus was shifting from foot to foot like a man possessed. Fabricius struggled to master his exasperation. Probably all that kept Flaccus' mouth shut was the desire not to breach military protocol by speaking out of turn, before the five senior tribunes.

Eventually, Publius grew impatient. 'Come now,' he said. 'Let us be frank. You may speak without fear of retribution. I want your honest opinions.'

Gnaeus cleared his throat. 'In theory, Hannibal should be confronted immediately. However, I wonder if it would be the right thing to do?'

'We know that his forces outnumber ours by at least two to one, sir,' added a senior tribune quickly. 'And if we suffered a setback, or even a defeat, what then? Massilia's defences aren't up to withstanding a siege. All of the other legions are occupied on other duties, either in Cisalpine Gaul, or in Sicily with Consul Longus. We have no support to call on.'

Sensible words, thought Fabricius. He was surprised to see Flaccus' face grow red with indignation.

Another senior tribune, an older man than the rest, stepped into view. 'Is the enemy's strength so important, sir?' he demanded angrily. 'Our legionaries are the finest soldiers in the world! They are used to winning victories against vastly superior numbers, and have done so against Carthaginian armies in the past. Why should they not do the same against this . . . *Hannibal?*' He filled the last word with contempt. 'I say we follow him, and stamp on the gugga serpent before it slides into Cisalpine Gaul and prepares to bite us in the heel.'

It was difficult to respond to the tribune's fierce words without seeming unpatriotic, and the first speakers sealed their lips. Even Gnaeus looked unsure. Naturally, Flaccus beamed and nodded in agreement, turning to his fellow junior tribunes for support. Cupping his chin with one hand, Publius gazed at the nearby fast-flowing water. Everyone waited for his response.

Roman soldiers are indeed without equal, thought Fabricius, but the Carthaginian forces who had left this camp were led by a man who, in less than a year, had conquered large areas of Iberia, passed through the mountains into Gaul and, despite fierce opposition, successfully crossed an enormous river, elephants included. Chasing after Hannibal could prove disastrous.

Publius held his counsel for an age. At length, he looked up. 'It seems to me that pursuing a larger enemy force into unknown territory would be most unwise. As some have already said, we are alone here apart from our Massiliote allies, who do not number more than a few thousand. We must reconcile ourselves to the fact that the Carthaginians will enter Cisalpine Gaul within the next two months.' Ignoring the shocked gasps this comment produced, Publius continued, 'Let us also not forget where Hannibal's main base is. If his access to that is cut off, his chance of supplies and reinforcements will be greatly reduced. With this in mind, I propose to hand the command of the consular army to my brother, and for him to lead it to Iberia.' Publius acknowledged Gnaeus' accepting bow. 'I myself will return to Italy with all speed. I intend to be waiting for Hannibal when he makes his descent from the Alps. In this way both our problems will have been addressed, the gods willing.'

Publius' decisive manner was good enough for most of the tribunes, who muttered in agreement. Only the older man and Flaccus seemed unhappy. The former was experienced enough to know when to keep quiet, but the latter was not. Ignoring Fabricius' warning look, Flaccus started forward. 'Think again, sir! Hannibal may win many allies among the discontented tribes in Cisalpine Gaul. The next time you meet his army, it could be far bigger.'

Publius' eyebrows rose at Flaccus' temerity. 'Is that so?' he said icily.

Fabricius was impressed by his future son-in-law's insight, but it was time to shut up. Angering a consul was not an intelligent thing to do. Again, however, Flaccus ignored his pointed stare.

'It is, sir! For the honour of Rome, you must follow Hannibal and defeat him. Think of the shame of a foreign enemy, especially a Carthaginian one, setting his foot on Italian soil.' Seeing his fellow officers' horrified expressions, Flaccus faltered. Then he looked for support. Finding none among his compatriots, his gaze finally fell on Fabricius. 'You agree with me, don't you?'

Suddenly, Fabricius was the centre of attention. He did not know what to say. Agreeing would make him party to Flaccus' insult to the consul. Refusing to agree would, in effect, renege on the newly founded alliance between his family and the Minucii. Both choices seemed as bad as the other.

To his intense relief, Publius leaped in. 'At first I thought you courage-ous for speaking your mind. Now I see that it was your arrogance. How dare you speak of Rome's honour when you have never drawn a sword in her defence? The only one here who has not, I might add.' As Flaccus' cheeks flushed crimson, Publius continued. 'Just so you know, I too hate the idea of an enemy on Roman soil. Yet there is no shame in waiting to face an opponent on the best terms possible, and in Cisalpine Gaul we shall have the entire Republic's resources behind us.'

'I'm sorry, sir,' Flaccus muttered. 'I spoke out of turn.'

Publius did not acknowledge the apology. 'Next time you place your foot in your mouth, do not try to redeem yourself by asking a junior officer such as Fabricius to disagree with a consul. *That* is a shameful act.' He stalked off with Gnaeus. The other tribunes fell to talking among them-selves. They pointedly ignored Flaccus.

Fortunately, Flaccus' outrage was so great that he assumed Fabricius was of the same opinion as he. Complaining bitterly about the public humiliation he had just suffered, he accompanied Fabricius back to the legions. For his part, Fabricius was content to remain silent. He had dismissed Atia's concerns out of hand before, but Flaccus' rash action revealed monstrous arrogance, but also a worrying lack of awareness. What else was he capable of?

Chapter XV: The Alps

Hunching his shoulders against the early-morning chill, Bostar emerged from his tent. He gazed in awe at the towering mountains that reared up before him. The range stretched from north to south above the fertile plain, and occupied the entire eastern horizon. A dense network of pine trees covered the lower slopes, concealing any potential routes of ascent. The sky was clear, but the jagged peaks above were hidden yet by shrouds of grey cloud. Despite this, they were a magnificent sight.

'Lovely to look at, eh?'

Bostar jumped. Not many of the soldiers were stirring, but it was no surprise that his father was already up. 'They are incredible, yes.'

'And we've got to cross them.' Malchus grimaced. 'Our passage of the River Rhodanus seems trivial now, doesn't it?'

Bostar's laugh was a trifle hollow. If anyone had made such a statement a few weeks before, he wouldn't have believed it. Looking at the harsh slopes above, he knew that his father might well be correct. Expecting more than fifty thousand men, thousands of pack animals and thirty-seven elephants to climb into the realm of gods and demons bordered on genius – or madness. Feeling disloyal for even thinking the latter, Bostar glanced around. He was surprised to see Sapho approaching. After the Rhodanus, the brothers had ostensibly patched up their relationship, but the reconciliation had been little more than a façade for their father's benefit. The two avoided each other if at all possible. Bostar forced a smile. 'Sapho.' Try as he might, he could not help but feel hurt when his brother silently responded with a salute.

'That's not necessary, is it?' Malchus' tone was sharp.

'Sorry,' said Sapho offhandedly. 'I'm still half asleep.'

'Yes, it's not exactly your time of day, is it?' retorted Bostar acidly. 'That would be more like midday.'

'Enough!' barked Malchus before Sapho could respond. 'Why can't you at least be civil to each other? There's far more at stake here than your stupid feud.'

As always, their father's outburst silenced the brothers. Unusually, it was Sapho who made the first effort. 'What were you talking about?' he asked.

His attempt made Bostar feel obliged to reply. 'Those.' He pointed at the mountains.

Sapho's face soured. 'Ill fortune awaits us up there. Countless men will be lost, I know it.' He made the sign against evil.

'We've had such good fortune since the Rhodanus, though,' protested Bostar. 'The Romans didn't pursue us. Then the Cavares gave us gifts of food, shoes and warm clothing. Since we entered their territory, their warriors have kept the Allobroges at bay. Who's to say that the gods won't continue to smile on us?'

'The year's practically over. Winter will be here soon. It will be a super-human task.' An impossible task, thought Sapho dourly. Hell awaits us. He had never liked heights, and the prospect of ascending the Alps – especially in late autumn – filled him with a murmuring dread. Of course he could not admit to that, nor to his resentment of Hannibal for choosing such a difficult route, or for favouring Bostar above him. He jerked his head towards the south. 'We should have travelled along the coast of Gaul.'

'That would have meant a pitched battle with the forces our cavalry encountered near the Rhodanus, which was something Hannibal wanted to avoid.' Despite his robust words, Bostar felt his spirits being dragged down. With the friendly Cavares returning to their homes, and nowhere to go other than up, there was no denying what they had let themselves in for. He was grateful when his father intervened.

'I want to hear no more talk like that. It's bad for morale,' growled Malchus. He had similar concerns, but he wouldn't admit them to anyone. 'We must keep faith with Hannibal, as he does with us. His spirits were high last night, weren't they?' He glared at his sons.

'Yes, Father,' Sapho conceded.

'He doesn't *have* to wander around his men's campfires for half the night, sharing their poxy rations and listening to their miserable life stories,' Malchus continued sternly. 'He doesn't sleep alongside them, wrapped only in his cloak, for the good of his health! Hannibal does it because he loves his soldiers as if they were his children. The least we can do is to return that love with utmost fealty.'

'Of course,' Sapho muttered. 'You know that my loyalty is beyond question.'

'And mine,' added Bostar fervently.

Malchus' scowl eased. 'I'm glad to hear it. I know that the next few weeks will be our toughest test yet, but it's officers such as we who will have to give an example. To lead the men when they falter. We must show no weakness, just a steely resolve to reach the top of whichever pass Hannibal chooses. Don't forget that from there, we will fall upon Cisalpine Gaul, and after it, Italy, like ravening wolves.'

Finally, the two brothers gave each other a pleased look. It lasted only an instant before they broke eye contact.

Malchus was already ten strides away. 'Get a move on. Hannibal wants us all to see the sacrifice.'

The brothers followed.

The flat, well-watered land where the Carthaginians were camped had provided respite to man and beast before the rigours that were to come. It also offered, Bostar realised, a place where Hannibal could address his troops, as he had at New Carthage before they'd left. Even though his forces were now considerably smaller, there were still far too many soldiers to be able to witness personally their general make an offering to the gods. That was why the commanders of every unit in the army had been ordered to bring a score or more of their men to the ceremony.

They made their way past rank-smelling Balearic slingers clad in animal skins and slender, dark-skinned Numidians with oiled ringlets in their hair. Burly scutarii and caetrati in sinew helmets and crimson-edged tunics stood with their arms folded. Alongside was Alete with twenty of his Libyan spearmen. Groups of bare-chested Gauls, their necks and arms decorated with torcs of gold, eyed the others present with supercilious stares.

Before the gathered soldiers stood a strongly built low wooden platform, and upon it a makeshift altar of stone slabs had been erected. In front stood fifty of Hannibal's bodyguards. A ramp led from the foot of the dais to the top, and beside it, a large black bull had been tethered. Six robed priests waited with the beast, which was snorting with unease. As Malchus led them to a position within a dozen steps of the soothsayers, Bostar shivered. In their gnarled hands – through the divination to come – lay the power to raise the army's morale, or to send it into the depths. Gazing at the nearby soldiers, Bostar saw the same concern twisting their faces that he was experiencing. There was little conversation; indeed an air of apprehension hung over the entire gathering. Bostar glanced at Sapho, whom he could read like a book. His brother was feeling the same way, or worse. Bostar sighed. Despite the ease of the last few days, the mountains' physical immensity had cast a shadow over men's hearts. There was only one person who could cast out that gloom, he thought. Hannibal.

The man himself bounded into view a moment later, ascending the ramp as if he were on the last lap of a foot race. A loud cheer met his arrival. Hannibal's bronze helmet and breastplate had been polished until they shone as if lit from within. In his right hand his falcata sword glinted dangerously; in his left, he carried a magnificent shield emblazoned with the image of a prowling male lion. Without a word, Hannibal strode to the edge of the platform and lifted his arm so everyone could see his blade. He let the troops focus on it before he pointed it to his rear.

'After so long, there they are! The Alps,' Hannibal cried. 'We have halted at our enemies' very gates to prepare for our ascent. I can see by your faces that you are worried. Scared. Even exhausted.' The general's eyes moved from soldier to soldier, daring them to hold his gaze. None could. 'Yet after the brutal campaign in Iberia, and the crossing of the Rhône, what are the Alps?' he challenged. 'Can they be anything worse than high mountains?' He paused, glancing around questioningly as his words were translated. 'Well?'

Bostar felt worried. Despite the truth in Hannibal's words, few men looked convinced.

'No, sir,' Malchus answered loudly. 'Great heaps of rock and ice is all they are.'

Hannibal's lips tightened in satisfaction. 'That's right! They can be climbed, by those with the strength and heart to do so. It's not as if we will be the first to cross them either. The Gauls who conquered Rome passed by this same way, did they not?'

Again the delay as the interpreters did their work. Finally, there was a mutter of accord.

'Yet you despair of even being able to get near that city? I tell you, the Gauls brought their women and children through these mountains! As soldiers carrying nothing but our weapons, can we not do the same?' Hannibal raised his sword again, threateningly this time. 'Either confess that you have less courage than the Romans, who we have defeated on many occasions in the past, or steel your hearts and march forward with me, to the plain which stands between the River Tiber and Rome! There we will find greater riches than any of you can imagine. There will be slaves and booty and glory for all!'

Malchus waited as the general's words were translated into Gaulish, Iberian and Numidian, but as a rumble of agreement began to sweep through the assembled troops, he raised a fist into the air. 'Hannibal!' he roared. 'Hannibal!'

Quickly, Bostar joined in. He noted that Sapho was slow to do the same.

Shamed by their general's words, the soldiers bellowed a rippling wave of approval. The Gauls chanted in deep voices, the Libyans sang and the Numidians made shrill ululating sounds. The cacophony rose into the crisp air, bouncing off the imposing walls of rock before the gathering and thence up into the empty sky. The startled bull jerked futilely at the rope tethering its head. No one paid it any heed. Everyone's gaze was locked on Hannibal.

'Last night, I had a dream,' he cried.

The cheering quickly died away, and was replaced by an expectant hush.

'I was in a foreign landscape, which was full of farms and large villages. I wandered for many hours, lost and without friends, until a ghost appeared.' Hannibal nodded as his words spread and the superstitious soldiers glanced nervously at each other. 'He was a young man, handsome, and clad in a simple Greek tunic, but there was an ethereal glow about him. When I asked who he was, he laughed and offered to guide me, as long as I did not look back. Although I was unsure, I accepted his proposal.'

Hannibal had everyone's attention now, even that of the priests. Men were making the sign against evil, and rubbing their lucky amulets. Bostar's heart was thudding off his ribs.

'We walked for maybe a mile before I became aware of a loud crashing noise behind us,' Hannibal went on. 'I tried not to turn and see what was going on, but the sound grew so great that I could not help myself. I glanced around. What I saw made my throat close with fear. There was a snake of wondrous size following us, crushing every tree and bush in its path. Black thunderclouds sat in the sky above it, and lightning bolts flashed repeatedly through the air. I froze in terror.' Hannibal paused.

'What happened next, sir?' cried one of Alete's Libyans. 'Tell us!'

An inchoate roar of agreement followed. Bostar found himself shouting too. Visions like this – for surely that was what Hannibal had had – could portend a man's future, for good or ill. Dread filled Bostar that it was the latter.

Sapho could not dispel his unease about what lay before them. 'He's making it up. So we'll follow him up into those damn mountains,' he muttered.

Bostar gave him a disbelieving glance. 'He wouldn't do that.'

Sapho's jealousy of his brother grew. 'Really? With so much at stake?' he retorted.

'Stop it! You'll anger the gods!' said Bostar.

Belatedly scared by what he'd said, Sapho looked away.

'Wait,' hissed Malchus. 'There's more.'

'The young man took my arm, and ordered me not to be afraid,' shouted Hannibal suddenly. 'I asked him what the snake signified, and he told me. Do you want to hear what he said?'

There was a short pause.

'YES!' The bellow exceeded anything that had gone before.

'The devastation represents what will happen to Rome at the hands of my army!' the general said triumphantly. 'The gods favour us!'

'Hurrah!' Bostar was so thrilled that he threw an arm around Sapho's shoulders and hugged him. His brother tensed, before stiffly returning the gesture. The exhilaration in the air was infectious. Even Malchus' normal solemnity had been replaced by a broad smile.

'HANN-I-BAL! HANN-I-BAL! HANN-I-BAL!' yelled the delighted soldiers.

While his troops cheered themselves hoarse, Hannibal made a gesture to the priests. With the aid of a dozen scutarii, the bellowing bull was hauled up the ramp until it stood in front of the altar. Hannibal stood to one side. At once the applause died away, and the worried looks returned to men's faces. Success was by no means guaranteed yet. The omens from the sacrifice also had to be good. Bostar found himself clenching his fists.

'O Great Melqart, accept this prize beast as a sacred offering, and as a gesture of our good faith,' intoned the high priest, an old man with a grey beard and fleshy cheeks. His companions repeated his words. Raising the hood on his robe, the priest then accepted a long dagger. The bull's head was pulled forward, stretching its neck. Without further ado, the old man extended his arm and yanked it back, drawing the blade across the underside of the bull's throat with savage force. Blood gouted from the large wound, covering the priest's feet. The kicking beast collapsed to the platform, and the unneeded scutarii were waved back. Swiftly, the old man moved to kneel between the bull's front and back legs. With sure strokes, he slit open the skin and abdominal muscles. Steaming loops of bowel slithered into view. The priest barely glanced at them as, still gripping the dagger, he shoved both his arms deep into the abdominal cavity.

'He's seen nothing bad so far. That's good,' whispered Bostar.

It's probably all been arranged in advance, thought Sapho sourly, but he no longer dared speak his mind.

A moment later, the old man stood up to face Hannibal. His arms were bloodied to the shoulder, and the front of his saturated robe had turned crimson. In his hands, he held a purple, glistening lump of tissue. 'The beast's liver, sir,' he said gravely.

'What does it tell you?' There was the slightest trace of a quaver in Hannibal's voice.

'We shall see,' replied the priest, studying the organ.

'Told you!' Bostar gave Sapho a hefty nudge. 'Even Hannibal is unsure.'

Sapho looked at Hannibal, whose face was now etched with worry. If their general was an actor, he was a damn good one. Fear suddenly clogged Sapho's throat. What was I thinking to call Hannibal's dream into question? Sapho couldn't think of a better way to call down the gods' wrath than to say what he just had. And there was Bostar, beside him, who was unable to put a foot wrong. Bitterness coursed through his veins.

'It is very clear,' the priest announced loudly.

Every man present craned his neck forward, eager to hear.

'The passage of the mountains will be difficult, but not impossible. The army will descend upon Cisalpine Gaul, and there allies will flock to our cause. The legions that come to meet us will be swept away, as the mightiest of trees are by a winter storm. Victory awaits!'

'Victory! Victory! Victory!' chanted the soldiers.

Raising his hands for silence, Hannibal stepped forward. 'I told you of my dream. You have heard the soothsayer make his pronouncement. Now, who will follow me across the Alps?'

The watching troops surged forward, shouting their acceptance.

Looking elated, Malchus and Bostar were among them. Sapho followed, telling himself that everything would be all right. The knot of fear and unease in his belly told another story, however.

Four days later, Sapho was beginning to wonder if his misgivings had been overblown. While the Carthaginians had encountered some resistance from the Allobroges, it had been swept aside by Hannibal's fierce response. Life in the mountains had settled into a reassuring routine, the same as they'd followed for months. Rise at dawn. Strike camp. Eat a cold breakfast. Assemble the men. Assume position at the head of the enormous column. Join the path eastwards. March. Sapho was immensely proud that Hannibal had picked his unit to lead the army. Let Bostar suck on that, he thought. His brother's phalanx marched behind his. Malchus and his soldiers were with the rearguard, more than ten miles back down the stony track.

His duty carried with it huge responsibility. Sapho was on the lookout for danger at all times. For the thousandth time that morning, he eyed the heights around the flat-bottomed valley in which they currently found themselves. Nothing. Intimidated by Hannibal's seizure of their main settlement and, with it, all their supplies, the Allobroges had vanished into the bare rocks. 'Good enough for the cowardly scumbags,' muttered Sapho. He spat contemptuously.

'Sir!' cried one of the guides, a warrior of the Insubres tribe. 'Look!'

To Sapho's surprise, the figures of men could be seen appearing on the track ahead. Where in the name of hell had they come from? He lifted his right arm. 'Halt!' At once the order began passing back down the line. Sapho's jaw clenched nervously as he listened to it. He was stopping the progress of the entire army. It had to be done, however. Until proven otherwise, every person they encountered was an enemy.

'Should we advance to meet them, sir?' asked an officer.

'Not bloody likely. It could be a trap,' Sapho replied. 'The fuckers can come to us.'

'What if they don't, sir?'

'Of course they will. Why else do you think they've slunk out of their rat holes?'

Sapho was right. Gradually, the newcomers approached: a group of perhaps twenty warriors. They were typical-looking Gauls, well built with long hair and moustaches. Although some wore tunics, many were bare-chested under their woollen cloaks. Baggy woven trousers were ubiquitous. Some wore helmets, but only a handful had mail shirts. All were armed with tall, oval shields and swords or spears. Interestingly, the men at the front were carrying willow branches.

'Are the dogs coming in peace?' asked Sapho.

'Yes, sir,' answered the guide. 'They're Vocontii, I think.' He saw Sapho's blank look. 'Neighbours – and enemies – of the Allobroges.'

'Why doesn't that surprise me?' sneered Sapho. 'Do any of you Gauls get on with each other?'

The guide grinned. 'Not too often, sir. There's always something to fight over.'

'I'm sure,' Sapho said dryly. He glanced to either side. 'Front rank, shields up! First and second ranks, ready spears!'

Wood clattered off wood as the spearmen obeyed his command. An instant later, the phalanx presented a solid wall of overlapping shields to its front. Over the shield rims, scores of spear tips poked forward like the spines on a forest of sea urchins.

Looking alarmed, the warriors stopped.

Sapho's lips peeled upwards. 'Tell them that if they come in peace, they have nothing to fear.'

'Yes, sir.' The guide bellowed a few words in Gaulish.

There was a brief pause, and then the Vocontii continued walking towards them. When they were twenty paces away, Sapho held up his hand. 'That's close enough.'

The guide translated his words, and the tribesmen dutifully halted.

'Ask them what they want,' Sapho ordered. He fixed his attention on the one man who had answered all the guide's questions. A fine mail shirt covered the middle-aged warrior's barrel chest, and three gold torcs announced his wealth and status. What Sapho didn't like, or trust, was the man's wall-eye and permanent leer.

'They have heard of the size of our army and of our victories over the Allobroges, sir, and wish to assure us of their friendship,' said the guide. 'They want to guide us through their territory, to the easiest pass over the Alps.'

'How charming,' Sapho replied caustically. 'And why in Melqart's name should we believe them?'

There was a shifty smile from the wall-eyed warrior as the guide interpreted. A wave of his hand saw several fat heifers herded into view.

'Apparently, they have a hundred of these to offer us, sir.'

Sapho didn't let his pleasure show. That quantity of fresh meat would be very welcome. 'The beasts don't count for much if the Vocontii steal them straight back. Hannibal needs far more assurance than that. What kind of guarantee of safe passage can the dirtbags offer?'

A moment later, fully half of the tribesmen took a step forward. Most obvious was the wide-faced young warrior with blond pigtails and finely made weapons. He looked decidedly disgruntled. An explanation from the deputation's leader followed.

'Apparently, the youngster is the chieftain's youngest son, sir. The rest are high-ranking warriors,' said the guide. 'They are to be our hostages.'

'That's more like it,' said Sapho. He turned to the nearest of his officers. 'Go and find the general. Tell him what's happened. I think he'll want to hear their offer for himself.' As the officer hurried off to do his bidding, Sapho resumed his study of the heights above. The fact that they were bare did not reassure him in any way. Gut feeling told him that the Vocontii were as trustworthy as a nest of snakes.

It wasn't long before Hannibal appeared. When he wasn't marching near the army's head, the general was to be found at its tail, and today it was the former. Sapho was flattered that Hannibal was not accompanied by any of his senior officers. He saluted crisply. 'Sir!'

'Sapho.' Hannibal reached his side. 'So this is the deputation from the Vocontii, eh?'

'Yes, sir,' Sapho replied. 'The shifty-looking bastard over there is the leader.'

'Tell me again what they've said,' Hannibal ordered, scanning the warriors.

Sapho obeyed.

Hannibal rubbed his chin. 'A hundred cattle and ten hostages. Plus the guides who will stay with us. It's not a bad offer, is it?'

'No, sir.'

'You're not happy,' said Hannibal with a shrewd look. 'Why?'

'What's to stop them from simply rustling the beasts back from us, sir?' Sapho answered. 'Who's to say that the hostages aren't peasants, whom the Vocontii chieftain wouldn't ever miss if they were executed?'

'Should I reject their offer?'

Sapho's stomach did a somersault. Give the wrong answer now, and Hannibal probably wouldn't ask him to lead the army again. Give the correct one, and he would rise in the general's estimation. Sapho was desperate for the latter. 'There's no point, sir.'

'Why not?' Hannibal demanded.

Sapho met his general's fierce gaze. 'Because if you did, we'd have to fight our way through their territory, sir. If we play along instead, there's a reasonable chance of anticipating possible attacks while continuing the march without hindrance. If they prove to be trustworthy, so much the better. If not, then we at least gave it a try.'

Hannibal did not reply immediately, and Sapho began to worry that he'd said the wrong thing. He was thinking of retracting his words when the general spoke.

'I like your thinking, Sapho, son of Malchus. It is easier to avoid treading on a serpent that is watched than to find it under any one of a thousand stones. It would be foolish not to take steps to prevent disaster, though. The baggage train and the cavalry must be moved to a position just behind the vanguard. They're the most vulnerable to being cut off.'

At the front that could never happen, thought Sapho. 'Yes, sir.' He tried not to feel disappointed that Hannibal was taking charge. At least he'd led the army for a few days.

Hannibal surprised him. 'We still need infantry to lead us. You've been doing an excellent job, so I want you to continue in your position.'

Sapho grinned. 'Thank you, sir!'

'I also want you to guard the hostages. At the slightest sign of treachery, you know what to do.'

'I'll have them tortured and then crucified in full view of their compatriots, sir.'

'Excellent. Do whatever you see fit.' Hannibal clapped him on the arm. 'I'll have the cavalry move up to your position at once. Start marching again as soon as they're in place.'

'What about the mules, sir?'

'Getting them into position would be far too awkward now. We'll keep our fingers crossed for today and do it tomorrow.'

'Yes, sir. Thank you, sir.' Delighted, Sapho watched his general disappear back down the track. The passage of the mountains was proving to be far more rewarding than he could have anticipated.

For two days, the party of Vocontii led Sapho through their lands. The cavalry and baggage train followed slowly behind them, and after them came the rest of the army. Although there had been no attacks on the column, Sapho's distrust of the tribesmen who guided him remained. It grew stronger when, on the morning of the third day, the Vocontii chose a track that entered a valley much narrower than that in which they'd been marching. There was barely enough room for the ubiquitous pine trees to grow up its steep sides. Halting his soldiers, Sapho summoned the wall-eyed warrior. 'Why aren't we staying on this path?' Sapho indicated the larger way to the right, which continued off into the distance. 'It's wider, and the terrain looks to remain flatter.'

The guide repeated his words in the local tongue.

The warrior launched into a long, rambling explanation, which involved much pointing and gesticulating.

'Apparently it ends in a sheer cliff face about five miles away, sir. We'd just have to turn around and come back here. This narrow one, on the other hand, leads gradually upwards and will take us to the lowest pass in the area.'

Sapho glared at the warrior, who simply shrugged. One of his eyes was looking at him, while the other was staring off into the sky. Sapho found it infuriating. It also made judging whether the warrior was lying exceptionally hard. He made up his mind. Sending a runner to ask Hannibal, who was with the rearguard, would entail a delay of three hours or more. 'Fine,' he growled. 'We'll do as he says. Tell him, though, that if there's any trickery, he'll be the first to die.' Sapho was pleased to see the warrior's throat work nervously when his threat was translated. He led the way confidently enough, however, allaying Sapho's concern a fraction.

His unease soon returned. It wasn't the stony and uneven track. That was much the same as those they'd followed since entering the Alps. No, thought Sapho, it was the sheer rock faces that pressed in from both sides. They went on and on with no sign of widening out. It created a feeling of real claustrophobia. He didn't know exactly how high the cliffs were, but it was enough to reduce significantly the light on the valley floor. Sapho wasn't alone in disliking the situation. He could hear his men muttering uneasily to each other. Behind, there were indignant brays from the mules. Many of the cavalrymen were dismounting in order to lead their reluctant horses forward.

Sapho set his jaw. He had committed the army to this route. With a ten-mile column following, there was no turning back now. They just had to get on with it. Loosening his sword in his scabbard, Sapho ensured that he stayed close to the wall-eyed warrior. If anything happened, he *would* carry out his threat.

Pleasingly, they made slow but continuous progress for what remained of the morning. Men's spirits rose, and even the animals grew used to the confined space. Sapho remained on edge, constantly scanning the skyline above for any sign of movement. He tried to ignore the crick that was developing in his neck from always looking straight up in the air.

What attracted Sapho's attention first was not motion, but sound. One moment all that he could hear was the noises he'd heard daily since leaving New Carthage. Soldiers gossiping with each other. An occasional laugh, or curse. Officers barking orders. The creak of leather and jingle of harness. Hacking coughs from those with bad chests. The sound of men spitting. Brays from mules. Horses' whinnies. The next moment, Sapho's ears rang with a terrible, screeching resonance. He flinched instinctively. It was the noise of rock scraping off rock. With a terrible sense of dread, he looked up.

For a moment, Sapho saw nothing, but then the irregular edge of a block of stone appeared at the edge of the cliff far above. Frantically, Sapho raised a hand to his mouth. 'We're under attack! Raise shields! Raise shields!' In the same instant, his head was turning, searching for the wall-eyed warrior.

As the air filled with panicked shouts, Sapho saw the man had already elbowed past his comrades and was shouting at them to follow him. 'You treacherous bastard!' Sapho shouted, drawing his sword. He was too late. Enraged, he watched as the Vocontii disappeared into a fissure in the rock not twenty paces away. Sapho cursed savagely. He had to stay where he was, and do what he could for his men. If he wasn't killed himself. One thing was certain: if any of the hostages, who were kept deep in the middle of his phalanx, survived, they would die the instant he could get to them.

The air filled with a rumbling thunder and Sapho glanced upwards again. It was a terrifying sound, amplified a thousand times by the confining valley walls. Awestruck, he watched as several boulders, each the size of a horse, were pushed over the edge high above them. They picked up speed fast, and tumbled with ever-increasing speed down the vertiginous cliff face. Relief battled with horror as Sapho realised that none would strike him. Loud screams rose from the soldiers directly underneath the rocks, who could do nothing but watch their death hurtle towards them. Their cries revealed their awful, helpless terror. Aghast, Sapho could not take his eyes off the plummeting pieces of stone. A hot tide of acid flooded the back of his mouth as they struck their targets with deafening thumps, silencing their victims for ever.

Their ordeal wasn't over, either. Further down the cliff tops, in a position over the cavalry and the baggage train, Sapho could see more boulders being pushed towards the edge. He groaned. There was nothing he could do for those men and beasts either. Sapho took a deep breath. Best see to the injured, he thought. At least those can be helped.

The scream of battle cries filled their ears before they could do a thing. To Sapho's fury, files of Vocontii warriors came spilling from the fissure into which their guides had just vanished. More issued from another one alongside it. A red mist of rage replaced Sapho's dismay. He recognised the wall-eyed man and others of their guides among their number. Raising his spear, he roared, 'Eyes front! Enemy attack!' His soldiers responded with alacrity. 'Shields up! Ready spears!'

From the shouts behind them, Sapho could tell that the column had been attacked in other places too. 'Rear five ranks, about turn!' he bellowed. 'Advance to meet the enemy. Engage at will.' That done, Sapho spun to face the Vocontii before them. The tribesmen were closing in fast, weapons held high. Sapho levelled his spear at the wall-eyed warrior. 'You're dead meat, you stinking whoreson!'

His answer was an inarticulate snarl.

To Sapho's frustration, he did not get to close with the other. The phalanx's rigid structure meant that he could not move from his position, and the warrior was heading for a different part of the front rank. Sapho had to forget about him, as a tribesman with a dense red beard thrust his sword at his face. Rather than ducking below his shield rim, thereby losing sight of his enemy, Sapho jerked his head to one side. The blade whistled past his left ear, and Sapho thrust forward with his spear. There was a grating feeling as it slipped between two ribs, and then it ran deep into the other's unprotected chest. Sapho had no chance to pull free his weapon from the dying man's flesh. Releasing his grip on the shaft, he dragged free his sword. The warrior slumped to the ground, a disbelieving expression still twisting his features, and was immediately replaced.

Sapho's second foe was a bellowing bull of a man with a thick neck and hugely muscled arms. To Sapho's shock, the triangular point of his enemy's spear punched clean through the bronze and leather facing of his shield and smacked into his cuirass. A ball of agony exploded from Sapho's lower belly, and he reeled several steps backwards, dropping his sword. Fortunately, the soldier behind was ready, and leaned forward, thereby preventing Sapho from falling over. Jammed in Sapho's shield, the tribesman's weapon was no longer usable. Quick as a flash, however, he ripped out a long dagger and reached over the top of Sapho's shield to lunge at his throat. Desperately, Sapho jerked his head backwards. Slash after slash followed, and he knew that it would only be a moment before his throat was ripped open by the wickedly wielded blade.

It was with the utmost relief that Sapho saw a spear come in from the side to pierce the warrior's throat. It stabbed right through, emerging scarlet-tipped from the right side of his neck. A dreadful, choking sound left the Gaul's gaping mouth. It was followed by a tide of bright red blood, which spattered the front of Sapho's shield and, below, his feet. The spear was withdrawn, letting the dead warrior collapse on top of Sapho's first opponent.

'Gods above,' Sapho muttered. He'd never been so close to death. He turned his head to regard his saviour. 'Thank you.'

The spearman, a gap-toothed youth, grinned. 'You're welcome, captain. Are you all right?'

Sapho reached a hand under the bottom edge of his cuirass, which had a great dent in it. He probed upwards, wincing at the pain this caused. When he pulled out his fingers, he was relieved to see that there was no blood on them. 'I seem to be,' he answered with relief. He stooped to pick up his sword. Returning his gaze to the fight, Sapho was gratified to see that the Vocontii charge had smashed apart against the phalanx's solid wall of shields. He wasn't surprised. While a few of his men might have been killed, it would take more than a charge by disorganised tribesmen to break them. It was time to lead a counter charge, thought Sapho. All reason left him, however, as he saw the wall-eyed warrior no more than twenty steps away, stooping to kill an injured Libyan even as he himself retreated. Dropping his useless shield, Sapho leaped forward. His desire to kill the deceitful tribesman gave him extra speed and he had covered maybe a third of the ground between them before the other even saw him. The warrior took one look and fled for his life. So did his comrades.

'Come back, you fucking coward!' Sapho screamed. He was oblivious to the fact that the phalanx's front-rankers had followed him. He increased his pace to a sprint, aware that if the other reached the gap in the rock, any chance of catching him would disappear. It was no good. The warrior seemed to have winged heels. But then fate intervened, and Sapho's enemy tripped on a protruding rock. He stumbled and fell to one knee. Sapho was on him like a dog cornering a rat. Instead of killing the tribesman, he smashed the hilt of his sword across the back of his head. Straightening, Sapho was able to slash another warrior's arm as he ran past. With a howl, the man blundered into the fissure and out of sight.

'Don't go in there!' Sapho shouted as the first of his spearmen arrived and made for the gap in the rock. 'It's a death trap.'

The soldiers reluctantly obeyed.

'I want twenty men stationed right here to make sure they don't try a counter attack.' Sapho kicked the wall-eyed warrior, who groaned. 'Someone, pick up this sack of shit. Find any of his compatriots who are alive, and tie them all up.'

'What are you going to do with them, sir?' asked an officer.

'You'll see,' Sapho replied with a wolfish smile. 'First, though, we need to see what's going on behind us.'

By the time they had reached the rear of the phalanx, the Vocontii who had been attacking there were gone. The corpses of fifteen or more warriors were sprawled on the ground, but that was of little satisfaction to Sapho. In this small section alone, at least fifty Carthaginian soldiers had been critically injured or crushed to death. Just beyond, so had the same number of mules and cavalry mounts. The ground was covered with blood, and the mangled bodies of men and beasts lay everywhere. The screaming of the injured, especially those who had been trapped when the boulders finally came to rest, was awful. Sapho closed his ears to their clamour, and concentrated on finding out what else had happened. Bostar was among the officers who reported to him.

Panicked by the falling rocks, an elephant had dashed three men to death with its trunk, before charging backwards into the column, there to cause untold damage. Fortunately, its companions had been kept calm by their mahouts. The most frustrating discovery was that the Vocontii had stolen dozens of mules, leading them up the same precipitous paths that had served to launch their daring attack. They had even seized some captives. Despite this, Sapho knew that there was no point in pursuing the raiders. Moving on was more important than trying to save a few unfortunate soldiers. Once the dead and the blocks of stone had been rolled out of the way, the column would have to resume its advance.

Before that, however, there was something that Sapho had to do.

He made his way back to where the Vocontii prisoners were. With the ten hostages, they had twenty-two in total, sitting together and surrounded by a ring of spearmen. The only one who did not look fearful was the wall-eyed warrior, who spat at Sapho as he approached.

'Shall we execute them, sir?' asked an officer eagerly.

An angry mutter of agreement went up from the Libyans.

'No,' Sapho replied. He ignored his men's shocked response. 'Tell them that despite their brethren's treachery, they are not to be killed,' he said to the interpreter. As his words were translated, Sapho was gratified to see traces of hope appear in some warriors' faces. He waited for a moment, enjoying his power.

'Please, sir, reconsider!' an officer enjoined. 'They can't go unpunished. Think of our casualties.'

Sapho's lips peeled into a snarl. 'Did I say that they would go unpunished?'

The officer looked confused. 'No, sir.'

'We shall do to them what they did to us,' Sapho pronounced. 'Do not translate that,' he snapped at the interpreter. 'I want them to watch, and wonder.'

'What do you want us to do, sir?'

'Tie the shitbags in a line. Next, get one of the elephants. Use it to shift a large rock. A rock so big that no men could ever move it.'

A slow smile spread across the officer's face. 'To dash out their brains, sir?'

'No,' reproached Sapho. 'We're not going to kill them, remember? I want the boulders dropped on their legs.'

'And then, sir?'

Sapho shrugged cruelly. 'We'll just leave them there.'

The officer grinned. 'It'll be dark before their scumbag companions can return. They'll be begging for death by that stage, sir.'

'Precisely. They might think before attacking us a second time.' Sapho clapped his hands. 'See to it!'

He watched as the Vocontii prisoners were forced to lie down by a rocky outcrop. Sapho intervened to make sure that the wall-eyed warrior was last in the line. There was a short delay as an elephant was brought up from its position with the baggage train. Sapho waited with the interpreter by the first of the warriors, whose eyes were now bulging with fear.

Sapho looked up at the mahout. 'Can you shift that boulder there?' He pointed.

'Yes, sir. Where?'

'On to these men's legs. But they mustn't be killed.'

The mahout's eyes widened. 'I think so, sir.'

'Get on with it, then.'

'Sir.' Leaning forward, the mahout whispered in his huge mount's ear before tapping it behind the ear with his hooked staff. The elephant lumbered up to the stone that Sapho had indicated, and gripped the top of it with its trunk. There was a moment's silence before the slab began to move out of its resting place. The mahout muttered another command, and the elephant stepped up to rest the front of its head against the boulder, preventing it from picking up speed. Slowly, the beast reversed towards the prisoners, controlling its load's progress down the slight slope. Realising at last what was about to happen, the Vocontii warriors began to wail in fear.

Sapho laughed. He scanned the heights above, and fancied he saw movement. 'Yes, you fuckers,' he screamed. 'Look! We're about to give your friends a dose of their own medicine.'

Several steps from the captives, the mahout made the elephant pause. He looked at Sapho questioningly.

'Do it.'

A murmured word in its ear, and the elephant moved aside, letting the stone roll on to the first three warrior's legs. Strangled screams shredded the air. The sound was met by an immense cheer from the hundreds of watching Carthaginian soldiers. This, in their eyes, was vengeance for their dead comrades. Meanwhile, the tribesmen's companions struggled uselessly against their bonds, which had been pegged to the ground.

'Tell them that this is Hannibal's retribution for double-crossing us,' Sapho thundered.

Pale-faced, the interpreter did as he was told. His words were met by a gabble of terrified voices. 'Some are saying that they didn't know that we would be attacked,' he muttered.

'Ha! They're liars, or fools, or both.'

'They're asking just to be killed.'

'Absolutely not.' Sapho waved a hand at the mahout. 'Do it again. Don't stop.'

Rock after rock was lowered into place, smashing the legs of all but the last Vocontii warrior. When the elephant had manoeuvred the final piece of stone into place, Sapho ordered the mahout to wait. Clicking his fingers to make sure that the interpreter followed him, he made his way to where the wall-eyed warrior lay. Purple-faced with rage, the tribesman spat a string of obscenities.

'Don't bother,' said Sapho with a sneer as the interpreter began to speak. 'I know what he's saying. Tell him that this is repayment for his deceit, and that a coward like him will never reach the warriors' paradise. Instead, his soul will rot for all eternity in hell.' He eyed the mahout. 'When he's finished, let the stone fall.'

The elephant driver nodded.

'What in the name of all the gods is going on?' Somehow Bostar's voice penetrated the cacophony of screams echoing throughout the narrow gorge.

The interpreter stopped speaking. The mahout sat motionless atop his beast. Stiff-backed with fury, Sapho turned to find his brother regarding him with an outraged expression. He inclined his head mockingly. 'I'm punishing these worthless whoresons. What does it look like?'

Bostar's face twisted. 'Could you think of a crueller way to kill them?'

'Several ways, actually,' Sapho replied amiably. 'They all took too long, though. This method might be crude, but it's effective. It will also send a strong message to the rest of their pox-ridden, louse-infested tribe that to fuck with us carries a heavy price.'

'You've already made your point!' Bostar indicated the line of screaming men. 'Why not just stab this man in the throat and have done?'

'Because this one' — and Sapho kicked the wall-eyed warrior in the head — 'is their leader. I've saved him until last, so he could watch his comrades suffer, and anticipate his own fate.'

Bostar recoiled. 'You're sick,' he spat. 'I command you to halt this outrage.'

'You might outrank me still, *brother*, but Hannibal entrusted the vanguard to me, not you,' Sapho said in a loud voice. 'I'm sure that our general would love to hear why you countermanded his orders.'

'Hannibal ordered you to kill any prisoners like this?' Bostar muttered in disbelief.

'He said I was to do as I saw fit,' snarled Sapho. 'Which I am doing. Now stand back!' He was delighted when, with slumped shoulders, Bostar obeyed. Sapho looked down for a final time at the wall-eyed warrior, who tried to spit at him again. Inspiration seized Sapho and he drew his dagger. Kneeling down, he shoved the tip into the man's right eye socket. With a savage wrench, he hooked out the eyeball. His victim's courage disappeared and a shriek of pure agony ripped free of his throat. Wiping his bloody hands on the warrior's tunic, Sapho stood. 'I'm leaving him one eye so that he can watch the mightiest army in the world pass by,' he said to the interpreter. 'Tell him that.' He glanced at Bostar. 'Watch and learn, little brother. This is how enemies of Carthage should be treated.' Without waiting for a response, Sapho jerked his head at the mahout. 'Finish it.'

Full of impotent anguish, Bostar walked away. He was unwilling to watch. Unfortunately, he couldn't block out the screams. What had his older brother become? he wondered. Why was Hanno the one who had been carried out to sea?

For the first time, Bostar allowed himself that thought without guilt.

Chapter XVI: Journeys

N aturally, the via Appia, the main road to Rome, led straight out
of Capua. Not wishing to enter the town, Quintus first bypassed
his father's farm and then took a smaller, cross-country track that
meandered through a number of hamlets and past countless farms to join
the larger way some miles to the north. Quintus rode his horse. As a
supposed slave, Hanno sat on the back of an irritable mule, which was also
laden down with equipment. They travelled in silence for the first hour.
Both had much to think about.

Quintus now felt confident of finding his father. He was sad to have
left Aurelia behind, but that was the way of the world. Their mother
would look after her well. However, Quintus felt uneasy. Once their
objective – that of finding his father – had been achieved, Hanno would
depart to join the Carthaginian forces. Did that mean that they were
already enemies? Thoroughly unsettled by this notion, Quintus tried not
to think of it.

Hanno prayed that Suniaton would be all right and that they would find
Fabricius swiftly. Then he would be free. He asked to be reunited with his
father and brothers. If they were still alive, of course. Hanno tried to be
upbeat, and concentrated on imagining marching to war against the Romans.
At once, however, another disquieting image popped up. Quintus and
Fabricius would be serving in the legions. Unknowingly, Hanno had the
same disturbing thought as Quintus, and buried it deeply in the recesses
of his mind.

Not long after they had joined the Via Appia, they came upon a party
of infantry marching south.

'Oscans,' said Quintus, relieved to have something to talk about. 'They're
heading for the port.'

Hanno knew that the River Volturnus ran in a southwesterly direction past Capua to terminate at the coast. 'To be transported to Iberia?'

Ill at ease again, Quintus nodded.

Hanno ignored him, focusing instead on the approaching group. Apart from Fabricius' escort, he hadn't seen many soldiers in Italy. These were socii, not regular legionaries, but such men would constitute up to half of any army that faced Hannibal's. They were the enemy.

Some of the Oscans were bareheaded, but most wore bronze Attic helmets decorated in striking fashion with horsehair or feathers, which were dyed red, black, white or yellow. Their short wool tunics were also eye-catching, ranging from red to ochre to grey. Few wore shoes or sandals, but all had a broad leather belt covered in bronze sheeting, which was fastened with elaborate hooks. The soldiers were armed with light javelins and thrusting spears of different lengths; the rare men with swords carried the slashing kopis, a curved weapon originally used by the Greeks. The majority of their shields were similar to *scuta*, concave and ribbed, but smaller.

'It wasn't many generations ago that they were fighting Rome,' Quintus revealed. 'Capua has only been under Roman rule for just over a century. Many locals think it should reclaim its independence.'

Hanno goggled. 'Really?'

'Yes. It's a favourite argument between Martialis and my father, especially when they've been drinking.' Quintus frowned, wondering if his mother felt similarly. She'd never said as much, but he knew that she was fiercely proud of her heritage.

Hanno was fascinated. His knowledge of the Republic's structure, and its relationship with the non-Roman cities and peoples of Italy, was patchy at best. It was interesting that natives of such a large and important city were unhappy being ruled by Rome. Could there be others who felt the same way? he wondered.

As one of the junior tribunes of a legion, Flaccus should have accompanied his unit to Iberia. After his foolish outburst in front of Publius, it would also have been wise for him to lay low for a time. As Fabricius rapidly discovered, that was not his way. Discovering that, in addition to Fabricius' cavalry, the consul was taking a single cohort back to Italy,

Flaccus begged to be included. One tribune was needed to command the legionaries, he reasoned. Why should it not be he? To Fabricius' utter amazement, Publius did not explode at the request. While clearly annoyed, the consul acceded. 'By Jupiter, but you have a brass neck,' he muttered. 'Now get out of my tent.'

Fabricius took a mental note of the incident, which revealed how far the power of the Minucii stretched. Although it mattered little which tribune accompanied Publius, Flaccus' gall in asking would have been punished had he been anyone else. Rather than punishment, though, he had got his wish. As he said smugly to Fabricius later, the Minucii had a finger in every pie. 'By the time we arrive in Italy, the clan will probably know about Hannibal's intentions.' The only way that could happen, thought Fabricius, was if you had sent a message ahead of us. He couldn't believe that was the case. Had Atia been right about Flaccus? Wishing that his prospective son-in-law were less of a braggart, Fabricius consoled himself by imagining how his family would benefit from the Minucii's influence once Aurelia was married.

For his part, Fabricius was delighted to be heading for Italy. Although there would be plenty of action there, he wanted to be part of the army that faced the main threat. Naturally, this was Hannibal, not the commander he had left in Iberia.

Sapho's brutal treatment of the prisoners did not stop the Vocontii from mounting further attacks. If anything, it increased their ferocity. More rocks were rolled down the slopes, causing heavy casualties among the soldiers and pack animals. During the late afternoon, the fighting grew so intense that the vanguard, including the cavalry and the baggage train, became separated from Hannibal and the bulk of the infantry. It remained so for the duration of the night. The following morning, to everyone's relief, the Vocontii had disappeared. Most supposed that their losses had eventually become heavy enough to make stealing supplies pointless. Yet the tribesmen had wreaked more than simple physical damage on the army. The terrifying ordeal helped morale to plummet among the less motivated units. Each night, hundreds of men vanished under cover of darkness. Hannibal had ordered that no one was to stop them. 'Soldiers who are coerced into fighting make poor comrades,' he said to Malchus.

The host marched on.

For eight days, the miserable, cold and footsore Carthaginians climbed. Their enemies were no longer the Vocontii or the Allobroges, but the elements and the terrain, which grew ever more treacherous. Wind chill, frostbite and exposure began to take their toll. From dawn until dusk, soldiers dropped to the ground like flies. At night they simply died in their sleep. They were weakened by hunger, exhaustion, insufficient clothing, or a combination of all three.

Hannibal's response to Sapho's robust defence of the vanguard had been to promote him. He had also left Sapho in charge of leading the column. Despite his joy at being equal to Bostar in rank, his responsibility was a double-edged sword. It was down to him and his men to act as trailbreakers, which was an utterly exhausting task. Boulders had to be moved. The track regularly needed repairing or strengthening. Casualties among Sapho's men soared. By the eighth night, he was on the point of physical and mental collapse. His dread of their passage of the mountains had been proved well founded. In his mind, they were all doomed. They would never find the promised pass that marked the high point of their journey. All that kept Sapho going was his pride. Asking Hannibal to relieve him of his command would be worse than jumping off a cliff. Yet Sapho didn't want to do that either. Incredibly, life was still better than death. Wrapped in five blankets, he huddled over a lukewarm brazier in his tent and tried to feel grateful. None of his men had the luxury of fuel to burn.

After a while, Sapho stirred. Although he didn't want to, it was time to check the sentries. It was also good for morale for him to be seen. He shed his blankets, pulled on a second cloak and wrapped a scarf around his head. As he unlaced the leather ties and opened the tent flap, a gust of bitingly cold wind entered. Sapho flinched, before forcing himself outside. Two sentries, Libyans, stood by the entrance. A pitch-soaked torch held upright by a small pile of stones cast a faint pool of light around them.

The pair stiffened to attention as they saw him. 'Sir,' they both mumbled through lips that were blue with cold.

'Anything to report?'

'No, sir.'

'It's as cold as ever.'

'Yes, sir,' the nearest man replied. He doubled over as a paroxysm of coughing took him.

'Sorry, sir,' said his companion nervously. 'He can't help it.'

'It's all right,' Sapho replied irritably. He eyed the first soldier, who was wiping bloody sputum from his lips. A dead man walking, he thought. Sudden pity filled him. 'Take the wretch inside to the brazier. Try and get him warm. You can stay there until I get back from my rounds.'

Stunned, the second Libyan stammered his thanks. Sapho grabbed the torch and stalked off into the darkness. He would only be gone for a quarter of an hour, but it might provide the sick man with some relief. A sour smile traced his chapped lips. I'm getting soft, like Bostar. Sapho hadn't seen his brother since their argument over the Vocontii prisoners. As far as he was concerned, that was fine.

Taking great care on the icy ground, Sapho traced his way past his soldiers' tents. He glanced at the pair of elephants Hannibal had ordered to stay with the vanguard. The miserable beasts stood side by side, trying to maximise their warmth. Sapho even pitied them. Soon after, he reached the first sentries, who were stationed some two hundred steps from his tent. They were in a line across the path where the advance had stopped for the night. Exposed on three sides, it was the worst place to stand watch in the whole army. No fire could survive in the vicious, snow-laden wind that whistled down from the peaks. In order that the soldiers here didn't all die from exposure, Sapho had ordered their periods on duty shortened to just an hour at a time. Even so, he lost men every night.

'Seen anything?' he shouted at the officer in charge.

'No, sir! Even the demons are in bed tonight!'

'Very good. As you were.' Pleased by the officer's attempt at humour, Sapho began to retrace his steps. He had only to check the sentries at the rear of the phalanx, and then he was done. Peering into the gloom, he was surprised to see a figure emerging around the corner of the outermost tent. Sapho frowned. The cliff might be twenty steps from the tent lines, but the wind was so powerful that a man could easily be carried over the edge. He had seen it happen several times already. Consequently, everyone walked between the tents, not around them. The man was carrying a torch, which meant that he was no enemy. Yet he'd just taken the most dangerous route past his phalanx. Why? What had he to hide?

'Hey!' Sapho shouted. 'Stop right there!'

The figure straightened, and the hood of his cloak whipped back. 'Sapho?'

'Bostar?' said Sapho incredulously.

'Yes,' his brother replied. 'Can we talk?'

Sapho staggered as a particularly savage gust of wind struck him. He watched, aghast, as it buffeted an unsuspecting Bostar sideways and on to one knee. As he struggled to stand up, another blast of air hit, carrying him backwards and out into the blackness.

Sapho couldn't believe his eyes. He ran to the edge of the precipice, where he was astonished to find his brother clinging desperately to the protruding branch of a stunted bush several steps below him.

'Help me!' Bostar shouted.

Silently, Sapho stared down at him. Why should I? he asked himself. Of what benefit is it to me?

'What are you waiting for?' Bostar's voice cracked. 'This damn branch will never hold!' Seeing the look in Sapho's eyes, he blanched. 'You want me to die, don't you? Just as you were happy when Hanno was lost.'

Sapho's tongue stuck to the roof of his mouth with guilt. How could Bostar know that? Still he didn't act.

The branch split.

'Fuck you to hell and gone!' screamed Bostar. Letting go with his left hand, he threw himself forward, searching for a fingerhold on the track. There would only be a moment before his body weight pulled him backwards and into the abyss. Knowing this, Bostar scrabbled frantically to gain any kind of purchase in the rock-hard, ice-covered earth. He found none. With a despairing cry, he started to slide backwards.

Sapho's gut instinct took over, and he leaned forward to grab his brother by the shoulders. With a great yank, he pulled him up and over the edge. A second effort saw them several paces away, on safer ground. They lay side by side for a few moments, their chests heaving. Bostar was the first to sit up. 'Why did you save me?'

Sapho met his gaze with difficulty. 'I'm not a murderer.'

'No,' Bostar snapped. 'But you were glad when Hanno vanished, weren't you? With him out of the way, you had a chance to become Father's favourite.'

Shame filled Sapho. 'I—'

'It's strange,' said Bostar, interrupting. 'If I had died just now, you'd have Father all to yourself. Why didn't you let me slip into oblivion?'

'You're my brother,' Sapho protested weakly.

'I might be, but you still stood there, looking at me when I first fell,' Bostar retorted furiously. He regained control of himself. 'Yet I have you to thank for saving my life. I am grateful, and I will repay my debt if I can.' He carefully spat on the ground between them. 'After that, you will be dead to me.'

Sapho's mouth gaped. He watched as Bostar got up and walked away. 'What will you tell Father?' he called out.

Bostar turned, a contemptuous expression twisting his face. 'Don't worry. I'll say nothing.' With that, he was gone.

Right on cue, a blast of icy wind hit Sapho, chilling him to the bone. He had never felt more alone.

Quintus' and Hanno's departure left Aurelia feeling abandoned. Finding an excuse to head off to visit Suniaton was far from easy. She could not confide in her mother for obvious reasons, and she didn't like, or trust, her old Greek tutor. She was friendly with Elira, but the Illyrian had been in a bad mood recently, which made her poor company. Julius was the only other household slave Aurelia could be bothered with. After the excitement of her trips to the woods, however, discussion about what was on next week's menu was of little interest. Inevitably, she spent most of her time with her mother, who, since they'd been left alone, had thrown herself into household tasks with a vengeance. It was, Aurelia supposed, Atia's way of coping with Quintus' disappearance.

Foremost among their jobs was dealing with the vast amount of wool stockpiled in one of the sheds in the yard. It had been shorn from the sheep during the summer, and in the subsequent months, the women slaves had stripped the twigs and vegetation from the fleeces, before dyeing them a variety of colours: red, yellow, blue and black. Once dyed, the wool was ready for spinning, and then weaving. Although the majority of this work was done by slaves, Atia also contributed to the effort. She insisted Aurelia did so as well. Day after day, they sat in or walked around the courtyard, distaffs and spindles in hand, retreating to the atrium only if it rained.

'It's the job of a woman to keep the house and work in wool,' said Atia one crisp morning. Deftly pulling a few unspun fibres from the bundle on her distaff, she attached them to her spindle and set it spinning. Her eyes lifted to Aurelia. 'Are you listening, child?'

'Yes,' Aurelia replied, grateful that Atia hadn't noticed her rolling eyes. 'You've told me that a thousand times.'

'That's because it's true,' her mother replied primly. 'It's the mark of a good wife to be proficient at spinning and weaving. You'd do well to remember that.'

'Yes, Mother,' said Aurelia dutifully. Inside, she imagined that she was practising with a gladius.

'No doubt your father and Quintus will be grateful for any cloaks and tunics that we can send them too. I believe that the winters in Iberia can be harsh.'

Guiltily, Aurelia applied herself to her task with more vigour. This was the only tangible way of helping her brother. She was shocked to find herself wishing that she could do the same for Hanno. He's one of the enemy now, she told herself. 'Has there been any more news?'

'You know there hasn't.' There was an unmistakable trace of irritation in Atia's voice. 'Father will have no time to write to us. With the gods' blessing, however, he'll have reached Iberia by now.'

'With luck, Quintus will find him soon,' Aurelia responded.

Atia's composure cracked for an instant, revealing the sorrow beneath. 'What was he thinking to go on his own?'

Aurelia's heart bled to see her mother so upset. Until now, she hadn't mentioned that Hanno had left with her brother. Saying nothing made things far simpler. Now, though, her resolve wavered.

A discreet cough prevented her from saying a word. Aurelia was annoyed to see Agesandros standing by the atrium doors.

In the blink of an eye, Atia's self-possession returned. 'Agesandros.'

'My lady,' he said, bowing. 'Aurelia.'

Aurelia gave the Sicilian a withering look. Since his accusation of Hanno, she had avoided him like the plague. Now he had stopped her from consoling her mother.

'What is it?' asked Atia. 'A problem with the olive harvest?'

'No, mistress.' He hesitated. 'I have come to make an apology. To Aurelia.'

Atia's eyebrows rose. 'What have you done?'

'Nothing that I shouldn't have, mistress,' said Agesandros reassuringly. 'But the whole business with the Carthaginian slave was most . . . unfortunate.'

'Is that what you call it?' Aurelia interjected acidly.

Atia raised a hand, stalling her protest. 'Continue.'

Publius was incensed, upon his arrival in Pisae nearly a week later, to be greeted by a messenger from the Senate. The consul's only thought was to travel north, to Cisalpine Gaul, and there take control of the legions presently commanded by a praetor, Lucius Manlius Vulso. Yet the note Publius was handed suggested in no uncertain terms that it would be judicious to report to the Senate before taking further action against Hannibal. This was necessary because, as Publius spat at Flaccus, he had '"exceeded his consular remit, by deciding not to proceed to Iberia with his army".'

Flaccus innocently studied his fingernails.

'Someone must have sent word before we left Massilia,' Publius raged, staring pointedly at Flaccus. 'Yet nowhere do I see any mention of the word *provocatio*. In other words, I could ignore this disrespectful note. I probably should. With every day that goes by, Hannibal and his army march closer to our northern borders. Sempronius has no chance of travelling from Sicily quicker than I can reach the north. Journeying to Rome will delay me by two weeks, or more. If Hannibal turns up during that time, the result could be catastrophic.'

'That would scarcely be my fault,' Flaccus replied smoothly.

Publius' nostrils flared white with fury. 'Is that so?'

Flaccus had the sense not to answer.

Reading the missive again, Publius composed himself. 'I will return to Rome as asked, but any responsibility for what happens because of the delay will fall on the heads of the Minucii, and on you particularly. Should Hannibal already be in the area when I eventually reach Cisalpine Gaul, I will make sure to position you in the front line every time we encounter the Carthaginians.' Flaccus looked up in alarm, and Publius snarled, 'There you can win all the glory you desire. Posthumously, I expect.' Ignoring Flaccus' shock, Publius turned to Fabricius. 'We shall take but a single turma to Rome. I want two spare horses for every rider. Your other men can buy new mounts, and then head north to join Vulso with the cohort of infantry. See to it. We ride out in an hour.'

Flaccus followed Fabricius as he supervised the unloading of the mounts and equipment. The quayside at Pisae was a hive of activity. Freshly disembarked soldiers retrieved their equipment from piles on the dock and formed up in lines under their officers' eagle eyes. Fabricius' cavalrymen watched as specially constructed wooden frames lifted their horses out of the ships' bellies and on to dry land once more. Grooms stepped in, reassuring their unsettled charges, before leading them off to one side where they could be readied for the impending journey. As soon as the opportunity presented itself, Fabricius rounded on Flaccus. 'What in the name of Hades is going on?'

Flaccus made a show of innocence. 'What do you mean?'

'Any fool knows that the best thing is not for Publius to go to Rome, but to Cisalpine Gaul, and with all haste. Yet you have conspired to make sure that he does the former.'

Flaccus looked shocked. 'Who's to say that I had anything to do with the news reaching Rome? Anyhow, I cannot answer for the actions of more senior members of my clan. They are men greater than you or I, men whose only interest is that of Rome. They also know Publius for an arrogant individual whose main aim is to gain glory for himself; his recent actions prove this. He must be brought to book by his fellows and reminded of his position before it's too late.

'It's not as if we are without forces in the north,' Flaccus went on persuasively. 'Lucius Manlius Vulso is already in the area with a full-sized consular army. Vulso is an experienced commander, and I have no doubt that he is skilled enough to face, and beat, the rabble Hannibal will lead out of the mountains. Would you not agree?'

Fabricius felt his position waver. Publius' confident decision to send his army on to Iberia while he himself returned to Italy had certainly been out of the ordinary. Initially, Fabricius had thought Publius was showing genuine foresight, but Flaccus' words sowed doubt in his mind. It was hard to credit that a faction in Rome would endanger the Republic just to score points over a political rival. The Minucii must have their reasons for demanding to see Publius, he reasoned. In theory, the legions in Cisalpine Gaul were fully capable of defending their northern border. Fabricius glanced at Flaccus, and saw nothing but genuine concern. 'I suppose so,' he muttered.

'Good. Let us travel to the capital without worrying about Hannibal, and see what our betters in the Senate would say to Publius,' said Flaccus earnestly. 'The gugga can be dealt with immediately afterwards, if Vulso has not already wiped him from the face of the earth. Are we agreed?' He stuck out his right arm in the soldier's fashion.

Fabricius felt uneasy. One moment Flaccus was talking as if those in Rome always acted unselfishly, and the next he was implying that Publius' recall was a political tactic made with scant consideration of the danger posed by Hannibal. There was far more going on here than met the eye. In Fabricius' mind, the sole issue at hand was Hannibal, and how to deal with him. Those who sat in the Senate obviously did not appreciate that. Yet did it really matter, he wondered, if they went to Rome before Cisalpine Gaul? If Hannibal did succeed in crossing the Alps, his army would need a prolonged period of rest to recover from their ordeal. Forewarned, Vulso would be ready, and Publius would not take long to travel from the capital. 'We are agreed,' he said, accepting Flaccus' grip.

'Excellent.' Flaccus' eyes glittered with satisfaction. 'By the way, don't take anything my brother says to heart. He is greatly looking forward to meeting you in private.'

Feeling rather out of his depth, Fabricius nodded.

Hannibal's army reached the top of the pass the next day. Thrillingly, the watery sunshine revealed flat plains far below. The distant image could have been a mirage for all the use it was to them, thought Bostar bitterly. The slopes that led down towards Cisalpine Gaul were covered in frozen snow, which entirely concealed the path. Achieving a secure footing from now on would be more difficult than ever, and the price of failure was no less lethal than it had been since they'd entered the mountains.

To relieve his troops' suffering, Hannibal let them rest for two days at the summit. Of course there was more to his decision than simple kindness. Hundreds of stragglers, soldiers who would have died otherwise, managed to catch up with their comrades in this time, where they were greeted with relief but little sympathy. Even if they'd wanted to speak of their ordeal, few would have found an audience. Despair clawed constantly at men's hearts, rendering them insensible to the suffering of others.

Remarkably, hundreds of mules that had gone missing during the ascent also made their way into the camp. Although the majority had lost their baggage, they were still a welcome sight. In an effort to raise morale, Hannibal allowed the weakest beasts, numbering two hundred or more, to be slaughtered on the last evening before the descent. The fires needed to cook this meal consumed most of the army's remaining wood, but for the first time in weeks, his soldiers went to sleep with fresh meat in their bellies.

Bostar's deeply held hope that Hanno was still alive, and the presence of his father, were what sustained him through the agonies of the following day and night. He tried not to think of Sapho at all, instead concentrating on helping his soldiers. If Bostar had thought that the journey through the mountains up to that point had been difficult, then the descent was twice as bad. After more than a week above the snow line, the troops were chilled to the bone. Despite the Cavares' gifts of clothing and footwear, many were still not suitably attired for the freezing, hazardous conditions. Slowed by the cold, the Carthaginians stumbled over the slightest obstacles, walked into snowdrifts and collided with each other. This, when a simple trip meant death, instantly from the fall, or by slipping away into a sleep from which there was no wakening.

The soldiers died in other ways as well. Sections of the path cracked away under the weight of snow and men, sending hundreds into oblivion, and forcing those behind to repair the track in order to continue. The unfortunate mules were now prone to panic at the slightest thing, and their struggles were the cause of more casualties. Bostar found that the only way not to go mad in the face of so much death and destruction was to act as if nothing had happened. To keep putting one foot in front of the other. Step by grim step, he plodded on.

Just when he thought that things could get no worse, they did. Late the next morning, the vanguard arrived at a point where a landslide had carried away the track for a distance of one and a half stades. Sapho sent word back that neither man nor beast could proceed without losing their life. Here the drop was at least five hundred paces. Undeterred, Hannibal ordered his Numidians to begin constructing a new path across the obstacle. The rest of the army was ordered to rest as best it could. The news made many soldiers break down and weep. 'Will our suffering never end?' wailed one of Bostar's men. Bostar was quick to issue a reprimand. Morale was painfully low, without being made worse by open despair.

All they had to go on were the garbled messages occasionally passed back from the vanguard. Bostar didn't know which to believe. The cavalry mounts were useful in pulling large boulders out of the way. Most of the work had to be done by bare hand. Hannibal had offered a hundred gold pieces to the first man over the obstacle. Ten men had fallen to their deaths when a section of the track had given way. It would take a week or more to clear the way for the elephants.

As darkness fell, Bostar's spirits were raised somewhat by a Numidian officer who was passing through Bostar's phalanx as he returned to his tent.

'Progress was good today. We've laid a new path over more than two-thirds of the landslide. If things proceed like this tomorrow, we should be able to continue.'

Bostar breathed a huge sigh of relief. After nearly a month in the mountains, Cisalpine Gaul would be within reach at last.

His optimism vanished within an hour of work resuming the following morning when the cavalrymen exposed a huge boulder. It completely blocked the way forward. With a diameter greater than the height of two men, the rock was positioned such that only a few soldiers could approach at a time. Horses weren't strong enough to move it, and there was no space to lead an elephant in to try.

As time passed, Bostar could see the last vestiges of hope disappearing from men's eyes. He felt the same way himself. Although they weren't speaking, Sapho looked similarly deflated. It wasn't long before Hannibal came to survey the problem. Bostar's usual excitement at seeing his general did not materialise. How could anyone, even Hannibal, find a way to overcome this obstacle? As if the gods were laughing, more snow began to fall. Bostar's shoulders slumped.

A moment later, he was surprised to see his father hurrying to speak with Hannibal. When Malchus returned, he had a new air of calmness about him. Bostar squinted at the soldiers who were hurrying back along the column. He grabbed his father's arm. 'What's going on?'

'All is not lost,' Malchus replied with a small smile. 'You will see.'

Soon after, the soldiers returned, each man bent double under a pile of firewood. Load after load was carried past and set carefully around the base of the rock. When the timber had been piled high, Malchus ordered it lit. Still Bostar did not understand, but his father would answer no questions. Leaving his sons to observe with increasing curiosity, he returned to Hannibal's side.

The soldiers who could see were also intrigued, but after the fire had been burning for more than an hour without any result, they grew bored. Grumbles about wasting the last of their wood began. For the first time since leaving New Carthage, Bostar did not immediately react. His own disillusionment was reaching critical levels. Whatever crackpot idea his father had had was not going to work. They might as well lie down and die now, because that was what would surely happen when night fell.

Bostar missed the construction of a wooden framework that allowed a man to stand over the top of the rock. It was only when the first amphorae were carried past that he looked up. Finally, his curiosity got the better of his despair. The clay vessels contained sour wine, the troops' staple drink. Bostar saw his father gesturing excitedly as Hannibal watched. Quickly, two strapping scutarii climbed the frame. To combat the extreme heat now radiating from the rock, they had both soaked their clothes in water. The instant they had reached the top, the pair lowered ropes to the ground. Men below tied amphorae to the cables, which were hauled up. Without further ado, the scutarii cracked open the wax seals and poured the vessels' contents all over the boulder. The liquid sizzled and spat, sending a powerful smell of hot wine into the faces of those watching. Realisation of what they were trying to do struck Bostar like a hammer blow. He turned to tell Sapho before biting his lip and saying nothing.

The empty containers were discarded and replaced by full ones, and the process was repeated. There was more loud bubbling as the wine boiled on the superheated rock, but nothing else happened. The scutarii looked uncertainly at Malchus. 'Keep going! As fast as you can!' he shouted. Hastily, they obeyed, upending two more amphorae. Then it was four. Still the rock sat there, immovable, immutable. Malchus roared at the soldiers who stood close by to add more fuel to the blaze. The flames licked up, threatening to consume the platform upon which the scutarii stood, but they were not allowed to climb down. Malchus moved to stand at the frame's base, and exhorted the soldiers to even greater efforts. Another two amphorae were emptied over the boulder, to no avail. Bostar's hopes began to ebb away.

A succession of explosive cracks suddenly drowned out all sound. Chunks of stone were hurled high into the air, and one of the scutarii collapsed as if poleaxed. His skull had been neatly staved in by a piece of rock no bigger than a hen's egg. His panicked companion jumped to safety, and the soldiers who had been tending the fire all retreated at speed. More cracking sounds followed, and then the rock broke into several large parts. Parts that could be moved by men, or smashed into pieces by hammers. The cheering that followed rose to the very clouds. As word spread down the column, the noise increased in volume until it seemed that the mountains themselves were rejoicing.

Elated, Bostar and Sapho rushed separately to their father's side. Joyfully, they embraced him one by one. They were joined by Hannibal, who greeted Malchus like a brother. 'Our ordeal is nearly over,' the general cried. 'The path to Cisalpine Gaul lies open.'

The two friends' first sight of the capital was formed by the immense Servian wall, which ringed the city and dwarfed Capua's defences. 'The fortifications are nearly two hundred years old,' Quintus explained excitedly. 'They were built after Rome was sacked by the Gauls.'

May Hannibal be the next to do so, Hanno prayed.

'How does Carthage compare?'

'Eh?' said Hanno, coming back to reality. 'Many of her defences are much more recent.' They're still far more spectacular, he thought.

'And its size?'

Hanno wasn't going to lie about that one. 'Carthage is much bigger.'

Quintus did his best not to look disgruntled, and failed.

Hanno was surprised that within the walls, Carthage's similarities with Rome grew. The streets were unpaved, and most were no more than ten paces across. After months of hot weather, their surfaces were little more than an iron-hard series of wheel ruts. 'They'll be a muddy morass come the winter,' he said, pointing. 'That's what happens if it rains a lot at home.'

'As in Capua,' agreed Quintus. He wrinkled his nose as they passed an alleyway used as a dung heap. The acrid odour of human faeces and urine hung heavy in the air. 'Lucky it's autumn and not the height of summer. The smell then is apparently unbearable.'

'Do many buildings have sewerage systems?'

'No.'

'It's not much different to parts of Carthage,' Hanno replied. It was strange to feel homesick because of the smell of shit.

The fuggy atmosphere was aided by the fact that the closely built structures were two, three and even four storeys tall, creating a dimly lit, poorly ventilated environment on the street. Compared to the fresh air and open spaces of the Italian countryside, it was an alternative world. Most structures were open-fronted shops at ground level, with stairs at the side that snaked up to the flats above. Quintus was shocked by the filth of it all. 'They're where the majority of people live,' he explained.

'In Carthage, they're mostly constructed from mud bricks.'

'That sounds a lot safer. The *cenaculae* are built of wood. They're disease-ridden, hard to heat and easy to destroy.'

'Fire's a big problem, then,' said Hanno, imagining how easy it would be to burn down the city if it fell to Hannibal's army.

Quintus grimaced. 'Yes.'

Along with its sights and smells, the capital provided plenty of noise. The air was filled with the clamour of shopkeepers competing for business, the shrieks of playing children and the chatter of neighbours gossiping on the street corners. Beggars of every hue abounded, adding their cries for alms to the din. The clang of iron being pounded on anvils carried from smithies, and the sound of carpenters hammering echoed off the tall buildings. In the distance, cattle bellowed from the Forum Boarium.

Of course Rome was not their main destination: that was the port of Pisae, from which Publius and his army had set sail. Yet the temptation of visiting Rome had been too much for either of the friends to resist. They wandered through the streets for hours, drinking in the sights. When they were hungry, they filled their bellies with hot sausages and fresh bread bought from little stalls. Juicy plums and apples finished off their satisfying meal.

Inevitably, Quintus was drawn to the massive temple of Jupiter, high on the Capitoline Hill. He gaped at its roof of beaten gold, rows of columns the height of ten men and façade of brightly painted terracotta. He came to a halt by the immense statue of a bearded Jupiter, which stood in front of the complex, giving it a view over much of Rome.

Feeling resentful, Hanno also stopped.

'This must be bigger than any of the shrines in Carthage,' said Quintus with a questioning look.

'There's one which is as big,' Hanno replied proudly. 'It's in honour of Eshmoun.'

'What god is that?' asked Quintus curiously.

'He represents fertility, good health and well-being.'

Quintus' eyebrows rose. 'And is he the leading deity in Carthage?'

'No.'

'Why has his temple the most prominent position then?'

Hanno gave an awkward shrug. 'I don't know.' He remembered his father saying that their people differed from the Romans by being traders first and foremost. This temple complex proved that Quintus' kind placed power and war before everything else. Thank all the gods that we have a real warrior in Hannibal Barca, he thought. If fools like Hostus were in charge, we would have no hope.

Quintus had come to his own conclusion. How could a race who gave pride of place to a fertility god's temple ever defeat Rome? And when the inevitable happens, what will happen to Hanno? his conscience suddenly screamed. Where will he be? Quintus didn't want to answer the question. 'We'd better find a bed for the night,' he suggested. 'Before it gets dark.'

'Good idea,' replied Hanno, grateful for the change of subject.

Agesandros gave a tiny nod of thanks and turned to Aurelia. 'I should have handled the matter far better. I wanted to apologise for it, and ask if we can make a new start.'

'A new start?' Aurelia snapped. 'But you're only a slave! What you think means nothing.' She was pleased to see pain flare in his eyes.

'Enough!' Atia exclaimed. 'Agesandros has served us loyally for more than twenty years. At the least, you should listen to what he has to say.'

Aurelia flushed, mortified at being reprimanded in front of a slave. She was damned if she'd just give in to her mother's wishes. 'Why would you bother apologising now?' she muttered.

'It's simple. The master and Quintus may be gone for a long time. Who knows? It could be years. Perhaps you'll have more of a hand with the running of the farm.' Encouraged by Atia's nod of acquiescence, he continued, 'I want nothing more than to do my best for you and the mistress here.' Agesandros made an almost plaintive gesture. 'A good working relationship is essential if we are to succeed.'

'He's right,' said Atia.

'You owe me an explanation before I agree to anything,' said Aurelia angrily.

The Sicilian sighed. 'True. I did treat the gugga slave harshly.'

'Harshly? Where do you get the gall?' Aurelia cried. 'You were going to sell a man to someone who would make him fight his best friend to the death!'

'I have my reasons,' Agesandros replied. A cloud passed across his face. 'If I were to tell you that the Carthaginians tortured and murdered my entire family in Sicily, would you think differently of me?'

Aurelia's mouth opened in horror.

'They did what?' demanded her mother.

'I was away, fighting at the other end of the island, mistress. A surprise Carthaginian attack swept through the town, destroying all in its path.' Agesandros swallowed. 'They slaughtered everyone in the place: men, women, children. The old, the sick, even the dogs.'

Aurelia could scarcely breathe. 'Why?'

'It was punishment,' the Sicilian replied. 'Historically, we had sided with Carthage, but had switched to give our allegiance to Rome. Many settlements had done the same. Ours was the first to be captured. A message had to be delivered to the rest.'

Aurelia knew that terrible things happened in war. Men died, or were injured terribly, often in their thousands. But the massacre of civilians?

'Go on,' said Atia gently.

'I had a wife and two children. A girl and a boy.' For the first time, Agesandros' voice cracked. 'They were just babies. Three and two.'

Aurelia was stunned to see tears in his eyes. She had not thought the vilicus capable of such emotion. Incredibly, she felt sorry for him.

'I found them some days later. They were dead. Butchered, in fact.' Agesandros' face twitched. 'Have you ever seen what a spear blade can do to a little child? Or what a woman looks like after a dozen soldiers have violated her?'

'Stop!' Atia cried in distaste. 'That's quite enough.'

He hung his head.

Aurelia was reeling with horror. Her mind was filled with a series of terrifying images. It was no wonder, she thought, that Agesandros had treated Hanno as he had.

'Finish your story,' Atia commanded. 'Quickly.'

'I didn't really want to live after that,' said Agesandros obediently, 'but the gods did not see fit to grant my wish of dying in battle. Instead, I was taken prisoner, and sold into slavery. I was taken to Italy, where the master bought me.' He shrugged. 'Here I have been ever since. That pair were some of the first guggas I had seen for two decades.'

'Hanno is innocent of any crime towards your family,' Aurelia hissed. 'The war in Sicily took place before he had even been born!'

'Let me deal with this,' said her mother sharply. 'Were you seeking revenge the first time that you attacked the Carthaginian?'

'Yes, mistress.'

'I understand. While it doesn't excuse your actions, it explains them.' Atia's expression hardened. 'Did you lie about finding the knife and purse among the slave's belongings?'

'No, mistress! As the gods are my witness, I told the truth,' said the Sicilian earnestly.

Liar, thought Aurelia furiously, but she dared say nothing. Her mother was nodding in approval. A moment later, her worries materialised.

'Agesandros is right,' Atia declared. 'Things will be hard enough in the months to come. Let us all make a new start.' She stared expectantly at Aurelia. Agesandros' expression was milder, but mirrored hers.

'Very well,' Aurelia whispered, feeling more isolated than ever.

Chapter XVII: Debate

Having found a cheap bed for the night, the two friends hit the nearest tavern. Drinking seemed the adult thing to do, but of course there was a darker reason behind it: their thoughts about the outcome of the war. Both felt more awkward than they had since falling out during Flaccus' visit. Aurelia was not there to mediate, so wine would have to do. Their tactic worked to some extent, and they chatted idly while eyeing the prostitutes who were working the room for customers.

It didn't take long before the wine began to affect them both. Neither were used to drinking much. Fortunately, they grew merry rather than morose, and the evening became quite enjoyable. Encouraged by a hooting Hanno, Quintus even relaxed enough to take one of the whores on to his lap and fondle her bare breasts. He might have gone further, but then something happened that took all their attention away from wine and women. Important news didn't take long to spread through cities and towns. People simply carried the word on foot, from shops to taverns, and market places to houses. Naturally, the accuracy of such gossip could not always be relied upon, but that did not mean there wasn't some truth to it.

'Hannibal is leading his army over the Alps!' cried a voice from outside the inn. 'When he falls upon Italy, we shall be murdered in our beds!'

As all conversation ceased, the two friends stared at each other, wide eyed. 'Did you know about this?' Quintus hissed.

'I had no idea,' Hanno replied truthfully. 'Why else would I have agreed to travel with you to Iberia?'

A moment later, a middle-aged man with a red face and double chin entered. His grubby tunic and calloused hands pointed towards him being a shopkeeper of some kind. He smiled self-importantly at the barrage of questions that greeted him. 'I have seen Publius the consul with my own eyes, not an hour since,' he announced. 'He has returned from Massilia with this terrible news.'

'What else did you hear?' shouted a voice. 'Tell us!'

A roar of agreement went up from the other patrons.

The shopkeeper licked his lips. 'Running through the streets is thirsty work. A cup of wine would wet my throat nicely.'

Hurriedly, the landlord filled a beaker to the brim. Scurrying over, he pressed it into the newcomer's hand.

He took a deep swallow and smacked his lips with satisfaction. 'Tasty.'

'Tell us!' Quintus cried.

The shopkeeper smiled again at his temporary power. 'After landing at Massilia for supplies, Publius heard word that Hannibal might be in the area. He sent out a patrol, which stumbled upon the entire Carthaginian army.' He paused, letting the shocked cries of his audience fill the air, and draining his cup. The innkeeper refilled it at once. The man raised a hand. Instantly, silence fell. 'When he heard, Publius led his army north with all speed, his aim to force the enemy into battle. But when they arrived, Hannibal had gone. Vanished. His only intention can be to cross the mountains and enter Cisalpine Gaul. Before invading Italy.'

Wails of terror met his final remark. The room descended into chaos as everyone screamed to be heard. Some customers even ran away, back to their houses. Quintus' face bore an expression of total shock, while Hanno struggled to control his exhilaration. Who else could be so daring, other than Hannibal? He wondered if his father had known about this tactically brilliant plan, and said nothing? At one stroke, his priorities had been changed utterly.

Quintus had realised the same thing. 'I suppose you'll be leaving now,' he said accusingly. 'Why travel to Iberia now? Just head to Cisalpine Gaul.'

Feeling guilty for even entertaining the idea, Hanno flushed. 'This changes nothing,' he replied. 'We are going to Iberia to find your father.'

Quintus looked Hanno in the eyes, and saw that he meant it. He hung his head. 'I'm sorry for doubting your honour,' he muttered. 'It's shocking to hear news like this.'

Their conversation was interrupted again. 'Do you not want to know why the consul has returned?' bellowed the messenger, who was already on his fourth cup of wine. He waited as the room grew quiet once more.

'Publius has been recalled by the Senate because he sent his army on to Iberia rather than pursuing Hannibal. They say that the Minucii want him replaced with one of their own. Tomorrow, he will attend the Curia to explain his actions.'

All thoughts of leaving Rome at dawn vanished from the pair's heads. What did it matter if they delayed their departure for a few hours to witness this drama unfold?

Whatever Publius' reception in the Senate might be, he was still one of the Republic's two consuls. At the walled gate that signalled the end of the Via Ostiensis, the road from Ostia, a fine litter borne by six strapping slaves awaited his arrival. He, Flaccus and Fabricius clambered aboard. A dozen lictores bearing fasces preceded the litter into the city. As soldiers under arms, Fabricius' thirty cavalrymen had to remain outside but this did not delay the party's progress. The lictores' mere presence, wearing their magnificent red campaign cloaks rather than just their usual togas, and with the addition of axes to their fasces, was enough to clear the streets. All citizens, apart from Vestal Virgins or married women, were obliged to stand aside, or face the consequences. Only the strongest and tallest men were picked to join the lictores, and they had been taught to use their fasces at the slightest opportunity. If ordered to do so, they could even act as executioners.

Fabricius had been to Rome several times, and always enjoyed the spectacle provided by the capital. The lictores' presence ensured that he gained the best possible impression of the city. People pushed inside the shops and into the alleyways to get out of the way. It was all a far cry from Capua, and even further from Fabricius' farm, and yet it felt very similar. He tried to ignore the feeling of homesickness that followed. Their rapid progress to the Forum Romanum ensured that he had no time to wallow in the emotion.

As they entered the Forum, Fabricius' eyes were drawn to the Curia, the home of the Senate. Unremarkable apart from its great bronze doors, it was nonetheless the focal point of the Republic. He picked out the Graecostasis, the area just outside, where foreign embassies had to wait until they were called in. Today, accompanying one of the two most important men in the land, there was no such delay. The lictores swept up to the entrance, scattering the crowd of senators' sons who were hovering outside, listening to the debates within. Publius alighted right before the portals; so too did Flaccus and Fabricius. All three were clad in their finest togas. Naturally, Publius wore the grandest, a shining white woollen garment with a purple border.

Before leaving, Fabricius had secreted a dagger in the folds of his toga. After months on campaign, he felt naked without a weapon, and had scooped it up without even thinking. Yet it was a risky move: the lictores alone were allowed to bear arms within the Curia. Now, Fabricius cursed his impulsive decision. There was no way of getting rid of the dagger, though. He would have to carry it inside and hope for the best. His heart began to pound. Publius had asked him to be present because he was the only Roman officer to have seen Hannibal's army. His testimony was vital for Publius' defence. 'I'm relying on you,' the consul had said. 'I know you won't let me down. Just tell them what you saw at the Carthaginian camp.' Fabricius had promised to do so. He sneaked a glance at Flaccus, who looked rather pleased with himself. Confusion filled Fabricius. What role would he play in the drama to come?

The most senior lictor spoke with the guards before entering to announce Publius' arrival. A hush fell inside. Upon the man's return, the twelve lictores re-formed in six columns of two. With a measured tread, they led the way into the Senate. Fabricius followed Publius and Flaccus. He had to stop himself from staring like an excited boy. He'd never entered the seat of the Republic's democracy. Light flooded in through long, narrow windows set high in the walls. Running the length of the rectangular room, three low steps were lined by marble benches. Rank upon rank of standing toga-clad senators filled this space. To a man, their gaze was locked on Publius and his companions. Struggling to control his awe, Fabricius kept his eyes averted from the senators. At the end of the chamber, he saw a dais upon which sat two finely carved rosewood chairs. These, the most important positions, were for the consuls.

The lictores reached the platform and fanned out to either side, leaving a space for Publius to assume his seat. Flaccus and Fabricius remained at floor level. As Publius sat down, the lictores smacked the butts of their fasces off the mosaic. The clashing sound echoed off the walls and died away.

There was a long pause.

Glancing sideways, Fabricius saw a tiny, satisfied smile flicker across the consul's lips. It was obviously up to Publius to begin proceedings, and, in a pointed reminder of his rank, he was making the men who had recalled him to Rome wait. On and on the silence went. Soon Fabricius could see senators muttering angrily to one another. None dared to speak, however.

Finally, Publius opened his mouth. 'As I speak, the greatest threat to Rome since the barbarian Brennus approaches us through the Alps.' He let his shocking words sink in. 'Yet instead of letting me fulfil my duty, that of defending the Republic, you would have me return to explain my actions. Well, I am here.' Publius extended his arms, as if to welcome interrogation, and fell silent.

A deluge of questions followed. Practically half the senators present tried to speak at the same time. Many of their queries involved Brennus, the Gaulish chieftain who had led his fearsome warriors to the Capitoline Hill itself, and sacked Rome. In the process, he had left a weeping sore deep in the Roman psyche, a source of eternal shame. Fabricius did not know if Hannibal was truly that dangerous, but merely by mentioning Brennus, Publius had scored the first points. Before the Minucii could make a single accusation, the Senate's attention had been neatly diverted to something far more primeval.

Publius wasn't finished. Lifting a hand, he waited for quiet. 'I want to know why I was summoned here. Only then will I tell you anything of Hannibal and the enormous Carthaginian army which follows him.'

Cries and protests filled the air, but Publius simply folded his arms and sat back on his chair.

Second round to Publius, thought Fabricius. His respect for the consul was growing by the moment.

Both young men were up late the next morning. A brief visit to the public baths helped to ease their pounding heads. Fortunately, both also had the wits to drink copious amounts of water. Relieving themselves was not an issue: all they had to do was dart up one of the many alleyways that contained dung heaps. Breakfasting on bread and cheese, they made their way to the Forum Romanum. Naturally enough, conversation was limited until they reached their destination.

Quintus soaked up the sight of the long, rectangular space. 'It used to be a marsh, but now it's the largest open area within the city walls. This is the heart of the Republic,' he said proudly. 'The centre of religious, ceremonial and commercial life. People come here to socialise, to watch court cases or gladiator fights, and to hear important public announcements.'

'It has a lot in common with the Agora,' said Hanno politely. Although it's not half as big, he thought.

Hundreds of shops lined the Forum's perimeter. They ranged from ordinary butchers, fishmongers and bakers to the grander premises of lawyers, scribes and moneylenders. Crowds of people thronged the whole area.

Quintus had been taught the Forum's layout. 'There are the shrines of Castor and Pollux, and Saturn,' he cried as they walked along. 'And the circular temple of the Vestal Virgins.'

'What's that?' asked Hanno, pointing at a grubby building along the northern side of the Forum.

'I think it's the *comitium*,' Quintus replied. 'It's a temple which was built during the foundation of Rome more than five hundred years before.' His voice lowered. 'Inside it is the *lapis niger*, a stubby pillar of black stone which marks the spot where Romulus, the founder of Rome, ascended to heaven. Beside is the rostra, the speaker's platform, which is decorated with the prows of captured ships.' Quintus flushed and fell silent. The most recent additions were from Carthaginian triremes that had been captured in the last war.

Realising, Hanno glowered.

The friends soon discovered that they had arrived just after Publius had entered the Curia, but consoled themselves with the fact that they would be close at hand when he emerged. Huge crowds were already present. The news about Hannibal had spread all over the city by now. Everyone in Rome wanted to know what would happen next. Wild rumours swept from one end of the gathering to the other.

'Hannibal has a host of more than a hundred and fifty thousand men,' cried a man with red-rimmed eyes.

'He has a hundred elephants, and twenty-five thousand Numidian cavalry,' wailed another.

'They say that Philip of Macedon has mobilised his army and is about to attack us from the northeast,' shot back the first man. 'He's going to join with the Carthaginians.'

'So is every tribe in Cisalpine Gaul,' added a third voice.

Hanno's anger over the rostra was replaced by delight. If only a fraction of the gossip was true, Rome faced a catastrophe of enormous proportions. He glanced at Quintus, who was staring rigidly at the Curia, pretending to ignore what was being said.

An awkward silence fell.

A hush fell in the Senate as a stocky figure with wavy black hair and a ruddy complexion made his way into view. Bushy eyebrows sat over a pair of calculating blue eyes and a prominent nose. The senators around him moved deferentially out of the way. Flaccus gave the man a tiny nod, and Fabricius knew at once who it was. He was Marcus Minucius Rufus, a former consul, and Flaccus' brother. This was the pre-eminent member of the Minucii clan, and one of the most powerful men in Rome. No doubt he was the person responsible for the letter to Publius.

'Consul,' said Marcus, inclining his head in recognition. 'We thank you for returning to Rome. It is an honour to see you once more.' With the niceties over, his expression turned hawkish. 'We were alarmed to hear that your brother was leading your legions to Iberia. This, so that you could return to Italy. We have asked you back to explain your extraordinary about turn, which goes completely against the Senate's decision made here not six months ago. You and Longus, your co-consul, have supreme command of the Republic's military forces. That is beyond doubt. Yet neither of you are immune to challenge, should that be necessary.' Marcus half turned, smiling at the mutters of agreement that were becoming audible. 'Clearly, I am not the only one to hold such an opinion.'

One of Publius' eyebrows arched. 'And what opinion might that be?' he asked in a silky smooth tone.

Marcus' reply was urbane. 'I speak of course, of the power of provocatio.'

Some of the senators hissed with disapproval at this, but others shouted in agreement. Fabricius felt a nerve twitch in his face. He'd never before heard of one of the Republic's supreme magistrates being threatened with a criminal charge. He shot a glance at Flaccus, but could glean nothing from his face. Why were the Minucii seeking to depose Publius during his consulship? Fabricius wondered. What purpose would it serve?

'Have you nothing to say?' Marcus asked, taking a smug look around the room. Like a tide that had just turned, the noise of those who supported him began to grow.

Fabricius glanced at Flaccus again. This time, he saw the same self-satisfied expression as the one adorning Marcus' face. Then it hit him. Flaccus had believed Publius' account of the threat posed by Hannibal and, in his letter, told his brother of his concerns. Now Marcus, a previously successful general in his own right, wanted to become consul so that he could claim the glory of defeating the Carthaginians instead of leaving it to Publius. This possibility, no, probability, Fabricius thought angrily, defied belief. All that mattered was defeating an enemy who posed a serious threat to the Republic. Yet to some of these politicians, it was more about making a name for themselves.

Bizarrely, Publius laughed. 'I find it remarkable', he said, 'that I should be accused of exceeding my remit when in fact I have done more than my duty in fulfilling it. My army has been sent to Iberia as ordered; its commander, my brother Gnaeus, has a proven record in the field. Furthermore, upon realising the implications of Hannibal's march across the Alps, and knowing that my colleague Longus would not have time to react, I returned to Italy with the intention of facing the Carthaginians myself. Immediately. Does that not prove my loyalty to Rome? And what should we think about those who would prevent me from doing my duty?'

In the uproar that followed, Publius and Marcus stared at each other with clear dislike. But Marcus' response was swift. 'I take it that you have seen Hannibal's "enormous" army with your own eyes? Made a realistic estimate of the number of enemy troops?'

'I have done neither,' replied Publius in an icy tone.

'Are you a soothsayer, then?' Marcus asked, to gales of laughter from his supporters.

'Nothing like that.' Publius coolly indicated Fabricius. 'I have with me the veteran cavalry officer who led the patrol that reconnoitred the Carthaginian camp's perimeter. He will be happy to answer any questions you may have.'

Marcus regarded Fabricius with thinly disguised contempt. 'Your name?'

Meeting Marcus' stare, Fabricius steeled his resolve. Whatever the other's rank, and however intimidating the scene, he would tell the truth. 'Gaius Fabricius, sir. Equestrian and landowner near Capua.'

Marcus made a dismissive gesture. 'Have you much military experience?'

'I spent nearly ten years in Sicily, fighting the Carthaginians, sir,' replied Fabricius proudly. He was delighted by the response of some of those watching. Many heads nodded in approval; other senators muttered in each other's ears.

Marcus pursed his lips. 'Tell us what you saw, then. Let the Senate decide if it truly poses the threat that Publius would have us believe.'

Taking a deep breath, Fabricius began the tale of his patrol. He did not look at Marcus or anyone else. Instead he kept his gaze fixed on the bronze doors at the far end of the room. It was a good tactic, and he warmed to his topic as he continued. Fabricius spared no detail of the Carthaginian encampment, and was particularly careful to stress the number of enemy cavalry, the River Rhodanus' immense width and the Herculean effort of ferrying the elephants across it. Finishing, he looked to Publius. The consul gave an approving nod. Flaccus' expression had soured. Had his prospective son-in-law thought that having to appear before the entire Senate would be too much for him? From the alarmed looks many senators were now giving each other, the opposite was true. Suddenly, Marcus seemed to be on the back foot.

Seizing the initiative, Publius moved to the front of the dais. 'Fabricius estimated the Carthaginian host to be greater in size than two consular armies. I'm talking about fifty thousand men, of whom at least a quarter are cavalry. Numidians, who bested our troops in Sicily on countless occasions. Do not forget the elephants either. Our combat record against *them* is less than valiant. We also have to consider the leader of this army. Hannibal Barca, a man who has recently conquered half of Iberia and taken an impregnable city, Saguntum, by storm. A general who is unafraid of leading his soldiers across the Alps in late autumn.' Publius nodded as many senators recoiled. 'Many of you know the praetor Lucius Manlius Vulso, as I do. He is an honourable and able leader. But is he capable of beating a force twice the size of his, which also possesses superior numbers of horse, and elephants?' He looked around. 'Is he?'

A brief, disbelieving silence cloaked the room. Then, sheer pandemonium broke out. Hundreds of worried voices competed with each other, but no individual would listen to what another was saying. Marcus tried to calm those around him, but his efforts were in vain. Fabricius couldn't believe it. Here were the men who ruled the Republic, squabbling and shouting like frightened children. He glanced at Publius, who was watching the spectacle, waiting for an opportunity to intervene. Impulsively, Fabricius pulled out his dagger and handed it over. 'It's yours, sir,' he said passionately. 'Like the sword of every citizen in Italy.' Publius' initial surprise was replaced by a wolfish smile. He accepted the blade before muttering an order to his lictores. The hammering of fasces on the floor drew everyone's attention.

Publius raised the dagger high. 'I have been handed this by Fabricius, who has broken the law by carrying it into the Curia. Yet he did it only because of his loyalty to the Republic. To show his willingness to shed his blood and, if necessary, to die in the struggle to overcome Hannibal. With determined soldiers like this, I promise you victory over the Carthaginian invaders! Victory!'

As a flock of birds seamlessly alters direction, the senators' mood changed. Their panic vanished, to be replaced by a frenzy of excitement. Spontaneous cheering broke out, and the atmosphere lightened at once. Publius had won, thought Fabricius delightedly. Nobody but a fool would try and depose the consul now.

A moment later, Flaccus sidled over. 'Happy?' he hissed.

Fabricius had had enough. 'What was I supposed to do? Lie about what I saw?' he retorted. 'Hannibal's army is huge. It's well armed, and led by a very determined man. We underestimate it at our peril.'

Flaccus' expression grew softer. 'Of course, you are right. You spoke well. Convincingly,' he said. 'And the danger must be addressed fast. Clearly, Publius is still the man to do it. The resolve he has shown here today is admirable.'

Looking at the displeasure twisting Marcus' face, Fabricius had difficulty in believing Flaccus' words. He shoved his disquiet away. Such things were no longer of importance.

All that mattered was defeating Hannibal.

Fabricius wasn't surprised when Publius ordered him to proceed back to the city gate, there to ready his men. They would leave for Cisalpine Gaul within three hours. Flaccus would be with them too. Publius rolled his eyes as he said it. 'Some things cannot be changed,' he muttered.

Fabricius was relieved to be given his orders. He had seen enough of politics for a lifetime, and was uncertain what to think of Flaccus and his brother. Maybe Atia had been right? he wondered. Deciding to inform her of what had transpired by writing a quick letter before they set off, Fabricius exited the bronze doors and headed across the Forum.

Chapter XVIII: Cisalpine Gaul

There were only two occasions when the two friends heard something of what was going on inside. The first was when alarmed shouts rang out; the second, which followed directly after, was the sound of loud cheering. Almost at once, news spread through the assembled crowds that the Senate had given Publius its resounding support. Now the consul was to head north with all speed, there to confront Hannibal. Before the pair had time to take the momentous information in, several figures hurried from the Curia. Suddenly, Quintus came to life. He gave Hanno a violent nudge. 'Look,' he hissed, taking a step forward. 'It's Father!'

'So it is,' Hanno muttered. He was even more shocked than Quintus. Why was Fabricius here? His next thought was far more worrying. How would Quintus explain his presence? A wave of terror struck him. What chance was there of Fabricius accepting Quintus' grant of freedom? Precious little. Hanno couldn't help thinking he should walk away into the crowd. He would be lost to sight in an instant. Free to make his own way north. Hanno wavered, but then his pride took over. I am no coward who runs away and hides.

Glancing around, Quintus sensed his unhappiness. Despite his excitement, he pulled himself up short. 'It's all right,' he said gently. 'I'm not going anywhere.'

'Eh? Why not?' Hanno cried. 'This is a perfect opportunity for you.'

'Maybe so, but it isn't for you.'

Hanno coloured. He didn't know what to say.

Quintus pre-empted him. 'What possibility is there that Father will honour your manumission?'

'I don't know,' Hanno muttered. 'Not much, I suppose.'

'Exactly,' Quintus replied. 'Which is the reason I'm staying right here. With you.'

'Why would you do that?' asked Hanno, caught off guard.

'Have you forgotten last night already?' Quintus cuffed him on the side of the head. 'You promised to accompany me to Iberia, even though you no longer had any need to go there. Plus you didn't make a run for it just now, which most people would have done. I have to repay your honour. Fair's fair.'

'It's not that simple.' Hanno indicated Fabricius, who was about to disappear from view. 'Maybe he's not going with the consul.'

'I'd say he is, but you're right. We should make sure.' Quintus strode off. 'Come on, let's follow him.'

Hanno hurried to catch up. 'What if he's going back to Iberia?'

'We'll talk about that afterwards,' Quintus answered. 'In that eventuality, I suppose it would make sense to split up. Otherwise, I'm travelling with you to Cisalpine Gaul.'

Hanno chuckled. 'You're crazy!'

'Perhaps.' Quintus gave him a lopsided smile. 'But I still have to do the right thing.'

'And once we get there?' Hanno asked uneasily.

'We'll part company. I'll find Father, and you' – there was an awkward pause – 'can seek out Hannibal's army.'

Hanno gripped Quintus' arm. 'Thank you.'

Quintus nodded. 'It's the least I can do.'

The army that straggled down into the green foothills of the Alps was a shadow of what it had been. All semblance of marching formation had long gone. Gaunt-faced, hollow-cheeked figures stumbled along, holding on to each other for support. The ribs on every surviving horse and mule stood out like the bare frame of a new-built ship. Although few had died, the elephants had suffered extraordinarily too. Bostar thought that they now looked like nothing more than giant skeletons covered by sagging folds of grey skin. The heaviest toll, however, was the number of men and beasts that had been lost during the passage of the mountains. The scale of it was hard to take in, but it was impossible to deny. Hannibal had insisted on a tally as his troops entered the flat plain where, exhausted beyond belief, they had first camped. Even when a margin of error was allowed for, the count revealed that perhaps 24,000 foot soldiers and more than 5,000 pack animals had deserted, run away or perished. Approximately 26,000 men remained, just a quarter of the number that had left New Carthage, and little more than one Roman consular army.

It was a sobering figure, thought Bostar worriedly, especially when there were peoples to fight other than the Romans. He was standing with other senior officers outside the fortified walls of Taurasia. It was the main stronghold of the Taurini, the hostile tribe into whose lands Hannibal's force had descended. To his left was Sapho's phalanx, and to his right, his father's. Alete was positioned beyond Malchus. Fully half of the Libyans were present: six thousand of Hannibal's best troops.

'Gentlemen.'

At the sound of Hannibal's voice, Bostar turned. He scarcely recognised the shambling figure before him, clad in a ragged military cloak. Dank tresses of brown hair fell from under a simple bronze helmet, framing a gaunt face streaked with filth. The man sported a padded linen cuirass, which had clearly seen better days, a thrusting spear and an old, battered shield. He was the worst dressed Libyan spearman Bostar had ever seen, and he stank to high heaven. Bostar glanced at the other officers, who appeared as stunned as he. 'Is that you, sir?'

The belly laugh was definitely Hannibal's. 'It is. Don't look at me as if I am mad.'

Bostar flushed. 'Sorry, sir. May I ask why are you dressed like that?'

'Two reasons. Firstly, as an ordinary soldier, I'm far less of a target to the enemy. Secondly, being anonymous allows me to mix with the troops and assess their mood. I've been doing that since we came down out of the mountains,' Hannibal revealed. He turned to include all those present. 'What do you think I've heard?'

Most of the officers, Bostar included, took a sudden interest in their fingernails, or a strap on their harness that needed tightening. Even Malchus cleared his throat awkwardly.

'Come now,' said Hannibal in a bluff tone. 'Did you really think that I wouldn't find out how low morale really is? Spirits are high amongst the cavalry, but that's because I looked after them so well in the mountains.

Far fewer of them died. But they're unusual. Many of the men think we'll be annihilated the first time we encounter the Romans, don't they?'

'They'll fight anyway, sir!' Malchus cried. 'They love you as no other.'

Hannibal's smile was warm. 'Worthy Malchus, I can always rely on you and your sons. I know that your soldiers will stay true, and so will the bulk of the army. But we require an immediate victory to raise the men's spirits. More importantly, we need food to put in their bellies. Our intelligence tells me that the stores behind those walls' – he indicated the fortress – 'are full of grain. I would have bought it from the Taurini, but they rejected my overtures out of hand. Now they will learn the price of their foolishness.'

'What shall we do, sir?' Sapho asked eagerly.

'Take the place by storm.'

'Prisoners?'

'Leave none alive. Not a man, woman or child.'

Sapho's eyes lit up. 'Yes, sir!'

His words were echoed by a rumble of agreement from the others.

Hannibal stared at Bostar. 'What is it? Are you unhappy with my command?'

'Must everyone die, sir?' Terrible images from the fall of Saguntum filled Bostar's mind.

Hannibal scowled. 'Unfortunately, yes. Know that I order this for a particular reason. We are in a very fragile position. If a Roman army presented itself tomorrow, we would indeed struggle to defeat it. When they hear of our weakness, the Boii and Insubres will think twice before giving us the aid that they so eagerly promised last year. If that happens, we will have failed in our task before it has even begun. Is that what you want?'

'Of course not, sir,' Bostar replied indignantly.

'Good,' said Hannibal with a pleased look. 'Slaughtering the inhabitants of Taurasia will send a clear message to the area's tribes. We are still a lethal fighting force, and they either stand with us, or against us. There is no ground in between.'

Humbled, Bostar glanced down. 'I'm sorry, sir. I didn't understand.'

'Some of the others probably didn't either,' answered Hannibal, 'but they didn't have the courage to ask.'

'I understood, sir,' Sapho snarled.

'Which is the reason you're standing here today,' said Hannibal grimly. 'Monomachus too.' He nodded at a squat man with a bald head. 'The rest of you are present because I know that, as my finest officers, you will do exactly what I have ordered.' He pointed his spear at the fortress walls. 'I want the place reduced by nightfall. After that, your men can have the rest they so well deserve.'

Bostar joined in the cheering with more enthusiasm this time. He caught a sneering Sapho trying to catch his eye, and ignored him. He would follow Hannibal's orders, but for a very different reason to his brother. Loyalty, rather than sheer bloodthirstiness.

Despite Quintus' generosity in accompanying him north, Hanno found the journey grating. He still had to act like a slave. Quintus rode a horse, while he had to sit astride a cantankerous mule. He could not eat with Quintus, or share the same room. Instead, he had to take his meals with the domestic slaves and servants of the roadside inns they frequented, and to bed down in the stables with the animals. Oddly, Hanno's physical separation from Quintus began to restore the invisible differences between them.

In a bizarre way, both were relieved by this. What they'd seen and heard in Rome had hammered reality home as never before, shredding the camaraderie that had developed on the farm. They were travelling to a place where there could be no friendship between Carthaginian and Roman, only combat and death. Not speaking to each other obviated the need to think about what might happen in the future. Of course their silently adopted tactic did not work. Both felt great pain at their impending separation, which in all likelihood would be permanent.

The three hundred miles from Rome to Placentia dragged by, but the pair finally reached their destination having encountered few problems. All the empty ground outside the town was taken up with vast temporary encampments, full of legionaries, socii and cavalry. The tracks were jammed with units of marching men and ox carts laden with supplies. Stalls lined the margins of every way, hawking food, wine and equipment. Soothsayers offered their services alongside blacksmiths, butchers and whores. Musicians played drums and bone whistles, acrobats jumped and tumbled, tricksters promised a cure for every ailment under the sun. Snot-nosed children darted to and fro, playing with scrawny mongrels.

It was utter chaos, thought Hanno, but there was no denying that Hannibal had set himself a Herculean task. There were already tens of thousands of Roman troops in the area.

Quintus wasted no time. He hailed a passing centurion. 'Has the consul arrived from Rome?'

'You're behind the times! He got here four days ago.'

Quintus was unsurprised. Unlike them, Publius and his party would have been changing their mounts every day. 'Where are his headquarters?'

The centurion gave him an odd look, but did not ask why. While young, Quintus was clearly an equestrian. He pointed down the road. 'That way. It's about a mile.'

Quintus nodded his thanks. 'What news of Hannibal?'

Hanno stiffened. This was the question he had been burning to ask.

The centurion's face darkened. 'Well, believe it or not, the whoreson succeeded in crossing the Alps. Who'd have thought it?'

'Amazing.' Quintus did not want to look at Hanno in case he was gloating. 'What has he been up to since?'

'He attacked the Taurini stronghold of Taurasia, and massacred its inhabitants. Apparently, he's now on his way here, to Placentia. We're blocking his route to the scumbag Boii and Insubres, see?' The centurion half drew his gladius from its scabbard and slammed it home again. 'There'll be one hell of a fight very soon.'

'May Mars and Jupiter keep us in the palm of their hands,' said Quintus.

'Aye. Now, I'd best be off, or my tribune will string me up by my balls.' With a cordial nod, the centurion marched away.

Quintus and Hanno looked at each other. Neither spoke.

'You're taking up half the fucking road. Get out of the damn way!' shouted a man leading a train of mules.

They led their mounts to one side and into a gap between two stalls.

'This is it, then,' said Quintus unhappily.

'Yes,' Hanno muttered. He felt awful.

'What will you do?'

Hanno shrugged. 'Travel west until I run into some of our forces.'

Your forces, thought Quintus, not mine. 'The gods grant you a safe passage.'

'Thank you. May you find your father quickly.'

'I don't think that will be a problem,' Quintus replied, smiling.

'Even you would find it hard to get lost now,' joked Hanno.

Quintus laughed.

'I wish that we could part under different circumstances,' said Hanno.

'So do I,' answered Quintus passionately.

'But we both have to do our duty by our people.'

'Yes.'

'Maybe we'll meet again one day. In peacetime.' Hanno cringed inwardly. His words sounded false even to his own ears.

Quintus did not rebuke him, however. 'I would like that too, but it will never happen,' he said gently. 'Go well. Stay safe. May your gods protect you.'

'The same to you.' At last, Hanno's eyes filled with tears. Clumsily, he reached out and embraced Quintus. 'Thank you for saving me and Suniaton. I will never forget that,' he whispered.

Quintus' emotions welled up. He awkwardly clapped Hanno on the back. 'You saved my life too, remember?'

Hanno's nod was jerky.

'Come on,' said Quintus, growing businesslike. 'You need to get as far from here by nightfall as you can. No point having to try and explain yourself to one of our patrols, is there?'

Hanno drew back. 'No.'

'Help me up.' Quintus lifted his left foot.

Grateful for the distraction, Hanno linked his hands together so that Quintus could step up and climb on to his horse's back. When it was done, he forced a smile. 'Farewell.'

'Farewell.' Quickly, Quintus pulled his horse's head around and urged it on to the roadway.

Hanno watched as his friend was swallowed up by the mass of men jostling along on the muddy track. It was only when he could no longer see Quintus that Hanno realised he had forgotten to send a last farewell to Aurelia. Sadly, he clambered aboard his mule and headed in the opposite direction. Despite the inevitability of their parting, Hanno felt a void inside. Let us never meet again, he prayed. Unless it happens in peacetime.

A hundred paces away, Quintus felt the same way. Only now could he allow himself to grieve the loss of a friend. They had been through a great deal together. If Hanno were a Roman, Quintus thought, I would be proud to stand beside him in battle. Sadly, it was only the opposite that could ever come to pass. Jupiter, Greatest and Best, never let this happen, he prayed.

Not long after, Quintus found the consul's headquarters, a large pavilion surrounded by the cavalry tent lines. The *vexillum*, a red flag on a pole, made sure that every soldier could see Publius' position. A few questions guided Quintus in the direction of his father, whom he found outside his tent, talking to a pair of decurions. To his relief, Fabricius did not immediately explode. Instead he quietly dismissed the junior officers. The moment that they were gone, however, he rounded on Quintus. 'Look who it is!' Sarcasm dripped from his voice.

'Father.' Feeling distinctly nervous, Quintus dismounted. 'Are you well?'

'I'm fine,' Fabricius replied. His eyebrows arched. 'Surprised, though. Annoyed and disappointed too. You should be at home, looking after your mother and sister, not here.'

Quintus shuffled his feet.

'Not going to answer that charge?' his father snapped. 'Why are you not on a ship to Iberia? After all, that's where I should be.'

'I travelled to Rome first,' Quintus muttered. 'I was there when Publius spoke in the Curia. I caught a glimpse of you outside.'

Fabricius frowned. 'Why in Jupiter's name didn't you come up to me there?'

'The press was too great to reach you, Father. I didn't know where you were staying, or even that you were heading north with the consul,' Quintus lied. 'I found out later. It was easy enough to follow you.'

'I see. Fortuna must have been guiding your path. The tribesmen around here aren't the friendliest,' said Fabricius dourly. 'It's a shame that you didn't make yourself known to me in Rome. You'd already be in Capua by now, or my name isn't Gaius Fabricius.' His dark eyes regarded Quintus carefully. 'And so you travelled up here alone?'

Quintus cursed inwardly. This was going even worse than he'd expected. He was such a poor liar when asked a direct question. 'No, Father.'

'Who was with you? Gaius, probably. He listens to Martialis as little as you do to me.'

'No,' Quintus mumbled.

'Who, then?'

Dreading his father's response, Quintus said nothing.

Fabricius' anger bubbled over. 'Answer me!'

'Hanno.'

'Who?'

'One of our . . . your . . . slaves.'

Fabricius' face purpled. 'That's not enough! Do you expect me to remember the name of every damn one?'

'No, Father,' Quintus said quickly. 'He's the Carthaginian that I bought after the bear hunt.'

'Oh, him. Where is the dirtbag? Putting up your tent?'

'He's not here,' replied Quintus, stalling for time.

Fabricius' eyes opened wide with disbelief. 'Say that again.'

'He's gone, Father,' Quintus whispered.

'Louder! I can't hear you!'

A passing officer glanced over, and Quintus' mortification soared. 'He's gone, Father,' he said loudly.

'What a surprise!' Fabricius cried. 'Of course he was going to run away. What else would the dog do with a host of his countrymen so near? I bet that he waited until the very last moment before disappearing too. Congratulations! Hannibal has just gained himself another soldier.'

Quintus was stung by the truth in his father's words. 'It's not like that,' he said quietly.

'How so?' retorted Fabricius furiously.

'Hanno didn't run away.'

'He's dead then?' Fabricius demanded in a mocking tone.

'No, Father. I set him free,' Quintus blurted.

'*What?*'

With ebbing confidence, Quintus repeated himself.

Astonishment and disbelief mixed with the anger on Fabricius' face. 'This goes from bad to worse. How dare you?' Stepping closer, he slapped Quintus hard across the face.

He reeled backwards from the force of the blow. 'I'm sorry.'

'It's a little late for apologies, don't you think?'

'Yes, Father.'

'It is not within your power to act in this manner,' Fabricius ranted. 'My slaves belong to me, not you!'

'I know, Father,' Quintus muttered.

'So why did you do it? What in Hades were you thinking?'

'I owed him my life.'

Fabricius frowned. 'You're referring to what happened at Libo's hut?'

'Yes, Father. When he came back, Hanno could easily have turned on me. Joined the bandits. Instead, he saved my life.'

'That's still no reason to free him on a whim. Without my permission,' Fabricius growled.

'There's more to it than that.'

'I should damn well hope so!' Fabricius looked at him enquiringly. 'Well?'

Quintus snatched the brief respite from his father's tirade. 'Agesandros. He had it in for Hanno from the first moment I bought him. Don't you remember what happened when the Gaul hurt his leg?'

'An over-enthusiastic beating is no reason to free a slave,' Fabricius snapped. 'If it was, there would be no servile labour in the whole damn Republic.'

'I know it isn't, Father,' said Quintus humbly. 'But after your letter arrived in the spring, Agesandros planted a purse and a dagger among Hanno's belongings. Then he accused him of stealing them, and planning to kill us all before he fled. He was going to sell Hanno to the same owner who had bought his friend. They were to be forced to fight each other as gladiators at a munus, he said. And it was all a complete lie!'

Fabricius thought for a moment. 'What did your mother have to say?'

'She believed Agesandros,' Quintus answered reluctantly.

'Which should have been good enough for you,' Fabricius thundered.

'But he was lying, Father!'

Fabricius' brows lowered. 'Why would Agesandros lie?'

'I don't know, Father. But I'm certain that Hanno is no murderer!'

'You can't *know* something like that,' replied Fabricius dryly. Quintus took heart from the fact that some of the rage had gone from his voice. 'Never trust a slave totally.'

Quintus rallied his courage. 'In that case, how can you depend on Agesandros' word?'

'He's served me well for more than twenty years,' his father replied, a trifle defensively.

'So you'd trust him over me?'

'Watch your mouth!' Fabricius snapped. There was a short pause. 'Start at the beginning. Leave nothing out.'

Quintus realised that he had been granted a stay of execution. Taking a deep breath, he began. Remarkably, his father did not interrupt at all, even when Quintus related how Aurelia had set a fire in the granary, and how he and Gaius had freed Suniaton. When he fell silent, Fabricius stood, tapping his foot on the ground for several moments. 'Why did you decide to help the other Carthaginian?'

'Because Hanno would not leave without him,' Quintus answered. Then he added, passionately, 'He is my friend. I couldn't betray him.'

'Hold on!' interrupted Fabricius, ire creeping back into his voice. 'We're not talking about Gaius here. Freeing a slave without the permission of his owner is a crime, and you have done it twice over! This is a very serious matter.'

Quintus quailed before his father's fury. 'Of course, Father. I'm sorry.'

'Both of the slaves are long gone, if they have any sense,' mused Fabricius. 'Thanks to your impetuosity, I have been left more than a hundred didrachms out of pocket. So has the official's son in Capua.'

Quintus wanted to say that Gaius had tried to buy Suniaton, but his father's temper was at fraying point. Buttoning his lip, he nodded miserably.

'As your father, I am entitled to punish you how I choose,' Fabricius warned. 'Even to strike you dead.'

'I'm at your mercy, Father,' said Quintus, closing his eyes. Whatever might happen next, he was still glad that he'd let Hanno go.

'Although you and your sister have behaved outrageously, I heard the truth in your words – or at least the belief that you were speaking the truth. In other words, you did what you thought was right.'

Startled, Quintus opened his eyes. 'Yes, Father. So did Aurelia.'

'Which is why we'll say no more about it for the moment. The matter is far from settled, however.' Fabricius pursed his lips. 'And Agesandros will have some explaining to do when next I see him.'

I hope I'm there to see that, thought Quintus, his own anger at the Sicilian resurfacing.

'You still haven't explained why you abandoned your mother and sister to make your way here.' Fabricius pinned him with a hard stare.

'I thought the war might be over in a few months, like Flaccus said, Father. I didn't want to miss it,' Quintus said lamely.

'And that's a good enough reason to disobey my orders, is it?'

'No,' Quintus replied, flushing an ever deeper shade of red.

'Yet that's precisely what you did!' accused his father. He stared off into the distance. 'It's not as if I haven't got enough on my plate at the moment.'

'I'll get out of your way. Return home,' Quintus whispered.

'You'll do no such thing! The situation is far too dangerous.' Fabricius saw his surprise. 'Publius has decided to lead his forces over the river Padus, into hostile territory. A temporary bridge has already been thrown over to the far bank. Tomorrow morning, we march westward, towards Hannibal's army. No Roman forces are to be left behind, and the local Gauls can't be trusted. You'd have your throat cut within five miles of here.'

'What shall I do, then?' asked Quintus despondently.

'You will have to come with us,' his father replied, equally unhappily. 'You'll be safe in our camp until an opportunity presents itself to send you back to Capua.'

Quintus' spirits fell even further. The shame of it! To have reached Publius' army only to be prevented from fighting. It wasn't that surprising, though. His actions had stretched his father's goodwill to the limit. At least Hanno had got away, Quintus thought, counting himself lucky that Fabricius hadn't given him a good hiding.

'Fabricius? Where are you?' cried a booming voice.

'Mars above, that's all I need,' muttered Fabricius.

Astounded by his father's reaction, Quintus turned to see Flaccus emerge into view.

'There you are! Publius wants another meeting about—' Flaccus stopped in astonishment. 'Quintus? What a pleasant surprise!'

Quintus grinned guiltily. At least someone was pleased to see him.

'You sent for Quintus, I presume?' Flaccus didn't wait for Fabricius to answer. 'What an excellent idea! His timing is impeccable too.' He raised a clenched fist at Quintus. 'Tomorrow, we're going to teach those bastard guggas a lesson they'll never forget.'

'I didn't send for him,' answered Fabricius stiffly. 'He saw fit to leave his mother and sister on their own and turn up here without so much as a by your leave.'

'The rashness of youth!' demurred Flaccus with a smile. 'Nonetheless, you'll let him ride out with us in the morning?'

'I hadn't planned on it, no,' said Fabricius curtly.

'What?' Flaccus threw him an incredulous look. 'And deny your son a chance to blood himself? To take part in what could be one of our greatest cavalry victories ever? Publius' boy is to come along, and he's no older than Quintus here.'

'It's not that.'

'What is it, then?'

'It's none of your concern,' said Fabricius angrily.

Flaccus barely blinked at the rebuff. 'Come now,' he cajoled. 'Unless the lad has committed murder, surely he should be allowed to be part of this golden opportunity? This could be the glowing start to his career – a career that will only blossom once your family is allied to the Minucii.'

Furious, Fabricius considered his options. They were in this situation purely because of Flaccus' pushiness, yet it would look rude now for him to turn down Flaccus' proposal. It might also jeopardise Quintus' chances of advancement. Even when wedded to Aurelia, Flaccus would be under no legal obligation to help his brother-in-law. It was all down to goodwill. He made a show of looking pleased. 'Very well. I'll ask the consul for his permission to let Quintus join my unit.'

'Excellent!' cried Flaccus. 'Publius won't turn down a cavalryman of your son's quality.'

Quintus couldn't believe the change in his fortunes. 'Thank you,' he said, grinning at both men. 'I won't let you down, Father.'

'Consider yourself lucky,' Fabricius growled. He stabbed a finger into Quintus' chest. 'You're not out of trouble yet either.'

'The glory he'll win tomorrow will make you forget anything he's done,' declared Flaccus, giving Quintus a broad wink. 'Now, we'd best not keep Publius waiting any longer.'

'True,' replied Fabricius. He pointed at a nearby tent. 'There's an empty space in that one. Tell the men in it that I said you were to bunk in with them. We'll get you some equipment later.'

'Yes, Father. Thank you.'

Fabricius did not reply.

'Until tomorrow,' said Flaccus. 'We'll cover the field with gugga bodies!'

Instantly, an image of Hanno appeared in Quintus' mind's eye. Forcing a grin, he did his best to shove it away. Defeating the Carthaginians was all that mattered, he told himself.

Chapter XIX: Reunion

anno did not dare to try crossing the makeshift bridge over the Padus with his mount. He had tempted fate enough by riding out of the camp alone on his mule, a likely slave. There had to be at least two centuries of legionaries guarding the road that ran up to the crossing. No matter how dull their duty, Hanno doubted that they were stupid enough to let a dark-skinned man who spoke accented Latin pass by without question. He therefore rode west along the southern bank, searching for a suitable place to ford the river.

Winter gales had stripped the leaves from the trees, leaving the flat landscape stark and bare. It made it easy to spot movement of any kind. This suited Hanno down to the ground. Unarmed apart from a dagger, he had no desire to meet anyone until he crossed the river into the territory of the Insubres. They were mostly hostile towards the Romans. Even there, however, Hanno wanted to avoid human contact. In reality, he could trust no one but his own people, or the soldiers who fought for them. Although he was by no means safe yet, Hanno could not help feeling exhilarated. He could almost sense the presence of Hannibal's army nearby.

Hanno hardly dared to wonder if his own father and brothers were still alive, or with the Carthaginian forces. There was absolutely no way of telling. For all he knew, they could yet be in Iberia. Maybe they had been posted back to Carthage. What would he do if that were the case? Whom would he report to? At that moment, Hanno did not overly care. He had escaped, and, gods willing, would soon place himself under Hannibal's command: another soldier of Carthage.

For two days and nights, Hanno travelled west. He avoided settlements and farms, camping rough in dips and hollows where there was little chance of being discovered. Despite the severe cold, he forbore from lighting fires.

His blankets were sufficient to prevent frostbite, but not to allow much sleep. It didn't matter. Staying alert now was critical. Despite Hanno's weariness, each new day of freedom felt better than the last.

His luck continued to hold. Early on the third day, Hanno reached a crossing point over the Padus. A collection of small huts huddled around the ford, but there was no one about. The days were short, and work on the land had ceased until spring. Like most peasants at this time of year, the inhabitants went to bed shortly after sunset and rose late. Nonetheless, Hanno felt very vulnerable as he stripped off by the water's edge. Placing his clothing in his pack, he rolled up the oiled leather tightly and tied it with thongs. Then, naked as the day he was born, he led the protesting mule into the river. The water was shockingly cold. Hanno knew that if they didn't cross it fast, his muscles would freeze up and he would drown. Winter rainfall ensured that its level was high, however, and for a time, his mount struggled against the current. Hanno, who was holding on to its reins and swimming as hard as he could, felt panic swelling in his chest. Thankfully, the mule possessed enough strength to carry them both into the shallows on the far side, and from there, on to the bank. The biting wind struck Hanno savagely, setting his teeth to chattering. Fortunately, only a small amount of water had entered his pack, meaning that his clothes were mostly dry. He dressed quickly. Then, wrapping his blanket around himself for extra warmth, he remounted and resumed his journey.

The day wore on and Hanno's excitement grew. He was deep in Insubres territory; Hannibal's army could not be far away. Since he'd been captured by the pirates, it had seemed impossible that he would ever be in such a position. Thanks to Quintus, it was now a reality. Hanno prayed that his friend would come through the impending war unharmed. Naturally enough, he quickly returned to thoughts of a reunion with his family. For the first time, Hanno's attention lapsed.

A short time later, he was brought back to reality with a jolt. Halfway down into a hollow, Hanno heard a blackbird sounding its alarm call, sharp and insistent. Scanning the trees on either side, he could see no reason for its distress. Yet birds did not react like that without cause. Acid-tipped claws of fear clutched at his belly. This was the perfect place for an ambush. For bandits to attack and murder a lone traveller.

Terror filled Hanno as, in the same instant, a pair of javelins scudded out of the bushes to his left and flew over his head. Praying that his attackers were on foot, he dug his heels into his mule's sides. It responded to his fear, and pounded gamely up out of the dip. Several more javelins hissed into the air behind them, but when Hanno glanced over his shoulder, his hopes vanished entirely. A group of mounted figures had emerged from the cover on each side. Six of them at least, and on horses. There was no chance of outriding his pursuers on a mule. Hanno cursed savagely. This was surely the cruellest turn of fate since he'd been washed out to sea. To have gone through all that he had, only to be murdered by a bunch of brigands a few miles from where Hannibal's forces lay.

He wasn't surprised when more horses and riders appeared on the road ahead, blocking it entirely. Gripping the dagger that was his solitary weapon, Hanno prepared to sell his life dearly. As the horsemen approached, however, his heart leaped. He had not seen any Numidian cavalry since leaving Carthage, but there could be no mistaking their identity. What other mounted troops scorned the use of saddles, bridles and bits? Or wore open-sided tunics even in winter?

Even as he opened his mouth to greet the Numidians, another flurry of javelins was hurled in his direction. This time, two barely missed him. Frantically, Hanno raised both his hands in the air, palms outwards. 'Stop! I am Carthaginian,' he shouted in his native tongue. 'I am Carthaginian!'

His cry made no difference. More spears were launched, and this time one struck his mule in the rump. Rearing in pain, it threw Hanno to the ground. The air shot from his lungs, winding him. He was vaguely aware of his mount trotting away, limping heavily. Within the blink of an eye, he had been surrounded by a ring of jeering Numidians. Three jumped down and approached, javelins at the ready. What a way to die, Hanno thought bitterly. Killed by my own side because they don't even speak my language.

From nowhere, inspiration hit him. He'd learned a few words of the sibilant Numidian tongue once. 'Stop,' Hanno mumbled. 'I . . . friend.'

Looking confused, the trio of Numidians paused. A barrage of questions in their tongue followed. Hanno barely understood one word in ten of what the warriors were saying. 'I not Roman, I friend,' he repeated, over and over.

His protests weren't enough. Drawing back his foot, one of the tribesmen kicked Hanno in the belly. Stars flashed across his vision, and he nearly passed out from the pain. More blows landed, and he tensed, expecting at any moment to feel a javelin slide into his flesh.

Instead, an angry voice intervened.

The beating stopped at once.

Warily, Hanno looked up to see a rider with tightly curled black hair standing before him. Unusually for a Numidian, he was wearing a sword. An officer, thought Hanno dully.

'Did I hear you speaking Carthaginian?' the man demanded.

'Yes.' Relieved and surprised that someone present spoke his tongue, Hanno sat up. He winced in pain. 'I'm from Carthage.'

The other's eyebrows rose. 'What in Melqart's name are you doing alone in the middle of this godforsaken, freezing land?'

'I was sold into slavery among the Romans some time ago,' explained Hanno. 'Hearing the news of Hannibal's invasion, I escaped to join him.'

The Numidian didn't look convinced. 'Who are you?'

'My name is Hanno,' he said proudly. 'I am a son of Malchus, who serves as a senior officer among our Libyan spearmen. If I reach Hannibal's army, I hope to be reunited with him, and my brothers.'

There was a long silence, and Hanno felt his fear return. Do not desert me now, great Tanit, he prayed.

'An unlikely story. Who's to say that you are not a spy?' the officer mused out loud. Several of his more eager men lifted their javelins, and Hanno's heart sank. If they killed him now, no one would ever know.

'Hold!' snapped the officer. 'If this man has really spent much time among the Romans, he may be useful to Hannibal.' He grinned at Hanno. 'And if you are telling the truth, I suspect that your father, whether he is with the army or no, would rather see you alive than dead.'

Hanno's joy knew no bounds. 'Thank you,' he said.

The officer barked an order and the Numidians swarmed in, hauling Hanno to his feet. His wrists were bound with rope, but he was offered no further violence. As the warriors mounted up, Hanno was picked up and thrown roughly across the neck of a horse, in front of its rider. He didn't protest. With his mule injured, there was no other way of returning to the Carthaginian camp at speed. At least they weren't dragging him behind one of the mounts.

As the Numidians began to ride west, Hanno gave thanks to every god he could think of, but most importantly to Tanit, whom he'd forgotten to address before leaving his home in Carthage.

He wasn't out of the woods yet, but he felt that she was smiling on him once more.

Upon reaching Hannibal's camp, Hanno was lowered to the ground. He gazed around him in wonderment, absolutely exhilarated to see a Carthaginian host so near the Italian border. His heart throbbed with an unquenchable joy. He was back with his people! Yet Hanno was concerned by the army's size. It was far smaller than he'd expected. He was alarmed too by the soldiers' faces. Suffering was etched deep into every single one. Most had unkempt beards, and looked half starved. The pack animals, and particularly the elephants, looked even worse. Hanno shot a worried glance at the Numidian officer. 'The crossing of the Alps must have been terrible,' he said.

'You cannot even imagine it,' the Numidian replied with a scowl. 'Hostile natives. Landslides. Ice. Snow. Starvation. Between desertions and fatalities, we lost nearly twenty-five thousand men in a month. Practically half our army.'

Hanno's mouth fell open in horror. Immediately, he thought of his father and brothers, who could easily be among the dead. He caught the Numidian watching him. 'Why tell me this?' he stuttered.

'I can say what I like. The Romans will never find out,' replied the other amiably. 'It's not as if you could escape my men on foot.'

Hanno swallowed. 'No.'

'Just as well you were telling the truth about who you were, eh?'

Hanno met the Numidian's gimlet stare. A sudden pang of terror struck him. What if no one could be found to vouch for his identity? 'Yes, it is,' he snapped, praying that the gods would not dash the cup of success from his lips at this late stage. 'Take me to the Libyans' tent lines.'

With a mocking bow, the Numidian led the way. He hailed the first spearman they met. 'We are looking for an officer by the name of . . .' He looked questioningly at Hanno.

'Malchus.'

To Hanno's utter joy, the man jerked a thumb behind him. 'His tent is three ranks back. It's bigger than the rest.'

'So far, so good,' said the officer, dismounting gracefully. He indicated that Hanno should follow him. Three of his warriors took up the rear, their javelins at the ready. Carefully, they weaved their way between the closely packed tents.

'This looks like the one.' The officer came to a halt outside a large leather pavilion. It was held up by multiple guy ropes staked into the ground. A pair of spearmen stood on guard outside.

A volcanic wave of emotion battered Hanno. Terror that his father would not be within. Joy that he might. Relief that, after all his ordeals, he was perhaps about to be reunited with his family. He turned to the officer. 'Stay here.'

'Eh? You're not in charge,' the Numidian growled. 'Until I hear otherwise, you're a damn prisoner.'

'My hands are tied! Where am I going to go?' Hanno snapped back. 'Stick a fucking spear in my back if I even try. But I'm walking over there on my own.'

The Numidian saw the steel in Hanno's eyes. Suddenly, he realised that his captive might outrank him considerably. There was a gruff nod. 'We'll wait here,' he said.

Hanno made no acknowledgement. Stiff-backed, he walked towards the tent.

One of the spearmen started forward. 'What's your business?' he demanded in a brusque tone.

'Are these Malchus' quarters?' asked Hanno politely.

'Who wants to know?' came the surly reply.

The last of Hanno's patience ran out. 'Damn your insolence,' he snarled. 'Father? Are you there?'

The spearman, who had advanced a step, stopped in his tracks.

'Father?' called Hanno again.

Someone coughed inside the tent. 'Bostar? Is that you?'

Hanno began to grin uncontrollably. Bostar had also survived!

A moment later, Malchus emerged, fully dressed for battle. He looked at his guards first, and frowned. 'Who called my name?'

'It was I, Father,' answered Hanno joyfully, stepping forward. 'I have returned.'

Malchus went as white as a sheet. 'H-Hanno?' he stuttered.

With tears of happiness filling his eyes, Hanno nodded.

'Praise all the gods. This is a miracle!' cried Malchus. 'But what are you doing, tied up like this?'

Hanno jerked his head at the Numidians, who were looking decidedly awkward. 'They weren't sure whether to believe my story or not.'

Drawing his dagger, Malchus sawed at the ropes that bound Hanno's wrists. The instant they had dropped away, he drew his son into his arms. Great shudders of emotion racked his frame, and for long moments, he clung to Hanno with a grip of iron. Hanno delightedly returned the embrace. Finally, Malchus stepped back to study him. 'It is you,' he breathed. A rare smile split his face. 'How you've grown. You're a man!'

In contrast, Hanno could not get over how his father had aged. Deep lines now creased his forehead and cheeks. There were bags of exhaustion under his eyes, and his hair was more grey than black. But Malchus had a new lightness about him, an air Hanno had not seen since well before his mother's death. It was, he realised with a thrill, because of his return. 'I heard you call out Bostar's name. Is Sapho here too?'

'Yes, yes, they both are. The pair of them should be back any moment,' Malchus replied, filling Hanno with more joy. He glanced at the Numidians. 'To whom do I owe my thanks?'

Saluting, the officer hurried forward. 'Zamar, section leader, at your service, sir.'

'Where did you find him?'

'About ten miles east of here, sir.' Zamar shot an uneasy glance at Hanno. 'I'm sorry for the rough treatment, sir.'

'It's all right,' Hanno replied. 'Your men couldn't be expected to know that I was Carthaginian. At least you stopped them from killing me, and listened to my story.'

Zamar dipped his head in gratitude.

'Wait here,' ordered Malchus. Hurrying into the tent, he emerged with a large leather purse. 'A token of my appreciation,' he said, handing it over.

Zamar's eyes widened as he accepted the clinking gift, and his men exchanged excited looks. It didn't matter what was inside. The bag's obvious weight spoke volumes. 'Thank you, sir. I am delighted to have been of service.' Zamar made a deep bow, and withdrew.

'Come inside,' Malchus muttered. Ushering Hanno within, he fussed over him as he hadn't done in years. 'Are you hungry? Thirsty?'

Gratefully accepting a cup of wine, Hanno took a seat on a three-legged stool he remembered from their house in Carthage. Malchus sat opposite. Neither could take their eyes off the other, or stop smiling. 'It's wonderful to see you,' Hanno said.

'Likewise,' Malchus murmured. 'I had given you up for dead. To first of all survive a storm at sea . . . well, Melqart must have laid his hand upon you and Suniaton.' His brows lowered. 'Is Suni dead?'

Hanno grinned. 'No! He couldn't travel because he was injured, but he is being cared for by a friend. Soon he will be making his way to Carthage.'

Malchus' frown cleared. 'The gods be thanked. Now, you must tell me what happened.'

Hanno laughed. 'I could say the same thing, Father, seeing you here, on the wrong side of the Alps.'

'That is a story worth hearing,' Malchus agreed. 'But I want to listen to yours first.' He cocked his head. The sound of approaching voices carried inside, and he smiled. 'I guess it will have to wait a while. You won't want to be telling it twice.'

Hanno's face lit up. 'Is that Sapho and Bostar?'

'Yes.' His father winked. 'Just sit there. Don't say a word until they see you.'

Hanno watched excitedly as Malchus moved towards the front of the tent.

A moment later, two familiar figures entered. Hanno had to grip his stool to stop himself leaping up to greet them. 'Good news, Father. Apparently, more than ten thousand Gaulish warriors are on their way to join us,' Bostar announced.

'Excellent news,' Malchus replied offhandedly.

'Aren't you pleased?' asked Sapho.

'We have an unexpected visitor.'

Sapho snorted. 'Who could be more interesting than that information?'

Silently, Malchus turned and indicated Hanno.

Sapho blanched. 'Hanno?'

'No!' Bostar exclaimed. 'It cannot be true!'

Hanno could not contain himself any longer. He leaped up and ran to greet his brothers. Laughing and crying at the same time, Bostar wrapped him in a huge bear hug. 'We thought you were dead.'

Laughing too, Hanno managed to extricate himself from Bostar's grip. 'I should be, but the gods did not forget me.' He reached out to Sapho, who awkwardly drew him into an embrace. Surely he can't still be angry about what happened in Carthage? Hanno wondered.

Sapho stepped back after only a moment. 'How in hell did you get here?' he cried.

'Where is Suniaton?' Bostar demanded.

A stream of questions poured from their lips.

Malchus intervened. 'Let him tell the whole story.'

Hanno cleared his throat. All he could think of was the manner in which he'd left the family house on that fateful morning. He looked guiltily at Malchus. 'I'm sorry, Father,' he said. 'I ought never to have run off like that. I should have stayed to do my duty.'

'The meeting was of small consequence anyway. Like most of them,' Malchus admitted with a sigh. 'If I had been more understanding, you might have been less bored by such things. Put it behind you, and tell us how you survived that storm.'

Taking a deep breath, Hanno began. His father and brothers hung off his every word. When he explained how he and Suniaton had been captured by the pirates, Sapho let out a grim chuckle. 'They got their just deserts eventually.'

'Eh?' Hanno gave his brother a confused look.

'I'll explain later,' said Malchus. 'Go on.'

Quelling his curiosity, Hanno obeyed. His family's fury over the pirates was as nothing compared with their reaction to his purchase by Quintus.

'Roman bastard!' Sapho spat. 'I'd love to have him here right now.'

Hanno was surprised by the defensive feelings that flared up at once. 'Not all Romans are bad. If it wasn't for him and his sister, I wouldn't be here.'

Sapho scoffed. Even Bostar looked unconvinced. Malchus alone did not react.

'It's true,' Hanno cried. 'You haven't heard all of my story yet.'

'True,' admitted Bostar.

Sapho raised an eyebrow. 'Surprise us,' he said.

Amazed by the speed at which his customary anger towards his eldest brother had returned, Hanno continued with his story. He emphasised how Quintus had engineered not only his escape, but that of Suniaton, and how the young equestrian had accompanied him to Cisalpine Gaul rather than be reunited with his father in Rome.

'He sounds like a decent person. So does his sister, for all that she is a child. That in turn means that their father must be an honourable man,' Malchus agreed. His jaw hardened. 'It is a shame that the Roman Senate does not possess the same morals. You heard from the horse's mouth how the whoresons demanded Hannibal be handed over to receive Roman "justice", how they lied about us breaking the treaty which confined us to the area below the River Iberus. Their arrogance is without parallel! That's before dragging up Sicily, Sardinia and Corsica.'

Sapho and Bostar growled in agreement.

Hanno felt a momentary sadness. Yet it was time to forget the kindness he had received. His father's words had made old resentment bubble up from the depths. He took a deep breath and exhaled slowly. Finally, I am where I longed to be, he thought. With my family. With Hannibal's army. And I am a soldier of Carthage. The Romans are our enemies. So be it. 'You're right, Father. What is Hannibal's plan?'

Malchus gave him a wolfish smile. 'To attack! We continue our march east tomorrow, in search of their legions.'

'I know exactly where they are,' Hanno replied, trying, and failing, not to think of Quintus.

'We'd best take you to Hannibal then,' said Malchus, looking pleased.

'Really?'

'Of course. He'll want to hear everything you know.'

Hanno turned to his brothers. 'I'm to meet Hannibal!' he cried delightedly. Bostar grinned, but Hanno caught Sapho shooting him a sour glance. Old emotions flared up yet again. 'What?' he demanded. 'Are you not pleased?'

Sapho blinked. 'Yes,' he muttered.

'It doesn't look like it,' said Hanno hotly.

'That's because he isn't,' Bostar growled. 'Our older brother gets jealous of anyone who might win favour from our general.'

The veins in Sapho's neck bulged with fury. 'Fuck you,' he snapped.

'Sapho!' shouted Malchus. 'Curb your tongue! You too, Bostar. Can we not forget our differences for once, on this most joyful of days?'

Shame-faced, Sapho and Bostar nodded.

Taking Hanno by the hand, Malchus led him away. 'Come on,' he ordered over his shoulder. Pointedly ignoring each other, Sapho and Bostar followed.

Hanno couldn't get over the level of animosity between his brothers. What on earth had happened between them? He was amazed too at the ease with which Sapho still got his back up. Seeing Hannibal's tent in the distance, Hanno put his concerns from his mind. He was going to meet the finest Carthaginian general in history. The man who dared to attack Rome on its own territory.

With a ragtag, half-starved army, his cynical side added. Hanno could not let go of this worrying thought as his father led him and his brothers onward. How could they ever match the numbers of soldiers Rome could call upon?

Soon they had reached a large open area before their general's head-quarters. The place was thronged. Hanno's eyes widened. Flanking the perimeter were hundreds of soldiers from all over the Mediterranean, men whom he'd heard much about, but never seen. Numidian and Iberian infantry mixed with Lusitanians. Spiky-haired, bare-chested Gauls stood shoulder to shoulder with Balearic slingers and Ligurian warriors. There were several nationalities of cavalrymen: Iberian, Gaulish and Numidian. Outside the main tent stood a large group of senior officers, resplendent in their polished muscled cuirasses, pteryges and crested helmets. Hannibal's purple cloak made him easy to pick out. A group of musicians was pos-itioned nearby, their instruments at the ready: curved ceramic horns and carnyxes, vertical trumpets made of bronze, each topped by a depiction of a wild boar.

Hanno glanced at his father. 'What's going on?'

Even Sapho and Bostar looked confused.

Frustratingly, Malchus did not answer. He walked on, up to the party of officers. A quick word in the ear of one of Hannibal's bodyguards saw them led straight to their leader's side. Recognising Malchus, Hannibal smiled. Hanno felt as if he were in a dream come true.

Malchus saluted. 'A word, if I may, sir?'

'Of course. Make it quick, though,' Hannibal replied.

'Yes, sir. You know two of my sons, Sapho and Bostar,' said Malchus. 'But there is a third, Hanno.'

Hannibal gave Hanno a curious look. 'I seem to remember a tragedy at sea in which he'd been lost.'

'You have a fine memory, sir. I discovered afterwards, however, that by some miracle, Hanno had not been drowned. Instead, he and his friend were found adrift by some pirates. They sold both into slavery. In Italy.'

Hannibal's eyebrows rose. 'This couldn't be him?'

Malchus grinned. 'It is, sir.'

'Gods above!' Hannibal exclaimed. 'Come here!'

Self-conscious in his ragged, filthy clothes, Hanno did as he was told.

Hannibal appraised him for several, breath-holding moments. 'You have the look of Malchus all right.'

Hanno didn't dare reply. His heart was thumping off his ribs like that of a wild bird.

'How did you escape?'

'My owner's son let me go, sir.'

'Did he, by Melqart's beard? Why?'

'I saved his life once, sir.'

'Intriguing.' Hannibal stroked his chin. 'Have you travelled far?'

'No, sir. He released me near Placentia.'

'You are welcome. Your father and brothers are valuable officers. I hope that you will be too.'

Hanno made an awkward half-bow. 'I will do my best, sir.'

Hannibal made a gesture of dismissal.

'Wait, sir,' said Malchus eagerly. 'Hanno's awe at meeting you has curdled his brains. He didn't say that Placentia is where Publius and his army were camped.'

Hannibal's face came alive with interest. 'Publius, you say? One of the Scipiones?'

'Yes, sir,' Hanno replied, aware that every officer within earshot was now listening. 'After missing you at the Rhodanus, he returned to Italy with all speed.'

There was a general gasp of dismay.

'Has he brought his entire army with him?' asked Hannibal softly.

'No, sir. He sent it to Iberia, under the command of his brother.'

'A shrewd general, then.' Hannibal let out a slow breath. 'Hasdrubal and Hanno will also have a fight on their hands. It is to be expected, I suppose.' He fixed Hanno with his dark eyes again. 'What of Publius now?'

'He has thrown a bridge over the Padus, and was intending to march west on the day I fled.'

Hannibal leaned forward. 'When was that?'

'Three days ago, sir.'

'So he cannot be far away. Excellent news!' Hannibal smacked a fist into his palm. 'What of his forces?'

Hanno did his best to recount all that he had seen and heard since leaving Rome.

'Well done, young man,' said Hannibal when he was done, making Hanno flush beetroot. 'We shall face the first of our great tests soon. What we are about to observe now seems even more apt. Stay here with me and watch, if you will.'

Stuttering his thanks, Hanno stood with Hannibal, Malchus and his brothers and watched as dozens of prisoners were led out into the open area before them.

'Who are they?' Hanno asked.

'Allobroges and Vocontii, prisoners taken during the passage of the Alps,' replied his father.

Hanno's stomach clenched. The men looked terrified.

A fanfare from the musicians' horns and carnyxes prevented any further conversation. Hannibal stood forth when it finished. At once an expectant hush fell over the gathered troops. Everyone watched as a line of slaves carried out bronze trays, some of which were laden with glittering mail shirts. On others, helmets were piled high. There were gold arm rings and torcs, fine cloaks decorated with wolf fur and gilt-handled swords.

Hannibal let the prisoners feast their eyes on the treasure before he spoke. 'You have been brought here to make a simple choice.' He paused to allow his message to be relayed to the captives. 'I will offer six men the chance to win their freedom. You will divide into pairs, and fight each other to the death. The three who survive will receive a good horse, their choice of everything on show and a guarantee that they will ride out of here unharmed. Those who do not volunteer will be sold as slaves.' Again Hannibal waited.

A moment later, the warriors began shouting and raising their clenched fists in the air.

The lead interpreter turned to Hannibal. 'They all want the honour, sir. Every last one.'

Hannibal smiled broadly. 'Announce that to my troops,' he ordered.

A loud sigh of appreciation rose from the watching soldiers as the Allobroges' reply was translated.

Malchus bent to whisper in Hanno's ear. 'Single combat to the death is much revered among the Gauls. This end is far superior to a life of slavery.'

Hanno still didn't understand.

'I will not allow every man to do this,' Hannibal proclaimed. 'Form up in two lines.' He waited as the prisoners were shoved into position. 'Pick out every fourth man until you have six,' he bellowed. His command was obeyed at once, and the remainder of the captives were shepherded to one side. The half-dozen warriors who had been chosen were each handed a sword and shield and, at a signal, were ordered to begin fighting. They went at each other like men possessed, and soon first blood had been spilled on the rock-hard ground.

'What's the point of this?' Sapho muttered after a few moments. 'We should just kill them all and have done.'

'Your damn response to everything,' Bostar retorted angrily.

'Shhh!' hissed Malchus. 'Hannibal does nothing by accident.'

Again Hanno was surprised by the degree of acrimony between his brothers, but he was granted no chance to dwell on this troubling development.

The duels were short, and savage. Before long, three bloodied warriors stood over the bodies of their opponents, waiting for Hannibal's promise to be fulfilled. And it was. Each man was allowed his choice of the rich goods on the trays, before selecting a horse from those tethered nearby. Then, with the cheers of everyone present ringing in their ears, they were allowed to leave.

'Even more than this can be yours,' shouted Hannibal to his men. 'For you the prize of victory is not to possess horses and cloaks, but to be the most envied of mankind, masters of all the wealth of Rome.'

The immense roar that followed his words rose high into the winter sky.

Impressed by Hannibal's tactic, Hanno glanced at Bostar.

'He will take us to the enemy's very gates,' said his brother.

'That's right,' declared Malchus.

'Where we'll slaughter every last one of the whoresons,' Sapho snarled.

Hanno's spirits soared. Rome *would* be defeated. He felt sure of it.

Chapter XX: Setbacks

Some days later, Quintus was huddled around a campfire with a group of his new comrades. It was a dank, cold afternoon. A gusty wind set lowering clouds scudding over the camp, threatening snow and increasing the general misery.

'I still can't believe it,' moaned Licinius, a garrulous Tarentine who was one of Quintus' tent mates. 'To have lost our first battle against the guggas. It's shameful.'

'It was only a skirmish,' said Quintus morosely.

'Maybe so,' agreed Calatinus, another of the men who shared their tent. Sturdily built, he was a year older than Quintus, but of similar outlook. 'It was a damn big one, though. I bet you're all glad to be sitting here now, eh?' He nodded as his companions shook their heads in agreement. 'Look at our casualties! Most of our cavalry and hundreds of *velites* killed. Six hundred legionaries taken prisoner, and Publius gravely injured. Hardly a good start, was it?'

'Too true,' said Cincius, their last tent mate, a huge, ruddy-faced man with a shock of red hair. 'We've also retreated since. What must Hannibal think of us?'

'Why in Hades did we even pull back?' Licinius demanded. 'After the bridge had been destroyed, the Carthaginians had no way of crossing the Ticinus to get at us.'

Calatinus made sure no one else was in earshot. 'I reckon the consul panicked. It's not surprising, really, with him being out of action and all.'

'How would you know what Publius thinks?' Quintus challenged irritably. 'He's far from a fool.'

'As if you'd know what the consul's like, new boy,' Cincius snapped.

Quintus scowled, but had the wisdom not to reply. Cincius looked ready for a fight, and he was twice Quintus' size.

'Why didn't Publius take his chance when Hannibal offered battle before our camp?' Cincius went on. 'What an opportunity to miss, eh?'

There was a gloomy mutter of agreement.

'I say it's downright cowardly,' said Cincius, warming to his theme.

Quintus' anger flared. 'It's best to fight on the ground of one's choosing, at a time of one's choosing,' he declared, remembering what his father had said. 'You all know that! At the moment, we can do neither, and with Publius injured, that position is unlikely to change in the near future. It made far more sense to remain in a position of security, here in the camp. Consider what might happen otherwise.'

Cincius glared at Quintus, but, seeing the others subside into a grumpy silence, chose to say no more for the moment.

Quintus felt no happier. While Publius' courage was in little doubt, that of Flaccus was a different matter. It had taken a sea change in his view of his prospective brother-in-law as a hero even to countenance such a thought, but the reality of what had happened at the Ticinus could not be denied. Flaccus had ridden out with the cavalry on the ill-fated reconnaissance mission at his own request. Still ecstatic about being allowed to accompany the patrol, Quintus had been there too. He and his father had seen Flaccus as the clash began, but not after that. He hadn't reappeared until afterwards, when the battered remnants of the patrol retreated over the River Ticinus and reached the Roman camp. Apparently, he'd been swept out of harm's way by the tide of battle. Seeing that the Carthaginians had the upper hand, Flaccus had ridden for help. Naturally, the senior tribunes had declined to lead their legions, an infantry force, across a temporary bridge to face an enemy entirely made up of cavalry. What else could he have done? Flaccus had earnestly asked.

Of course there was no way of questioning Flaccus' account. Events were moving apace. They would just have to accept it. While Fabricius had not said as much to Quintus, he was clearly troubled by the possibility that Flaccus was a coward. Quintus felt the same way. Although he'd been terrified during the fight, at least he had stood his ground and fought the enemy. Aurelia must not marry a man, however well connected, who did not stick by his comrades in battle. Quintus poked a stick into the fire and tried not to think about it. He was annoyed to realise that the others had resumed their doleful conversation.

'My groom was drinking with some of the legionaries who guard Publius' tent,' said Licinius. 'They said that a huge Carthaginian fleet has attacked Lilybaeum in Sicily.'

'No!' exclaimed Cincius.

Licinius nodded mournfully. 'There's no question of Sempronius Longus coming to our relief now.'

'How can you be so sure?' demanded Quintus.

'The soldiers swore on their mothers' graves it was true.'

Quintus gave him a dubious look. 'Why haven't we heard it from anyone else, then?'

'It's supposed to be top secret,' muttered Licinius.

'Well, *I* heard that the entire Boii tribe is marching north to join Hannibal,' interjected Cincius. 'If that's right, we'll be caught in a pincer attack between them and the guggas.'

Quintus remembered what his father had told him. A monstrous calf, which was somehow turned inside out to expose all of its internal organs, had been cut out of a cow that could not give birth on a farm nearby. The damn thing had been alive too. An officer whom Fabricius knew had seen it while on patrol. Stop it, thought Quintus, setting his jaw. 'Let's not get overexcited,' he advised. 'These stories are all too far-fetched.'

'Are they? What if the gods are angry with us?' retorted Licinius. 'I went to the temple of Placentia to make an offering yesterday, and the priests said that the sacred chickens would not eat. What better evidence do you need?'

Quintus' anger overflowed. 'Should we just surrender to Hannibal?'

Licinius flushed. 'Of course not!'

Quintus rounded on Cincius, who shook his head. 'Shut your damn mouths, then! Talk like that is terrible for morale. We're equestrians, remember? The ordinary soldiers look to us to set an example, not to put the fear of Hades in their hearts.'

Shame-faced, the others took a sudden interest in their sandals.

'I've had enough of your whingeing,' Quintus growled. He got up. 'See you later.' Without waiting for a response, he stalked off. His father would be able to shed a more positive light on what was going on. Quintus hoped so, because he was struggling with a real sense of despondency. He hid it well, but the savage clash with Hannibal's deadly Numidian horsemen had shaken him to the core. They were all lucky to have survived. No wonder his comrades were susceptible to the rumours sweeping the camp. Quintus had to work hard not to let his own fear become overwhelming.

His father was not in his tent. One of the sentries said that he'd gone to the consul's headquarters. The walk would do him good, Quintus decided. Blow out the cobwebs. His route took him past the tents of the Cenomani, local Gaulish tribesmen who fought for Rome. There were more than two thousand of the tribesmen, mostly infantry but with a scattering of cavalry. They were a clannish lot, and the language barrier compounded this difference. There was, however, a palpable air of comradeship between them and the Romans, which Quintus had come to enjoy. He hailed the first warrior he saw, a strapping brute who was sitting on a stool outside his tent. To his surprise, the man looked away, busying himself with the sword he was oiling. Quintus thought nothing of it, but a moment later, the same thing happened again. A bunch of warriors not ten steps from where he was walking gave him cold, stony stares, before turning their backs.

It's nothing, Quintus told himself. Scores of their men were killed the other day too. Half of them have probably lost a father or a brother.

'Aurelia! Aurelia!'

Atia's voice dragged Aurelia reluctantly from a pleasing dream, which had involved both Quintus and Hanno. Importantly, they'd still been friends. Despite the impossibility of this situation, and the urgency in her mother's tone, she was in a good mood. 'What is it, Mother?'

'Get out here!'

Aurelia shot out of bed. Pulling open her door, she was surprised to see Gaius standing in the atrium with her mother. Both looked decidedly serious. Suddenly self-conscious, Aurelia darted back and threw a light tunic over her woollen nightdress. Then she hurried out of her bedroom. 'Gaius,' she cried. 'How nice to see you.'

He bobbed his head awkwardly. 'And you, Aurelia.'

His grave manner made Aurelia's stomach lurch. She glanced at her mother and was horrified to see that her eyes were bright with tears. 'W-what is it?' Aurelia stammered.

'Word has come from Cisalpine Gaul,' said Gaius. 'It's not good.'

'Has our army been defeated?' Aurelia asked in surprise.

'Not exactly,' replied Gaius. 'But there was a big skirmish near the River Ticinus several days ago. Hannibal's Numidians caused heavy casualties among our cavalry and velites.'

Aurelia felt faint. 'Is Father all right?'

'We don't know.' Her mother's eyes were dark pools of sorrow.

'The situation is still very confused,' muttered Gaius. 'He's probably fine.'

'Heavy casualties,' repeated Aurelia slowly. 'How heavy, exactly?'

There was no answer.

She stared at him in disbelief. 'Gaius?'

'They say that out of three thousand riders, perhaps five hundred made it back to camp,' he answered, avoiding her gaze.

'How in the name of Hades can you say that Father is alive, then?' Aurelia shouted. 'It's far more likely that he's dead.'

'Aurelia!' barked Atia. 'Gaius is just trying to give us some hope.'

Gaius flushed. 'I'm sorry.'

Atia reached out to take his hand. 'There's nothing to apologise for. You have ridden out here at first light to bring us what information there is. We're very grateful.'

'I'm not! How could I be grateful for such news?' Aurelia yelled. Sobbing wildly, she ran towards the front door. Ignoring the startled doorman, she pulled it open and plunged outside. She ignored the cries that followed her.

Aurelia's feet led her to the stables. They had long been her refuge when feeling upset. She went straight to the solitary horse of her father's that had been left behind. A sturdy grey, it had been lame at the time of his departure. Seeing her, it whinnied in greeting. At once Aurelia's sorrow burst its banks and she dissolved in floods of tears. For a long time, she stood sobbing, her mind filled with images of her father, whom she would never see again. It was only when she felt the horse nibbling at her hair that Aurelia managed to regain some control. 'You want an apple, don't you?' she whispered, stroking its nose. 'And I've stupidly come empty-handed. Wait a moment. I'll get you one.'

Grateful for the interruption, Aurelia went to the food store at the end of the stables. Picking the largest apple she could find, she walked back.

The horse's eagerly pricked ears and nickers of excitement made her sorrow surge back with a vengeance, however. Aurelia calmed herself with the only thing she could think of. 'At least Quintus is safe in Iberia,' she whispered. 'May the gods watch over him.'

Fabricius was closeted with Publius, so Quintus didn't manage to meet with his father until later in the afternoon. When told about Quintus' comrades' scaremongering, Fabricius' reaction was typically robust. 'Despite the rumours, Publius is doing fine. He'll be up and about in a couple of months. The rumour about a Carthaginian fleet attacking Sempronius Longus I also know to be untrue. Publius would have mentioned it to me. It'd be the same if he'd had any intelligence about the Boii rising up. As for these bad omens – has a single one of your companions actually witnessed one?' Fabricius laughed as Quintus shook his head. 'Of course not. Apart from that calf, which was just a freak of nature, no one ever has. The chickens in Jupiter's temple might not be eating, but that's to be expected. Poultry are frail bloody creatures. They're forever falling sick, especially in weather like this.' He pointed to his head, and then his heart, and last of all at his sword. 'Trust in these before you worry about what other men say.'

Quintus was heartened by Fabricius' attitude. He was also grateful that his father no longer mentioned sending him home. Nothing had been said since the defeat at the Ticinus. Whether it was because of the number of riders who had fallen, or because Fabricius had become reconciled to the idea of him serving in the cavalry, Quintus did not know – or care. His good humour was added to by the bellyful of wine and hearty stew that his father had provided, and he left in much better spirits than he'd arrived.

His good mood did not last long, however. The currents of air that whipped around Quintus as he struggled back towards his tent were even more vicious than earlier in the day. They cut clean through his cloak, chilling his flesh to the bone. It was so easy to imagine the gods sending the storm down as punishment. There was an awful inevitability about the snow that began falling a moment later. His worries, only recently allayed, returned with a vengeance.

What few soldiers were about rapidly vanished from sight. Quintus couldn't wait to climb beneath his blankets himself, where he could try to forget it all. He was amazed, therefore, to see the Cenomani tribesmen outside. They stood around blazing fires, their arms around each other's shoulders, singing low, sorrowful chants. The warriors were probably mourning their dead, thought Quintus, shivering. He left them to it.

Licinius was first to catch Quintus' eye when he entered the tent. 'Sorry about earlier,' he muttered from the depths of his blankets. 'I should have kept my mouth shut.'

'Don't worry about it. We were all feeling down,' Quintus replied, shedding his damp cloak. He moved to his bedroll. It lay alongside that of Calatinus, who also gave him a sheepish look. 'You might be interested to know that Publius knows nothing of a Carthaginian fleet attacking Sicily.'

An embarrassed grin creased Calatinus' face. 'Well, if he hasn't heard of it, we have nothing to worry about.'

'What about the Boii?' challenged Cincius aggressively.

Quintus grinned. 'No. Good news, eh?'

Cincius' glower slowly faded away.

'Excellent,' said Calatinus, sitting up. 'So we just have to wait until Longus gets here.'

'I think we should raise a toast to that day,' Cincius announced. He nodded at Quintus as if to say that their disagreement had been forgotten. 'Who's interested?'

There was a chorus of agreement, and Quintus groaned. 'I can feel the hangover already.'

'Who cares? There's no chance of any action!' Cincius leaped up and headed for the table where they kept their food and wine.

'True enough,' Quintus muttered. 'Why not, then?'

The four comrades were late getting to sleep. Despite his drunken state, Quintus was troubled by bad dreams. The most vivid involved squadrons of Numidian horsemen pursuing him across an open plain. Eventually, drenched in sweat, he sat up. It was pitch black in the tent, and freezing cold. Yet Quintus welcomed the chill air that moved across his face and arms, distracting him from the drumbeat pounding in his head. He squinted at the brazier, barely making out the last glowing embers. Yawning, he threw back the covers. If the fire was fed now, it might last until morning.

As he stood, Quintus heard a faint noise outside. Surprised, he pricked his ears. It was the unmistakable crunching of snow beneath a man's feet, but rather than the measured tread of a sentry, this was being made by someone moving with great care. Someone who did not want to be heard.

Instinctively, Quintus picked up his sword. On either side and to the rear, the next tents were half a dozen paces away. In front, a narrow path increased that distance to perhaps ten. This was where the sound was coming from. Quintus padded forward in his bare feet. All his senses were on high alert. Next, he heard whispering. Adrenaline surged through him. This was not right. Groping his way back through the darkness, Quintus reached Calatinus and grabbed his shoulder. 'Wake up,' he hissed.

The only answer he got was an irritated groan.

At once the noise outside stopped.

Quintus' heart thumped with fear. He might have just attracted the attention of those on the other side of the tent leather. Letting go of Calatinus' tunic, he frantically pulled on his sandals. His fingers slipped on the awkward lacing, and he mouthed a savage curse. Finally, though, he was done.

As Quintus straightened, he heard a soft, choking sound. And another. There was more muttering, and a stifled cry, which was cut short. He rushed to Licinius' bedroll this time. Perhaps he wasn't so pissed. Placing a hand across the Tarentine's mouth, Quintus shook him violently. 'Wake up!' he hissed. 'We are under attack!' He made out the white of the other's shocked eyes as they opened. Licinius nodded in understanding, and Quintus took away his hand. 'Listen,' he whispered.

For a moment, they heard nothing. Then there was a strangled moan, which swiftly died away. It was followed by the familiar, meaty sound of a blade plunging in and out of flesh. Quintus and Licinius exchanged a horrified glance and they both leaped up. 'To arms! To arms!' they screamed in unison.

At last Calatinus woke up. 'What's going on?' he mumbled.

'Damn it, get up! Grab your sword,' Quintus shouted. 'You too, Cincius. Quickly!' He cursed himself for not raising the alarm sooner.

In response to their cries, someone pushed a blade through the front of the tent and sliced downwards. Ripping the leather apart, he stepped inside. Quintus didn't hesitate. Running forward, he stabbed the figure in the belly. As the man folded over, bellowing in pain, a second intruder entered.

Quintus hacked him down with a savage blow to the neck. Blood spattered everywhere as the intruder collapsed, screaming. Unfortunately, a third man was close behind. So was a fourth. Loud, guttural voices from outside revealed that they had plenty of back-up.

'They're fucking Gauls!' yelled Licinius.

Confusion filled Quintus. What was happening? Had the Carthaginians scaled the ramparts? Ducking underneath a swinging sword, he thrust forward with his gladius, and was satisfied by the loud cry this elicited. Licinius joined him. Side by side, they put up a desperate resistance against the tide of warriors trying to gain entry. It was soon obvious that they would fail. Their new enemies were carrying shields, while they were in only their underclothes.

More ripping sounds came from Quintus' left and he struggled not to panic. 'The whoresons are cutting their way in. Calatinus! Cincius! Slash a hole in one of the back panels,' he shouted over his shoulder. 'We've got to get out.' There was no response, and Quintus' stomach clenched. Were their comrades already dead?

'Come on!' Calatinus screeched a moment later.

Relief flooded through Quintus. 'Ready?' he bellowed at Licinius.

'Yes!'

'Let's go, then!' Quintus delivered a desperate flurry of blows in the direction of his nearest opponent before turning and sprinting for the rear of the tent. He sensed Licinius one step behind. Quintus reached the gaping hole in the leather in a few strides. He hurled himself bodily through it, landing with a crash at the feet of the others. As they hauled him up, he peered inside, and was horrified to see Licinius – almost within arm's reach – trip and fall to his knees. Quintus had no time to react. The baying Gauls were on his comrade like hounds that have cornered a boar. Swords, daggers and even an axe chopped downwards. The poor light was not enough to prevent Quintus seeing the spurts of blood from each dreadful, mortal wound. Licinius collapsed on to the tent's floor without a word.

'You bastards,' Quintus screamed. Desperate to avenge his friend, he lunged forward.

Strong arms pulled him back. 'Don't be stupid. He's dead. We have to save ourselves,' Cincius snarled. Quickly, he and Calatinus dragged him off into the darkness.

There was no pursuit.

'Let me go!' Quintus shouted.

'You won't go back?' insisted Calatinus.

'I swear it,' Quintus muttered angrily.

They released him.

Quintus gazed around with horrified eyes. As far as he could see, pandemonium reigned. Some tents had been set on fire, vividly illuminating the scene. Groups of Gaulish warriors ran hither and thither, cutting down the confused Roman cavalrymen and legionaries who were emerging, half-clothed, into the cold night air. 'It doesn't look like an all-out attack,' he said after a moment. 'There aren't enough of them.'

'Some of the whoresons are already running away,' swore Calatinus, pointing.

Quintus squinted into the glow cast by the burning tents. 'What are they carrying?' His gorge rose as he realised. A great retch doubled Quintus over, and he puked up a bellyful of sour wine.

'The fucking dogs!' cried Cincius. 'They're heads! They've beheaded the men they've killed!'

With watering eyes, Quintus looked up. All he could see were the trails of blood the Gauls had left in the dazzling white snow.

Cincius and Calatinus began to moan with fear.

With great effort, Quintus pulled himself together. 'Quiet!' he hissed.

To his surprise, the pair obeyed. White-faced, they waited for him to speak.

Quintus ignored his instincts, which were screaming at him to search for his father. He had two men's lives in his hands. For the moment, they had to be the priority. 'Let's head for the *intervallum*,' he said. 'That's where everyone will be headed. We can fight the whoresons on a much better footing there.'

'But we're both barefoot,' said Cincius plaintively.

Quintus bridled, but if he didn't let the others equip themselves with caligae from nearby corpses, frostbite beckoned. 'Go on, then. Pick up a *scutum* each as well,' he ordered. A shield was vital.

'What about a mail shirt?' Calatinus tugged at a dead legionary. 'He's about my size.'

'No, you fool! We can't afford the time. Swords and shields will have to do.' Twitching with impatience, he waited until they were ready. 'Follow me.' Keeping an eye out for Gaulish warriors, Quintus set off at a loping run.

He led them straight to the intervallum, the strip of open ground that ran around the inside of the camp walls. Normally, it served for the legion to assemble before marching out on patrol or to do battle. Now, it allowed the bloodied survivors of the covert attack to regroup. Many had had the same idea as Quintus. The area was packed with hundreds of milling, disorganised legionaries and cavalrymen. Not many were fully dressed, but most had had the wits to pick up a weapon as they fled their tents.

Fortunately, this was where the discipline of officers such as centurions came into play. Recognisable even without their characteristic helmets, there were calm, measured figures everywhere, shouting orders and forming the soldiers into regular lines. Quintus and his companions joined the nearest group. At that point, it didn't matter that they were not infantry. Before long, the centurions had marshalled a large force together. Every sixth soldier was issued with one of the few torches available. It wasn't much, but would do until the attack had been contained.

At once, they began sweeping the avenues and tent lines for Gauls. To everyone's frustration, they had little success. Their desire for revenge could not be sated. It appeared that as soon as the alarm had been raised, the majority of the tribesmen had made their getaway. Nonetheless, the search continued until the entire area had been covered.

The worst discoveries were the numerous headless bodies. It was common knowledge that the Gauls liked to gather such battle trophies, but Quintus had never witnessed it before. He had never seen so much blood in his life. Enormous splashes of red circled every corpse, and wide trails of it ran alongside the Gauls' footprints.

'Jupiter above, this will look like a slaughterhouse in daylight,' said Calatinus in a hushed voice.

'Poor bastards,' replied Cincius. 'Most of them never had a chance.'

An image of his father sleeping in his tent made Quintus retch again. There was nothing left to come up except bile.

Calatinus looked concerned. 'Are you all right?'

'I'm fine,' Quintus barked. Forcing down his nausea, he carefully scanned each body they came across. He begged the gods that he would not find his father. To his immense relief, he saw none who resembled Fabricius. Yet this did not mean a thing. They had covered but a small part of the camp. Only when daybreak came could he be sure.

The centurions kept every soldier on high alert for what remained of the night. The sole compromise they would make was to allow each makeshift century in turn to go to their tents and retrieve their clothing and armour. Fully prepared for battle, the legionaries and cavalrymen then had to wait until dawn, when it became clear that there would be no further attack. The men were finally allowed to stand down, and were ordered to return to their respective units. The cleaning-up operation would take all day. Disregarding this, Quintus went in search of his father. Miraculously, he found him in his tent. Tears came to his eyes as he entered. 'You're alive!'

'There you are,' Fabricius declared, waving at the table before him, which was laid out for breakfast. 'Care for some bread?'

Quintus grinned. Despite his father's nonchalance, he had seen the flash of relief in his eyes. 'Thank you. I'm famished. It's been a long night,' he replied.

'Indeed it has,' Fabricius replied. 'And more than a hundred good men are gone thanks to those bastard Cenomani.'

'You're certain that's who it was?'

'Who else could it have been? There was no sign of the gate being forced, and the sentries on the walls saw no one.'

Realisation struck Quintus. 'That's why they were so surly yesterday!' Seeing his father's confusion, he explained.

'That clarifies a great deal. And now they've fled to the Carthaginian camp. No doubt their "trophies" will serve as an offering to Hannibal,' said Fabricius sourly. 'Proof that they hate us.'

Quintus tried not to think of Licinius' headless corpse, which he'd found in the wreckage of their tent. 'What will Publius do?'

Fabricius scowled. 'Guess.'

'We're to withdraw again?'

His father nodded.

'Why?' cried Quintus.

'He thinks it's too dangerous on this side of the Trebia. After last night, that's hard to argue with.' Fabricius saw Quintus' anguish. 'It's not just that. The high ground on the far bank is extremely uneven, which will stop any chance of attacks by the Carthaginian cavalry. We'll also be blocking the roads that lead south through Liguria to the lands of the Boii.'

Quintus' protests subsided. Those reasons at least made sense. 'When?'

'This afternoon, as it's getting dark.'

Quintus sighed. The very manner of their retreat seemed cowardly, but it *was* prudent. 'And then we sit tight?' he guessed. 'Contain the Carthaginians?'

'Exactly. Sempronius Longus is travelling here with all speed. His forces will arrive inside a month.' Fabricius' expression grew fierce. 'Hannibal's forces will never stand up to two consular armies.'

For the second time since the Cenomani attack, Quintus had a reason to smile.

'There you are. Your mother's been worried. She thought you'd be here.'

At the sound of Elira's voice, Aurelia turned. The Illyrian was framed in the doorway to the stable. All at once, she felt very childish. 'Is Gaius still here?'

'No, he's gone. Apparently, his unit is to be mobilised soon. He said that you would be in his thoughts and prayers.'

Aurelia felt even worse.

Elira came closer. 'I heard the news,' she said softly. 'Everyone did. We all feel for you.'

'Thank you.' Aurelia threw her a grateful look.

'Who's to know? Your father may well be alive.'

'Don't,' Aurelia snapped.

'I'm sorry,' said Elira quickly.

Aurelia forced a smile. 'At least Quintus is still alive.'

'And Hanno.'

Aurelia shoved away the pang of jealousy that followed Elira's words. Mention of Hanno inevitably made her think of Suniaton. She hadn't taken him any food for four days. He'd be running out of provisions. Aurelia made her mind up on the spot. Seeing Suni now would cheer her up. She squinted at Elira. 'You liked Hanno, didn't you?'

Twin dimples formed in the Illyrian's cheeks. 'Yes,' she whispered.

'Would you help him again?'

'Of course,' Elira answered, looking puzzled. 'But he's gone, with Quintus.'

Aurelia smiled. 'Go to the kitchen and fill a bag with provisions. Bread, cheese, meat. If Julius asks, tell him that they're rations for our foraging trip. Fetch a basket too.'

'What if the mistress wants to know where you are?'

'Say that we're going to look for nuts and mushrooms.'

Elira's face grew even more confused. 'How will that help Hanno?'

'You'll see.' Aurelia clapped her hands. 'Well, get on with it then. I'll meet you on the path that leads up to the hills.'

With a curious glance, Elira hurried off.

Aurelia hadn't been waiting long before Elira came hurrying through the trees towards her. A small leather pack dangled from one hand, a cloak that matched her own from the other.

'Did anyone ask what you were doing?' Aurelia asked nervously.

'Julius did, but he just smiled when I told him what we were doing. He said to be careful.'

'He's such an old woman!' declared Aurelia. She looked down and realised that she'd come out without her dagger or sling. It doesn't matter, she told herself. We won't be gone for long. 'Come on,' she said briskly.

'Where are we going?' asked Elira.

'Up there,' replied Aurelia, waving vaguely at the slopes that loomed over the farm. Abruptly, she decided that there was no further need for subterfuge. 'Did you know that Hanno had a friend who was captured with him?'

Elira nodded.

'Suniaton was sold to become a gladiator in Capua.'

'Oh.' Elira didn't dare to say more, but her muted tone spoke volumes.

'Quintus and Gaius helped him to escape.'

The Illyrian was visibly shocked. 'Why?'

'Because Hanno was Quintus' friend.'

'I see.' Elira frowned. 'Has Suniaton got something to do with where we're going now?'

'Yes. He was injured when they rescued him, so the poor thing couldn't travel. He's much better now, thank the gods.'

Elira looked intrigued. 'Where is he?'

'At the shepherd's hut where Quintus and Hanno fought the bandits.'

'You're full of surprises, aren't you?' said Elira with a giggle.

Aurelia's misery lifted a fraction and she grinned.

Talking animatedly, they walked to the border of Fabricius' land. The fields on either side were empty and bare, lying fallow until the spring. Jackdaws were their only company; flocks regularly flew overhead, their characteristic squawks piercing the chill air. Soon they had entered the woods that covered the surrounding hills. The bird cries immediately died away, and the trees pressed in from all sides with a claustrophobic air that Aurelia did not like.

When Agesandros stepped out on to the path, she screamed in fright. So did Elira.

'I didn't mean to scare you,' he said apologetically.

Aurelia tried to calm her pounding heart. 'What are you doing here?' she demanded.

He raised the bow in his hands. An arrow was already notched to its string. 'Hunting deer. And you?'

Aurelia's mouth felt very dry. 'Looking for nuts. And mushrooms.'

'I see,' he said. 'I wouldn't stray too far from the farm on your search.'

'Why not?' asked Aurelia, trying desperately to sound confident.

'You never know who might be about. Bandits. A bear. An escaped slave.'

'There's little chance of that,' Aurelia declared boldly.

'Maybe so. You're unarmed, though. I could come with you,' the Sicilian offered.

'No!' Instantly, Aurelia regretted her vehemence. 'Thank you, but we'll be fine.'

'If you're certain,' he said, stepping back.

'I am.' Jerking her head at Elira, Aurelia walked past him.

'It's a bit late for mushrooms, isn't it?'

Aurelia's step faltered. 'There are still a few, if you know where to look,' she managed.

Agesandros nodded knowledgeably. 'I'm sure.'

Aurelia's skin was crawling as she walked away.

'Does he know?' whispered Elira.

'How could he?' Aurelia hissed back.

But it felt as if he did.

Many days passed by, and it became evident that there would be no battle. As Fabricius had said, no commander would choose to fight unless he could select the time and place. Publius' refusal to move from the high ground and Hannibal's unwillingness to attack his enemy's position produced a stalemate. While the Carthaginians roamed at will across the plain west of the Trebia, the Romans stayed close to their camp. Hannibal's cavalry now severely outnumbered their horsemen. Patrols were so risky that they were rarely sent out. Despite this, Quintus found it hard to remain equable about their enforced inactivity. He was still suffering nightmares about what had happened to Licinius. He hoped that in battle he could purge himself of the disturbing images. 'I'm going crazy,' he told his father one night. 'How much longer do we have to wait?'

'We'll do nothing until Longus arrives,' Fabricius repeated patiently. 'If we marched down to the flat ground today and offered battle, the dogs would cut us to pieces. Even without the difference in cavalry, Hannibal's army outnumbers us man for man. You know that.'

'I suppose so,' Quintus admitted reluctantly.

Fabricius leaned back in his chair, satisfied that his point had been made.

Quintus stared gloomily into the depths of the brazier. What was Hanno doing at this very moment? he wondered. It didn't seem real that they were now enemies. Quintus also thought of Aurelia. When would his recently composed letter reach her? If Fortuna smiled on them both, he might get a reply within the next few months. It was a long time to wait. At least in the meantime he was serving alongside his father. His sister, on the other hand, was not so lucky. Quintus' heart ached for her.

'Here you both are!' A familiar booming voice broke the silence.

Fabricius made a show of looking pleased. 'Flaccus. Where else would we be?'

Quintus jumped up and saluted. What does he want? he wondered. Since the debacle at the Ticinus, they had hardly seen Aurelia's husband-to-be. The reason, all three knew, was Flaccus' conduct during that disaster. It was hard to dispel suspicion once it had taken root, thought Quintus. Yet he could not shake off his feeling. Nor, it appeared, could his father.

'Quite so, quite so. Who would be out tonight apart from the sentries and the deranged?' Chuckling at his own joke, Flaccus proffered a small amphora.

'How kind,' Fabricius murmured, accepting the gift. 'Will you try some?'

'Only if you will,' Flaccus demurred.

Fabricius opened the amphora with a practised movement of his wrist. 'Quintus?'

'Yes, please, Father.' Quickly, he fetched three glazed ceramic beakers.

With their cups filled, they eyed each other, wondering who would make the toast. At length, Fabricius spoke. 'To the swift arrival of Sempronius Longus and his army.'

'And to a rapid victory over the Carthaginians thereafter,' Flaccus added.

Quintus thought of Licinius. 'And vengeance for our dead comrades.'

Nodding, Fabricius lifted his cup even higher.

Flaccus beamed. 'That's fighting talk! Just what I wanted to hear.' He gave them a conspiratorial wink. 'I've had a word with Publius.'

Fabricius looked dubious. 'About what?'

'Sending out a patrol.'

'Eh?' asked Fabricius suspiciously.

'No one has been across the river in more than a week.'

'That's because it's too damn dangerous,' Fabricius replied. 'The enemy controls the far bank in its entirety.'

'Hear me out,' said Flaccus in a placatory tone. 'When Sempronius Longus arrives, he'll want fresh intelligence, and information on the terrain west of the Trebia. After all, that's where the battle will be.'

'What's wrong with waiting until he gets here?' demanded Fabricius. 'Some of his cavalry can do his donkey work.'

'It needs to be now,' urged Flaccus. 'Presenting the consul with all the information he needs would allow him to act fast. Just think of the boost it would provide to the men's morale when we come back safely!'

'We?' said Fabricius slowly. 'You would come too?'

'Of course.'

Not for the first time, Fabricius wondered if it had been a good idea to betroth Aurelia to Flaccus. Yet how could he be a coward and offer to take part in such a madcap venture? 'I don't know,' he muttered. 'It would be incredibly risky.'

'Not necessarily,' Flaccus protested. 'I've been watching the Carthaginians from our side of the river. By *hora decima* every afternoon, their last patrol has vanished from sight. It's at least *hora quarta* the following morning before they return. If we crossed at night, and rode out before dawn, we'd have perhaps two hours to reconnoitre the area. We would be back across before the Numidians had finished scratching their lice.'

Quintus laughed.

Fabricius scowled. 'I don't think it's a very good idea.'

'Publius has already given his approval. I could think of no one better to lead the patrol, and he agreed,' said Flaccus. 'Come on, what do you say?'

Damn you, thought Fabricius. He felt completely outmanoeuvred. Refusing Flaccus' offer could be seen as a snub to Publius himself, and that was not a wise course of action. Furious, Fabricius changed his mind. 'It could only be a small patrol. One turma at most,' he said. 'It would have to be under my sole command. You can come along – as an observer.'

Flaccus did not protest. He turned to Quintus. 'Your father is a shining example of a Roman officer. Brave, resourceful and eager to do his duty.'

'I'm coming too,' said Quintus.

'No, you're not,' snapped his father. 'It will be far too dangerous.'

'It's not fair! You did things like this when you were my age – you've told me!' retorted Quintus furiously.

Flaccus stepped in before Fabricius could reply. 'How can we deny Quintus such a chance to gain valuable experience? And think of the glory that will be heaped upon the men who brought Longus the information that helped him to defeat Hannibal!'

Fabricius looked at his son's eager face and sighed. 'Very well.'

'Thank you, Father,' said Quintus with a broad smile.

Fabricius kept showing a brave face, but inside he was filled with fear. It will be like walking past a pride of hungry lions, hoping that none of them sees us, he thought. Yet there was no going back now.

He had given his word to lead the mission.

Chapter XXI: Hannibal's Plan

One morning, not long after the Carthaginians had driven the Romans back over the Trebia, Malchus was ordered to Hannibal's tent. While this happened regularly, he always felt a tremor of excitement when the summons arrived. After so many years of waiting for revenge on Rome, Malchus still thrilled to be in the presence of the man who had finally begun the war.

He found Hannibal in pensive mood. The general barely glanced up as Malchus entered. As ever, he was leaning over his campaign table, studying a map of the area. Maharbal, his cavalry commander, stood beside him, talking in a low voice. A thin man with long, curly black hair and an easy grin, Maharbal was popular with officers and ordinary troops alike.

Malchus came to a halt several steps from the table. He stiffened to attention. 'Reporting for duty, sir.'

Hannibal straightened. 'Malchus, welcome.'

'You asked to see me, sir?'

'I did.' Still deep in thought, Hannibal rubbed a finger across his lips. 'I have a question to ask you.'

'Anything, sir.'

'Maharbal and I have come up with a plan. An ambush, to be precise.'

'Sounds interesting, sir,' said Malchus eagerly.

'We're hoping that the Romans might send a patrol across the river,' Hannibal went on. 'Maharbal here will organise the cavalry that will fall upon the enemy, but I want some infantry there too. They will lie in wait at the main ford, and prevent any stragglers from escaping.'

Malchus grinned fiercely. 'I'd be honoured to take part, sir.'

'I didn't have you in mind.' Seeing Malchus' face fall, Hannibal explained,

'I'm not losing one of my most experienced officers in a skirmish. I was thinking of your sons, Bostar and Sapho.'

Malchus swallowed his disappointment. 'They'd be well suited to a job like this, sir, and I'm sure delighted to be picked for it.'

'I thought so.' Hannibal paused for a moment. 'And so to my question. What about your other son?'

Malchus blinked in surprise. 'Hanno?'

'Is he battle-ready yet?'

'I put him into training straight after he returned, sir. Not being in Carthage, it was a little improvised, but he performed well.' Malchus hesitated. 'I'd say that he's ready to be commissioned as an officer.'

'Good, good. Could he lead a phalanx?'

Malchus gaped. 'Are you serious, sir?'

'I'm not in the habit of making jokes, Malchus. The crossing of the mountains left many units without officers to command them.'

'Of course, sir, of course.' Malchus gathered his thoughts. 'Before Hanno was lost at sea, I would have had grave reservations.'

'Why?' Hannibal's gaze was as fierce as a hawk's.

'He was a bit of a wastrel, sir. Only interested in fishing and girls.'

'That's hardly a crime, is it?' Hannibal chuckled. 'I thought he was too young to serve in the army back then?'

'He was, sir,' Malchus admitted. 'And, to be fair, he was excellent when it came to lessons in military tactics. He was skilled at hunting too.'

'Good qualities. So, has your opinion changed since his return?'

'It has, sir,' Malchus replied confidently. 'He's changed. The things he experienced and had to live through would have broken many boys, but it didn't Hanno. He is a man now.'

'You're sure?'

Malchus met his general's gaze squarely. 'Yes, sir.'

'Fine. I want you and your three sons back here in an hour. That'll be all.' Hannibal turned back to Maharbal.

'Thank you, sir.' Grinning with excitement, Malchus saluted and withdrew.

Confusion filled Hanno when his father told him the news.

'What does he want with a junior officer like me?'

'I couldn't say,' Malchus replied neutrally.

Hanno's stomach twisted into a knot. 'Are Sapho and Bostar also to be present?'

'They are.'

That did little to reassure Hanno. Had he done something wrong?

'I'll leave you to it,' said Malchus. 'Make sure you're there in half an hour.'

'Yes, Father.' With a racing mind, Hanno set to polishing his new helmet and breastplate. He didn't stop until his arms burned. Then he rubbed his leather sandals with grease until they glistened. When he was done, Hanno hurried to his father's tent where there was a large bronze mirror. To his relief, Malchus wasn't there. He scowled at his reflection. 'It'll have to do,' he muttered.

As he walked to Hannibal's headquarters, Hanno was grateful that none of the soldiers hurrying to and fro gave him a second look. It wasn't until he reached the scutarii who stood guard outside the large pavilion that he became the focus of attention.

'State your name, rank and business!' barked the officer in charge of the sentries.

'Hanno, junior officer of a Libyan phalanx, sir. I'm here to see the general.' Hanno blinked, half expecting to be told to get lost.

Instead, the officer nodded. 'You're expected. Follow me.'

A moment later, Hanno found himself in a large, sparsely furnished chamber. Apart from a desk and a few hide-backed chairs, it held only a weapons rack. Hannibal was there, surrounded by a circle of his commanders. Among them were his father and brothers.

'Sir! Announcing Hanno, junior officer of the Libyan spearmen!' the officer bellowed.

Hanno flushed to the roots of his hair.

Turning, Hannibal smiled. 'Welcome.'

'Thank you, sir.'

'You all know about Malchus' prodigal son?' asked Hannibal. 'Well, here he is.'

Hanno's embarrassment grew even greater as the senior officers studied him. He could see Bostar grinning. Even his father had the trace of a smile on his lips. Sapho, on the other hand, looked as if he'd swallowed a wasp. Hanno felt a surge of annoyance. *Why is he like that?*

Hannibal looked at each of the brothers in turn. 'You're probably wondering why I summoned you this morning?'

'Yes, sir,' they answered.

'I'll come to my reason in a moment.' Hannibal looked at Hanno. 'You've heard no doubt of our severe casualties, suffered during the crossing of the Alps?'

'Of course, sir.'

'Since then, we've been short of not just men, but officers.'

'Yes, sir,' Hanno replied. What was Hannibal getting at? Hanno wondered.

The general smiled at his confusion. 'I'm appointing you to the command of a phalanx,' he said.

'Sir?' Hanno managed.

'You heard me,' replied Hannibal. 'It's a huge leap, I know, but your father assures me that you've returned a man.'

'I . . .' Hanno's gaze flickered to Malchus and back to Hannibal. 'Thank you, sir.'

'As you know, a phalanx should number four hundred men or so, but yours now barely musters two hundred. It's one of the weakest units, but the men are veterans, and they should serve you well. And, after your extraordinary ordeals, I have high expectations of you.'

'Thank you, sir,' said Hanno, acutely aware of the huge responsibility he'd just been handed. 'I am deeply honoured.' Bostar winked at him, but he was irritated to see that Sapho's lips were pursed.

'Good!' Hannibal declared. 'Now for the reason I called you all here today. As you probably know, there's been no action since we sent the Romans packing over the Trebia. Nor is there much chance of any in the near future. They know that our cavalry greatly outnumbers theirs, as does our infantry. From our point of view, it would be pointless to attack their camp. It's on such uneven ground that the advantage our horsemen grant us would be negated. The Romans know that too, so the mongrel bastards are happy just to block the road south and wait for reinforcements. We may have to wait until those forces arrive, but I'm not happy to sit about doing nothing.' Hannibal turned. 'Maharbal?'

'Thank you, sir,' said the cavalry commander. 'To try and encourage the enemy to send some men over the river, we've been giving the impression that our riders have become quite lax. Do you want to know how?' he asked.

'Yes, sir,' the three brothers replied eagerly.

'We never appear on our side of the Trebia until late in the morning, and we always leave well before dark. Understand?'

'You want them to try a dawn patrol, sir?' asked Bostar.

Maharbal smiled. 'Exactly.'

Hanno felt his excitement grow. He didn't feel confident enough to ask a question, however.

Sapho did it for him. 'What else, sir?'

Hannibal took over once more. 'Maharbal has five hundred Numidians permanently stationed in the woods about a mile from the main ford over the river. If the Romans take the bait, and send out a patrol, they'll have to ride past our men. Not many of the dogs will escape when the Numidians fall on them from behind, but some might. Which is where you and your Libyans will come in.'

Hanno shot a glance at Bostar and Sapho, who were grinning fiercely.

'I want a strong force of infantry to remain hidden near the crossing point. If any Romans do cross, they're not to be hindered, but when they return . . .' Hannibal clenched a fist. 'I want them annihilated. Is that clear?'

Hanno glanced at his brothers, who gave him emphatic nods. 'Yes, sir!' they cried in unison.

'Excellent,' declared Hannibal. His gaze hardened. 'Do *not* fail me.'

Shortly after darkness had fallen the following evening, Hanno and his brothers led their units out of the Carthaginian camp. As well as their tents and sleeping rolls, the men carried enough rations for three days and nights. To Hanno's delight, the Numidians who were to guide them into position were led by no less than Zamar, the officer who'd found him near the Padus. Following the horsemen, the phalanxes quietly marched to the east, following little-used hunting tracks. As the sound of rushing water filled everyone's ears, Zamar directed them to a hidden dell which lay a couple of hundred paces from the area's main crossing point over the River Trebia. It was a perfect hiding place. Spacious enough to contain their entire force, but sufficiently close to the ford. 'I'm leaving you six riders as messengers. Send them out the moment you see anything,' Zamar muttered before he left. 'And remember, when the Romans come, none are to be left alive.'

'Say no more,' Sapho snarled.

Although Bostar said nothing, Hanno saw a look of distaste flicker across his face. He waited until Zamar was out of sight before turning to his brothers. 'What's going on?' he demanded.

'What do you mean?' asked Sapho defensively.

'You two are permanently like a pair of cats in a bag with each other. Why?'

Bostar and Sapho scowled at each other.

Hanno waited. The silence dragged on for a few moments.

'It's really none of your business,' said Bostar at length.

Hanno flushed. He glanced at Sapho, whose face was a cold mask. Hanno gave up. 'I'm going to check on my men,' he muttered and stalked off.

They waited in vain through what remained of the night. By dawn, the Carthaginians were chilled through and miserable. To avoid any possibility of being spotted, no fires had been lit. While it hadn't rained, the winter damp was pervasive. Following strict orders, the soldiers remained in the clearing during daylight. The sole exceptions to this were a handful of sentries, who, with blackened faces, hid themselves among the trees lining the riverbank. Everyone else had to stay put, even when answering calls of nature. While some found the energy to play dice or knucklebones, most men stayed in their tents, chewing on cold rations or catching up on lost sleep. Still annoyed by his brothers' pettiness, Hanno spent his time talking to his spearmen, trying to get to know them. He knew by their muted reactions that his efforts would mean little until he'd led them into combat, but it felt better than doing nothing.

The day dragged past without event.

Night fell at last, and Hanno took charge of the sentries, who were stationed along the river's edge for several hundred paces either side of the ford. He spent his time wandering the bank, his eyes peeled for any enemy activity. There was little cloud cover. The myriad stars above provided enough light to see relatively well, yet hours went by without so much as a flicker of movement on the opposite side. By the time dawn was approaching, Hanno had grown bored and annoyed. 'Where are the fuckers?' he muttered to himself.

'Still in their beds, probably.'

Hanno jumped. Turning, he recognised Bostar's features in the dim light. 'Tanit above, you scared me! What are you doing here?'

'I couldn't sleep.'

'You should have stayed under your blankets anyway. It's a damn sight warmer than out here,' Hanno replied.

Bostar crouched down beside Hanno with a sigh. 'To be honest, I wanted to apologise about what happened yesterday with Sapho. Our argument shouldn't affect our dealings with you.'

'That's all right. I shouldn't have poked my nose where it didn't belong.'

A more comfortable air settled about them.

'We've actually been fighting for over a year,' Bostar admitted a moment later.

Hanno was grateful for the darkness, which concealed his surprise. 'What, the usual stuff with him being pompous and overbearing?'

Bostar's teeth glinted sadly in the starlight. 'I wish it was just that.'

'I don't understand.'

'It started when you'd been lost at sea.'

'Eh?'

'Sapho blamed me for letting you and Suniaton go.'

'But you both agreed to do so!'

'That's not how he saw it. We hadn't patched things up by the time I was posted to Iberia, and it flared up again the instant he and Father arrived from Carthage months later.'

'Why?'

'They'd had news of what had happened to you and Suni. Sapho was furious. He blamed me all over again.'

'You mean the pirates?' Suddenly, Hanno remembered Sapho's comment the day he'd returned, and his father's promise to tell him what had happened. 'I'd forgotten.'

'There was so much going on,' said Bostar. 'All that mattered was that you had returned.'

'We've got plenty of time now,' retorted Hanno. 'Tell me!'

'It was a few weeks after you'd disappeared. Thanks to one of his spies, Father got wind of some pirates in the port. Four of them were seized and taken in. Under torture, they admitted selling you and Suni into slavery in Italy.'

Vivid images flashed through Hanno's mind. 'Do you know any of their names?'

'No, sorry,' said Bostar. 'Apparently, the captain was an Egyptian.'

'That's right!' said Hanno, shivering. 'What happened to them?'

'They were castrated first. Then their limbs were smashed before they were crucified,' Bostar replied in a flat tone.

Hanno imagined the terrible scene for a moment. 'Not a good way to die,' he admitted.

'No.'

'But they deserved it,' declared Hanno harshly. 'Thanks to those whoresons, Suni and I should have died in the arena.'

'I know,' said Bostar with a heavy sigh. 'Yet seeing what happened to the pirates changed Sapho in some way. Ever since, he's been much harder. Crueller. You saw how he reacted to what Zamar said. I know that we have to kill any Romans who might cross the river. Orders are orders. But Sapho seems to take pleasure in it.'

'It's not nice, but it's not the end of the world, surely?' said Hanno, trying to make light of his brother's words.

'That's not all,' muttered Bostar. 'He thinks that I'll do anything to curry favour with Hannibal.' Quickly, he related how he'd saved Hannibal's life at Saguntum. 'You should have seen the expression on Sapho's face when Hannibal congratulated me. It was as if I'd done it to make him look bad.'

'That's crazy!' Hanno whispered. 'Are you sure that's what he thought?'

'Oh yes. "The perfect fucking officer" he's taken to calling me.'

Hanno was shocked into silence for a moment. 'Surely, it hasn't been all him? There are always two sides to every argument.'

'Yes, I've said some nasty things too.' Bostar sighed. 'But every time I try to sort it out, Sapho throws it back in my face. The last time I tried . . .' He hesitated for a heartbeat before shaking his head. 'I've given up on him.'

'Why? What happened?' asked Hanno.

'I'm not telling you,' said Bostar. 'I can't.' He looked away, out over the murmuring river.

Troubled by what Bostar had said, Hanno did not press him further. He tried to be optimistic. Maybe he could act as a mediator? Imagining a world in which Carthage was at peace once more, Hanno pictured himself hunting with his brothers in the mountains south of their city.

Bostar nudged him in the ribs, hard. 'Pssst! Do you hear that?'

Hanno came down to earth with a jolt. He leaned forward, listening with all his might. For a long time, he could make out nothing. Then, the jingle of harness. Hanno's senses went on to high alert. 'That came from across the water,' he muttered.

'It did,' replied Bostar excitedly. 'Hannibal was right: the Romans want information.'

They watched the far bank like wolves waiting for their prey to emerge. An instant later, their patience was rewarded. The sounds of horses, and men, moving with great care.

A surge of adrenaline pulsed through Hanno's veins. 'It has to be Romans!'

'Or some of their Gaulish allies,' said Bostar.

It wasn't long before they could make out a line of soldiers and mounts, winding their way down the track that led to the ford.

'How many?' hissed Bostar.

Hanno squinted into the darkness. An accurate head count was impossible. 'No more than fifty. Probably less. It's a reconnaissance patrol all right.'

Stopping, the Roman riders gathered together in a huddle.

'They're getting their last orders,' said Hanno.

A moment later, the first man quietly walked his horse into the ice-cold water. It gave a gentle, dissenting whinny, but some muttered reassurances in its ear worked wonders, and it continued without further protest. At once the others began to follow.

Bostar unwound his limbs and stood. 'Time to move. Go and tell Sapho what's happening. The Numidians must be alerted immediately. Clear?'

'Yes. What are you going to do?'

'I'll go along the bank to the next sentry, and keep an eye on them until they're out of sight. We need to be sure that no more of the bastards are going to cross.'

'Right. See you soon.' Hanno backed away slowly until he was behind the cover of the trees. Treading lightly on the hard ground, he sped back to their secret camp. He found Sapho pacing the ground before his tent. Quickly, he filled his brother in.

'Excellent,' said Sapho with a savage grin. 'Before long, you will get to blood your men's spears, and perhaps your own. A special moment for you.'

Hanno nodded nervously. Was he imagining Sapho's lasciviousness?

'Well, come on then! This is no time for standing around. Get your men up. I'll send out a few of the Numidians, and get my phalanx ready. Bostar will do the same no doubt, when he eventually gets here,' said Sapho.

Hanno frowned. 'No need for that,' he said. 'He'll be here any moment.'

'Of course he will!' Sapho laughed. 'Now get a move on. We'll need to move into position the instant the Romans have gone.'

Hanno put his head down and obeyed. He didn't understand the feud between his brothers, but one thing was certain: Sapho still liked telling him what to do. Irritated, Hanno began rousing his men. When he heard a man grumbling, Hanno lambasted him from a height. His tactic seemed to work; it didn't take long for the soldiers to assemble alongside Sapho's phalanx.

Soon after, Bostar's shape emerged from the gloom that hung over the trees that lined the riverbank. 'They've gone,' he declared. He whistled at the last three Numidians. 'Ride out at once. Trail the dogs from a distance. Return when the ambush has been sprung.'

With a quick salute, the cavalrymen sprang on to their horses' backs. They headed off at the trot.

Bostar approached his brothers. 'Our time here was not in vain,' he said with a smile.

'Finally,' drawled Sapho. 'We've been waiting for you.'

Why is he needling him like that? thought Hanno.

Bostar's jaw bunched, but he said nothing. Fortunately, his soldiers had heard their comrades getting up, and were doing the same. When he was done, the trio convened in front of their men.

'How are we going to work this?' asked Hanno.

'It's obvious,' said Sapho self-importantly. 'The phalanxes should form three sides of a square. The fourth side will be completed by the Numidians, who will drive the Romans into the trap. They'll have nowhere to go. All we have to decide is which phalanx holds each position.'

There was a momentary pause. Each of them had reconnoitred the ground around the crossing point several times. The left flank was taken up by a dense patch of oak trees, while the right was a large swampy area. Neither constituted ground that horses would choose to ride over if given the choice. The best place to stand was on the track that led to the ford. That was where any action would take place.

As the youngest and most inexperienced, Hanno was content to take whichever of the flanks he was given.

'I'll take the central side,' said Bostar abruptly.

'Typical,' muttered Sapho. 'I want it as well. And you don't outrank me any more, remember?'

The two glowered at each other.

'This is ridiculous,' said Hanno angrily. 'It doesn't matter which one of you does it.'

Neither of his brothers answered.

'Why don't you toss a coin?'

Still neither Bostar nor Sapho spoke.

'Melqart above!' exclaimed Hanno. 'I'll do it, then.'

'That's out of the question,' snapped Sapho. 'You've got no combat experience.'

'Exactly,' added Bostar.

'I've got to start somewhere. Why not here?' Hanno retorted. 'Better this, surely, than in a massive battle?'

Bostar looked at Sapho. 'We can't stand around arguing all morning,' he said in a conciliatory tone.

Sapho gave a careless shrug. 'It would be hard for Hanno to get it wrong, I suppose.'

Feeling humiliated, Hanno looked down.

'That's unnecessary,' barked Bostar. 'Father has trained Hanno well. Hannibal himself picked him to lead a phalanx. His men are veterans. The chances of him fucking up are no greater than if I were in the centre.' He paused. 'Or you were.'

'What's that supposed to mean?' Sapho's eyes were mere slits.

'Stop it!' Hanno cried. 'You should both be ashamed of yourselves. Hannibal gave us a job to do, remember? Let's just do it, please.'

Like sulky children, his brothers broke eye contact. In silence, they stalked off to stand before their phalanxes. Hanno waited for a moment before realising that it was up to him to lead the way. 'Form up, six men wide,' he ordered. 'Follow me.' He was pleased by his soldiers' rapid response. Many of them looked pleased by what had happened, which encouraged him further.

The three phalanxes deployed at the ford, in open order. Once they closed up, the spearmen would present a continuous front of overlapping shields. No horse would approach such an obstacle. The forest of spears protruding from it promised death by impalement to anyone foolish enough to try.

Hanno marched up and down, muttering encouraging words to his men. He was grateful that his father had advised him to recognise as many of his soldiers as possible. It was a simple ruse, yet not a man failed to grin when Hanno spoke to him by name. His efforts didn't take long, though, and soon time began to drag. Muscles that had been stirred into activity by their movement into position grew cold again. A damp breeze blew off the river, chilling the waiting soldiers to the bone. Allowing them to warm up was not an option, nor was singing, a common method of raising morale.

All they could do was wait.

Dawn came, but banks of lowering cloud concealed the sun. The sole sign of life was the occasional small bird fluttering among the trees' bare branches; the only sound the murmur of the river at their backs. Finally, Hanno's grumbling belly made him wonder if they should order an issue of rations. Before he could query this with his brothers, the sound of galloping hooves attracted everyone's attention. All eyes turned to the track leading west.

When two Numidians came thundering around the corner, there was a massed intake of breath.

'They're coming!' one shouted as he drew nearer.

'With five hundred of our comrades hot on their tails!' whooped the other.

Hanno scarcely heard. 'Close order!' he screamed. 'Ready spears!'

Chapter XXII: Face to Face

Quintus had hoped that his unease would dissipate as they left the Trebia behind them. Far from it. Each step that his horse took further into the empty landscape felt as final as if he had crossed the Styx to penetrate the depths of Hades itself. The eagerness he'd felt in his father's tent, with a belly full of wine, had totally vanished. Quintus said nothing, but a glance to either side confirmed that he was not alone in his feelings. The other riders' faces spoke volumes. Many were throwing filthy glances at Flaccus. Everyone knew that he was responsible for their misfortune.

At the front, Fabricius had no idea, or was choosing to ignore, what was going on. It was probably the latter, Quintus decided. These were some of the most experienced men in his command. Yet they were unhappy. Why had his father accepted the mission? Quintus cursed. The answer was startlingly simple. How would it look to Publius if Fabricius had refused a duty like this? Terrible. Quintus eyed Flaccus sourly. If the fool hadn't put the idea in the consul's head, they'd all still be safe on the Roman side of the river. Guilt soon replaced Quintus' anger. By being so eager, he had probably helped push his father into accepting the suicide mission.

For, despite the fact that there was no sign of the enemy, that is what it felt like.

Quintus waited for only a short time before urging his horse forward to his father's position. Flaccus was riding alongside. He gave Quintus a broad wink. It wasn't entirely convincing.

He's frightened too, thought Quintus. That made up his mind.

Fabricius was intent on scanning the landscape. His rigid back told its own story. Quintus swallowed. 'Maybe this patrol was a bad idea, Father.' He ignored Flaccus' shocked reaction. 'We're visible for miles.'

Fabricius dragged his gaze around to Quintus. 'I know. Why do you think I'm keeping such a keen eye out?'

'But there's no sign of anyone,' protested Flaccus. 'Not even a bird!'

'For Jupiter's sake, that doesn't matter!' Fabricius snapped. 'All the Carthaginians need is one alert sentry. If there are any Numidians within five miles of here, they'll be after us within a dozen heartbeats of any alarm.'

Flaccus flinched. 'But we can't go back empty-handed.'

'Not without looking like fools, or cowards,' Fabricius agreed sourly.

They rode in silence for a few moments.

'There might be a way out,' Flaccus muttered.

Quintus was ashamed to feel a flutter of hope.

Fabricius laughed harshly. 'Not so keen now, are you?'

'Are you doubting my courage?' demanded Flaccus with an outraged look.

'Not your courage,' Fabricius growled. 'Your good judgement. Haven't you realised yet that Hannibal's cavalry are lethal? If we so much as see any, we're dead men.'

'Surely it's not that bad?' protested Flaccus.

'I should have refused this mission, regardless of how it looked to Publius. Let you lead it on your own. If anyone would follow you, that is.'

Flaccus subsided into a sulky silence.

His father's outburst revealed the depths of his anger; Quintus was amazed.

Fabricius relented a fraction. 'So what's your bright idea? You might as well tell me.'

'We will report that the enemy cavalry was present in such numbers that we were unable to proceed far from the Trebia,' said Flaccus with bad grace. 'It's not cowardice to avoid annihilation. Who will gainsay us? Your men certainly won't talk about it, and no one else will be foolish enough to cross the river.'

'Your capacity for guile never ceases to amaze me,' snarled Fabricius.

'I . . .' Flaccus spluttered.

'But you're right. It's better to save the lives of thirty men in the way you suggest rather than throw them away through foolish pride. We will return at once.' Fabricius reined in his mount, and turned to issue the order to halt.

Quintus sagged down on to his horse's back. His relief lasted no more than a heartbeat. From some distance away came the unmistakable sound of galloping hooves.

The eyes of every man in the turma turned to the west.

A quarter of a mile distant, a tide of riders was emerging from behind a copse of trees.

'Numidians!' Fabricius screamed. 'About turn! Ride for your lives!'

His soldiers needed no urging.

Trying not to panic, Quintus did the same thing. The ambush might have been sprung early, but it remained to be seen if they could make it back to the Trebia before the enemy horsemen reached them.

It soon became clear that they would never reach the river in time. The Numidians were physically smaller than the Romans, and their mounts were faster. They were operating to a plan too. While some continued riding in direct pursuit from the south, others angled their path outwards and to the west, effectively hemming the patrol against the Trebia. The Romans had to flee northwards. Naturally, they made for the ford. There was no other option. It was the only one for miles in either direction.

'Get to the front,' Fabricius shouted at Quintus and Flaccus. 'Stay there. Stop for nothing.'

Flaccus obeyed without question, but Quintus held back. 'What about you?'

'I'm staying at the rear to prevent this becoming a complete rout,' snapped Fabricius. 'Now go!' His steely gaze brooked no argument.

Fighting back tears, Quintus urged his horse into a full gallop. It soon drew ahead of the other cavalrymen. Never had he been more glad of his father's insistence on taking the best mount available, or more ashamed that he could feel such relief. Quintus did not want to die like a rabbit chased down by a pack of dogs. With this dark thought fighting for supremacy, he leaned forward over his horse's neck and concentrated on one thing. Surviving. With luck, some of them would make it.

They had covered nearly a mile before the first Numidians had closed to within missile range. Riding bareback, half-clothed, the lithe, dark-skinned warriors did not look that threatening. Their javelins' accuracy proved otherwise. Every time Quintus looked around, another cavalryman had been struck, or fallen from his mount. Others had their horses injured, and were no longer able to keep up with their comrades. No one saw their swift, and inevitable fate, yet their strangled cries followed in the survivors' wake, sending terror into their hearts. The Roman riders could not even respond. Their thrusting spears were not made to be thrown.

By the time Fabricius' men had covered another mile, the Numidians were attacking from three sides. Javelins were scudding in constantly, and Quintus could count only ten riders apart from himself, his father and Flaccus. At the bend in the track that led around and down to the ford, that number had been reduced to six. Desperately, Quintus urged his mount to even greater efforts. He didn't know why, but they seemed to have drawn slightly ahead of their pursuers. Perhaps they still had a chance? he wondered. With their horses' hooves throwing up showers of stones, they pounded around the corner and on to the straight stretch that led to the Trebia, a mere two hundred paces away.

All Quintus' hopes evaporated on the spot.

The tribesmen had held back in order to close the trap. Blocking the way ahead was a massed formation of spearmen. Their large, interlocking shields formed three sides of a square, leaving the open side towards him. Quintus' eyes flickered around in panic. A dense network of trees lined the right-hand side of the road. There was no escape there. On the left was a large area of boggy ground. Only a fool would try to ride across that, he thought.

Yet one of the cavalrymen took this second option. He swiftly learned his lesson. Within twenty paces, his horse was belly deep in glutinous sludge. When the rider tried to dismount, the same happened to him. Screaming with terror, he had soon sunk to his armpits. At last he stopped struggling, but it was too late. The best the man could hope for was an accurately thrown enemy javelin, thought Quintus bitterly. It was that, or drown in the mud.

Fabricius' voice snapped him back to the present. 'Slow down! Form a line,' he ordered in a stony voice. 'Let us meet our death like men.'

One of the five remaining cavalrymen began to make a low, keening noise in his throat.

Suddenly, Quintus' fear became overwhelming.

'Shut your fucking mouth!' Fabricius shouted. 'We are not cowards.'

To Quintus' amazement, the rider stopped wailing.

'Form a line,' Fabricius ordered again.

Moving together until their knees almost touched, the eight men rode forward. Wondering why he hadn't had a javelin in the back by now, Quintus turned. The Numidians had slowed to a walk. We're being herded to the slaughter like so many sheep, he thought in disgust.

'Keep your eyes to the front,' Fabricius muttered. 'Show the whoresons that we are not afraid. We will look our fate in the eyes.'

About 150 paces separated the Romans from the phalanxes. To Quintus, the distance felt like an eternity. Part of him wished that the travesty would just end, but he was also desperate not to die. Inexorably, the gap narrowed. A hundred paces, then eighty. Terrified now, Quintus glanced at his father. All he received in the way of reassurance was a tight nod. Quintus took a deep breath, forcing himself to be calm.

I am a boy no longer. How I face my death is my decision alone. I will make it as brave an end as possible.

'Ready spears,' Fabricius ordered.

Quintus shot a look at Flaccus and was faintly pleased by his jutting chin. For all his arrogance, he was *not* a coward.

Sixty steps. They were nearing the distance of a long volley from the spearmen. As they crossed this invisible line, every one of the eight flinched. It was impossible not to. Yet nothing happened. Fabricius felt a new determination. They could ignore this torture if they wished. 'Let's take some of the bastards with us! At the trot. Choose your targets!' he yelled, pointing his spear at a bearded Libyan.

Relieved that the movements of his horse concealed his shaking arm, Quintus took aim at a man with a notched helmet. Let it be over soon, he prayed. May the gods look after Mother and Aurelia. He heard the shout of orders as the Carthaginian officers prepared their soldiers for a final volley, saw hundreds of men's torsos twist as their right arms went back. Quintus closed his eyes. The darkness this granted was somehow comforting. He was aware of his pounding heart, and his mount between his knees. Bounded on each side by its companions, it would not stray from its course. All he had to do was hold on.

'Quintus?' bellowed a voice.

With a jerk, Quintus opened his eyelids. That shout had come from

377

within the Carthaginian ranks. He glanced at his father. 'Stop! You must stop!'

Something in Quintus' tone penetrated Fabricius' battle madness, and his fierce expression cleared. He raised his spear in the air. 'Halt!'

Pulling hard on their reins, the Romans screeched to a halt ten paces from the forest of bristling spear tips. Unsettled, their horses tried to shy away. More than one Libyan shoved his weapon forward in an attempt to reach them. Quintus heard a familiar voice cry out in Carthaginian. Goosebumps rose on his arms. Ignoring his companions' confusion, he scanned the enemy ranks. He couldn't believe it when Hanno, clad in a Carthaginian officer's uniform, elbowed his way out of the phalanx a moment later. Quintus lowered his spear. 'Hanno!'

'Quintus.' Hanno's tone was flat. He spoke in Latin. 'What are you doing here?'

'We were on a patrol,' he replied. 'A reconnaissance mission.'

Hanno made a sweeping gesture with his right arm. 'We control the whole plain. You must know that. What kind of fool would order an undertaking like that?'

'Our consul,' Quintus muttered. He wasn't going to reveal Flaccus' involvement.

Hanno gave a derisory snort. 'Enough said.'

Quintus had the sense not to reply. He glanced at his father and saw that he too had recognised Hanno. Sensibly, Fabricius also said nothing. Flaccus and the cavalrymen looked baffled, and fearful. Quintus turned back to Hanno. He tried to ignore the fierce stares of the enemy soldiers.

'Hanno!' cried an angry voice. A torrent of Carthaginian followed as two more officers emerged, one from the phalanx on either side. The first was short and burly, with thick eyebrows, while the other was tall and athletic, with long black hair. Their features were too similar to Hanno's to be coincidence. They had to be his brothers, thought Quintus. 'You found your family, then?'

'I did. And they want to know why you're still alive.' Turning to his siblings, Hanno launched into a long explanation. With his stomach knotted in tension, Quintus watched. Their very lives depended on what was said. There was plenty of shouting and gesticulating, but eventually Hanno seemed satisfied. The shorter of his brothers looked most unhappy, however. He continued muttering loudly as the taller brother approached the Romans. His face was hard, but not without kindness, thought Quintus warily. He had to be Bostar.

'Hanno says that he owes his life to you twice over,' Bostar said in accented Latin.

Quintus nodded. 'That's true.'

'For that reason, we have agreed not to slay you, or your father.' At this, Sapho launched into another tirade, but Bostar ignored him. 'Two lives for two debts.'

'And the others?' asked Quintus, feeling sick.

'They must die.'

'No,' Quintus muttered. 'Take them as prisoners. Please.'

Bostar shook his head and turned away.

Cries of fear rose from the cavalrymen. Flaccus, however, sat up straight on his horse, gazing with contempt at the Libyans.

Quintus' gaze shot to Hanno, and found no pity there. 'Show them some mercy.'

'We have our orders,' said Hanno in a harsh voice. 'But you and your father are free to go.' He snapped out a command, and the phalanx behind him split open, opening a passage to the ford.

An idea struck Quintus. 'There is one other family member here.'

Hanno turned. 'Who?' he demanded suspiciously.

Quintus indicated Flaccus. 'He is betrothed to Aurelia. Spare him also.'

Hanno's nostrils flared in belated recognition. 'If they are not married, he is not yet part of your family.'

'You would not deprive Aurelia of her prospective husband, surely?' Quintus pleaded.

Hanno was shocked to feel resentful. 'You ask for more than you know,' he said from between gritted teeth.

'I ask it nonetheless,' replied Quintus, meeting his gaze.

Hanno stalked closer to Flaccus. If the truth be known, he did not want to withdraw the hand of friendship so fast, but this *was* one of the enemy.

Incredibly, Flaccus spat a gob of phlegm at his feet.

Rage filled Hanno, and his hand fell to his sword. Before he could draw it, however, Sapho had stepped past. There was a spear gripped in his fists. Without saying a word, he shoved the blade deep into Flaccus' groin, below his armour, before ripping it out again. As his victim fell screaming to the ground, Sapho spun around. He aimed his bloody spear tip at Hanno. 'We're not here to be friendly with these fucking whoresons,' he snapped. 'You and Bostar might have overridden me over releasing two of them, but you're not setting another one free!'

Hanno pointed grimly at the ford. 'Go.'

Quintus stared helplessly at Flaccus, who was clutching his wound while blood spurted from between his fingers. There was already a large pool beneath him. We can't just leave the poor bastard to die, Quintus thought. But what other choice have we?

Fabricius took the initiative. 'May you meet each other in Elysium,' he muttered to the cavalrymen. 'Your family will be told that you died well,' he said to Flaccus. Then, without so much as a backward glance, he rode towards the river. 'Come on,' he hissed at Quintus.

Trying to think of what to say, Quintus took a last look at Hanno. Rather than meet his gaze, the Carthaginian stared right through him. There was to be no farewell. Gritting his teeth, Quintus followed his father. At once his ears were filled with the cries of the five unfortunate cavalrymen, who were promptly surrounded and dispatched by the clamouring Libyans.

Father and son made their way unhindered to the ford, and into the water.

On the other side, it finally sank in that they had escaped.

A long, shuddering breath escaped Quintus' lips. Never let me meet Hanno again, he prayed. His former friend *would* try to kill him: there was no doubt about that. And Quintus realised that he would do the same. As cold misery gripped his heart, he stared back across the river. The Libyans were already marching away. They had left the crumpled forms of the Roman dead on the riverbank. The sight caused Quintus' shame to soar. Everyone deserved to be buried, or burned on a pyre. 'Maybe we can retrieve the bodies tomorrow,' he muttered.

'We'll have to try, or I'll never be able to look Aurelia in the eyes again,' replied his father. *And the moment that the damn moneylenders hear that Flaccus is dead, they'll be all over me like a rash.* He glanced at Quintus. 'It's all my damn fault. Flaccus and thirty good men are dead, because I agreed to lead the damn patrol. I should have refused.'

'It's not up to you to make tactical decisions, Father,' Quintus protested. 'If you'd said no, Publius could have demoted you to the ranks, or worse.'

Fabricius shot Quintus a grateful look. 'I'm only alive because of you. Helping the Carthaginian to escape and then manumitting him were good decisions. I'm grateful.'

Quintus nodded sadly. His friendship with Hanno might have saved their lives, but this was not the way he'd have wanted it to end. There was nothing he could do to change things, however. Quintus hardened his heart. Hanno was one of the enemy now.

Fabricius rode straight back to the camp, and from there to the consul's command tent. Leaping from his horse, he threw his reins at one of the sentries and started towards the entrance. Quintus watched miserably from the back of his mount. Publius would not want to speak to a low-ranking cavalryman such as he.

His father stopped by the tent flap. 'Well?'

'You want me to come in?'

Fabricius laughed. 'Of course. You are the sole reason we're still breathing. Publius will want to hear why.'

Re-energised, Quintus jumped down and joined his father. The sentries at the entrance, four sturdy *triarii* – veterans – wearing highly polished crested helmets and mail shirts, stood to attention as they passed. Quintus' chest swelled with pride. He was about to meet the consul! Until now, his only interactions with Publius had been to salute and return a polite greeting.

They were ushered through various sections of the tent by a junior officer until they reached a comfortable area lined with carpets. The space was lit by large bronze lamps and contained a desk covered in parchments, ink pots and quills, various iron-bound chests and several luxurious couches. Bolstered by cushions, Publius was reclining on the biggest. His face was still an unhealthy grey colour, and bulky dressings were visible on his injured leg. His son stood attentively behind him, reading from a half-unrolled manuscript. Publius' eyes opened as they approached, and he acknowledged their salutes. 'Well met, Fabricius,' he murmured. 'Is that your son?'

'Yes, sir.'

'What's his name again?'

'Quintus, sir.'

'Ah, yes. So, you have returned from your patrol. Did you meet with any success?'

'No, sir,' Fabricius replied tersely. 'In fact, the complete opposite. Before getting anywhere near the Carthaginian camp, we were ambushed by a hugely superior enemy force. They pursued us right to the riverbank, where a strong force of spearmen was waiting.' He indicated Quintus. 'We are the only survivors.'

'I see.' Publius' fingers drummed on the arm of his couch. 'How is it that you were not also killed?'

Fabricius met the consul's scrutiny with a solid gaze. 'Because of Quintus here.'

Publius' brows lowered. 'Explain.'

Prompted by his father's nudge, Quintus told the story of how he had been recognised by a former slave of the family, whom he had befriended. He faltered when it came to explaining how Hanno had been freed, but encouraged by Publius' nod, Quintus revealed everything.

'That is an incredible tale,' Publius acknowledged. 'The gods were most merciful.'

'Yes, sir,' Quintus agreed fervently.

The consul looked up at his son. 'You're not the only one able to rescue his father,' he joked.

The younger Publius blushed bright red.

Publius' face turned serious. 'So, a whole turma has been wiped out, and we know no more about Hannibal's disposition than yesterday.'

'That's correct, sir,' Fabricius admitted.

'I see little point in sending further patrols across the Trebia. They would meet the same fate, and we have few enough cavalry as it is,' said Publius. He pressed a finger against his lips, thinking. Then he shook his head. 'Our main priority is to block the passage south, which we are already doing. The Carthaginians will not attack us here, because of the uneven terrain. Nothing has changed. We wait for Longus.'

'Yes, sir,' Fabricius concurred.

'Very good. You may go.' Publius waved a hand in dismissal.

Father and son made a discreet exit.

Quintus managed to contain his frustration until they were out of earshot. 'Why doesn't Publius *do* something?' he hissed.

'You want revenge for what happened at the ford, eh?' asked Fabricius with a wry smile. 'I do too.' He bent close to Quintus' ear. 'I'm sure that Publius would have moved against Hannibal again if he weren't . . . incapacitated. Of course he's not going to admit that to the likes of us. For the moment, we just have to live with it.'

'Will Longus want to fight Hannibal?'

'I'd say so,' replied his father with a grin. 'A victory before the turn of the year would show the tribes that Hannibal is vulnerable. It would also reduce the number of warriors who plan on joining him. Defeating him soon would be far better than leaving it until the spring.'

Quintus prayed that his father was correct. After all the setbacks they'd suffered, it was time for the tables to be turned. The quicker that was done, the better.

Chapter XXIII: Battle Commences

Bostar waited until they'd got back to the Carthaginian camp before he launched his attack. The moment that their men had been stood down, he rounded on Hanno. 'What the hell was that about?' he shouted. 'Don't you remember our orders? We were supposed to kill them all!'

'I know,' muttered Hanno. The sad image of Quintus and his father riding down to the Trebia was vivid in his mind's eye. 'How, though, could I kill the person who had saved my life, not once, but twice?'

'So your sense of honour is more important than a direct order given by Hannibal?' Sapho sneered.

'Yes. No. I don't know,' Hanno replied. 'Leave me alone!'

'Sapho!' Bostar snapped.

Sapho raised his hands and stepped back. 'Let's see what the general says when we report to him.' He made a face. 'I presume that you are going to tell him?'

Hanno felt a towering fury take hold. 'Of course I am!' he cried. 'I've got nothing to hide. What, were you going to tell Hannibal if I didn't?' His mouth opened as Sapho flushed. 'Sacred Tanit, you fucking were! Where did you get to be so poisonous? No wonder Bostar doesn't like you any more.' He saw Sapho's shock, and despite his anger, felt instant shame. 'I shouldn't have said that. I'm sorry.'

'It's a bit late,' retorted Sapho. 'Why should I be surprised that you've been talking about me behind my back? You little dirtbag!'

Hanno flushed and hung his head.

'I'll see you at the general's tent,' said Sapho sourly. 'We'll see what Hannibal thinks of what you've done then.' Pulling his cloak tighter around himself, he walked away.

'Sapho! Come back!' Hanno shouted.

'Let him go,' advised Bostar.

'Why is he being like that?'

'I don't know,' said Bostar, looking away.

Now you're the one who's lying, thought Hanno, but he didn't have the heart to interrogate his older brother. Soon he would have to explain his actions to Hannibal. 'Come on,' he said anxiously. 'We'd best get this over with.'

Hanno was relieved to find that Sapho had not entered Hannibal's tent, but was waiting outside for them. Zamar, the Numidian officer was there too. Announcing themselves to the guards, they were ushered inside.

Hanno slipped to Sapho's side. 'Thank you.'

Sapho gave him a startled look. 'For what?'

'Not going in to tell your version of the story first.'

'I might disagree with what you did, but I'm not a telltale,' Sapho shot back in an angry whisper.

'I know,' said Hanno. 'Let's just see what Hannibal says, eh? After that, we can forget about it.'

'No more talking about me behind my back,' Sapho warned.

'It's not as if Bostar said much. He commented that after the pirates' capture, you had changed.'

'Changed?'

'Grown tougher. Harder.'

'Nothing else?' Sapho demanded.

'No.' What in Tanit's name happened between you two? Hanno wondered. He wasn't sure he wanted to know.

Sapho was silent for a moment. 'Very well. We'll put it behind us after we've reported to Hannibal. But understand this: if he asks me my opinion about the release of the two Romans, I'm not going to lie to him.'

'That's fine,' said Hanno heatedly. 'I wouldn't want you to.'

Their conversation came to an abrupt halt as they entered the main part of Hannibal's tent.

The general greeted them with a broad smile. 'Word of your success has already reached me,' he declared. He raised his glass. 'Come, taste this wine. For a Roman vintage, it's quite palatable.'

When they all had a glass in hand, Hannibal looked at them each in turn. 'Well?' he enquired. 'Who's going to tell me what happened?'

Hanno stepped forward. 'I will, sir,' he said, swallowing.

Hannibal's eyebrows rose, but he indicated that Hanno should continue.

Shoving away his nervousness, Hanno described their march to the Trebia, and the long wait in the hidden clearing. When he got to the point where the Roman patrol had crossed, he turned to Zamar. The Numidian related how his men had carried word to him of the enemy incursion, and of how the ambush had been sprung early by an overeager section leader. 'I've already stripped him to the ranks, sir,' he said. 'Thanks to him, the whole thing might have been a disaster.'

'But it wasn't, thankfully,' Hannibal replied. 'Did any make it to the river?'

'Yes, sir,' said Zamar. 'Eight.'

Hannibal winked. 'That didn't leave much work for nine hundred spearmen!'

They all laughed.

'Did you find any documents on the Roman commander?'

Hanno didn't know how to answer. 'No, sir,' he muttered. From the corner of his eye, he could see Sapho glaring at him.

Hannibal didn't notice Hanno's reticence. 'A shame. Still, never mind. It's unlikely that they would carry anything of importance on such a mission anyway.'

Hanno coughed awkwardly. 'I didn't manage to search him, sir.'

'Why not?' asked Hannibal, frowning.

'Because I let him go, sir. Along with one other.'

The general's eyes widened in disbelief. 'You had best explain yourself, son of Malchus. *Fast.*'

Hannibal's intense stare was unnerving. 'Yes, sir.' Hanno hastily began. When he had finished, there was a pregnant silence. Hanno thought he was going to be sick.

Hannibal eyed Sapho and Bostar askance. 'Presumably, he consulted with you two,' he snapped.

'Yes, sir,' they mumbled.

'What was your reaction, Bostar?'

'Although it was against your orders, sir, I respected his reason for wanting to let the two men go.'

Hannibal looked at Sapho.

'I violently disagreed, sir, but I was overruled.'

Hannibal regarded Zamar. 'And you?'

'I had nothing to do with it, sir,' the Numidian replied neutrally. 'I was a hundred paces away with my men.'

'Interesting,' said Hannibal to Hanno. 'One brother supported you, one did not.'

'Yes, sir.'

'Is this what I am to expect in future when I issue a command?' demanded Hannibal, his nostrils flaring.

'No, sir,' protested Bostar and Hanno. 'Of course not,' Hanno added.

Hannibal didn't comment further. 'Do I detect that there was quite an amount of disagreement?'

Hanno flushed. 'You do, sir.'

'Why was that?'

'Because we were given orders to let none survive, sir!' cried Sapho.

'Finally, we come back to the nub of the issue,' said Hannibal. In the background, Sapho smiled triumphantly. 'Under ordinary circumstances, this situation would be black and white. And if you'd disobeyed my orders as you have done, I would have had you crucified.'

His words hung in the air like a bad smell.

Fear twisted Sapho's face. 'Sir, I . . .' he began.

'Did I ask you to speak?' Hannibal snapped.

'No, sir.'

'Then keep your mouth shut!'

Humbled, Sapho obeyed.

Hanno wiped his brow, which was covered in sweat. I still did the right thing, he thought. I owed Quintus my life. Sure that, at the very least, a severe punishment was about to follow, he resigned himself to his fate. Beside him, Bostar was clenching and unclenching his jaw.

'Yet what transpired happens but once in a host of lifetimes,' said Hannibal.

Stunned, Hanno waited to hear what his general said next.

'A man can't go killing those who have helped him, even if they are Roman. I cannot think of a better way to anger the gods.' Hannibal gave Hanno a grim nod. 'You did the right thing.'

'Thank you, sir,' whispered Hanno. He'd never been so relieved in his life.

'I will let you off, Bostar, because of the unique nature of what happened.'

Bostar stood rigidly to attention and saluted. 'Thank you, sir!'

Hanno glanced at Sapho. His fear had been replaced by a poorly concealed expression of resentment. Did he want us to be punished? Hanno wondered uneasily.

'As well as satisfying your honour, your lenient gesture fulfilled another purpose,' Hannibal continued. 'Those two men will speak of little but the excellence of our troops. Some of their comrades will be demoralised by what they hear, which helps our cause. Despite your disobedience, you have achieved the result I wanted.'

'Yes, sir.'

'That's not all,' said Hannibal lightly.

Hanno's fear returned with a vengeance. 'Sir?'

'There can be no repeat of such behaviour.' Hannibal's voice had grown hard. 'You have paid off your obligation to this *Quintus*. Should you see either him or his father again, you can act in only one way.'

He's right, screamed Hanno's common sense. How can I remain friends with a Roman? Despite everything, his heart felt differently. 'Yes, sir.'

'Trust me, those men would bury a sword in your belly as soon as look at you. They are the enemy,' growled Hannibal. 'If you meet either again, you will kill them.'

'Yes, sir,' Hanno said, finally giving in. *But never let it happen.*

'Understand too that if any of you disobey my orders again, I will *not* be merciful. Instead, expect to end your miserable lives screaming on a cross. Understand?'

'Yes, sir,' replied Hanno, shaking.

'You're dismissed,' said Hannibal curtly. 'All of you.'

Muttering their thanks, Zamar and the three brothers withdrew.

Sapho sidled up to Hanno outside. 'Still think you did the right thing?' he hissed.

'Eh?' Hanno gave his brother an incredulous look.

'We could all be dead now, thanks to you.'

'But we're not! And it's not as if such a thing will ever happen again, is it?' demanded Hanno.

388

'I suppose not,' Sapho admitted, taken aback by Hanno's fury.

'I'm as loyal as you or any man in the damn army,' Hanno snarled. 'Line me up some Romans, and I'll chop off all their fucking heads!'

'All right, all right,' muttered Sapho. 'You've made your point.'

'So have you,' retorted Hanno angrily. 'Did you want us to be punished in there?'

Sapho made an apologetic gesture. 'Look, I had no idea he might crucify you.'

'Would you have said anything to Hannibal if you had?' challenged Bostar.

A guilty look stole across Sapho's face. 'No.'

'You're a fucking liar,' said Bostar. Without another word, he walked off.

Hanno glared at Sapho. 'Well?'

'Do you really think I'd want the two of you to die? Please!' Sapho protested. 'Have some faith in me!'

Hanno sighed. 'I do. I'm sorry.'

'So am I,' said Sapho, clapping him on the shoulder. 'Let's forget about it, eh? Concentrate on fighting the Romans.'

'Yes.' Hanno glanced after Bostar, and his heart sank. His other brother looked angered by the friendly gesture Sapho had just made. Gods above, he thought in frustration, can I not get on with the two of them?

It appeared not.

Saturnalia was fast approaching. Despite Atia and Aurelia's melancholy, preparations for the midwinter festival were well under way. It was a way, Aurelia realised, of coping with the void both of them felt inside at her father's probable death, and the lack of word from Quintus. Life had to go on in some fashion, and losing themselves in mundane tasks had proved to be an effective method of maintaining normality. There was so much to be done that the short winter days flashed by in a blur. Atia's list of things to do seemed never-ending. Each evening, Aurelia was worn out, and grateful that her exhaustion meant deep slumber without any bad dreams.

One night, however, Aurelia did not fall asleep as usual. Her mind was racing. She and her mother were going to Capua in two days on a final shopping expedition. Dozens of candles were still required as gifts for their family friends and the guests. Not all of the food for their impending feasts had been ordered yet – there had been a mix-up with the baker over what was needed, and the butcher wanted far too much money for his meat. Atia also wanted to purchase pottery figurines; these were exchanged on the last day of the celebrations.

Despite her best efforts, Aurelia found herself thinking about Suniaton. After meeting Agesandros, she and Elira had made their way to the hut without any difficulty. Pleasingly, Suni's leg had healed enough for him to leave. He's long gone, thought Aurelia sadly. Suniaton had been her last link with Hanno, and in a strange way, Quintus and her father. It was entirely possible that she would never see any of them again. On the spur of the moment, she decided to visit the isolated dwelling one more time. What for, Aurelia wasn't sure. Perhaps the gods would offer her some kind of sign there. Something that would make her grief more bearable. Keeping this idea to the forefront of her mind, she managed to fall asleep.

Waking early the next morning, Aurelia dressed in her warmest clothes. She was relieved to find only a finger's depth of snow covering the statues and mosaic floor in the courtyard. Pausing to tell a sleepy Elira where she was going, and to raise the alarm if she was not back by nightfall, Aurelia went to the stables and readied her father's grey horse.

She had never ridden so far from the farm in the depths of winter before, and was stunned by the beauty of the silent countryside. It was such a contrast to the spring and summer, when everything was bursting with life. Most of the trees had lost their leaves, scattering them in thick layers upon the ground, layers that were now frozen beneath a light covering of snow. The only movement was the occasional flash of wildlife: a pair of crows tumbling through the air in pursuit of a falcon, the suggestion of a deer in the distance. Once, Aurelia thought she saw a jackal skulking off into the undergrowth. Gratifyingly, she heard no wolves, and saw no sign of their spoor. Although it was rare for the large predators to attack humans, it was not unheard of. The chances of seeing them grew as she climbed, however, and Aurelia was grateful that she had taken a bow as well as her sling.

Her anticipation grew as she neared the hut. Its peaceful atmosphere would assuage her worries about her loved ones. With a growing sense of excitement, Aurelia tied up her horse outside. She scattered a handful of oats on the ground to keep it happy, and stepped towards the door. A faint sound from inside stopped her dead. Terror paralysed Aurelia's every muscle as she remembered the bandits whom Quintus and Hanno had fought. What had she been thinking to travel alone?

Turning on her heel, Aurelia tiptoed away from the hut. If she made it onto her saddle blanket, there was a good chance of escaping. Few men possessed the skill with a bow to bring down a rider on a galloping horse. She had almost reached her mount when it looked up from its oats, and gave her a pleased whinny. Frantically stroking its head to silence it, Aurelia listened. All she could hear was her heart pounding in her chest like that of a captured beast. Taking a good grip of the horse's mane, she prepared to scramble on to its back.

'Hello?'

Aurelia nearly jumped out of her skin with fright.

A moment passed. The door did not open.

Aurelia managed to calm herself. The voice had been weak and quavering, and certainly not that of a strong, healthy man. Gradually, her curiosity began to equal her fear. 'Who's there? I'm not alone.'

There was no response.

Aurelia began to wonder if it was a trap after all. She vacillated, torn between riding to safety and checking that whoever was inside did not need help. At length, she decided not to flee. If this was an ambush, it was the worst-laid one she could think of. Gripping her dagger to give her confidence, she padded towards the hut. There was no handle or latch, just a gap in the timbers to pull open the portal. With trembling fingers, Aurelia flipped the door towards her, placing her foot against the bottom edge to hold it ajar. She peered cautiously into the dim interior. Instead of the fire she might have expected, the round stone fireplace was full of ashes. Aurelia gagged as the acrid smell of human urine and faeces wafted outside.

Finally, she made out a figure lying sprawled on the floor. She had taken it first for a bundle of rags. When it moved, she screamed. 'S-Suni?'

His eyes opened wide. 'Is that you, Aurelia?'

'Yes, it is.' She darted inside and dropped to her knees by his side. 'Oh, Suniaton!' She struggled not to weep.

'Have you any water?'

'Better than that: I have wine!' Aurelia ran outside, returning with her supplies. Gently, she helped him to sit up and drink a few mouthfuls.

'That's better,' Suniaton declared. A tinge of colour began to appear in his cheeks, and he cast greedy eyes at Aurelia's bag.

Delighted by his revival, she laid out some bread and cheese. 'Eat a little at a time,' she warned. 'Your stomach won't be able to take any more.' She sat and watched him as he devoured the food. 'Why didn't you leave after my last visit?'

He paused between mouthfuls. 'I did, the next day. About half a mile down the track, I tripped over a jutting tree root and landed awkwardly. The fall tore the muscles that had just healed in my bad leg. I couldn't walk ten steps without screaming, never mind reach Capua or the coast. It was all I could do to crawl back to the hut. My food ran out more than a week ago, and my water two days after that.' He pointed at the hole in the roof. 'If it hadn't been for the snow that came through that, I would have died of thirst.' He smiled. 'They took their time, but the gods answered my prayers.'

Aurelia squeezed his hand. 'They did. Something told me to come up here. Obviously, you were the reason why.'

'But I can't stay here,' Suniaton said despairingly. 'One heavy fall of snow and the roof will give way.'

'Don't worry,' Aurelia cried. 'My horse can carry both of us.'

His expression was bleak. 'Where to, though? My leg will take months to heal, if it does at all.'

'To the farm,' she replied boldly. 'I will tell Mother and Agesandros that I found you wandering in the woods. I couldn't just leave you to die.'

'He might remember me,' Suniaton protested.

She squeezed his hand. 'He won't. You look terrible. Totally different from that day in Capua.'

Suniaton scowled. 'It's obvious that I am an escaped slave.'

'But there won't be any way of proving who you are,' Aurelia cried in triumph. 'You can act mute.'

'Will that work?' he asked with a dubious frown.

'Of course,' Aurelia declared robustly. 'And when you're better, you can leave.'

A spark of hope lit in Suniaton's weary eyes. 'If you're sure,' he whispered.

'I am,' Aurelia replied, patting his hand. Inside, however, she was terrified.

What other choice had they, though? her mind screamed.

More than two weeks later, Quintus was wandering through the camp with Calatinus and Cincius. The general mood had been improved dramatically seven days before by the arrival of Tiberius Sempronius Longus, the second consul. His army, which consisted of two legions and more than 10,000 socii, infantry and cavalry, had swelled the Roman forces to nearly 40,000 men.

Inevitably enough, the trio found their feet taking them in the direction of the camp headquarters. So far, there had been little news of what Longus, who had assumed control of all Republican forces, planned to do about Hannibal.

'He'll have been encouraged by what happened yesterday,' declared Calatinus. 'Our cavalry and velites gave the guggas a hiding that they won't forget in a hurry.'

'Stupid bastards got what was coming to them,' said Cincius. 'The Gauls are supposed to be their allies. If they go pillaging local settlements, it's natural that the tribesmen will come looking for help.'

'There were heavy enemy casualties,' Quintus admitted, 'but I'm not sure it was the total victory Longus is claiming.'

Both of his friends looked at him in astonishment.

'Think about it,' urged Quintus. It was what his father had said to him when he'd raved about the engagement. 'We had the upper hand from the start, but things changed immediately once Hannibal came on the scene. The Carthaginians held their ground then, didn't they?'

'So what?' Cincius responded. 'They lost three times more men than we did!'

'Aren't you pleased that we finally got the better of them?' demanded Calatinus.

'Of course I am,' said Quintus. 'We shouldn't underestimate Hannibal, that's all.'

Cincius snorted derisively. 'Longus is an experienced general. And in my book, any man who can march his army more than a thousand miles in less than six weeks shows considerable ability.'

'You've seen Longus a few times since his arrival. The man positively exudes energy,' added Calatinus. 'He's keen for a fight too.'

'You're right,' said Quintus at last. 'Our troops are better fed, and better armed than Hannibal's. We outnumber the Carthaginians too.'

'We just need the right opportunity,' declared Cincius.

'That will come,' said Calatinus. 'All the recent omens have been good.'

Quintus grinned. It was impossible not to feel enthused by his friends' words, and the recent change in their fortunes. As always when Quintus thought of the enemy, an image of Hanno popped into his mind. He shoved it away.

There was a war on.

Friendship with a Carthaginian had no place in his heart any longer.

Several days passed, and the weather grew dramatically worse. The biting wind came incessantly from the north, bringing with it heavy showers of sleet and snow. Combined with the shortened daylight, it made for a miserable existence. Hanno saw little of either his father or brothers. The Carthaginian soldiers huddled in their tents, shivering and trying to stay warm. Even venturing outside to answer a call of nature meant getting soaked to the skin or chilled to the bone.

Hanno was stunned, therefore, by the news that Sapho brought one afternoon. 'We've had word from Hannibal!' he hissed. 'We move out tonight.'

'In weather like this?' asked Hanno incredulously. 'Are you mad?'

'Maybe.' Sapho grinned. 'If I am, though, so too is Hannibal. He has ordered Mago himself to lead us.'

'You and Bostar?'

Sapho nodded grimly. 'Plus five hundred skirmishers, and a thousand Numidian cavalry.'

Hanno smiled to cover his disappointment at not also being picked. 'Where are you going?'

'While we've been hiding in our tents, Hannibal has been scouting the whole area. He discovered a narrow river that runs across the plain,' Sapho revealed. 'It's bounded on both sides by steep, heavily overgrown banks.

We have to lie in wait there until the opportunity comes – if it comes –
to fall upon the Roman rear.'

'What makes Hannibal think that they'll cross the river?'

Sapho's expression grew fierce. 'He plans to irritate them into doing so.'

'That means using the Numidians,' guessed Hanno.

'You've got it. They're going to attack the enemy camp at dawn. Sting
and withdraw, sting and withdraw. You know the way they do it.'

'Will it drag the whole Roman army out of camp, though?'

'We'll see.'

'I wish I'd been chosen too,' said Hanno fervently.

Sapho chuckled. 'Save your regrets. The whole damn enterprise might
be a waste of time. While Bostar and I are freezing our balls off in a ditch,
you and the rest of the army will be warmly wrapped up in your blankets.
And if a battle does look likely, it's not as if you'll miss out, is it? We'll
all have to fight!'

A grin slowly spread across Hanno's face. 'True enough.'

'We'll meet in the middle of the Roman line!' declared Sapho. 'Just
think of that moment.'

Hanno nodded. It was an appealing image. 'The gods watch over you
both,' he said. I must go and speak to Bostar, he thought. Say goodbye.

'And you, little brother.' Sapho reached out and ruffled Hanno's hair,
something he hadn't done for years.

Quintus was in the middle of a fantasy about Elira when he became aware
of someone shaking him. He did his best to stay asleep, but the insistent
tugging on his arm proved too much. Opening his eyes irritably, Quintus
found not Elira, but Calatinus crouched over him. Before he could utter a
word of rebuke, he heard the trumpets sounding the alarm over and over.
He sat bolt upright. 'What's going on?'

'Our outposts beyond the camp perimeter are under attack. Get up!'

The last of Quintus' drowsiness vanished. 'Eh? What time is it?'

'Not long after dawn. The sentries started shouting when I was in the
latrines.' Calatinus scowled. 'Didn't help my diarrhoea, I can tell you.'

Smiling at the image, Quintus threw off the covers and began scrambling into his clothes. 'Have we had any orders yet?'

'Longus wants every man ready to leave a quarter of an hour ago,' replied Calatinus, who was already fully dressed. 'I've been shouting at you to no avail. The others are readying their mounts.'

'Well, I'm here now,' muttered Quintus, kneeling to strap on his sandals.

Before long, they had joined their comrades outside, by their tethered horses.

It was bitterly cold, and the north wind was whipping vicious little flurries of snow across the tent tops. The camp was in uproar as thousands of men scrambled to get ready. It wasn't just the cavalry who had been ordered to prepare themselves for battle. Large groups of velites were being addressed by their officers. Unhappy-looking *hastati* and *principes* – the men who stood in the legion's first two ranks – left their breakfasts to burn on their camp-fires as they ran to get their equipment. Messengers hurried to and fro, relaying information between different units. On the battlements, the trumpeters kept up their clarion call to arms. Quintus swallowed nervously. Was this the moment he had been waiting for? It certainly felt like it. Soon after, he was relieved to see his father's figure striding towards them from the direction of the camp's headquarters. Excited murmurs rippled through the surrounding cavalrymen. As one, they stiffened to attention.

'This is no parade. At ease,' said Fabricius, waving a hand. 'We ride out at once. Longus is deploying our entire cavalry force, as well as six thousand velites. He wants this attack thrown back across the Trebia without delay. We're taking no more nonsense from Hannibal.'

'And the rest of the army, sir?' cried a voice. 'What about them?'

Fabricius smiled tightly. 'They will be ready to follow us very soon.'

These words produced a rousing cheer. Quintus joined in. He wanted this victory as much as anyone else. The fact that his father hadn't mentioned Publius must mean that the injured consul agreed with his colleague's decision, or had been overruled by him. Either way, they weren't going to sit by and do nothing.

Fabricius waited until the noise had died down. 'Remember to do everything I've taught you. Check your horse's harness is tightly fastened. Take a leak before you mount up. There's nothing worse than pissing yourself in the middle of a fight.' Hoots of nervous laughter met this comment, and Fabricius smiled. 'Ensure that your spear tip is sharp. Tie the chin-strap on your helmet. Watch each other's backs.' He scanned the faces around him with grave eyes. 'May the gods be with you all.'

'And with you, sir!' shouted Calatinus.

Fabricius inclined his head in recognition. Then, giving Quintus a re-assuring look, he made towards his horse.

For the third time since dawn, Bostar scrambled up the muddy slope towards the sentry's position. More than anything, he wanted to warm up. Unfortunately, the climb wasn't long enough to shift the chill from his muscles. He glanced down at the steep-sided riverbank below him. It was filled with Mago's men: 1,000 Numidians and their horses, and 1,000 infantry, a mixture of Libyan skirmishers and spearmen. Despite the fact that the warmly dressed soldiers were packed as tightly as apples in a barrel, it seemed an eternity since they had arrived. In fact, it was barely five hours. Men are not supposed to spend a winter's night outdoors in this godforsaken land, thought Bostar bitterly. His bones ached at the idea of the warm sunshine that bathed Carthage daily.

Reaching the top of the bank, Bostar crouched down, using the scrubby bushes that regularly dotted the ground as cover. He peered into the distance, but saw nothing. There had been no movement since the Numidian cavalry had quietly passed by, heading for the Roman side of the river. Bostar sighed. It would be hours before anything of import-ance happened. Nonetheless, he had to keep his guard up. Hannibal had given them the most important task of any soldiers in his army. For what felt like the thousandth time, Bostar slowly turned in a circle, scan-ning the landscape with eagle eyes.

The watercourse that formed their hiding place was a small tributary of the Trebia, and ran north–south across the plain that lay before the Carthaginian camp. Following Hannibal's instructions, they had secreted themselves half a mile to the south of the area upon which he wished to fight. The general's reasons were simple. Behind them, the ground began to climb towards the low hills that filled the horizon. If the Romans took the bait, they were unlikely to march in this direction. It was a good place to hide, thought Bostar. He just hoped that Hannibal's plan worked, and that they weren't too far away from the fighting if, or when, the time came to move.

He found Mago lying alongside the sentry in a shallow dip, seemingly oblivious to the cold. Bostar liked the youngest Barca brother. Like Hannibal, Mago was charismatic and brave. He was also indomitably cheerful, which provided a counterweight to Hannibal's sometimes serious disposition. Smaller than Hannibal, Mago reminded Bostar of a hunting dog: lean, muscular and always eager to be slipped from the leash. 'Seen anything, sir?' he whispered.

Mago turned his head. 'Restless, aren't you?'

Bostar shrugged. 'The same as everyone else, sir. It's difficult waiting down there without a clue what's going on.'

Mago smiled. 'Patience,' he said. 'The Romans will come.'

'How can you be sure, sir?'

'Because Hannibal believes that they will, and I trust in him.'

Bostar nodded. It was a good answer, he thought. 'We'll be ready, sir.'

'I know you will. That's why Hannibal picked you and your brother,' Mago replied.

'We're very grateful for the opportunity, sir,' said Bostar, thinking sour thoughts about Sapho. He and his older brother hadn't spoken since Hannibal's reprimand. Bostar felt regret that he'd only had the briefest of words with Hanno before they'd left the camp. He'd been angry that his younger brother seemed to be friendly with Sapho. Really, it was none of his business.

Mago got to his feet. 'Have the men eaten yet?'

'No, sir.'

'Well, if I'm famished, they must be too,' Mago declared. 'Let's break out the rations. It won't be a hot breakfast, like the lucky dogs back at camp will get, but anything's better than nothing. A man with a full belly sees the world with different eyes, eh?' He glanced at the sentry. 'You won't miss out. I'll send someone up to relieve you soon.'

The man grinned. 'Thank you, sir.'

'Lead on,' Mago said.

Bostar obeyed. Mention of the encampment brought his father and Hanno to mind. If it came to a battle, they would be in the front line. Not quite in the centre – that honour had been given to Hannibal's new recruits, the Gaulish tribesmen – but still in a dangerous position. The fighting everywhere would be intense. He sighed. The gods protect us all, he prayed. If it comes to it, let us die well.

Combining his riders with Publius' depleted horsemen gave Sempronius Longus just over four thousand cavalry. The moment that the assembled turmae had heard their orders, they were sent out from behind the protection of the fortifications. Fabricius and his men were among the first to exit the camp.

Quintus blinked with surprise. Beyond the sentry posts lay open ground that rolled down to the river. It was normally empty of all but the figures of training soldiers or returning patrols. Now, it was occupied by thousands of Numidian tribesmen. Waves of yelling warriors were galloping into the Roman positions and loosing their javelins, before wheeling their horses in a tight circle and retreating. The unfortunate sentries, who only numbered four or five per outpost, received no respite. Scarcely had one set of Numidians disappeared before another arrived, whooping and screaming at the top of their lungs.

'Form a battle line!' Fabricius shouted. His call was already being echoed by other officers who were emerging from the camp.

With a pounding heart, Quintus obeyed. So did Calatinus, Cincius and his comrades, each turma fanning out six ranks wide and five riders deep. The instant they were ready, Fabricius shouted, 'Charge!'

His men went from the trot into a canter. This was followed immediately by a gallop. For maximum impact, they had to hit the Numidians at full speed. That was if the enemy riders stayed to fight, thought Quintus suspiciously. His experience with the fierce tribesmen had taught him otherwise. Yet Longus was doing the right thing. He could not just let his sentries be massacred within sight of his camp. Hannibal's men had to be driven off. With six thousand velites following hot on their heels, that would not be difficult.

The thunder of hundreds of hooves drowned out all sound except the occasional encouraging shout from Fabricius: 'Forward!' As they closed in, each man let go of his reins and transferred the spear from his left hand, which also held his shield, to his right. From here on in, they would guide their horses with their knees. Now the months of careful instruction they had received would pay off. For all his comrades' skill, Quintus was still wary of the Numidians, who learned to ride almost before they could walk. He was heartened by the thought of the velites. Their help would make all the difference.

'Look! They've seen us!' shouted Calatinus, pointing at the beleaguered sentries, whose terrified expressions were being replaced by elation. 'Hold on!'

'The poor bastards must have got the shock of their lives when the Numidians suddenly appeared,' replied Quintus.

'We're coming none too soon,' Calatinus added. 'Many of the outposts have no defenders left.'

They had closed to within fifty paces of the enemy.

'Time to even up the score,' cried Quintus, picking out a slight Numidian with braided hair as his target.

Cincius' lip curled. 'They'll turn and run any moment now, the way they always do.'

Instead, to their amazement, the enemy riders turned and began driving their horses straight at the Roman cavalry.

'They're going to fight, not run.' Quintus felt faintly nauseous, but he kept his eye on the Numidian, who was riding straight at him. Oddly, it seemed the warrior had also chosen him.

'Pick your targets,' Fabricius shouted, praying that the outcome of this clash proved different to the one at the Ticinus. 'Make every spear count.'

Seeing the Numidian loose a javelin in his direction, Quintus panicked. Fortunately, it missed, sailing between him and Calatinus. Quintus cursed savagely. The Numidian still had two javelins. Even as the thought went through his mind, the next one scudded his way. He bent low over his horse's neck, hearing it whistle overhead. Claws of desperation tore at him. How long would his luck hold out? He was fewer than twenty paces from his enemy. At that range and closing, the warrior could hardly miss.

The Numidian held on to his last javelin until he was practically on top of Quintus. His error meant that Quintus was able to catch the missile in his shield. He had to discard the useless thing, but he was also able to stab his spear deep into the Numidian's belly as he rode past. Side by side, Quintus and Calatinus struck the enemy formation. At once the world shrank to a small area in their immediate vicinity. Quintus' ears rang with the clash of arms and men's screams, a deafening cacophony that added hugely to the confusion. The press of opposing riders pushing against each other meant that he seldom fought the same opponent for more than a couple of strokes. Quintus' first opponent was a young Numidian who nearly took his eye out with a well-aimed javelin. He jabbed his spear unsuccessfully at the warrior before being swept twenty paces away, never to see him again.

In quick succession, Quintus fought two more Numidians, stabbing one in the arm and plunging his weapon into the other's chest. Next he went to the aid of a Roman cavalryman who was being attacked by three enemy riders. They fought desperately for what seemed an age, barely able to defend themselves against the Numidians' lightning-quick javelin thrusts. And then, like wraiths, the warriors were gone, galloping off into the distance. All across the battlefield, Quintus could see their companions doing the same. It was done with the ease of a shoal of fish changing direction. Unexpectedly, though, the Numidians reined in several hundred paces away. They began shouting insults at the Romans, who responded loudly and in kind.

'Mangy bastards!' shouted Cincius.

'Come back, you goat-fuckers!' roared Calatinus.

Quintus grinned. 'We've driven them a good distance from the camp already.'

'Yes,' agreed Calatinus, whose face was drenched in sweat. 'Time for a rest. I'm bloody exhausted.'

'And me,' added Cincius.

Fabricius and his fellow officers let the Roman cavalry catch their breath for a few moments. Clouds of condensation hung above the mass of horsemen, but were soon dispersed by the heavy sleet that began to fall.

'Time to move before you all freeze to death,' bellowed Fabricius.

Quintus glanced at Calatinus and Cincius. 'Ready for another bout?'

'Definitely,' they snarled in unison.

Right on cue, Fabricius' voice bellowed the command. 'Hold the line! Advance!' The call was repeated by all along the front rank. The Roman horsemen needed little encouragement, and urged their mounts forward. Once again, the ground shook as thousands of horses pounded across the soft ground. This time, the Numidians fought for only a short time before retreating. Yet the tribesmen did not go far. Instead, they turned to fight again. Without pause, the Roman cavalrymen charged at their enemies. Keeping up the momentum of an attack was vital.

Their confidence was boosted by the sight, to their rear, of six thousand velites pouring to their aid. The fact that they were on foot did not take away from the skirmishers' value. They would first consolidate and hold the area that had been taken back from the Numidians. If the enemy horsemen decided to stand their ground, the velites could support their comrades and tilt the balance in their favour. If, on the other hand, the Roman cavalrymen were driven back, then the velites would provide a protective screen for them to fall back through. It was a win-win situation, thought Quintus jubilantly.

At daybreak, the horns that normally signalled the Carthaginian troops to get up remained silent. Used to army routine, most men were already awake. Hanno smiled as he listened to the rumours filling the tents around him. The rank-and-file troops had no idea yet why they had not been ordered from their beds. The majority were happy not to enquire, but some of the more eager ones poked their heads outside. Their officers told them that nothing was wrong. Not wanting to pass up such a rare opportunity, the soldiers duly returned to the comfort of their blankets. For half an hour, an unusual calm fell over the encampment. To the Carthaginians, it was a small dose of heaven. Despite the inclement weather, they were dry, warm and safe.

Finally, the horns did sound. There was no alarm, just the normal notes that indicated it was time to rise. Hanno began moving from tent to tent, encouraging his men.

'What's going on, sir?' asked a short spearman with a bushy black beard.

Hanno grinned. 'You want to know?'

'Yes, sir,' came the eager reply.

Hanno was fully aware that every soldier within earshot was listening. 'The Numidians are attacking the Roman camp even as we speak.'

A rousing cheer went up, and Hanno raised his hands. 'Even if the whoresons take the bait and follow our cavalry, it will take them an age to cross the Trebia. You have plenty of time to get ready.'

Pleased mutters met this comment.

'I want you to prepare yourselves well. Stretch and oil your muscles. Check all your equipment. When you're ready, lay your arms aside and prepare a hot breakfast. Clear?'

'Yes, sir,' his men shouted.

Hanno retired to his own tent in search of food. When that was done, he lay down on his bed and instantly fell asleep. For the first time since leaving Carthage, Hanno dreamed of his mother, Arishat. She did not seem concerned that Malchus and her three sons were in Hannibal's army. Hanno found this immensely reassuring. His mother's spirit was watching over them all.

Soon after, he was roused by the horns sounding the call that meant 'Enemy in sight'.

Hanno sat bolt upright in bed, his heart racing. The Romans *had* followed the Numidians! He and every man in the army were about to be given their first chance to punish Rome for what it had done to his people.

They would grasp it with both hands.

Little more than an hour later, eight thousand of Hannibal's skirmishers and spearmen, with Hanno among them, had been deployed about a mile and a half east of their camp. Behind this protective screen, the rest of the army was slowly assuming battle formation. Hearing that the entire enemy host was crossing the Trebia, the Carthaginian general had finally responded. Hanno was delighted by Hannibal's ingenuity. Unlike the Romans, who had not eaten and were even now fording chest deep, freezing water, Hannibal's soldiers had full bellies and came fresh from their fires. Even at this distance, the chill air was filled with their ribald marching songs. He could hear the elephants bugling too, protesting as they were taken from their hay and sent out to the flanks.

Hanno was positioned at the easternmost point of the defensive semi-circle, nearest the River Trebia. It was where contact with the Romans would first be made. To facilitate the Numidians' withdrawal, gaps had been left between each unit. These could easily be closed if necessary. Five score paces in front of the Libyans' bristling spears, hundreds of Balearic slingers waited patiently, the leather straps of their weapons dangling from their fists. The tribesmen didn't look that impressive, thought Hanno, but he knew that the egg-sized stones hurled by their slings could travel long distances to crack a man's skull. The ragged-looking skirmishers' volleys could strike terror into an advancing enemy.

The wind had died down, allowing the grey-yellow clouds to release heavy showers of snow on the waiting troops. They would have to bear with it, Hanno decided grimly. Nothing would happen for a while. The Numidians were still retreating across the Trebia. When the Roman cavalry arrived, they probably wouldn't attack the protective screen. He was correct.

Over the following half an hour, squadron after squadron of Numidians escaped between the phalanxes. Soon after, Hanno was pleased to recognise Zamar approaching. He raised a hand in greeting. 'What news?'

Zamar slowed his horse to a walk. 'Things go well. I wasn't sure if the Romans were up for a fight to start off with, but they poured out of their camp like a tide of ants.'

'Just their cavalry?'

'No, thousands of skirmishers too.' Zamar grinned. 'Then the infantry followed.'

Thank you, great Melqart, thought Hanno delightedly.

'We fought and withdrew repeatedly, and gradually led them down to the river. That was where we took most of our casualties. Had to make it look as if we were panicking, see?' said Zamar with a scowl. His face lifted quickly. 'Anyway, it worked. The enemy foot soldiers followed their cavalry into the water and started wading across. To cap it all, that was when the snow really started falling. You could see the fuckers' faces turning blue!'

'Did they turn back?'

'No,' replied Zamar with a grim pleasure. 'They didn't. It might take the whoresons all day to get here, but they're coming. Their whole damn army.'

'This really is it then,' Hanno muttered. His stomach churned.

Zamar nodded solemnly. 'May Baal Saphon protect you and your men.'

'And the same to you,' Hanno replied. He watched sadly as the Numidian led his riders to the rear. Would they ever see each other again? Probably not. Hanno didn't wallow in the emotion. It was far too late for regret. They were all in this together. He and his father. Sapho and Bostar. Zamar and every other soldier in the army. Yes, bloodshed was inevitable. So too were the deaths of thousands of men.

Even as he saw the first files of Roman legionaries filing into view, Hanno believed that Hannibal would not let them down.

Chapter XXIV: At Close Quarters

With the Numidians gone, Fabricius regrouped his riders on the near riverbank. The mass of horsemen crossed together and went pounding up the track, past the spot where their patrol had been annihilated by Hanno and his men. Trying not to think about what had happened, Quintus squinted up at the low-lying cloud. For the moment, the snow had stopped. He tried to feel grateful. 'What time is it?' he wondered. 'It has to be *hora quinta* at least.'

'Who cares?' growled Calatinus. 'All I know is that I'm parched with thirst, and bloody famished.'

'Here.' Quintus handed over his water bag.

Grinning his thanks, Calatinus took a few deep swallows. 'Gods, that's cold,' he complained.

'Be grateful you're not a legionary,' advised Quintus. He pointed back towards the Trebia, where thousands of soldiers were already preparing to follow the cavalry across.

Calatinus scowled. 'Aye. Fording that was unpleasant enough on a horse. I pity the poor bastard infantry. The damn river must be chest deep.'

'It's the winter rain,' said Quintus. 'Even the parallel tributaries are waist high, so the poor bastards will have to immerse themselves repeatedly. It doesn't bear thinking about.'

'A fight will soon warm them up,' declared Cincius stoutly.

Quintus and his two comrades were among the first to emerge from the trees' protection. They reined in at once, cursing. Their chase was over.

A quarter of a mile away, stretching from left to right as far as the eye could see, stood the figures of thousands of waiting men. Carthaginian troops. 'Halt!' bellowed Fabricius. 'It's a protective screen. No point committing suicide.' Cheated of the chance for further revenge on the Numidians, his men shouted insults after the retreating enemy riders.

Fabricius found Quintus a moment later. He smiled to see his son unharmed. 'Quite a morning so far, eh?'

Quintus grinned. 'Yes, Father. We've got them on the run, eh?'

'Hmmm.' Fabricius was studying the brown-yellow clouds above. He frowned. 'There's more snow coming, and we're going to have a long wait before the real fight begins. The legions and the socii will take hours to get in position. By that time, the men will be half dead with cold.'

Quintus glanced around. 'Some of them don't even have cloaks on.'

'They were too keen to engage with the enemy,' replied Fabricius grimly. 'What's the betting that they didn't feed and water their horses?'

Quintus flushed. He hadn't remembered that most basic of duties either. 'What should we do?'

'Do you see those trees?'

Quintus eyed the dense stand of beech a short distance to their left. 'Yes.'

'Let's take shelter there. Longus might not like it, but he's not here. We'll still be able to respond fast if there's any threat to the legionaries. Not that that's likely. Hannibal threw out this protective screen deliberately. He wants a proper battle today,' Fabricius declared. 'Until the fighting starts, or orders come to the contrary, we should try to keep warm.'

Quintus nodded gratefully. There was more to war than simply defeating an enemy in combat, he realised. Initiative was also important.

And so, while the rest of the cavalry and the velites milled about uncertainly, watching the legionaries wading across the Trebia, Fabricius led his riders under cover.

By the time two hours had passed, Hanno was shivering constantly. His soldiers were in the same condition. It was absolute torture standing on an open plain in such bitter weather. Although the snow showers had died away, they had been succeeded by sleet, and the wind had recovered its viciousness. It whistled and whipped at Carthaginian and Roman alike with an unrelenting fury. The only opportunity Hanno's men had been given to warm up was when the instruction had come to withdraw towards their camp.

'Look at the whoresons!' cried Malchus, who had come over from his phalanx. 'Will they never stop coming?'

Hanno eyed the ground opposite their position, which was being filled with a plodding inevitability. 'It must be the entire Roman army.'

'I'd say so,' answered his father bleakly. Abruptly, he laughed. 'However cold you think your men are, those fuckers are in a far worse state. In all likelihood, they've had no food, and now they're all drenched to the skin too.'

Hanno shuddered. He could only imagine how cold the wind would feel on wet clothing and heavy mail, both of which carried heat away from the body anyway. Demoralising. Energy-sapping.

'Meanwhile,' his father went on, 'we're ready and waiting for them.'

Hanno glanced to either side. As soon as the Numidians had retreated safely, he and his men had pulled back to Hannibal's battle formation, which consisted of a single line of infantry in close order. The slingers and Numidian skirmishers were arrayed some three hundred paces in front of the main battle line. Their general had not placed his strongest infantry – the Libyans and Iberians – in the centre. Instead, that space was filled by about eight thousand Gauls. 'Surely we should be standing there?' he asked crossly. 'Instead, it's our newest recruits.'

Malchus gave him a calculating look. 'Think about it. Listen to them.'

Hanno cocked his head. The war cries and the carnyx blasts emanating from the Gauls' ranks were deafening. 'They're delighted with the honour that Hannibal has granted them. It will increase their loyalty.'

'That's right. To them, pride is everything,' answered Malchus. 'What could be better than being given the centre of the line? But there's another reason. The heaviest fighting, and the worst casualties will be there too. Hannibal is saving us and the Iberians from that fate.'

Hanno gave his father a shocked glance. 'Would he do such a thing?'

'Of course,' replied Malchus casually. 'The Gauls can easily be replaced. Our men, and the scutarii and caetrati, cannot. That's why we're on the wings.'

Hanno's respect for Hannibal grew further. He eyed the seventeen elephants standing just in front of their position. The rest were arrayed on the other wing, before the Iberian foot soldiers. Further protection for the heavy infantry, he realised. Outside, on each flank, sat five thousand

Numidians and Hannibal's Iberian and Gaulish horse. The Carthaginian superiority in this area would hopefully afford Hannibal a good chance of winning the cavalry battle. Meanwhile, the Gauls would have to resist the hammer blow delivered by the Roman legions to the centre of the Carthaginian line. 'Will the Gauls hold?' he asked anxiously.

'There's a decided chance that they will not,' Malchus replied, clenching his jaw. 'They might be brave, but they're poorly disciplined.'

Hanno stared over at the tribesmen. Few of them wore armour. Even in this weather, most preferred to fight stripped to the waist. There was no denying that the legionaries' mail shirts and heavy scuta would provide them with a severe test. 'If they don't break, however, and our cavalry are successful . . .'

Malchus' grin was wolf-like. 'Our troops on each side will have a god-given opportunity to attack the sides of the Roman formation.'

'That's when Mago's force will appear.'

'We must hope so,' said his father. 'For all of our fates will lie with them.'

Hanno could hardly bear it. 'So many small things have to succeed for us to win the day.'

'That's right. And the Gauls will have the hardest task of any.'

Hanno closed his eyes and prayed that everything went according to plan. *Great Melqart, you have helped Hannibal thus far. Please do the same again today.*

In the event, Fabricius spotted one of the consul's messengers well before Quintus and his comrades had warmed up. He rode to confer with him, and returned at the double.

'Longus wants all citizen cavalry positioned on the right flank, and the allied horse on the left. We've got to ride north, to the far end of the battle line.'

'When?' asked Quintus irritably. His earlier excitement had been sapped by the mind-numbing cold.

'Now!' Fabricius called out to his decurions: 'Have the men form up. We ride out at once.'

As the cavalrymen emerged from the trees, Quintus could have sworn that the wind hit them with a new vigour, stripping away any of the warmth that they had briefly felt. That settled it, he thought grimly. The sooner the fighting began, the better. Anything rather than this torture.

Fabricius led them through the gaps in the three lines of soldiers to the front of the army. By the time they had reached open ground, Quintus had gained a good appreciation of the entire host. Longus had ordered the legions to deploy in traditional pattern, with a hundred paces between each line and the next. The veteran triarii were at the rear, in the middle were the principes, men in their late twenties and early thirties, and next came the ranks of the hastati, the youngest of the infantry. At the very front stood the exhausted velites, who, despite their recent travails, would be forced to engage the enemy first.

All three lines were composed of maniples. Those of hastati and principes comprised two centuries of between sixty and seventy soldiers. There were fewer triarii, however, and their maniples were made up of just two centuries of thirty men each. The units in each line did not yet form a continuous front. Instead, they were positioned one century in front of the other, leaving gaps equal to the maniple's frontage between each unit. The units of the second and third lines stood behind the spaces in front, forming a quincunx configuration like the '5' face on a gaming die. This positioning allowed a rapid transition to combat formation when the rear century in each maniple would simply run around to stand alongside the front one. It also permitted soldiers to retreat safely from the fighting, allowing their fresher comrades access to the enemy.

It was a long way to the edge of the right flank, so Quintus also had time to study the Carthaginian forces. These were arrayed about a quarter of a mile distant, sufficiently near to appreciate the enemy's superior numbers of cavalry, and the threatening outlines of at least two dozen elephants. The blare of horns and carnyxes carried through the air, an alien noise compared to the familiar Roman trumpets. It was clear that Hannibal retained fewer troops than Longus, but his host still made for a fearsome, if unusual, sight.

At length Quintus began to feel quite exposed. Fortunately, he didn't have to wait much longer. They passed the four regular legions, spotting Longus and his tribunes at the junction between these and the allied troops of the right wing. Finally, Fabricius' unit reached the Roman cavalry, which, with their arrival, numbered just under a thousand. There was more ribaldry as the assembled riders demanded to know where they had been.

'Screwing your mother!' shouted a wit among Fabricius' men. 'And your sisters!'

Angry roars rose from the joke's victims, and the air filled with insults. A smile twitched across Fabricius' lips. He glanced at Quintus and registered his surprise. 'Many of them are going to die soon,' he explained. 'This takes their minds off it.'

The mention of heavy casualties made Quintus feel nauseous. Would he survive to see the next dawn? Would his father, Calatinus or Cincius? Quintus looked around at the familiar faces, the men he had come to know over the previous weeks. He didn't like all of them, but they were still his comrades. Who would end the day lying bloodied and motionless in the cold mud? Who would be maimed, or blinded? Quintus felt the first fingers of panic clutch at his belly.

His father took his arm. 'Take a deep breath,' he said quietly.

Quintus shot him a worried glance. 'Why?'

'Do as I say.'

He obeyed, relieved that Calatinus and Cincius were deep in conversation with each other.

'Hold it,' Fabricius ordered. 'Listen to your heart.'

It wasn't hard to do that, thought Quintus. It was hammering off his ribs like that of a wild bird.

His father waited for a few moments. 'Now let the air out through your lips. Nice and slowly. When you've finished, do the same again.'

Quintus' eyes flickered around nervously, but nobody appeared to be watching. He did as he was told. By the third or fourth breath, the effect on his pulse was noticeable. It had slowed down, and he wasn't feeling as scared.

'Everyone is frightened before battle,' said his father. 'Even me. It's a terrifying thing to charge at another group of men whose job it is to kill you. The trick is to think of your comrades on your left and right. They are the only ones who matter from now on.'

'I understand,' Quintus muttered.

'You will be fine. I know it.' Fabricius clapped him on the shoulder.

Steadier now, Quintus nodded. 'Thank you, Father.'

With his army in place, Longus had the trumpeters sound the advance. Stamping their numb feet on the semi-frozen ground, the infantry obeyed.

Loud prayers to the gods rose from the ranks, and the standard-bearers lifted their arms so that everyone could see the talismanic gilded animal that sat atop the wooden poles they bore. Each legion had five standards, depicting respectively an eagle, Minotaur, horse, wolf and boar. They were objects of great reverence, and Quintus wished that his unit possessed them too. Even the allied infantry bore similar standards. For reasons unclear to him, the cavalry didn't.

Victory will be ours regardless, he thought. Urging his horse on with his knees, he rode towards the enemy.

It was imperative that their enemies marched beyond Mago's hidden position. Consequently, the entire Carthaginian army had to stay put as the Romans approached. It was a nerve-racking time, with little to do other than pray or make last, quick checks of equipment. Imitating his father, Hanno had given his men a short address. They were here, he'd told them, to show Rome that it could not trifle with Carthage. To right the wrongs it had done to all of their peoples. The spearmen had liked Hanno's words, but they cheered loudest when he reminded them that they were here to follow Hannibal's lead and, most importantly, to avenge their heroic comrades who had fallen since their departure from Saguntum more than six months before.

Their racket was as nothing compared to that of the Gauls, however. The combination of drumming weapons, war chants and wind instruments made an incredible din. Hanno had never heard anything like it. Musicians stood before the assembled warriors, playing curved ceramic horns and carnyxes at full volume. The tribesmen's frenzied response was to clatter their swords and spears rhythmically off their shields, all the while chanting in unison. Some individuals were so affected that they broke ranks, stripped naked and stood whirling their swords over their heads, screaming like men possessed.

'They say that at Telamon, the ground shook with their noise,' his father shouted.

But they still lost, thought Hanno grimly.

The tension mounted steadily as the Roman battle line drew closer. It was immensely long, stretching off on both sides until it was lost to sight. The Carthaginian formation was considerably narrower, which threatened immediate flanking. Hanno's worries about this were forgotten as Hannibal ordered his skirmishers forward.

The Balearic slingers and Numidian javelin men bounded off, eager to start the battle proper. A vicious and prolonged missile encounter followed, from which the Carthaginians emerged clear victors. Unlike the wet, tired velites, who had been fighting for hours and had already thrown the majority of their javelins, Hannibal's men were fresh and keen. Stones and spears whistled and hummed through the air in their hundreds, scything down the velites like rows of wheat. Unable to respond in similar fashion, the Roman light troops were soon put to flight, retreating through the gaps in their front line. Hannibal immediately recalled his skirmishers, whose lack of armour made them vulnerable to the approaching hastati. As they trotted back through the spaces between the various Carthaginian units, they received a rousing cheer.

'A good start,' Hanno yelled to his men. 'First blood to us!'

A moment later, the Romans charged.

'Shields up!' Hanno yelled. From the corner of his eye, he was dimly aware of their Iberian and Gaulish cavalry, as well as the elephants, charging at the enemy's horsemen. He had literally an instant to pray that they succeeded.

Then the Roman *pila*, or javelins, began to arrive. Each hastatus carried two of the weapons, which gave their front line fearsome firepower. The missiles were thrown in such dense showers that the air between the two armies darkened as they flew. 'Protect yourselves!' Hanno screamed, but it was only those in the front rank who could do as he said. The phalanx's formation packed men together so tightly that it prevented the rest from raising their large shields. As the javelins came hammering down, they gritted their teeth and hoped not to be hit.

Topped by a pyramidal point, the pila were fully capable of punching through a shield and piercing its bearer's flesh. And they did exactly that: killing, wounding, cutting tissue apart with ease. Hanno's ears rang with the choking cries of soldiers who could no longer talk thanks to the iron transfixing their throats. Screams rang out from those who had been struck elsewhere. Wails of fear rose from the unhurt as they saw their comrades slain before their eyes. Hanno risked a look to the front and cursed. While their first volley flew, the hastati had continued to advance. They were now less than forty paces away, and preparing to release again. He couldn't help admiring the legionaries' discipline. They actually slowed down or even stopped to throw their pila. As he already knew, it was well worth the effort to make an accurate shot. Lesser foes would have already broken and run beneath the rain of iron-tipped terror. Hanno was grateful that he was commanding veterans. While his men had suffered terribly, their lines remained steady. His father's phalanx looked rock solid too.

To his left, the Gauls were also suffering heavy casualties. Hanno could see some of them wavering, a worrying sign so early. But their chieftains were made of sterner stuff, shouting and exhorting their followers to stand fast. To Hanno's relief, the tactic worked. As the second shower of javelins was launched, the Gauls swiftly lifted their shields. While their response reduced the number of wounded and killed, it stripped many of the warriors of their main protection. Few things were more useless than a shield with a bent pilum protruding from it. Weirdly, this looked more to the Gauls' liking. Shouting fiercely, they prepared to meet the hastati head on.

Many of the men at the front of Hanno's phalanx were also now without shields. He cursed savagely. The gaps would provide the legionaries with opportunities too good to pass up, but there was nothing Hanno could do to remedy the problem. 'Close order!' he shouted. As the command was repeated all along the line, he felt the shields of the men on either side slide against his to form a solid barrier. 'Front two ranks, raise spears!' Scores of wooden shafts clattered off each other as those in the second row shoved their weapons over the shoulders of the soldiers in front. Hanno gritted his teeth. 'This is it!' he roared. 'Hold fast!'

He could pick out individuals now: there a stocky figure with a pock-marked face; beside him a young man wearing a pectoral breastplate who couldn't have been more than eighteen. His own age. He looked a bit like Gaius, Martialis' son. Unsettled, Hanno blinked. Naturally, he was mistaken: Gaius was a noble, and would serve in the cavalry. Who cares? he thought harshly. They are all the enemy. Kill them. 'Steady,' he roared. 'Wait for my command!'

The hastati screamed as they closed in. Each man clutched a gladius in his right fist, and in the other he carried a heavy, elongated oval scutum with a metal boss. Like Hanno's men's shields, many Roman ones had designs painted on their hide covers. Bizarrely, Hanno found himself admiring the charging boars, leaping wolves and arrangements of circles and spirals. They contrasted strongly with the more ornate patterns favoured by the Libyans.

Nervous, the man beside him shoved his spear forward too soon, and Hanno's attention snapped back to the present. 'Hold!' he ordered. 'Your first thrust has to kill a man!'

One heartbeat. Two heartbeats.

'Now!' Hanno roared at the top of his voice. In the same moment, he thrust forward with his weapon, aiming it at the face of the nearest hastatus. On either side, hundreds of Libyans did the same. Hanno's speed caught the legionary off guard, and his spear tip skidded over the top of the other's scutum to take him through the left eye. Aqueous fluid spattered everywhere and an agonising scream ripped free of the hastatus' throat. Hanno's instinct was to shove his spear even deeper, making the blow mortal, but he stopped himself. The man would probably die of his injury. More importantly, he would not take any further part in the battle. With a powerful twist, Hanno pulled the blade free. Iron grated off bone as he did so and the bellowing hastatus collapsed.

Hanno barely had time to breathe before another legionary came trampling over his first opponent and deliberately barged straight into him. If it hadn't been for the fact that his shield was locked with that of the man on either side, Hanno would have fallen over. As it was, he was knocked off balance and struggled to regain his footing. This was precisely what the hastatus had intended. Bending his right elbow, he stabbed his gladius over the top of Hanno's shield. Frantically, Hanno twisted his head to one side, and the blade gouged a deep line across the cheekpiece of his bronze helmet before skimming through the hair on the side of his head. The hastatus snarled with anger and pulled back his weapon to deliver another blow. Hanno struggled to use his spear, but his opponent was too close to reach him easily. Panic bubbled in the back of his throat. The battle had hardly started, and already he was a dead man.

Then, out of the blue, a spear took the hastatus through the throat, making his eyes bulge in shock. He made a choking gasp as the blade slid out of his flesh, and dropped like a stone, sending gouts of blood all over Hanno's shield and lower legs. 'My thanks!' Hanno shouted at the soldier behind him. He couldn't turn around to express his gratitude, because another hastatus was already trying to kill him. This time, Hanno managed to fend off his attacker with his spear. Cursing loudly, they traded blows back and forth, but neither could gain an advantage over the other. Things were taken out of both their hands a moment later when a man a few steps to Hanno's right, who had discarded his pilum-riddled shield, was killed. Two hastati forced their way into the space at once, shouting at their comrades to follow them. Hanno's opponent knew that this was too good a chance to pass up. In the blink of an eye, he had shoved his way after his fellows. To Hanno's relief, he was granted a brief respite.

Panting heavily, he glanced to either side. Claws of worry raked at his insides. The phalanxes were holding their own, but only just. To his left, the Gauls were struggling to contain the same intense assault. Worryingly, the hastati there had already been joined by the principes. The Gauls had even less prospect of holding back these legionaries, thought Hanno sourly. Most of the principes wore mail shirts, making them much harder to kill. Thus far, however, the tribesmen were not retreating. Despite their lack of armour, they persisted in fighting to the death. Already the ground beneath their feet was a churned-up morass of corpses, discarded weapons, mud and blood.

Desperately, Hanno cast his eyes to the Roman left flank. His heart lifted. Thanks to the Iberians and Gauls, it had been shorn of its cavalry protection. There was no sign of Hannibal's heavy cavalry, however, which meant it was still pursuing the Roman horse. Hanno's worry increased tenfold. If that battle hadn't been won, they might as well all give up now. Then his attention was drawn by hundreds of figures who were swarming towards the enemy's left flank. To his delight, he saw that they were hurling javelins and firing sling stones. It was the Carthaginian skirmishers!

A yelling hastatus jumped into the attack, preventing Hanno from any further thought. He fought back with renewed determination, using the greater length of his spear to stab at the Roman's face. The fight wasn't over by any means. There was hope yet.

As they rode towards the Carthaginians, Quintus forgot his father's reassuring words. He felt sick to the stomach. How could a thousand men prevail against what looked like more than five times that number? It simply wasn't possible.

Calatinus also looked unhappy. 'Longus should have split our horsemen equally,' he muttered. 'There are nearly three thousand allied riders on the other flank.'

'It's not fair,' moaned Cincius.

'The figures still don't equate,' Quintus replied wearily.

'I suppose. It's not even as if the bastards coming towards us will be scared. They've already tasted victory over us.' Calatinus cursed the consul heartily.

'Come on! We should be able to stall the enemy attack,' encouraged Quintus. 'Hold the line, and stop the enemy from having free rein over the battlefield.'

Calatinus' grunt conveyed all types of disbelief. Cincius didn't seem convinced either.

'Listen to our infantry,' cried Quintus. The noise of their tread was deafening. 'There are more than thirty-five thousand of them. How can Hannibal with his little army, made up of a hodgepodge of different nationalities, prevail against that type of might? He can't!'

His comrades looked a trifle more confident.

Wishing that he felt as certain as he sounded, Quintus again fixed his gaze to the front.

The first of the enemy riders were now very close. Quintus recognised them as Gauls by their mail shirts, round shields and long spears. He squinted at the small, bouncing objects tied to their horses' harnesses. To his horror, he realised they were severed human heads. These warriors could be some of their so-called allies, and the heads those of his former comrades. Of Licinius, perhaps.

Calatinus had seen the same thing. 'The fucking dogs!' he screamed.

'Yellow-livered sons of whores!' Cincius bellowed.

A towering rage also filled Quintus. He wasn't going to flee from cowards like these. Men who would kill others as they slept. I would rather die, he thought. Quintus raised his spear and chose a target, a warrior on a sturdy grey horse. The magnificent gold torc visible over the top of the Gaul's mail shirt revealed him to be an important individual. So did the three human heads bouncing off his mount's chest. He would be a good start, Quintus decided.

However, the tide of battle swept Quintus away from the Gaul he'd aimed for. In hindsight, it was a good thing. The tribesman was immensely skilled. Quintus watched in horror as a Roman rider fewer than twenty paces away was skewered through the chest by the Gaul's weapon. The force of the impact punched the man off his saddle blanket, dropping him dead to the dirt below. The horse behind stumbled over the corpse, unbalancing its rider, and rendering him easy prey for the Gaul, who was now swinging a long sword. He took off the cavalryman's head with a great sideways lop. Quintus had never seen blood spray so high in the air. Gouts of it went everywhere as the panicked horse galloped off. It was perhaps a dozen steps before its dead rider toppled off.

At once the Gaul sawed on his mount's reins and jumped down. Quintus' amazement turned to disgust. The warrior was after another head. He would have given anything just then to be able to reach the Gaul, but it was not to be. He nearly lost his own head to a swinging sword, managing to dodge it only because its bearer uttered a loud war cry as his killing stroke came down. As it was, Quintus nearly fell off his horse. With a speed born of utter desperation, he managed to regain his seat in time to parry his opponent's next powerful blow.

Fortuna was smiling on him in that instant, for the warrior was even younger than he, and, as Quintus realised, far less skilled. A more experienced man would have already despatched him. The Gaul was not lacking in bravery, however, and they hammered fiercely at each other for a few moments before Quintus found an opportunity to strike. The other's wild swings left his right armpit exposed. Taking a gamble that he could react faster than his enemy, Quintus did not defend against the next strike. Instead, bending low over his horse's neck, he listened to it whistle overhead. While the Gaul was still coming to the end of his swing, Quintus came up like a striking snake. He buried his spear in the other's side, sliding it neatly into the armhole of his mail shirt. With nothing but a tunic to stop its progress, the blade slid between the man's ribs, through one lung and into his heart. It was as clean a stroke as Quintus had ever made, killing instantaneously. He would always remember it not for that, however, but for the brief burst of shock and pain in the Gaul's eyes before they went dark for ever.

When Quintus looked up, he quailed. Most of the nearby Roman riders had been cut down. The others were fleeing. There was no sign of Calatinus,

Cincius or his father. Quintus' vision was filled with Gauls. Behind them came hundreds of Iberians. He would be dead long before those riders arrived, however. Three Gaulish warriors were heading straight for him. Despairing, Quintus picked the man he thought would reach him first. It would make little difference, but he didn't care. His father was dead, and the cavalry battle half lost. What did it matter if he also fell? Raising his spear, Quintus screamed a final cry of defiance. 'Come on, then, you bastards!'

The trio of warriors roared an inarticulate response.

A horrifying image of his own head as a trophy filled his mind. He banished the image. Just let the end be quick, Quintus prayed.

Chapter XXV: Unexpected Tactics

Bostar had barely been able to contain himself since the sentry's report that the enemy were crossing the river. He and Sapho had clambered up the bank to lie beside Mago, who was trembling with excitement. With every nerve stretched taut, they'd watched as the Roman cavalry and velites were gradually followed by the allied infantry and the regular legionaries. Only then did it sink in.

'The Roman commander has no interest in nibbling at the bait,' muttered Mago excitedly. 'He's swallowed it in one great bite. That's his whole fucking army!'

They exchanged nervous grins.

'The fighting will start soon,' said Sapho eagerly.

'It's not time to move yet,' interjected Bostar at once.

'That's right. We have to wait until the perfect moment to fall upon the Romans' rear,' warned Mago. 'Moving too early could cost us the battle.'

Knowing that Mago was correct, the brothers reluctantly stayed put. The wait that followed was the longest of Bostar's life. Mago's incessant twitching and the savagery with which Sapho bit his nails told him that they felt the same way. It was no more than three to four hours, but at the time it seemed like an eternity. Naturally, the news that the Romans were on the move had spread through their two thousand soldiers like wildfire. Soon it became difficult to keep them silent. It was understandable, thought Bostar. There was only so long that one could take pleasure in being out of harm's way rather than facing mortal danger – especially when one's comrades were about to fight for their lives.

Even when the clash of arms became audible, Mago did not move. Bostar forced himself to remain calm. The rival forces of skirmishers would meet first, and then pull back. Sure enough, the screams and cries soon abated.

They were replaced by the unmistakable sound of thousands of feet tramping the ground in unison.

'The Roman infantry are advancing,' said Mago in an undertone. 'Melqart, watch over our men.'

A knot of tension formed in Bostar's belly. Facing so many of the enemy would be terrifying.

Beside him, Sapho shifted uneasily. 'The gods protect Father and Hanno,' he whispered. Their enmity momentarily forgotten, Bostar muttered the same prayer.

The crashing sound that reached their ears a moment later was as deafening as thunder. Yet there were no threatening storm clouds above, no flashes of lightning to sear their eyeballs. It was something altogether more lethal. More terrifying. Bostar trembled to hear it. He had witnessed terrible things since the war started: the immense block of stone that had nearly killed Hannibal; the scenes at the fall of Saguntum; avalanches sweeping away scores of screaming men in the Alps. But he had never heard the sound of tens of thousands of soldiers striking each other for the first time. It promised death in any number of appalling ways, and Hanno and his father were caught up in it. Somehow Bostar kept still, trying his best to block out the screams that were now discernible amid the crescendo of sound. His tactic didn't work for long. He looked at Mago, who gave him a tiny encouraging nod.

'Is it time yet, sir?' Bostar asked.

Mago's eyes glittered eagerly. 'Soon. Prepare your men to move out. Tell the same to the officer commanding the Numidians. At my signal, bring them up.'

'Yes, sir!' Bostar and Sapho grinned at each other as they hadn't done in an age, and hurried to obey.

From then on, time moved in a blur, a continuum that Bostar could only remember afterwards in a series of fractured images. The frisson of excitement that shivered through the waiting soldiers when they heard their orders. Mago's head silhouetted as he peered over the riverbank, and his beckoning arm. Reaching the top, and being awestruck by the colossal struggle going on over to their left. Who was winning? Was Hanno still alive? Mago shaking his arm and telling him to keep focused. Telling the men to unsling their shields from their backs and ready their weapons.

Assembling their phalanxes in open order. Watching the thousand Numidians split, placing half their number on each side of the infantry. Mago's raised sword pointing at the enemy and his cry, 'For Hannibal and for Carthage!'

And the run. Bostar would never forget the run.

They did not sprint. It was more than half a mile to the battlefield. Exhausting themselves would give away all the advantage they had been granted. Instead they moved at a fast trot, leaving plumes of exhaled breath in their wake. The cold air was filled with the low, repetitive thuds of horses' hooves and men's boots and sandals on the hard ground. No one spoke. No one wanted to. Everyone's eyes were locked on what was unfolding before them. Amid the confusion, one thing was clear. There was no sign of the enemy's cavalry, which meant that the Iberian and Gaulish horsemen must have driven them off. On the Roman flanks, the allied infantry were struggling against the Carthaginian elephants, skirmishers and Numidian horsemen. In itself, these were major achievements, and Bostar wanted to cheer. But he did not utter a word. The battle's outcome still hung in the balance. As they drew closer, he saw that the fighting in the centre was incredibly fierce. The legionaries there had actually moved in front of their wings, which meant that they had pushed the Gauls who formed the central part of Hannibal's line backwards.

They had come not an instant too soon, thought Bostar.

Mago came to the realisation at the same time. 'Charge!' he screamed. 'Charge!'

With a wordless roar, Bostar, Sapho and his soldiers obeyed, increasing their speed to a dangerous, breakneck pace. Any man who tripped now risked breaking an ankle or a leg. But no one cared. All they wanted to do was to start shedding their opponents' blood. To bury their weapons in Roman flesh.

The last moments of their run were surreal. Exhilarating. Thanks to the deafening sounds of battle, there was no need to worry about how much noise they made. The triarii in the enemy's third rank — their targets — were not looking behind them. Unsurprisingly, the veterans were engrossed by the bitter struggle going on to their front, and were preparing to join in. They had no idea that two thousand Carthaginian soldiers were about to strike their rear at a full charge. Bostar would always remember the first faces that turned, casually, for whatever reason, to look around. The sheer disbelief and terror that twisted those faces to find a group of the enemy fewer than thirty paces away. The hoarse screams as the small number of triarii who were aware tried to warn their comrades of their deadly peril. And the satisfaction as they smashed into the Roman ranks, drawing their weapons down on the backs of men who did not even know they were about to die.

For the first time in his life, Bostar was overcome by battle rage. In the red mist surrounding him, it was easy to lose count of the number of men he killed. It was like stabbing fish in a rock pool off the coast of Carthage. Thrust forward. Run the blade in as deep as possible. Withdraw. Select another target. When eventually his blunted spear stuck in a triarius' backbone, Bostar simply discarded it and pulled out his sword. He was vaguely aware that his arm was bloody to the elbow, but he didn't care. *I'm coming, little brother. Stay alive, Father.*

Eventually, the veteran legionaries managed to turn and face their attackers. The fight became harder, but the advantage was still with Mago's men, who could now see that the enemy's flanks had broken. Bostar exulted. The combined wave of Carthaginian troops and cavalry on the allied infantry's undefended side had proved too much. Prevented from wheeling to face the threat, they had been mercilessly hacked to pieces.

Now, dropping their weapons, the survivors turned and ran for the Trebia. Bostar threw back his head and let free an animal howl of triumph. To the rear, he glimpsed thousands of their cavalrymen waiting for just such an eventuality. The allied troops would not go far. Suddenly, a veteran with a notched sword blade drove at him and Bostar was reminded that their own task was not over. Although the triarii were suffering heavy casualties, the rest of the legionaries were still moving forward into, and through, the lines of Gauls. Like a battering ram, they could only be resisted for so long. Bostar's elation died away as he realised that some of the Libyan phalanxes had also given way. They quickly crumbled before the legionaries' relentless assault. Catching Sapho's attention, Bostar pointed. His brother's face twisted in rage. With renewed energy, they both threw themselves at the triarii.

'Hanno! Father!' Bostar shouted. 'We're coming!'

Too late, his heart screamed back.

* * *

When Aurelia entered the bedroom, her mother barely stirred. Elira, who was sitting by the bed, turned.

'How is she?' Aurelia whispered.

'Better,' the Illyrian replied. 'Her fever has broken.'

Some of the tension went from Aurelia's shoulders. 'Thank the gods. Thank *you*.'

'Hush,' murmured Elira reassuringly. 'She was never that ill. It's a bad winter chill, that's all. She'll be up and about by Saturnalia.'

Aurelia nodded gratefully. 'I don't know what I'd do without you. It's not just caring for Mother these past few days. You made all the difference in Suni's—' She looked over her shoulder guiltily. To her relief, there was no one in the atrium. 'I mean Lysander's recovery.'

Elira waved a hand in dismissal. 'He's young, and strong. All he needed was some food and warmth.'

'Well, I'm thankful to you nonetheless,' said Aurelia. 'So is he.'

Elira bobbed her head, embarrassed.

Things had moved on since she had returned to the farm with a half-conscious Suniaton two weeks previously, thought Aurelia, looking down at her sleeping mother. Fortunately, Atia had not questioned her story of finding him in the woods. In a real stroke of luck, a heavy snowstorm later that night had concealed the evidence of her tracks up to the hut. Unsurprisingly, everyone had taken Suniaton for a runaway slave. As agreed, he had pretended to be mute. He also put on a good show of appearing simple. Agesandros had been suspicious, of course, but there had been no trace of recognition in his eyes at any stage.

Aurelia had given the Sicilian no chance to have anything to do with Suniaton. Any master who wanted his property back could come looking for the boy, she had said to her mother. Until then, she was going to keep him. 'Lysander, I'll call him, because he looks Greek.'

Atia had smiled in acceptance. 'Very well. If he even survives,' she'd joked.

Well, he had, thought Aurelia triumphantly. Suni's leg had recovered enough for him to limp about the kitchen under Julius' instruction. For the moment, he was safe.

What frustrated Aurelia most was the fact that she could rarely talk to him. The best they could manage was an occasional snatched conversation in the evenings, when the other kitchen slaves had gone to bed. Aurelia used these moments to ask Suni about Hanno. She now knew much about his childhood and family, his interests, and where he had lived. Aurelia's reason for wanting to know about Hanno was quite simple. It was a way of not thinking about her betrothal. Even if Flaccus had been killed with her father, her mother would soon find her another husband. If Flaccus had survived, they would be wed within the year. One way or another, she would have an arranged marriage.

'Aurelia.'

Her mother's voice jerked Aurelia back to the present. 'You're awake! How do you feel?'

'Weak as a newborn,' Atia murmured. 'But better than I did yesterday.'

'Praise all the gods.' Tears leaped unbidden to Aurelia's eyes.

Finally, things were looking up.

Her mother's improvement lifted Aurelia's mood considerably. For the first time in days, she went for a walk. The chill weather meant that the snow that had fallen over the previous few days had not melted. Aurelia didn't want to go far from her mother or Suni. Just venturing a short distance along the track towards Capua felt wonderful, however. She relished the crunch of the frozen snow beneath her sandals. Even the way her cheeks rapidly went numb felt refreshing after all the time she'd spent indoors. Feeling more cheerful than she had in a while, Aurelia let herself picture a scenario in which her father had not been killed. She imagined the joy of seeing him walk through the front doors.

With this optimistic thought uppermost in her mind, she returned to the house.

As Aurelia crossed the courtyard, she saw Suniaton. He had his back to her, and was carrying a basket of vegetables into the kitchen. Her spirits lifted even higher. If he was able to do that, his leg must have improved further. She hurried after him. Reaching the door, Aurelia saw Suniaton lifting his load on to the work surface. All the other slaves were busy in other parts of the room. 'Suni!' she hissed.

He didn't react.

'Pssst! Suni!' Aurelia stepped inside the kitchen.

Still he did not respond. It was then that Aurelia noticed his stiff-backed stance. Claws of fear raked her belly. 'Sunny, it's so sunny outside,' she said loudly.

'I could have sworn you said S-u-n-i,' Agesandros purred, stepping from the shadows beside the kitchen door.

Aurelia blanched. 'No. I said it was sunny. Can't you see? The weather's changed.' She gestured outside at the blue sky above the courtyard.

She might as well have been speaking to a statue. 'Suni – Suniaton – is a gugga name,' said the Sicilian coldly.

'What's that got to do with anything?' Aurelia retorted desperately. Her gaze shot to Julius and the other slaves, but they were carefully pretending not to notice what was going on. Despair filled her. She wasn't the only one who was scared of the vilicus. And her mother was still sick in bed.

'Is this miserable wretch Carthaginian?'

'No. I told you, he's Greek. His name's Lysander.'

From nowhere, a dagger appeared in Agesandros' hand. He pricked it to Suniaton's throat. 'Are you a gugga?' There was no response, and the vilicus moved his blade to Suni's groin. 'Do you want your balls cut off?'

Petrified, Suniaton shook his head vehemently.

'Speak, then!' Agesandros shouted, returning the dagger to Suni's neck. 'Are you from Carthage?'

Suniaton's shoulders sagged. 'Yes.'

'You *can* talk!' crowed the Sicilian. He rounded on Aurelia. 'So you lied to me.'

'What if I have?' Aurelia cried, genuinely angry now. 'I know what you think of Carthaginians.'

Agesandros' eyes narrowed. 'It was odd when this scumbag arrived, half-dead. With a recently healed sword injury. I bet he's the runaway gladiator.' Like a hawk, he pounced on Suniaton's reactive flinch. 'I *knew* it!'

Think! Aurelia told herself. Quickly, she drew herself up to her full height. 'Surely not?' she snapped haughtily. 'That creature would have fled long ago.'

'He might have fooled you, but there's no drawing the wool over my eyes.' Agesandros leaned on his blade. 'You're no simpleton, are you?'

'No,' Suniaton mumbled wearily.

'Where's your friend?' the Sicilian demanded.

Don't say anything, thought Aurelia pleadingly. He's still not sure.

To her horror, Suniaton's courage flared one last time. 'Hanno? He's long gone. With any luck, he'll be in Hannibal's army by now.'

'Shame,' murmured Agesandros. 'You're of no further use, then.' Smoothly, he brought down his dagger and slipped it between Suniaton's ribs, guiding it into his heart.

Suniaton's eyes bulged in shock, and he let out a shuddering gasp of pain. His limbs went rigid before relaxing slowly. With an odd tenderness, Agesandros let him down. A rapid flow of blood soaked the front of Suni's tunic and spread on to the tile floor. He did not move again.

'No! You monster!' Aurelia shrieked.

Agesandros straightened. He studied his bloodied blade carefully.

Panicking, Aurelia took a step backwards, into the kitchen. 'No,' she cried. 'Julius! Help me!'

At last, the portly slave came hurrying to her side. 'What have you done, Agesandros?' he muttered in horror.

The Sicilian didn't move. 'I have done the master and mistress a service.'

Aurelia couldn't believe her ears. 'W-what?'

'How do you think he'd feel to discover that a dangerous fugitive – a gladiator – had contrived to join the household, placing his wife and his only daughter in danger of their lives?' asked Agesandros righteously. He kicked Suniaton. 'Death is too good for scum like this.'

Aurelia felt herself grow faint. Suniaton was dead, and it was all her fault. She could do nothing about it either. She felt like a murderess. In her mother's eyes, the Sicilian's actions would be completely justifiable. A sob escaped her lips.

'Why don't you attend to the mistress?' There was iron below Agesandros' apparent solicitousness.

Aurelia rallied herself. 'He's to have a decent burial,' she ordered.

The Sicilian's lips quirked. 'Very well.'

Aurelia stalked from the kitchen. She needed privacy. To wail. To weep. She might as well be dead, like Suniaton – and her father. All she had to look forward to from now on was her marriage to Flaccus.

Suddenly, an outrageous image popped into Aurelia's mind. It was of her, standing on the deck of a ship as it sailed out from the Italian coast. Towards Carthage.

I could run away, she thought. Find Hanno. He—

Leave everything you've ever known behind to find one of the enemy? Aurelia's heart shouted. That's madness.

It was only the bones of an idea, but her spirits were lifted by its mere existence.

It would give her the strength to carry on.

Quintus didn't notice Fabricius appearing by his side. The first thing he knew was when his reins were grabbed from his hands and his horse's head was yanked around to face to the rear. Using his knees to control his own mount, Fabricius headed east. Quintus' steed was happy enough to follow. Although it had been trained for cavalry service, the middle of a battle was still a most unnatural place to be. Quintus' initial joy at seeing his father alive exceeded his desire to fight for a moment, but then the balance reversed. 'What are you doing?'

'Saving your life,' his father shot back. 'Are you not glad?'

Quintus glanced over his shoulder. There wasn't a living Roman cavalryman in sight, just a swarming mass of enemy horsemen and riderless mounts. Thankfully, the Gauls who'd been heading for him had already given up the chase. Like their compatriots, they had dismounted to hunt for trophies. A huge sense of relief filled Quintus. Despite his decision to stand his ground, he *was* glad to be alive. Unlike poor Calatinus, Cincius and his other comrades, who were probably dead. Shame followed swiftly on the heels of this emotion. He grabbed back his reins and concentrated on the ride. On either side, scores of other cavalrymen were also fleeing for their lives.

Their common destination seemed to be the Trebia.

Off to one side, both sets of opposing infantry were now locked together in a bitter struggle, the outcome of which was totally unclear. On the fringes of the conflict, Quintus could see the shapes of the enemy's elephants battering the allied foot soldiers. The massive beasts were supported by horsemen, and he guessed it had to be the Numidians. It could only be a matter of time before the Roman flanks folded. Then Hannibal's soldiers would be free to swing around and attack their rear. That was even before the rest of the Carthaginian cavalry returned to the conflict. Quintus blinked away tears of frustration and rage. How could this have happened? Just two hours before, they had been pursuing an enemy in disarray over the Trebia.

Hoarse shouting dragged Quintus' attention back to his own surroundings. To his horror, the Gauls to their rear had resumed the chase. With their gory trophies taken, the tribesmen were eager for more blood. His stomach churned. In their present state, the nearest cavalrymen were in no state to turn, stand and fight. Nor was he, he realised with shame. Quintus wondered if it was the same on the other flank, where the allied horse had been positioned. Had they too broken and fled?

Fabricius had also seen their new pursuers. 'Let's head that way.' Surprisingly, he pointed north. He saw Quintus' questioning look. 'There'll be too many trying to ford the river where we crossed before. It will be a slaughter.'

Quintus remembered the narrow approach to the main crossing point and shuddered. 'Where should we aim for?'

'Placentia,' his father replied ominously. 'No point returning to the camp. Hannibal could take that with little difficulty. We need the protection of stone walls.'

Quintus nodded in miserable acceptance.

Doing their best to bring along as many others as they could, they turned their horses' heads. Towards Placentia, where they might find refuge.

It was ironic, thought Hanno, that his life had been saved by Roman efficiency. It wasn't because he and his men had been victorious. Far from it. The Libyans' position adjoining the Gauls meant that many of them had shared the tribesmen's fate. When the Gauls had finally crumbled before the mass of heavily armed legionaries, some of the phalanxes had been dragged in. The spearmen in question were slaughtered to a man. Sheer luck had determined that Malchus and Hanno's units had not been affected. Battered and bloodied, they had fought on, even as they were pushed to one side by the massive block of Roman soldiers.

Somehow, Hanno utilised the natural breaks in the fighting to regain better control of his phalanx. He ordered the spearmen to the rear to pass their shields forward. The same was done with spears, allowing his unit to resume, at the front at least, a more normal appearance. Malchus emulated Hanno. With their defensive shield walls restored, the two phalanxes were a much harder proposition to overcome. Without their pila, the Romans had to rely on their gladii, which were shorter than the Libyans' spears. It did not take the legionaries facing Hanno's unit long to realise this. Seeing the hastati and principes to their right advancing without difficulty through the remnants of the Gauls, they broke away to follow their comrades.

Hanno's exhausted men watched with a sense of stunned relief.

Then, quite suddenly, the Romans were gone. Oddly, they didn't wheel around to attack the rear of the Carthaginian line. Hanno couldn't believe it. There were still isolated pockets of fighting, small groups of legionaries who had been cut off from their comrades, but the vast majority of the enemy infantry had broken through Hannibal's centre. They showed no interest, however, in doing anything except beating a path to the north. As far as Hanno was concerned, they could go. His men weren't capable of mounting a meaningful pursuit. Nor were his father's. No command issued from the musicians stationed by Hannibal's side, proving that their general was of the same mind. Having arrayed his foot soldiers in a single line, he had no reserve to send after the retreating legionaries.

Chest heaving, Hanno studied the scene. There was no sign of the allied infantry. The combination of elephants, Numidians and skirmishers must have routed them from the field. Off to his right, which had been the phalanx's front until the Romans had pushed them sideways, the battleground was now almost devoid of life. Suddenly, Hanno was overcome with a heady combination of exhilaration and fear. They had won, but at what price? He looked up at the leaden sky and offered up a heartfelt prayer: Thank you, great Melqart, all-seeing Tanit and mighty Baal Saphon, for your help in achieving this victory. You have been merciful in letting both me and my father survive. I humbly beseech that you have also seen fit to spare my brothers.

He took a deep breath. *If not, let all their wounds be at the front.*

Soon there was an emotional reunion with his father. Blood-spattered and steely-eyed, Malchus said nothing when they drew close. Instead he pulled Hanno into a tight hug that spoke volumes. When he finally let go, Hanno was touched to see the moisture in his own eyes mirrored in his father's. Malchus had shown more emotion in the last few weeks than at any time since his mother's death.

'That was a hard fight. You held your phalanx together well,' Malchus muttered. 'Hannibal will hear of it.'

Hanno thought he would burst with pride. His father's approval meant ten times that of their general.

Malchus' businesslike manner returned fast. 'There's still plenty of work to be done. Spread your men out. Advance. Tell them to kill any Romans that they find alive.'

'Yes, Father.'

'Do the same for those of our men who are badly injured,' Malchus added.

Hanno blinked.

Malchus' face softened for a moment. 'They'll die in far worse ways otherwise. Of cold, a wolf bite, or exposure. A swift end from a comrade is better than that, surely?'

Sighing, Hanno nodded. 'What about you?'

'Those who are lightly wounded might survive if we can carry them from the field. It will be dark within the hour, though. I must act fast.' He gave Hanno a shove. 'Go on. Look for Sapho and Bostar as well.'

Did his father mean alive or dead? Hanno wondered nervously as he walked away.

His men responded with enthusiasm to the idea of killing more Romans. Unsurprisingly, they reacted less well to doing the same to their comrades. Few objected, however, when Hanno explained the alternatives to them. Who wanted to die the lingering death that awaited when night fell?

In a long line, they began advancing across the battlefield. Beneath the struggle of so many men, the ground had been churned into a sludge of reddened mud that stuck to Hanno's sandals. Only the tiniest areas of snow remained untouched, startling patches of brilliant white amid the scarlet and brown coating everything else. Hanno was stunned by the scale of the horror. This was but a tiny part of the battlefield, yet it contained thousands of dead, injured and dying soldiers.

Pitifully small figures now, they lay alone, heaped over one another and in irregular piles, Gauls entwined with hastati, Libyans beneath principes, their enmity forgotten in the cold embrace of death. While some still clutched their weapons, others had discarded them to clutch at their wounds before they died. Spears dotted the bodies of many Romans, while count-less pila were buried in the Carthaginian corpses. So many severed limbs were lying around that Hanno was soon sick. Wiping his mouth, he forced himself to continue searching. Again and again he saw Sapho and Bostar's faces among the slack-jawed dead, only to find that he was wrong.

Inevitably, Hanno felt his hopes of finding his brothers alive wither and die.

It was especially hard to look at the soldiers who had lost their extremities. The lucky ones were already dead, but the rest were screaming for their mothers while what blood was left in them spurted and dribbled out on to the semi-frozen earth. It was a mercy to kill them. Yet for every gruesome sight that Hanno beheld, there was another one to exceed it. It was the suffering of those of his own side that tore at his heart the most. He had to force himself to examine these unfortunates. It was his job to judge the severity of their injuries and make a snap decision if they should live or die.

It was usually the latter.

Gritting his teeth, Hanno killed men who were shuddering their way into oblivion, holding their intestines, the rank smell of their own shit filling their nostrils. Those who lay moaning and coughing up the pink froth that signified a lung wound also had to be slain. More fortunate were the men who wailed and thrashed about, clutching at the arm that had been sliced open to the bone, or the leg that had been hamstrung. Their reaction to Hanno and his soldiers, the lone uninjured figures among them, was uniform. It did not matter whether they were Libyan, Gaulish or Roman. They reached out with bloodied hands, beseeching him for help. Muttering reassurances to the Carthaginian troops, Hanno offered the enemy wounded nothing but silence and a flashing blade. It was far worse than the savagery of close-quarters combat, and soon Hanno was utterly sick of it. All he wanted to do was find his brothers' bodies and return to the camp.

When first the familiar voice of Sapho, and then Bostar, called out his name, Hanno didn't react. As their shouts grew more urgent, he was thunderstruck. There they were, not fifty paces away, in the midst of Mago's men. It was a miracle, Hanno thought dazedly. It had to be, for all four of them to survive this industrial-scale butchery.

'Hanno? Is that you?' Sapho demanded, unable to keep the disbelief – and joy – from his voice.

Hanno blinked away his tears. 'It is.'

'Father?' Bostar's tone was strangled.

'He's unhurt,' Hanno yelled back, not knowing whether to laugh or cry.

In the event, he did both. So did Bostar. An instant later, even Sapho had tears in his eyes as the three came together in a fierce embrace. Each stank of sweat, blood, mud and other smells too foul to imagine, but none of them cared.

Their arguments had been forgotten for the moment.

The only thing that mattered was that they were still alive.

At last, grinning like fools, the brothers pulled apart. Not quite believing their own eyes, they held on to one another's arms or shoulders for a long time afterwards. Inevitably, though, their gaze was drawn to the devastation all around. Instead of the din of battle, their ears rang with the sound of screams. The voices of the countless injured and maimed, men who were desperate to be found before darkness fell and a certain fate claimed them for ever.

'We won,' said Hanno in a wondering tone. 'The legionaries might have escaped, but the rest of them broke and ran.'

'Or died where they stood,' Sapho snarled, his customary hardness already creeping back. 'After what they've done to us, the whoresons had it coming!'

Bostar winced as Sapho gestured at the piles of dead, but he nodded in agreement. 'Don't think that the war has been won,' he warned. 'This is just the start.'

Hanno thought of Quintus and his dogged determination. 'I know,' he replied heavily.

'Rome must pay even more for all the wrongs it has done to Carthage,' intoned Bostar, raising his reddened right fist.

'In blood,' Sapho added. He reached up to clasp Bostar's hand with his own.

Both looked expectantly at Hanno.

An image of Aurelia, smiling, popped into Hanno's head, filling him with confusion. It took but an instant, however, before he savagely buried the picture in the recesses of his mind. What was he thinking? Aurelia was one of the enemy. Like her brother and father. Hanno could not truly bring himself to wish any of the three ill, but nor could they be friends. How could that ever be possible after what had gone on here today? On the spot, Hanno decided never to think of them again. It was the only way he could deal with it.

'In blood,' he growled, lifting his hand to enclose those of his brothers. They exchanged a fierce, wolfish smile.

That is what we are, thought Hanno proudly. Carthaginian wolves come to harry and tear at the fat Roman sheep in their fields. Let the farmers of Italy tremble in their beds, for we shall leave no corner of their land untouched.

Quintus' abiding memory of their ride to Placentia was the extreme cold. The wind continued to blow from the north, powerful gusts that threatened to dislodge an unwary rider from his seat. While it didn't succeed in doing that, the chill air penetrated every layer of Quintus' clothing. Initially, he had been kept warm by the effort and thrill of the chase, and latterly by the fear that kept his heart hammering off his ribs. Now, his sweat-soaked clothes felt as if they were about to freeze solid. Everyone was in the same position, of course, so he gritted his chattering teeth and rode on. After what they'd all been through, silence was best.

Lost in their own private worlds of misery, the twenty cavalrymen brought together by Fabricius simply followed where they were led. Hunched over their horses' backs, helmetless and with their sodden cloaks pulled tightly around them, they were a pathetic sight. It was as if each one knew that Hannibal's army had prevailed. Yet in reality, they didn't, thought Quintus. The battle had still been raging when they'd fled. It was hard to see how, though, with their flanks exposed, Longus' legions could have seized victory.

Quintus felt like a coward, but his fear had abated enough for him to consider fighting again. He'd ridden to the front of their little column a number of times, intent on remonstrating with his father.

Fabricius had been in no mood for conversation. 'Shut your mouth,' he snarled when Quintus had suggested turning back. 'What do you know of tactics?' A short while later, Quintus tried again. On this occasion, Fabricius let him have it. 'Once cavalry break, it's unheard of for them to rally and return to the fight. You were there! You saw the way they ran, the way I struggled to get this many men to follow me *away* from the battle. Do you think that in this weather, with night coming, they would turn and face the Gauls and Iberians again?' He glared at Quintus, who shook his head. 'In that case, what would you have us both do? Commit suicide by charging at the enemy alone? Where's the damn point in that? And don't give me the "death with honour" line. There's no honour in dying like a fool!'

Shaken by his father's anger, Quintus hung his head. Now he felt like a total failure as well as a coward.

They rode without speaking for a long time after that.

Fortuna finally lent the weary cavalrymen a hand, guiding them to a spot where the Trebia was fordable. By the time they'd reached the eastern bank, it was nearly dark. As miserable as he'd ever been in his life, Quintus looked back over the fast-flowing water into the gathering gloom. More snow was falling, millions of little white motes that clouded his vision even further. The scene was so peaceful and quiet. It was as if the battlefield had never existed. 'Quintus.' Fabricius' tone was gentler than before. 'Come. Placentia is still a long ride away.'

Quintus turned his back on the River Trebia. In a way, he realised, he was doing the same on Hanno and his friendship. Feeling hollow inside, he followed his father.

They reached Placentia about an hour later. Quintus had never been so glad to see the walls of a town, and to hear the challenge of a sentinel. The lines of frightened faces on the ramparts above soon distracted him from thoughts of sitting by a fire, however. Word of the battle had arrived before them. Despite the sentries' fear, Fabricius' status saw the gate opened quickly. A few barked questions at the officer of the guard revealed that a handful of cavalrymen had made it to the town ahead of them. Their garbled account appeared to have the entire army wiped out. There had been no sign of Longus or the infantry yet, which had only fuelled the fears of the soldiers who were manning the defences. Fabricius was incensed by the harm that the unsubstantiated reports would have already caused and demanded to see the most senior officer in the town.

Not long after, both men were wrapped in blankets and drinking warm soup in the company of no less than Praxus, the garrison commander. The rest of their party had been taken off to be quartered elsewhere. A stout individual with a florid complexion, Praxus barely fitted into his dirty linen cuirass, which had seen better days. He paced up and down nervously while father and son thawed out by a glowing cast-iron brazier. At length, he could hold in his concerns no longer. 'Should we expect Hannibal by morning?' he demanded.

Fabricius sighed. 'I doubt it very much. His soldiers will be in need of rest as much as we are. You shouldn't give up on Longus just yet either,' he advised. 'Last I saw, the legionaries were holding their own.'

Praxus winced. His Adam's apple bobbed up and down. 'Where are they then?'

'I don't know,' Fabricius replied curtly. 'But Longus is an able man. He will not give up easily.'

Praxus resumed his pacing and Fabricius left him to it. 'Worrying about it won't do any good. This fool won't be able to stop the rumours either. He probably started half of them,' he muttered to Quintus before closing his eyes. 'Wake me up if there's any news.'

Quintus did his best to stay alert, but it wasn't long before he too grew deliciously drowsy. If Praxus wanted his fireside chairs back, he could bloody well wake them up, Quintus thought as sleep claimed him.

Some time later, they were woken by a sentry clattering in, shouting that the consul had arrived at the gates. It seemed a miracle, but as many as ten thousand legionaries were with him. Quintus found himself grinning at his father, who winked back. 'Told you,' said Fabricius. Praxus' miserable demeanour also vanished, and he capered about like a child. His sense of self-importance returned with a vengeance. 'Longus will have need of my quarters,' he declared loftily. 'You'd best leave at once. One of my officers can find you rooms.' He didn't give a name.

Fabricius' top lip lifted at the sudden return of the other's courage, and his bad manners, but he got up from his chair without protest. Quintus did likewise. Praxus barely bothered to say goodbye. Fortunately, the officer who'd initially brought them from the gate was still outside, and upon hearing their story, agreed to let them share his quarters.

The three hadn't gone far before the heavy tramp of men marching in unison came echoing down the narrow street towards them. Torchlight flickered off the darkened buildings on either side. A surge of adrenaline shot through Quintus' tired veins. He glanced at his father, who looked similarly interested. Quintus' lips framed the word 'Longus'? His father nodded. 'Stop,' he requested. The officer complied, as eager as they to see who it was. Within a few moments, they could make out a large party of legionaries – *triarii* – approaching. The soldier at the outside edge of each rank carried a flaming torch, illuminating the rest quite well.

'Make way for the consul!' shouted an officer at the front.

Quintus sighed with relief. Sempronius Longus had survived. Rome had not lost all its pride.

The *triarii* scarcely broke step as they passed by. One of the two most important men in the Republic did not wait while a pair of filthy soldiers gaped at him. Especially on a night like this.

Quintus couldn't stop himself. 'What happened?' he cried.

His unanswered question was carried away by the wind.

They gave each other a grim look and resumed their journey. Soon after, they happened upon a group of principes. Desperate to know how the battle had ended, Quintus caught the eye of a squat man carrying a shield emblazoned with two snarling wolves. 'Did you win?' he asked.

The princeps scowled. 'Depends what you mean by that,' he muttered. 'Hannibal won't forget the legionaries who fought at the Trebia in a hurry.'

Quintus and Fabricius exchanged a shocked, pleased glance. 'Did you turn and fall on the Carthaginian rear?' asked Fabricius excitedly. 'Did the allied infantry throw back the elephants and the skirmishers?'

The soldier looked down. 'Not exactly, sir, no.'

They stared at him, not understanding. 'What then?' demanded Fabricius.

The princeps cleared his throat. 'After breaking through the enemy line, Longus ordered us to quit the field.' A shadow passed across his face. 'Our wings had already broken, sir. I suppose he wasn't certain that we could turn the situation around.'

'The allied troops?' Quintus whispered.

The silence that followed spoke a thousand words.

'Sweet Jupiter above,' swore Fabricius. 'They're dead?'

'Some may have escaped back to our camp, sir,' the princeps admitted. 'Only time will tell.'

Quintus' head spun. Their casualties could number in the tens of thousands.

His father was more focused. 'In that case, I think it's we who will be remembering Hannibal rather than the other way around,' he observed acidly. 'Don't you?'

'Yes, sir,' the princeps muttered. He threw a longing glance at his comrades, who were disappearing around the nearest corner.

Fabricius jerked his head. 'Go.'

In a daze, Quintus watched the soldier scuttle off. 'Maybe Praxus was right,' he muttered.

'Hannibal could be at the gates by dawn.'

'Enough talk like that,' his father snapped. His lips peeled back into a feral snarl. 'Rome does not give up after one defeat. Not with foreign invaders on her soil!'

Quintus' courage rallied a fraction. 'What of Hannibal?'

'He'll leave us to it now,' Fabricius declared. 'He will be content to gather support from the Gaulish tribes over the winter.'

Quintus was relieved by his father's certainty. 'And us?'

'We will use the time to regroup, and to form new legions and cavalry units. One thing Rome and her allies are not short of is manpower. By the spring, the soldiers lost today will all have been replaced.' *And I'll have won a promotion which will keep the moneylenders at bay.* Fabricius grinned fiercely. 'You'll see!'

At last Quintus took heart. He nodded eagerly. They would fight the Carthaginians again soon. On equal or better terms. There would be a chance to regain the honour that, in his mind, they had left behind on the battlefield.

Rome would rise again, and wrench victory from Hannibal.

Author's Note

I
t is an immense privilege to be accorded the opportunity to write a set of novels about the Second Punic War (218–201 BC). I have been fascinated by the time period since I was a boy, and I, like many, regard this as one of history's most hallowed episodes. The word 'epic' is completely overused today, but I feel that it is justified to use it with reference to this seventeen-year struggle, the balance of which was uncertain on so many occasions. If it had tipped but a fraction in the opposite direction during a number of those situations, life in Europe would be a very different affair today. The Carthaginians were quite unlike the Romans, and not in all the bad ways history would have us believe. They were intrepid explorers and inveterate traders, shrewd businessmen and brave soldiers. Where Rome's interests so often lay in conquest by war, theirs lay more in assuming power through controlling commerce and natural resources. It may be a small point, but my use of the word 'Carthaginian' rather than the Latin-derived 'Punic' when referring to their language is quite deliberate. The Carthaginians would not have used the term.

Many readers will know the broad brush strokes of Hannibal's war with Rome; others will know less; a very few will be voracious readers of the ancient authors Livy and Polybius, the main sources for this period. For the record, I have done my best to stick to the historical details that have survived. In places, however, I have either changed events slightly to fit in with the story's development, or invented things. Such is the novelist's remit, as well as his/her bane. If I have made any errors, I apologise for them.

The novel starts with a description of Carthage in all its magnificence. In the late third century BC, it was an infinitely grander city than Rome. I have taken the liberty of describing the fortifications present at the time of the Third Punic War (149–146 BC). I did this because we do not know what defences were in place in Hannibal's time. Because the incredible and impressive structures that held off the Romans in the final conflict were built sometime in the fifty years after Hannibal's defeat, I did not feel that using them was a major digression from fact.

Describing Carthaginian soldiers, both native and non-native, is a whole minefield of its own. We have little historical information about the uniforms that Carthaginian citizens and the host of nationalities who fought for them wore, or the type of equipment and weapons that they carried. Without several textbooks and articles, which I'll name later, I would have been lost. Another difficult area was Carthaginian names. In short, there aren't very many, or at least not many that have come down to us, more than 2,200 years later. Most of the ones that have survived are unpronounceable, or sound awful. Some are both! Hillesbaal and Ithobaal don't exactly roll off the tongue. Hence the main Carthaginian protagonist is called Hanno. There were important historical characters with this name, but I desperately needed a good one for my hero, and they were in very short supply.

The siege of Saguntum happened much as I've described. Anyone who visits Spain's eastern coast could do worse than climb the huge rocky outcrop near modern-day Valencia. It's such an impressive place that it's not hard to imagine Hannibal's soldiers besieging it. The formidable size of his army is attested by the ancient sources, as are the ways it was reduced by deaths, desertions and release from service. Whether any troops were left as garrisons in Gaul, we do not know. There has been much argument over which route the Carthaginian army followed after the Pyrenees, and where it crossed the River Rhône. The Volcae were surprised from the rear by a party of Carthaginians who had crossed upriver; their commander was one Hanno, not Bostar, however. The elephants were ferried over the river in the manner I've described.

The dramatic confrontation between the Roman embassy and the Carthaginian Council of Elders apparently took place as I've portrayed it. So too did the chance encounter between a unit of Roman cavalry and one of Numidians in the countryside above Massilia. I altered events, however, to take Publius back to Rome before he travelled to Cisalpine Gaul to face the invaders. Minucius Flaccus is a fictitious character, but Minucius Rufus, his brother, is not.

Most controversy over Hannibal's journey concerns which pass his host took through the Alps. Having no wish to enter into such debates, I merely used the descriptions which Polybius and Livy gave us to set the scene. I truly hope that I managed to convey some of the terror and elation that would have filled the hearts of those hardy souls who followed Hannibal up and over the Alps' lofty peaks. The speech he gave to his troops before they started climbing was very similar to the one I described. Although not every source mentions the scene with the boiling wine and the boulder, I felt that I had to include it.

The term 'Italy' was in use in the third century BC as a geographical expression; it encompassed the entire peninsula south of Liguria and Cisalpine Gaul. The term did not become a political one until Polybius' time (mid second century BC). I decided to use it anyway. It simplified matters, and avoided constant reference to the different parts of the Republic: Rome, Campania, Latium, Lucania, etc.

My description of the calf born with its internal organs on the outside is not a figment of my imagination – I have performed two caesarean sections on cows to deliver the so-called *schistosomus reflexus*. They were without doubt two of the most revolting things I've ever set eyes upon. On one occasion, the unfortunate calf was still alive. Although this happened only fifteen years ago, the farmer's superstition was obvious and he became extremely agitated until I had euthanased it. We can only imagine what kind of reaction such a creature might have provoked in ancient times.

The duels between the Carthaginian prisoners, and the rewards on offer to those who survived, are described in the ancient texts. So too is the fate of Taurasia. When it came to making a point, Hannibal was as ruthless as the next general. The Roman losses in the Ticinus skirmish were severe and the savage night attack by some of their so-called Gaulish allies only served as another knock to Publius' confidence. I invented the Carthaginian ambush at the River Trebia, but the details of the remarkable battle that unfolded afterwards are as exact as I could make them. Hannibal's victory on that bitter winter's day proved beyond doubt that his crossing of the Alps was no fluke. As the Romans would repeatedly discover in the months that followed, he was a real force to be reckoned with.

A bibliography of the textbooks I used while writing *Hannibal: Enemy of Rome* would run to several pages, so I will mention only the most important, in alphabetical order by author: *The Punic Wars* by Nigel Bagnall, *The Punic Wars* by Brian Caven, *Greece and Rome at War* by Peter Connolly, *Hannibal* by Theodore A. Dodge, *The Fall of Carthage* by Adrian Goldsworthy, *Armies of the Macedonian and Punic Wars* by Duncan Head, *Hannibal's War* by J. F. Lazenby, *Carthage Must Be Destroyed* by Richard Miles, *The Life and Death of Carthage* by G. C. & C. Picard, *Daily Life in Carthage (at the Time of Hannibal)* by G. C. Picard, *Roman Politics 220–150 BC* by H. H. Scullard, *Carthage and the Carthaginians* by Reginald B. Smith and *Warfare in the Classical World* by John Warry. I'm grateful to Osprey Publishing for numerous excellent volumes, to Oxford University Press for the outstanding *Oxford Classical Dictionary*, and to Alberto Perez and Paul McDonnell-Staff for their superb article in Volume III, Issue 4 of *Ancient Warfare* magazine. Thanks, as always, to the members of www.romanarmy.com, whose rapid answers to my odd questions are so often of great use. I also have to mention, and thank, the three Australian brothers Wood: Danny, Ben and Sam. Their excellent mini travel series, *On Hannibal's Trail*, couldn't have screened on BBC4 at a better time than it did, and was a great help to me when writing the chapter on crossing the Alps.

I owe gratitude too to a legion of people at my wonderful publishers, Random House. There's Rosie de Courcy, my indefatigable and endlessly encouraging editor; Nicola Taplin, my tremendous managing editor; Kate Elton, who was generous enough to welcome me into the big, brave world of Arrow Books; Rob Waddington, who ensures that my novels reach every possible outlet in the land; Adam Humphrey, who organises fiendishly clever and successful marketing; Richard Ogle, who, with the illustrator Steve Stone, designs my amazing new jackets; Ruth Waldram, who secures me all kinds of great publicity; Monique Corless, who persuades so many foreign editors to buy my books; David Parrish, who makes sure that bookshops abroad do so too. Thank you all so much. Your hard work on my behalf is very much appreciated.

So many other people must be named: Charlie Viney, my agent, deserves a big mention. Without him, I'd still be working as a vet, and plugging away at my first Roman novel. Thanks, Charlie! I'm very grateful to Richenda Todd, my copy editor, who provides highly incisive input on my manuscripts; Claire Wheller, my outstanding physio, who stops my body from falling to bits after spending too long at my PC; Arthur O'Connor, the most argumentative man in Offaly (if not Ireland), who also supplies excellent criticism and improvements to my stories. Last, but most definitely not least, Sair, my wife, and Ferdia and Pippa, my children, ground me and provide me with so much love and joy. Thank you. My life is so much richer for having you three in it.

Glossary

acetum: vinegar, the most common disinfectant used by the Romans. Vinegar is excellent at killing bacteria, and its widespread use in Western medicine continued until late in the nineteenth century.

Aesculapius: son of Apollo, the god of health and the protector of doctors. Revered by the Carthaginians as well as the Romans.

Agora: we have no idea what Carthaginians called the central meeting area in their city. I have used the Greek term to differentiate it from the main Forum in Rome. Without doubt, the Agora would have been the most important meeting place in Carthage.

Alps: In Latin, these mountains are called *Alpes*. Not used in the novel (unlike the Latin names for other geographical features) as it looks 'strange' to modern eyes.

Assembly of the People: the public debating group to which all Carthaginian male citizens belonged. Its main power was that of electing the suffetes once a year.

Astarte: a Carthaginian goddess whose origins lie in the East. She may have represented marriage, and was perhaps seen as the protector of cities and different social groups.

atrium: the large chamber immediately beyond the entrance hall in a Roman house. Frequently built on a grand scale, this was the social and devotional centre of the home.

Baal Hammon: the pre-eminent god at the time of the founding of Carthage. He was the protector of the city, the fertilising sun, the provider of wealth and the guarantor of success and happiness. The Tophet, or the sacred area where Baal Hammon was worshipped, is the site where the bones of children and babies have been found, giving rise to the controversial topic of child sacrifice. For those who are interested, there is an excellent discussion on the issue in Richard Miles' book, *Carthage Must Be Destroyed*. The term 'Baal' means 'Master' or 'Lord', and was used before the name of various gods.

Baal Saphon: the Carthaginian god of war.

bireme: an ancient warship, which was perhaps invented by the Phoenicians. It had a square sail, two sets of oars on each side, and was used extensively by the Greeks and Romans.

caetrati (sing. *caetratus*): light Iberian infantry. They wore short-sleeved white tunics with a crimson border at the neck, hem and sleeves. Their only protection was a helmet of sinew or bronze, and a round buckler of leather and wicker, or wood, called a *caetra*. They were armed with *falcata* swords and daggers. Some may have carried javelins.

caligae: heavy leather sandals worn by the Roman soldier. Sturdily constructed in three layers – a sole, insole and upper – *caligae* resembled an open-toed boot. The straps could be tightened to make them fit more closely. Dozens of metal studs on the sole gave the sandals good grip; these could also be replaced when necessary.

carnyx (pl. *carnyxes*): a bronze trumpet, which was held vertically and topped by a bell shaped in the form of an animal, usually a boar. Used by many Celtic peoples, it was ubiquitous in Gaul, and provided a fearsome sound alone or in unison with other instruments. It was often depicted on Roman coins, to denote victories over various tribes.

Carthage: modern-day Tunis. It was reputedly founded in 814 BC, although the earliest archaeological finds date from about sixty years later.

cenaculae (sing. *cenacula*): the miserable multi-storey flats in which Roman plebeians lived. Cramped, poorly lit, heated only by braziers, and often dangerously constructed, the *cenaculae* had no running water or sanitation. Access to the flats was via staircases built on the outside of the building.

Choma: the manmade quadrilateral area which lay to the south/southeast of the main harbours in Carthage. It was probably constructed to serve as a place to unload ships, to store goods, and to act as a pier head protecting passing vessels from the worst of the wind.

Cisalpine Gaul: the northern area of modern-day Italy, comprising the Po plain and its mountain borders from the Alps to the Apennines. In the third century BC, it was not part of the Republic.

consul: one of two annually elected chief magistrates, appointed by the people and ratified by the Senate. Effective rulers of Rome for twelve months, they were in charge of civil and military matters and led the Republic's armies into war. Each could countermand the other and both were supposed to heed the wishes of the Senate. No man was supposed to serve as consul more than once.

Council of Elders: Carthaginian politics, with its numerous ruling bodies, is very confusing. The Council of Elders was one of the most important, however. Its members were some of the most prominent men in Carthage, and its areas of remit included the treasury and foreign affairs. Another ruling body was the Tribunal of One Hundred and Four. Composed of members of the élite aristocracy, it supervised the conduct of government officials and military leaders; it also acted as a type of higher constitutional court.

crucifixion: contrary to popular belief, the Romans did not invent this awful form of execution; in fact, the Carthaginians may well have done so. The practice is first recorded during the Punic Wars.

decurion: the cavalry officer in charge of ten men. In later times, the decurion commanded a *turma*, a unit of about thirty men.

didrachm: a silver coin, worth two drachmas, which was one of the main coins in third century BC Italy. Strangely, the Romans did not make coins of their own design until later on. The *denarius*, which was to become the main coin of the Republic, was not introduced until around 211 BC.

Eshmoun: the Carthaginian god of health and well-being, whose temple was the largest in Carthage.

falaricae (sing. *falarica*): a spear with a pine shaft and a long iron head, at the base of which a ball of pitch and tow was often tied. This created a lethal incendiary weapon, used to great effect by the Saguntines.

falcata sword: a lethal, slightly curved weapon with a sharp point used by light Iberian infantry. It was single-edged for the first half to two-thirds of its blade, but the remainder was double-edged. The hilt curved protectively around the hand and back towards the blade; it was often made in the shape of a horse's head. Apparently, the *caetrati* who used *falcata* swords were well able to fight legionaries.

fasces: a bundle of rods bound together around an axe. The symbol of justice, it was carried by a lictor, a group of whom walked in front of all senior magistrates. The fasces symbolised the right of the authorities to punish and execute lawbreakers.

fides: essentially, good faith. It was regarded as a major quality in Rome.

fugitivarius (pl. *fugitivarii*): slave-catchers, men who made a living from tracking down and capturing runaways. The punishment branding the letter 'F' (for *fugitivus*) on the forehead is documented; so is the wearing of permanent neck chains, which had directions on how to return the slave to their owner.

Genua: modern-day Genoa.

gladius (pl. *gladii*): little information remains about the 'Spanish' sword of the Republican army, the *gladius hispaniensis*, with its waisted blade. It is not clear when it was adopted by the Romans, but it was probably after encountering the weapon during the First Punic War, when it was used by Celtiberian troops. The shaped hilt was made of bone and protected by a pommel and guard of wood. The *gladius* was worn on the right, except by centurions and other senior officers, who wore it on the left. It was actually quite easy to draw with the right hand, and was probably positioned like this to avoid entanglement with the *scutum* while being unsheathed.

gugga: in Plautus' comedy, *Poenulus*, one of the Roman characters refers to a Carthaginian trader as a 'gugga'. This insult can be translated as 'little rat'.

hastati (sing. *hastatus*): experienced young soldiers who formed the first ranks in the Roman battle line in the third century BC. They were armed with mail or bronze breast and back plates, crested helmets, and *scuta*. They carried two *pila*, one light and one heavy, and a *gladius hispaniensis*.

hora secunda, the second hour; *hora quarta*, the fourth hour; *hora undecima*, the eleventh hour: Roman time was divided into two periods, that of daylight (twelve hours) and of night-time (eight watches). The first hour of the day, *hora prima*, started at sunrise.

Iberia: the modern-day Iberian Peninsula, encompassing Spain and Portugal.

Iberus: the River Ebro.

Illyricum (or Illyria): the Roman name for the lands that lay across the Adriatic Sea from Italy: including parts of modern-day Slovenia, Serbia, Croatia, Bosnia and Montenegro.

intervallum: the wide, flat area inside the walls of a Roman camp or fort. As well as serving to protect the barrack buildings from enemy missiles, it could when necessary allow the massing of troops before battle.

kopis (pl. *kopides*): a Greek sword with a forward curving blade, not dissimilar to the *falcata* sword. It was normally carried in a leather-covered sheath and suspended from a baldric. Many ancient peoples used the *kopis*, from the Etruscans to the Oscans and Persians.

lictor (pl. *lictores*): a magistrates' enforcer. Only strongly built citizens could apply for this job. Essentially, lictores were the bodyguards for the consuls, praetors and other senior Roman magistrates. Such officials were accompanied at all times in public by set numbers of lictores (the number depended on their rank). Each lictor carried a fasces. Other duties included the arresting and punishment of wrongdoers.

Ligurians: natives of the coastal area that was bounded to the west by the River Rhône and to the east by the River Arno.

Lusitanians: tribesmen from the area of modern-day Portugal.

Massilia: the city of Marseille in modern-day France.

Melqart: a Carthaginian god associated with the sea, and with Hercules. He was also the god most favoured by the Barca family. Hannibal notably made a pilgrimage to Melqart's shrine in southern Iberia before beginning his war on Rome.

mulsum: a drink made by mixing four parts wine and one part honey. It was commonly drunk before meals and during the lighter courses.

munus (pl. *munera*): a gladiatorial combat, staged originally during celebrations honouring someone's death.

Padus: the River Po.

papaverum: the drug morphine. Made from the flowers of the opium poppy, its use has been documented from at least 1000 BC.

peristyle: a colonnaded garden which lay to the rear of a Roman house. Often of great size, it was bordered by open-fronted seating areas, reception rooms and banqueting halls.

pilum (pl. *pila*): the Roman javelin. It consisted of a wooden shaft approximately 1.2 m (4 ft) long, joined to a thin iron shank approximately 0.6 m (2 ft) long, and was topped by a small pyramidal point. The javelin was heavy and, when launched, all of its weight was concentrated behind the head, giving it tremendous penetrative force. It could strike through a shield to injure the man carrying it, or lodge in the shield, making it impossible for the man to continue using it. The range of the *pilum* was about 30 m (100 ft), although the effective range was probably about half this distance.

Pisae: modern-day Pisa.

Placentia: modern-day Piacenza.

praetor: one of four senior magistrates (in the years 228–198 BC approximately) who administered justice in Rome, or in its overseas possessions such as Sardinia and Sicily. He could also hold military commands and initiate legislation. The main understudies to the consuls, the praetors convened the Senate in their absence.

principes (sing. *princeps*): these soldiers – described as family men in their prime – formed the second rank of the Roman battle line in the third century BC. They were similar to the *hastati*, and as such were armed and dressed in much the same manner.

provocatio: an appeal on behalf of the Roman people, made against the order of a magistrate.

pteryges: also spelt *pteruges*. This was a twin layer of stiffened linen strips that protected the waist and groin of the wearer. It either came attached to a cuirass of the same material, or as a detachable piece of equipment to be used below a bronze breastplate. Although *pteryges* were designed by the Greeks, many nations used them, including the Romans and Carthaginians.

quinquereme: the principal Carthaginian fighting vessel in the third century BC. They were of similar size to triremes, but possessed many more rowers. Controversy over the exact number of oarsmen in these ships, and the positions they occupied, has gone on for decades. It is fairly well accepted nowadays, however, that the quinquereme had three sets of oars on each side. The vessel was rowed from three levels with two men on each oar of the upper banks, and one man per oar of the lower bank.

Rhodanus: the River Rhône.

Saguntum: modern-day Sagunto.

Saturnalia: a festival which began on 17 December. During the week long celebrations, ordinary rules were relaxed and slaves could dine before their masters; at this time, they could also treat them with less deference. The festival was an excuse for eating, drinking and playing games. Gifts of candles and pottery figures were also exchanged.

saunion: also called the *soliferreum*. This was a characteristic Iberian weapon, a slim, all-iron javelin with a small, leaf-shaped head.

scutarii (sing. *scutarius*): heavy Iberian infantry, Celtiberians who carried round shields, or ones very similar to those of the Roman legionaries. Richer individuals may have had mail shirts; others may have worn small breastplates. Many *scutarii* wore greaves. Their bronze helmets were very similar to the Gallic Montefortino style. They were armed with straight-edged swords that were slightly shorter than the Gaulish equivalent, and known for their excellent quality.

scutum (pl. *scuta*): an elongated oval Roman army shield, about 1.2 m (4 ft) tall and 0.75 m (2 ft 6 in) wide. It was made from two layers of wood, the pieces laid at right angles to each other; it was then covered with linen or canvas, and leather. The *scutum* was heavy, weighing between 6 and 10 kg (13–22 lbs). A large metal boss decorated its centre, with the horizontal grip placed behind this. Decorative designs were often painted on the front, and a leather cover was used to protect the shield when not in use, e.g. while marching. Some of the Iberian and Gaulish warriors used very similar shields.

Scylla: a mythical monster with twelve feet and six heads that dwelt in a cave opposite the whirlpool Charybdis, in the modern Straits of Messina.

socii: allies of Rome. By the time of the Punic Wars, all the non-Roman peoples of Italy had been forced into military alliances with Rome. In theory, these peoples were still independent, but in practice they were subjects, who were obliged to send quotas of troops to fight for the Republic whenever it was demanded.

stade: from the Greek word *stadion*. It was the distance of the original foot race in the ancient Olympic games of 776 BC, and was approximately 192 m (630 ft) in length. The word 'stadium' derives from it.

strigil: a small, curved iron tool used to clean the skin after bathing. First perfumed oil was rubbed in, and then the *strigil* was used to scrape off the combination of sweat, dirt and oil.

suffete: one of two men who headed the Carthaginian state. Elected yearly, they dealt with a range of affairs of state from the political and military to judicial and religious issues. It is extremely unclear whether they had as much power as Roman consuls, but it seems likely that by the third century BC they did not.

tablinum: the office or reception area beyond the *atrium*. The *tablinum* usually opened on to an enclosed colonnaded garden, the peristyle.

Tanit: along with Baal Hammon, the pre-eminent deity in Carthage. She was regarded as a mother goddess, and as the patroness and protector of the city.

Taurasia: modern-day Turin.

tesserae: pieces of stone or marble which were cut into roughly cubic shape and fitted closely on to a bed of mortar to form a mosaic. This practice was introduced in the third century BC.

Ticinus: the River Ticino.

Trebia: the River Trebbia.

tribune: senior staff officer within a legion; also one of ten political positions in Rome, where they served as 'tribunes of the people', defending the rights of the plebeians. The tribunes could also veto measures taken by the Senate or consuls, except in times of war. To assault a tribune was a crime of the highest order.

trireme: the classic ancient warship, which was powered by a single sail and three banks of oars. Each oar was rowed by one man, who on Roman ships was freeborn, not a slave. Exceptionally manoeuvrable, and capable of up to eight knots under sail or for short bursts when rowed, the trireme also had a bronze ram at the prow. This was used to damage or even sink enemy ships. Small catapults were also mounted on the deck. Each trireme was crewed by up to 30 men and had around 200 rowers; it could carry up to 60 infantry, giving it a very large crew in proportion to its size. This limited the triremes' range, so they were mainly used as troop transports and to protect coastlines.

triarii (sing. *triarius*): the oldest, most experienced soldiers in a legion of the third century BC. These men were often held back until the most desperate of situations in a battle. The fantastic Roman expression 'Matters have come down to the *triarii*' makes this clear. They wore bronze crested helmets, mail shirts and a greave on their leading (left) legs. They each carried a *scutum*, and were armed with a *gladius hispaniensis* and a long, thrusting spear.

tunny: tuna fish.

turmae (sing. *turma*): a cavalry unit of thirty men.

velites (sing. *veles*): light skirmishers of the third century BC who were recruited from the poorest social class. They were young men whose only protection was a small, round shield, and in some cases, a simple bronze helmet. They carried a sword, but their primary weapons were 1.2 m (4 ft.) javelins. They also wore bear- or wolf-skin headdresses.

Vespera: the first watch of the night.

vilicus: slave foreman or farm manager. Commonly a slave, the *vilicus* was sometimes a paid worker, whose job it was to make sure that the returns on a farm were as large as possible. This was most commonly done by treating the slaves brutally.

Vinalia Rustica: a Roman wine festival held on 19 August.

THIN AIR

THIN AIR

SUE GEE

First Published in 2002 by
HEADLINE BOOK PUBLISHING

A REVIEW hardback

10 9 8 7 6 5 4 3 2 1

British Library Cataloguing in Publication Data

Gee, Sue
Thin air
I.Title
823.9'14[F]

ISBN 0 7472 7494 0

Typeset by
Letterpart Limited, Reigate, Surrey

Printed and bound in Great Britain by
Clays Ltd, St Ives plc

HEADLINE BOOK PUBLISHING
A division of Hodder Headline
338 Euston Road
LONDON NW1 3BH

www.reviewbooks.co.uk
www.hodderheadline.com

For Danusia, Hazel, Norah and Polly,
in slightly different ways

Autumn 2000

I

Letters

1

***

The wind was getting up again, and William, tugging open the front door first thing in the morning and nearing – he knew, he could feel it – the closing years of his life, bent down for the milk on the top step and had his pyjama trousers whipped about his ankles. He straightened up, pulling his dressing gown to. Rain was blowing past the portico; it splashed on the steps and the unpruned rose at the gate, where a last, astonishing bloom collapsed. Glorious wet pink on soaking earth: he noticed that.

Below him, along the street, the first commuters banged their doors and fought with wild umbrellas. Dulwich to London Bridge: the 8.15. William had made the journey for over thirty years. Before him – standing there on the top step, clasping the bottle of semi-skimmed milk which his daughter had advised – were the tossing trees, the Impressionist umbrellas, silvered by the swirling rain. Behind, in the hall, the telephone was ringing.

'Hello?' On the hall table the milk bottle sank damply into the front-page photograph of floods.

'Global warming,' said Buffy, putting down her coffee cup in her flat in Notting Hill.

'What's that?' He sank into the chair by a tepid radiator, crossing his elegant legs. Eve had thought them elegant.

'This. This filthy wet. The floods, the storms, the breaking banks. It's up to the first floor in York.'

William, cradling the receiver, looked down at the front-page photograph. Was that York? No – an ancient stretch of meadow, glassy and perfect, set with ancient trees. The water had risen around them, and now, as if waiting for the dove, was still and pure. The milk bottle had ruined it. Without his glasses, it could be anywhere.

'The world has changed,' said Buffy, pouring, he could hear it, another piping cup. 'The climate is in chaos – we've destroyed our *climate*, William. Nothing can ever be the same again.'

'You'd say that whatever the weather.' William ran his hand along the radiator, which, like him, was very cold. And less than tepid. 'It's our age, Buffy. Everything feels ghastly.'

'But this is *apocalyptic*. Your age,' added Buffy. 'I'm not in my dotage yet. What are you doing today?'

'Keeping to the house,' said William, swinging his leg for exercise and watching, against his ancient foot, the elegant flap of wine-coloured leather mules from Austin Reed. From Eve, one distant Christmas. They'd lasted well, as they were meant to. 'Phoning a plumber,' he added, feeling the chill at his back. 'And you?'

'It's Thursday,' said Buffy. 'My singing class.'

'That'll cheer you up.'

'It would if I could get there.'

'London isn't flooded.'

'It's only a matter of time. It's grinding to a halt. I'm not going to stand in the pouring rain for a bus that never comes.'

'Get the Tube.'

'I hate the Tube. You know I hate the Tube. I hate everything.' There was a chink of the coffee cup. 'Sorry.'

'Poor old Buffy.'

'I hate being poor old Buffy.' A little pause, then: 'Sorry,' she said again. 'I shouldn't go on to you like this, William. You've got far more important things to worry about.'

'I've got the central heating to worry about, certainly,' said William, as the letterbox banged. He peered at the mat. Was that a square of white, among the bills? 'Tell you what,' he said, getting stiffly to his feet, 'when all this clears up, I'll take you to the flicks. How does that sound?'

'Very nice,' said Buffy. 'If there were anything one wanted to see.'

'Now come on – we'll find something. And anyway—' He felt in his dressing-gown pocket for his glasses, which weren't there. 'I'll be seeing you on the stall on Saturday.'

'I know, I know, it's always fun. You're such a tonic, William, sorry to moan.'

'I'll see you very soon,' he said, craning his neck with the telephone lead at its fullest extension. 'I'd better get on now.'

The hall, lit only by the fading apricot silk of the table lamp, was darkened by the rain. He made his way past the curtained drawing room and bent to pick up the reminder for his TV licence, an envelope printed with violently coloured pound signs and, yes, a square of white. Mr William Harriman, Esq – dear, dear. A wild hand, a cheap, thin envelope. He took it all, with the milk and paper, down to the kitchen, where Danny, still in his basket, opened half an eye. *Thought for the Day* was murmuring. William searched for his glasses, half listening to a soothing bishop from the studio in Bristol, where sandbags had been heaped along the Severn.

Here were the glasses, still on the morning tea tray. The phone rang again as he gazed at dreadful handwriting. Now what?

He climbed back up to the hall, sank into the telephone chair once more, peering at the postmark on his letter.

'Daddy?'

'Who do we know in Shropshire?'

'What?' Claire, as so often, sounded sharp.

'Shropshire. I've got a letter here.'

'I've no idea. I've rung about Matthew. It's Thursday.'

'So it is,' said William, thinking of Buffy's journey through the rain to sing Handel oratorios in a bright upper room of the Mary Ward Centre. And thinking, collecting himself, of Matthew.

'Is something wrong?'

Asking this, as from time to time it was necessary to ask – when a doctor or social worker or, once, the police telephoned or rang the doorbell – brought back, always, those days when they'd been forced to face it: that, yes, something was terribly wrong.

'What is it?' he asked steadily, as the dark rain lashed the world.

'Nothing's wrong with *him*, don't panic. But I should be visiting, shouldn't I? It's my day. And Geraldine's got an ear infection. We've been up half the night.'

'Oh, dear.' Dimly, he could recall such nights, waking at some god-forsaken hour to see the landing light on, and hear Eve's gentle voice, up on the top floor, with one of the children. Generally ears or sick bowls. Generally the sick bowl for Matthew, ears with Claire.

'Anything I can do?' He'd stagger up there, to pale, tear-stained faces; Eve, in her pink wool dressing gown, being sweet.

'No, no, darling, you go back to bed.'

He doubted that Claire said this often to Jeremy, no matter what kind of day lay ahead.

'Anyway,' she was saying, above a little wail, 'I'm taking her to the doctor and I'm keeping her off nursery. I'm not going to cart her off to see Matthew on a day like this when she's ill. Am I?'

'No, no, of course not.'

'So can you go?'

'Yes, yes, of course.'

'I mean,' said Claire, as the wailing increased in pitch, 'he probably won't notice either way, but—'

'Don't give it another thought. Poor little Geraldine.'

'We'd better get going, it's emergencies only.'

'Give her my love.'

"Bye.'

"Bye, darling.' But she had already rung off.

William looked at the rain, trickling down the stained-glass panels of the front door, emerald and bottle green and violet. Would it ever stop? No matter, he'd get there. He went back down to the kitchen, where Danny was stirring, and about time too. 'We're going to visit Matthew,' he told him, putting the kettle on, and Danny, who knew that this word meant the acres of hospital grounds, and lots of racing about, thumped his dachshund tail and stretched. 'Out,' said William, unbolting the back door. 'Go on, make a dash for it.'

The wind and rain blew in as Danny made his reluctant exit, aided by William's slippered foot. He banged the door to, rinsed out the coffee pot. 'Shropshire,' he said again, looking at crazed uneven capitals. 'Oh, God, it's Mary.'

The last of the yellow leaves on the willow tree blew madly about the garden. William watched from the window above the sink. He and Eve used to have tea beneath that willow, on summer afternoons.

'*They fly forgotten, as a dream/Dies at the opening day*—' he heard himself humming, as a minister pronounced on climate change from a radio car in central London and Danny scrabbled frantically at the door. William let him in, shook biscuits into his bowl, made coffee, put the toast on, slit open the thin white envelope. Of course it was Mary, who else would it be? 'I must be worse than I think,' he murmured, settling down, unfolding the cheap lined pages, with their startling hand. 'What on earth does she want?'

2

'You'd like it in London,' said Mary Harriman, stirring tea. 'Bit going on.'

'I expect there is,' said Janice, watching two more spoonfuls of sugar go into the Coronation mug.

'Not much going on here.' Mary dug out the teabag and hurled it into the sink. 'Suit you, down there.'

'Possibly.' Janice leaned back in the kitchen chair and watched the rain stream down the little windows. At the front, the towering hedge obscured the lane, and most of the light, further obscured by the rows of china dogs. At the back, a disconsolate fowl was huddled on the sill, muddy white, with a drooping comb. Mary gazed, as Janice gazed, at the broken cement and churned-up mud in the yard, with its chicken-wire pens and flung-together coops and kennels, from whose open doorways the dogs stood staring out. It had rained for three days.

'Mind you,' said Mary, drinking, 'I haven't set eyes on William since I don't know when. Mother's funeral, I think.'

'Fifteen years ago,' said Janice. 'I know. You said.'

'And he's only a second cousin,' said Mary. 'Or third. Not as if we'd keep up much anyway.' She put down her tea. 'Sure you won't have another cup?'

'Certain,' said Janice. 'I should be on my way.'

'Can't go in this.'

'I know.'

Early this morning the rain had been light; it had stopped for over an hour, and the sky had cleared. During this lull, Janice had set out to do her deliveries, the bicycle panniers filled with the shopping of three households. She went slowly at first; as the load grew lighter, and she

9

approached her second drop, she picked up speed, spinning along between the hedges, glimpsing the misty hills through field gates. Then, as she came to the Dog Museum, it had started to chuck it down again.

'Been waiting for you,' Mary had said at the front door, taking the carrier bags of tins and sliced white Mother's Pride. 'Come along in.'

Across the yard, the rain was beating down on Ernie's caravan. Janice could see him, morose and smoking, at his table by the dingy Perspex window. Broken guttering let down a stream of water, just above his front door. It would rot the steps.

'Those dogs will go mad if they don't get out soon.'

'I think it's easing off.' Janice got up, and peered out of the window at the front. Her bike leaned dripping against the gate.

'You need a van.'

'I know. One day.'

'Make a lot of money in London.'

'Doing what?'

Mary didn't know. She finished her tea. Sophie came in from the snug.

'What do you want?' asked Mary.

'We've visitors,' said Sophie, in her pink-and-blue print pinafore, and spaniel hair slide.

'Where?'

'Down the lane.'

Mary and Janice went back to the window, to look. A family of three in cagoules and wellingtons was approaching the gate: middle-aged parents with a plumpish boy. They stopped at the sign, and looked at the house. The man walked on a little, passing the kitchen window. He stopped again, and beheld the rows of china Alsatians, terriers, poodles with curly china topknots, greyhounds with red china ribbons, eager Labradors. He saw Mary and Sophie and Janice looking back at him, and started. Rain dripped from his hood.

'Come in out of the wet,' shouted Mary, banging on the window. 'Only a pound.'

Janice watched them all confer. Then they clicked open the gate. Somebody usually did.

'Fancy going for a walk in this,' said Sophie.

'An ill wind,' said Mary, going to the back door. 'That's three pounds we've got here.'

'Two-fifty,' said Sophie. 'Family membership.'

Mary gave her a look.

'I must be off,' said Janice.

'I'll let you know when I hear,' said Mary. 'I'm sure William will put you up.'

'Thanks.' Janice nodded to the visiting family as she zipped up her jacket, pulled down her knitted hat and strode across the yard. They were gazing bemusedly at the sisters: Sophie in her pinafore, chopped-off hair held back with the hair slide, and Mary in pond-green cardigan, drooping skirt and ankle socks, their sixty-year-old faces as fresh and scrubbed and pure as Blyton children.

Mary held out the Jubilee tin. Across the yard the dogs had come out of their sheds and were up by the chicken wire, tails beating hopefully in the wet. Janice saw the boy's eyes widen as he took in their number, the ranges of breeds, and half-breeds.

'Are they all yours?'

'They are,' said Mary. 'Rescued, every one. Rescued from terrible homes and looking for good ones.' She shook the Jubilee tin. 'Do you like dogs?'

'Some dogs.' He went towards the wire.

'Martin,' said his mother, her voice uncertain, as Janice climbed on to her bike.

'They're good dogs,' said Sophie, peering from the dim-lit porch. 'They won't bite.'

'Some will,' said Mary. 'Any dog will, when roused.'

'Martin—'

Martin's father took control. 'Martin, come here. What kind of museum do you have?' he asked Mary, feeling in his pocket, as she rattled the Queen about.

'A Dog Museum,' she told him, prising the lid off.

'It says so at the gate,' said Sophie. 'On the notice.'

'I know, but—'

'Two pounds fifty,' said Mary. 'Family membership.' She nodded towards more creosoted huts, set at some distance, with cobwebbed windows. 'Everything's in there.'

'Would you like a guided tour?' asked Sophie, giving her little laugh.

Nobody took any notice.

'That's fifty, three pounds, and two is five.' Mary was firmly counting out change.

11

'Thanks. Well – we'll go and have a look.' He turned to his wife and child. 'All right?'

'What do we get for family membership?' asked Martin.

'Entrance,' said Mary, observing him with dislike. 'Entrance to the museum.'

'Do you have a newsletter?'

'That's a good idea,' said Sophie.

'No, it isn't.'

'Can I Adopt a Dog?'

His parents were shifting from foot to foot.

Mary's manner changed. 'What kind of dog would you like? We've terriers, lurchers, greyhounds – greyhounds make lovely pets, very gentle. We've whippets and cross-bred Labradors and spaniels—'

'We'd love to have a dog.' The boy turned to his mother, as the rain splashed down. 'Wouldn't we? You're always saying, because I'm an Only Child.'

'Yes, but—'

'But it's out of the question,' said Martin's father.

'We live in London,' explained his mother sadly.

'London?' said Mary. 'Do you, now?' She looked towards the gate in the hedge, but Janice had long since gone.

There was a sound from within the rain's swift pattering. Ernie had opened his plywood door and was standing on the top of his caravan steps, holding a roll-up in yellowed fingers.

'You stay there!' yelled Mary.

William, after breakfast, found a plumber in the Yellow Pages and phoned him. He ran a tepid bath, he dressed, came down again, drew back the drawing-room curtains. The windows at back and front were high, almost floor to ceiling, and in summer the room was filled with graceful light. It was one of the things they'd fallen in love with, looking for somewhere to settle and have a family, all those years ago. The house, then, had needed much doing to it; over the years they had had things done. Now they needed doing all over again, and he hadn't the heart. Mrs T., on her one day a week, almost a part of the furniture, kept dust at bay and silver polished. That was quite enough. He drew back the heavy old velvet curtains Eve had found in the sixties, their rust brown faded to mushroom in the folds, their calico lining in ribbons. He unlooped the tasselled silk ropes she had found in the Liberty sale, tied the curtains back, and stood looking out, down through the front garden to the wet black railings and the rainswept street.

'Lucky you caught us,' the plumber had said. 'We was just on our way to a call.'

Now he stood reading his letter again.

It's ever such a long time since we were all together, William, wrote Mary, dotting her capital Is and looping extraordinary Ts. *I think it must have been at Mother's funeral, God rest her soul. She did suffer, William, it was a Blessing in the end. We are all keeping well and the Dogs are a Comfort. We have a girl who does the shopping who wants to come to London. Going to waist, up here. I thought you might know of a Job and Lodgings. You are always welcome here yourself, of course, if you ever fancy a visit. Ernie I know would be glad of a Visit. Looking forward to hearing from you soon. The girl is called Janice Harper, she is twenty-three I think and Tall and Fit.*

A van turned into the street at the far end and came along slowly. William waved.

'That was quick,' he said, opening the front door to the two men climbing the steps. Beside him, Danny shimmied about.

'Morning, mate. Morning, sausage.'

They wiped their feet and tramped in.

'I'm Jim and this is my boy Darren. What's the problem?'

William indicated the stairs down to the kitchen, the boiler. They dropped their bags and stood before it, awestruck. Danny gazed up with them.

'What's that, circa Domesday Book?' asked Jim. He got out a screwdriver and attacked the casing. Falls of soot came away with the front.

'Dear oh dear oh dear. How long since you had a service?'

William couldn't remember.

'Dangerous. People die from less.'

Darren sniffed, pushing back his baseball cap. 'Wunsamunf,' he said, twisting his earring.

'I'm sorry?'

'That's what we was told at college. Check it out wunsamunf.'

'Once in a very blue moon, this looks like,' said Jim. 'Pass us that spanner.' Danny was nosing in the bag. 'Nothing in there for you, mate.' He stroked his ears. 'Bright, aren't you? Bright as a button. Getting a bit grey round the chops. How old are you, then?' Danny licked his horny hand.

'He's very old,' said William. 'Like me. He was really my wife's dog.'

'Is that right?' Jim straightened up, and turned back to the boiler, now exposed. Soot clung to every visible surface. 'You was lucky,' he said. 'Got a dustpan?'

Martin and his parents entered the first of the museum huts and fumbled for the light switch. A single naked bulb hung from a frayed flex in the centre, spotted with long-dead insects.

'Gordon Bennett,' said Martin's father, pushing his hood back and looking about him. 'Fucking hell.'

'Derek!' said his wife.

'It's *sweet*,' said Martin, approaching the first of many booths. Within, a team of stuffed huskies strained at the leash towards him. They were made of fake fur, and wore fierce expressions, felt tongues lolling over plastic teeth, glass eyes bright in the gloom. Behind them, next to a sled heaped high with parcels, an Eskimo just a bit taller than Martin stood stiffly in his fake fur suit, smiling broadly. From one gloved hand hung a whip, from the other a brilliant fish, its papier-mâché body marked out with felt-tip scales, its mouth agape. As backdrop, on the three tall walls of the booth, a painted scene of pinned-up lining paper depicted dazzling snow, a polar bear, a fiery melting sun. A small Eskimo child bent over a pool in the ice with a fishing rod, where a seal had obligingly popped its head up. A little puff of blue smoke rose from an adjacent igloo.

'They *made* this?' asked Jenny, leaning closer to gaze at fake-fur seams. 'Martin, don't touch.'

'But they're sweet.'

'I know.'

Derek was taking a look at the booth next door.

'Blimey oh flaming Reilly.'

'What? What?' Martin went to see. A vast St Bernard with a dear little keg of brandy round its neck was nosing a prone figure in a fantastic heap of snow. Martin gingerly put out a toe and a million grains of polystyrene shifted.

'Martin!'

'Sorry.'

The man in the snow wore climbing boots and held a pickaxe. A wicked coil of rope was clipped to his waist and a great big bloody gash ran down his cheek. But he was still breathing, you could tell. St

14

Bernard had got there just in time. Beyond them, on the pinned-up paper walls, the mountains of Switzerland rose in jagged peaks, their snow-topped summits lit by a blood-red disc.

He could do pictures like this, he could get a job here.

'I could get a job here,' he told his parents.

'You don't have to be barking mad to work here, but it helps,' said his father. 'Ha, ha.'

Martin looked at him pityingly. Jenny giggled.

'Is it all winter dogs?' she asked, feeling the half-term holiday perk up. It could be hell, with just the three of them.

'What other winter dogs are there?' asked Martin, moving along the aisle.

Nobody knew.

'Look!' he said suddenly. 'Come and look!'

Derek and Jenny, united as they had not been for days – well, ages, really, thought Jenny – followed to where their only child was pointing.

A mighty waterfall roared down a great ravine. African animals prowled in the burning distance, beneath an African sun. And here, in the tumbling darkness of the pool, a child was drowning, a white child, brought here no doubt by her missionary-explorer parents, circa 1870. But help was at hand, for while her parents were off with their Bibles, heedless of Africa's teeming dangers, the family dog, a yellow retriever, had leapt into the boiling pool and was tugging the little girl to safety. Flaxen hair streamed out behind her, her ribboned hat bobbed wildly, a pale little hand was flailing in the foam. But the dog had her blue-and-white dress in his grip, and the rocks were but feet away.

'Fantastic,' said Derek, wiping his glasses. 'Bloody fantastic.'

Martin, gazing into the distance beyond the top of the falls, made out a cheetah, a wildebeest, a rhino. He could have done that rhino, easily.

'What are they called, these things?' he asked.

'Dogs,' said Derek, putting his glasses back on.

'No, stupid, the things – the—' He made a gesture to embrace it all, each scene, each recreation.

'I suppose they're diorama,' said Jenny, who'd been a primary-school teacher before she had Martin, and often wished she was still. 'Aren't they?'

'What's a diorama?'

'A prehistoric grass-eating animal.' Derek blew his nose.

'You think you're so funny.'

'I know.'

'But they *can't* have done all this,' said Jenny, as they wandered on. 'No one could do all this.'

'Not so much could, as why.'

'Why not?' asked Martin, and there they could not answer him.

And so the soaking-wet morning passed. In hut after hut they marvelled: at hunting dogs, bringing limp game across autumn fields; at Lassie, leaping a ravine; at guide dogs, in the second hut, leading blind men through the traffic; dogs for the deaf alerting deaf house-wives to the phone; circus dogs leaping through hoops, beheld by lions on stools, while scarlet-coated moustachioed ringmasters cracked their fearsome whips. Finally, and perhaps most magnificent of all, were the hounds streaming after the outstretched fox – 'I think that's a real fox,' said Martin, and it was – while the painted hunt leaped over the five-barred gate. It was a toss-up between this and the panting Border collie, crouched low before his swirling flock of sheep. He was pretty good, and the sheep were real wool.

'Enjoying yourselves?' called Mary, as they stepped over puddles to the last hut. Rusting bits of cars were heaped up by the fence that bordered the field; a dismal-looking hen was crouched beneath a mudguard.

'It's wicked,' said Martin.

'What's that?'

'Don't bother,' said Derek, as Jenny began to explain. He held the hut door open for her. 'Shall we have lunch in the pub?'

'What about Martin?'

'There'll be a games room somewhere.'

He smiled down at her; she smiled up at him, feeling so much better than this morning. She followed their only child inside, to shelf upon shelf of Dinky Toys.

Janice, on leaving the Dog Museum, cycled between high hedges to her last delivery: Albert Page, living alone at 3 Rushock Bank with his cat and his arthritis, living on Winter Vegetable soup, struggling with the ring-pull.

'You could try packets,' said Janice once, watching him.

'Packets? Packet soup? What do you think I am?'

'Or those cartons,' said Janice. 'They're nice.'

'What's that, then?'

'Carrot and coriander. Vichyssoise.'

'How much do they want for that?'

She told him, setting down tins and Rich Tea biscuits. Why did you have to be over ninety to enjoy a Rich Tea biscuit?

'Because they're cheap, that's why,' said Albert, stirring at the stove. 'How much did you say them cartons were?'

She told him again.

'One pound *eighty*? One pound eighty for a carton of soup?'

'I know,' said Janice, 'but they are nice.'

'I should think they blooming are. One pound eighty. I should cocoa.' He tipped the cat off his chair and sat down, trembling.

'It's never going to stop,' he told her today, as she set the carrier bag down on his table.

'What's that, Albert?'

'This rain. Do you think it's ever going to stop?'

'I think it's clearing,' said Janice, glancing through his kitchen window, which, like Mary and Sophie's, was in need of a good clean. 'Want me to do your windows for you, Albert?'

'Why? Short of a bob?'

'I'll do them for nothing,' she said, folding the carrier bag. 'I like cleaning windows.'

'You're a good girl' he told her, as she sprayed out a cloud of Mr Muscle. 'Isn't she, Tibs?'

'Only people on the telly have cats called Tibs,' said Janice, rubbing with the duster. 'People in adverts.'

'Old crocks like me,' said Albert, stroking Tibs's magnificent head. 'You're doing a good job there.'

'Can you tell?'

'Don't be cheeky.'

Janice rubbed away the last smears, and stood back. The duster was black. 'That's better. Now you can see when the sun comes out.'

'It won't.'

'It might. Right, then, I'd better be off.'

'Where you off to?'

'My other job.'

Albert gave a filthy laugh.

'Do you mind?' And she was gone, leaving him in his snug little kitchen, with the chill of the unheated cottage, in which nothing had been changed or touched since 1959, all around him. The garden at the front was nice, though, a proper cottage garden, which he still managed himself, though now it was a sodden mess.

She cycled away with a farewell ring on the bell, tyres whirring splashily, rounding the corner to where the road began to climb. She settled to it, head down, bike lighter with the last load gone, panting but determined. Three bends to go. The land on either side, glimpsed here and there through gates, stretched over soaking fields and clumps of woodland to fall away down to the valley, dotted with sheep, and rise again to the far wooded hills of Leinthall Ridge, brushy and autumnal, with great dark patches of fir. The storms had done dreadful damage, they'd been talking in the pub about it, and here, as she rounded the last bend, up on her pedals and gasping, a ripped-off branch was lying halfway across the road. She pulled up, wet brakes squealing. When had this come down? Somebody could have been killed. And here, in the middle of the morning, somebody still could be. She laid the bike down on the verge and walked up to the fallen bough.

The rain had stopped, but was still in the air, and it was windy up here, always. She felt the cold, driving across the valley and churned-up fields, stirring in the bare branches of the oak at the gate, where a great yellow gash showed where the limb had been torn away. A crow, drinking from a puddle, looked up at her sharply, then bent to drink again. Janice put her gloved hands round an upper branch and tugged. A few remaining leaves shook on the twigs, and twigs crunched underfoot. The bough was enormous: how come no one had reported this? She heaved and pulled and at last got it moving, inch by inch, over the road and on to the verge, where it was harder to move for the last pull, dragging on the bumpy wet grass, and she had to stop and draw breath. Phew. She clapped her gloved hands, flexed her fingers, tried again. There. Done it.

She walked back to the place where the bough had lain, and kicked away the last long bits of branch. That crow was up on the gate now, watching her, beady old thing, and in the silence of the morning, disturbed only by the rising wind, she heard the sudden chatter of a couple of magpies, hopping about in the oak. Their glossy green-and-purple plumage was caught in a fitful, unexpected glance of sunlight, gone as quickly as it had come, but still – two for joy, that was something. And here, coming up the hill from the far side, was the yellow council lorry: she waved, and it drew up beside her.

'Had to pull it out of the road myself,' she told the young man leaning out of his cab window. She gestured down the road.

'Did you, now?' He glanced to where the huge bough lay. 'You must be strong.'

'I am,' said Janice, sniffing in the wind and feeling for a hanky. 'Lucky, isn't it, or someone might've been killed.'

'We've had that many calls. Can't do everything at once.' He grinned down, meaningfully, and she blew her nose with some force. She walked alongside as the driver put his foot down again, and when they drew up by the bough said, 'Right, I'll leave you to it, then,' and crossed to pick up her bike, as they parked and got down, lifting out the power saw.

'Where d'you drink, then?' called the young man, as she got on.

'That'd be telling,' she said, and rode away, on the flat at last, with the wind on her face, and the whining saw behind her, and the smell of the wood, and the sawdust – a good strong cheerful smell, which made her think cheerful thoughts. Could do with a few of those.

This was the pattern of Janice's week. Deliveries in the morning to a load of old lunatics and loners. Once she'd done a couple, word had seemed to spread – the first was just as a favour, a friend of her gran's, then it was a friend of the friend, then the friend's neighbour, and so on. Three pounds a week she charged them, saving all that effort in town. Peanuts, but cash. In the afternoons she worked in Cloud Nine, the café up on the hill, where she'd had her first weekend job while she was still at school, and where she might as well stay on, really.

'What's the matter with you?' her dad demanded, when she went down to the Jobcentre and came back saying she didn't fancy anything much. 'Nice bright girl like you. You should be working in the bank.'

'No I shouldn't,' said Janice, sixteen and horrible to live with. They both said so.

'You need to go to college, get your A-levels,' said her mother, watching the toaster.

'Why?'

'So you can go to university.'

'I don't want to go to university.'

'Turning your nose up. Wish I'd had the chance. Get a proper job, then, something in Shrewsbury.'

'There's a nice pet shop in Shrewsbury,' said Janice, who'd hung out in the back streets when bunking off. 'White doves, fantails. And exotics. Perhaps I could get a job there.'

'Work in a pet shop? What d'you want to do that for?' Her mother took out hard white toast.

'You do it too high,' said Janice, taking her slice. 'You should set it at three, I keep saying.'

'There's children in Africa,' said her mother, pulling her chair out.

'I know.'

Anyway, she hadn't gone to work in Shrewsbury, neither in the pet shop nor the bank. Nor had she gone to college, to do her A-levels, though she went on reading, like she always had. She just did deliveries and dog-walking. Her parents had gone on and on till she said she'd leave home, and they said good riddance, and then they all got fed up with this; so long as she was paying her way, which she just about was, making a contribution, anyway. Later, she thought she might like to go to horticultural college: she wasn't bad in the garden. Sometimes she did the old lunatics' gardens, when they were getting past it.

But now she was twenty-three, and getting nowhere. Bored with it all. Bored with eking out a pint and wispy roll-ups. Fed up – you could say that again – with living at home. Thirty-three Curlew Gardens, a 1950s estate out the back of the bypass. Why didn't it just fall into a hole in the road?

One day, something would happen.

Not if you don't make it, said a voice inside her, as she stopped outside Cloud Nine, saw it was empty, and wheeled the bike round the back. There was a garden here: in summer, customers sat outside at the picnic tables, looking out over the hills, scattering cake crumbs for the birds. Janice made the cakes – at least she could turn her hand to things, her mother said, defending her at home when necessary. She did a nice lemon drizzle, coffee-and-walnut, good plain fruit and a delectable chocolate.

'Should be working in a hotel,' said her dad, wiping his mouth. 'Should have done Hotel and Catering.'

'I'm happy as I am,' said Janice. 'I like my independence.'

'I suppose the next thing you'll be saying is you don't want to get married.'

'Who's there to marry, round here?'

'Other people manage. Look at Tracy Keenan.'

'Please.'

Janice, outside the back of the café, opened her pannier and took out the last remaining item, a double tin (Oxfam, £1.20) with chocolate in the bottom and iced jam sponge on top. She carried it up the path to the side door, and let herself into the kitchen.

'That you?' Steve, proprietor of Cloud Nine and proud of it, was behind the counter.

'All right?'

'Quiet,' said Steve. 'Not a dicky bird.'

In summer, walkers strode over the hills and cluttered the café with rucksacks. Carloads of families bought endless cans and crisps, lesbian teachers read paperbacks in corners. In autumn the walkers kept up; by now, mid-November, weekday customers were like winter migrants: nowhere to be seen.

'Cuppa tea?'

'Please. And I'll make a sandwich.' Janice took her things off, hung them on the hook on the kitchen door and rummaged about in the fridge for her own supplies. There was a stove in here, a mottled old grey thing which ran on Calor gas and reminded her of something she'd had in her doll's house, now up in the loft. There was a kettle, which sat on the top. But Steve, behind the counter, had a fantastic tea urn, his pride and joy, which simmered and hissed and sent clouds of steam boiling romantically about his cropped blond head, and the heads of his customers, waiting for their good strong pot, or herbal tisane. Rows of sickly smelling, sweetly coloured boxes stood on the shelf: bilberry and blackcurrant, lemon and tangerine, raspberry leaf.

'I prefer PG Tips myself,' said Janice, adding her soya milk.

'Most normal people do.'

Steve's urn had been given him by his mother, when the Ludlow WI were having a turnout. He, having been to university, told Janice it came from the pages of a novel by Virginia Woolf.

'Which one?'

'*Jacob's Room*. It's always hissing away. It carries clouds of eternity within.'

Janice had read *Mrs Dalloway* and some of the *Diaries*. At least she read, said her mother. She reads too blooming much, said her dad. Why hadn't she gone to university, if she liked reading so much?

'Because I was a free spirit,' said Janice, pulling her jacket on.

21

'What's a clever young man like Steve Bounds doing running a café?' asked her mother.

'Because he likes it. Anything wrong with that?'

'Why isn't he teaching?'

'He doesn't like teaching.'

'Why isn't he married? Why don't you marry him? You're always up there, you might as well.'

'Because he's gay,' said Janice. 'Why do you think?'

She heard her father groan.

The pot of tea was waiting on the counter when she carried her sandwich through.

'Thanks.'

'Good morning?' asked Steve, joining her at a corner table.

'Same as usual.' She told him about the family, arriving at the Dog Museum in the downpour, looking aghast.

'I'm not surprised,' said Steve, pouring two large mugs. Janice, tucking into her peanut-butter and soya spread sandwich, realised she was starving. All that exercise.

'Mary Harriman thinks I should go to London,' she said, between mouthfuls.

'London? Whatever for?'

'Work. Stimulus. Not to mention money.'

'You can't go to London.' Steve was adamant. 'How would I manage?'

'There's nobody here in winter. It's hardly worth keeping it open.'

'Yes it is. People come. You know they come. It's a service, up here, people are glad of us. And in summer I really need you.' He looked at her, across the red-checked tablecloth. 'Please don't go.'

'Well,' said Janice, finishing her sandwich. 'I don't suppose I will.' She sipped her tea. 'God, I needed this.'

'What does old Mary know about London, anyway? I shouldn't think she's ever been there.'

'Neither have I. She's got a cousin there, or something. She's written him a letter.'

'Can she write?'

'Sort of. A bit.'

'Well, anyway,' said Steve sadly, 'I don't want you to go.'

The clock on the wall chimed once, melodiously. The deal in winter was that Steve did mornings, and Janice afternoons.

'I'm going into Welshpool,' he told her. 'You'll lock up and every-thing?'

'Will do.'

When he had gone, she settled herself with more tea and another sandwich. She got out her roll-ups, and smoked with her tea, and her book, a second-hand collection of Emily Dickinson which she'd found, as it happened, in Welshpool, in the bookshop down the alley behind Iceland.

> It's all I have to bring today –
> This, and my heart beside –
> This, and my heart, and all the fields –
> And all the meadows wide –

Sometimes she thought that she should have been someone like Emily, brilliant and alone and yearning.

> Out of sight? What of that?
> See the bird – reach it!
> Curve by Curve, Sweep by Sweep –
> Round the Steep Air –
> Danger! What is that to Her?

The café door swung open, striking the bell. Janice looked up. The rain had quite cleared, and in forgotten sunshine the glass door was shining with drops. A young man stood there, his motorbike helmet under his arm, his leather jacket zipped to the top against the wind. He wiped his enormous boots, put the helmet on a table, and went up to the counter.

'It's me,' said Janice, getting up. She lifted the flap and went behind. 'What can I get you?'

He unzipped his jacket, and ran his eye down the chalk-written board at the back.

'I'll have a tea and a toasted ham-and-cheese, on brown.'

'Come far?' she asked him, slicing granary bread.

'Just Ludlow.' He had a light growth of dark stubble, and his eyes were very blue. As water hissed into the china pot, steam hung about him like a nimbus.

'Been working here long?' he asked her, as she reached in the fridge.

'Too long.' She closed the fridge door and unpeeled the packet of ham. 'I'll bring this to you, if you want to sit down.'

He went to the table where he'd parked his helmet, glancing at her book as he passed. She took him his tea, and then the sizzling sandwich.

'Mind – it's very hot.'

She went to the door and breathed in the freshness of it all: the sky rinsed clear and the distant clouds sailing over the hills like departing ships. His motorbike was parked on the verge, a metallic green, gleaming. A jackdaw was perched on the telegraph wire, preening wet feathers.

'What are you doing tonight?' he asked her, when she went back inside.

3

William walked up Denmark Hill. The rain had blown away after lunch, which he'd eaten on a tray in the drawing room, listening to *The World at One* while the men went on banging about. They finally left at two. William wrote out a cheque for a hundred and thirty-five pounds and said he hoped that would be it for a good long while.

'Like I said,' Jim told him, pocketing the Coutts cheque. 'You're lucky to be here, mate.'

'Wunsamunf,' said Darren, stroking Danny's ears.

'Once every six, that's for sure,' said Jim. 'Lucky you didn't have to have a new boiler. Expertise, that's what you got here.'

William thanked him, and saw them off on the steps. The sky was still cloudy, but light and high. He wrapped up, and fetched Danny's lead. 'Right, then. We're off.'

Still windy. Wet leaves blew along Denmark Hill. November, thought William, approaching the hospital. London in November. The place and month had always held for him a particular light, a particular sensation: as a boy, playing on the Dulwich rugby pitch; as a young man at UCL, hurrying across the quad in the fading afternoons; as a civil servant, looking out from his Treasury desk along Whitehall; now, in widowhood, in his life's winter. Such a strange, undefinable feeling, every year: the sky smoky; the bus such a clear bright red; the air, like a piece of music, melancholy, shot through with something sharper.

At the hospital gates he stopped to let an ambulance pass, then walked slowly across to the glass doors. He tied Danny up to the hook. 'Shan't be long.' People were coming and going: doctors with clipboards, women with flowers. He hadn't brought anything today. Inside, in the shop, he picked up the *TLS* and a Twix. One could only try. He made his way down the endless corridors.

John Ogden had been in here once. No, twice. As he often did, William imagined Ogden's huge bulk and trembling fingers coming to rest before the piano, pulling the stool out, starting to play. He imagined Beethoven and the showers of Schumann, the Brahms, spilling out into the grounds from open windows. Hours passed in a trance; then he slept.

William and Eve used to listen to Ogden; before his breakdown, they'd gone to hear him: at the proms, at the Festival Hall. They used to put him on in the drawing room, settling down with an LP after supper.

Matthew was in the day room, staring at a quiz show. William tapped on the glass. One or two people looked up through the clouds of smoke, and looked away again. He pushed the door open, and coughed.

'Hello, Matthew.'

Matthew turned. His face was pallid and expressionless; there were soup stains down his jumper. William had thought on his last visit that he needed a haircut; now it was worse.

'Hello, darling. Want to come out for a bit?'

Matthew turned back to the screen. Enormous scores were flashing in white and gold, and a gong sounded.

·'Danny's outside,' said William. 'We could go for a turn in the grounds.' He felt in his pocket and pulled out the Twix. 'Do come.'

'I'm wearing pink knickers today,' said Patricia, who often told people this. She gazed up at him from her plastic armchair, a long snake of ash on her cigarette just about to fall.

'Are you, now?' said William. He put an ashtray under her hand, and she winked.

'You're a very nice young man.'

'I was once.' He waved at the smoke, and went over to Matthew. 'Have a bit of choc.' Matthew took the Twix very slowly, and held it. The doors to the garden were closed, but unlocked. Beyond them, a man walked up and down, deep in conversation with an invisible companion, gesturing. Beyond the cedars a bonfire was smoking. November, thought William again, feeling a tug at his heart.

'I can't stay in here,' he said, through the clouds of cigarettes. 'Do come outside for a bit.' He felt in the other pocket. 'I've brought the *TLS*.'

Matthew sat with the Twix in his lap. William coughed again, and opened the door to the garden. Heads turned. He stepped outside on to the terrace, leaving the door open, and he walked up and down, smelling the bonfire and the autumn air. Clouds blew over the cedar trees. The eloquent man disappeared. After a while, Matthew got up, and came out.

'Shall we fetch your coat?' said William, kissing him.

He found a nurse, who unlocked the coat room. 'Having a walk with your dad?' he asked Matthew. Matthew held out his arms and allowed the coat to be pulled on, and a scarf to be put round his neck. 'Don't you look nice.'

They went round the front for Danny. 'Claire couldn't come today,' said William, undoing the lead. 'Geraldine's got earache. She sends her love.'

Matthew nodded. They returned to the huge expanse of grounds. Matthew threw a stick and it landed at his feet. William threw another and Danny went tearing off. The windy sky was full of racing clouds.

'I had a letter today,' said William, tucking Matthew's ungloved hand through his arm. 'From batty old Mary. Remember her?'

Matthew shook his head, frowning.

'We went there a couple of times when you were small. You and Claire used to chase the hens.'

There was a little smile. It always gave William hope.

'Fierce old cousin Edna,' he went on. 'The mother. Remember?'

He could feel the struggle, the swim through layers of time.

'Never mind,' he said after a little while, and patted the hand which once held a bow and soared through Schubert. 'I sold a rather nice old serving dish last week,' he told him, changing tack, keeping to everyday things. 'Mason's Ironstone. Fetched quite a bit.'

4

On Saturdays, William and Buffy had a stall in Camden Passage. They'd had it for years: since Eve's death, and long since William's retirement. Buffy had also retired. 'Thank God, thank *God* for that,' she'd said on her last Friday, in 1988, tipping the rubber bands and paper-clips and bits of fluff into the wastepaper basket, heaving the awkward drawer into the filing cabinet for the last time. They took her out to lunch and gave her a polyester scarf.

'How *could* they have thought I'd wear that?'

She gave it to Oxfam. 'At last I can do what I like,' she said on the phone to Eve, her one remaining schoolfriend. But then she got bored and lonely. She missed the ringing phones, the wasted-looking temps and Mr Lawson. Computerisation was coming in: she knew she could never have coped. 'Windows are what you look out of,' she said, when they sent her on a course. 'A mac is what you wear in the rain.' The time had come. She was glad the time had come. And yet—

'Not much fun,' she said to Eve on the phone. 'Bit miz, really. Didn't think it would be, but it is.'

She gazed from her third-floor sitting-room at the pigeons on the rooftops opposite; at her bright window-box geraniums.

'How come Buffy never married?' asked William, at supper, when Eve told him about all this. He poured them each a glass of Chablis, unfolded his napkin, and sniffed as Eve lifted the lid.

'She just didn't,' said Eve, ladling the chicken casserole. 'Some people just don't.'

'No one does, nowadays.'

'That's different.' She passed him his plate.

' "My partner," ' said William, thinking of Claire and Jeremy. 'Partners are people you set up a firm with.'

'You sound like Buffy.'

'Poor old Buffy. I wonder why she didn't. Marry.' He spooned out new potatoes. 'She isn't—'

'No.'

'Well, that's something.'

Later, when they were having coffee in the drawing room, Buffy rang again.

'I've had an idea,' she said.

Eve listened, the phone crooked on her shoulder while she carried on with her tapestry. 'That *is* a good idea.'

'What is?' asked William, looking up from his book.

'William's asking what the idea is,' said Eve to Buffy.

'Tell him,' he heard Buffy say. 'See what he thinks.'

He thought it was brilliant. Pottering round the country sales, bringing the stuff back. Just china, said Buffy. China and glass. They should specialise. 'We could do it together,' said Eve.

'I'll join you,' said William. 'Now I'm retired I can do as I like.' Forty years in the Treasury: enough for any man, and now he had his pension. 'Sounds like fun.'

It *was* fun. Looking through *Country Life* and *Miller's Guide*, setting off early on Saturday mornings with rugs and a flask and Danny in the back. They became experts, turning over Coalport plates and Minton coffee cups, checking for chips and rivets, learning the manufacturers' marks from Cushion & Honey's *Handbook*: that was a world in itself. They wandered round marquees, set out on the lawns of listed houses, they bid in dusty salesrooms, they loaded it all into boxes, wrapping each piece in *The Times*.

'Another thing that isn't what it was,' said William, thinking of his own long-dead father, and breakfast in the morning room.

At first, they had a stall in Portobello, because it was close to Buffy's flat. It had all been her idea in the first place, and you could make a fortune there, not that William and Eve were in need of that. 'But I need every penny,' said Buffy, and anyway, it was fun being there, quite a different part of London; it did them both good to leave the sedate acres of Dulwich, where William had, after all, lived all his life.

They set off at the crack of dawn, much as if they were going down to a sale in Wiltshire or Gloucester – just to get across London, but you had to, on Saturday, just to get a parking space. They set out the

stall and sat, on summer afternoons, listening to extraordinary music –
heavy metal, said Buffy, who had been forced, through proximity, to
learn this – and watching anorexic young women, still out of their
heads from last night's substances and sex, wander dreamily in and out
of the traffic, on and off the pavement, trailing silk and velveteen.
'Don't they get awfully *hot*?' asked Buffy. Wide-eyed American tourists
gazed after them, then came, with some relief, to the antiques.

'Worcester,' said Buffy firmly, watching manicured male hands
hover above a fruit bowl. 'Royal Worcester, 1870s.'

'Is that so? Honey? Honey, come and take a look . . .'

And Honey came. 'How about these little coffee cups?' she asked.

'Those are Royal Doulton,' said Eve, with her sweet soft smile.
'Pretty, aren't they?'

'They certainly are. Do you take American Express?'

It was all most satisfactory.

Not everything they bought and sold was of this class, of course.
Amongst the triumphant finds in the sales, and special pieces bid for at
the auctions – 'You can do the bidding, William,' said Eve, and he did
it to the manner born – there were plenty of things which they bought
just because they loved them: unmarked blue-and-white eggcups; a
little blue-and-white tea set which might have been Copenhagen but
wasn't, though quite as pretty; any number of cups and bowls and
single serving dishes. Tureens. Tureens with ladles. And then there was
the glass, which became Eve's passion, and the Spode, which became
Buffy's.

'I don't think I can bear to part with this,' she said, cradling a
breakfast cup and saucer, circa 1830 and without a chip. Its perfect
diameter was a full six inches, a serious, proper breakfast cup, with a
heavenly handle. They were down at a sale near Cirencester, a liquid
spring morning bedewing the grounds beyond French windows, the
trestle tables nicely spaced, a buzz in the air.

'Keep it,' said Eve, watching her. 'You deserve it.'

And so Buffy's collection began. The whole enterprise was going
swimmingly. They joined the Antique Collectors Club, took out
subscriptions to specialist magazines, couldn't have enjoyed themselves more.

Then Matthew came home with a first from Durham, and shut
himself into his room.

☆

'Darling? Matthew? Are you coming down for lunch?'

'Matthew? Want to pop out for a drink?'

At first they thought he'd had his heart broken.

'You can tell me,' said William, sitting on the edge of the bed. 'I can remember. Just.'

'Fuck off,' said Matthew.

He lost a stone and the house stank: of his unwashed body, his cigarettes.

'He's ill,' said Claire, furious. 'Surely you can see he's really ill.' She sat with him while they rang his tutors, who had all gone off for the summer. They rang the university counsellor and got an answerphone. When the counsellor picked up the message and rang, she said that Matthew had been in to see her a year ago, but it was confidential. She did say that the classic age for a schizophrenic breakdown was between sixteen and twenty-four. Matthew was twenty-two: he'd had a gap year, teaching in Ghana. He'd come back strained and silent. Had it begun then? I think it began when he was in his teens, said Claire, only *you* two never noticed.

Matthew went into hospital on a perfect September morning in 1991, the trees in the grounds just turning crimson and ochre, the air invigorating. William and Eve held hands, fighting back their tears. Matthew sat on the edge of his bed, his head cocked, his eyes glazed.

'We love you so much,' said William. 'You'll soon be home.'

'We'll come tomorrow,' said Eve. 'We'll come whenever you want.'

'Fuck off,' said Matthew.

'You're crowding him,' said Claire, and stalked outside.

In the carpark they clung to one another.

'He'll be all right,' said William, wiping his eyes. 'They'll pull him through.'

Eve wept. 'Poor little Matthew. He looks so—'

At home, William poured them each a brandy.

'How is he?' asked Buffy, phoning that evening.

'Not very good,' said Eve. 'I'm not sure about the stall this week. I'm so sorry.'

'Don't give it a thought.'

Two weeks later, Eve went for a routine mammogram with the NHS Mobile Screening Service, set up in the carpark in Lewisham Hospital. She came out to where William was waiting in the car, listening to Mozart from St John's, Smith Square. She was later than

31

he'd expected, since there'd hardly been a queue. 'People don't show up,' said the receptionist in her cubby-hole. 'They really should. Anyway, you're here, dear.' She ticked off Eve's name on a list and gestured to a curtain. 'Undress to the waist. You can keep your jewellery on.'

'I feel like a gypsy,' said Eve with a little laugh. 'I've always wanted a caravan.'

'Have you really?' asked William, and then, as she disappeared, 'I'll be waiting outside.'

Eve, when she came out at last, looked pale.

'Everything all right?'

'I think so. They took a couple of shots more than once.' She put her hands over her navy wool jacket, and the crimson and cream and indigo scarf which he loved.

'Bit sore?' he asked her, kissing her cheek. It sounded ghastly, he couldn't imagine it.

She shook her head. 'It'll wear off. Let's go.'

Ten days after that she had a letter, and went, without telling him, he later realised, down to the surgery.

Three months later, she'd gone.

'She won't see the baby,' Claire sobbed. 'She won't see the *baby*.'

'I will,' said William, 'I'm longing for that.'

Matthew, at the funeral, stood like a ghost, pale and vacant. He let William kiss him, and didn't tell anyone to fuck off, but they said that he shouldn't come home. Not yet. After a while, they let him.

He wandered in and out of rooms. He cradled Danny for hours, sitting in Eve's place on the sofa, watching television. He did not go near the piano, or pick up his violin.

'Shall we have that off for a bit?' asked William, as daytime soap followed daytime quiz. His head felt as if it would burst. 'How about a bit of music?'

He switched the television off, put on Schubert's Piano Trio No. 1, found himself in tears. Matthew got up and went up to his room, right at the top of the house.

'Please come down,' said William, reliving the sickening misery of when it had all begun. Eve had been there then, they had had one another. 'Come down and have a spot of supper.' Danny gazed up at him; beneath the bedclothes his tail began to thump. 'See?' said

William. 'Danny wants supper. Come on, old chap.' Matthew turned away. William sank down on the edge of the bed and put his head in his hands. Matthew kicked him off. William went out, and down to the kitchen, Danny following. He held him in his arms and sobbed.

Dreadful, dreadful days.

After a little while, Matthew perked up. He came down to breakfast and looked at the paper. He started to talk about the news. William found he was having a conversation. His heart began to lift, as if someone had unloosed a great weight – he found himself watching, in some obscure place within, a kite, bobbing about in the clouds above the common, while he and Matthew, as a little boy, watched it, hand in hand.

'He's getting better,' he told Claire on the phone. 'I really think he's turning a corner.'

A day or two later, he came into the drawing room to find Matthew laughing wildly at a nature programme. Lemurs clambered about in swaying trees. They made William smile, but they didn't make him clutch his sides. He looked at Matthew and a little rivulet of anxiety ran through him. That night he woke to a fearful crashing about downstairs, and realised, as he ran down there, that Matthew had perked up because he'd stopped taking his pills.

'Oh, Christ,' he said, as the dining-room glass went splintering. The door was open: inside, he saw a madman. Then Matthew turned, and his face was murderous. He came towards him, his hand upraised, holding one of his grandfather's heaviest silver candlesticks. William fled. He ran upstairs and dialled 999. Then he barricaded himself into the bathroom, hearing the dining-room table overturned, waiting for the sirens, and the flashing, sickly blue.

Matthew went back to the hospital, raving, and was put out for hours. Next day, when William and Claire went to see him, he could not speak.

Gradually, he got better. Months later, with the promise of a visit from the district nurse each day, William had him back. It was pretty grim. They played draughts, where they used to play chess. They played Chinese chequers. Each game took hours. The television roared. Matthew, between games and programmes, wandered about. William thought he was looking for Eve. He could sense how much it disturbed him being back here, even on the medication.

After a while it was decided that, until he could cope on his own, Matthew should be based in the hospital and come home now and then, for as long as they both enjoyed it.

This, for a long time now, had been the pattern of things.

And later, much later, when Buffy cautiously suggested that perhaps – only when he felt up to it, of course – they might resume their old activity, and have a little stall, William said he would like that, and yes, it would probably do him good.

But not in Portobello. Would she mind that dreadfully? It was just the thought of travelling right across London, it was just the thought of being there, where Eve had been – was he being terribly selfish?

Of course not, said Buffy, it would do her good to have a change of scene: she'd been thinking about it herself. How about Camden Passage, a good halfway place for the two of them, and a very good pub for lunch. People came flocking on Saturdays. And Wednesdays.

'Let's just say Saturdays for now,' said William, refilling her glass. 'Would Saturdays suit you?'

'Very well indeed,' said Buffy, who by now had long since booked herself into the Mary Ward Over-Sixties Club.

'My dear,' she told the receptionist, 'I'm over seventy.'

'That doesn't matter at all, my love.'

'My name is Buffy Henderson. Please don't call me love.'

She went to the choir and the art class, she even did a little training on the Internet.

Life had begun, at last, to look up again.

It had begun to look up for William, too. And this, for a long time now, had been the pattern of things.

5

———————

N ow, on a November morning, he set up the Camden Passage stall with Buffy. It was bitter. Danny was curled up in an ancient anorak beneath the trestle; Buffy, in her fingerless gloves, unwrapped a Staffordshire teapot, and put it next to an unmarked milk jug, patterned in green and blue.

'What do you think?'

'Perfect.' William was unwrapping the newspaper from six little Victorian glasses, engraved on the rim with a garland of grapes.

'You did wash them?'

'Of course I washed them.'

They sat sipping coffee from Thermos cups, waiting for the crowds.

'Five weeks to Christmas,' said Tom, on the next stall. 'Things should pick up a bit now.'

'That's a nice little set of spoons,' said William, having a look.

'Seventeen-ninety,' said Tom. 'Very nice.'

'You should be inside, with something like that,' said Buffy. 'You should be in the Arcade.' She finished her coffee and got out her lipstick. 'You're getting too classy for us.'

'It's the overheads,' said Tom. 'It's the overheads, or I would be.'

'I like those earrings,' said William, noticing, as Buffy looked in her little mirror.

'Liberty sale. You've seen them before.'

'Have I really?' He watched her pursing her lips. Tendrils from her bun were escaping a knotted scarf; the fingers in fingerless gloves were blunt and reddened; a trellis of broken veins embroidered her nose and cheeks beneath visible powder. She was wearing the deep-pocketed, hairy grey jacket she always wore in winter: it made him think of yaks, and stony paths. Sometimes, watching Buffy set things

35

out on the stall, he thought of the careful way Eve had unwrapped and set things out – not that Buffy was ever clumsy, it was different, that was all. Eve's touch was delicate, Buffy's workmanlike – professional, perhaps, was the better word. In quiet moments he'd find himself moving from the memory of Eve's hands, and the sheen of her nails, to her pink-and-white skin, its softness and opacity, her silken white hair, the scent she wore, whose name he could never remember, and which he had to ask Claire about each Christmas.

'Why don't you write it *down*?'

After Eve's death, when he tried, once, to go through her clothes, a drawer he pulled open released a ghostly cloud of that scent, clinging to petticoats and stockings. That had been one of the worst days. Now, on the whole, in daytime, he tried not to think of any of this.

The traffic on the Essex Road was building up. A hesitant sun shone briefly on the plate glass of Waterstone's, behind the Green. Pigeons conversed on the top of the war memorial; the sun touched the six Victorian glasses, set out in a circle.

'Those will have gone by lunch-time,' said Buffy, settling back in her fold-up chair.

'Have I told you about my letter?' asked William. 'I seem to be telling everyone.'

'You haven't told me.'

'From my second cousin in Shropshire,' he said. 'Second cousin twice or thrice removed, if I remember rightly. She's a rather extra-ordinary old thing – well, they're a pretty rum lot.' He stopped, remembering cousin Edna's funeral, held in St Michael of All Angels, up in the hills. It had rained then, too, blowing in great windy gusts across the churchyard, where the little group of mourners had assem-bled round a precipitous grave while the vicar struggled with his surplice. Claire and Matthew had not been among them, could even then remember Great-Cousin Edna only dimly, from the one or two visits when they were little, when she had shouted at them.

'Anyway,' said Eve, making arrangements for them to stay overnight with schoolfriends, 'they're far too young to attend anyone's funeral.' So he and Eve had gone up there, and stood beneath his black umbrella on one side of the grave while Mary, Sophie and Ernie, Edna's children, stood on the other. What a strangely affecting sight they made. It seemed probable that none had visited what one might call a clothes shop for many years: their buttoned-up, belted overcoats,

36

in murky shades of flecked maroon and camel, the sisters' pulled-down berets and Ernie's knitted scarf and hat, all looked as if they had drooped from hooks on the crumbling plaster of the kitchen passage since circa 1959. Sophie had wanted to wear Mother's court shoes, bought some years before from the Sue Ryder shop in Oswestry, but Mary, looking out at the rain as the hearse drew up at the gate, had bullied them all into wellingtons, now thick with Shropshire graveside mud.

In the chill of the church, they had sung *Abide with Me* in mournful whispers; watching them clutching their hymn books, William wondered how on earth they would all manage, released from Edna's maternal grip, which had been fearsome. Ernie's long yellow finger-nails picked at a thread in his greenish scarf; his wispy untrimmed hair straggled here and there from beneath the woollen hat; he had not, for a long time, met anyone's eye.

Afterwards, William drove them all back to the house, the three of them squeezed in the back, seeing, through the swishing wipers, two trudging figures arriving at the gate.

'That'll be Win,' said Mary, leaning forward. 'And Johnny.'

'They should've come to the church,' said Sophie, shifting. 'They was good friends to Mother.'

'People don't like funerals,' said Ernie, the first remark he had made throughout the journey.

Indoors, greeted by two lurchers and a rheumy-eyed spaniel, they assembled in the kitchen, beneath a slatted airer hung with strange-looking underwear and a quantity of socks.

'Your health,' said Johnny, raising his teacup. 'She was a good strong woman, your mother.'

'She did suffer in the end,' said Mary. Ernie gazed out of the window at the ceaseless fall of rain. Sophie passed round a plate of ginger nuts and another of digestives. Win had made a fruitcake.

Describing all this to Buffy, as the market began to fill up, and one or two people paused to consider her 1940s Dartmouth Pottery tea plates, William wondered how, indeed, the cousins had all continued to occupy that long, half-lived-in house, where paper peeled in damp shards from every upstairs room – he knew, he'd been up to the icy bathroom, had a look into desolate bedrooms – and nowhere, surely, was bearable in winter except the kitchen. Christmas cards over the years had told him that Ernie now lived out in a caravan in the yard, and that they had taken in more dogs. Beyond this, he knew nothing.

'Now Mary's written out of the blue. Can I help a young woman who wants to come to London,' he said. 'She wants a job and lodgings, as Mary puts it.'

'Bit of a tall order.'

'Do you think I should have a lodger?' He moved his cold feet to embrace the sleeping Danny.

'Not someone you've never met.'

'Claire thinks I should sell, and buy a flat. She's always saying it.'

'I must say,' said Buffy, 'I don't think I could cope with anything more than a flat, now. On the other hand—'

'Quite,' said William, who knew that they would have to carry him out of that house, in which everything in his life that had ever been important had occurred.

'But I do sometimes think I should have someone about the place,' he said. 'I mean – you never know.'

Buffy's attention had been diverted to the middle-aged woman in a raincoat whose eyes were on a 1920s cow creamer, and also a very pretty butter dish, patterned in Marguerite.

'May I?' She made to lift the lid, and realised it was Sellotaped.

'I'll show you, if I may.' Buffy turned it over. 'Winton.' She indicated the mark. 'Nineteen thirties. Rather nice, isn't it?'

'It's sweet.' The raincoated woman put on her glasses, and peered at the label. 'Does that say sixty-five pounds?'

'It does.'

'And the creamer?'

'That we can do for thirty-five.'

'Oh, isn't Christmas dreadful? All so tempting, but—'

William pointed out the ceramic toast racks. 'These make nice presents. And they won't break the bank.' He lifted one whose sections were gently scalloped. A little sprig of juniper was painted on the front, and the end had a stripe of juniper green. 'Now this is also Winton, but we could do it—' He picked it up, and looked at the label. 'Well, it says twelve pounds, but I'm sure we could knock something off for you.'

The woman put her glasses on again, and had a look. 'It is quite sweet. It's just that the creamer is *so* sweet.'

Buffy and William waited. A young couple stopped to look.

'Oh, those are nice,' they said, looking at the toast racks.

In the end, they sold the creamer to the woman in the raincoat, knocking off £6.50, and a 1920s shell-design toast rack to the couple.

'You were saying,' said Buffy, as they disappeared into the throng. It was getting quite busy now, and also quite a bit colder.

'Where was I?' William turned up his collar, round his sea-green woollen scarf.

'Contemplating a lodger,' said Buffy. 'That colour does suit you, I must say.'

'The thing is,' he said, contemplating the sound of a key in the lock at the end of the day, and a friendly drink by the fire now and then, 'the thing is Matthew, of course.'

'Is he coming home for Christmas?'

'I hope so. He does find strangers unsettling. I don't think it would really do.'

'Perhaps in the New Year.'

'We'll see.' William leaned back in his chair. 'One day, of course, I hope Matthew will be home for good. That's the plan.'

Buffy didn't answer. Then she said, 'What about Claire? Would she like a lodger? Au pair, sort of thing. Does she like children, this girl?'

'I have no idea. And you know what Claire's like – especially with the children. She has her own ideas; she doesn't really like suggestions.'

'Oh, well, just a thought.'

'Rather a good one. Any more coffee?'

Buffy poured out the last cupfuls.

'What are you doing for Christmas?' he asked her. 'Any plans?'

'Not quite sure yet,' said Buffy, moving a couple of candlesticks. She finished her coffee, and stood up. 'Time for a little wander.'

6

'I'm going out with a tree surgeon,' said Janice.
'That won't do you any good,' said Mary.
'It might.'

Sophie was unpacking the groceries; tins of bulk-buy mushy peas were piled upon the table. Outside, the holm oak in the sodden field behind the museum huts was tossing in the wind. Inside, a heap of dogs lay snoring in front of the range.

'Perhaps your young man could come and do some surgery here,' said Sophie. 'If that tree comes down we'll be ruined.'

Janice glanced across to the back window. Ernie's caravan, parked alongside the field fence, was, she realised, really quite close to the oak. She said so.

'That tree,' said Mary, stirring in three spoons of sugar, 'has been there since I was a girl.'

'I was a girl then, too.' Sophie's fingers strayed to her hair slide, this morning a small enamelled sheepdog, black and white and friendly, with a nice red collar. 'Does he work for the council, your young man?' she asked Janice.

'No,' said Janice, remembering the bloke in the council lorry that day she'd pulled half a tree across the Ridge. Was he a tree surgeon? If so, she might have met two in one day, something of a first. 'He works for himself,' she told Sophie. 'He's called Eric. I'm not sure—'

Did a drink after work, a dizzying ride round the lanes on his bike, and a sudden, liquefying kiss, back in the pub carpark, make someone your young man? They were seeing each other again tonight. She thought of his stubbled cheek grazing hers, beneath a stormy sky, and had to put her mug down.

'What you need,' said Mary, 'is a change of scene. Bright young woman like you.'

'You sound like my mother.'

'Mother knows best,' said Mary, and Sophie's gaze, which had been upon the last lumpy carrier bag, strayed to the photograph upon the mantelpiece, next to the Coronation tin. On the other side of Mother, Charles and Diana smiled down from their transfer-printed mug, on the day of their engagement. What a dreadful business that had been. That poor, poor girl.

'What *I* need,' said Mary briskly, 'is help with walking these dogs. Does he like walking, your Eric?'

'He rides a Harley-Davidson,' said Janice, thinking of her cheek pressed against his leathered back, her arms tight round his waist. 'Anyway,' she said, looking out once again at the weather, 'if I'm going to walk them now, I'd better get going.'

A tail thumped behind her. 'He heard us,' said Mary. 'Didn't you, Ned? Off you go, then.'

'You haven't heard from your cousin, then?' Janice got up. 'In London.'

'I haven't, but that doesn't mean to say I won't. He's a good man, William.'

'Blood is thicker than water,' said Sophie, and started to tell Janice just how William and they were all related, on their mother's side. Janice rinsed out the mugs at the sink, pretending to listen.

'Walk,' said Mary to the heap of dogs on the hearth-rug, and the kitchen was suddenly filled with swirling chaos. From outside in the pens came a manic barking.

'Quiet, you hounds!'

Mary opened the back door: they all streamed out, and the pens went wild. Sophie gave Janice a handful of leads from the passage hooks. Outside, she bent to fasten them. The windy morning air was filled with yelps and yaps and howling; the sky, after last night's downpour, was full of high, fast-moving cloud. Everything felt bright and clear and hopeful.

'Right, then.' Mary unbolted the gate, looking up the lane for visitors. You never knew. Janice was dragged through by two straining Labradors, a whippet, a greyhound and three collie-cross. Up in the hills she could let them off. 'Have a good time,' shouted Mary.

'Heel!' shouted Janice.

41

The lane was full of soughing trees and gurgling ditches, the wind was whipping across the fields. More rain was on the way, they all knew that.

William was having Sunday lunch with Claire and the family.

'Sit down, please, Hugo,' said Claire. 'Geraldine, please sit down. Where's Piers?' She went to the bottom of the stairs. 'Piers!'

Jeremy was lifting a cast-iron casserole from the hotplate to the table. 'Mind! Hands off the table, please, Geraldine.'

Piers came down the stairs and into the kitchen, looking flushed and hot.

Claire sat down again. 'About time, too.'

'Hello, old chap,' said William, reaching out an arm.

'Hello.' Piers slid into his seat.

Rain was streaming down the window behind the settle.

'Now, then.' Jeremy lifted the lid. A heavenly smell wafted into the air: chicken, tarragon, white wine, cream. Courgettes and parsley and slivers of carrot were all detectable as he ladled out the first helping, and Claire prepared to serve potatoes from a stoneware dish. Everyone perked up.

'That smells *yummy*.' Geraldine half rose from her seat to look and was told to sit down again.

'How's that poor old ear?' William asked her, unfolding his napkin. She looked at him blankly.

'That was ages ago,' said Claire. 'She's forgotten all about it.'

'I'm glad to hear it. Oh, look who's here.'

Danny, until now being good in a cardboard box by the Rayburn, had, with the lifting of the casserole lid, begun to take an interest. He came trotting up.

'Danny!' said Hugo. 'Danny! Here, boy.' He bent down from across the table and peered beneath, patting his leg. Danny was there like a shot.

'Hugo!'

'Oh, come on, he only wants a little bit, can't he have just a little bit?'

'No.' Claire glared at William.

'Come on, Danny.' He bent to look beneath the table. Danny, sitting firmly between Hugo's feet, looked back at him unflinchingly. 'Come on,' said William again. Hugo's feet tightened their grip. Plates were going round the table. As William pushed his chair back and bent down farther, he caught the edge of the cloth, and a splash of the glorious-smelling sauce fell on to it.

'Daddy!'

'Oh, dear, I'm so sorry. Now, Danny, come here at once.' He reached across and took hold of his collar. Danny yelped, and stood his ground. Hugo was shaking with laughter.

'Hugo!'

Geraldine bent down to see what was going on. 'Oh, look at him, he's so *lovely*. Aren't you, Danny?'

'Geraldine!'

'What's he doing?' asked Piers, moving his bit of the cloth aside.

'Children!' Claire was going pink. '*Will* you all behave? We're trying to have *lunch*.' She looked at their father. 'Jeremy!'

Jeremy had set down the ladle. 'I'm certainly not going to serve any more until everyone's calmed down.'

'Thank you. Now, Daddy, will you please take charge.'

'Of course, of course, I'm so sorry.' William, now on his hands and knees, took hold once again of the collar, and Hugo at last gave in. His feet suddenly moved apart, Danny came skidding across the hardwood floor, and as William released him he went on skidding, flying past the Rayburn, until he hit his box.

The children were helpless.

'Look at him – *look* – he's like a *cannonball*!'

Danny righted himself and shook himself violently. He looked across at them all, and gave a little bark.

'He wants you to do it again. Oh, go on, Grandpa, do it again.'

'I'm not sure he does,' said William, conscious of Claire's fury at his elbow. 'And I think it's time we all enjoyed this delicious lunch, don't you? Now, basket, Danny. Basket!'

Danny got into the box, and looked out sorrowfully.

'Poor Danny.' Hugo was gazing at him. 'I *wish* we had a dog.'

Claire's hand came smartly down on the table. Pepper and salt pots shook.

'If I hear one more word . . . Will you *please* all settle down.'

'Why are you always so *grumpy*?' asked Hugo.

'I'm not.'

'You are.'

'I must say, this looks like the best lunch I've had for a long time,' said William, and meant it. Cooking for one – it was pretty dismal. Even now. Perhaps Buffy was right – a lodger might be a good idea. Then again – he certainly wouldn't want to be cooking all the time, and laying tables. There was something to be said for a tray in front of the television.

'Have I told you about my letter?' he said to Claire. She didn't answer. 'Darling?'

She was scarlet, tight lipped. Tears spilled on to the tablecloth.

'Darling—' he said again, and put out a hand. She shook it off.

'Oh, dear.'

Silence fell round the table.

'My fault,' said William. 'I shouldn't have brought him.'

'This is going to get cold,' said Jeremy, helplessly. 'Perhaps you could pass the potatoes.'

'Anything I can do?' asked William, later. The rain had stopped; they were walking across the park. Ahead, the children were hurling sticks for Danny. Jeremy, due in court first thing tomorrow, had stayed behind.

'Do you mind?' he'd asked them, as they put on their macs in the hall and the children had a skirmish about who should clip on Danny's lead. 'It's the one chance of a quiet hour.' Already, he was straying towards the stairs, and the desk in their bedroom, piled high with briefs and files.

'Of course not,' said William. 'You go ahead.'

'Do whatever you like,' said Claire, wrenching open the front door. Danny strained towards it, panting. 'Out!' she said to them all.

The street was full of the silence after the rain, the quietness of a Sunday afternoon in London. The children and Danny swiftly broke it, racing towards the park gates. The trees dripped; deep puddles lay everywhere.

'Not that I want to interfere in the least,' William went on carefully. Oh, how careful one had to be with Claire – more so than with Matthew, he often felt, in spite of everything. Even Eve had had to tread round her sometimes, and still had her head snapped off. And then, when she died, Claire had been inconsolable, and sobbed after Piers was born as if her heart would break.

'I want her to *be* here, I want her to *see* him—'

Gradually the weeping stopped, and the mantle of motherhood

44

settled on her shoulders. She drew it tight around her. She trained to be a counsellor with the National Childbirth Trust, trained to be a breast-feeding counsellor, decided, after all, not to return to the solicitors through whom she had met Jeremy, and who had given her maternity leave.

'The law can do without me. We can manage. My place is here,' she told William, come to admire his grandson on a summer afternoon. Danny sat in the shade at a required distance; Piers lay in his grandfather's arms, gazing up at him. Gazing back, flooded with mingled love and grief, William listened, or half listened, as Claire talked of Winnicott, and bonding, and feeding on demand. He tried to remember whether Eve had gone on in quite this way, at quite such length; could only remember the two of them watching Claire sleep, saying how perfect she was. And so had Matthew been, and who could have ever predicted what hell lay waiting for him, as summery light and shade played over his pram beneath the trees?

'Claire?' he said to his daughter now, watching the children racing about with Danny in the cold damp air.

'What?'

'As I say,' he said, skirting a puddle, wishing he could take her arm and the two of them could walk companionably, father and daughter talking things over, on a Sunday afternoon. 'I don't want to butt in—'

'Then don't,' said Claire briskly. 'I'm just a bit overtired, that's all.'

'It's a lot for you,' said William, watching Piers and Hugo haring over the soaking grass, with Danny leaping joyously after them. Geraldine was struggling to keep up, shouting, 'Wait for *me*!' Eternal cries of childhood, and that was one of the most potent.

'Boys!' called Claire. 'Hugo! Piers!'

There were other families, other London dogs, let off the lead, claws clicking along the wet black paths, lifting their legs on empty flower-beds, sniffing elaborately at one another, shouted at. It was starting to rain again: umbrellas went up.

'God, will it ever stop?'

'I've had a letter from mad old Mary,' said William, trying again, putting up his own umbrella. He held it over his daughter and she didn't move away. He started to tell her about this missive, as the rain began to fall faster, and then gave up, as everyone fled for the trees and bandstand. The children grabbed Danny and climbed the steps; half a dozen Dulwich families stood in its shelter, gazing out across grass and tarmac at the downpour. Teal and mallard quacked from the lake; Claire saw a mother she knew, and began a conversation about school governors. William picked up Geraldine, whose hand he found in his.

'What do you want for Christmas?'

'Danny. I wish he could live with us.'

'I'm afraid I'd be rather lonely without him,' he said, and in the chill of the darkening afternoon, with the rain falling like a punishment, on and on and on, had a sudden glimpse of how true that was, the big house cavernous around him. He gave a little shake: this wouldn't do.

'What were you saying about Mary?' asked Claire, getting the tea. They'd come back soaking, everyone making a dash for it across the park, and the hall was full of wet shoes. The children were all watching television, Danny snuggled in among them on the sofa; Jeremy had shown his face and taken it away again; the kettle was simmering on the hob.

William told her, watching her move about the kitchen, competent and unhappy. It was so: clearly it was so.

'Buffy had a thought,' he said, leaning back in his chair.

'Don't do that.'

'What?'

'Lean back on your chair – I'm always telling the children. You can break the chair and you can break your back. Jeremy had a client that happened to: no insurance, nothing. What was Buffy's thought?'

William tipped himself forward again, and told her. 'You know, mother's help. Sort of thing. Perhaps if things are getting a bit on top of you—'

'They're not.' She went out to the bottom of the stairs. 'Jeremy! Tea, if you want a cup.'

'Shall I take it up to him? I know what it's like when you're deep in something.'

Claire looked at him. 'He still has the use of his legs.'

William gave up. He took the cup that was offered to him, beheld his son-in-law, grey about the gills with overwork, come down for his, and retreat once more; he listened to the synthetic chirrup of cartoons from the sitting room.

'There's no real drama on any more,' said Claire. 'Nothing of substance.' She sat down, and reached for the paper, turning the pages

46

of the Culture section, sighing. William picked up the travel pages, and ran his eye over Christmas breaks in the Seychelles. Parakeets skimmed the treetops, silvery fish leapt from ink-blue waters. If Eve were still here, they could be planning things.

Next door, the cartoons came to a violent conclusion. Channels were flipped, and voices rose. Claire got up and went through. From somewhere in Tunisia's New Year weekend for two, William became aware of discord: Sunday night homework still to be done, general insubordination. Voices grew louder, Danny came through.

'Hello, old chap.' He reached down to fondle his ears. Claire reappeared, and drew the curtains on the rain-soaked afternoon, now turning into a filthy wet evening.

'Time we were off,' said William, rising. 'Thanks for a lovely lunch.'

'That's all right.' Claire put the teacups into the dishwasher, where the lunch things waited. Danny, sniffing the remains, went after her with interest. 'Nothing for you,' she told him sharply, and went to the bottom of the stairs. 'Jeremy! Are you coming to say goodbye?'

In the hall, with his coat and scarf and umbrella, and Danny clipped to his lead once more, William kissed the children in turn, shook hands with Jeremy and brushed Claire's cheek, which was all that seemed possible.

'Think about it,' he said, and opened the front door on to sheets of rain and darkness. 'Someone to help you out a bit.'

'Help you do what?' he heard Geraldine asking, as he made his way to the car beneath their streetlamp. Silver rain drummed on the roof. 'Nothing,' said Claire. 'It's bathtime.'

''Bye,' he called to the closing door, getting his keys out, and sensed, as the door banged to, family life closing in on itself, his visit over and done with even before he drove away: on with the next thing, and then the next. Another day over. Was this how Claire wanted to live?

He started the car and pulled out, the wipers at full tilt. The street was curtained, porch lights shone through the drowning world.

'God Almighty,' said William aloud, all at once washed through with desolation. He hadn't felt as bad as this for a long time.

7

'He says he doesn't know. He says something might turn up in the New Year.' Fountain pen flowed across creamy pages; Mary put the letter down, next to its thick lined envelope. Sophie turned it over wonderingly.

'This looks nice.'

'William's always done things nicely.' Mary looked across the table at Janice, rolling up a few shreds. 'Do you good,' she said. 'Bit of class.'

'I've got that already,' said Janice, thinking of last week. Eric lived up in the hills, in an abandoned shepherd's hut he rented from a farmer. The beam of his Harley-Davidson headlamp cut through the driving black rain and showed, on the winding road, a one-storey dwelling of stone and patched-up slate set among boulders and empty sheep pens. Miles from bloody anywhere. They got off the bike, and she ran for the door and stood shivering while he wheeled the bike under a lean-to of galvanised iron. When he switched off the ignition everything went pitch black. She heard the rain soaking into the turf, and battering the slates; she heard his footsteps squelching up to the front.

'Don't you have a torch?'

'Don't need one when I'm on my own. Know it by heart.'

He unlocked the door and felt for the light switch. 'This is it.'

Janice blinked. 'It's nice.'

One room: table and a couple of chairs, open fire, sink, cooker. Bed. She hung her soaking jacket and woollen hat on the back of the door; he put down his helmet, lit a candle in a bottle on the table, and nodded towards a door. 'In there, if you want it.'

'I'm all right for now.'

Eric poured whisky into a couple of tumblers. 'Cheers.'

'Cheers.'

He lit the fire and they sat drinking. The wind rattled the door and windows, the rain came down in torrents, they heard a slate shift on the roof.

'That's another one gone,' said Eric. 'I'll have to get up there.'

'Not now.'

He looked at her. 'No.'

When they'd finished their whisky he got up and kissed her. They took each other's clothes off and lay before the fire. The floor was stone flags, with a couple of rugs.

She shut her eyes, thinking about it. She'd thought of nothing else for days.

'Look at you,' said Mary, putting the letter from London back in its envelope. 'Fit for nothing.'

'Oh, I don't know.'

Janice gazed dreamily across the kitchen. It wasn't raining; in fact it was brightening up. Across the yard she could see the door of Ernie's caravan pulled open, and then he appeared on the steps, having a bit of a look-round. Poor old bugger.

'If it stays fine, we might have visitors,' said Sophie, stirring her tea. 'We might do a Christmas party.'

'And pigs might fly,' said Mary.

Ernie was coming down the rotting steps. One day he was going to break his leg. He stood sniffing the sky and the dogs in the pens came forward: Janice watched him go over and greet them. Their tails wagged wildly, they licked his hand through the wire. That was the good thing about dogs, they didn't care what you looked like: she supposed that was half the point.

Ernie was crossing the yard, skirting the puddles so as not to let in the wet. Where were his wellingtons, silly old fool? The wind blew his jacket and scarf about, wisps of hair straggled out under his woolly hat. Dreadful. She heard him open the back door and slip off inadequate footwear. Then he came creeping up the passage.

'What do you want?' demanded Mary.

'Just looking in. Bit brighter today.' He padded over the kitchen flags, long yellow toenails poking through his holey socks. 'Any tea?'

A tail or two thumped on the hearth. He bent to give his greetings. 'Good boy, there's a boy. Any tea?'

'It's gone cold,' said Mary.

'I'll make a fresh pot,' said Sophie, rising.

'Nice and strong.' He straightened up, and beheld Janice, drinking and smoking her roll-up. 'I'm right out of baccy,' he told her.

'Is that right?' She reached for her Rizlas and tin.

He watched her prise it open. 'Good little tin, that.'

'Much the same as yours, isn't it?'

'Mine's old. Like me. And empty.' He shuffled to the chair by the hearth and eased himself on to it, rubbing his hands. 'Christmas is coming. Ta very much,' he added, taking the wafer-thin roll-up. 'Got a light?'

'Always cadging,' said Mary, as Janice passed him her lighter. 'Always on the scrounge.'

'If it wasn't for me,' said Ernie, inhaling happily, 'there'd be no museum, no income, nothing.' He pulled a shred of tobacco from his lip.

'That was a long time ago you did all that.'

'Lasted, though, hasn't it?' He watched Sophie stirring the pot. 'Still pulls the crowds. Any biscuits?'

'You old bugger,' said Mary, levering open the tin.

'How many visitors have you had this year, then?' asked Janice, remembering the dismal trio who'd been there the previous week.

'We had a good summer.' Sophie gave Ernie his mug. 'We've entered it all in the book.'

'You mean I have,' said Mary, getting up and fetching it from the back windowsill. 'It's me who keeps the records.'

'You was always the learner,' said Ernie.

'You *were* always the learner,' Mary corrected him.

'No I wasn't. I was always the one at the back.' He gave Janice a dreadful wink. 'It was my art that saved me. Saved the family fortunes.'

Mary pulled out the last of a little row of scarlet Woolworths exercise books, wedged between years of *Yellow Pages* and a shelfful of 1950s *Dairyman's Days*.

'Who did those belong to?' asked Janice, noticing them for the first time.

'Them was Father's.' Ernie sipped his tea. 'He was dairyman to Broxwood Hall for years.'

'That's how he met Mother,' said Sophie reverently. 'When she were in service.'

'Was in service.' Mary sat down again, smoothing out lined pages.

Janice looked at the deep-scored Biro, the columns of dates and figures, and at the letter from London, with its exquisite hand. She felt a stirring of curiosity, of interest even. Did such a hand betoken such a life? Was bossy old Mary right – should she stretch her wings next year? Just as she and Eric . . .

Just as she and Eric what?

The fact was, she hadn't seen him since the soaking-wet morning which followed that wild, soaking-wet night. He'd driven her down from the hills and left her, that was the fact of the matter, back in Cloud Nine, where Steve gave her a quizzical look.

'Mind your own business,' she told him, wiping down the counter. The Harley-Davidson had roared away, and it hadn't roared back again. Not once, in a week. Pretty poor show, her dad would have called it, had he the chance.

'And where were you last night?' her mother had demanded, as she reappeared for her microwaved tagliatelle for three. Ugh. God, what was she doing still living at home? She might be up in the hills, in a shepherd's hut, spread-eagled before the fire at the hands of a tree surgeon. An expert in the field, as it were.

Cut to the quick though she was, Janice heard herself give a sudden bark of laughter.

'Whatever's got into you?' asked Mary, looking up from her counting. 'I make it fifty-five to date, with July and August the peaks.'

'Summer holidays,' said Ernie sagely. 'That's what brings them.'

'You don't say.'

'And how much money has that made you?' asked Janice, returning herself to the present with a wrench. 'If it's not rude to ask.'

'Almost a hundred pounds. Family discount is what brings it down.' Mary pursed her lips.

'But it is an attraction,' said Sophie. 'You can't deny it.'

'Was it your idea?' Janice asked her, sensing the glow of pride.

Sophie gave a modest little smile. She was wearing one of her prettiest hair slides today, a pair of leaping dolphins in turquoise blue, smiling benignly down on pudding-basin trim, green turtleneck and a pinafore patterned in floral pink and red. Little daisies, or marguerites, perhaps. A bias-binding trim.

'Where do you get those slides?' asked Janice.

'In Healing Arts, down behind the cathedral,' said Sophie promptly. 'They do a lovely range.'

'Frippery and con tricks,' said Mary. 'One-to-one herbal teas. Reflexology. Psychodynamic star signs. Counselling.' She gave a violent sniff. 'Holistic beeswax.'

Ernie snorted.

'Well, they do very nice hair slides, anyway,' said Sophie. 'And they're always very kind to me, I must say. I'm hoping to pick up something nice for Christmas.'

'Bit late for that,' said Ernie, pulling tobacco shreds off the tip of his tongue. 'Now if I had my time again—' He cast a meaningful look at Janice, and flicked the tobacco towards the hearth. It landed on a greyhound, and stayed there. There was a little, irritable twitch of skin.

'Your time came and went and nobody even noticed,' said Mary, closing the museum accounts in an access of irritation.

'Not even me,' said Ernie. 'Heh, heh. Oh, well.' He drained his Charles & Diana mug with a flourish. 'Didn't do them two much good, neither.'

'*Either*.' Mary stood up. 'If you want to make yourself useful you can get in the back parlour and do some de-fleaing. Otherwise, out you go.'

Ernie rose resignedly. 'Where's the powder?'

'Out on the passage shelf, where it always is. Now bugger off.'

He shuffled out, returned with a giant tin and moth-eaten brush and waved it at the hearth. 'Come on, now. Then it's a walk.'

They leapt and shook themselves. Claws clicked over the flags. Ernie lured them through the back parlour door and closed it. There was a sudden cacophony.

'Quieten down! Quieten down, you curs!' His voice when raised was like a punctured organ pipe, whistling and wheezing, with sudden forceful peals. 'Down, I say!'

'Holy Moses,' said Janice. She packed up her papers and tin, put her mug down next to the letter. How could there be a commonality of blood between the erudite, elegant William Harriman and this trio of Harriman crackpots? How distant could cousins be?

'Did Ernie really do all the dioramas?' she asked, pushing her chair back, thinking of straining huskies, racing across the sunlit snow, and brave St Bernards, beneath the mountain peaks.

'He did,' said Mary, passing the empty mugs to Sophie and gesturing at the sink. 'He did have a way with it all, I'll give him that. Not that it lasted, but for a while it kept him busy.'

52

'It kept him very happy,' said Sophie, rinsing the mugs beneath the brass cold tap. She put them on the draining board, alive with silverfish. 'He was at his best, in those days. We put up the huts with Mother's legacy and Ernie filled the lot.'

Janice pulled on her woollen hat. 'And does it run in the family? I mean—' She indicated the letter, with its glimpse of another world. 'I mean, is your cousin William artistic?'

'He's clever,' said Mary. 'He's a civil servant, or I should say he was. Very clever with money.'

'Was it the Post Office he worked in?' Sophie asked, setting down the last cracked, tea-stained mug. 'Was that it?'

'The Treasury, you fool.'

'The Treasury,' sighed Sophie. 'Isn't that a lovely word?'

Oswestry was Christmassy, with lights around the lampposts. Puddles reflected red and green and gold, the windows of Past Times were full of amber silk cushions and goblets engraved with holly leaves and Latin. Janice met Tracy Keenan coming out of Lo-Cost with feverish toddlers and a pushchair.

'And another on the way,' she said, nodding down at a bright acrylic bulge.

'Well done,' said Janice. 'Fantastic.'

'It's hard work,' said Tracy, 'but it's worth it.'

Janice knew how she herself must look – like a biker, which she was, in one aspect of her being: tall, lithe, irresponsibly selfish and carefree, in her black Lycra leggings and Doc Martens, her zipped-up jacket and nifty close-fitting woollen cap. She clapped the ringless hands of singlehood and beamed down at the infants, who shifted from foot to foot with streaming noses.

'What do you want for Christmas?' she asked them, and they began their frightful list. Perhaps it was different if they were your own.

'What about you, then?' asked Tracy, moving them all aside for an old bat on a Zimmer frame. What was she doing out here in the cold and wet? Perhaps she'd like some Christmas shopping done. Janice found herself checking this thought abruptly. Enough of old bats with their tins and Rich Tea biscuits. Enough of serving toasted sandwiches and walking packs of dogs. Was this all that the millennium had had to offer her?

Something's happened to me, she thought, standing among the

milling shoppers, hearing the Rotary Club rattle its Rotary Tin and churn out 'Hark the Herald' from its Rotary Camper Van. In 2001 it's tree surgeon or bust.

'What are you up to, then?' asked Tracy, whose mother used to hang out with Janice's mother, in distant, unimaginable days when both were girls with hippie beads and joss-sticks.

'I'm still working in Cloud Nine and all that,' said Janice. 'You know. Shopping. Dogs. Same old things. I'm going out with a tree surgeon,' she added, hoping it was true.

'Get you,' said Tracy. 'What's his name?'

'Eric.' Janice thought of Keith, Tracy's electrician husband, with his funny teeth and coils of flex in the van. 'He's ever so good looking,' she said cruelly.

'Not Eric Lammering,' said Tracy. 'Not that Eric Lammering with the bike.'

'Why? What's wrong with him?'

'Oh, nothing. Just he's a bit of a one, that's all.'

'I like a bit of a one,' said Janice, possessed by unstoppably sickening feelings. 'What do you mean?'

'Oh, nothing. You know how these things get around. Just he's a bit of a . . . well, like I say.' Beside her, the children were starting up. 'Mum, Mu-um.'

'I'd better go before they catch their deaths,' said Tracy, beaming. 'It's ever so nice to see you again. Ta-ra, see you later, merry Christmas.'

She wheeled the pushchair around and disappeared into the throng.

'Ta-ra,' said Janice, watching her go.

Well. Well, how about that, then? What was a bit of a one when it was at home? She stood on the main street as the light began to fade, and the rain to fall once more, swirling past the Christmas lights in pretty colours. 'Hark the Herald' had turned into 'We Three Kings'.

One in a taxi, one in a car, she heard within herself from irreverent schooldays. Now it sounded somehow rather plaintive.

One on a scooter, blowing his hoo-ooter . . .

I've given myself to a love-rat, thought Janice, with not an item of shopping done, Christmas or otherwise. She turned up her collar and strode into Lo-Cost, as dismally fluorescent a shoppers' hell as anyone could wish for. There might indeed be something to be said for a total change of scene.

☆

'What did you say you were doing for Christmas?' William asked Buffy the next weekend. They were sitting at the stall, where holly and mistletoe had been placed cheerfully here and there in little sprigs and vases. Danny, curled up on a folding chair, had a scarlet ribbon tied to his collar. This alone, William knew, enabled him to put an extra five quid on every single thing on the stall.

'Oh, isn't he *sweet?*' said every single punter.

'I didn't say,' Buffy answered, moving a set of eggcups. 'What about you?'

'Oh—' William let his response die unfinished. He thought of Claire and Jeremy, the fury across the turkey, the children over-wrought, ignoring him. He thought of his darling boy, vacant before Christmas television, the two of them pulling a hopeless cracker. Dismal. It shouldn't be, but this year it was. Had he been in denial, all the other Christmases since Eve had gone? Why should this one feel so especially terrible?

'Don't suppose you'd like to come over to me?' he said, watching the careful arrangement of bone china. Not very practical, for egg-cups. 'We could light the fire, raise a glass. Even a couple of glasses.'

'Oh, William.' Buffy's hands, in their fingerless hairy gloves, hovered like moths above the stall. 'Would you really—'

'I'd love it,' said William. 'Do come. Only if you're free, of course.'

'Since Mother died in 1989 I've been freer than I care to remember,' said Buffy, recalling the fall of the Berlin Wall and she before the television, suddenly horribly loud, as November afternoon drew in to November night. 'It would be heavenly, William.'

Christmas came and Christmas went, and was infinitely more enjoy-able than William had imagined. The house was warm, the boiler roaring. Buffy arrived on Christmas Eve with a basketful of parcels, including a pudding, which she had made herself, listening to *Any Questions*, and a tin of mince pies, likewise, but with *Home Truths*. He met her at the station and held his umbrella over her all the way down the street, awash with the worst downpour for days. Fairy-lit trees stood in rain-lashed windows, the gutter gurgled.

'I tell you, William,' said Buffy, shifting her basket from one arm to the other, while he carried her overnight bag, 'I tell you, your grandchildren will live to curse us.'

'Don't say that.'

'But it's true. Our sins and foolishness visited upon the heads of generations. A hole in the ozone layer the size of Timbuktu, rivers foaming with detergent and dead fish, the globe warmed up to boiling point.'

'Oh, come, come.'

'Desertification. Rainforests ruined. Oestrogen in the drinking water, men no longer men . . .' A great lake lay before her in the dip in the pavement.

'Here, take my arm,' said William, guiding her into the streaming street.

'You see? We can't even walk on the *pavement*. Floods, William, floods and pestilence lie ahead.'

'Well, Noah got through it,' said William. 'Now do buck up.'

Indoors, he took her soaking coat and fake-fur Russian hat, and hung them to drip in the hall. Danny got up from his place by a crackling fire, which she glimpsed through the open door of the drawing room. At once, she began to feel better.

'Now you settle yourself in that chair,' said William, 'unless you want to spend a penny first—'

'Well, perhaps I'll just pay a little visit.'

In the downstairs cloakroom Buffy took out her tortoiseshell combs and put them in again, and pursed her lips over the last – the very last – of her Lizzie Arden Petal Pink. There. She powdered her nose, took one last look. Well. Too late to do much about it now.

'Come and have a drink,' said William, as she returned.

Decanter and glasses winked in the firelight; there was an enormous bowl of nuts.

'Heaven,' said Buffy, settling down with her whisky mac, and Danny at her feet.

'Cheers,' said William.

'Cheers, William. And thank you so much.'

'Absolutely my pleasure. You've saved the day.' He eased himself into his own chair, on the other side of the hearth. Buffy knew that they now occupied the positions which he and Eve had held all their married life, when they weren't hand in hand on the sofa watching television. Oh, dear. Oh, well. She raised her glass again.

'What have you done today?' she asked him.

'This morning I got in a quantity of drink and a small organic bird.

This afternoon I listened to the *Nine Lessons and Carols* and made some chestnut stuffing.'

'I say, did you really? How glorious.'

'It was very pleasant.' William did not add that he had wept with the very first notes of 'Once in Royal David's City', dissolving with that pure sweet treble and the thought of Matthew, who'd sung in the school choir so beautifully and whom music now left cold. He'd pulled himself together with the first lesson, then sobbed aloud through 'O Little Town of Bethlehem', Eve's favourite. Had he not had the prospect of Buffy arriving at the station in the wet at half past five, he didn't know what he'd have done. Phoned the Samaritans, perhaps: he found himself thinking this, and then felt ashamed, when he had so much to be thankful for.

'How would you feel about midnight Mass?' he asked Buffy, refilling her glass.

'Oh, stop, William, I shall be drunk as an owl,' she said happily. 'Well, it's entirely up to you, dear. I'd like it, of course, provided I'm not legless by then.'

'Let's see what the weather's like. Not if it's chucking it down. Now then, supper. I thought we'd have something light. I've got in a bit of wild salmon . . .'

How delightfully the evening passed. Supper. *Christmas from Around the World*. And the rain eased off, miraculously, and at a quarter past eleven, drunk and warm and purposeful, they staggered down the steps and off to St Matthew's, which was packed and full of bonhomie.

'The only thing is,' said William, as they found two places near the back, 'I'm afraid I might get a bit tearful. It's that treble solo that does it – those first six notes of "Once in Royal" and I'm a goner. If it happens, you must take no notice: I'm just a sentimental old fool.'

'Join the club,' said Buffy, and held herself erect. It was a long time since she'd allowed herself a good cry, and she really, really didn't want to make a fool of herself now.

In the end, tears streamed down both their faces as the choir processed by candlelight, the cross held high and gleaming. Then they'd recovered, and got into the spirit of things, and Buffy, her voice well exercised by the Mary Ward Over-Sixties choir, sang her heart out.

As they made their way out up the aisle, greeting people William had known all his life, he suddenly saw Jeremy, whom he had missed entirely, standing right at the back, looking tired and legal.

'Hello, old boy!' William clapped his arm. 'Good to see you.'

'And you,' said Jeremy, moving with them through the throng to the porch and the smiling deacon. 'Claire said I might see you here.'

'She's home with the children. Of course. Do you know Buffy Henderson, my old friend and fellow stallholder? My son-in-law, Jeremy Wright.'

'Of course. We've met several times.' Leather glove met knitted glove in Christmassy enthusiasm.

'Have you really met? I must be losing it,' said William. 'Anyway, looking forward to seeing you on Boxing Day, old chap, if that's still all right?'

'Yes, yes, of course.'

They were out in the churchyard, where recorded bells were ringing and the rain was falling fast. Up went everyone's umbrellas.

'Matthew's joining us tomorrow,' said William. 'I expect Claire's told you.'

'Yes, indeed. Hope it all goes well. And happy Christmas.'

And he shook hands again and loped away.

'What a sad-looking chap,' said Buffy, as they made their way home across the common. 'Whatever's happened to him?'

'Don't know,' said William. 'Don't quite know. The stress of modern life or something more sinister. I'm trying not to think the worst.'

'One should never think the worst.'

'Thus speaketh the prophetess of doom.'

'That's different. Global disaster is not on a par with domestic distress.'

'Oh, I don't know.'

But Christmas Day passed happily. Bacon and eggs for breakfast, presents by the fire. Buffy gave William a Friends of the Earth calendar and a tea towel with a scarlet border and a Christmas goose in the snow. Also a bottle of Scotch, and a packet of chocolate Canine Treats.

'I say, Danny, have a look at these.'

He needed no second bidding.

William gave Buffy the millennial edition of Lyle's *Antiques Review* – 'Oh, how splendid, I shall pore over this for hours' – and a Crabtree & Evelyn casket of Elizabethan Garden soap and foaming bath oil. 'Oh, what luxury. And there's a *mitt*, look.'

'Good gracious.' He gazed at it, china blue and rather on the small side. 'Do you use mitts?' he wondered.

'I do now.' She got up to kiss him. 'Thank you, William. Lovely, lovely.'

'You've been much too generous. Look at this Scotch. Do you think—' He glanced at the carriage clock on the mantelpiece.

'We can't start drinking at half past *ten*,' said Buffy.

'Are you sure?'

By the time they came to put in the bird they were well away.

'I must sober up,' said William. 'I'm fetching Matthew at twelve.'

'Have a black coffee. I'll do the sprouts.' Buffy put on last year's Greenpeace apron, which she'd brought for this very moment. The previous night, unpacking in the spare bedroom, which Eve had made both restful and full of charm, she had thought herself a mad old fool, bedecking her bosom in sperm whales and ice floes. But better than a floral pinny, surely. She hung it up next to her dressing gown, made, incredibly, from the hair of the Pyrenean mountain dog and dyed powder blue. That morning, the apron came into its own, perfect for peeling and basting and steaming, over her Jaeger jumper from the previous year's sales.

'Don't worry about a thing,' she told William, pouring coffee into a Copeland Spode mug for him. 'This is pretty.' She had a closer look: Spode blue watering cans, trowels and rollers. Even a little fork.

'Their Gardeners range,' said William, taking it from her. 'My birthday present from Claire.'

'She has taste.'

'Oh, Claire has always had a good eye. The house is perfect.'

'Something wrong there. A house with three children shouldn't be perfect. Is it three?'

'It is.' He drained scalding coffee and rose from the kitchen table. 'See you about one o'clock.'

'We should have waited. With the presents? I have got Matthew something.'

'No, no. It's too much for him, all that carry-on, we've tried it before. Much better to keep it simple. A couple of little things by the fire at teatime – he'll love that.'

Matthew came up the steps on William's arm. Around them the garden dripped and somewhere in the street a blackbird was singing, joyous and pure.

'Listen to that,' said William. 'Here we are, then.' He fished out his keys on the top step and unlocked the front door. A delicious smell of roasting bird came wafting out to greet them. 'Buffy!' he called, and turned back to a still and silent Matthew. 'Come on in, darling, welcome home.'

Matthew stepped into the hall, and looked about him. Holly hung over the pictures, drawing-room firelight leapt. 'Danny?' called William. 'Look who's here.'

Danny came trotting out, saw Matthew and rushed to greet him. Matthew gave a slow, sweet smile which tore at William's heart with love and hope. 'Well, well. Here we all are. In you come by the fire; let me take your things.'

Matthew's hands went up to his scarf and stayed there. Buffy came up from the lower depths. 'Here we are,' said William again. 'Matthew, do you remember our friend Buffy?'

'Hello, Matthew.' Buffy was flushed from the oven, still wearing the sperm whales, her hair drifting out of her combs and bun. 'Happy Christmas. How nice to see you again.'

Matthew's hands were still on his scarf, his coat damp.

'Come on through to the fire,' said William, leading him gently by the elbow. 'You can take your things off there. Buffy—'

'I'll join you in a moment.'

Progress was infinitesimally slow. It took ten minutes to get Matthew into the drawing room, allow him time to gaze round and issue, once more, that heartbreaking smile of recognition, take off his gloves and his scarf and coat, hang them up, return to find him still in exactly the same position, lead him to a fireside chair and settle him with a glass. He looked at it, holding it before him in mid-air, perfectly still.

'Nothing alcoholic,' said William. 'It's called Norfolk Punch. Lots of herbs and spices. Rather good.' He went to the door. 'Buffy!'

'Coming!'

They raised their glasses. 'Happy Christmas.'

'Cheers.'

'Happy Christmas, darling.' William's glass touched Matthew's. 'Going to try a drop?'

The Norfolk Punch went slowly to his lips. He sipped minutely, then again.

'Thought you'd like that. Thought so. Just the ticket, eh?' William heard himself, being hearty and going on. If Claire were here, there'd be a sharp reproof. Well, she wasn't. Face all that tomorrow. 'Cheers,' he said again, and then: 'How are things below deck?'

'Coming along nicely,' Buffy told him, without turning her gaze from Matthew, who was inching his Norfolk glass towards the fireside table. Then she came to, and said brightly, 'I'll summon you both in a bit.'

'Anything I can do? I don't want you slaving away.'

'I'll call you to take out the bird.'

Lunch was perfect: the bird sweet and tender, the sprouts crisp, potatoes just right with all the scrunchy bits, the stuffing, though he said it himself, magnificent. Buffy's gravy slipped down like wine, which was scarcely surprising, since that was mostly what it was, thick with giblets and mushrooms. William poured claret into lead crystal glasses, and white Amé for Matthew, and prepared to feel Christmassy and content, his old friend at the other end of the polished dining table, laid with silver candlesticks and holly, his dog by the fire, his son come home.

'Wonderful to have you here,' he told him. 'Wonderful to have you both.'

Matthew nodded. It took him half an hour to eat half a potato, two sprouts and a sliver of bird. Between each of these mouthfuls he laid down his knife and fork and gazed before him – at the candles, at china, at a speck of dust, spinning in the heat from candlelight.

'Try a little bit more,' said William. 'Just a little bit.'

It took him back to the days in the high chair. Claire had eaten every scrap, thrown rusks about with abandon. Matthew had picked.

'Not enough to keep a bird alive,' said Eve, white with anxiety. 'How will he grow?'

Had it all started, even then? A turning away from food, from life, retreating into another kind of world? When he started school it got better. Soon he was eating like a horse. They forgot all about those crumbs of meals, until he came home from Durham.

'Matthew! Lunch-time! Are you coming down?'

A dreadful silence.

Watching him now, staring at specks of nothingness, spearing a sliced mushroom in infinite slow motion, William asked himself, for the millionth time, whether it still had to be like this. Was it the illness, or was it the drugs? Was Matthew, without his medication, still capable of murder?

☆

'He's drugged out of his skull,' said Buffy later. 'I'm sorry to say so, but it's true.'

'Ssh!'

'My dear, he can't hear you. I'm not sure he can hear you when he's awake.'

It was late afternoon. Lunch had at last been completed, with crumbs of pudding and teaspoons of cream for Matthew, who'd gazed at the flaming brandy as if at the Holy Grail. They'd had coffee by the fire, and the tail-end of the Queen's Speech before presents. Matthew had fallen asleep, while letting William help him unwrap a pair of leather gloves with fleecy linings.

'For winter walks,' said William, indicating the dog, the winter sky beyond the window. Matthew nodded, and did not raise his head. Gently William took his present away, and eased the head into a comfortable position against the wing of the chair. 'Have a good sleep, old chap,' he murmured. 'Do you good.'

Now it was almost dark, the blackbird, incredibly, starting up once more, but closer, perhaps even in his own front garden.

'Listen to that.'

'I know,' said Buffy. 'The most beautiful of all the songbirds. Almost the last – we're poisoning our wildlife. When did you last hear a song thrush?'

William couldn't think. He looked at sleeping Matthew. 'Do you think I should wake him? Or perhaps he needs his sleep.'

'He's drugged out of his skull,' Buffy said then. 'Surely you can see that, William. I'm sorry to say so, but it's true.'

William winced. 'Ssh. *Sotto voce*.' He looked at his son, his once fine features – the Harriman nose, the generous, sensitive mouth, Eve's delicate brows – blurred with years of suffering.

'He could have been a professional,' he said quietly. 'He could have had anything he wanted. He went to Durham on a music scholarship.' His voice broke.

'I know,' said Buffy gently. 'I know. I'm so dreadfully sorry.'

William shook his head. 'Do you really think he's overdosed? I mean, that they're overdosing him?'

'It doesn't seem right.' Buffy put down her empty coffee cup. 'He moves like—' She stopped herself saying it, undead. 'Like a robot,' she said carefully. 'He hardly speaks. I mean, surely in this day and age—'

62

'They have tried, though. Over the years it's all gone up and down. Sometimes he's been a bit better, but if they lower it too much he gets so restless and unhappy. He doesn't sleep, and that makes everything worse, and then—' He broke off. 'Oh, I don't know.'

'Why don't you have another word with them? In the New Year. See if they can't try just a *little* less.'

'I will,' said William. 'I'll ask for a review. The whole team. We haven't had one of those since ... since I don't know when. I do wonder if perhaps it's all taken for granted now. Long-stay patient, no trouble, you know.'

'Yes,' said Buffy. 'I should have a word. Now, shall I make a pot of tea?'

'I will.' William rose. 'You've done more than enough. Have we room for Christmas cake, do you think?'

'Sinful,' said Buffy. 'Why not? And what about this dog? Shouldn't he take a turn or two before tea?'

'He should.' William whistled. 'Come on, old chap.'

Dog and master made their way to the lower depths. She heard the door to the garden pushed open with difficulty, warped with wet weather, and then banged to again. Distantly she heard the kettle filled, and then, from the front garden, the blackbird's song, renewed once more, soaring into the winter afternoon.

Buffy got up. She went to the huge high windows and looked out. There he was, on the topmost branch of the magnolia, perfect from tip to tail, a bird out of every book of her childhood – singing through A.A. Milne and E.H. Shepard, dark amidst the apple blossom; warbling in James Reeves's water meadows, on Grahame's riverbank. Oh, how thrilling and sad it felt.

'You're beautiful,' said Buffy aloud, as the last of the Christmas light drained from the sky and rain trickled down the darkening glass. 'You're everything you should be.'

Behind her came a little sound. She turned and saw Matthew, awoken, gazing at her. 'Come and listen to this,' she said, and went to take his hand. He let her. Slowly he unfolded his long, once elegant limbs – his father's limbs, well made and perfectly proportioned – and let her lead him to the window. And they stood there, as the blackbird's liquid voice explored the trill, the rill, the fluty phrase, the whole full-throated miracle.

'You're musical,' said Buffy, at last, turning to Matthew. 'Your father says you're very gifted.'

'I was musical once,' said Matthew slowly, the most lucid and complex sentence he had uttered all day. She realised his hand was still in hers. This was what it might have been like, to have a grown-up son you cared for.

William's son.

She checked the thought before it even formed itself, turning as he came in with the tea tray, seeing his look of astonishment and delight, as the blackbird opened his throat in a last abandoned ascension of joy, and darkness fell.

2001

II

Visits

8

And then it stopped raining, and the big freeze came. Just before New Year William woke to a different light, felt stillness all around him, and drew back his bedroom curtains on to snow. Garden and rooftops and trees transformed: he stood there, thinking of Monet and Pissarro, whose paintings of *Winter at Giverny* and *South Norwood under Snow* had been reproduced on several Christmas cards that year. He thought of the children, in years when it had seemed to snow more often, out there building snowmen, racing down the street and through the park, pelting him and Eve with snowballs, shrieking. When was the last fall?

He stood there in his dressing gown, counting years – not a good thing to do at his age. Where had they gone, and how had they gone so quickly? But he counted back and thought that the last time when snow – real, proper snow – had fallen in London was in January 1990, when Eve had been dead two months and Piers, his first grandson, was not yet born. So this must be the boy's first sight of it – extraordinary. His own childhood seemed always to have been filled with snow, every winter.

It began to fall again, light but insistent. How entirely beautiful it was, and how fortunate that he had had the boiler fixed. Time for breakfast. Put something out for the birds. Perhaps later he'd take Danny up to the hospital, get Matthew out in the grounds, in his Christmas-present gloves. White fields. Snow light. Good for the soul.

For a moment, watching the tumble of flakes – thicker and faster now – work their other-worldly magic on the garden, William remembered the look on Matthew's face, lit up on Christmas Day by the blackbird's stream of song. My love, he thought, with a little twist of longing. We'll have you right again.

Down in the kitchen the kettle boiled. Upstairs the paper fell on the mat. Out in the garden Danny was sniffing the air, excitedly shaking off snowflakes. The willow tree, each branch outlined, was exquisite. As always – in boyhood; with his own children; on every occasion except in the black year after Eve's death, when Matthew had tried, incredibly, to kill him – William felt with the snow a lift of the heart, a sudden rush of hope.

By New Year the country was in the grip. The television showed stranded cars in Northern Ireland and Glasgow; in London the temperature had dropped ten degrees below freezing; blizzards were sweeping in from the west. The news every hour grew worse: patches of freezing fog, black ice, stretches of the motorway closed.

'Thank God we're not going anywhere,' William said to Danny, turning the boiler up. 'That's one good thing about getting old: you don't have to go anywhere.' He lit the fire and poured a large measure of Buffy's Christmas Scotch. 'Cheers, old boy. Happy New Year.'

He rang the family: Claire answered.

'Happy New Year, my darling.'

'Oh, hello.'

'How are you all getting on?' he asked her, and thanked her again for Boxing Day, which had been a strain.

'You don't have to keep thanking me,' she said.

'What are you all doing tonight?'

'People are coming in for drinks. Most of the terrace.'

'That sounds fun.'

She didn't answer.

'Claire—'

'What?'

'Just . . . happy New Year,' he said again, hesitantly. 'I mean – I hope it's a really good year for you, darling. Less . . . well, you know—'

'Less what?'

'Well, fraught,' he said, and saw in his mind's eye a wintry skater, venturing much too close to the Danger sign.

Claire said tightly: 'I do wish you wouldn't. I do *wish* you wouldn't. If I need your platitudinous words of wisdom, I'll ask for them.'

William watched the ice beneath his skater crack, over terrible blackness. For a moment he couldn't speak.

Then he said quietly: 'Very well.' He wanted to speak to Jeremy, to wish his son-in-law, for whom he and Eve had always been thankful, and of whom he had grown genuinely fond, a very good New Year, but he knew that he mustn't ask for him. In any case, he did not trust himself to utter another word.

There was silence. Then Claire said: 'Well. Happy New Year. I must get on,' and put the phone down.

William replaced the receiver, trembling.

Buffy rang just after ten. 'I'm not staying up until midnight,' she said briskly. 'Had to do it last year, had to see the wretched millennial thing. This year I'm bedding down at a sensible hour.'

'Quite right.' William, still shaky, leant forward to turn down the television.

'What are you watching?'

'I really couldn't tell you.'

'William? Is everything all right? You sound a bit—'

'I'm fine,' he said, as firmly as he could. 'Let me wish a happy New Year to a good old friend.'

'And a very happy New Year to you, William. And thank you again for Christmas – it was perfect.'

'It was good, wasn't it? Did me a power of good. We must do it again.'

'Well – lovely.' Buffy's voice was cautiously warm. Why the caution, he wondered, but hadn't the strength to enquire. 'And how are the family? Have you spoken to Claire?'

'I have.'

'William? Something's wrong, isn't it? Tell me.'

'Oh – you know. Families.'

'You mean Claire.' Buffy was brisk again. 'Now what's she done? She's hurt you, I can tell.'

William leaned back in his chair and closed his eyes. He felt tears rise – good God, he was getting like a girl, waterspouts at the slightest thing. He swallowed hard, cleared his throat.

'William?'

'Just a little tickle.'

'That girl,' Buffy said forcefully, 'needs a good hard smack. I'm sorry, dear, I don't mean to interfere, but I don't like to think of you upset.'

'It's all right. He wiped his eyes. 'I expect it's the time of year. A

71

seasonal disorder. Everyone's too emotional. Or hormonal. You know. Women's sort of thing.'

'I'm a woman, but I don't think I've gone around upsetting people in quite the way Claire manages. She needs a counsellor or something.'

'UHT, perhaps.'

'That's *milk*, William. You mean HRT. Honestly.' She gave a snort of laughter.

William at once began to feel better. He blew his nose and chucked another log on to the fire. 'Do let's change the subject. Isn't the snow glorious?'

'It's bloody cold.'

'I thought you said we were warming up. Globally.'

'Don't mock. You're burying your head in the sand.'

'Or the snow,' said William wittily.

'It isn't *funny*.'

Sometimes she sounded like Claire. But different. Buffy had a bedrock, always had done, he knew that. Claire, who looked as if she was embedded in every kind of rock on earth, lived, he now realised, above a morass of violent misery.

But why? Did she not have everything she had ever wanted?

Janice sat up in her bedroom in 33 Curlew Gardens. The room was small and, in winter, stuffy. She propped her pillows up against the wall and leaned against them on the narrow bed, writing a letter. It was Sunday afternoon, and downstairs the telly was roaring. Outside, the New Year snow had muffled everything, and it felt as though no one in the entire world would ever do anything, ever again.

Dear Mr Harriman, she wrote, *I wonder if you can help me. I am thinking of coming down to London, in order to change my life.*

She crossed this out at once.

Dear Mr Harriman, If I don't get out of this place I shall go—

How on earth should she write? Probably she should go through it all with Steve, but the Ridge was impassable, the café shut up, and Steve gone off for a week to Marrakech. All right for some.

Dear Mr Harriman, We have never met, but I think your loopy old cousin has written to you about me. I am thinking of coming to London, and—

And what?

Dear Mr Harriman, I hope you won't mind me writing when we have never met, but your cousin Mary kindly suggested that you might be able to help me.

72

There. That sounded pretty normal, didn't it? She was pretty normal, wasn't she?

Janice put her pen down and gazed out of the window. God, it was dead out there. No hum from the bypass, no sheep on the hills. Perched on the bed like this she could see only the snow-covered tops, beneath a relentless opaque grey sky. Somewhere in a fold beneath was Eric, in his shepherd's hut, toasting his feet in thick wool walkers' socks before a fantastic fire.

She ripped the sheet from its pad and tore it into pieces.

9

Everything slowed down with the snow. The skies, after the first fall, were dark and low; the milk came late, likewise the paper. The post barely came at all. For two or three days, in freezing weather, William kept to the house, feeling himself in shut-down mode, not minding. He put out some food for the birds, lit fires, played Brahms and Schubert. He stood browsing at the bookshelves, pulling out forgotten volumes. Recalling Monet and Pissarro, the morning he had awoken to a new white world, he dipped in and out of the art books on which he had, in his time, spent a fortune. For a whole afternoon he sat reading a life of Matisse, who, during a youthful illness, distraught at the prospect of life as a small-town lawyer, was given a box of paints by his mother.

'From the moment I held the box of colours in my hand, I knew this was my life . . .'

William turned the pages, losing himself in windows on to the sea, the shaded garden; in scarlet, green and Prussian blue interiors – rugs, screens, samovars; he gazed at women in silken patterned robes, or naked on daybeds, naked beneath the trees. Here was the shimmer of lemons in a blue-glazed dish; here was the Cartier-Bresson photograph everyone knew: Matisse in old age, in a corner of his sunlit studio, glasses upon his nose, cap on his head, tranquil dove in his hand while he drew. The dove's companions, released from their cage, sat watching, murmuring. Old age; a contented morning; working until the end.

When William looked up, he saw it was almost dark, the snowy trees ghostly in the fading afternoon, everything muffled and still. Not a bird, not a footstep. He got up to draw the curtains, looked out on the empty street. Matisse's radiant interiors receded: this was an oil from a

London painter, whiteness smudged into grey in the dusk, here and there a lighted window. *Winter Street*, something by one of the Camden Town Group, perhaps – London in the twenties, in a muted palette. Whistler would have dissolved it all, to black and white and gold. I might have been a painter, William thought, recalling lost afternoons in classes, decades ago, before he was told to concentrate on serious subjects. I might not just have looked at everything, I might have picked up a brush. And he stood where Matthew, at Christmas, had stood, briefly transfigured by the blackbird's song, letting the depth of the afternoon sink into him.

That evening, he sat at his desk – his father's old desk – in the corner of the drawing room, and wrote to Matthew's consultant, asking for a meeting. The letter began as a brief request, and became an impassioned plea – for a young life going to waste, brilliance occluded, gifts which must be rediscovered. He read it through, remembering how busy he himself had been, in the old Treasury days, wanting letters and memoranda to keep to the point, to let him get on. For a moment he considered tearing it up, writing just a brief note. Then he signed and sealed it, and gave it a first-class stamp.

Leaning back in his chair – his father's old chair, a Windsor – tapping his fountain pen against his lips, hearing the fire crackle, and Danny sigh before it, he wondered whether to write to Claire. Would that make things better between them?

I don't want to intrude, my darling, but I'm here if you need me, I'm always here, for both of you.

No. He could feel her irritation even as he considered it. Let her be, let her come to him, when she was ready. That was best.

Over supper, soup on a tray, he realised that he had not spoken to anyone for two days, and had not minded. The snow had done that: falling like a meditation, enclosing the house, and him. In bed, in the dark, in utter silence, he closed his eyes on Matisse's windows, Matisse's women – fully aware of their beauty, keeping it to themselves. It had been a long time since William had thought of female beauty – of skin, unclothed, of a glance, a touch – in relation to anyone but Eve, who all his life had made him happy, just to look at her. In bed he was almost always aware, still, of her absence, of the place where she should be, beside him, feet tucked beneath his feet, arm round his middle as they fell asleep. Now, on this winter night, he began to contemplate not her, not even an individual, but an idea of something perfect – a room, a figure, clothed or naked, an arrangement of colour.

I have been nourished, he thought, his hands behind his head, listening to the tick of the clock. Perhaps these tranquil, unexpected moments, after all the emotion of Christmas and New Year, were what was meant by the accommodation of old age – and reached without speaking to a soul.

In particular, he had not spoken to Claire. Was this why such calm had come upon him?

Have I lost her? he wondered, turning over, pulling the pillow down. For so long he had felt he had lost his son – but his love for him had remained, grown deeper even: pure, piercing, unswerving. With Claire – how hard she was to care for. As he sank into sleep, the images of remote, secret but untroubled womanhood swam once again before him. Claire, in new motherhood, had briefly had something of these qualities – a certainty about her place in the world, about her physicality. Now ... He sank into sleep, before he could work it out.

Next morning, the skies had cleared: by the time William had done with the paper, over a late breakfast, the snowy garden was lit by brilliant sun. He finished his coffee, made a shopping list, took down the lead from its hook.

'Walk,' he announced, as if he needed to, for Danny, at the first chink of the chain, was racing up the stairs.

The hall was full of light, streaming in through the lintel glass and through the stained-glass panels, coloured lozenges falling on to the tiles. Picking up his letter to the consultant from the table, William, in his winter coat, caught sight of himself in the mirror and thought, for a startling moment, that he had seen his father. He almost greeted him aloud – Father? Then he stood there, taking a good look at himself, as the dust in the flooding sunlight danced against the glass.

Thinning white hair but a well-made head – he'd give himself that. The Harriman nose, strong and bony; eyes a faded blue, with the pale circle round the iris which everyone developed as they got older – once it came, that was it: you knew you were on your way. But still – he wasn't there yet, and, like his father, had in old age a decently handsome face, he allowed himself, tucking his scarf in, pulling on his gloves.

Danny was gazing up, alert and waiting.

'What do you think?' he asked him. 'Still pass muster?'

Dachshund tail beat on Victorian tiles. William reached for his hat on the hook, glanced back in the mirror. 'Hello,' he said, to his father's eyes, and saw his father smile. Beside him, there was a little bark of anxiety: how much longer could this take?

'Right.' Hat, shopping bag. 'We're off.'

Snow was already melting on the steps: he took them carefully, clipping on Danny's lead at the gate. The air was invigorating, but very cold: he took a deep breath and at once began to cough. Better take it slowly: he set off, wondering whether he should have a flu jab, something he had always resisted, as a mark of frailty, when he was still active and fit.

People were out and about in the streets, setting off for the shops, like him, scraping snow from garden paths. There was Edith Horsley, at number seventeen, doing just this, in her woollen gloves and wellingtons. He raised his hat, and they agreed that it was a beautiful morning. The sound of shovel on stone rang through the air, a train came into the station and doors slammed. William walked on. The scarlet of the post-box on the corner was still trimmed with white: he posted his letter to the consultant, and thought of Matthew, in the overheated day room, turning – he hoped – from the television to gaze out at the stretch of grounds, firs dark against the glittering white.

He had reached the main road. The 14 was rumbling through the slush; the queue at the bus stop moved forward quickly; people were hurrying in and out of the shops in the cold. How busy everyone was. After his days of seclusion he found himself wondering whether he might see anyone he knew. He went to the bank, where Danny was allowed, and to Spar for basics, where he wasn't, and thence to the delicatessen, which a dachshund always found interesting, even from his hook outside.

Full-roasted coffee was grinding; the ham slicer slid smoothly back and forth. Time for an interesting lunch or two, a bit of company again, a root about in the sales. Time for a concert, a visit to a gallery. William, in the queue at the counter, wondered that the smells of coffee, marinated olives, salami and cheese and fresh bread could so quicken the blood, but so it was: he made his purchases, including a carton of spinach-and-nutmeg soup for lunch, and a small pannetone cake in a blue-ribboned box for tea.

Who might join him for tea? Or supper, come to that?

If Buffy didn't live right on the other side of London; if he were able to drop in, now and then, on his daughter and grandchildren, as one might hope to do, without it being always the wrong moment; if Matthew, darling Matthew—

He tucked his wallet back in his inside pocket and made for the door. Danny, on the pavement, leapt up in an abandonment of joy. And William, greeting and unhooking him, running gloved hands over beloved glossy head, felt again the sudden, unexpected prick of tears.

Now what? Where was the tranquillity of his retreat, where the joyous quickening of the blood?

I am alone too much: he almost said it aloud.

Life had its routine, and its satisfactions. The china stall was the heart of the week, the outings to sales delightful. There were times – he had just had one – when solitude was divine.

But with the children lost to him—

He straightened up, blew his nose, gathered himself and his shopping together.

'We need something to happen, old boy,' he said, as Danny looked brightly up at him. 'Not giving up yet.'

Then he set off home, down the street where the thaw was just beginning, the snow on the pavements pockmarked with drips from the trees, the railings black again, and shining; and let himself into the empty house: finding, on the mat, a letter.

Dear Mr Harriman . . .

He stood with his back to the empty grate, the sun-filled drawing room smelling of cinders and wood ash. The letter was on good paper, in a pleasing, youthful hand.

Dear Mr Harriman,

I wonder if you would be kind enough to help me. I know we have never met, but your cousin Mary has said you might know of a job. I am twenty-three and though I have no proper qualifications I am able to turn my hand to most things. At present I am working as a dog-walker, shopper and general help. I have been shopping for the Dog Museum for about three years. I also work in a café, and make good cakes, though I say it myself, though I am not really a cake-making sort of person, to look at.

Although I do not know London, I think it is time I did. Mary and Sophie have talked about you, and although I have never met anyone like you I don't know where to begin, or anyone else to ask. If you know anyone with a spare room who needs some general assistance, perhaps you could tell me. I am practical but not brainless.

I hope you are well, and look forward to hearing from you.

Yours sincerely,

Janice Harper

William, in his long winter coat, in the great high space that was his drawing room, filled with books and paintings, china in alcoves, and a walnut desk, the light from the thawing snow pouring through high windows, read this letter twice.

What was a Dog Museum? What, in God's name, could it be, and why would it need shopping done for it?

Ill-written words from another letter, arriving before Christmas in floods and driving rain, came all at once to mind.

The Dogs are a Comfort, Mary had written, capitalising at will.

He had assumed, not really thinking about it, that she meant the two or three living beasts last seen after Edna's funeral, but they must be long since gone. Had she had them stuffed? Or was this some other place entirely, a Heritage Britain venture of some kind? He shook his head, trying to imagine it.

More to the point, here was this young woman. Living in Curlew Gardens – how charming.

He tried to imagine her – someone who did not look like a cake-maker and who, he recalled, Mary had in her letter described as Tall and Fit. And clear minded – he felt that from the letter he now held in his hand: someone who knew herself, and knew how to get what she wanted.

Well.

Danny was sitting at the front window, in the fall of sun on pale worn carpet and Persian rug, looking out at the street and garden. Small though he was, the window was low enough for him to do this, and now and then his ears pricked up, as something of interest appeared. The possibility of cats was essentially the focus, but today, William knew, he was aware of the change in the weather, enjoying the intriguing little falls, now and then, of clumps of melting snow, from the magnolia tree and the extravagant stems of unpruned roses. Up went the ears, this way and that, out went the eager nose, and in the sunshine his chestnut coat gleamed like a polished antique.

'What do you think?' asked William, walking across the room in his unbuttoned coat, laying the letter on the open walnut desk. Danny turned to glance up at him, then looked back at the garden, where a blue tit had suddenly arrived, and was swinging on the last of the bag of nuts. William stood watching it too – such a beady, compact, bright little bird – trying to imagine, in his house, a lodger, an energetic young woman breezing in and out, turning her hand to things, chatting away, while the smells of baking wafted up from the kitchen.

'Oh, God, I don't know.'

On the one hand the prospect of companionship, conversation, help when needed. But with what? He didn't need help – not yet, not really. Shopping was perfectly manageable, a focus to the day. Twice-weekly mornings with Mrs T. had for years kept the domestic wheels oiled. The house was dilapidated in corners, but clean; his shirts were ironed, the silver polished. And anyway, Janice Harper was not offering herself as a cleaner.

It wouldn't do, it wasn't suitable.

A lodger was one thing, coming and going, with a job outside the house. An ever-present young woman: no. Someone wanting to talk, while he wanted to read: no.

Had he grown selfish, living alone all this time?

'Can't get it right,' he told Danny, and it was true. He swung from contentment to loneliness, unstable as an adolescent.

Well – this was life without Eve. Even now, even after all these years. If you were essentially monogamous, this was widowhood: nothing ever quite right.

Perhaps he had better just accept it, live with it. A lodger could only bring complications.

And anyway – there was Matthew. Up at the top of the house was his old room, along the upper landing from Claire's; there were his books and music and violin, shut in its case. One day, when he was well enough, he'd be back here – that, at William's time of life, was who should be living here.

So they'd have to see. Any other arrangement now could only be pro tem.

The blue tit flew up from the last of the nuts and was gone. Danny, bored now, looked round, awaiting instructions.

'Lunch-time,' said William, and they made their way out to the hall, where the bag of shopping, including the very good soup, was propped against the table, while Janice Harper's letter lay on the antique desk in the sun, amongst old fountain pens, and letters from the past.

10

'He's written back,' said Janice, heaving in provisions. She set the bags on the kitchen table, and numberless dogs on the hearth got up, stretched, and came to have a look.

'William?' asked Mary, turning from the sink. Enormous and impenetrable heaps of washing filled it; her sleeves were rolled up to her elbows, her pinafore soaking.

'Yes. You need a machine,' Janice added, nudging away three hairy lurchers and the red-eyed bassett-hound. She unpacked the tins of Saversoup, and flimsy economy packs of toilet rolls: she stacked up tins of Chum. 'No one on the planet washes by hand any more.'

'More fool them.' Mary held up a pair of Ernie's trousers. Pitch-black water streamed from the turn-ups.

'Ugh,' said Janice. 'Yuk. How can you?'

'Pounding and beating,' said Mary, flinging them back in the sink. 'That's what gets the dirt out, and we can't afford a machine.'

'Rubbish.' Janice piled up the tinned steamed puddings, put the bags of dog biscuits in their corner, pushing away a narrow-nosed collie. 'I've told you a million times you can get them on instalments. Argos. Curry's. Anywhere, for God's sake.'

'Hire purchase.' Mary was full of distaste. 'The beginning of the end.'

'You don't even have to pay interest. Not any more.'

'Why don't they give them away, then?'

Footsteps sounded on the creaking boards above, and came down the stairs, with their dangerous carpet, rodless and frayed. The latch on the bottom was raised with a click: dogs padded over at once.

'What have you been doing up there all morning?' demanded Mary.

Sophie closed the door and smiled sweetly at Janice, from within the circle of hounds. She was wearing a sky-blue nylon polo neck beneath a pinafore trimmed in purple, and her hair was hooked up with a cheerful new slide on which two cockatoos with vast yellow combs swung on a perch beneath an arch of brilliant foliage.

'You look nice,' said Janice, taking out custard creams and Bourbons.

'Titivating.' Mary sloshed violently in the sink. 'Preening in the mirror. Who cares? Who cares what you look like? There's work to be done down here.'

'You could have a washing machine and time to titivate, too.' Janice shook out the last of the carrier bags and folded it.

Mary sniffed. 'It's been a long time since I sat looking in mirrors.'

'Just as well.' Ernie's sepulchral voice sounded from the passage. A blast of snow-laden air blew behind him and all the dogs rushed towards it. He banged the door to.

'Oh, let them out,' Mary shouted, and yanked up the plug from the sink.

'Good day for washing, I must say.' Ernie came padding across the floor as the dogs all raced past him.

'Why don't you do it, then?' she asked him, wrenching on the taps. They leapt about unnervingly.

'Why don't you buy a machine?' asked Janice again.

'Debt!' yelled Mary, and they all stepped back. 'Debt and the poorhouse!'

Sophie's hands went to her mouth.

'What's this?' asked Ernie, making for his chair.

'Mother,' said Sophie, biting her lip. 'Mother taught us never, never—'

'Never to get into debt,' said Mary, and turned off the gushing taps with determination. 'And she was right.'

'She was.' Ernie settled into his chair and those dogs remaining, a small brown creature of indeterminate breed, and Flossie, the ancient spaniel-cross, settled down at his feet with a sigh. 'When we want, we wait,' he told Janice.

'The credit card is not for us,' said Sophie, eyeing the Bourbon biscuits.

'Neither a borrower nor a lender be.' Mary turned back to her rinsing with finality.

'Don't suppose you've got any baccy,' Ernie enquired of Janice.

83

'No,' she said, tugging open the ill-fitting drawer in the kitchen table, stuffing the folded bags inside. 'I don't suppose I have.'

London had got to be better than this.

'Doesn't anyone want to hear about my letter?' she asked, a little later, when everyone had calmed down. The house dogs were outside, sniffing about in the patches of snow, nosing up at those in the pens, skimpy little old ones shivering inside the porch. Beyond the fence, the field was a map of white and green, the last snowy islands shrinking beneath the morning sun.

In here, the tea was made, the range refilled, and Sophie had swept the floor of dog hair. The desperate heaps of washing lay inert in the sink and Mary was at last sitting down, reaching for the sugar. Janice had given Ernie a shred or two of Golden Virginia, so he was happy now. She felt in her pocket and pulled out the letter from William Harriman.

'*Dear Miss Harper,*' she read aloud, and they all settled back to listen. She had at once a vision of them all as children – a state of being curiously close to them still: three pre-war children, stuck out here in the back of beyond without even any electricity, sitting round the table – could it have been this table? – waiting for bread and jam, and being good.

'*Thank you so much for your letter, to which I have given much thought.*'

What a lovely, graceful line. It fell upon the snow-lit kitchen, and upon the strangeness of the lives within it, like a phrase of music.

'*I should very much like to be able to help you, and since I live alone, in a roomy old family house, and am not as young as I was, it would make perfect sense for me to have a lodger . . .*'

'There!' Mary was triumphant.

'A roomy old family house,' murmured Sophie, gazing about her.

'Bit different from this one, I expect,' said Ernie. He rubbed his knees. 'It's freezing, out there in that trailer.'

'Don't start.' Mary looked at Janice with flinty bright eyes. 'Carry on.'

'*However,*' read Janice, wondering again how Ernie did, indeed, survive in his leaky tin dwelling, '*I have to confess to some mixed feelings. Chiefly, these relate to my son, Matthew, whom my cousins may remember from one or two childhood visits.*' She looked up, enquiringly.

'Dear little boy,' said Sophie.

'Him and his sister.' Ernie blew smoke into the air and watched it dissolve, and vanish.

'*Since the death of my dear wife, Eve, Matthew and my daughter and her family have become the chief focus of my life, and about Matthew I have particular anxieties. He suffered a breakdown some years ago, and has for a long time been in hospital.*'

Janice looked up, to see the effect of this news, and was met with total incomprehension all round. 'Hospital,' said Sophie sadly, at last, and touched the two bright cockatoos on her slide, swinging on their perch.

'Go on,' said Mary, reaching for the teapot.

'*He still is not well enough to live on his own,*' read Janice. '*My hope and dream is that one day he will come home, and if that were to happen I don't think I should want to have to worry about anything else. On the other hand, I have, as I say, plenty of space here now, in which I rattle about, with my wife's little dog, Danny. Like me, he has seen the last of his youth, but I think there is life in both of us yet.*'

'There was always life in William,' said Mary.

'He sounds a dear little thing,' said Sophie. 'Danny. What breed, I wonder?'

Janice turned the page. The handwriting was like no other handwriting she had ever seen – it made her think of museums, and manuscripts, and shafts of light.

'Dachshund,' Mary said briskly. 'That's what I seem to recall. Smooth-haired.'

'*I am not without interests,*' the letter continued, '*as you yourself clearly are not. (I do like the sound of your cakes.) I run an antiques stall – china and glass – with my dear wife's oldest friend, which is great fun. I read a great deal, and am thinking of taking up painting. I see my grandchildren as often as I can. In other words I am not, I hope, someone who needs to "get a life", as I think the phrase is nowadays.*'

'More than you can say here,' said Ernie, stubbing out the last shred of roll-up on the hearth with the heel of his stockinged foot.

'Don't do that!' Mary was on to him at once. 'No wonder they're all in holes.' She turned back to Janice. 'So what's the top and tail of it, then? What's he decided?'

'*So what am I saying?*' Janice read out, each of them hanging on every word. '*I think the position is that I could offer you temporary accommodation, while you find your feet in London. You could stay in the spare room, for minimal*

rent, for, let us say, a period of three months. I should expect you to look for a job – I did have something in mind, with my daughter's family, but my daughter must speak for herself, and I don't know if it would suit either of you. Essentially—'
Here there was a long, elegant dash. *'Essentially I am used to having the house to myself, and am perhaps a little cautious at the idea of sharing it. So if this does not sound too unwelcoming, and you would be happy to settle for bed and breakfast and supper on occasion – I could give you your own kitchen cupboard, of course – then by all means do come and stay.*

'I shall wait to hear from you, and, if all this sounds acceptable, I look forward very much to meeting you. I am really a very friendly person, and Danny is certainly a very friendly dog. Yours sincerely, William Harriman.'

'There!' Mary said again, and put down her mug. 'Just the ticket.'

'I don't know why you're so anxious to be rid of me,' said Janice, laying the letter down. 'Who will do all your shopping?' She pictured them, standing at the bus stop in all weathers, in their belted coats and ancient headwear; trudging through Oswestry or Shrewsbury with plastic holdalls, hauling sacks of dog biscuits. Poor old bats. And all that dog walking: how would they manage that?

'There's a PS,' she added, and read it out to them. *'Do tell me – what is a Dog Museum?'*

Sophie was filled with wonder. 'To think he doesn't know.' She turned to Mary, fingering her slide. 'Didn't you tell William? When you wrote? Doesn't he know what we do?'

'He knows we have dogs,' said Mary shortly. 'I can't remember what else I've said.' She got up, and went to look out of the back window, where snow was sliding in clumps down the corrugated-iron roofs of the huts, shut up for the winter. No one came in winter, ever: couldn't expect it. But in the spring—

The dogs outside sensed her presence, and came over, in twos and threes. They stood in the snow beneath the window, looking up at her. Flossie barked. She was a poor old thing who'd had too many litters. Mary had found her shut up in a barn on old Jim Walsh's land – he was a wicked old bugger. She'd been out with the pack on a summer afternoon in 1997, and heard a whining. When she broke into the barn she knew at once there were puppies, could sense it, and saw them all, right at the back without even a piece of sacking, and the bitch sucked dry and thin as a bone. 'You come with me,' said Mary, and took the lot of them, the puppies in her holdall and the bitch called Flossie – she generally knew their names as soon as she saw them – slipping in

86

at once with the pack, her tail between her legs, drooping dugs swinging back and forth, pattering weakly down the lane. The sun was high and the air still; the lane was full of cowpats. Mary led them all home and gave Flossie a vast bowl of milk. The four pups were almost beyond saving, but she saved them, all except one, which Ernie buried. He was used to that, though he didn't like it. She found homes for two, and the last was here now: Jip, with his mother, just as it should be, both with their operations done, and that cost a fortune, every time. But this was her life's work, the work of all of them, and she wouldn't have it any other way.

'We'll manage,' she said to Janice, turning to look at them all, two weaklings, both a bit soft in the head, and a fit young girl. 'You get a life,' she told her. 'Seize your chances.'

Janice went walking, up in the hills. Her black woollen hat was pulled down as low as it would go, her scarf wound tightly round her mouth. She wore two pairs of gloves, and a vest, T-shirt and two jumpers under her army surplus jacket, lined with dung-coloured fleece. It weighed a ton. There were two pairs of socks inside her walking boots, one thin, one thick. She knew how to dress for the country, for walking this lot: she was boiling now, though high up the snow was still thick and looked likely to freeze tonight. The dogs were off their leads, which she'd slung round her neck, or stuffed in her pockets. They'd gone streaming off in all directions, and though one or two little ones wanted carrying she wouldn't give in, not yet – they needed exercise, do them good, bit of snow wouldn't hurt them.

In summer, the problem was always the sheep. Mostly, the dogs were well trained and not all that interested, but there were two or three you had to keep an eye on all the time. No question, with any of them, of going through the fields, lambs or no lambs, but up here it was generally OK. A couple of heads would come up in the bracken, or you'd round a corner and hear them, cropping the turf. They'd take one look at the dogs and scatter, bouncing off up the slope, or down into a dip. Janice would whistle and shout, the dogs would wheel round to her, and the ewes would pick up grazing as if nothing had happened. Now they were almost all down on the lower slopes, or inside for lambing, though now and then you'd suddenly see a tough old blackface with tight horns and mad yellow eyes come looming out of the snow at you. She supposed there might be one or two buried in drifts, but the thaw was on its way: they'd come out, look around, and trot away, as if nothing had happened. Thick. She knew about sheep, like she knew about old people, now.

Some old people, anyway. This lot. Her gran, and her gran's friends. Albert Page. She didn't know about William Harriman, who had seen the last of his youth but still had life in him. She strode along the hillside track, the letter in its vellum envelope tucked back inside her trouser pocket.

I should very much like to be able to help you, and since I live alone, in a roomy old family house . . . I am a little anxious at the prospect of sharing it . . .

Was that what he had said? Something like that. She realised that though she did not have the letter quite by heart, already his style, and the rhythms of his prose, had begun to feel familiar, though she knew no one else who wrote, or spoke, like that. Steve, when he flew back from Marrakech, was probably the only other person she knew who would appreciate it.

Since the death of my dear wife, Eve . . . I run an antiques china stall, read a great deal, and am thinking of taking up painting . . .

A voice from another age, urbane and courteous. A fountain pen, flowing over the creamy pages, from his roomy London house. Something which Janice had not known was missing from her life was answered by all of this. She strode along the wintry track, watching the dogs race up and down the slopes, slipping in falls of snow, barking and shaking themselves, and turned over well-made phrases in her mind.

And what did you wear in London? she wondered, boiling in her layers and fleecy lining. Not army surplus, that was for sure. Would she look a right idiot down there? Would she sound a right idiot, every time she opened her mouth?

The sky was cold and clear, though cloud was gathering. Janice rounded a bend and stood looking down the hillside.

Ah. There it was.

Preoccupied as she had been with the prospect of another life, it had not escaped her attention that she was in the folds of the hills of Wenlock Edge wherein lay Eric Lammering's shepherd's hut.

There it was, nestled in the snow, with his bike parked under the lean-to.

She could see, from her vantage point up here, the rising plume of smoke from the chimney, set on the sloping patched slate roof. He was there, the bastard, there by the roaring fire with his glass of whisky and who knows what poor fool of a girl, taking her clothes off on a winter afternoon, thinking the snow and the firelight so romantic, just as she, Janice Harper, idiot, had thought the drumming rain and howling wind.

She bent down, and from the melting snow picked up a stone. She rubbed it against her jacket, and then she hurled it, up in an arc, and watched its distant, symbolic fall on the lower slopes.

'So much for you!' she shouted, and at once the dogs were all round her, barking, looking out to the place where the stone had fallen and back at her, tongues hanging out, eyes eager.

Serve him right if she unleashed the lot of them down there. Set a pack of dogs on him, that's what she should do.

Instead—

'Come on,' she called to them, and turned, whistling them to heel, not looking back. They all swerved to follow, and then race past her, as she bent and threw another stone, as far as she could, back along the way they had come, back towards the museum. Off they all went after it, except for little Pip, Ernie's Yorkie, who stood there trembling in the snow, looking up at her beseechingly.

This time she took pity, bent down and picked him up, wrapping him deep inside her heavy jacket, striding after Doberman and Dalmatian-cross, collie and lurcher, greyhound and spaniel and God knows what, streaming away through the Shropshire hills as the winter sun slipped down.

That night, in her stuffy bedroom, with its Anaglypta wallpaper, Marks & Spencer tie-back curtains and louvred cupboards from Homebase, she wrote to William Harriman, thanking him for his kind offer.

I will look for a job and try not to get in your way, she wrote. *PS The Dog Museum is run by your cousins as a charity to support their work with rescued strays. It is probably unique. I will tell you all about it. PPS I am a vegan.*

'I've done it,' William told Buffy. The snow had gone, the rain had returned, they were sitting at the stall on Saturday morning. Things felt pretty much back to normal.

'What's that?' asked Buffy, unscrewing the Thermos.

'Arranged for the lodger. The Shropshire lass.'

'Oh.' Buffy poured scalding coffee into the plastic beaker with concentration. Her grip was not as it used to be. She passed the beaker to William. 'Well. There's a thing. And when's she coming?'

'In a couple of weeks – I expect she's got things to sort out up there, and I'll have to get ready, too. Clear out the cupboards and things.'

'Yes, yes, of course.' Buffy sat back with her cup. The stall was a little thin today, and the market quiet. No one was spending much after Christmas and then the sales. And now the bloody rain again. Even Danny, curled up on William's old jacket on the fold-up chair beside her, looked a bit glum. She gave him a little pat.

'Which room are you giving her?' she asked, thinking of the pretty spare room where she had spent Christmas, with its soft satin eiderdown, and curtains from Ruffle and Tuck.

'Claire's room,' said William, stretching his long legs out beneath the stall. 'I think that'll do. I want to hang on to the spare room, just in case, and of course she can't have Matthew's.'

'No, of course not. Claire won't mind, will she?'

'I shouldn't think so. Why should she?' William put down the beaker, and looked at Buffy. 'Do you think she will? Do you think I should make it the spare room?'

'Oh, William. No. Do what you want, dear, it's your house. Claire has her own life now – how could she possibly mind?'

William was silent. 'I'd hate to upset her again,' he said at last.

'You won't,' said Buffy firmly. 'And anyway, it's not going to be for ever, is it?'

'No, no, it's a temporary arrangement. I've made that quite clear. Just while she finds a job and gets settled. She won't want to hang around with an old codger like me once she's got into the swing.'

Buffy touched his hand, with her fingerless knitted gloves. 'No one,' she said, 'in a million years, could ever call you an old codger.'

He gave her his meltingly beautiful smile.

A week later, Janice said goodbye to Steve, back from Marrakech and perky, until she told him.

'You can't,' he said. 'You haven't even given notice.'

'I'm giving it now,' said Janice, lighting up. The snow had all gone and now it was raining again, great dark sweeps of it blowing over the Ridge. The windows of Cloud Nine were almost black, and the tea urn had never hissed more comfortingly. 'Let's face it,' she said, inhaling deeply, 'no one is going to come here for weeks. You don't need me. You do not need me,' she said again with emphasis, seeing his face. 'If you can't make tea and sandwiches twice a week you're not fit to call yourself proprietor.'

'The cakes,' he said sadly. 'What about the cakes?'

'There's two in the fridge.'

'I've never really understood,' he said, suntanned and gorgeous beneath spiked hair, 'how you could be a vegan and make them. Cakes are the hardest thing. There's no substitute for eggs, in a cake.'

'Tell that to Albert Page,' said Janice. 'He lived on dried egg through two world wars.' She had felt sorry, saying goodbye to him.

'I might never see you again,' he said, trembling at the door.

''Course you will,' she told him, giving him a peck on his papery old cheek. 'And the social worker will be in tomorrow.'

'Social.' He snorted. 'I don't want no social. They'll put me in a home.'

'No they won't,' said Janice, knowing they probably would.

'Dried egg is still egg,' said Steve. 'How can you cook with eggs and dairy foods and call yourself a vegan?'

'Vegan is as vegan does.' Janice sipped her tea. 'I don't *eat* all that stuff. It does not pass my lips.'

'Not what I call proper vegan.'

'I have to live, don't I? Stop going on about it. Who did you meet in Marrakech?'

'No one.' He took her hand. 'Please stay.'

Janice looked at the hand. 'I thought you were gay.'

'I am. I just like you, that's all.'

'I like you too, and I'm going to London.'

She said goodbye to Mary and Sophie and Ernie, and that was hard.

'But you're doing the right thing,' said Sophie bravely. She was wearing the dolphins today, leaping joyously out of crested waves. 'You'll have a good time, I expect.'

''Course she will,' said Ernie. 'Don't get too posh.'

'She'll do what she wants,' said Mary.

They all crowded into the porch. Rain dripped from the tiles, the dogs stood looking out. Janice counted nine heads, poking their noses in the gaps between pinafore and frayed tweed jacket.

91

'Goodbye and good luck,' she said quickly. 'I'll probably be back in a week, let's face it.'

She turned and ran ducking through the rain to her bike, and rode away in great sprays of water.

'Dulwich?' said her mother. 'Who lives in Dulwich?'

'William Harriman. He's a retired civil servant. From the Treasury. He has a dachshund and two grown-up children and collects old china.'

'And how did you find him?'

Janice explained and her parents whitened.

'A relative of those barmy old—'

'He's different,' said Janice. 'He's completely different and I'm going and that's that.'

They saw her off at the station, on a windswept afternoon. Rain blew in drifts from the platform roof and dripped from the baskets of trailing ivy. Janice, on her Apex single ticket, sat in a corner of the only smoking carriage, and waved with the greatest sense of relief she had ever felt in her life.

11

'Now, then,' said Buffy, starting the day. 'Now, then.'
What a business it was, getting going. She sat on the bedroom chair, and tugged.

The thing was to keep to a routine: she'd realised that years ago, almost as soon as she'd retired. While you were working, the prospect of unfettered days, with a lie-in whenever you wanted, was perfect bliss. It hadn't taken long to realise that lie-ins, and laxity, were a great mistake. She looked back on those early days – gazing mournfully out at the traffic, and pigeons on rooftops, tending her window-box geraniums as if they were the only thing that mattered – with something approaching horror. The china stall had saved her, a whole new lease of life begun, and the Mary Ward Over-Sixties Club had been a revelation.

Had she wanted, she could have filled every day with activities in Queen Square: Keep Fit, Computer Skills, Sculpture, Writing for Pleasure, Making Music, Circle Dancing. There were even trips to Paris. She opted for Choral Singing, and for Computer Skills – which, had she had them, might have delayed her retirement, but she'd felt such a fool, in the office, peering at the screen, trying to click in the right place and always missing, while people sighed, and said they must go to lunch. Once she could go at her own pace, with none of it mattering, not the way it did when you were getting paid for it, she found she was rather a whizz. Well, she could do it: get on to the Web, type things and print them, set up files and even send attachments, though this last was of minimal interest: she had nothing to attach, and no one to send it to anyway. She did, however, now have an e-mail address: buffy@hotmail.com. At first, she used this for very little, opening it up in the computer room at Mary Ward on Wednesdays and finding nothing there except, now and then, an encouraging word from her tutor.

Good morning, Buffy. Nice to have you with us today.

It was meant very kindly, but she had hoped for more. Who from? Who might she send to? No one she knew was on e-mail at home, and although once or twice she had triumphantly sent word to the office, where everyone now sat gazing all day at their screens, and though Mr Lawson sent back *Hello, Buffy! Wonderful to hear from you electronically! How is retirement?*, she knew she must let them get on. Nothing worse than clinging like a mollusc: once you had gone, you had gone. That was work for you. Forty years, and nobody gave a damn. Anyway, e-mail was just for fun, she didn't *need* it.

Then, one afternoon, just as she'd got home from the Mary Ward and was putting the kettle on, the telephone rang.

'Good afternoon. Is that Miss Henderson?'

The voice was young, and rather nice, and male.

'Who's that?' asked Buffy, her mind racing.

'This is the Friends of the Earth,' said the voice. 'My name's Nick, I'm calling from our fund-raising department. Is this a convenient moment?'

Buffy looked at the receiver, just as they did in films. Now she knew why.

'How did you get my number?' she demanded.

'From the phone book,' nice Nick said mildly.

'What do you want?'

'I was coming to that. We're looking for new subscribers, people who really care about the environment and want to make the world a better place. Do you know about our work?'

Buffy said: 'This is outrageous.' She could hear the kettle coming to the boil; she was dying for a cup. 'What do you mean, telephoning people out of the blue, intruding on people's privacy?'

'I'm dreadfully sorry,' said Nick. 'Would you prefer to have something sent in the post? It's just that people get so much mail these days – sometimes they prefer a personal call.'

'Well, I don't,' said Buffy, hearing the kettle click. 'I think it's a nerve. It's like those people selling double-glazing, or damp-proofing, who ring just as you're getting the supper. "We're in your area, this is a courtesy call." '

'That's different,' said Nick, in his nice young voice. 'This is something important.'

And she knew, all at once, that it was.

That had been the beginning. Before she knew it, Buffy, who for much of her life had felt on the edge of things – working at jobs she didn't much care for, helping her mother look after her father, then looking after her mother – found herself with interests and a cause. Packing up her mother's flat, washing and putting the china in boxes, she had realised that china was something she had always really loved, and the idea for the stall had come to her, just like that. Now she knew all about Spode. At Mary Ward she found she could click a mouse, and sing. She came home humming Handel, let herself go in the bath with Hubert Parry, learned to like Britten.

Then, with Friends of the Earth, her eyes were opened. What use to sing, when the songbirds choked on pesticide? There was lead in petrol, there were oil spills in oceans. The hole in the ozone layer was growing larger, chemicals seeped into the soil from which harvests grew. Even bread was risky.

She threw herself into it all.

Caught up with campaigning, collecting on corners and leafleting every household in W8, had saved, if not the world, then Buffy herself, in the long dark months after Eve's so sudden, dreadful descent into illness and death. Poor Eve, sweet Eve – her oldest and most loyal friend. Poor, poor William, who, at the funeral, with that broken boy beside him, and Claire sobbing her heart out, had looked quite haunted. His companion of a lifetime gone – there had, for William, never been anyone but Eve. Fortunate Eve, Buffy allowed herself to think later, as she had thought on their wedding day, throwing confetti after the departing car, going home for tea with Mother. And poor me, she thought, though she hated self-pity.

But without the cheery Saturdays in Portobello, without the drives out to the sales, boxes and hamper in the back – how bleak the week felt now, all of a sudden. There was nothing like old friends. There was nothing like finding, on some dusty trestle, a perfect Minton bowl without a chip. 'I say – do come and look at this.' So companionable, such fun. Of course, she could run the stall by herself, but it wasn't the same: she tried it, and it felt quite horribly lonely, packing up afterwards, carrying boxes back to the empty flat.

Environmental campaigning saw her through. As secretary to her local FoE group, she was in touch with other groups, on mailing lists for meetings. When she opened up her e-mail, there were lots.

Looking back, Buffy thought now that those days in the eighties had been quite innocent, compared with what went on now. She had joined Friends of the Earth before Genetically Modified was – as it were – on anyone's lips; before BSE; before Dolly had been cloned or the weather, so unnervingly, had begun to change.

'We're ruining the *climate*, William,' she told him. Why couldn't he see?

Recently, however, it was not just – just! – the ceaseless rain, and the television pictures of storm-lashed coasts and burst embankments, which kept Buffy awake at night. Her body, to which, for decades, she had given little thought, was making itself known to her in divers troublesome ways. Even without a hot drink last thing – and she missed the comforting cocoa – she was forever getting up in the night. Staying with William at Christmas, she'd had to stumble along to the bathroom in the small hours, wondering whether she was waking him with the flush: not once, but twice. So embarrassing, though of course he was so well bred that he would never have mentioned it.

Now – horrors – she seemed to be suffering from constipation. She had never thought she might gaze at a bottle of Senakot as if it were a friend, but so it was. Even this didn't always do the trick. And her clothes felt uncomfortable, in more than the usual after-Christmas way. She found herself wearing her skirts unbuttoned at the waist, and, on coming home after classes, desperate to put her feet up. Her feet weren't quite right, either – even K shoes needed stretching. She felt the cold much more: sitting at the stall on Saturdays required layer after layer, and a rug right over her knees. And her knees weren't right – oh, what an effort to climb the stairs to her singing class, to climb the stairs to the flat.

In short, my dear, she told herself this morning, struggling into her tights, in short you are not as you were. Not that that had ever been anything much to write home about.

She got to her feet, heaving up M & S sixty-denier over her bulging bottom. The curtains were still drawn; the bedside lamp cast its glow upon the room, reflecting, in the wardrobe mirror, the heap of quilt, the tea tray, *Antiques Review* and cold hot-water bottle, and Buffy, getting dressed. She caught sight of herself, and was, for a moment, horrified. Surely she didn't really look like that. Surely her tummy had never been – and wasn't now – so vast. She moved quickly to open the wardrobe door, to take out her skirt and Jaeger cardigan. Generally speaking, she considered this mirror her friend. Certainly, it showed her, in the familiar privacy of her bedroom, an infinitely kinder version of herself than the one you were liable to behold in the all-round glass of a John Lewis cubicle, where, frankly, until you had the garments on, it was better simply not to look. To see oneself at every *angle*, beneath that unforgiving neon—

Buffy zipped up her skirt, as far as it would go. No question of the waistband button – *how* had she got so fat?

'I think of myself as medium-sized,' she said aloud, and put on, over her thermal vest, her pin-striped shirt, and grey cashmere cardigan. Then she swung the door to again, and had another look. There – that was better, that wasn't too bad at all. Couldn't go wrong with cashmere, couldn't go wrong with grey, and silver earrings. She brushed her hair into its knot, with its tortoiseshell slide, put on her strand of pearls, worn every day for perhaps a dozen years – it didn't matter, it was a classic, classics were a part of you – and put in her earrings. When she'd done her face, she could face the world. Do it after breakfast; she could feel her tummy rumbling.

She drew back the curtains, looked out on to the rainswept road. Half past eight on a Wednesday morning, and London going to work, as for forty years Buffy had done, queuing at the bus stop, fighting through the Tube – never, never again – buying her poppy-seed cream cheese rolls in the sandwich bar at lunchtime, eating them at her desk with Anita Brookner – *that* was someone she would never read again – clattering away for years on Remington, Adler, Olivetti, in the days before Olivetti sounded like something you'd have for lunch in Islington. Taking down shorthand and typing it up again, for all those men – surveyors, solicitors, property developers, insurance brokers. Not one had asked her out. No, that wasn't true. There had been birthday lunches – their birthdays – and sometimes a quick drink at the end of the day. On the whole, though – no. Mr Lawson, to whom, for her last ten years in the saddle, she had been quite a good PA: he had been kind, the only one ever to ask when *her* birthday was, though he had forgotten the very next year. But he himself led a less than vigorous life, she could tell. Up and down for thirty-five years to Haywards Heath: what kind of life was that for a man?

Anyway, it was all long since behind her now, and watching the scurry of Notting Hill below her, the snow all gone and the rain just pouring down, Buffy was glad. She watched the mad dash from the newsagent's, the rush down the steps of the Tube, the soaking-wet wait for the bus, and then she took her tray and cold hot-water bottle through to the little kitchen, put on the wireless and boiled herself a very nice free-range egg.

Wednesday was Choral Singing: heaven.

'Blest pair of sirens, pledges of heav'n's joy . . .' sang Buffy, washing up.

The class began at two, and when it had finished they all had tea downstairs. Surely the graceful, interconnecting houses in Queen Square which made up the Mary Ward Centre gave room to one of the happiest places in London. From the art studio on the top floor to the ground-floor vegetarian café, it was alive and bustling with activity. In the writing class you could hear the choir; on the stairs – broad, shallow, but an effort, it had to be said – you could smell oil paint and baking. In the spring you glimpsed people with learning disabilities contentedly potting petunias; in summer, with the windows open wide, you could hear, as you walked through the square, the drifting notes of piano and recorder. People learnt French and Italian; you could do TEFL and ESOL and TESOL, and receive free legal advice. The girls on the desk were kind and smiling, the tutors cheerful.

Now and then a melancholy stray student or two wandered in for a meeting: these came from a nearby college of London University, where they took things more seriously. One of the most lugubrious-looking men Buffy had ever seen in her life turned out, at the Christmas party, to be studying Psychoanalysis & Literature. He started to talk about Freud, and she hurried away.

'Where the bright Se-ra-phim, in burning row, / Their loud, up-lifted angel-trumpets blow . . .' she sang now, washing up the breakfast things. She put away eggcup and saucer, and went into the sitting room.

A mailshot awaited: the desk was piled high, leaflets on one side, envelopes on another, stamps, and the long list of names and addresses, in the middle. That would keep her busy until lunch-time, and no mistake. After which, rain or no rain, she would set off.

She tidied up a bit, and settled down.

Greenhouse gas emissions – do you care?

Buffy sat licking and sticking, in her small west London flat, in her lamplit sitting room, with its walls of antique rose, and plumped-up cushions. The bedroom wasn't large, and the kitchen and bathroom bordered on the poky, but the sitting room, with its comfortable sofa before the television and china wall plates, with Mother's inlaid desk, and the Sutherland table up against the wall – things in here, thought Buffy, writing out an address in Shropshire, certainly could be worse.

The excessive burning of oil, gas and coal is raising our planet's thermostat to unacceptable levels . . .

Would they realise, in Shropshire, just how bad things were? Buffy wondered, putting the envelope on to the pile. In Herefordshire, the floods had been fearful – two years ago a whole pig farm had been drowned. But Shropshire? She pictured a place a little less dramatic, softer, less ancient, and more prosperous.

The battle against the carbon-belching corporations has begun . . .

Buffy reached for the next envelope, crossed off the last address. Now where was she? Northumberland. Bare craggy hills, sheep huddled in snowdrifts, grey stone farmhouses, thick-walled barns. That was the pleasant thing about mailing lists – you could, in a more frivolous frame of mind, travel all over the country in a single morning.

The rain splashed into her window boxes, where the first shoots of crocuses and narcissi were nosing up.

'Hymns devout and ho-ly, devout and ho-ly psalms,' sang Buffy, and picked up the ringing phone.

'Good morning, Buffy.'

'William.' She put down her pen. 'How nice to hear you.'

'Filthy morning.'

'Isn't it? I'm doing a mailing list, about greenhouse gas emissions.'

'Ah. I'm interrupting you.'

'No, no,' she said quickly, 'I didn't mean that at all. How are you?'

'Fine. Very well. I thought I'd let you know she's arrived.'

For a moment, her mind full of fossil fuels and the Kyoto Summit, Buffy couldn't think what he meant.

'The lodger,' said William. 'The Shropshire lass. She got here last night. I rather like her.'

'Oh.'

'She's absolutely not a London person, but I think she'll fit in quite well. Danny likes her. She says she's used to dogs.'

'Oh. Good.'

'I'll probably take her out and about a bit later, so she can get her bearings.'

99

'That's a good idea.'

She pushed her pen back and forth on the blotter, letting all this sink in. 'Tell me a bit more about her.'

'Well,' said William, with some enthusiasm, 'she's quite nice to look at. Tall, and pretty supple, I suppose. She's done a lot of cycling. Short dark hair, nice country skin – I don't know what else. But easy on the eye, in a boyish sort of way.'

'Boyish,' said Buffy.

'Sort of. Perhaps that's not the right word – she's certainly not what I'd call masculine.' He gave a little laugh. 'If Claire were here she'd say I was obsessed with gender.'

'Is that the kind of thing she says these days? No wonder she's unhappy.' Buffy could hear herself sounding sharp.

'Are you all right?' asked William.

'Fine.'

'Only you sound a bit—'

'I'm fine. Perhaps I'd better get on – I've got to get this in the post, and it's my singing this afternoon.'

'What a busy person you are – I'll let you go. See you on Saturday. I've found a rather pretty little jug and sugar bowl.'

'Very good,' said Buffy, and put the phone down. She picked up the next leaflet.

The icecap in the Arctic Ocean is melting fast . . .

She stuffed it into the Northumberland envelope, and put on a stamp. The glue was beginning to make her feel queasy – she should have one of those little sponges in a dish. Well, she hadn't. She turned in her chair, to take a breather. The rain was falling faster and the sky was black as pitch. She'd put another light on. Lights on in the *morning* – what a waste, and it all contributed. The icecap was melting, and she, who cared, was using electricity in daylight. It was all a vicious circle.

Buffy got up, and switched on the lamp by the sofa. That was a bit better. But oh – how quiet it was, up here. Only the falling rain, the tick of Mother's carriage clock. She looked at her desk, with its heaps of dreadful news. Walking back to it, she caught sight of herself in the mirror over the Sutherland table, saw such a grey-looking person without her lipstick, someone to whom you wouldn't give a second glance. She licked her lips, which were dry with stamp glue.

'I was feeling quite happy,' she said aloud.

☆

'Where the bright Se-ra-phim, in burn-ing row, / Their loud, up-lift-ed an-gel Trum-pets blow...'

Their voices rose into the brightly lit upper room; the piano was triumphant; the rain was blowing away across Queen Square.

'Oh, may we *soon* a-gain re-*new* that *song,* / and *keep* in tune with Heaven...'

Michael, their young conductor, was in rapture, urging them on.

'To live with *Him,* and sing in *end*-less morn / of light...'

But this, like the beginning, was in eight parts, and Buffy found herself stumbling.

'To live with *Him*...'

An A sharp or A natural? Whatever it was, she couldn't get it.

And she gave up, and let the voices all round her soar confidently and joyously towards the ceiling.

'And sing in end-less *morn,* in *end*-less morn, in / *end*-less *morn*...'

'Right!' said Michael, looking at his watch. 'That's it – well done, see you all next week.' And they all trooped down to the café.

'Such a *tonic,*' said Sylvie Strauss, standing next to Buffy in the queue at the counter. 'Don't you just love Parry?' Sylvie was from New York, had come to London when her husband had relocated his business, in the seventies, and just fallen in love with it. Poor Ray had passed away in 1992, but she had made a good life for herself here, and hardly thought at all about going back.

'I do like it,' said Buffy, picking up a piece of carrot cake, 'but I'm afraid I'm not quite up to the eight-part sections.'

'You're a second alto? You know, I think that's harder. Up at the front with the firsts – I think we're that little bit stronger in numbers. I'll have an Earl Grey, please,' Sylvie said to the girl at the counter. 'Just a dash of milk, that's perfect, thank you so much.'

They carried the trays to the last remaining window seats. Dorothy and Stanley were already there, their macs slung over the chairs; all around them, the tables were filling up, and they could hear the front door bang open and shut, and the thunder of feet up and down the uncarpeted stairs. Stanley, who used to work for Camden Council Parks and Gardens, was staying on for Circle Dancing; had already, in the morning, done Life Drawing with Elsbeth Fermor, who'd trained at the Slade. He opened his shoulder bag, laying it flat on the table to put away his music. Buffy glimpsed within it a tin of pencils, a recorder, a pad of drawing paper and a heap of cassettes. He zipped it all up with a flourish, and took it away from the teacups.

'Such a dear old boy,' Buffy had said to William, describing the various members of the choir at Christmas, as they'd walked up the street after midnight Mass, under his umbrella. 'Left school at fourteen, all his life out in all weathers, never married, never done anything much – and now: he's an inspiration.'

'Sounds splendid,' said William, unlocking the front door. 'Rather like you, dear. How about a nightcap before we turn in?'

They'd sat before the banked-up fire with their brandy, yawning.

Oh well, thought Buffy now, shaking her sweetener into her tea. Oh well. Never mind.

The rain had gone but the light was fading: she sat looking out at the darkening square, and the toings and froings of students in the street. A group of young Italians was smoking out on the steps: they were lissom and dark and stylish, casually draping their arms over one another's shoulders, stubbing out their cigarettes, leaning against the wet railings, laughing.

'Are you all right?' asked Dorothy, the oldest soprano in the choir.

Buffy turned to her, saw a kindly look.

'Not quite yourself today?'

'I'm absolutely fine,' said Buffy, pulling herself together, and she was, why ever shouldn't she be? 'And I must give you all one of these.' She rummaged in her bag for the leaflets, and put them on the table, brushing crumbs away. 'Do take one – I'm on a new subscription drive.'

Amidst the tea cups a fierce plume of burning oil rose into the sky. Choking dark smoke blew over a tiny moon.

12

He had met her on the platform. She knew him at once, as the train pulled in: the tall, greying, well-proportioned man in his winter coat and stylishly knotted sea-green scarf, waiting in the grey afternoon with the bright little dachshund on his leash. And William, as the doors banged open and shut, saw a lean young woman in jeans and black woollen hat heave out a nylon grip and come striding down towards him – and of course this must be her, who else? He waited, the nervous excitement he had felt all morning subsiding suddenly as a lifetime's courtesy took over.

'Miss Harper?' He held out his leather-gloved hand.

'That's me.' She was fresh faced and fit, and she shook hands properly, not like some limp-wristed girl.

'William Harriman. How do you do.'

'I'm fine, thanks,' said Janice.

'May I take your bag?'

'No, no, that's OK, I'm used to lugging things about.'

She looked down at Danny, alert and bright eyed. 'Hello.' She bent down to give him a pat, as people moved past them to the gate, and the train pulled out again. 'You're nice.' Danny's ears were up, and he barked, once.

'He loves visitors,' said William, 'but he's not a yapper.'

'That's good.' She straightened up again, and they walked along the platform. 'Where I come from, there's quite a bit of yapping.'

'You have dogs at home?'

'No, no, there's only my mum's goldfish. I mean at the Dog Museum. Your cousins.'

'Ah, yes, indeed,' said William. 'This I must hear about.'

They came out of the station, and walked along the tree-lined street. Janice looked about her, taking in the tall, well-presented houses, with their tiled paths, window boxes, well-painted, solid front doors. She opened her mouth to say it was posh here, and shut it again.

'And that's us,' said William, nodding towards the cross-street at the end. Janice beheld the glossy row of arrow-head railings, the flights of steps, the wintry lilac and tulip trees.

'Wow.' She couldn't help it.

'We're the black front door, and the magnolia.' William was tugging Danny to heel. 'That's quite a sight, in the spring.'

'I bet.'

The January afternoon was growing darker; lights were coming on.

'Time for tea,' said William, getting his keys out.

'That sounds good.' And it did – not just the prospect of Earl Grey in bone china; she knew that was what it would be – but the phrase itself: orderly and graceful. She could hear her mother yell out across the back garden – 'Janice, your tea's on the table!' She could see Mary Harriman stirring the brown enamel teapot amidst the tins of Chum. As they climbed the steps she caught sight, through a gleaming high window, of firelight and a vast gilt mirror, deep in an endless room.

'Do you like muffins?' asked William, unlocking the door.

He showed her to her room, and explained that it had been his daughter's, that both the children had been up here, at the top of the house, once they were out of babyhood.

'Claire has her own family now, of course,' he said, opening white-painted cupboard doors. 'But she still keeps a few things here.'

There was a little shelf of books, and another of dolls in costume – a flamboyant Spanish dancer with a fan, a Highlander with bagpipes, kilt and tiny sporran. 'I remember buying that,' said William, following Janice's gaze. 'On her tenth birthday – we stayed in a house on a loch on the West Coast. Lovely summer – except for the midges, of course.' He closed the cupboard doors. 'Hope you'll have enough space for everything. Come down when you're ready – no rush.'

'Thanks.' Janice heard him go slowly down again, and along the broad landing where, he had shown her, were his room, the spare room – 'my wife used to sew in there' – and the bathroom. 'There's a cloakroom downstairs,' he added, 'so we won't be too much on top of one another.' She heard him murmuring to Danny, and then she

104

couldn't hear anything, as they descended into what at home they'd have called a basement, but which William had described as the bowels of the earth.

She stood in the attic room and took it in. He had put a little bunch of snowdrops on the chest of drawers: she sniffed them and was at once transported to Shropshire woodland days. There was a nursery rug by the bed – heavy cotton in pale blue and white, with a border of animals, going into the ark, over and over again. The bed itself was white and narrow, set beneath the sloping ceiling with a pale blue quilt and a bedside lamp on a white-painted locker. A china Benjamin Bunny was on the windowsill, in his Tam o'Shanter and red spotted handkerchief, with his string of onions. Beatrix Potter had been part of Janice's childhood, too. The window was curtained with more animals: pandas chewing bamboo on sky-blue chintz.

Janice, twenty-three years old, a country girl of independent spirit but limited experience of travel, stood in the room of someone else's childhood and wondered that William had put her in here, rather than the spare ex-sewing room. How strange, to give a stranger your daughter's old room, when you didn't have to. Perhaps he thought it would be comforting. You shouldn't need comforting, at twenty-three. But it sort of was.

She went to the window, overlooking the street. The sky was quite dark now, and she could see in it, everywhere she turned, the sodium glow of the city. In winter, when she looked out of her room in Curlew Gardens, she could see only the blackness of the empty fields across the road, and sometimes starlight. The bypass beyond was unlit at night, and the Shrewsbury streetlamps distant. Here, even in this secluded patch, the vast stretch of London pressed upon you.

Could you hear it, too, the city? She opened the window, and leaned out. Only a train, rattling away from the station: when it had gone, it was dead quiet. Except – she listened. Yes, there it was again, the soft, hollow hoot of an owl. A London owl, but that did feel like home. She listened, but he didn't call again, and it was getting cold. She shut the window, drew the cheerful pandas, unzipped her nylon bag, and put her Lycra leggings and walkers' socks into Claire's old chest of drawers.

They had tea by the fire, and the muffins were served in a proper silver muffin dish with a lid.

105

'Just for fun,' said William. 'I don't live like this every day.'

'No. Right. Thanks.' She helped herself, sitting on the edge of a fireside chair whose springs had long since gone and whose loose covers were frayed and worn. This was the only thing about the house which put her in mind of the cousins, though the covers here had clearly once been very good. She spread strawberry jam and sat back a bit, looking around. Being tall, Janice generally felt pretty large indoors – they were always standing back for one another in Curlew Gardens, and the lounge with the three of them in it always felt crowded. In Eric's shepherd's hut . . . She refused to think of this. At Albert's she had to duck in the doorways; in Cloud Nine the kitchen was tiny. At the Dog Museum – well, it was full of dogs. But here—

'No butter?' William asked.

'I'm a vegan, remember,' she said. 'That's why I said no milk.'

'Oh, dear,' said William. 'Oh, dear. I'm afraid I don't know much about vegans. I'd rather put this aspect of things to the back of my mind.'

'Never mind,' said Janice, wondering whether the muffins had whey in them. Well, she couldn't ask to see the packet now, not when she'd just arrived. 'I'm sure we'll manage.'

'But—' He watched her, sipping milkless Earl Grey tea, from a pink-and-green Minton cup: his favourite tea set. 'How are we to—' He'd have to think about every ingredient. What was he to do about supper? He'd been in the kitchen all morning, and a liver-and-bacon casserole had just gone into the oven. 'I'm getting old and forgetful,' he said. 'I pretend it isn't so, but I'm clearly losing it.'

He looked so distressed that Janice said quickly, 'Please – please don't worry. I'm not expecting you to cook for me. And I've brought some stuff to start me off.'

'Stuff?' wondered William, reaching for the teapot.

'Soya milk. Soya protein and spread.'

'But isn't it all—' He poured them both more tea, thinking all at once of Buffy. 'Isn't it all genetically modified?'

'Not *all*. It says on the labels, doesn't it: GM free. Where's your nearest health shop?'

William had no idea.

'I'll find it,' said Janice. 'There's bound to be one somewhere.'

'The certainty of youth.' He lifted the lid of the muffin dish, as his mother had done all through his own youth. 'Do have another.'

'I'm fine, thanks.' She leaned back in the chair, surprisingly comfortable, and tried to take in the room. Fitted bookcases, crammed with hardbacks; gently lit alcoves of china cups and saucers, jugs and coffee pots; a carved oak corner cupboard, overflowing desk, worn sofa, the fireplace with its clock, and candlesticks, dark woven rugs on old pale carpet, the flickering fire, the heavy curtains – and the height of those windows, the space of it all. She could see herself walking slowly from one end to the other, stopping at a bookcase, reading on the sofa for whole afternoons, space and quiet all about her. She could feel how you might, in such a room, expand your whole sense of yourself, in ways which until now she had only ever glimpsed when cycling over the hills in summer, the valley stretching away below and the sky magnificent. She put down her cup, and felt suddenly excited.

'More tea?' asked William, watching her.

'No, I'm fine, thanks,' she said again.

Between them, on the hearth-rug, Danny gave a little twitch in his sleep, and then another. She reached down to pat him, and he opened a contented eye.

'Seems funny having only one dog.'

'Now, this museum,' said William. 'Tell me.'

So she did. She told him about the dilapidated huts, with their extraordinary interiors: the scenes of hunting, of dramatic rescues and domestic help; the vivid painted backdrops in the booths, and stuffed-toy enormities of dog and handler: huntsman, housewife – deaf housewife, she added – ringmaster, Eskimo. She described the vast St Bernard, with his felt tongue, furry ears and keg of brandy, guarding the fallen climber in a heap of polystyrene snow; and the burning African veldt, beyond the drowning daughter.

'And *Ernie* did all this?' asked William, putting down his teacup. '*Ernie*?' he said again.

'He did,' said Janice. 'A long time ago. Now he lives in a manky old caravan out in the yard.'

And she told him about the pens, the makeshift kennels, the countless dogs up at the wire, whom she took walking, with the house dogs—

'*How* many?' William interrupted. 'How many all in all?'

'About forty? Fifty? It changes all the time, they come and go, they're always looking out for homes, they have an ad in the *Shropshire Star* every week, in the Pets column.'

'Who pays for that?'

'God knows. Scrimps of pension, I suppose, with the three of them. And in summer they do get visitors. We have an ad for them up in Cloud Nine.'

'Cloud Nine?'

So she described the hilltop café, too, but briefly because he was naturally more interested in the poor old cousins, who at this moment would be shutting up the hens for the night, and taking the house dogs out for a last run down the lane.

'You don't walk all those dogs all at once?'

'No, no, in shifts.'

'And they're all strays.'

She could see him trying to imagine it all. 'Pretty much. Some were born there – it's expensive getting them spayed, and besides—' She stopped, remembering a morning the previous spring when Ernie had come out to greet her with two soft-faced puppies nestling inside his jacket. She had never seen him look so happy.

'They can't resist the puppies?' William guessed. He shook his head. 'Well, well, well. And what's the house like these days?'

Janice had never been upstairs, could only wonder about the bedrooms, didn't want to think about the bathroom. She painted a picture of the kitchen, the heaps of dogs snoring on the hearth, Mary washing extraordinary garments at the sink, Sophie mopping the tiled floor. The walls were bulging and the paintwork gone; now and then you met a hen, nesting on a heap of local papers, and the draining boards ran with silverfish.

'Good Lord,' said William. 'Dear, oh dear, oh dear.'

'Sophie's tried to explain how you are related,' said Janice, stroking Danny's haunches with her foot. 'I couldn't quite get it.'

'You're not alone there,' he said. 'Some distant ancient alliance – I've never really focused on the exact connection, I'm afraid. But anyway—' He looked at her, from across the fireside, and gave her a little smile. 'Here you are, my dear, by a strange concatenation of circumstances. And what shall we do about supper?'

Winter. Whole blimming world shut down by teatime. Ernie, out in the trailer, lit the paraffin lamp and stirred his enamel mug. Both objects had been in the family for generations: his dad and his granddad had swung that lamp in them pitch-dark lanes, setting off for the milking at some ungodly hour, tramping through iced-up puddles and frozen mud with its beam going this way and that before them; hanging it up on the hook in the Broxwood milking parlour and a lot of other cowsheds, too: they'd had to go where the work was, though Dad had been lucky to settle at Broxwood in the end, good steady job to finish up with. But blimming heck, what a life, week in, week out in all weathers.

> Oh, the country, the country,
> The country gets you down.
> There's nothing like the country
> To make you want the town . . .

Good little song, that, though he couldn't think where he'd heard it. Something on the wireless, no doubt, and he reached out and turned it on, waiting through some daft short story for the news, smoking and sipping his tea. Must be forty years old, this mug, carried with the sandwiches down to the farms, going up to the house for a fill. 'Thank you very much, ma'am.' They'd manners, in them days.

Beneath the table, Pip lay at his feet, and took the chill off; through the window he could see across the yard to the house, where a single light was on in the kitchen, and old Mary was at the table, scraping out tins into bowls and shouting. They'd all be round her, and supplies was getting low. He watched her shake out scraps from a pan, eking it all out till they got into town again.

Have to do it all themselves, now. None of that cheerful ring of the bike bell coming up the lane, none of that striding into the kitchen with the bags. None of that chat, the sharing a bit of a smoke.

'What did she want to go and do that for?' he said, nudging Pip with his foot. 'We was going on all right.'

William had the casserole, Janice had wholewheat pasta. He opened a bottle of wine; they ate in the kitchen.

'Would you mind if I smoked?' she asked him afterwards, as he poured coffee beans into the grinder.

This was something else he had not considered. Had she mentioned smoking in her letters? He folded down the packet of Dark Italian Roast, and put it back in the tin – a rather nice tin, black and gold and Chinese red. 'I'd rather you didn't smoke in the bedroom.'

'Oh, I won't,' said Janice, who had imagined just that – a long quiet unwinding with her tin and her book, on the blue-and-white quilt. 'I won't smoke now, if you don't like it.'

'No, no. Go ahead. Please.' He found her an ashtray, switched on the grinder. The room filled with the pleasantly mingling smells of the casserole, the last of a very good claret, freshly ground coffee, and cigarette smoke. He watched her lean back in her chair, inhaling on a roll-up, taken ready made from her Golden Virginia tin. She looked completely at home.

'And what are your plans?' William asked her, as they sat over tiny Coalport coffee cups, last used at Christmas, with Buffy and Matthew, sitting at the polished dining-room table, in the candlelight. Janice held hers with enormous care: this was pleasing, and she had good hands, he noticed, strong and slender, with flat, well-kept nails.

'I'm not sure yet,' she said, putting the cup down. 'It's rather early days.'

'Yes, yes, of course. No rush. But is there anything you'd like to do tomorrow?'

'Get my bearings a bit? Have a look round the shops?' She yawned. 'Sorry. I suppose I should look at the papers. Find some kind of agency.'

'Agency,' said William. 'The papers. Yes – I suppose that's right. I wonder if perhaps my daughter . . . well, we'll see. More coffee?'

'I think I'll turn in, if that's all right.' Janice took a last puff, and stubbed out the roll-up. 'Can I wash up?'

'No, no, we have a machine.' He watched her pick up her tin, and get to her feet. 'I'm sure you'd like a bath, after your long day. Do help yourself to things up there. Did you find the towels?'

'Yes, I did.' She gave him an easy smile. 'Thanks for everything. It's all great.'

'Very nice to have you here. Sleep well.'

Upstairs, Janice lay in a foaming scented bath and watched the clouds of steam rise past painted tiles. The soap lay in a scallop, on whose edge knelt a smiling cherub. Sprigged wallpaper was peeling away from the corners, and the white-painted bookcase next to the towel rail was full of the kind of old green and orange Penguins you found in the second-hand bookshop in Welshpool: here, they looked as if they'd been untouched for decades, their spines stained with steam. Part of the furniture, like the white wicker chair; part of Claire and Matthew's childhood, she supposed.

Apart from the brief introductions to the costume dolls, they had hardly talked about William's children since her arrival. There were photographs in the drawing room, but she had not taken them in, and he had not shown her. They had talked, in fact, almost entirely about people he had not seen for twenty years, and whose strangeness he must be struggling to imagine.

After less than twenty-four hours, she found it hard to imagine them all herself.

She swished hot scented water around her. Whose scent? She looked through the clouds of steam at the pretty glass bottles on the corner of the bath. An old bath, with limescaled taps and chipped enamel. And rather old bath oil, now she came to look at it, the labels faded, and the bottles almost empty. Could they have belonged to William's wife? Hadn't she died years and years ago?

Getting out, drying herself on an enormous lavender towel, Janice knew that the bottles must, indeed, have belonged to Eve, who, like William, had clearly known how to buy things that aged well, that lasted.

But fancy keeping your wife's old bath oils. Did he – no, surely he didn't – he didn't use them, did he? Flushed with her hot bath, the towel wrapped around her, Janice bent to look at the bottles more closely. Their glass stoppers were tight; she had taken one out with some difficulty, she recalled. No – he wasn't using them, just kept them to look at, and remember.

How touching.

How fantastic, to love someone like that.

She pulled on her nightshirt, brushed her teeth, brushed her damp hair, rubbed away the film of steam on the mirror, and looked at herself. She looked completely different from how she looked at home.

Some time later, after he had done all his jobs – loaded the machine, booted Danny out into the garden, put out the milk bottles, whistled Danny in again, locked up, raked the fire, put the guard up; God, what a lot you had to do, just to go to bed – William slowly climbed the stairs, switching lights off. He stopped on the landing, suddenly assailed with memory and longing.

Darling?

He almost called out, but he didn't, just stood there, while Eve, years and years ago, had her bath, the wireless murmuring, her bath scent wafting out, drifting, like her laughter at a play – in the days when there were plays you could laugh at – along the landing, into their bedroom, where he got undressed, and pulled on pyjamas and dressing gown and went along to brush his teeth and sit on the bathroom chair, and chat.

Oh, sweetheart.

He closed his eyes, as the last threads of steam, filled with roses and lavender and something indefinable, entire unto itself, floated through his house in winter, and disappeared.

13

Within three days, Janice had found a job. She was working in a wine bar in the Village, where, as chance would have it, a Polish girl called Danuta, who wanted to make experimental films, had been taken on by a small independent production company the very week before.

'Too good a chance,' the manager told Janice, when she had her interview. There'd been a notice for part-time staff in the window. I could do that, thought Janice. Easy. And in she walked, and got it, just like that. 'They're called Egret Films,' said the manager, a woman in her forties called Sandra, who had smoked and drunk too much all her life. You could see, soon as you saw her – open pores, bags beneath the eyes. 'Have you ever heard of them?' Janice said she hadn't. 'Very hip,' said Sandra darkly. 'I expect she sees herself at the London Film Festival, with some erotic little short.' Janice didn't know what she was talking about. 'Anyway, she was off, with two days' notice. In the week it's not so much of a problem, but the weekends—' She blew out smoke expressively, indicating crowds and drama. 'What do you know about wine?'

'Not a lot,' said Janice, 'but I'm a fast learner. And I've got a lot of experience of restaurant work. I'm good with customers. All sorts,' she added, for it was true.

'References?'

'On their way.'

'P45?'

'What?'

'P45 – from your last employers.'

'Oh, right, yes, of course. I've been self-employed, on the whole.' And she gave an edited version of her working life to date, highlighting charity work, and volunteering. And that was that. Friday to Sunday, lunch-times and evenings. And Tuesday and Thursday evenings, when it wasn't so busy. 'We're closed on Mondays, and the lunch-times I can manage, on the whole; it's pretty quiet. On Wednesdays I have a young man. As it were. Good.' She held out her hand, bedecked with designer steel. 'See you tomorrow. In at the deep end, but you look pretty competent.'

'I am,' said Janice. 'Is this your own place?' she asked, as they walked out of the smoke-filled back office, across the hardwood floor. There were little marble tables, each with a slender vase, and a spray of white freesias, and the bar was high and swish looking. Everything was neutral, or white on white, and the chairs were black and chrome.

'It is now,' said Sandra, pausing to straighten a chair. 'I bought it with my husband, but he left me for a girl of twenty, the bastard. I made sure I got this in the settlement, though he got the flat, the shit. Now I live over the shop.' She yanked open the plate-glass door. 'He was always touching up the staff. Danuta told me he'd tried it on with her, once, but she's a tough little thing, got her eyes on something a bit more than a failed actor.' She stepped aside for the first lunch-hour arrivals. 'Be with you in just a moment. She flashed them a smile. 'Anyway, good riddance, that's how I feel now,' she said to Janice. 'Thank Christ we had no kids.' She looked at her, about to reimmerse herself in the cold, pulling on her black woollen cap once more. 'He'd have had more sense than to try it on with you.'

'Yeah, well, right,' said Janice, not sure how she should take this. 'See you tomorrow.'

''Bye now.' And Sandra closed the door.

Janice went off through the Village. She bought a spinach-and-onion samosa and a small bar of Green & Black vegan chocolate at the health shop, and she went to the library and asked how to enrol, and whether they had books about wine, which they assured her they had. She walked home, eating the chocolate.

'I've got a job,' she told William, at lunch-time. 'And can you sign this, as a proof of address?'

'How clever you are,' said William, putting his glasses on. 'And this is for the library?'

'I've finished *Great Expectations*, and I've got to find out about wine.'

'Wine,' said William, happily. 'Now there I can tell you all you need to know.'

☆

Within a week, a routine, and a way of life, were established. Janice stocked up her shelves in the kitchen cupboard, which William had cleared of a quantity of long-forgotten jars of Marmite, ancient stock cubes, curry powder, jams with a growth of pale furry mould. 'Good Lord.' He chucked it all away, and asked Mrs T. if she wouldn't mind getting up on a chair and giving the whole thing a good scrub. He thought there were weevils.

'There would be,' she said, clambering up for a look. 'I'd be surprised if you didn't have mice.'

'All old houses have mice,' said William firmly, making her tea. 'It's part of their character.'

Now the shelves were full of packs of organic raisins, wholewheat noodles, bags of soya mince, chick peas, lentils, and tins of beans. This last, at least, he recognised. His semi-skimmed milk stood in the fridge beside cartons of soya milk enriched with vitamins and calcium. A box of sunflower spread, a cheerful yellow, rested on top of soya sausages, in Country Herb and Tomato & Garlic guises. A Cranks wholemeal load was in the bread bin, and the vegetable rack was fuller than it had ever been. He'd never seen so many swedes and parsnips. As for the fruit bowl—

'I must say you do look well on it all,' he told Janice, over their breakfast of coffee and toast and fresh orange juice.

'It's a very healthy diet,' she said. 'People don't realise.'

'But the iron,' he muttered, thinking of his liver casserole.

'There's loads of iron in spinach.'

He thought of Popeye, and the children rolling about.

'You must meet my daughter,' he said, reaching for the coffee pot. 'And my son.' What a lot there was to arrange, and think about. 'And one day you must come and visit the stall. You'd love it. And we must show you something of London, after all.'

After breakfast, they went their separate ways, though on the first weekend they'd gone together to the park, for Danny's constitutional. 'Now you know where it is,' said William, throwing a stick, 'you might like to bring him here yourself, when you feel like a breath of fresh air.'

'I thought I'd put my dog-walking days behind me,' said Janice, bending to pat Danny's eager little shape, as he came running back. But she did take him now and then, needing to stretch her legs after the unaccustomed days spent reading, or working in the wine bar. She strode beneath the trees in her zipped-up navy jacket, leggings and vegan-version Doc Martens, her hat pulled down, Danny's expensive lead in her gloved hands.

'You can get fabric leads,' she told William, on her return. 'They don't have to be leather.'

'I'm a leather sort of person,' he said, with finality, and that was that.

He spent two evenings telling her about wine, pulling down books about French vineyards, the wine-growing regions of Italy, the soil, the sun. Of course, he told her, there were fine Australian and Californian wines, no doubt about it, but the European wines – now there, there was *history*. And he told her about summer holidays with his wife, motoring down to the Auvergne, staying in sun-baked villages, lunching for hours; about the cheeses, the old boys playing boules beneath the trees, the peeling, faded blue shutters. 'I'm sorry,' he said at last, closing the books and throwing a log on the fire. 'I'm getting carried away.'

Once Janice started working, they pretty much stopped eating together. She came down late, long after William had breakfasted with the paper, and taken Danny out to the shops. On Wednesday he was on the Camden Passage stall – you could come then, he said, since it's your day off, and she said that she would, one day, and he sensed that he might be crowding her, and left it for a bit. But he came home from the stall that evening to find the house full of an interesting smell, and put down his boxes of china in the hall and went down with Danny to find Janice in the kitchen, and the red-checked tablecloth laid for two. A pan of parsnip soup stood piping on the stove, and a dish of pasta was in the oven. 'Well, well,' he said, pulling the cork of a bottle of 1998 Beaujolais, 'this is a bit of all right.' He told her about the stall, and the sale of a 1976 Denby thatched cottage for £65.

'Sounds like the kind of thing my gran used to have,' said Janice, ladling the soup, which he found perfectly delicious. After that, she cooked a vegan supper for him every Wednesday. They settled down, and it felt as if he'd always known her.

And then, at last, he had a reply from Matthew's consultant, apologising for the delay, offering an appointment at the end of February. He looked at the calendar. Then he rang Claire, to tell her – something specific to talk about, so it didn't seem as if he was pestering. He realised, dialling the number, that they hadn't spoken for almost three weeks. Good Lord.

'Hello, darling.'

'Oh. Hello.'

'Just thought I'd ring for a chat. How are you?'

'Fine. How are you?'

'Very well,' he said, and meant it. 'Very well indeed. Couple of bits of news.' And he told her about the hospital letter, reading it out to her as he sat in the hall, swinging his foot. 'I don't suppose you'd like to come?' he said tentatively. 'Someone else in the family – give a proper picture of how Matthew used to be.'

'They know how he used to be, you've told them often enough.'

William took a long, deep breath.

'What other news did you have?' asked Claire. 'Only I've got to go out in a minute.'

'I've got a lodger,' he told her, as the key turned in the lock. Ah, here she was, coming in with Danny close behind, and an armful of library books. And here, right behind her, came Mrs T. puffing up the steps. Quite a houseful.

'What?' She was suddenly alert.

'I've got a lodger,' he said again, smiling at everyone, as Janice went on up the stairs with a cheerful nod, and Mrs T. and Danny went down to the kitchen. And he told her all about it. 'Remember the mad old cousins?'

'Yes,' she said curtly. 'I do. And where's this girl sleeping?'

He felt a little twist of anxiety. 'I've put her in your old room,' he said brightly.

'What?'

'It's so nice and sunny up there. You know what the spare room is like. Those rooms at the back never get the sun.'

'They get plenty of sun. That's my room.'

'Oh, darling—'

'Don't darling me. How dare you let my room without permission?'

'Oh, come, come—'

'Come, come nothing. It's *my* room.'

William, though it was barely lunch-time, felt the strong urge for a glass of Scotch. And for conversation with Buffy. 'That girl,' he could hear her saying briskly, 'needs a good smacked bottom.' He'd ring her at teatime.

'It's only for a little while,' he said to Claire now, keeping his voice steady.

'What's a little while? A lodger's a lodger. Has she got a job?'

'She has, as a matter of fact.' He started to tell her about the wine bar, but Claire cut him off.

'She's obviously *dug in*. If she comes from those crackpots in Shropshire we'll never get rid of her.'

This, William realised, with a different kind of painful little twist to the heart, was the first time for years that he could recall his daughter conjoining them with this pronoun. We, he thought longingly, swinging his foot more slowly now. How long is it since we've been that?

'I'm coming over,' said Claire. 'I'll come after lunch and meet her.'

'I thought you were going out.'

'This is more important. I'll come before picking up Geraldine.'

'How is she?'

'Perfectly well.' And she put the phone down.

William went into the drawing room, and poured himself the Scotch. The room was full of pale February sunshine, wintry but lighter, definitely lighter, and he realised it had not rained for days. Or had it? He hadn't been so much aware of the weather these last few weeks. He held up his glass to the light with a trembling hand.

'You *mustn't* let her get to you,' he could hear Buffy saying, but how could he help it? Your children were your children – everything they did was important, everything mattered. And if they turned against you—

'Mr Harriman? Fancy a tin of soup?' Mrs T. was in the doorway. She was wearing a knitted maroon cardigan today, with a cable-knit front, and pockets. She'd always been a terrific knitter; she and Eve used to discuss patterns, polishing the silver together.

He put his hand across his eyes.

'There's winter veg or tomato,' Mrs T. went on, impervious.

'I think—' He knew there was fresh leek and potato, made by Janice yesterday, with coriander and dill snipped in, but he hadn't the energy or heart to say so.

'Anything.' And he took his glass to the window, turning his back.

For a moment Mrs T. was silent. Then she said, 'We'll have the tomato, then,' and stumped off.

☆

118

He rallied. Scotch always helped. At lunch, he announced to Janice, taking her leek-and-potato soup from a blue Cornish Ware bowl, and to Mrs T., dunking her bread in the Heinz tomato, 'Claire's coming over this afternoon.'

'Is she? That's nice.' Mrs T. wiped the bread round her empty bowl, and got up. 'Cuppa tea, anyone?'

'Not for me, thanks.' Janice reached for the fruit bowl. 'She doesn't mind me having her old room, does she?' she asked William.

'No, no, of course not—' For what could he say? 'Why ever should she?'

'She might. People have special feelings about childhood rooms, don't they?' Not that she'd care who had her room in Curlew Gardens, they were welcome to it.

'Do they?' He supposed they did. Certainly he would never have considered letting Matthew's room, but that was different, Matthew was coming home one day. Oh, dear, how thoughtless he had been about Claire – no wonder he drove her mad.

And did she speak the truth, about their family? Was it really possible that he hadn't known Matthew at all? Was that really why he—

'Anyway, I'm glad I'm meeting her,' said Janice. 'Then I'm going out.'

'Where?' Oh, dear – how rude that sounded.

'Think it's time I crossed the water, saw the sights.' She was munching on an organic apple. 'They'll never believe at home that I've been to London, otherwise.'

'How are they all? At home? Getting on all right without you?'

'Oh, yes.'

They'd spoken once, on the phone.

'What's it like?' Her mother was breathless with anxiety.

'It's great, it's really nice.' She was standing in the spacious hall, light flooding through the stained-glass panels. 'It's . . . I'll write and tell you.'

'He isn't mad? He isn't like—'

'No,' said Janice. 'He absolutely isn't.'

And looking at William now, across the kitchen table – a little out of sorts today? – she thought how clever old Mary had been, to know that she'd like it here, and would, improbable as it seemed, fit in.

The doorbell rang just after two.

'Want me to get that?' shouted Mrs T., still in the kitchen.

'No, no, it's all right.' William, bracing himself by the fire, got to his feet. He supposed, if Claire and he had been closer, she'd have had a key – she did have one, surely she did; when Eve was alive she used to come and go, letting herself in, hugging her mother in the hall. 'Sorry I snapped.' 'Darling, it doesn't matter, I understand. You've got a lot to think about.' She hadn't even had the children then.

He was in the hall; he could see her square, determined shape at the door.

'Darling, come on in.'

'Hello.' She was brushing past him, looking around. She was wearing a grey jacket, and a long grey scarf – a good scarf, perfectly good, but it made her look like a schoolgirl, somehow, or at least a student, though the rest of her looked like exactly what she was: a clever, nicely heeled middle-class mother, just past her best. Hard to remember what Claire's best had looked like, quite – for a wild, disloyal moment, following her into the drawing room, he found himself thinking of Clare Short, then checked this at once. But certainly she had nothing of Eve's delicate bones, or pink-and-white skin, or gentle manner. Matthew had the Harriman height, the nose. Before he was ill, he had had the charm – still had it, buried somewhere, visible now and then with that sweet, vague smile.

But Claire—

'Well?' She was looking around the drawing room. 'Didn't you say I was coming to meet her?'

'She's upstairs – I'll call her.'

'She's in my room.'

'Oh, darling—' He strode back into the hall. 'Janice! Janice, can you hear me? Do come down for a minute.'

'Coming!' yelled Janice, who had been opening the window to get rid of the smell of cigarette smoke. Had it done the trick? She left it open, the early afternoon sun, infused with just the faintest hint of spring, falling on to the blue-and-white bed, the blue-and-white animals, going round and round the ark. It was the kind of thing you might put by your own child's bed, having loved it all through your childhood, made up names for the animals, knelt on it to say your prayers, if you said them. But Claire had left it here.

'Coming!' she called again, with a last wave at the lingering Golden Virginia, and she ran downstairs.

☆

Bloody hell, she looked just like Mary.

'My daughter Claire,' said William, his hand hovering behind her shoulders. 'Claire, this is Janice Harper.'

'How do you do?'

'Fine, thanks,' said Janice, stepping forward. She shook Claire's hand in the firm and friendly fashion which was partly instinctive and partly intentional, in that she knew it won her over to people. 'How are you?'

'Oh – I'm well, thank you,' said Claire.

There was a little pause, in which the sharp smell of Flash came powerfully into everyone's consciousness, as Mrs T. did her stuff downstairs. They could hear her, pulling chairs out, sloshing away.

'Well, now,' said William. 'Well, now. Coffee?'

'Not for me, thanks,' said Janice.

'You won't be able to make it, will you?' said Claire. 'Not with Mrs T. down there. Anyway, I've just had some.'

Janice regarded her sharp brown eyes, her furious tension. Mary to the life.

'It's ever so nice of your dad to let me stay here,' she tried, and meant it. 'Can't be easy, sharing the house when you've been on your own a long time.'

'It's doing me a lot of good,' William said warmly. 'Very nice to have a young person about the place again.'

'I hear you're working locally,' said Claire, still in full override mode, still looking at Janice.

'Yeah, that's right. In this wine bar. It's good.'

'In the Village? Not Drake's?'

'That's it. Do you go there?'

'Very occasionally. You don't go to wine bars much when you have three young children.'

'No, I bet.'

They were all still standing in the middle of the room. Down in the lower depths, Mrs T. had started singing.

'Oh, I want to be alone, oh I want to be alone, / Oh, I want to be alone with Mary Brown . . .'

'Goodness,' said William, 'that's going back a bit. I can remember my father singing that in the bath.' He looked at the two women, the one so square and fearsome, the other tall and leggy, so full of youth and promise.

'When I *see* her in the park, when I *kiss* her in the dark, / Then I tell her she's the nicest girl in town . . .'

Mrs T. was in full throttle.

'We used to play that on seventy-eights,' he said wistfully. 'Don't suppose you'd have met a seventy-eight,' he added to Janice.

'Bit before my time. We're all digital now.'

'Are we really?'

'Oh, for God's sake,' said Claire, but she sounded just marginally less violent, and looking at her sudden, softening smile, Janice was put in mind of Mary in milder mode, patting one of the smaller dogs, or greeting them all when they came home for walks.

'Hello, my beauties, that's it, wag, wag, wag.'

'I say, do sit down everyone,' said William, coming to. 'What are we all doing, standing about?'

'I told you I was just dropping in,' said Claire, her eyes on Janice. 'My father says you're renting my old room,' she went on, but though William inwardly flinched at what this might turn into, her tone was less querulous and shrill. Janice had this effect on people, he realised, hearing her easy 'Yes, that's right'. I felt at ease with her at once, she's a good fitter-in.

'Must seem a bit funny,' she went on. 'Do you want to come up and see it? I've not changed anything, just sort of put my things there.'

'As one would,' said Claire kindly. She looked at her watch. 'I'm picking up my youngest in half an hour.'

'How old's your youngest, then?'

'Just four. She's still at nursery, going into reception in September.'

'That's nice.'

'Geraldine,' said William. 'Lovely child. And how are the boys?' he asked Claire, then rather wished he hadn't, as she launched into a full account of SATs, standards, underlying anxieties manifesting themselves in rudeness, calling on all one's parental skills.

God, had there ever been such mothers as there were now? When he and Eve had been young parents they'd never gone on like this, he was sure of it. School was school, and home was home, and that was it, wasn't it? What a fuss these days.

And *that* was why Matthew broke down, he could hear Claire accusing him, over and over again. Because *you* never noticed *anything*.

'I told you I'd heard from Matthew's consultant, didn't I?' he said absently, staunching the flow.

'Yes, you did, you know you did, and no, I don't want to come to a meeting at the moment.' She turned back to Janice, who had been listening politely. 'Right, then. Let's have a look.'

'After you,' said Janice, stepping aside at the door.

'No, go ahead – it's your room now.'

'Not really.'

'Well, you know what I mean.'

Somehow they entered the hall.

'On Ilkley Moor bah't'at,' sang Mrs. T., lugging the Hoover upstairs. 'Oh, hello, Claire, haven't seen you for a long time. Going on all right?'

They climbed the stairs, with their worn eau de Nil carpet beneath brass runners. The walls were hung, all the way up, with watercolours, little oils, sepia family photographs. 'This is my father, just after he was called to the Bar,' William had told Janice, taking her up through them all one evening.

'After what?' she said, looking at the weird white wig and cravat.

'Ah,' he said, with his nice kind smile. 'A different kind of bar from the one you're working in, of course,' and he explained, in the nicest way. Anyone else might have made you feel an idiot.

'And this is Eve's grandmother . . .' He pointed to a delicate young woman with her hair piled up, in a beautiful dress, all soft and cloudy. 'Chiffon – those were the days. I don't suppose any of you young things wear it now.'

'No,' said Janice, in her Lycra jacket with the yellow stripe. 'Not really.'

There were no photographs of the cousins, and she had remarked on this. William shook his head. 'Don't know why. I'm sure we had one of Edna somewhere . . . Edna's their mother, of course,' he added.

'Yes,' said Janice, recalling the fearful, hatchet-faced visage on the museum mantelpiece.

And had there been pictures of Edna, or of her curious offspring, she realised now, following Claire up to the top floor, then William might have noticed the unmistakable family resemblance between Mary Harriman and his daughter, now she was grown up. In childhood, of course, it was hard to tell just who anyone was going to turn out like. Which perhaps was just as well.

'Gosh, what a climb,' said Claire, on the top landing. 'We used to race up and down these stairs.' The winter afternoon sun was spilling from the open door of Janice's room on to the carpet. Claire glanced at Matthew's room, the door of which was closed. For a moment, Janice detected a fleeting, quite different expression on the well-defined features – a sadness, a tenderness, and something indefinable, which was at once shut down as she gestured to her own long-uninhabited bedroom.

'Go ahead,' she said, with a little twisting smile.

And Janice went ahead, and pushed the door wide, and held it aside – what a lot of this there was today; she couldn't remember feeling so self-conscious, so mindful of her manners – and Claire crossed the threshold.

For a moment she did not speak. She stood looking about her: at the shelf of Beatrix Potter books, and Ardizzone's *Little Tim*, at the costume dolls smiling blankly into the sunlight, at the rug with its ark and animals, the open window on to the town garden, and the blackbird's song, which downstairs no one had noticed, what with Mrs T., though Janice had become aware of his visits, his perch high up on the magnolia, set amidst mossy flags.

'Well,' said Claire at last. 'Well, at least you haven't ruined it.'

'I hope not,' said Janice carefully. She saw with Claire's eyes the heap of books on the bedside table – Emily Dickinson, brought from home, and *Great Expectations*, likewise, and the Dulwich library books – Peter Ackroyd's *London*, and *Hawksmoor*, and William's books on wine, which he'd lent her, and which, she knew, she was the first person to open for years and years. The ashtray had been washed, and slipped into the drawer, and there wasn't the faintest trace of smoke. She saw Claire's eyes flicker over the spines of the books, the jackets hung on the back of the door, her hat on the top hook, the trainers and boots in the corner, a few papers on the desk, and really nothing else to see, was there? She'd hardly been in the place five minutes.

'All right?' she asked, and Claire said quietly, 'Yes, of course, it's fine.' She walked across to the narrow bed, and made to sit down, then quickly drew back. 'Sorry, what am I thinking of?'

'It doesn't matter. It's fine, really.'

But Claire was looking at her watch again. 'I must be going. I hate to keep Geraldine waiting.'

'Must be a lot of work,' said Janice politely. 'Three children.'

'You can't imagine. I must say, I had no idea.' Claire was at the casement window, looking down. 'There used to be bars on here, when we were little,' she said. 'I made them take them off, when I was ten.' She leaned out, past Benjamin Bunny, shining in the sun with his red-spotted handkerchief. 'It's quite a drop, I must say.' For a second her voice held a real chill; then she had moved away, was back in the middle of the room, and smiling at Janice, warm and direct.

'Thanks for letting me have a look. Old times' sake and all that.'

'It's a pleasure,' said Janice. 'Any time.' Beyond the open window, the still winter air and quiet, empty street were filled with the blackbird's song – gosh, but that bird could sing, she hadn't imagined a London bird could sound so—

Claire was at the door, checking the time again. They went back down the stairs.

'I don't suppose,' she said, as they came to the lower landing, 'that you'd ever be free for some baby-sitting? I expect that wine bar keeps you pretty busy.'

'It does,' said Janice, rounding the corner. 'But yeah – one day, why not?'

Her heart leapt when she heard his voice.

'My dear. How nice to hear you.'

'Hello, Buffy,' William said again, warmly. 'Hello, old girl.'

She did wish he wouldn't call her that.

'How are things?' she asked him, leaning forward to turn the television down. It was the wildlife slot: zebra were thundering past a crouching lion, to ghastly technomusic. In a moment, they'd show the whole kill, she knew it: the rending of limbs, the shriek, the rolling eye – sometimes it looked as if they'd planted a camera right under the lion's chin. She wouldn't put it past them. In the old days, with David Attenborough, they used to cut away at the kill, move to flamingos or something. Gnus. And the music was proper music, too. Now you had to see every dreadful moment, all with this awful hiss-buzz-buzz, as if you were in a club.

'What did you say?' she asked him, one eye on the screen.

'I said things are pretty good,' said William, and she could sense he was holding a glass, as she was. She raised it to him.

'Cheers.'

'Cheers.' He did sound bright. 'Just thought I'd give you a ring – had quite a day.'

'Oh?' It was Monday, Mrs T.'s day, if she remembered rightly. What sort of a day could you have with Mrs T.? Something to do with that girl, she thought, the Shropshire lass, and braced herself.

'Claire came over,' William was saying. 'She'd got in a frightful state on the phone, you know what she's like – thinking of you, old thing, was the only way I got through it.'

Still have my uses, then, thought Buffy. And she cradled her drink, as jackals crowded round the carcass, and looked away, and listened.

'She's quite a girl,' said William, finishing the story. 'By the time Claire went she was a different person, quite won over. Even kissed me goodbye.' In truth it had been the merest brush of the lips, barely a peck – but still. This was progress – this, considering the phone call, was something of a miracle. He'd stood on the step, watching her hurry out of the gate and get in the car, turning to raise her hand and nod, before she drove away. And he went on standing there, as the light began to go, hearing the blackbird, liquid and exquisite, with Danny beside him on the step. From deep in the house came the sound of the Hoover, and footsteps, running down the stairs. It almost felt like the old days – everyone getting on with things, civilised and affectionate.

Was that how it had been?

'I'm off now,' said Janice, and he turned to see her, pulling her gloves on in the hall.

'It's getting dark,' he told her, putting out a hand. 'Surely you don't want to go up to town in the dark.'

'Oh, I shan't be long, I don't suppose. I would've gone earlier, but—'

'We delayed you. I'm so sorry.'

'No, no, it was great. Right, then.' She bent to give Danny a pat.

'I'll walk you up to the station,' said William. 'He's longing for a little turn, aren't you, old chap?'

'There's no need—'

'It's no trouble.' And he took down the lead, and his things from the coatrack, and off they set, the blackbird singing his heart out behind them, and the lights everywhere coming on for tea.

'Should get the three forty-five,' said William checking his watch. 'I was hoping to show you some of the sights myself. What are you going to do?' For she was, after all, a young woman of twenty-three, and he mustn't fuss round her, mustn't feel anxious about her, setting off into the city, as darkness fell.

'Just thought I'd look round, really.'

'A splendid skyline from London Bridge,' he told her. 'St Paul's, the NatWest Tower. And the Millennium Bridge, of course, not that anyone can use it.' And he started to explain: about the disconcerting creak and sway, the sudden closure.

'Gosh,' said Janice, and then: 'Look! There's a train! 'Bye!' And she ran off like a hare, up the last stretch of the street and through the station gate, and was gone.

'Quite a sprinter,' he said to Buffy now, reaching for the whisky. He leaned back in his chair. The fire was lit, and the house smelled pleasingly of furniture polish.

'We're out of Hoover bags,' Mrs T. had told him, taking her money.

'I'll get some tomorrow.' He saw her off with a cheery wave.

Buffy had gone rather quiet, he noticed, refilling his glass. 'Hello?' he said to her.

The wildlife programme was over, and now it was *Panorama*: that theme tune, Wagner at his most stirring. Quite unexpectedly, her eyes were full of tears.

'Buffy? You still there, old girl?'

'Yes,' she said quietly. 'I'm still here.'

And the next thing was Matthew. William thought about the hospital meeting with another lift of the spirits. Snowdrops were everywhere in the garden – in clumps beneath the magnolia at the front, between the flagstones; in corners beneath the trailing dark ivy on the walls, and in the rose bed; in heart-stopping drifts across the grass at the back, and there, just there, at the foot of the willow tree. He couldn't remember the last time they had looked so dense, so white and green, so snowy. He bent down to pick them, running his finger over the pure perfect drops, the petals still tightly furled; he watched them come out, in the warmth of the house, the outer petals like wings around the tiny bell of the centre, edged with two delicate little green hearts, conjoined.

Sitting at his desk, gazing at them in the fluted glass vase he thought he had found in a sale, but which might have belonged to his mother, he found himself reaching for pencil and paper, making a drawing. He propped it up against a pigeonhole full of bills. Not bad. Rather pretty, though he said it himself.

Should they be pretty? Mackintosh would have stylised them into something austere. And Dürer – ah, well, Dürer.

Perhaps he would be better painting them. Where were his water-colours? He opened drawers, found files and newspaper cuttings, and the children's school reports, tied up with pink solicitor's ribbon. No paints, no brushes. Perhaps he might buy some, next time he was in town – call in at Cornelissen's, what a treat, while he was taking Janice to the British Museum.

Did she want to go to the British Museum? He sat there, half listening to *Composer of the Week*, making a list of all the things she might want to see, all the things she should see. British Museum, V & A, the Tate. He stopped. Not 'the Tate' any more. Tate Britain – he thought that was probably for him. Tate Modern – probably for her. He still hadn't been.

Wallace Collection, National Gallery. The Courtauld: he pictured them walking across the frosty courtyard of Somerset House, the fountains splashing on to the cobbles, him taking her arm. They'd spend the whole morning with Cézanne, Monet, Pissarro; then they'd have lunch, walk by the freezing river, come home for tea.

He sat there, tapping his pencil against his lips.

It was a Tuesday morning, and Janice was walking Danny in the park. No wine bar today: when she came back, they'd have lunch, and then—

Greenwich Maritime Museum, he wrote down, and found himself thinking of the Dog Museum, so truly strange.

'I like walking Danny,' Janice said. 'It brings it all back, keeps me in touch with the whole canine experience.' She flashed a smile, taking down the lead.

What could he show her that wasn't about dogs?

The *Cutty Sark*, he wrote, keeping close to home. Those jars of ship's biscuits. Scurvy. The Dome. He crossed this off at once: it was up for sale, it should never have happened. 'I knew,' he'd said to Buffy many times, 'I knew it would never work.' 'And why is that?' she asked him, Sellotaping the lid on a butter dish, stacking art deco tea plates.

'Because a dome,' said William, 'sits on top of something. That's the whole point. It surmounts. It's the crowning glory; the architectural summit, as it were. It's a miracle of arches, tension, buttresses. St Paul's. Wren.' He waved his hands. 'Brunelleschi, Florence, Prague. St Petersburg. A *dome*, for God's sake – a gilded dome. How can it squat on the ground? With all those silly things sticking out, like a flying saucer. It's ludicrous.'

'You're absolutely right,' said Buffy.

Right, then. No Dome. Good riddance.

Chris de Souza was murmuring on the hi-fi in the corner. The morning concert: what had they got today? There was the usual tuning up, and settling down, the coughs, de Souza burbling on, and then the sudden applause, his voice rising above it, as the conductor entered, and—

And all at once the winter room, with the leafless trees beyond the high clear glass, was filled with unutterable beauty.

William leaned back in his chair at his desk, and closed his eyes, and let the Kreutzer Sonata flood him.

He saw himself and Eve, at autumn concerts; he saw Matthew, at his music stand, here, in the middle of the room, his face intent, his long hand on the bow, graceful and exquisitely articulated, fingers running over the strings, the phrases soaring.

He sat there until the end of the first movement, and then, in the pause, the renewed coughs and rustling, wrote down: the Wigmore Hall. Purcell Room. Festival Hall. He thought for a moment, then added the Proms. Well, why not? If she stayed, why not?

Was she musical? Well, if she wasn't, he would teach her. He would take her to concerts, and play her things, and teach her.

And Matthew—

I have been a fool, thought William, as the second movement opened. I have colluded in this – this apathy, this half-deadness, this entirely lost persona. I have gone up to that bloody hospital, and dragged him down here, and never once, not for years, have I ventured farther. There's a world. There are galleries and concerts. I shall take him with me – I shall reawaken him. I shall take them both—

The key was in the front door. He looked round from his chair as she came in, fresh from the cold and full of energy, letting Danny off the lead to run and be welcomed home. The music was—

'I must introduce you to Matthew,' he said. 'We can't delay.'

III

Intimations

14

'Valentine's Day,' said Ernie, stumping round the shops. 'Blimming Valentine's Day.'

Sophie's hand fluttered over her hair slide, a keen young pointer, with jewelled yellow eyes.

'Forget it,' said Ernie. He shifted a five-kilo bag of dog biscuits from one hand to another. 'Don't even think about it.'

Inside the post office, he slipped out of the queue and had a look at the card racks. He gazed at cushiony satin hearts, ran his eyes over elaborate verses. What about the rude ones? The rude ones were all right. He found them further down, and stood there pulling them out, one by one, and laughing.

'Stop it,' said Sophie. 'People are looking.' She tugged him back into the queue.

'I could write some of them verses,' he said, fingering his wispy beard. 'Easy. I could do some of them drawings.'

Sophie took no notice. She waited for the nice voice to tell them it was their turn at last.

'Cashier number six, please!'

'My sister couldn't come today,' she said, pushing Mary's pension book beneath the glass.

'What a shame,' said the woman cheerfully. She counted out £68.34 and stamped the book. 'There you go.' And she pressed her buzzer.

'Cashier number six, please!'

''Bye,' said Sophie. 'Thanks ever so much.' She counted it all out into her purse.

'I'll look after that,' said Ernie.

Every week they went through this. Two of them came into town on market day, and one had to stay and look after the Museum.

'It can never be left unattended,' said Mary, and they knew she was right. Each week one of them signed the pension book, giving permission for another to collect the funds: Mary in her wild, capitalised Biro, Sophie with her enormous looped S and H, and Ernie in his good clear hand. Ernest William Harriman, read Ernie's signature, and you'd think that behind it stood a person of some education, an architect, perhaps, or an artist.

'Which is what I am,' he said, from time to time. 'I should have gone to college. Should have gone to the Royal College of Art, in London.'

'They'd never have taken you, you old crackpot,' said Mary.

Today it was she who was minding the house. Generally the sisters took it in turns: with Janice gone, Ernie was needed to carry the bulk. He and Sophie went back outside, and stood in the freezing-cold high street, ticking off their list. Biscuits for human and canine consumption. Tea bags. Toilet rolls. When things got tight, they made do with torn-up pieces of the *Shropshire Times*, just as their parents had had to, during the war, when they were children. Not all the pieces flushed away: sometimes Ernie, having a pee in his Elsan, would find himself peering at a bit of a headline, mad odd words still floating in the pan. In his time, he'd peed on Livestock, Red-Handed, Fifty Happy, Toddler.

Now they ticked off beans, Saversoup, Mother's Pride and Chum. Cheese, streaky bacon, cookers. Light bulbs. Washing powder. Mushy peas. Sugar. Sardines. Spotted dick.

Even in Lo-Cost there were Valentines.

'Mind out,' said Ernie, pushing his trolley at a pair of giggling girls. 'I said mind out the way.'

They turned and stared at him, then turned back to the cards, in fits.

'I'm going to have a look-round,' said Sophie, up at the till.

'Oh no you're not.' He stacked tins on to the conveyor belt.

'I am,' she said stubbornly.

'You'll have us all in the poorhouse.'

'I've saved up every penny.'

This conversation took place every few weeks. In the intervening period, the jam jar on Sophie's dressing table filled up with tiny bits of change.

'Go on, then,' said Ernie, outside in the cold again. 'I'll get my baccy.'

'See you at the bus stop.' And she was off, away from the main streets and into the cathedral close, past all the tourists, and the jackdaws on the grass; bobbing at the clergy; smelling, on the other side, down in the tucked-away alley, the heady mix of lavender and tea tree, old rose and rosemary, sandalwood and myrrh.

She pushed the door open and breathed it all in. Healing Arts. Lovely.

Crumbling joss-sticks stood in little brass holders; there were boxes of soaps, racks of sensual oils: everything in here was healthy and healing and kind. She stood there, in her belted green coat and mud-brown beret, taking it all in.

Natural loofahs, dried flowers, natural peppermint foot cream. Soothing tape recordings, helpful books. Stress, Deep Massage, Bio-Massage, Anxiety and Depression, Phobias, Herbalism, Crystals, Star Signs. Homoeopathy. Aromatherapy. Bio-energetic Therapy. Eating for Life. You could cure yourself of anything in here.

And there, on the counter, were all the little pretty things: lavender bags, lucky ladybirds, stick-on glittery moons and stars. The cards of hair slides.

'Good morning, Sophie.'

Oh, they were so nice in here.

'And how are you today?'

'Keeping well,' said Sophie, as one or two people moved away. 'Mustn't grumble.' Her fingers in frog-green knitted gloves hovered over the slides, went back to her lips, returned decisively. She could feel her heart begin to race. No other shop in the world had things like this. Poodles and boxers and a fabulous great Dane. He was new. Her fingers trembled. He was splendid: from the top of his sleek grey tail to his brilliant ears, muscles rippling beneath the mushroom sheen – what a magnificent beast.

'Have you seen the birds?' asked Daphne behind the counter, in her warm, expensive voice. 'We've had some new ones in.'

Sophie looked. Not just cockatoos and parrots and budgies but swooping swallows and cooing white doves. Pairs of darting bluebirds – lovebirds. Was that what they were? She peered.

'Aren't they pretty? Specially for Valentine's Day – we've sold quite a few.'

'Bit late for me to think about Valentines,' said Sophie, facing facts.

'Oh, don't say that. It's never too late for love.' Well-kept hands took

135

the card down from the rack; silver-ringed fingers removed elastic thread. 'There. Why don't you try them on?' And she placed the pair of lovebirds in Sophie's outstretched hand. They lay on the frog-green bobbles like spirits from another world.

'What did you get?' asked Ernie, smoking in the market bus shelter. The winter air was full of the smell of sheep and cattle. Bits of straw, chip papers and cigarette butts blew about in the icy wind; they could hear the clanging pens, the shouts, the lowing and bleating. Tom's Trailer was serving hot teas and soup, but they hadn't a farthing left.

'Well,' confided Sophie. 'It was a toss-up.'

Ernie snorted.

'A Great Dane or lovebirds,' she told him. Oh, how she lingered over that Great Dane. 'I'll keep him for you, if you like,' said lovely Daphne. 'You can buy him next time you're in.' And she put him in a paper bag and tucked him beneath the counter. Sophie knew that Mary would look on this as on a par with Credit, but how could she refuse?

'I got the lovebirds,' she said, and reached into her pocket.

'Show me on the bus,' said Ernie, as it rumbled towards them.

They clambered on, heaving up bag after bag. It started to rain. A tin rolled out on to the ground.

'That Janice,' he said. 'That blimming Janice Harper.'

She had sent them a beautiful card of the Tower of London.

'I'm waiting for my Valentine from that girl,' he said, settling into his seat.

The wipers began to swish back and forth across the muddy windscreen; Sophie pulled out the birds, in their tissue-paper wrapping, and showed him.

He raised his eyes to the heavens. 'Long way they'll get you.'

'Did you get anything?'

'I might have done.'

'What? Go on, I won't tell.'

But he pulled out the paper, and buried himself in the market prices.

All the way home, looking out through the streaming windows at the sodden, grey-green fields, she thought about the choice she'd made, fingering iridescent blue wings and tenderly entwined beaks, recalling powerful shoulders and hindquarters, a noble head.

He was a prince, and that, when she got him home at last, was what she would call him.

It rained for the rest of the day. Ernie, after a lunch of cut-price cream crackers, mild Dutch Edam and a mug of tea, locked his ill-fitting front door and settled down. The paraffin stove was lit, and a nice fug was building up. He sat at his Formica-topped folding table by the window, and opened the brown paper bag.

There. Just the ticket.

The Yorkie at his feet turned round twice, and settled. He started to snore. Ernie ran his fingers over the shiny tin lid. Quite a good size, quite a bargain. He lifted it, with his yellowing fingernails; he drew a little breath.

Yes.

Ultramarine. Cerulean. Moss green. Winter green. Pillar-box red, blood red, amber and umber and ochre. Blackboard black. Chalk white.

And here, in the shiny tin groove at the front, two brushes.

If Ernie had gone to the Royal College of Art in London, he'd have had squirrel, he knew it. Squirrel or even sable, for the really delicate stuff. He'd done out the huts with a job lot of Dulux – no choice, working on such a grand scale, what else was he supposed to use? But now—

He picked up the slender red handles, and ran the brushes between cracked finger and thumb. Soft as a smooth-haired puppy, soft as a puppy's ear. He peered. Probably synthetic, probably nylon, the world was going to the dogs – ha.

Never mind. It would do for now.

From the other recycled brown paper bag he slipped out the pad. It wasn't the quality art paper he deserved, but it would do. For what he had in mind, for starters.

Ernie stood at his sink, and rinsed out a jam jar. The sink was made of stainless steel, but you'd hardly know it. About once a year Mary came across the yard in a fury, bearing a tin of Vim and a scouring pad. Generally in the spring: there was generally a bit of a turnout all round in the spring. He looked out of the back window on to the rainswept field: come April it brought a bob or two, with grazing. He'd be bringing in a bob or two himself, come summer, once he got going. He could see it now, a nice little show in a teashop somewhere, called on by all the nobs.

Ernie wiped the jam jar on his sleeve and took it across to the table. For a moment, sitting there with everything before him, all set out and ready, he knew the purest pleasure. He reached for his baccy tin, rolled up, lit up; he closed his eyes. An image of Janice Harper swam before him, the only smoking companion he'd had for years, coming in so bright and cheerful – breath of fresh air. Every dog in the place perked up, even an old dog like him. Ha. He felt himself begin to drift, came to with a practised start. Fall asleep in here with a cig and you'd be done for.

Right, get a grip. There was the paint-box, there were the brushes and paper and water. Just like the old days. The very old days. Puffing on his roll-up, looking at it all, Ernie beheld a long-forgotten scrap of a boy, up at the front in the art class, the radiators banging away, the schoolroom crammed with kids and smelling of sweat and farmyards. Powder paints and primary colours – mix 'em, that was the thing.

Mix 'em up and make green and gold and purple. All around him kids were sniffing and kicking each other, slopping the water from 1940s jam jars and being told off. Up at the front, high on the teacher's desk, draped in blackout cloth, stood a jar of catkins, and a jug of buttery daffodils. Spring had come at last. Pale sun shone through the schoolyard windows, a thrush was up in the apple tree, they had half an hour till the dinner bell. He dipped his brush, he peered at the jug, the jar, the catkins: he began.

When was the last time he had been so happy?

Rain drummed on the caravan roof; beneath the fold-up table Pip sighed and snored. Ernie reached down from his chair, pulled him out, set him upon the window seat.

Wake up, he told him, you've got a job to do. Now, look at me.

Sunday morning. The rain had blown away, the day was brighter, church bells rang. In the old days, with Mother, they'd always gone to church. Before Father passed away they'd all gone together, regular as clockwork, walking down the lane in order: them two at the front; then Ernie; then she and Mary, holding hands, keeping an eye on Ernie. At this time of year it would still be parky, but you'd hear the lambs, stop to look at them through the gates, see an early bird or two with a bit of hay, bit of twig, darting in and out of the hedges. And the bells were lovely, hopeful and happy. Not like those dreadful funeral bells that had tolled for Father, then Mother. You wouldn't want to hear those again.

But with Mother's passing, the going to church had passed, too. Not straight away. No one really talked about it, or decided, but there were always jobs to be done from the week which now they could do on a Sunday. Cleaning out the pens, cleaning the huts – that was a job and a half. The dogs could be walked on a Sunday morning, as well as the afternoon: they could do shifts. She'd been the one who'd wanted to keep up the churchgoing, but somehow they just . . . stopped.

It was the hymns she missed the most.

Sophie sat up in her bedroom, before her dressing table. This, like much of the household furniture, was postwar utility, made of varnished plywood. Over the years, some of the varnish had worn away, leaving thin furrows. Sometimes these made her think of a ploughed field, sometimes of a desert after a sandstorm, the sand whipped into ridges, which she had seen on a poster, once, in the window of a Shrewsbury travel agent, beneath a lovely sunset. Sometimes, as she dreamed away up here, the scratches put her in mind of the sand on a beach, the ridges left by retreating waves, hard on bare feet as you ran. It was a long time since Sophie had run anywhere, but as children they had once been taken by Father and Mother on a seaside holiday: it had left a lasting impression. She remembered the sand, and the leathery dark purse of a dogfish, lying upon it; she remembered the mysterious depths of a rock pool, and the fronded, sucking mouth of the sea anemone, wherein she had not dared to place her finger, in spite of Ernie's urgings, and Mary's scorn. She sometimes thought, still, of her ruched bathing costume, which had been very pretty, and of Mother yanking down her white rubber bathing cap, the painful stuffing up of her hair beneath it, the tightness of the strap and buckle beneath her chin.

Somewhere in the house was a photograph album, with tiny black-and-white photographs of this holiday in gluey paper corners. There they all were, lined up and smiling into the sun with Rover, their very first dog, eating their sandy sandwiches.

They'd had a good time, then.

Sometimes, sitting before her mirror, Sophie would run the point of a nail file over the varnish, scraping it away still further, making lakes and lagoons, and foreign countries. Mary, coming in once and finding her, miles away, scraping back and forth, had accused her of vandalism, and idleness, and shouted. Since then, Sophie had tried to desist. It was, after all, her favourite piece of furniture, something she felt had been made exclusively for her.

139

There was a three-fold mirror. Plain as it was, the glass fixed to the plywood back by rusting clips, this felt like luxury. To see oneself from every *angle* – to look this way and that to see if things were right, without having to crane, or peer, or ask someone else to hold a mirror behind you: it was like being a film star. There was also the endlessly interesting activity of angling the side panels so that, when you leaned in and looked to left or right, your reflection went on and on, endlessly repeated. She had done this when she was little, and she sometimes did it now, setting the panels and leaning forward, turning her head, and – there! Sophie after Sophie after Sophie returned her gaze, stretching back and back – as if to the very place where she, Sophie Harriman, had begun.

What a peculiar thought.

The dressing table had two levels, and was in three sections; this, too, felt like something of a luxury. In the lower, middle section, she had arranged her hairbrush, comb, and a small Pyrex bowl with a lid, in which were kept hairpins, buttons, suspenders, poppers – anything still waiting to be reunited with its place of origin. On the raised sections on either side, each with a little drawer, were her jam jar of change, and the small china boxes, collected over many years, and each with a distinct personality. These were for the slides, and one held brooches.

Bells were ringing; somewhere along the landing, something dripped.

'Dear Lord and Fa-ather of Mankind, / Forgive our foolish ways,' Sophie sang quietly, lifting the lid of the china box, patterned in pink roses. This was where the birds were kept, and now she had a new addition. Lovebirds – what a lovely word. Just to think of it made you feel happy. She picked them up tenderly, held them in her cupped hand, stroked their blue-blue wings. How they swooped and darted, how they billed and cooed. Lovebirds. Bluebirds. Both such pretty things.

'Re-clothe us in our right-ful mind, in purer lives Thy ser-vi-ice find . . .'

She unfastened the clip, leaned forward, and slipped the slide into a strand of dark hair. Wonderful, really; she hadn't gone grey. Still young at heart; still a girl, at heart.

She pressed the clip shut, tidied a few strands of hair; she leaned into the depths of the three-fold mirror. And there she was, retreating

THIN AIR

with the birds into infinity, reflected over and over, on and on, going deeper and deeper, far, far away, but never – no, never; she felt a sudden racing of the blood, a rush of terror – vanishing into thin air.

Janice was seeing the sights. On her first trip she had taken herself to London Bridge – a wonderful place to start, as William had indicated, if you wanted to soak up the new Thames atmosphere. London! She wasn't in Oswestry, or Welshpool, or in a council estate on the back of the Shrewsbury bypass, was she? She had left home. At last, thank God, at last.

It was already dark. She stood outside the station beneath a streetlamp, her head bent over the *A–Z*. She was between two monumental buildings: Guy's Hospital, sprawling hugely across the road, and Southwark Cathedral. Well. She wasn't going to go prowling round a hospital, was she? Even if it was famous. Nor did she fancy, in the darkness, entering a cathedral. Choral singing by candlelight? No thanks, not today. Anyway, it would probably be locked. What else? The Old Operating Theatre (Mus). Instruments of torture, no anaesthetic – please. The Clink Prison? What had she stepped into?

But all along the Embankment suits were hurrying into pubs and wine bars, getting out of the cold. She took another look. Shakespeare's Globe. Ah. Steve would like to know about that. But it was quite a walk, and anyway... She had a sudden vision of herself, in jacket and jeans and vegan-version Doc Martens, striding into a foyer filled with posh people, all dressed up and talking about Shakespeare. Perhaps another time. As she heard herself think this, she knew it was just the sort of phrase which William used. She could hear him saying it, with a little smile.

Right, then. What should she do?

'Got a light, love?'

Janice looked up at the balding man before her. He grinned, in a horrible, intimate way, and she said coolly, 'No, I haven't, and don't call me love,' and stood there, willing him to go.

'Be like that, then, you fucking cow.' And as he walked off she knew in a concentrated instant exactly why her mother had not wanted her to come to London. But he'd gone, and she could hack it, she'd be OK.

And she turned, and walked down to the river, which took her through side streets, but she made sure she always had people in view.

And when she leaned on a railing and looked out over the water, where lay the illuminated hulk of HMS *Belfast*, she began to breathe steadily again, and to feel in control of things. She felt in her jacket pocket for her tin, and lit up. That was better. Barges chugged to and fro, and the water washed against the wall beneath her; the moon was rising, the Thames was silver and black. And to right and to left it was magical. William was right. The floodlit dome of St Paul's, the skyscrapers and arches of the bridges – and there, far down to the right, was Tower Bridge. This picture-postcard sight, familiar from every book about London she had ever opened, now filled her with excitement and satisfaction. She was here, she'd seen it. The mighty stone walls of the Tower itself were bathed in floodlight – God, this was fantastic.

And she leaned on the railing, letting it all sink in, the smoke from her roll-up drifting out across the water and a river-boat hooting, deep and sonorous, into the London sky.

Where next?

'I'd like to take you to the Dulwich Picture Gallery,' said William. 'I'd like to take you to the Horniman Museum, when it's a bit warmer – lovely gardens. Wonderful glasshouse. We could have tea.'

'That'd be nice.'

They were having a drink by the fire. Janice, used to halves in the pub, and a game of darts, was beginning to get used to William, on the evenings she was at home, lighting the fire at about six, having a look in the drinks cupboard, bringing out a couple of glasses.

'Whisky? Sherry? Do you young things drink sherry? Or would you rather have a glass of wine? There's a rather nice Chablis in the fridge, if I remember rightly. Or a little Beaujolais Nouveau?'

'Not all wine's vegan, you know,' said Janice, and explained about blood, and eggs, and cochineal, made from crushed insects.

'Good Lord.' He watched her, sipping her whisky and ginger, rubbing her foot along Danny's spine, before the fire.

'There are all the concert halls,' he said, setting non-vegan wines aside. 'What I really want to do, when it brightens up a bit, is take you and Matthew to a concert. Of course' – he gave a thoughtful smile – 'I'll have to introduce you, first.'

'That'd be nice,' said Janice, again. 'I don't know much about music,' she added. 'Not classical music, not really.'

'Well, we can put that right.' He got up, went over to the hi-fi, ran his fingers over the shelves of LPs.

'You can't buy those any more,' she told him. 'Don't you have CDs?'

'A few. But I love my old collection. Eve and I used to listen all the time – some of these recordings go back decades. Nothing wrong with that. Some of them are famous – von Karajan, Kurt Masur, Lorin Maazel – great names.'

She'd never heard of any of them, but it didn't matter. That was the thing about William: he made everything easy; you felt you could say anything, pretty much, and he'd take it all in his stride.

'What sort of music do you like?' he asked her, but she knew, as she started to tell him, that he wasn't taking it in.

'Now,' he said, slipping an LP from its sleeve and setting it on the turntable – it was like the Ark here, 'what do you think of this?'

The first few phrases sounded, piano and violin, and a ripple ran through her. In part this was recognition – had she heard this before? Must've done – Steve often used to put on Classic FM in the Cloud Nine kitchen. She leaned back in the chair, let it wash over her, heard it begin to soar—

God. Yes – yes, she had heard it before, she remembered stopping washing up, or whatever, and listening to this fantastic music, looking out over the sunlit hills, where swifts were wheeling and—

She shut her eyes.

'The Kreutzer Sonata,' said William quietly, going back to his chair, and then: 'Matthew used to play this.'

God, did he really?

The violin was a living thing, exquisite, tender and wild, like rain on a river, like—

For the whole of the first movement they listened together in silence, something Janice had never done before in her life, never even thought about doing, though it felt quite natural now. Then, when the last notes had died away, she opened her eyes and saw William watching her, as the firelight played over the scattering of ash in the hearth, the fender, and the sleeping dog.

He raised an eyebrow. She nodded.

'Yeah, it's great.'

'You're musical,' he told her, leaning forward to throw on another log.

Well. That was something else she hadn't known.

Then the next movement began.

143

☆

Within a week he had taken her to the Dulwich Picture Gallery and the National Maritime Museum at Greenwich. At the Dulwich, reached by a pleasant walk through the village, they tied Danny up to a ring outside.

'This is the first purpose-built art gallery in England,' William told her, straightening up. 'Designed by Sir John Soane in 1811. So now you know.' It was cold, and Danny, sensing abandonment, began to whimper. 'We shan't be long, old chap.'

Janice was glad to hear this, and William sensed it.

'I know,' he said, ushering her through the blue-painted door, set in its pale stone arch. 'Galleries can be exhausting. We'll just have a look at one or two things. Now then—' And he had picked up a plan at the desk and was leading her into the first room.

Polished floors and gilded frames: she looked about her, half listening to William talking of Canaletto, Watteau, Poussin – painters she had never heard of, and none of whom did it for her, with their great dull buildings, overstocked flower-beds, soppy girls in gardens, and oversized nymphs and river gods, draped in pink and blue.

'No?' asked William, seeing her face.

'No,' she said. 'Sorry.'

'No need to be sorry. See what you make of the Dutch. I think they'll be more to your taste.'

And he was right. For a start, she'd seen some of these on birthday cards: huge great soaring skies reflected in the still waters of the dykes in that flat, flat land – you'd have to be dead from the neck up not to like those. And the quiet courtyards in faded brick, the women with their plain black dresses and neat white caps, talking together: you could almost hear their voices, as they went about their work, sweeping and washing and sewing in the sun.

'Better?'

She nodded.

'Let's have a look at the Rembrandt, and then have lunch.'

The Rembrandt he showed her was called *Girl at the Window*. It was dark, and painted in close-up, the girl with her untidy hair and plain cotton blouse and jacket taking up almost all the canvas, as she leaned from a shadowy dark background on a rough stone windowsill. She was – what? Fifteen? Maybe a bit more. She was completely human – not like those simpering girls and nymphs, but sturdy and practical.

There was also something about her which Janice couldn't quite put her finger on, but was to do with the way she was lit, from that shadowy background: made to look both ordinary and special.

'I thought you'd like her,' said William.

At the National Maritime Museum they let Danny off the lead in the hilly grounds and threw sticks. He went racing after them, until they reached the bottom. It was still cold and pretty windy: clouds raced over the rooftops and a fitful sun played over the pillared façades and struck the glass Observatory.

'Now that,' said William, 'is what I call a dome.'

They crunched across the gravel, and tied Danny up once more. This time William had put his dachshund coat on, and he fished out a dog chew from his pocket. Danny ignored it, and barked until they were out of sight.

Inside, in the vast main building, they wandered through rooms full of models and maps, sextants, uniforms, flags. They went to the exhibition of polar expeditions, and Janice, who had, with her father, watched an amazing programme about Shackleton and the *Endurance* the previous autumn, now gazed at the photographs again: the skeletal, ice-encrusted masts and rigging, the frostbitten men and the husky puppies, born at sea, gambolling over the snowy wastes.

'God,' she said suddenly. 'You know what this makes me think of?'

'What's that?'

'Ernie,' she said, and began to laugh. 'One of the huts. The Eskimos. I told you about them.'

'So you did. What would old Ernie make of this, I wonder?'

'Can't really see him here, somehow.'

But how strange, she thought, as they walked on, to think of these separate but similar Harriman passions – museums, galleries, pictures, in their oh-so-different guises.

'The Observatory?' asked William, as they left Scott and Shackleton behind. 'Have you the strength for the twenty-eight-inch telescope and Meridian Line?'

'Just about.'

They unclipped Danny, and walked him across to the Observatory building, leaving him outside once more. Inside they beheld the Line, walked over it, walked back.

'Do you realise,' said William, reading from the guide, 'that until the late nineteenth century a cup of tea at half-past four in London might be taken at five in Norwich? With nothing and no one to put you right.'

'How weird,' said Janice, imagining the strange disharmony of bells and chimes throughout the land. Mind you, the Dog Museum would always be out of step.

'Whereas now,' said William, 'all is in order. More or less.' And he reset his watch, on its pigskin strap, with its plain white face, Roman numerals and fine gold hands and rim. 'My father's,' he told Janice, watching him. 'I must have changed the strap a good few times, but I've worn this watch since the day he died. Day after, anyway.'

He glanced at her wrist, where her digital watch from Argos kept perfect, pulsing time.

'Doesn't it wear you out?' he asked her. 'All that flashing?'

'No, not really.' She had never given it a thought.

'I'd find it very tiring. Let's go and have some tea.'

The days went by. She was getting to know her way around. Up in her bedroom, at Claire's white-painted desk, she made a list of other places to go to, north of the river.

Tate Modern. The London Eye. She pictured herself and William, slowly revolving through the cloud-filled sky.

15

Valentine's Day: the whole country on alert. Few, apart from brazen schoolgirls, admitted this, but it was true. Hope dies hard, and even in old people's homes there was a little joke, a little flutter of the heart. Would there be – could there be – one for me?

William and Eve had rarely sent one another Valentines, but he had always bought her flowers, and taken her out, and generally marked the occasion. After her death, he had found the day so painful that he had, in a sense, abolished it, quickly turning the pages of the paper past the columns of sentimental gush and mild pornography which these days passed for romance. After a while, the abolishing was so successful that he rarely gave the day a thought, except to use it to put the prices up on the stall. Marvellous how a scarlet satin ribbon could lift the dullest jug, or sell a stack of rather ordinary saucers. Tie them up, cut the price tag into a heart, and bob's your uncle.

'Go on, make her happy,' he urged with a winning smile. 'Just the thing to put under flowerpots.'

A romantic to his bones, William generally put a flowerpot on the stall, planted by the Dulwich florist with miniature daffs or narcissi – heavenly scent of spring, cheering everyone up, worth at least a couple of quid on everything. Romance without a head for business – where did that get you?

'There we are,' he said to Buffy at the end of the day, divvying up the takings. 'Not a bad day's work.' He carried the boxes to the car and drove her home. But although they certainly had, after Eve's death, shared many a supper, they did not, she noticed, do so on Valentine's Day. He carried her china up the stairs, he stayed for a drink, and then he had to be off, baby-sitting for Claire and Jeremy, in the early days, or just . . . going.

Buffy had never had a Valentine in her life. She told herself she had long since come to terms with this, no longer gave it a thought. This year—

This year, in the days of the run-up, she gave herself up to mingled misery and hope. The night before, she sat knitting before the television. She brought through a mushroom omelette and a glass of Sauvignon on a tray, and left most of the omelette; she had a hot bath and read, in bed, two chapters of *The 1940s House*, which she and William, at opposite ends of London, were both enjoying, on the screen and on the page. And all the while there ran through her bloodstream the insistent, hopelessly insistent, little line of enquiry. Would there be – could there be – might he, perhaps—

She fell into a restless sleep, waking at two with a heavy head, and went urgently to the bathroom. The heating was off, of course, and it was bloody cold. Everything, at two in the morning, in the middle of February, felt completely bloody.

'How is it,' William asked Janice, as the day approached, 'that a nice young girl like you has no boyfriend?'

They were having a late breakfast: she was off today. He looked at her over the top of the paper, wherein he could beat a retreat if he had overstepped the mark.

'Young woman,' said Janice, slicing a banana on to her bowl of high-fibre cereal. 'No one's a girl any more.'

Was this really so? How dreadful. He lowered the paper, frowning.

'Unless,' she said, licking her fingers, 'you're talking girl power, of course.'

'And what is that?'

'Power,' said Janice, getting up to drop the banana skin in the bin. She came back, and sprinkled on brown sugar. 'Doing what you want. Not taking no for an answer. Getting what you want. Like, always.' Not that there had been an enormous amount of empowerment in Shropshire. Not so as you would notice.

'An enviable state of affairs,' said William. He looked at her, fresh skinned and still a bit sleepy, munching away. It was true – she wasn't a girl, not what he understood by the term. Girl was – how could he put it? – girl was romantic, wore dresses, was light on her feet, was like –

148

he searched his memory – the girls in blue muslin running along the pier in that painting by Philip Wilson Steer in the Tate. Tate Britain, rather. Girl was like those young things laughing and holding down polka-dot dresses in a seaside summer breeze in that wonderful fifties photograph taken by . . . taken by—

He gave up, and looked at the young woman before him, tipping up her bowl to finish the soya milk, sensible and organised, eating a healthy breakfast.

'How is it that a young woman like you, if I may so rephrase it, is without a boyfriend?'

'Search me,' said Janice. 'Toast?'

'Let me—' he made to rise.

'It's all right, I'll do it.' She got to her feet, and opened the bread bin. 'One slice or two?'

'Two, please.' He watched her wield the bread knife. 'Was there perhaps some young man in Shropshire?'

'Like, mind your own business?' said Janice, and dropped two slices of Honey & Sunflower Stoneground into the toaster.

William retreated to the paper, as men, throughout the ages, have been wont to do.

After breakfast, they went their separate ways.

Upstairs, in her bedroom, she sat at Claire's old desk and took out the Valentine's card from the paper bag. She drew it out of its Cellophane and looked at it. It was the coolest she had been able to find: just dead plain white, with a single word, in small red letters: Hello? Inside, it was blank, except for the smallest red heart. She took out a stamp and stuck it on the envelope. That was the easy bit. Then she picked up her Biro. Of course, people were probably e-mailing Valentines these days, from some cool Internet café, or loft, or office desk. No one she knew at home was on e-mail, but it was only a matter of time. Everyone here was, except for William, of course. Sandra, in her office at the back of the wine bar, was forever scrolling through messages and swearing, puffing away.

'What's he on about, the fucking idiot?'

Would Sandra get a Valentine?

Would Janice?

Her fingers hovered, over the letter E. E for Eric. Not much call for e-mail, up in a shepherd's hut, or up a tree.

Should she?

Would he?

What did Hello? mean, with a little heart?

Hello, remember me? Hello, long time no see, but I still—

Did she? And even if she did, should she tell him?

If she didn't put her address, he couldn't answer. If she put her address she'd start looking out for letters. And if he didn't write—

Of course, he could always send one to 33 Curlew Gardens, might already have posted it, in which case it wouldn't arrive here, forwarded on, until at least a day later. So she needn't think about looking on the mat until the 15th or 16th, by which time anything could have happened.

Oh, yeah?

Like what?

Well, like—

She cast her mind's eye round the wine bar, drew a blank. So far, anyway. So far, she'd been chatted up in light-hearted fashion by an estate agent, until his girlfriend arrived, and by the guy from the wine wholesalers, leaning his clipboard on the bar, and giving her the eye while they waited for Sandra, who soon put a stop to that. 'Want to come into the office, Jon? Janice, make us a cup of coffee, will you?' That was it, unless you counted the bearded bloke called Derek who vaguely reminded her of someone, and who told her he was a freelance graphic designer, whatever that was. He leaned rather heavily upon the bar until his wife showed up. Other than that – solicitors came and solicitors went, and likewise accountants, and not one of them had the smouldering, sinewy, all-dissolving *presence* which Eric—

She'd almost said his name aloud, and almost doing so – just almost doing so – put her in a spin.

No. She leaned back in the chair, in her sweater from Gap, which was new, and bought with her first week's wages, and refused to succumb. She'd come down to London to get away, remember? To find something new, something different. She'd made a good start.

Right, then.

No spins. No casting yearning glances at the past, with its rain-soaked night of passion.

And she leaned forward again, and with her pen wrote, inside the card:

150

Dear Steve,

Remember me? I do miss you and Cloud Nine, and everything, and I hope you're getting on OK. It's good here, and I'm glad I came. Why don't you come and visit one day?

Lots of love – Janice

There. Written without a second thought, and safe as houses. And she addressed and stuck down the envelope and felt much better.

But it was a pity, she thought later, dropping the card into the postbox on the way to work, that not a single person she'd met so far had proved of real interest. Not lasting, I-want-to-get-to-know-you-better, I-wonder-what-this-might-lead-to interest.

Except, of course—

And at this thought Janice stopped, and stood for a moment quite taken aback, and then, pulling herself together, walked briskly on.

William spent the morning looking through the catalogues of sales-rooms and auctioneers, with an open diary. He'd marked in Guildford already, which he and Buffy had yet to go to; now he entered Chichester, and, in early March, a house sale in Ippenham, a fair. He looked through the Phillips and Sotheby catalogues, circled a couple of things in each, wondered whether Janice might like to go to an auction, just for the experience. He made a cup of coffee, looked through the new programme of the National Theatre, just arrived, considered an evening of dramatised Proust, and was just about to whistle up Danny for a spot of shopping when it started to rain. They'd go after lunch, then. He made another coffee, and took it to the bookshelves. Was there anything else in the wine department which Janice might find useful? He ran his fingers over the spines, found himself, after a little while, straying towards the art shelves, taking down Matisse once more, and turning the pages, as the rain fell faster, and the sky darkened. He switched on a light.

Girls or young women?

Not for a moment would he call these creatures girls. They leaned back on ottomans, half naked, with their arms behind their heads; they sat at dressing tables, languid and long limbed; they unfolded them-selves beside a folding screen, draped in vermilion and lemon and blue – oh, those singing colours.

151

He could not begin to place here any girl, or young woman, or woman, that he had ever known. Certainly Janice, with her easy stride, and roll-ups, and kind of – innocence? – did not belong here.

But they were . . . they were—

They must be something I never knew I wanted, he thought, settling into the armchair, just as the telephone rang. He got up to answer it. Danny followed.

'Hello?'

'That girl,' said Claire. 'Your lodger. Is she there?'

'She's not, as it happens. Hello, darling. How are you?'

'Fine, thanks. Could you ask her to give me a ring? She said she might like to do some baby-sitting.'

'Did she really? I'll be happy to baby-sit for you, any time – I'd love it. You have only to ask.'

'Yes. Well. If she's not free, perhaps. Anyway, could you ask her?'

'Yes, yes, of course.'

'Thanks. 'Bye.'

And that was that, and it was almost lunch-time. He left Janice a note on the hall table, and went down to open a tin.

Valentine's Day. The wine bar was packed. A single red rose in an opaline vase on every table, floating candles, a Valentine's Special – a spritzer, blood red with kirsch, and Sandra in something very short, and very low. Janice, from the moment she arrived, was rushed off her feet, which was just how she wanted it, since there had, of course, been no card on the mat that morning, and she had been unable to suppress the sudden plummet of disappointment, even though she'd known all along, hadn't she?

By now, she knew quite a few of the regulars, and chatted cheerfully away as she uncorked chilled Chardonnay, filled ice buckets, let champagne corks go whizzing across the room. This was all right. She refilled the bowls of olives, the dips and crudités, she nipped in and out of the marble-topped tables with a snow-white napkin over her arm and felt quite the business. Someone let off a party popper; Sandra, behind the bar, was flirting with Jonty, who was helping out; a couple were kissing with abandon on one of the banquettes, and here was the door opening again, and here was Derek, the graphic designer, with his sad little wife, all dressed up.

For a moment, watching them cast around for a table, and find one, and settle in, she thought they looked familiar, as she had thought before, the first time he came in. She went to take their order.

'Don't I know you from somewhere?' she asked them, and at once regretted it, as Derek's eyes lit up at this age-old opening line, and his wife began to shrink.

'Well, well, I've been trying to place you ever since we met,' he began. 'Do you recognise this young lady, Jenny?' But fortunately, just as he started to explore the limitless dead-end possibilities, the door opened once again and in came Claire Harriman, looking less like Mary, and with her – well, it must be him – her nice-looking husband.

'Excuse me just one moment,' said Janice, and, leaving Derek and Jenny with the wine list, she went to say hello.

'Janice.' Claire greeted her with a warm smile. 'I wondered if this was one of your nights. Let me introduce you—'

'Jeremy Lewis,' said the nice tall husband, and shook her hand. 'I've heard about you. You're staying with William.'

'I am, it's great.' And she pulled out their chairs, and took their coats.

'Did my father leave you a message?' asked Claire, handing her a very good silk scarf. She watched Janice tuck it into the sleeve of her coat, as Sandra had shown her was the thing to do. 'About baby-sitting?' she added, sitting down.

'Great balls of fire,' said Janice, embarrassed. He had, indeed he had. 'Sorry. I've been a bit preoccupied. But yeah, sure. When were you thinking of?'

'Oh, there were a couple of dates,' said Claire. 'Let's not bother about it now, you're so busy.' And she turned back to Jeremy, who was scanning the wine list. 'What shall we have?'

It wasn't until much later in the evening that Janice, helping everyone get drunk, getting a bit drunk herself, had a chance just to stand behind the bar and hazily observe proceedings. She observed the couple on the banquette stagger out, helpless with laughter and desire, and considered how pleasant this must be. She observed a row brewing between Derek and Jenny, and remembered where, incredibly, she had seen them before. In the Dog Museum, in the pouring rain the previous autumn. They had turned up with their child, a round-faced boy, just as she was leaving. It had been half-term, a filthy day, and they had been almost the only visitors. God, how weird. Well – she wasn't going to remind them. But thinking about that day, and about her life then, she felt a sudden wave of nostalgic longing for it all: places and people she knew by heart; all the old bats in the rainswept hills and valleys, the bicycling and dog-walking and cake-making, and Steve, and even her parents, who weren't really all that bad, just boring, like all parents were.

And yet, she thought, leaning on the bar and watching Sandra make a fool of herself, I wouldn't have missed coming down here for the world. She helped herself to a couple of olives, and took an order from a young man swaying like a tree in the wind on Leinthall Ridge. She wanted to tell him he had had enough, but it was none of her business, and anyway, what the hell. It was Valentine's Day, for God's sake: someone had to enjoy themselves. She was enjoying herself, in a funny kind of way, more than she'd thought she would, anyway. And she lit up a proper cigarette, for once, offered by the inebriate young man, and watched him walk back with incredible care to his table, where sat another young man. Which made her think of Steve, again, and wonder what he was doing tonight. Not much call for Valentine's parties, up in Cloud Nine of a February night. He'd be down the pub with everyone, as she would have been, had she stayed.

It was growing incredibly noisy and smoky and loud. Janice poured herself another glass while Sandra, sitting on somebody's lap, leaned back and roared with unbecoming laughter. She observed, beholding the throng once more, that Claire and Jeremy also knew Derek and Jenny, and were avoiding them. There had been a waving of the wine list by Derek, and a cheery 'How's school?' from Jenny, and then – after the little nod of acknowledgement, the smiles – a definite retreat. Well, you would retreat from Derek, wouldn't you? Hard to say quite why, but you would. No reason why a freelance graphic designer should be boring, but—

Claire and Jeremy were in conversation. Janice leaned on the bar and enjoyed her cigarette and glass of wine, and watched them. They didn't, Claire had told her, get out very much, with their three young children. She had made it clear, both to Janice and William, that life, with three young children, was a fearful strain. So you'd think that now they were off the leash they'd be—

Well, perhaps this was what marriage and three kids and overwork did for you. God, he looked knackered. It must be awful, being a barrister. But he also had a sweet, kind sort of look, and as he listened to Claire, and yawned, she wondered that they were not holding hands,

154

or . . . well, laughing, or something. Perhaps one of the children was ill, or had failed an exam, or perhaps they'd discovered dry rot in the cellar, or whatever it was that gave people with mortgages sleepless nights. Or perhaps—

Smoke drifted here and there through the crowded room. The roses on the tables had opened in the warmth, and their scent was everywhere, mingling with the wine, and cigarettes; Billie Holiday, through the sound system, was unbearably husky and alone.

Claire looked up. She glanced towards the bar, and rested her eyes upon Janice, who was leaning upon it, with her cropped dark hair and her drink and smouldering cigarette held between her slender fingers. For a moment their eyes met. For a moment her smile was full of warmth and friendship. And then, as if recollecting herself – for Claire, Janice knew, was a terrible snob, and unlikely to allow herself to indulge in familiarity with her father's lodger, and anyway was a difficult, complicated person – then she returned her gaze to her husband, and took his hand, and he, with a little start of pleasure, leaned forward and kissed her cheek.

Valentine's Day. It came. It went. There was nothing but bills on the mat for Buffy, and for an instant she felt quite sick with disappointment. And straightening up, with her National Trust reminder for renewal, and the quarterly service charges from the landlord, she leaned against the wall in a sudden little spasm of giddiness.

Dear, dear, this wasn't right. She made her way cautiously back to the kitchen and sank on to her chair, her head in her hands. After a little while, everything stopped spinning, and with a few sips of tea she felt that wonderful rush of warmth and wellness which can follow a nasty turn. She slit open the National Trust envelope, looked through the booklet offering soaps and scarves and bird-life tea towels which accompanied the bill and gradually recovered herself.

But she only had one slice of toast, no room anywhere for another crumb, and as she washed up the breakfast things and thought about the day ahead – the getting across town to the Angel, the walk down to Camden Passage, the setting up of the stall, and the morning sitting out there, in the February cold and wet – it all felt almost daunting. Even though she was seeing William, even though this was the highlight of the week – she was tired, she was terribly tired.

But why? Was it all the getting up in the night, the trouble spent getting back to sleep afterwards? Was she doing too much? No more than she had ever done. Then was it, perhaps, something psychological?

Buffy had never had much time for the psychological. The closest she had come to interest, or insight, was with poor Matthew, whose suffering so tore at William's heart. Who knew what would become of that poor boy in the end, but at least, at Christmas, she'd had the good sense to wake William up to things, urge him to seek a review. Still, that hadn't taken much. Any fool could have seen things weren't right.

Buffy put away the toast rack. She put away the marmalade, and the butter back in the fridge. She considered her state of mind, which had, she knew, developed, as it were, a new strain, a new cast, since Christmas and New Year, when she had felt so happy. The nine o'clock news came on, and passed her by. She went into the sitting room, where sun was struggling through the rain. It lit the watery windowpane, the shoots in the window box, where the crocuses were just in bud; it filtered through the bright yellow poster for the Mary Ward concert, and fell upon her desk, where a pile of yellow concert fliers were waiting to be delivered. She always put them through her neighbours' letterboxes, and in the local shops, and the church, and she always took them to the stall. The Angel, after all, was not far from Bloomsbury, and people came, people liked to be told about musical events, it cheered them up.

But oh Lord, thought Buffy, putting them into an envelope, putting them into her bag, even the thought of the concert, the soaring Parry and the rousing Masefield and Kipling, somehow did not cheer her now.

'Hello, old thing.' William was in fine fettle, already setting up the stall, which she noticed had a different cloth upon it, a faded crimson damask, which set everything off a treat. He kissed her on both cheeks; he gestured to Danny, sniffing round other people's stalls, wearing a scarlet ribbon. 'That'll brighten up the punters, catch the mood.' He felt in a carrier bag on his folding chair, pulled out a pot of paper-white narcissi, and set it in the middle of the trestle. 'There. Springtime. Valentines. Love's young dream.'

'Where did you get that cloth?' asked Buffy, setting down her bag.

'Found it at the back of the press in the spare room. Woke up in the

156

middle of the night and thought: I know just the thing. Change from all that black — it sets off silver so nicely, but today—' He was rummaging in his cardboard boxes, taking out newspaper-wrapped packages, peeling off layers. 'What do you think of this?'

Buffy beheld a teapot, pale cream with fluted sides, wide spout and slender handle. Cabbage roses smothered it; the handle and the handle on the lid were dusty gold. 'Very nice,' she said, and it was. She lifted it and turned it over, clasping the lid until she saw he'd already taped it securely. 'Staffordshire. I thought so.'

'Did you really? That was clever.' William put his glasses on, and peered at the mark. 'It's about 1880. What do you think?'

'A good hundred,' said Buffy, on automatic now, getting into the swing again. It just went to show: you should never succumb. Moods. Tiredness. Out and about — that was the thing; getting on.

'Just what I thought,' said William. 'Shall we try one-twenty?'

'Why not?' And she set it down and waited for the next unwrapping. That, on good days, was one of the stall's delights. It wasn't just the shared days out, the sales in barns and country houses. It was the finding things individually, bringing them to show one another; the poking about on wet afternoons in little shops and salesrooms. Sometimes it was she who found something, poking about in the Chiswick Oxfam shop, the jumble sale, the West London auction rooms. Often there was nothing at all: there had, for instance, been nothing at all for a fortnight in Notting Hill, but sometimes—

'Now then,' said William, unwrapping something else. 'These I fell for.'

Traffic on the Essex Road was building up; people were running for the bus; the man in the Turkish antiques shop by the green was shaking out a kilim in the sun. The world felt normal and ordinary again, the morning's moment of distress, the dizzy spell and weakness, quite forgotten. After all, she had known William for years and years; friendship was what counted, in the end. It was simply silly to think of something more, it spoiled everything.

'There,' he said, and stood back for the effect.

Two white china doves lay side by side. Their feathery wings were folded, their heads tucked into their breasts, their eyes gently closed in sleep.

She picked one up. It was hollow: half a dove, in fact, the tail swept up into a smooth white fan, the body quite at rest.

'Jelly moulds,' said William. 'Nineteen thirties jelly moulds. Worth quite a bit.' He watched her set down again the one she had picked up. 'Especially today, don't you think?' And carefully, with his beautiful fingers, in the leather winter gloves she had always been so fond of, he moved the two birds close together, so that their sleeping heads could rest together tenderly, lovingly, as if for a lifetime.

'You've gone awfully quiet, old girl,' William said later. 'Everything all right?'

'Fine,' said Buffy. 'Absolutely fine.'

The Staffordshire teapot had been sold, knocked down to £75, to someone they'd thought was a dealer but had given the benefit of the doubt. Those darling doves had gone to a retired couple who still, in retirement, held hands as they walked away. Buffy watched them, then busied herself with the rearrangement of her rug. And so the whole wretched Valentine's Day went by, and then it was over, and a good thing too.

William and Janice walked up the hill to the hospital. The morning was brighter, lighter, the air fresh: again, despite the cold, you could sense just a hint of spring.

'It's very good of you to come,' said William, tugging Danny out of a doorway. He had said this several times.

'It's fine,' said Janice, as she had kept saying. 'Honestly.'

'I mean, of course it would have been much nicer for you to have met at home,' he went on, 'and I very much hope he'll come for Sunday lunch or something, soon, but I can never be completely sure if it unsettles him. At least we know he feels safe here.'

They had come to the open gates; he stopped, put a hand on her arm as a car turned in. Then they went through.

Danny, on familiar territory, trotted briskly ahead on the lead, making for the grass alongside the tarmac path. William drew him back. 'You'll have to wait a bit, old chap, same as usual.'

Janice, gloved hands in her jacket pockets, looked about her. She'd never been to a loony bin before. Was that what this was? She imagined, when the weather got warmer, the patients would be out and about, doing gardening therapy, or painting therapy, or playing ball games – was that the sort of thing they got up to? Now there were only the lawns, the huge dark firs, with a scattering of cones on the grass beneath, and a gardener working in the flower-beds, where bulbs were pushing up. Oh, and there was a squirrel, leaping towards the fir cones. Danny saw it too, gave a sudden yelp of excitement, and it was up on the trunk in a flash, round it and gone, just like that. Again, for a minute, she was tugged back to Shropshire, and loads of old squirrels, everywhere in the woods, and the sheep up in the hills, suddenly looming at you round a bush or a boulder, or scattered like stones on the slopes, with a crow or two flapping across the valley.

'Here we are,' said William.

Plate-glass doors were before them, one or two visitors coming out, one or two going in. She glimpsed a white coat, a nurse, an endless corridor, stretching away beyond the reception area; she heard, in the distance, the sudden blare of an ambulance. And for the first time, as William bent to clip Danny's lead to the hook on the wall, with the dish of water beneath, she felt a rush of nerves. What really went on in here? What the hell did she know about mental illness? How ill was Matthew, and did she, really, even want to meet him?

'All right?' asked William, straightening up.

'Yeah, sure.'

He stepped aside as a doctor came out with a sheaf of notes; an anxious-looking woman was with him and they stood and conferred a few paces away, by a bench beneath a window, their voices low.

William was beside her again, his hand on her shoulder. 'You'll be all right,' he said. 'We needn't stay long, if you don't want to.'

She glanced up at him, saw the warmth in his eyes, considered for the umpteenth time the decades that lay between them.

Then he was ushering her through, as the automatic doors slid back, and she smelt that smell which distinguishes all hospitals, which she could recall from visiting Albert Page two years back, after a fall had put him briefly into Shrewsbury Hospital: disinfectant, flowers, school meals and cleaning fluid, and somewhere forbidden cigarettes. God, she could do with one now.

The Friends Coffee Shop was busy and bright; the flower shop likewise, full of greenhouse tulips and early daffs in buckets. The corridor running endlessly ahead was lined with paintings; a porter was wheeling an old girl along in a hospital chair; the phone on the reception desk was ringing, and was picked up. So far, so familiar; so far she might be in any old hospital.

Then she heard it. Then she saw it.

A man in his forties – fifties? – was coming down the corridor towards them. His hair was the texture of fibreglass or something – lifeless and faded and dry, neither white nor a proper colour, and his mouth was open, fixed like that, like he was dead: a gaping black hole in a face the colour of tallow, quite without expression. He was walking with a stiff, strange gait, and every now and then an arm was flung out, or a hand was flung across his face, or his head jerked wildly, as if yanked by a string. And from the gaping, deathlike hole of a mouth came intermittent shouts, or cries, very loud, as if he were right out in the open, out on the hills or something, in some lost age, lost place, calling across from hillside to hillside, a madman abandoned to die out there, among stones and sheep and circling birds.

She felt herself go pale.

'It's all right,' said William steadily, and he put his hand beneath her elbow and led her along the corridor, with its still lifes and landscapes and London scenes.

They came to a crossroads, as it were: more corridors, running to right and left, signs up for wards, for clinics and departments.

'This way,' said William, and they turned to the right. A nurse pushed open a double door, and Janice glimpsed a little group, in a circle, sitting in silence. Then the door swung to.

'Are you all right?' he asked her.

'Yeah, sure. Terrific.'

'Nearly there. I know it's distressing when you first come here.'

'I need a cigarette, to be honest.'

'Ah.' William smiled. 'You'll be in good company, then.'

'Will they—' She hesitated. How should she put it?

'Will they be like the poor chap we just saw? No.'

They walked on in silence. William asked himself: Why am I doing this? Why on earth am I bringing this poor girl here? Whatever was I thinking of?

Janice thought: if Claire made me think of Mary Harriman, what about Matthew? For a second she had a wild glimpse of Ernie, shuffling into the kitchen at the Dog Museum, in his grubby old jacket and holey socks, laughing and cadging a fag. She felt a rush of affection: what a strange old thing he was. Wispy as a dandelion clock, but sharp as a ferret. No flies on Ernie, though when you saw him out and about in town he looked ... well, he looked pretty barmy, didn't he?

160

'Don't make that face,' she heard her mother say suddenly, as she sat at the kitchen table, being annoying at seven or eight. 'If the wind changes, you'll get stuck like that.'

If the wind had blown a bit harder, a bit longer, over the Shropshire hills, Ernie, let's face it, could have been that poor bloody sod they'd just seen, his mouth stuck open, yelling from the back of some dreadful dark cave of the mind, treading the barren wastes of the world, stony and dry.

And Sophie—

'Here we are,' said William.

And she came back to earth with a bump, as they entered the open doorway of a ward with the usual stuff — beds, lockers, nurses' desk, flowers in horrible vases.

A girl — a young woman — of nineteen or twenty was sitting quite still on the side of her bed. Her hair was scraped up in a knot on the top of her head; bright pink mules hung on bare feet; she was wearing a pink flowery dressing gown over a white nightshirt. Her skin was pasty and pale. The left-hand sleeve of the dressing gown was drawn up, and she was gazing intently at her arm, fingering a long line of . . . clusters of—

Christ.

'We'll find him in the day room,' said William, his arm around her, and she made to accompany him, but her legs were like jelly.

Christ. Did people really—

The top half of the door to the day room was of glass, and plate-glass doors lay beyond it, leading to the grounds. As they approached, this area of the ward was therefore full of light. And looking back, much later, Janice could remember of these moments — this turning point in the whole occasion, in the whole of her time in London — a sudden flood of light, of whiteness: from the walls of the ward, from the sudden striking through the cloud of the February sun, illuminating the winter grass, the great dark trees, the faces of those who sat smoking and thinking — of what? — around the leaping colours of the television screen, with its images of another world, a million miles away. The horrible sights of that screaming mouth, that burned-up, gouged-out arm, were still within her; she knew she was shocked, and shaking, and perhaps — looking back — more open to anything, more vulnerable, than she had ever been in her life. But around her, in this place of broken souls, there was now, all at once, this light, this radiance, as she stepped with William across the threshold of the day room, and a man who looked just like him, but decades younger, turned from his chair and saw them, and with an incredible beauty slowly smiled.

16

'Foot-and-mouth,' said Buffy. She was trembling with distress. 'Foot-and-mouth – look at this.' She flung the newspaper down on to the stall, where William was setting out a ring of eggcups.

'I know,' he said. 'It's ghastly.'

'It's unspeakable. Do stop fiddling about. Do you realise what's been going on all this time?' She dropped her bag on her folding chair and stood there, twisting the ends of her woollen scarf this way and that.

William glanced at the paper. Buffy, of course, took the *Guardian*, while he still clung to *The Times*, changed as it was from its days of grandeur. Still, in the coverage of this catastrophe there wasn't that much to choose between them.

'Gone are the days,' said Buffy, twisting her scarf. 'Gone are the days when a farmer lambed his ewes, and drove them to the local market, and sold them locally, and had them . . . well, slaughtered, in a local abattoir. Now they go up and down the country. They're sent off to Europe, they're sent to the ends of the earth. Do you realise that a lamb born in Northumberland can end up in *Beirut*?'

William unscrewed the Thermos.

'And we're importing so much – why do we need to *import*? Why do our sheep have to make horrible journeys while other meat comes in? Infected meat in the food chain, and this is the result. Now we're having to slaughter fit, healthy livestock – those pyres, those dreadful pyres, have you seen them on the news? I can't bear it, William, I simply can't bear it.'

William took her bag off the folding chair and set it down. He put a hand on her arm, and indicated the coffee.

'My father,' he said, 'was never without his hip flask. Very wise. If I had one now, I'd add a little nip to this. You look as if you need it, dear. Do sit down.'

'A little nip?' She gestured wildly at the plastic coffee cup, and almost sent it flying. 'You think one can feel better about a thing like this with a little *nip*? Honestly, William, sometimes I despair.'

It was still early, not many people about, and Buffy's outrage was beginning to carry across the covered stalls. One or two heads were turning; William coughed. He pulled the chair out farther, patted her arm again.

'Do not,' said Buffy, 'pat me. Please do not.' She sank on to the folding chair, and shook her head.

'Poor Buffy,' said William. 'How you feel things.'

'Please don't tell me you don't feel things.'

'More the ones close to home,' he said. 'I fear that that's the truth of it. I don't have your wider vision. I wish I had.'

'How can you have spent your entire career in the heart of the country's most powerful institution, and not have a sense of the wider world?' Buffy, a little calmer, sipped her hot coffee and felt it do her good. 'No, don't answer. In the answer to that lie all this country's problems.'

'It isn't *quite* like that.'

'It's not far off it,' said Buffy. 'The blinkered civil servant.' She picked up the paper, revealing beneath it the pile of Winton dinner plates which had remained unsold last week. William, she noticed, had knocked the price down. Probably wise. Until spring came, this was a quiet season. In spring, with everyone perking up, you could charge almost anything. She finished her coffee, held out the cup for more. A biting wind was playing around her ankles. She should be wearing her boots – how foolish to think, with a gleam of sunshine, that she'd be all right in these old K flatties.

She folded the paper, with its heartbreaking photographs of soft-faced lambs, and maps of fearful journeys, and put it in her bag. Danny, beneath the trestle, poked his head out, draped in crimson damask. She bent to stroke his ears. 'Hello, old boy, how's things?'

Other stallholders were arriving, parking for five minutes on the double yellows, heaving their boxes out before the warden came sauntering along. Normal life in London. Not so normal in the countryside, with its sealed-off gates and footpaths, and disinfected straw in every gateway.

'Oh, dear,' she said aloud. 'Oh, dear.' And then, because this could not go on all morning, she turned to William and reminded him about the concert at Mary Ward, in three weeks' time. 'I gave you a flier last week,' she said. 'Remember?'

'Indeed you did,' said William, who had loyally put it up in his drawing-room window, though he knew, let's face it, that no one in Dulwich was going to trek up to Bloomsbury just to hear the old dears warble away. He'd been to these concerts, often. He knew what they were like.

Then he was struck by a thought. Something gentle, for Matthew to start with. Somewhere where people knew him. Buffy knew him well enough.

'I might bring Matthew,' he said, pouring his own second cup. 'I might bring Matthew and Janice. I was going to tell you – they've met.'

'Oh?'

'I took her up to the hospital.'

'Oh.'

'Bit of a risk, plunging her in at the deep end, but actually—' He stopped, remembering that rare, meltingly beautiful smile, and the way in which Janice, entirely out of her element, had stepped into the day room, with its smoke and blaring daytime television, smiling back, and as William introduced them had taken Matthew's hand, and knelt down beside him, and said: 'It's really good to meet you.'

'Actually she coped with it perfectly well?' said Buffy, and leaned forward to rearrange a pair of art deco vases. Plaster parrots. She had never liked them.

'She did,' said William. 'I mean, there were patients who disturbed her, I think – you can see some very sad sights in there, of course. But with Matthew – they seemed to hit it off, somehow. We went for a little walk in the grounds with Danny, had a bit of lunch, then we saw him into his OT class and said goodbye.'

'Very nice,' said Buffy. 'And what are they getting up to in OT these days? Basket weaving?'

'No,' said William, wondering at her tone. She could be quite sharp, old Buffy, especially when something had upset her. Foot-and-mouth – of course it was dreadful, but—

'They're painting at the moment,' he said. 'It makes me itch to pick up a brush.'

'Pick one up, then,' said Buffy. 'There's nothing to stop you.'

A woman was approaching the stall, her eye, quite clearly, drawn to the pair of parrots. Buffy fixed her with an uncompromising gaze. '*Good* morning,' she said brightly.

'I've had an idea,' Ernie told the girls. 'Bit of an inspiration.' It was Saturday lunch-time; they were gathered in the kitchen. Outside it was the usual filthy wet weather, but dogs were dogs, and needed walking, and he'd done his stint – been gouged out of doors by Mary just after ten, hammering on his window with one of Father's walking sticks, shouting and carrying on.

'Wake up, you old idler! Bestir yourself!'

'All right, all right, no need to shout.'

He came to the door and peered out. What a sight she was.

'What sort of time do you call this?' she demanded.

'Time for a bit of peace and quiet.' He stood his ground, the door open just a few inches. Have her in here and there'd be no stopping her, banging about with a mop and pail, hauling out his sleeping bag. 'I wasn't asleep,' he told her. 'I was working.'

She snorted. 'Working on what?'

'You wait and see.'

'Those dogs have been waiting since I don't know when. Come on, out you come, get your boots on.' She turned the stick upside down; he eyed the crook.

'You keep that thing away.'

He closed the door; he pulled his boots on, fetched down his waterproofs. Then he went out to the pens. Behind the wire the dogs leapt and scrabbled, barking joyously.

'Here I am, my darlings,' he told them, as Mary snapped open the padlocks. He bent to embrace them, kissing wiry coats. 'Off we go, then, off we go.'

And off they all went in the wet, noses down, tails beating, legs cocked at every corner.

'Mind out the way of that car! Flossie! Mind out the way!'

He bent to hold on to scruffs and collars, he tugged in the ones on the leads. Estate cars and Land Rovers slowed: he smiled and nodded, until they had gone. Then he shouted after them.

'Think you own the place! Have us all killed, you will!'

It had happened, once, to Jessie, a bright young springer: she'd slipped out of the pen in the days before the padlocks, and raced off, leaping the front gate and racing down to the bend just as—

It didn't bear thinking about.

He got them all over the stile, and into the rough empty pasture. Lambs'd be out soon, that'd be good, but it stopped them walking here. Make the most of it now. He squelched across, head down, the rain dripping off his waterproof hat, while they all enjoyed themselves.

Now it was lunch-time. Mary let him in. He'd done his stint of cheese and crackers: no man could live on blimming cheese and crackers. Time for a bit of hot soup. Time for a nice pork chop. That'd be the day. He settled himself at the table and waited, while she stirred.

'Where's Sophes?'

'She'll be down.'

He tried to picture her, doing things upstairs. He only ever went up there to have a bath, and that wasn't often: too blimming cold in that bathroom, too blimming draughty. When they were kids, of course, they'd all been up there together, put to bed at six by Mother, lights out, curtains drawn.

'And I don't want to hear a sound.'

All that giggling, after she'd gone. Them were the days.

Something settled itself on his feet beneath the table. He bent down to peer, saw the hen, kept quiet. He could have the egg for supper, if Mary didn't twig. He drummed his fingers on the table.

'Smells good.'

Mary sniffed. She went to the bottom of the stairs and shouted.

When Sophie came down, he told them.

The woman who bought the parrots was writing a book.

'I'm something of an expert on art deco,' she told them. 'Something of a collector.'

She tried to beat them down, but William would have none of it.

'Sorry, my dear,' he told her, with a winning smile, 'but I can't let anyone ruin me, not even you. Do tell me more about this book you're writing, it sound fascinating.'

When she had gone, he entered the sum in his book, and tucked her cheque away.

'Now then,' he said to Buffy, 'where were we?'

'I can't remember.'

The market was livening up a bit now, all the stalls set up and people wandering down past the Pizza Express on Upper Street, and the little Afghan café round the corner. But oh, how cold it was.

'Yes you can,' said William. 'I'm sure we were talking about something important.' He put his hands together, musingly. How clever and interesting he looked, thought Buffy, especially in that scarf. He *was* clever and interesting, even if he did have blind spots. She gave a small involuntary sigh.

'Oh, dear,' he said at once. 'What a sad sound. What is it, Buffy dear? Foot-and-mouth? Or something else?'

And the look he gave her was so tender and kind that she quite dissolved.

'William,' she began, with infinite caution.

'Got it!' he said suddenly. 'We were talking about Matthew and Janice. You know, I think she's really rather special. She's sensible and down to earth, but she's also much more sensitive than I'd given her credit for. And principled. Did I tell you she's a vegan?'

Buffy got to her feet. 'Yes,' she said. 'You did. More than once, if I remember rightly. I'm going to have a little look round, if you don't mind holding the fort.'

And she moved back her folding chair and stepped past him. Danny, beneath the table, was at once on the alert, and made to follow her, but William put down a restraining hand.

'Stay there, old boy,' he murmured. 'Stay put for now. I'm sorry,' he said to Buffy. 'I must be a crashing bore.'

But she couldn't answer him, and made her way with care among the stalls, until she had left the covered part of the market behind, and was walking with some difficulty along the crowded passage by the pub. Antique teddy bears gazed glassily at her from the tiny shop on the corner. One had particular character and distinction. For a dreadful moment she wanted nothing more than to hold him in her arms and weep into his comforting old fur.

'See?' said Ernie, warming to his theme. 'This could run and run.'

The table had been cleared of soup plates; he had been out to the trailer and come back, everything clutched to his chest in plastic carrier bags. He set it all up, propping against teapot and tin and jam jar, a proper exhibition, if you like, now that he'd mounted them on card. They sat there gazing: from Labrador Ned to little Pip; from greyhound to Jack Russell, from Flossie, so old, but still so precious, to

Benjy, so playful and bright. There was nothing like a boxer puppy, couldn't beat it for character. Mind you . . . Sophie leaned forward, and fingered the nose of a soulful young sheepdog. Was that Flash or Gerry? She tried to think.

'Mind,' said Ernie. 'Don't get crumbs on it.'

'I haven't got any crumbs,' said Sophie, withdrawing her finger. She looked again. 'Isn't that a lovely face?'

'What's that in your hair?' asked Mary suddenly. She leaned across and peered. 'When did you get that?'

Sophie's hand flew to the Great Dane. He was here at last, and how could she not wear him, now he was home?

'He wasn't very dear,' she said, and at once saw Mother, standing there with her rolling pin. 'Don't you lie to me, young lady!'

'Frippery,' said Mary. 'Endless frippery!' She banged on the table and everything leapt. 'We haven't the money, we haven't the funds.'

'Steady,' said Ernie, rescuing a collie-cross about to slip to the floor. He propped it up again. It was one of his best, though he said it himself. 'I don't want no arguing, I don't want no sniping. There's a body of work here, and I want some serious suggestions.'

Silence fell. He sat there, turning over the egg in his pocket.

'You're the one with the head for business,' he told Mary. 'Here I am, with a bold proposal, and all you can do is complain.'

'Tell us again what you had in mind,' said Sophie timidly.

'Concentrate, this time.' Blimey, how he needed a cig. Not a shred of baccy left, and not a penny till Monday. 'It's no good just dreaming and saying how pretty they are – we all know that, that's the point. The point is to reach a wider market. Make some serious money.'

'Serious money,' said Sophie, lingeringly.

'We need a business plan,' said Mary, averting her eyes from the Great Dane prancing through Sophie's pudding-basin hair.

'Now you're talking.'

'We need proper marketing.'

'We've always needed that.'

'We need a patron.'

'My plan,' he said again, watching Sophie's mind begin to wander already, 'is to start with a good show in town. Where, that's the thing. Teashop? Cinema? Town hall?'

'What about down in the parish? Parish hall would do nicely, they'll put up anything.'

Ernie regarded Sophie with scorn. 'In town, I said. Where people go. Then, when they see it, they pick up the leaflets.'

'The Perfect Present,' said Mary thoughtfully.

'Your Dog in Your Dining Room,' said Ernie. 'Commissions Undertaken.' He could see it all: the opening of the gate on to the gravel drive; the greeting at the door, the offer of coffee or tea. Admiring looks at the portfolio beneath his arm, the bounding up, the instant bonding. Shown into the drawing room, settled into a corner beside high windows on to a lawn. Out come the paints and brushes, down sits Rover, gazing up adoringly. The long contented hours. The mahogany door is quietly opened. '*May* I have a look?' Footsteps across the carpet, the small intake of breath. 'Oh, Mr *Harriman*—' His name is made, his name is on everyone's lips, he's charging – what? Fifty? A hundred? Put up the prices and people respect you, never let people think you're cheap.

'With You for Evermore,' he said aloud. 'Your Lasting Memory.'

'I know,' said Sophie, all at once. 'I know just the place.'

Buffy walked blindly up Camden Passage, past the Camden Head, where wonderful smells of hot lunch were wafting forth and bursts of cheerful laughter sounded. She passed the stalls of lace and linen, the maps and period postcards, period kitchen things. She passed without a glance the humbler offerings on mats set out on the ground – she knew those tins and trinkets, those plastic toys – and she marched past the grand glass-plated fronts of the real antique shops, with their fathomless interiors and fathomless prices. In the window of Beck's, that darling toyshop, the little Hornby train ran round and round, as it had done in all the years that she and William had had their stall here. They knew this place by heart, knew every shopfront and most of the dealers. In their time they'd had countless lunches in the Camden Head, pottered about among the shops and stalls, and bought things. They'd introduced Danny to Poppy, the West Highland who sat in her basket on Beck's counter, dear old girl; they'd browsed in the Angel Bookshop, after packing up the stall.

Happy days. Ordinary, contented days.

Buffy turned now into the second covered area, crammed with stalls of paper-knives, paper-weights, silly reproduction signs. Perhaps, if you were in the mood, they might raise a smile. She was not in the mood. She came into Pierrepoint Arcade, and walked along it, cold, and fighting misery. Tables were set out on the flagstones, outside tiny shops. Most of the arcade was china, and most she knew by heart. She slowed, her eye caught by a pretty green-and-gold tea set; automatically, she made a guess at the pottery, and date. She stopped, and stood at the window. It was crammed.

Inside was a space perhaps ten by six. A tiny heater burned in the corner; the owner was nowhere to be seen. Must have popped out to the loo – yes, there was the sign on the door: Back in a Tick. Could mean anything. Buffy pressed her face to the glass and peered. A comfy low chair with a cushion stood by the table, where rested an open book. There wasn't an inch of space uncovered: the tables, the walls, the mounted shelves were filled to the last inch.

And oh, how *warm* it looked, with that bright little flame, glinting on gravy boat and soup bowl. The cardigan hung on the back of the chair; what a nice chintz cushion. She could just see herself in there. With an inch more room, she could see William, too—

No, she couldn't. He was too tall, they'd need the same space all over again, to fit the two of them, and anyway—

'Excuse me.'

Someone was trying to get by her, as someone else came up the narrow passage. She pressed herself against the door, and a tall young woman strode past, in jeans and jacket.

Was that her? Surely not. Surely she wouldn't have come up here without warning; surely, if William had arranged it, he would have told her.

Buffy gazed after her. No – this girl was fair, and the Shropshire lass was dark, she remembered that. She breathed a sigh, and leaned against the door frame. It started to rain. She began to cry.

This was dreadful. Weeping in the open, on a Saturday morning. Going to pieces, in the middle of the day. What had become of her, where would all this lead?

She fumbled in her pocket, found a hankie. There. She blew her nose. There, that was better.

'My father,' she heard William say, in his kindly, beautiful voice, 'was never without his hip flask.'

She had snapped his head off, it was awful. And oh, how she could do with a little nip.

She made herself grow calmer. She would not let this happen. She wiped her eyes, and she knew that no one had noticed, for, let's face it, who would? She was out in the press of a busy Saturday, people getting on with their lives, looking at old china, not at old bats like her. And she turned from the door, and walked slowly on, seeing in her mind's eye – oh, it was dreadful, dreadful – a poor frightened ewe, stumbling up the ramp of a huge dark lorry with all her companions, shouted at, pressed up against other heaving sides, hearing the door slam, and the bolts pushed to; feeling the engine start up, and the long, long journey begin.

17

W illiam was out, with Danny. Janice was in. She took herself
down from her blue-and-white room at the top of the
house, past the family photographs, into the hall. It was
mid-afternoon, and she'd done her lunch-time shift; in a couple of
hours she'd be back for the evening. Now – the place was hers. She
could hear, in the quietness, the tick from the kitchen clock
downstairs.

'From my grandfather's schoolroom, I believe,' said William, winding it up each Sunday evening. He ran a finger over the mahogany
casing, pushed the door to, and touched the pendulum. Off it went,
steady and true; back went the big brass key on the top. 'There. I'd like
to say it kept perfect time, but it's slow, like me. Getting old.' He took
off his glasses, he gave her his smile. 'Now then, what shall we have
for supper?'

She could hear, now, the carriage clock on the drawing-room
mantelpiece, the little whirr of wheels, like an intake of breath, just
before it began to chime. One, two, three notes into the stillness. The
door was ajar; she went in.

Was it taking a liberty? Would he mind? He'd told her to make
herself at home. She let the door swing to; she stood there, drinking it
in, the size of it, the largest room she had ever been in, remembering
her feelings the day she'd arrived, and they'd sat taking tea by the fire:
that this was somewhere in which you could grow and expand, let your
mind roam, feel at peace. The carriage clock ticked softly; she walked
from end to end.

The winter afternoon was dull and cold; nothing in the sky today
held the promise of spring; in the gardens at front and back the
snowdrops were over, and although the beds and cracks in the

173

flagstones were speared by bulbs they were still tight and only inches high, not a bud visible: the frost had seen to that. Yet this room was filled with light: pale, even, but everywhere, from the immense high windows at back and front, and she walked up and down between them, over the creaking floor, smelling the ash from last night's fire, observing the patina on book jacket, china, desk and oak cupboard and piano, where photographs of the family were crammed, and needed dusting, and where Matthew, before his illness, had used to play. She stopped in front of it.

There they all were.

There were William and Eve on their wedding day, he in tails, she in a lily-white dress, with her veil thrown back and her hand tucked into the crook of his arm, and the two of them, you could see it, truly in love. 'That rare state of being' – was that how William would describe it? Something like that. They stood beneath that old stone arch, in a flood of sunlight, and . . . well, there they were, and it must have been—

Here were the children: Eve with her newborn baby Claire, bending over that wide-eyed face, the long snowy fall of shawl, the little fist. Here was Claire at two or three, squinting cheerfully into the sun, in a square-cut fringe and candy-striped sundress, buttoned on the shoulder, clutching a bear. Janice paused: was he upstairs, with all the other things left behind? No, she was sure not – he must have gone: into a new home, three children, married life. Then, a year or two later, came the baby brother, sleeping in his canopied pram beneath the trees, with Claire, on sandalled tiptoe, peering in.

And there, thereafter, were the two of them, always together, or almost: on the beach, with their buckets and spades; coming down the little slide in the garden, her arms round his waist; in a studio portrait, side by side and laughing – two healthy, contented, loved and well-dressed children, prepared for well-balanced, purposeful lives.

And here was Matthew, in a frame by himself, in his new school uniform. Janice picked it up.

What could you know from the face of a child, of what might lie ahead? He was open faced, though not in Claire's square-jawed, frank, determined mould. He smiled – and he looked, already, a little like William, you could see that at once, in his height, the easy way he carried himself, his charm. And was there, in those smiling eyes, beneath the clear brow, the tousled head of fair hair, a shadow? He was thin: that was noticeable, but that was all.

She put the photograph back; she picked up another, and another: Matthew at eight, with his violin; Matthew at twelve or thirteen, at the piano – this piano; at fifteen or sixteen, with his violin again, here, in the middle of the family drawing room, before his music stand, his chin resting lightly upon the instrument, extraordinary fingers on the keys, the bow drawn back in his long right hand, his eyes, for a moment, raised from the music, entirely intent, absorbed, lost to the world.

Janice carried the photograph to the window, and stood so the light, wintry and dull as it was, could fall upon it. She breathed upon the glass, which needed cleaning; she rubbed at it, and as the vapour cleared, Matthew looked back at her, and through and beyond her: a gifted and completely beautiful boy, for whom, at that moment, no human being mattered at all.

The phone was ringing. Somewhere the phone was ringing, and had been for ages, she realised, coming to with a start, and hurrying out to the hall, the photograph in her hand. She put it down on the hall table, and picked up the receiver.

'Hello?'

'Janice?' said Claire. 'Is that you?'

William threw a stick, and then another. Danny, each time, came scampering back, over the muddy stretch of grass, on to the path where he was pacing about. Winter afternoon, a weekday, an overcast sky – few people out and about in the park, and how wise they were, thought William, feeling the cold, clapping gloved hands together. He nodded to one or two other dog-walkers, known by sight for a long time now: the fey-looking woman with her Afghan, the old chap with his sharp-faced black-and-tan mongrel, lifting a leg in the empty rose beds, whistled away.

'Not getting any warmer.'

'Fearful, isn't it?' He bent to retrieve Danny's stick, and held it high. Danny watched, eager and waiting.

'Go on, off you go!' And he hurled it as far as he could, not bad for someone of his age, though he said so himself: life in the old boy yet. Danny raced off, and he walked on, beating his arms, keeping the circulation going.

Far above, London gulls were wheeling, sharp-eyed and hungry, over the leafless trees. Across the park a gardener had lit a bonfire: the last of the debris of leaves and pruning and fallen branches before spring came, if it ever came, burning into the afternoon, smoke into smoky cloud. And what did this remind him of, this dark plume rising?

Foot-and-mouth! Look at these pictures, William — have you been watching it on the news? Those pyres, those dreadful pyres — I just can't bear it.

Poor old Buffy: how she took things to heart. Had he imagined it, or had she, away from the stall, been weeping about it all? She wouldn't look at him when she came back.

'I'm sorry.' She sank heavily into her chair. 'I'm dreadfully out of sorts for some reason — please don't take any notice.'

He patted her arm. 'It's my fault — I talk about myself too much.'

'No, no, please don't say that. Let's just forget it, I'll be fine tomorrow.'

One or two punters came and went: they sold a Creamware jug, and a couple of Victorian tiles. Quite a good price for the tiles. But somehow — after all these years of friendship, the easy chat, the never having to think about a thing, just rubbing along so nicely — somehow all that was gone, today.

The rain fell harder; everything felt dismal.

'Let's call it a day,' he said at last. 'Let's go and have lunch.'

But the Camden Head was packed, and neither of them could face it: all that loud laughter, all those wet clothes.

'I'll treat you to Frederick's,' he said, as they came out into the wet. 'Come on, it'll do us both good.'

But Frederick's was booked solid, and at that point Buffy said: 'I'm fit for nothing anyway, William, I wouldn't enjoy it.' And she put up her umbrella and nothing he could say would dissuade her. He saw her to the bus stop, he saw her on to the bus, Danny tucked inside his coat, and she lifted a hand at the streaming window, but oh, so bleakly — not at all like spirited old Buffy.

'I'll phone you tonight,' he mouthed as the bus pulled away, but he didn't know whether she had seen. He went back to the car, parked in Duncan Terrace, the boxes piled up in the back, and a ticket on the windscreen. Raindrops clung prettily to the plastic envelope; he pulled it off, threw it into the glove compartment, and drove home feeling grim.

Janice was out; Mrs T. had been and gone, and though the house was clean it was also cold and empty. He put on the heating, had a hot bath, lit the fire. Restored, he phoned Buffy that evening, glass in hand.

'I'm fine,' she said, but she didn't sound it. 'Think no more about it, William, I'm having an early night.' And she hung up quite quickly, and that was that.

Oh, dear. He couldn't, as Mrs T. would say – so often – he couldn't make it out.

Oh, dear – and just when everything had been looking up.

And now—

Danny was running back again, stick clamped between his dachshund jaws. They were bred for hunting, of course; they were fierce, even ferocious working dogs by nature. For a moment, bending to take the stick – and that was enough now, it was simply too bloody cold to stay out a moment longer – he found himself thinking of the Dog Museum, with its great range of the canine: from stuffed to (presumably) working, to flat out by the fire. What a strange business it was. He clipped on Danny's lead, made his way to the gates.

There was nothing he could do about Buffy, not at the moment. And she'd rally, she always did. No – the next thing was Matthew, the meeting with Fisher at last: tomorrow as ever was.

Action. Teatime. He looked at his watch. Janice would still be at home, before her evening shift. He'd light the fire, put the kettle on, call her down.

'Come on, Danny. Homeward bound.' He tugged on the lead, walked faster.

But when he reached the house, he knew straight away that it was empty – no light at the top-floor window, in Claire's old room, and the silence in the unlit hall was palpable. He switched on the lamp, saw the note by the phone:

Gone to see Claire, then straight to work. Janice.

'Come in,' said Claire. 'You must be frozen.'

'I'm OK.' She wiped her feet on the mat and entered the roomy hall. Through living with William she had, even in this short time, grown to have a sense of the well-heeled London life, but in his house everything was worn, faded, had been lived in, unreplaced, for donkey's years. The place gathered itself around you: you could sink in, settle down, get on. Here, where there were three children, coats were neat upon the coatrack, shoes in the rack below; the well-brushed stairs ran up to a sparkling landing window, hung with heavy curtains, looped back with silky ropes and tassels. Bloody hell.

She tucked her hat and gloves into her pockets; she let Claire take jacket and scarf and hang them up; she followed her into the kitchen, which was huge. Acres of classy vinyl, patterned in terracotta tiles; gleaming Rayburn, clean tea towels on the rail; long family table laid with that wipe-clean fabric but in a pattern which looked like antique wallpaper; more shining windows on to well-planted window boxes and the garden. There, at least, were signs that things had got a bit out of hand: no one, in this winter's weather, could maintain the perfect garden.

'Do sit down.' Claire was putting the kettle on. She leaned against the Rayburn rail as Janice pulled out a chair, and smiled at her. 'It's very nice of you to come.'

'That's OK.'

'I just thought – if you do come and baby-sit, it would be nice to get to know one another.'

'Yeah.'

'And for you to get a feel of the house, and meet the children.'

'Yeah,' said Janice again. 'Sure.'

There was silence. The kettle came to life. Janice felt for her tin, which wasn't there. Just as well – who would dare to light up in a house like this? She found herself looking round for signs of animal life: a dog basket, a dish, put down for the cat. Even a hamster cage would do it. Even a cockatiel. She looked at the shelf of cookbooks, the labelled boxes of Lego and felt tips and Warhammer elves.

'What time do the kids get back?'

The slightest furrow creased Claire's intelligent brow. 'Just after four. They don't come back by themselves – I'm on a rota.'

'Oh.' She watched the careful rinsing of the pot, over a spotless white sink; the taking out of tea bags from a tin. Rather like William's tin: black and Chinese red – perhaps he had given it to her. Bit different from the caddy in the Dog Museum.

What was it with that frown, then?

'Did I say something stupid?' she asked. 'I don't really know much about kids.'

Again, that infinitesimal furrow, as Claire took expensive-looking mugs from hooks.

'I just have a thing about that word.'

'What word?'

'Kids.'

'Eh?'

'It's rather – I don't know – rather denigrating, somehow. It makes me think of *Time Out* special issues: Kidstuff. Where to Take the Kids. As if they were just a class of being. All those shrieking TV programmes – Kids! Everything so *cheerful*.'

'What do you call them, then?'

'Children,' said Claire, and took milk from the fridge. 'A proper word. Like childhood. You can't have *kid*hood.'

'You're just like your dad,' said Janice. 'I suppose I should call him your father.'

'I think you should, and I'm not at all like him.' She brought everything over, set it all down. 'Do you take sugar?'

'No. Nor milk,' Janice added, as Claire's hand moved towards a green-and-white jug which also put her in mind of William. 'I'm vegan, didn't he tell you?'

Claire sat, and looked at her.

'No, he didn't. We don't talk all that often, and anyway he's getting forgetful. How very principled of you. Would you like a slice of lemon?'

'If you've got it.'

'Of course.' And she rose, and took one from the vegetable rack, and sliced it into a cobalt-blue saucer with a thin gold rim. 'Here.'

'Thanks.'

And Claire poured the tea, and Janice dropped in a slice of lemon, and Claire asked, sitting back in her chair and observing her across the table, 'How long have you been a vegan?'

'Since I was a kid,' said Janice, giving what she knew was a winning, ironic little lift of an eyebrow, and the set of Claire's features, so uncannily like those of her fearsome distant cousin, dissolved all at once into a smile full of warmth and humour.

'I suppose I do need taking down a peg or two,' she said, and then, after a moment, sipping her tea: 'I certainly need something.'

'How do you mean?'

There was a pause. There was a look – as if she were on the brink

179

of something momentous. Then Claire shook her head, and waved a hand. 'Never mind.' She put down her mug, and the subject, whatever it may have been, was clearly closed. 'How are you getting on here? You seem to have settled in very well.'

'Yeah,' said Janice. 'I suppose I have. William – I mean your dad – I mean your father – he's been great. I really like him. And I was lucky to get the wine-bar job.'

'How did you get it?'

She snapped her fingers. 'Just like that.'

Claire smiled. 'How clever of you. And what else have you been doing?'

'Oh, you know – going to a few museums and stuff.' She described the outings to Greenwich, the Dulwich Picture Gallery. She felt Claire's eyes intent upon her. She looked down at her expensive mug of black tea, with its slice of lemon.

'And?' Claire prompted.

The lemon was floating, meditatively, from rim to rim. Janice, watching it, held the memory and image of Matthew within her, as she had done for days, not telling anyone, as if to talk about him would break a spell. But not to mention the visit – if Claire found out afterwards, she'd wonder, wouldn't she? Think it strange.

'We went to see your brother,' she said, and heard herself, for the first time, sound awkward.

'Oh.' There was a little pause. 'And how was that?'

'It was . . . I was a bit freaked out by the hospital. But Matthew – I liked him. I felt . . . OK with him, I suppose.'

'Good,' said Claire, but when Janice looked up she was frowning again.

'Do you mind me going to see him?' she asked, and remembered, all at once, the glance along the sunlit upper landing, in William's house, towards her brother's old room, a glance full of sadness, quickly erased.

'No,' said Claire, lifting her mug to her lips. 'No, of course not.'

Was she telling the truth? Was it a bit of a threat, a bit of an intrusion, having this stranger land in your midst, and start stirring things up?

Was that what she was doing?

'You were very close, weren't you?' she said. 'When you were young.'

Claire looked at her, and Janice felt herself begin to blush. There she had been, nosing about in the empty house, looking at family photographs without so much as a by-your-leave. Claire must realise – it must look dreadful.

'I mean,' she said, flounderingly, 'I mean that's what I imagine. I'm an only child, I don't know what it's like, I suppose . . .' Her voice trailed away.

'Are you?' asked Claire, a sister and mother of three. 'I've always thought only children are so interesting, I must say. Such a complex relationship with one's parents, so many inner resources.' She smiled, in full child-psychology mode, and Janice felt her blush begin to fade, the conversation steered, quite deliberately, away from the source of her embarrassment. 'You become so independent, I imagine. I certainly sense that about you.'

'Yeah, well. Yeah, I suppose so.'

'But your parents must miss you. Is this the first time you've lived away from home?'

'Yeah, yeah it is. Time I gave them another ring, I suppose.'

And where had Matthew got to in all this? Was it safe to mention him again?

'Do you mind me asking—' she began. 'About Matthew. I mean, like—' She didn't know how to go on.

For a moment Claire did not respond; for a moment, in the silence, Janice felt aware once more of something quite unfathomable. Then the rain began to fall again, and Claire said slowly, 'He's been ill for a very long time. You do realise that.'

'Yes,' said Janice, as the rain sank into the untended garden.

'And is unlikely to recover,' said Claire, with great deliberation.

'Is that—' Despite the lemon tea, her mouth felt dry. 'I mean – is that definite?'

'I wouldn't say anything in mental health was *definite*. But—' She spread her hands. 'He's schizophrenic. My father must have told you.'

'No,' said Janice. 'Not exactly.' And she felt something within her shift, like the plates of the earth or something.

The sky darkened, the rain fell harder, the children – as she must think of them – were dropped off from the school run.

'This is Janice,' said Claire, when they had hung up wet coats and bags and come trooping into the kitchen. 'She's staying with Grandpa.'

'Like, the lodger,' said Janice, getting to her feet. 'Hi.'

'Hi.'

'Piers, Hugo, Geraldine,' said Claire, and they each shook hands. They were bright looking, nice looking. She expected them all to go off and collapse in front of the telly, like normal kids after school, but they sat round the table and waited, as Claire made tea.

'Have you brought Danny?' asked Geraldine, looking around.

''Fraid not. He's good, isn't he?'

'He's wicked,' said Hugo. 'Remember the skidding? Whee!' And he made a sweeping gesture.

'Skidding?'

They started to describe it; Claire came over with sandwiches and drinks.

'Janice is going to do some baby-sitting,' she told them.

'We've got a baby-sitter,' said Geraldine, taking her beaker.

'We don't need a baby-sitter,' said Piers, reaching for a sandwich. 'Not being rude or anything.' He was tall and lanky and had a blurred, tired look which put Janice in mind of his father, last seen in the wine bar on Valentine's Day. 'I can baby-sit,' he said.

'Are you fourteen?' asked Janice. 'It's illegal if you're not fourteen.'

Piers shrugged, and was silent.

'Why do we need another baby-sitter?' asked Geraldine.

Janice looked at her watch. Why did they? 'I'd better be off in a minute.'

'Please come again,' said Claire, in the hall, as she pulled on her jacket and scarf. 'We'd love to have you. I'll phone.'

'Yeah. Sure. Thanks for the tea.'

'It's a pleasure.' She put out a hand, and rested it for a moment on Janice's arm. 'You mustn't be upset about Matthew. It's sad, but it's how things are. My father should have told you. He can be very thoughtless.'

'He wants to have him home,' said Janice, with a flash of how this might be. 'He often talks about it.'

Claire shook her head. 'I think that's extremely unlikely.' And then voices rose in the kitchen, and she pulled open the front door, saying: 'I'd better get on.'

Outside, it was dark, and chucking it down. 'Do let me lend you an umbrella.'

182

'It's OK,' said Janice, 'I'll make a dash for it. 'Bye.'

And she went out into the rain, silvered in the lamplight, feeling Claire's watchful gaze upon her, until the door slowly closed, and she began to run.

18

J anice sat drinking tea and smoking, at the table in the kitchen with its red-checked cloth. It was mid-afternoon; she was waiting for William to return from his hospital visit.

'I should be home by teatime,' he had said, buttoning his coat in the hall, adjusting the sea-green scarf before the mirror. 'That is if Fisher is prompt – you can never tell, these days.' Beside him, Danny was looking up brightly, full of anticipation. 'Sorry, old chap – not today.' He turned to Janice, waiting at the foot of the stairs. 'Sure you won't come?'

'I'll keep the home fires burning,' said Janice, stretching out a hand to Danny, who at once came trotting over. 'I'll give him a walk, and be here when you get back. I might bake a cake, if that's OK.'

'Very OK,' said William. 'Entirely satisfactory.' He turned up his collar, pulled on his gloves, reached for his umbrella from its stand. 'Well, now – wish me luck.'

'Good luck.' And she came over, Danny trotting back again, and he bent to kiss her: once, twice, as Londoners did, she kept noticing, and she felt the dry brush of his well-shaven skin against hers, and the warmth of his lips on her cheek.

'There.' He squeezed her hand with soft worn leather. 'I'm off.' And he strode to the door, and she held Danny back, feeling almost choked.

'I'm sure it'll be fine,' she said.

'You haven't told me about Claire.' He turned, suddenly, his fingers on the latch.

'Not much to tell.' He'd been in bed by the time she got home from the wine bar; today Mrs T. had been banging about until lunch-time, had only just gone, and his mind was all on Matthew. 'I might do some baby-sitting one day.'

'You met the children?' His face lit up.

'I did, they're great.' She looked at him, standing there, hovering, really, putting off the moment. 'Go on,' she said gently. 'You'll be late.'

And he nodded, and opened the door. She caught a glimpse of the tight buds on the magnolia, just in leaf, felt the cold come into the unheated hall, and then he was gone, and she buried her face in Danny's chestnut neck, noticing grey hairs.

'Come on.'

Down in the kitchen, she let him out into the garden, opened the cupboard doors. She shook raisins into a blue-and-white striped bowl, cracked eggs into another. Cornish Ware, William had told her, worth quite a bit these days. She'd seen bowls like this on Albert Page's dresser, cracked and yellow with age, like him. How was he getting on without her, poor old git?

She turned on the oven, put half a packet of organic soya spread to warm in a Creamware bowl within it, and opened more cupboard doors until she'd found a baking tin. She greased it, shook wholemeal flour over it, watched Danny, in the garden, sniffing and cocking a leg, looking up as a magpie suddenly arrived, landing on the wall and giving that hoarse cak-ak-cak she'd know anywhere, had heard all her life in the Shropshire woods and hills. He cocked his glossy head, and lifted his tail, his eye wicked and bright. Cak-ak-ak-cak, across the London garden, soaked by the endless rain into mud: no one but Danny had been out there for weeks.

One for sorrow.

Janice took out the Creamware bowl and beat brown sugar into the softened soya spread. She beat the eggs with a fork into a foaming froth, stirred them in with a wooden spoon, beat in wholemeal flour and raisins, and finely grated lemon and orange peel. But for the eggs it was vegan; she wouldn't eat it, she'd keep it for William, in a tin wrapped up in greaseproof paper, something he could have by the fire when he felt like it; something to take to the china stall and share with his old friend Buffy, whom she was waiting to meet. She spooned it all into the baking tin, put it in the oven, set the timer. Right: that was that. She washed up the bowls, partly because the largest was too big to go in the machine, and partly because, though it made her feel like the Harriman cousins, she wasn't used to dishwashers – not at home, nor at Cloud Nine, come to that. She wasn't used to a lot of things she'd met down here, but then that was the point of coming, wasn't it? To open up her life.

185

Cak-ak-ak-cak. Bright eyed, watchful, still there. Janice put the kettle on, and leaned on the sink and watched the bird and dog and fitful sun and cloud. Shropshire things, if you just made a list of them: she might have been in the kitchen in Cloud Nine, looking out over the hills at magpie and starling and blackbird, and the dogs of the visitors, hoping for biscuits. And she had a sudden memory of the morning during the storms of last November, of cycling up on Leinthall Ridge, finding a tree down and hauling boughs out of the way across the road, watched by a beady-eyed crow, and a couple of magpies. Two for joy – old wives' stuff, the kind of thing her gran was always saying, or one of the cousins, or Albert, but it had cheered her up, and that very day she'd met Eric.

Well. So much for that.

And now—

One for sorrow. What a harsh cry. And now he was up and away, on a sudden gust of wind, over to a tree in a neighbouring garden, where she could still hear him, and Danny, too, looking up and barking.

The kettle switched itself off; the kitchen, which had smelled of Flash, now filled with the smell of baking. Janice made tea in a blue-and-white Cornish Ware mug; she let Danny in again, sat down with her tin at the table. Would William mind if she smoked? Just one. And she rolled up and lit up, as Danny settled into his basket – she wasn't going to take him out, sorry, she'd done enough dog-walking to last a lifetime, and it was warm in here, and she needed to think.

And she thought about Claire, and yesterday afternoon: the intensity of that gaze, across that table, in that perfectly appointed kitchen.

I suppose I do need taking down a peg or two. I certainly need something . . .

And what is that? wondered Janice, inhaling Golden Virginia. What is it with this immaculate house and everything just right, but not right at all?

She thought about Matthew, as she had thought about him for days; of the silence when one tried to find out more.

You do realise he is very ill . . . he's schizophrenic . . . my father should have told you . . .

I couldn't have gone today, thought Janice now, drinking her milkless tea. Should she have done? Been a support for William, going off all alone to a meeting he dreaded? She knew that he did – she could tell; he must do. But she couldn't have faced that place again, without having some hope—

Of what?

And is unlikely to recover . . .

If William knew that—

How did Claire know that?

And she closed her eyes, and relived once again that moment of illumination, entire and complete and unlike anything else, when a man with a face like a sleeping angel had slowly turned, and seen her, and dissolved her with his smile.

William sat across the desk. Matthew's consultant pulled a file from a heap, and opened it. The room was cramped, the file was bulging. William read, upside down, snatched details of his son's confinéd life – the phrase came upon him, even as his eyes skimmed over the dosages of drugs, the reports and observations, his own impassioned letter.

My son's confinéd life—

The music of Shakespeare, or Donne. He pictured a winter garden, a man alone, in a hat and black buttoned coat, pacing up and down and writing, to ease his own distress.

'Well?' asked Fisher. He was of an age and type which William, from the quite different milieu of his Treasury days, knew well: over sixty, living a life of driven intensity, saved by a powerful mind from complete exhaustion. He thought it was Fisher who had signed the papers sectioning Matthew, all those years ago – confining him, indeed, lest he murder his own father.

'Well?'

William looked at shrewd pale eyes behind newly fashionable wire-rimmed spectacles.

He said, with difficulty: 'I'm very wound up. I've lost my concentration. Please forgive me. What were you saying?'

Fisher took off his glasses and leaned forward in his cushioned plastic chair. The shadow of a wing fell briefly upon William's letter, as a magpie flew past the window.

The sorrow of my son's confinéd life—

Fisher leaned on the desk, and pressed long, sixty-year-old fingers to his lips. His gaze met William's; William's eyes filled with tears.

'Forgive me,' he murmured again, and cleared his throat.

'You have been through a very great deal,' said Fisher, watching him. 'I understand your feelings – they are entirely natural.'

'But things have been getting much better,' said William, feeling for his handkerchief. 'Much.'

187

'You mean with Matthew?'

'Not exactly. I mean ... well, yes, in some ways. I have sensed potential, I have allowed myself to hope. I have wanted to—' he gestured, blew his nose. 'Have wanted to bestir myself – breathe some new life into the whole thing. Oh, dear.' He put his handkerchief back in his pocket, coughed experimentally. Yes: he was steady again.

'At Christmas—' began William, and explained a little about Buffy, an old friend with clear views, who had made her feelings about Matthew plain. Drugged to the eyeballs, if Fisher would forgive him. Turning into a zombie: Fisher would understand that this was only one person's view. But then – and he explained a little about the arrival of his lodger, a bright, original young woman who was livening up the household, who had put a spring in his step, lessened his loneliness, made him feel—

'Young again?' asked Fisher drily.

'And what is wrong with that?' asked William, recovering his spirit a little, now that his tongue had loosened.

'Nothing at all. It all sounds—' But he left the sentence unfinished, and lifted William's letter from the file, and ran his eyes over its distinctive hand once more, turning the pages.

'I brought Janice here,' said William. 'Last week. I introduced them.'

'And?' Fisher laid down the letter.

And William described the encounter: the radiant smile, the walk in the grounds, the way in which Janice and Matthew – curiously, quite unexpectedly – had seemed at ease with one another. It was something he could not account for, but it lifted his spirits.

'And you are proposing? Your wish is?'

William closed his eyes. There stole upon his inner eye a scene: Matthew in the drawing room, before his music stand. Violin and bow were in his hands; the one met the other, hesitantly, in a little scale. A smile played over his lips; Janice, perched on the piano stool, watched intently, swinging a foot. The scale rose and fell, and rose again. William, in his chair with Danny, leaned back and listened, feeling the old days begin anew.

He opened his eyes, saw Fisher's cool, clear-sighted gaze upon him. He asked carefully, 'What is the best we can hope for?'

Fisher's long fingertips were pressed together as if in prayer – did anyone but a doctor or priest ever make such a gesture?

'We can adjust his medication,' he said slowly. 'It's true he has been heavily sedated for perhaps too long. They're pretty much a sledge-hammer, the traditional drugs – Stelazine, that's what Matthew's been on, I think.' And he looked down at the file again. 'Yes. Well – we can ease him off that, we can try him on one of the new-generation pills. Respiradone.' He made a note.

'What does that do?' asked William. My darling boy, he thought, pumped through with all of this. My darling clever boy.

'Respiradone is still a sedative. But it's gentler, it's one of a group we call atypicals—' Fisher reached behind him, pulled down a pharmaco-poeia from the shelf, flicked through the index, found the page. 'We'll try it,' he said, still reading. 'We'll give it a go.'

'And will there be—' William tried to imagine it. 'Side effects? Withdrawal symptoms?'

'Probably.' Fisher closed the book. 'Almost certainly, I should think. But in time he might do much better. We'll have to see.'

'And if he does well?' asked William, with a little flare of hope.

'Then you could try a longer visit home, see how he responds. Is that what you would like?'

'It is,' he said fervently. 'I feel so certain that this is what he needs: familiar surroundings, stimulation, love . . .'

Fisher made another note in the file, and closed it. 'Of course,' he said carefully, 'there are those of a younger generation than I who'd throw all these drugs out of the window. They wouldn't even give Matthew this diagnosis. "Schizophrenia" – they say it's a label, an all-purpose, meaningless term. Psychosis can take many forms, have many causes. They'd look for a psychosocial model – they'd try to treat him with therapy. Cognitive behavioural therapy – have you heard of that at all?'

William had not. He recalled, with a horrible intensity, the night he tried never to think of: Matthew's unrecognisable hatred, and rage, the smashing, splintering glass and furniture, the upraised candlestick become a murder weapon.

Something had had to be done. Something had had to knock him out.

But now—

But why—

'It's all *your* fault,' he heard Claire say bitterly. 'Because *you* never notice anything—'

'Oh, dear,' he said aloud. 'Oh, God.'

Fisher put a hand across the desk. 'We can only try. If he picks up, we might try all sorts of things. But please – don't expect too much. Disappointment is hard to bear as one grows older.'

William looked at him, but there was no elaboration, and slowly he got to his feet.

'Thank you,' he said, as he had been saying for years. 'You've been very kind.'

And then they shook hands, and he opened the door on to the waiting area, the Tuesday clinic – oh, such a blessedly ordinary phrase – with its understated turmoil, its sea of troubled lives.

It was growing dark. William walked down the road, towards his home, where lamps were lit: in the hall, with its tattered apricot silk; in the drawing room, where firelight flickered. He quickened his step, beat the umbrella against his coat. God, it was cold.

The iron gate squeaked at his touch, and was stiff: something else that needed attending to, as soon as spring arrived. He closed it, climbed the stone steps, unlocked the door.

The house was warm, and the smell of baking wafted up from the lower depths. A fruitcake, with a hint of citrus. Heaven. He was about to call out, to whistle, to say he was back, but then he didn't want to – he wanted only to savour the moment, and he quietly closed the door and stood there, letting it all wash over him: a proper home, a proper tea, a place for Matthew to return to, now he was going to recover. For he would, he would.

The sorrow of my son's confinéd life / Is washed away, for he is well again . . .

The phrasing had run through his head during the entire long walk home, musical and haunting.

And what rhymes with life? he asked himself, leaning against the door in a flood of weary happiness, seeing her walk up the stairs, and smile, and come to greet him.

They stood in the middle of Healing Arts, and strange scents wafted over them. Ernie started to cough.

'Blimey. It's like a sweet shop.'

'Ssh,' said Sophie, tugging at his sleeve. 'Come along here. Come and say hello.'

Portfolio beneath his arm, he shuffled across to the counter, temporarily unattended. Baskets of soap wrapped in Cellophane stood next to jars of prettily coloured balls of bath oil.

'Thirty-five pence, for one of them? How much are them soaps?'

They were £2.60 each.

'Blimming rip-off. And what's a tea tree, when it's at home?'

'*Ssh!*'

There were little heaps of leaflets. He picked one up. It was pale green, and written in calligraphy, with a leafy border. He peered. There was a name, with a lot of letters after it. There was a photograph, of an intense-looking woman past her prime.

Are you suffering from tension, anxiety and stress?

Is insomnia ruining your life?

Are you a victim of compulsive habits?

I am a qualified Masseuse, Hypnotherapist and Counsellor.

I have many years of successful experience in treating phobias, depression, smoking, relationship problems and back complaints.

Unlock your hidden energy. Learn the secrets of an ancient healing force.

Restore your body's natural balance and rid yourself of toxins.

Private consultations and group work.

Your life is in my hands.

Ernie snorted. He picked up another, in raspberry pink. It offered a course in one-to-one life-focusing, in tranquil surroundings. Where was that, then? He peered at the address. That was old Ford's place, wasn't it? Who'd he sold up to, after all these years? Must've been someone with a bob or two, to do up that old ruin. He picked up another leaflet.

If you'd like to improve your ability to stay grounded and centred, to purify your working space and keep your energy clear, I may be able to help . . .

Sophie was gazing at the cards of hair slides and earrings. Her square, bitten fingers strayed towards a pair of dangling trout.

'*Good* morning!'

They both started.

'How are you, Sophie?' The woman behind the counter was bright and smiling. She wore a nice soft jumper in royal blue, with a scarf loosely knotted at the neck, and a cheerful lipstick. Ernie perked up. The last time he'd been in here they'd been served half-heartedly by a wan-looking girl whose grey-complexioned child slept in a pushchair. And not so much stock in here, neither: half-empty shelves. Under new management, that must be it. Rip-off. Profit. Just what he needed.

'This is my brother,' said Sophie, pushing him forward. 'Ernie. He's an artist.'

'How do you do?' she said kindly. 'I'm Daphne.'

'Pleased to meet you.'

'And what can we do for you today? I see you have your eye on those trout, Sophie. Aren't they pretty?'

'She's an old trout herself,' said Ernie. 'Heh, heh, heh.'

Mary would have swiped him good and proper, shop or no shop, but Sophie just gave him her look.

'We was wondering—' she began, and he put his portfolio on the counter with a flourish. Leaflets fluttered to the floor and a lucky magnetic ladybird dropped from the side of a jar and fell among the Cellophaned baskets. Daphne retrieved it. Sophie bent for the papers, and muddled them up. Customers stepped aside.

'Oh, dear.' Daphne lifted the portfolio in her manicured hands and leaflets swirled this way and that in the passage of air. Sophie's hand went to her mouth: he could feel her thinking, We should never have come.

'Like she says,' he began, with some authority. 'I'm an artist, and that there's my work. And some leaflets. We was thinking about a show.'

People were queuing. People began to cough. Daphne stood the portfolio behind the counter and looked firmly past them. They took themselves into a corner, and waited.

'Never give up,' said Ernie. 'That's my motto.'

'Well, now,' said Daphne, some while later. 'Well, now. These are rather—'

They were in her office; her part-time assistant had arrived, panting, and was now at the till. Ernie had unzipped the portfolio, and spread his work out on the desk. It smelled like a sweet shop in here, too: bunches of dried stuff hanging over his head and boxes of sickly soap and shampoo in every corner. Crystals were hung in the lancet window: it had started to rain. He stood next to Sophie, watching Daphne consider his portraits, one by one. Quality, that was the thing. It always told.

Daphne propped up a noble-headed Labrador in profile: that was Ned. She paused over Alfie the Westie, and Benjy the boxer-cross; she turned over Flossie and Pip, with their faithful eyes, and then turned back to them. He'd put in six profiles and six full-on – sock 'em with the lot.

'And them's the leaflets,' he said, pointing.

Daphne picked one up. Here was where quality told, as well: look at that hand and you'd know you were with a professional. He'd spent hours on it, writing it all out, taking account of the girls' suggestions.

Your Closest Friend Will Never Leave You.

There. Couldn't beat it. He'd pasted on Ned, gazing loyally, soulfully, upwards; he'd taken the sheet into CopyFast and done a hundred: 4p a throw. Nearly broke him. Still: there they were, and he was proud of them. Put that holistic beeswax in the shade, said Mary, and he knew she was right. Balance. Toxins. Crystals. Load of old cobblers. Dogs were the thing. Dogs had meaning. A dog would put you right.

'What do you think?' asked Sophie timidly. He gave her a look. Never ask. Let them come to you, like an animal. Make 'em wait.

'Well,' said Daphne again. 'Of course, it's not our usual thing at all, but actually—' She ran a finger along Ned's nose and Ernie knew he'd done it. 'I had a dog like this once,' she began, and he knew they were in at the kill.

'See?' he said to Sophie, as they made their way back through the close. 'What did I tell you?'

Fifty leaflets were on the counter, and Ned was on the wall, next to an astrology chart, and a poster of Britain's Butterflies. Most of them he hadn't seen for years.

'No,' said Sophie. 'I told *you*. It was me what thought of it.'

Rain was swirling over the lawns, the bells of the cathedral struck the hour. Lovely.

'Clever old you,' said Ernie. 'What a team we make.'

She flushed with pleasure.

Out in the street, outside the newsagent's, there were huge great numbers on billboards. In the window of Radio Rentals the lunch-time news was on, on a dozen screens. They stopped to look. This was the only time they ever saw the telly: might as well make the most of it. And they stood in the rain, and watched the man talk to them, as the fire behind him burned up carcass after carcass, and stiff legs pointed to the sky.

'It's bad,' said Sophie, her eyes widening. 'It's very bad.'

'It hasn't got to here,' said Ernie. He thought of their father, up every morning at six for the milking, taking his cap off the peg in the passage, pulling his boots on, walking off with his lamp to the farms in all weathers. He thought of the three of them, pressing in to watch on summer evenings: the smell of it all – a proper, animal smell. The munching on feed, the swish of the tails, the stream of the milk in the pail, his father's hands running down teats, the farm cat slipping in.

Foot-and-mouth. They'd had it before, but this was—

'Come on,' he said to Sophie, and tugged her away from the sight of it all, the cruel wicked sight of them hoofs, them lolling heads, them heaped-up, beautiful creatures.

IV

Home

19

'Everything's uncomfortable,' said Buffy. 'Everything's an effort.'

The surgery was packed: she'd been waiting for forty minutes beyond her appointment, leafing through the kind of magazines she only ever read in here, or at the dentist. Bright women beamed in their awful houses; there were long ghastly articles about sex.

'Well, now,' said the doctor, kindly. 'You're not *quite* as young as you were.'

'I haven't come to be told that,' Buffy said sharply. 'I know exactly how old I am, thank you. What I want is a diagnosis. Something's not right.'

He was new, he was a fool. They were all fools. No one knew anything any more.

He sat back and looked at her. 'Go on.'

So she went on. She told him about getting up in the night, and the giddy spells, three now, and her ever-expanding waistline. She told him how exhausted she felt, even just doing the shopping. She said there was nothing she wanted to eat, anyway; she'd lost her appetite. She said she would never eat meat again as long as she lived, and she started to say why, and began to cry.

'And I've got a pain,' she sobbed. 'That's new. It comes and goes, but it's there.'

'Where?'

She pointed. Her tummy felt like a football.

'Let's have a look.'

And she blew her nose on a man-size tissue from the box on his desk, and lay on the couch while he felt all over her.

'Here?' he asked, prodding and poking. 'Here?'

'What is it?' asked Buffy, when he had finished. 'What have I got?' She swung her legs off with enormous difficulty. Oh, how nice it would be to tuck down with a hot-water bottle and never have to do anything again.

The doctor was writing on her notes, in an illegible hand. She peered.

'It's probably nothing at all,' he said, turning them over. 'But perhaps we had better be sure.' He put down his pen, and smiled at her.

She tried to smile back: after all, she'd met worse, and at least he was thorough.

'I'm going to get you an appointment at the West London,' he said lightly. 'Just, as I say, to be sure.'

'With what department?' asked Buffy, but she wasn't a fool. She knew, she knew.

> Out of sight? What of that?
> See the Bird – reach it!
> Curve by Curve – Sweep by Sweep –
> Round the Steep Air –
> Danger! What is that to Her?

Janice lay on the blue-and-white quilt in her bedroom, revisiting Emily Dickinson. Smoke from her roll-up drifted through the open window into the cold March air, clouds drifted over a hesitant sun, she heard the beat of wings.

> Curve by Curve – Sweep by Sweep –
> Round the Steep Air –

She said the words aloud, felt herself climb with them, swept on through soaring currents, feeling the rush, the rise, the dizzying descent, the whirling up once more, into—

Into what danger, what treacherous place?

She put the book down. The last time she had read this verse was up in Cloud Nine on a gusty, rainy afternoon, with the place to herself, the rain beginning to die away at last, the sun to break through. It glistened on the wet glass door, which was all at once pushed open.

Had she been in danger then? She supposed she had been; she supposed she might have gone into free fall, picked up and taken to airy heights like that, then dropped like a plummeting stone. And thinking this she remembered all at once the stiff, gaping man in the corridor of the hospital, his mouth wide open as if to shriek the shrieks of madness, into echoing hill and stony valley.

Wild, unreachable places.

Janice drew on her cigarette once more, and laid it to rest in the ashtray by the bed. She let the image of Matthew's face swim before her again, sink into her again, as it had done ever since she first saw him, coming and going, leaving and returning, as if to the right place. She picked up the book again, hearing, from the magnolia, the blackbird's sudden rush of song.

> Danger! What is that to Her?
> Better 'tis to fail – there –
> Than debate – here –
>
> Blue is Blue – the World through –

Was that beautiful, or what?

She closed her eyes, let them rest on the blueness of calm and distant hills, and safety.

Buffy, after her visit to the doctor, took herself home. She went slowly down the surgery steps to the windy street, beneath the pollarded plane trees to the main road, where buses roared past and people did their shopping, and had their hair done, and lived their lives. She turned into the corner of her own street, and after some moments found herself at her own front door.

She felt in her bag for her keys and could not find them. Very carefully, she searched again, and there they were. She turned both latches, went into the communal hall. In the dimness, the atmosphere of closed doors, and everyone out, was almost palpable. She stood there, taking breaths. Then she climbed the stairs, pressing the time switch on the wall to turn the light on, feeling the wornness, where everyone had pressed it, going up, going down, year after year after year.

She let herself into the flat, the silence. After a moment or two, the light on the stairs went out.

199

☆

Ernie, in his pyjamas, put the kettle on the gas ring and looked out on the back field. It was March, it was spring, there were ewes and lambs out there – they'd woken him up with their racket, but he didn't care, just so long as they were safe. There were buds in the hawthorn hedge, the first hint of leaves on the trees. And about time too. He pulled on his jacket and went outside for a pee, round the back of the trailer. Good for the grass, and more natural: he got sick of using that smelly old Elsan all winter. Time to get out and about. Time for pastures new. And he smelled the cold spring air, and listened to the lambs, and banged his foot on the hollow gas canister, and swore. A hen beneath the trailer cocked her head. They liked it under there: nice and dark, bit of peace and quiet.

'Hello, old girl. Got a nice egg for my breakfast?' He rubbed his sore foot, bent down to feel beneath her in the mud. Not a dicky bird. Ha.

'Not much use, are you?' He straightened up, turned, and peed an arc, over the rotting fence and into the field. There – life in the old boy yet. He turned back, saw the brown hen watching. 'Wasn't bad, was it?' he asked her, and shuffled back inside.

The gas was flickering feebly. Another blimming thing to think about, another blimming thing to buy. Them canisters cost a fortune. He stood there listening to the weak putt-putt of the flame.

'Go on, give us a cuppa at least.'

The kettle was small and lightweight, like him. Like his old black wireless: he'd had them both for donkey's years, however many that was. And now, looking out at the lambs, waiting for his early-morning cuppa, he put the wireless on, fiddling with the coat-hanger aerial and dial until he heard the eight o'clock pips, and set it back on the table and listened, shaking his head.

The kettle, at last, approached the boil, just before the flame went out. He made his tea, he opened his tin, he sat smoking and drinking and watching the lambs, the butting and wriggling, and skipping about, as the clouds rolled back and the day broke properly. The wireless murmured beside him: that John Humphrys, talking about the crisis to that Nick Brown. What did any of them know, stuck in London? What was that Janice Harper doing, stuck down there?

The lambs, as lambs did – he knew, he'd been with them all his life – suddenly all took off, all together, haring round the field, up and down, round and round the trunk of the holm oak, just in bud. Look at them, look at that, what a sight for sore eyes. On the wireless, they were talking about emergency measures, and experts. If they sent any of them experts up here, if they started any of that culling up here—

Someone was throwing stones at the door.

He got up, opened up, saw Sophie at the bottom of the steps in her gumboots. Dogs were following, dogs were barking in the pens.

'Action stations,' said Sophie. 'She says are you up.'

'I don't need no chivvying,' said Ernie crossly. 'What's she on about?'

'She says we've got to walk them while we can.'

'We can't,' he said flatly. 'Haven't you heard the news? No one's going out anywhere. Not now.'

'She says we've got to. She says we're not an infected area.'

'She'll have to whistle. We can't.'

He looked down at the sea of eager faces, beating tails.

'Sorry,' he told them. 'Not today.'

Sophie, in her pinafore and gumboots, shifted from foot to foot.

'But how are we going to manage?' she asked him. 'What are we going to do?'

Janice walked into the hospital grounds. Daffodils blew in the flower-beds, a girl sat on the bench outside the main entrance, talking on her mobile. Her hair was lank, and her wrists were bandaged. She wore leopard-print mules and a big black cardigan. 'I'm going mad in here,' she said.

Janice went through the sliding doors, and took herself down into Matthew's ward, looking neither to left nor right. If the wilderness man was haunting the hills and corridors she did not wish to see him. She did not wish to encounter slashed wrists, or infected sores from cigarette burns, or to hear, from behind a screen, the sounds of some poor bastard throwing up his overdose. Sorry, can't handle that. So how come you think you can cope with Matthew? a part of herself enquired, and this she could not answer, except by being here.

She found the ward, and told the staff nurse who she had come to see, and that she was a friend, and had been before, with Matthew's father. 'I remember,' said the nurse, who wore a badge that said Eileen.

'How is he?'

'Up and down. We've changed his medication – did you know?'

'Oh, yes,' she said, remembering the conversations with William: his happiness, his hope, his taking of her hand. 'I'll go and find him,' she said, and turned to cross the floor to the light-filled day room, and saw a tall, stooping man walking slowly towards the nurses' desk, and was about to step aside when she thought he reminded her of someone she liked a lot, and realised who it was.

She stopped. 'Hello, Matthew.'

He inclined his head towards her, gave a hesitant smile. She sensed in it everything he had been brought up to be: well mannered, careful with other people's feelings, kind.

'Have we met?' he asked, with painful slowness.

'Yeah,' she said, and took his hand. 'I'm Janice, remember? I came here with your dad. We had lunch together.'

'Of course,' said Matthew. 'Of course we did. I remember now.' And his eyes moved away, and he withdrew his hand, and walked slowly to the nurses' desk. 'What day is it today?'

'It's Thursday,' said Eileen. 'All day. Are you going to talk to your visitor?'

'Visitor?' He looked round.

'Me,' said Janice. 'Would you like to go for a walk?'

He looked at her, and through and beyond her. She felt his remoteness, his utter apartness, his long, slow flailing about inside, like a stranded creature.

'I'm here,' she said. 'There's no hurry.' And she went over, and took his hand again, and led him towards the light.

'You know where the coats are?' called Eileen, and picked up the ringing phone.

'Where are they?' asked Janice, and his eyes roamed around the ward.

There was a pause.

'In there, I believe.' He gestured at a door, as if moving under water.

Slow though his speech was, he had, she realised, spoken more in the last few minutes than during the whole of previous visit.

Inside the cloakroom, she watched him move among the hooks, finding, at last, his own long winter coat. He took it down, handed it to her. She held it open for him, helped his beautiful hands slip into each sleeve.

'Great,' she said. 'That's brilliant. Right, we're off.'

And they went back through the ward, and through the blaring day room, and out into the grounds, which smelled of earth after rain, and fir. She slipped her hand through his arm; he looked down at her, from his father's height.

'I remember you,' he said. 'You've been here before.'

'Yes.'

'What day is it today?'

The cold spring wind stirred the boughs of the fir tree, the shadows of massive clouds moved over the grass.

'It's Thursday,' said Janice, and leaned her head against his shoulder. 'All day,' she added, watching a London blackbird rise and fall on the wind.

'Buffy!' said William. 'How are things?'

'Fine,' said Buffy. 'I was just about to phone you. Are you coming to the concert?'

'I am indeed. We all are.'

'All?' She reached to turn down the television.

'If there are tickets left. Is it a sell-out? Might we hope for three returns?'

He sounded positively buoyant.

'Three?' she asked him.

'I'm bringing Matthew. Do him good. And Janice – high time you two met.'

'Ah,' said Buffy. 'Well. I'll have them put on the door. Or did you want me to send them?'

'Send them? Can't you bring them to the stall?'

'The thing is—' Buffy began, and did not know how to proceed. 'The thing is—' she tried again, and felt the icy coldness which had taken root somewhere in her lower spine, ever since the visit to the surgery, begin to seep into every part of her. 'I've got to have a little check-up,' she said firmly. 'That's why I was about to ring – it's on Wednesday, as it happens. So I'm afraid I can't do the stall this week. I'm so sorry.'

'Check-up?' William was on the alert at once. 'What kind of check-up?'

'Only a little one.'

'For—' He hesitated. 'Don't want to pry, dear, but—'

'Women's things,' said Buffy. 'Nothing you need give a thought to.'

'Ah.' She could sense his relief. What babes men were. What fools. Even William. Even after Eve.

'So I'll see you at the concert,' she said cheerfully. 'I'm so glad you can all come.'

'So am I,' said William. 'Matthew's first outing for ages. All thanks to you, Buffy, dear. New pills. You were perfectly right.'

'I'm so pleased.' And she moved the receiver to her other ear, since this, like everything else, was heavier than it used to be, and listened, as William went on.

'Good,' he said, replacing the receiver. 'Very good.' He finished his whisky, poured another. Just a little nip more. 'A nippity nip,' he said aloud, moving the last of the ice around the glass. The curtains were drawn, the fire was lit, and Danny was snoring before it. He looked at his watch, turned on the Channel 4 news. Good chap, Jon Snow, always liked him – met him, once, at some do. He settled back into his chair.

There were over a thousand cases. Over a thousand. In Northumberland, in Cumbria, in Devon – in Devon they were almost under siege. Couldn't go anywhere, couldn't move a lamb.

'This is quite dreadful,' said William aloud, beginning to see what Buffy was on about. There were cases in Scotland, pyres in the Welsh borders. Herefordshire. Shropshire.

And how were the cousins coping with all this? He might give them a ring. As you were – he might drop them a line. 'They've never had a phone,' said Janice. 'Never had a washing machine. Nor telly.'

Well, they'd be spared the close-ups of dying lambs. Or perhaps there were sights like this all around them.

The phone was ringing: he picked it up, as the feature finally ended, and the advertisements began.

'Hello?'

'Is Janice there?'

'Hello, darling,' said William, realising that the second whisky, on an empty stomach, had perhaps been a mistake. 'All this foot-and-mouth,' he said. 'Isn't it frightful? Have you been watching the news?'

Claire gave an exasperated sigh. 'No,' she said shortly. 'I haven't. This coverage has got completely out of hand, the whole business is absurd. They're getting compensation, aren't they? What are they fussing about?'

'Oh, dear,' said William, feeling the chasm yawn open once more, but wider still.

'I was asking if Janice was there.'

'So you were. No, she isn't. She's working tonight. Shall I give her a message?'

'You could say I rang. I'll try her again.'

'How are the children?' asked William. 'Have I told you about the concert? One of Buffy's things – Matthew's coming. I'm so pleased. I don't suppose you'd like to join us? I can't remember the programme—' He felt among his papers. 'Parry, I think.'

After a moment, he realised he was talking to thin air.

'Hello, Janice.'

'Oh. Hello.'

Early in the week, Sandra's night off, and the wine bar pretty quiet. Janice, once she had served the one or two regulars, and polished up and put away the lunch-time glasses, had settled herself on the stool behind the bar with a glass of house red, her tin and her thoughts, which were many. Now she slid off, and prepared for action.

'I'm disturbing you,' said Claire.

'No you're not. What can I get you?'

'What are you drinking?'

'Plonk.'

'I'll have a glass of that.' Claire heaved herself up on a stool, and took out her purse. 'And what about you? Can I get you another?'

'I'm fine for now, thanks.' She turned to reach up for a glass, and filled it; she set it before Claire, and passed her the little bowl of olives, dressed with lemon and dill. 'That's two pounds fifty,' she said, and took Claire's fiver, gave her the change, and sat down again.

'Cheers,' said Claire, raising her glass.

'Cheers.' Janice took out her tin and set to work, teasing out strands. Nice to be able to afford a decent roll-up these days. She thought of poor old Ernie, eking out every shred. 'Not often you can get out on your own, is it?' she asked Claire, his distant cousin – how incredible was that? – and finished off, running the tip of her tongue along the paper. 'Who's looking after the kids? I mean the children,' she added, with a little smile, and reached for her lighter.

'Jeremy,' said Claire, smiling back, watching her. 'I've been at home all day – I just thought I'd have a breather, come and see how you were getting on.'

'That's nice.' Janice lit up, inhaled, took up her glass again, met Claire's intense dark eyes.

'And we must make a date,' said Claire. 'For you to come and baby-sit, when you've got time.'

'Yeah. Sure.'

Claire opened her bag again, and took out her diary. She leafed through its packed weeks, checking off aloud the picking up and dropping off of children, the after-school maths, the music lessons, swimming lessons, Geraldine's dance class, Jeremy's court appearances, people in for drinks. There were theatre tickets, secured with paper-clips, there were dinner dates, with sitters already booked.

This is Matthew's sister, Janice thought, as pages turned, and Claire went on and on. This was the little girl peering into the pram on tiptoe, smiling into the sun, clasping Matthew round the waist on the garden slide, leaning on the piano, watching him play.

She had kissed his cheek when they said goodbye, back on the ward from the windy grounds, hearing the bang of the trolleys for lunch, feeling the dryness of his skin beneath her lips.

'Nice to see you,' said Matthew, as he must have said many, many times in the past, saying goodbye, goodbye, see you soon, kissing his friends, his parents' friends, his sister.

'I'll see you at the concert,' she said.

'What day is that?'

'Saturday,' she told him, as she had told him twice before, walking beneath the towering fir trees, seeing squirrels leap. 'We'll come and pick you up.'

He nodded, smiled, turned away. Did she imagine it, or was he steadier in his walk since the first time they'd met, making his way along the ward to the tables with more certainty?

'How about the nineteenth?' asked Claire at last. 'That's the Thursday after Easter. We're going out to supper.'

'Yeah, maybe,' said Janice. 'I'll have to check here first.'

'Well, just let me know.' And she stuffed the diary back in her bag. 'The children would love to have you.'

Would they really? Why was that?

'Anyway.' Claire raised her glass again. 'How are you?'

'Fine.' Janice drew on her roll-up. 'Fine, thanks.' She hesitated, feeling Claire's gaze so intent upon her. 'I went to see Matthew yesterday,' she said, though she didn't want to, and she heard his name echoing, over and over again, as if in a chamber, with a grey-green sea at its entrance, rushing in, pulling back, drawing everything in its wake.

206

Claire frowned. 'Oh? How was he?'

'I think a bit better,' said Janice, and with every word she spoke sensed unease and disturbance and danger, though whether to her, or to Matthew, or Claire, she could not tell.

It's dark, it's raining, Claire is walking home. The Village is behind her, with its lit-up shops, and pubs, and shut-up library. She turns into her street, full of family houses, as the rain drums faster upon her umbrella, and drips from each sharp point. She takes out her keys, unlocks the door of her home, where her daughter and younger son are sleeping, and her husband and elder son are watching the news, Piers's dark head upon his father's shoulder, slaughter and death before them.

'Is that you?' calls Jeremy, hearing her footsteps in the hall.

'Yes, it's me,' says Claire, hanging up her wet mac, and she walks past the open sitting-room door and into the kitchen, so warm and welcoming, the heart of the family house, and puts the umbrella to dry before the Rayburn.

'It's me,' she says again.

The kitchen curtains are undrawn, the table lamp is lit, its reflection gleaming in the dark wet glass, and she leans to pull the curtains to, and catches sight of herself, whoever that might be.

20

———

Spring rain: more spring rain, splashing off the buds of London plane and hornbeam, soaking into the well-kept garden of Queen Square, the flower-beds of daffodils and tulips, the lawn and shrubbery. It's seven o'clock on a Saturday evening, and outside the confines of the square bus and taxi swish in the wet along Southampton Row, up to the Aldwych, and over Waterloo Bridge to the South Bank, to theatre, theatre bar and concert hall. Here in Queen Square the audience is arriving for the concert at the Mary Ward, shaking out umbrellas on the steps; pushing open the heavy front door on to the cramped but well-lit hall, with its pleasing black-and-white tiles; crowding into the lavatories, making the ascent up the broad shallow stairs with some difficulty, for it's a hell of a climb, quite frankly, when you're getting on.

But the concert is on the first floor, in rooms that are lovely and spacious. Tall rainswept windows overlook the square, and the atmosphere tonight is lively, with tables laid with light refreshments, programmes, jugs of spring flowers. Through the double doors the chairs are arranged in a sweeping semicircle, with notices of future events – the summer concert, summer party, summer trip to Bruges – on every one.

'Marvellous,' says William, ushering Janice and Matthew. 'Splendid. Let me get you a drink.'

He is a good head taller than anyone in the room, except for Matthew, and each, in different ways, attracts quick glances. William has always attracted glances, all his life, and never less than here, among the Over-Sixties, with his silver hair, his well-cut, well-worn clothes, his courtesy and charm, that smile. This evening he is wearing a Marie Curie paper daffodil in his buttonhole: it looks, on William, fresh and alive.

'Now then.' He scans the bottles of red and white, the elderflower, the orange juice, smiles at these good people offering all this, and Rosemary Barker, uncorking chilled Blue Nun, feels the evening's brightness fall, in particular, on her. 'What will you have?'

'I'll have the elderflower,' says Janice, holding Matthew's hand. Matthew, because of his medication, has not touched alcohol for years; she knows this, feels how cold his hand is in hers, sees one or two people look at him, and look away, as she asks him: 'Is the elderflower OK?' and he nods, with a vague, sweet smile which turns her over.

Matthew is his father's son. He is tall, and well made, and, as she took in the first moment she beheld him, beautiful. But the years of his illness, his drugs, his long confinement, have dulled the thick hair, dulled the eyes which once swept over Bach and Chopin; there is an invalid pallor to the skin on good Harriman cheekbones, a pinch to the Harriman nose. His circulation is poor, and his movements slow, and the long, slender fingers which ran over Beethoven and Schubert, which lifted violin and bow as if they were a part of him, now rest in hers cold and passive. And, after all these years, he is set apart: seeing him in a crowded room, on the crowded pavement, even out of the corner of an eye, you think at once – something's not right. Looking more closely, you know it. The beauty is damaged, the stone of the angel eroded.

But we will restore it, thinks William, passing drinks. We'll have you back in the world again. He raises his glass of Blue Nun. 'Cheers. Well done all round.' He moves them away from the crush at the table, and looks around, feeling extraordinarily happy. The first outing: they've done it, and here he is again, back with the old dears and looking forward to it.

The choir have been changing, behind the scenes. Now they emerge, one or two, in their concert clothes, and mingle.

'Buffy!' calls William. 'Over here!'

And she looks round, looking good, he observes, in her smart black skirt and fuchsia silk shirt and silver earrings, and sees him, and she feels oh, so many, many things as she moves through the crowd to this little knot of three.

'Buffy. You're looking marvellous.' He bends to kiss her, once, twice – as Londoners do, Janice notices again; he takes her hand, turns to his son. 'Matthew, you remember Buffy. We had the most marvellous Christmas.'

209

'Of course,' murmurs Matthew, as she reaches up to kiss him.

'Lovely to see you here,' she says brightly. 'Really lovely.'

'And this,' says William with joyful emphasis, 'is Janice Harper. Janice – my dear old friend Buffy Henderson. At last I've got you two together.'

'How do you do,' says Buffy, extending her hand, with its silver rings, which had once been Mother's, and its liver spots and wrinkles.

'I'm fine, thanks,' says Janice, clasping it in her strong young fingers. 'Great to meet you.'

'We're so looking forward to this,' says William, as the piano strikes up in the concert room, just a few scales, to tune up, and put them all in the mood.

'Me too,' says Buffy.

And she watches Matthew all at once raise his head, as the accompanist runs up and down the keyboard, and sees William and Janice both notice too, and exchange quite radiant smiles.

'We'd better go through,' she says, and turns away, going to line up with the altos, clearing her throat.

Janice is watching Matthew, so tall among the crowd, so close to her but so set apart. A frown plays over his features; she feels in his hand a tremor of movement, like an enquiry. Then he relinquishes his grip, and moves towards the double doors, slow but intent, listening. The scales run on, the choir is assembled, the audience is moving through.

'Give me those.' William is taking their glasses, smoothly depositing them on the long table, reappearing. They are ushered to their seats, and he raises his programme to Buffy in encouragement. The scales die away, there is a general settling, coughs, a hush. Within it, you can hear for a moment the patter of rain. Then Michael, the young conductor, makes his appearance, and bows; the first full chords of Parry's *Sirens* resound in a mighty opening, and with the choir's audible intake of breath the concert has begun.

Music and rain and upraised voices: for a moment, his programme resting on his long crossed legs, William feels a current of joyous excitement run through him, no less powerful than if he were in the stalls at the Festival Hall with Eve.

'Where the bright Seraphim, in burning row, / Their loud, uplifted angel trumpets blow . . .'

What stirring stuff it is, and what a good sound: dear things, how keen they are.

210

'Oh, may we soon again renew that song, / And keep in tune with Heaven, and keep in tune with / Heaven . . .'

Buffy is singing her heart out, silver earrings catching the light as she turns the pages, head uplifted. Dear girl. And he settles back, and glances at Matthew, to see what he is making of it all, now they are here at last.

Matthew is very still. He seems to listen as if from a great distance – to the first rumble of thunder, or the first fall of rain on the sea. It is, thinks Janice, sitting next to him, her upper arm touching, just, his upper arm, as if he were under water, and she sees again in her mind's eye a sea-filled chamber, his name resounding with each rush and retreat of the waves.

She is conscious of William's glance: she turns, and smiles at him, and he locks her gaze in the intensity of his joy – at seeing his son, from however far away, respond, once again, to music.

'To live with Him, and sing in endless morn of light . . .'

Janice watches the long musician's finger lift from his lap – just a little, almost imperceptibly – in hesitant response. And although she has never heard music like this in her life, and finds it incredible, really, that she should even be here, used as she is to hanging out at gigs down the pub, she finds herself quite swept up in it all: the stirring song, the turning pages, the sight of them all, singing their hearts out on a cold wet night in spring, the trees dripping in the square beyond the windows as the rain falls on and on.

The first song is over: she find herself clapping alone, looks round, sees William's kindly gaze. Oh, right, not till the interval, then. And they're off with another, and Matthew inclines his head.

'We're doing some rather marvellous songs in the second half,' says Buffy, in the interval. She settles herself on the row in front, turning in her chair to face them. 'Masefield,' she tells them. 'Masefield and Kipling and Whitman – lovely rousing songs, we've really enjoyed them.'

'Kipling,' says William, shifting his legs in the space between the rows, which isn't big enough. 'Haven't looked at him for years. Who reads him now, I wonder?'

'No one,' says Buffy. 'Certainly not me. But I think there's a new biography – did you see it in the papers?'

'Possibly.' He tries to remember.

'Dreadfully sad about his son,' she goes on. 'I think that's what they were saying. Kipling sent him off to the front, to make a man of him, and he was killed and Kipling could never accept it, tried for years to think he was missing, and would come back. It almost broke his heart...' She stops, her voice trailing away, then quickly recovers. 'Goodness, what am I thinking of, talking about such sad things? How are you enjoying it all?'

'Very much,' said William.

'It's great,' says Janice. She has dimly heard of Kipling, though Steve, in Cloud Nine conversations, never mentioned him, but she wonders that Buddy should, indeed, choose on this very evening to talk about sons, and death, and heartbreak. She touches Matthew's hand: he is gazing towards the window. 'You liked it, didn't you?' she asks him, and he slowly turns his head, and slowly nods, and a smile lifts his mouth for a moment and is gone again, as a cloud moves over the sun. She lets her hand rest on his, and he does not move it away.

She feels Buffy watching the two of them.

'Have you been singing with the choir for long?' she asks her, taking in the ageing face, bright clothes and sharp, bright gaze.

'Oh, for years,' says Buffy briskly. 'When you get to my age, you've been doing everything for years.'

'Oh, come, come,' says William gallantly, and then, to Janice, 'You really must come to the stall one day – we've certainly had that for ever, haven't we, Buffy, dear?'

'We have. How did you get on on Wednesday?'

'Rather well, if I remember rightly. Those teacups went.'

'The Marguerite? I knew they would. Remember I found those.'

'I remember perfectly well. And how did you get on with your little test?'

'I'm waiting for the results,' says Buffy. 'Nothing to worry about.' And then there is the sound of a handbell, and people are coming back to their seats, and she rises – with some difficulty, Janice notices – and says, 'Right. Back to business. We end with Tennyson.'

'Tennyson?' William picks up his programme. 'What Tennyson?'

' "Crossing the Bar." Very beautiful. And affecting, it must be said.'

And she pats William's arm, and makes her way back to her place, second row from the back. There is, once again, the settling, reassembling, clearing of throats, and then Michael is back, and bowing again, and they're off.

Buffy, in her place in the altos, sings the Masefield with vigour. It swings, it rouses, it takes her away on its tall ships, billowing sails and great winds sweeping the crew to sunlit islands. Marvellous, she can hear William say, and looks up to see him nodding in time, loving it all. He meets her eye, he smiles, and she sings on, lifted from Masefield's ships to Kipling's white road running, running, down through the grassy hills.

Everything's all right, she tells herself. Everything's all right. And she knows that as long as nobody knows, that as long as she can keep going, and being bright, she'll manage. She just doesn't want to tell a soul, that's all. All around her, voices are raised in joyful unison – how that white road runs, and how the white foam rolls across the sands!

And then there is a pause, and they turn to the last song, and the piano is sounding a pure and haunting note, as the Tennyson begins.

> Sunset and evening star,
> And one clear call for me!
> And may there be no moaning of the bar,
> When I put out to sea . . .
>
> Twilight and evening bell,
> And after that the dark!
> And may there be no sadness of farewell,
> When I embark . . .

Buffy, in the altos, in the place she has occupied for years and years, as she has done everything now, everything in her life familiar, and properly done, and interesting – yes, life at its best is *interesting* – feels herself borne now upon a great wave of mournful, tender sound, as if someone else is singing for her, so that she can look out across the room to where, among the audience, sits Janice Harper, who seems, on the face of it, a perfectly pleasant young woman; and Matthew, entirely filled with the beauty of the music – she can see this, it is just as William had hoped; and William himself, gazing across at her, absorbed, intent, tears glinting, knowing nothing of what she will, quite soon, have to tell him.

It's Mary's and Sophie's turn: they heave their bags round the shops.

'Will you come and have a look-see?' asks Sophie, when the last

Savers tin of beans, and Savers Swiss Roll and custard, have been stuffed into the bag with the broken zip. She shifts the weight from one hand to the other; Mary grunts.

'Might as well.'

They make their way to the cathedral, hearing from within, as they cross the precinct, the sudden, unexpected sounds of treble voices, soaring exquisitely. Beneath her coat, and cardigan, and nylon jumper, Sophie feels the prickle of hairs rise all up the back of her neck, and along her arm.

'Choir practice?' she wonders. 'On a Saturday morning?'

'Must be a wedding later,' says Mary, and they stand outside the great west door and listen: to the muted swell of the organ, those pure, sweet voices rising ethereally, and the crooning of a pair of pigeons from a lofty medieval niche.

'Love Divine, all loves excelling...'

Sophie is transported: some cloudy, half-dreamed place where bluebirds play in the balmy air awaits her, she can feel it, and she stands on the old stone flags with her bulging bags of Lo-Cost dog food, murmuring, 'A wedding...'

'Oh, don't be so daft,' snaps Mary, and as the last strains fade she pulls at her sleeve and drags her into the cloisters.

'No harm in listening,' says Sophie, mulishly. 'No harm in a bit of music.'

'Puts a lot of nonsense in your head.' Mary sets down the bags for a moment. 'There's quite enough of that in there already.'

Sophie does not reply; she puffs along half-empty cloisters. It's mid-morning, it's almost Easter, there should be lots of people, lots of tourists looking round and buying things. Postcards, cathedral tea towels, bookmarks with lovely prayers on. They should be coming down to Healing Arts, snapping up Ernie's pictures. Instead—

'Gone ever so quiet,' she says.

'What d'you expect?' Mary's eyes are like bright black coals. 'Remember Oswestry, in '67?'

But Sophie has never had a head for facts and figures. That was what had done for her at school, the facts and figures: she hadn't had Ernie's gift with Art, she hadn't had Mary's quick, sharp way with sums. She shakes her head, as she has shaken it all her life. Mary gives a snort.

They come out into the alley. As always, even from here, you can

214

smell the wafts of scent from Healing Arts – the gift-wrapped natural soaps, the natural creams and natural massage oils. And all those little bottles. Aromatherapy – isn't that a lovely word? Just to hear it makes you feel better.

Mary is wrinkling her nose. They pass the second-hand bookshop, and Cloisters Gallery, its window filled with oils in heavy frames.

'How about in there?' Sophie had thought suddenly, when they came to set up Ernie's exhibition. 'Would that be better?'

'That's posh,' he said, shifting his portfolio to under his other arm.

'Healing Arts is posh.'

'There's posh and posh,' said Ernie. 'Trust me.' And he marched up to Daphne's polished door and set his shoulder to it. Ting! In they went, and there was Daphne, smiling, with a space on the wall all cleared. Sophie hadn't seen him look so happy for years.

And it's all my idea, she told herself, following him inside. Got something right for once.

Now she is following Mary: inside the shop they set down their bags behind a window display of natural sponges from the depths of the seabed – that's what it says on the card. Pearly little balls of natural bath oils are strewn among them; there are tall glass jars of soap, with round glass stoppers. There are Easter chicks. There's a seahorse!

She tugs at Mary's arm, but Mary is looking fiercely around the empty shop, and coughing. For a moment Sophie wonders whether the bunches of dried herbs and flowers will bring on an early bout of her hayfever. It makes her savage, all red and streaming, and never enough handkerchiefs.

'Well? Where are they?'

Mary is building up to something, Sophie can tell, and sensing this she feels as anxious as she has ever done, all knotted up and fearful, as if she has – she feels a dreadful flush – as if she has wet the bed, and Mother is coming up the stairs.

You naughty girl—

Made to stand in the corner, the wet sheet over her head. Not for long, but long enough. And all that washing.

'They're over there,' she says, as helpfully as she can. And she points to the wall on the left, from where the British Butterflies have been removed, and the Wild Flowers. Now, in their place, are Ernie's paintings. 'Look.' She points again, to Ned's noble head, and Flossie's loving gaze, but Mary slaps her hand down.

SUE GEE

'No need to point. No need, ever, to point.' Goodness, how like Mother she can sound.

'Isn't it nice?' she whispers.

Mary is marching over, beetle-eyed. She stands full square and glares at every picture.

'Sophie! How nice to see you, dear.' And here is Daphne, coming out from the back with a box of pretty things. She sets it on the counter. Mary swings round.

'Are you in charge?'

Daphne – even she, nice and kind and always smiling – is taken aback. Sophie watches, twisting her fingers in their holey green gloves.

'I am,' says Daphne, staying behind the counter. 'Daphne Clark,' she adds. 'How do you do?' She looks across at Sophie, and back at Mary, wonderingly. 'Have we met?'

'We have not,' says Mary. 'Last time I was in here there was some pasty young girl at the till, with an undernourished baby. Born out of wedlock, no doubt.'

'Kirsty,' says Daphne faintly. 'That was a long time ago. And you are—?'

'Mary Harriman.' She nods violently at the paintings. 'The artist's sister.'

'And my sister,' says Sophie weakly, explaining. 'My brother. We're all related, see.'

Mary gives her a withering look. 'What I want to know,' she demands of Daphne, 'is where's all the red dots?'

Daphne gestures at the empty shop floor, with its baskets of sponges – more sponges! There must be a glut. Sophie, escaping, pictures a slender dark-haired boy diving down to the seabed, knife in hand, and bubbles streaming upward. Oh, those little Ladybird books! How she used to—

'I'm afraid it's been rather quiet,' Daphne is saying carefully. 'The crisis is hitting all of us, I'm afraid.'

'There's no foot-and-mouth in the city centre,' says Mary.

'No cows in the cloisters,' says Sophie under her breath, and claps her hand to her mouth, seeing just that: a dear old cow called Buttercup, munching on that nice trim grass, listening to the bells.

'It's a knock-on effect,' says Daphne, quiet but firm.

Mary glances at them both. 'Frivolity!' she snaps at Sophie. 'Frivolity in the midst of penury!' She swings back to Daphne. 'We need the

216

money,' she says. 'We've got mouths to feed.' She gestures at the paintings, beneath their lettered sign. Daphne had been doubtful about the sign, but Ernie had insisted.

Your Faithful Friend – With You For Ever – Commissions Undertaken.

'This is our livelihood,' Mary says with finality. 'Foot-and-mouth or no. I don't care what you have to do to sell them, but' – and she marches across to the counter, waving – 'sell them you must.' Her wild hands send a counter basket flying. Shell-shaped soaps tumble to the floor, Easter chicks are everywhere. 'Frippery!' shouts Mary. Her eyes rake the racks of healing oils. 'Holistic beeswax! Whisky and aspirin and an early night! That'll soon put you right. All this quackery—'

Sophie is awash with fear: she hasn't seen Mary so overheated for years. Whatever has got into her?

'Now, look—' says Daphne, and her own voice is beginning to rise.

Just then, the door tings open. Everyone swings round. A young man comes in, wiping his feet on the mat. His bicycle is leaning up against the window, his skin fresh and healthy, his earring catching the light.

'Hi,' he says, sounding lovely and cheerful and normal, and closes the door behind him.

Mary is beside him in a trice. 'Here,' she tells him, seizing his hand, and marching him across to the exhibition. Shell-shaped soaps crumble beneath her feet. 'You buy one of these.'

Later, after Daphne has threatened to call the police, and has taken every picture off the wall, after Sophie has swept up every soap crumb, picked up every trampled Easter chick, and said, over and over again, that she's sorry, they heave their bags out of the shop and make their way in dreadful silence back through the cloisters.

'Do you think you're coming down with something?' Sophie ventures, taking all her courage in her hands.

'If I am,' snaps Mary, 'I'll know where not to go to find a cure.' She gives a violent sniff, and quickens her pace.

Sophie trails miserably after her. The choirboys have finished their practice and are streaming out of the west door, in mufti, as Father would have said, ragging about before the afternoon wedding. How beautiful that will be, how happy. She starts to cry, very softly. Mary is on to her at once.

'No snivelling! Pull your silly socks up!'

Mother to the life.

They make their way through town to the market bus stop. Tom's trailer is selling soup and hot dogs, just as usual, but there isn't much of a queue, and the silence from the market is eerie. No shouts, no bleating or lowing, no clang of pens. No farmers. It's all shut up, just a few bits of straw blowing like ghosts across the carpark, and no one, in the queue at the bus stop, is talking of anything else.

Ernie is out in the huts. Blimming heck, it's like an ice house. Some of the newspaper stuffed in the gaps in the boards has been blown out by winter winds, and there's draughts everywhere. The concrete floor is sound, give or take a few cracks, but even he can smell damp, and no wonder. Rain getting in all winter, floods and storm and pestilence. Could have brought the whole lot down. He tramps about, inspecting. Spiders scuttle away, there are cobwebs everywhere. Time for a good spring clean, time for a good stiff brush, and mops and buckets. Might even do the trailer, before Mary starts going on: have a good sweep-out, beat a few rugs, wash the windows. The windows in here – blimming heck.

But despite the general dilapidation, he feels, as he shuffles from stall to stall, a swell of pride. Look at that Eskimo, look at them scales on that fish, them straining huskies. Shackleton would have been proud to have had a team like that, Scott would have shaken his hand.

I am going outside, and may be gone some time . . .

Them were the days: proper men, proper heroes. Expeditions, rations, ice picks; disappearing into the snowy wastes and no blimming mobile phone.

Hello? Hello, Darren, I'm in the toilet . . .

Ernie has actually heard someone say this once, down the pub: he snorts at the memory. End of civilisation. Bring back National Service – that'd sort 'em out. Go off on an expedition, and don't come back.

The cold spring wind blows through, newspaper dances over the floor, and there's something else – a whisk, a scampering. He stops, and his eyes dart everywhere. Well, what do you expect? Shut up all winter, cracks and gaps. So long as it's only mice – if it's rats, he'll set the dogs on them.

He strides across to Africa, feeling masterful. Look at that waterfall, look at that poor drowning girl. What were her parents thinking of, leaving her like that? Missionaries, Bibles, preaching to the natives –

what about their own little daughter? 'Course, Livingstone had had no children, nor Stanley neither, not that that made them what everyone nowadays would say it made them, nothing like that. Proper men, proper heroes, doing what they thought was right. Fever and swamps and quinine. Borne on stretchers, lips all cracked; snakes dropping down from the trees in lethal silence. 'Onward Christian Soldiers' and 'I Did It All For Thee'. Sun beating down on a simple wooden cross.

Ernie, walking from scene to scene, deep in thought, grows more thoughtful still.

Heroes.

Not just places, and themes, but a real sense of history in here.

He stands before the Swiss Alps, the sunset peeling away from the back, lets his hand stray over the noble head of the St Bernard, feels it all too soft to the touch, and watches sawdust stream to the heaps of polystyrene snow, from where the mice have gnawed. Right behind them furry ears. Dreadful. He bends to look, sees a blimming great hole, pokes about, hears squeaking, pulls out his fingers, sharpish. Blimming heck, right inside the head. Well, what can you expect, with no protection? Should have polythene sheeting wrapped round everything, all winter; should have poison down, and mouse traps.

And walking along to the hunt, and finding even old Foxy full of holes, and moth throughout the hunting coat, he feels a wave of mingled grief and shame.

Can't even afford a roll of polythene sheeting.

Can't even run to a flipping mouse trap.

Here he is, sixty-eight, the curator of a fine museum – unique, probably, nothing like it nowhere – falling to pieces before his very eyes.

Here he is, an artist to his fingertips, an exhibition in town, acclaim just round the corner, and all these works of art in here are on the brink of ruin.

Venice in Peril. Restoration. Trust funds.

What is to be done?

He lights up, though he knows he shouldn't, not in here, but a man has to have something. Ah, that's better. And he paces about, smoking, thinking furiously – always thinks better with a cig in his mouth, always has done – hearing drips, and scuttling, smelling the damp, the mice, the spiders; hearing, from outside, the wind in the trees, the birds, them darling little lambs, still safe, thank God; hearing the whines and sighs of them poor old penned-up dogs, and the wild triumphant cackle of a laying hen.

Something for lunch, then.

That was something.

Got it!

Heroes of yesteryear.

(*Dogs of Yesteryear?*)

No – heroes always pulls them in. He ticks them all off on his fingers, yellow with baccy stains, chapped and cracked with the cold.

Shackleton. Scott. Livingstone. Wellington. Nelson – must have had a dog, bound to, they'd never set sail without a good old sea dog for the rats. Who else? Hillary – must have had dogs at the base camp. Himalayan mountain dogs? Or is it Pyrenean? Look it up in the library, next time they're in town. He looks at his watch – Dad's watch, a proper heirloom. Mary had Mother's. How're they getting on in town today? All them red dots – that's what'll pay for this bold new venture.

Capital. Investment. Restoration funds.

Who else?

Lindbergh. No – he'd never have taken a dog up there.

I know that I shall meet my death, / somewhere in the clouds above. / Those that I fight I do not hate, / those that I guard I do not love . . .

Keats. Blimming marvellous, had to learn it by heart at school, had to recite it: he could remember it now, standing up and trembling.

Should've gone to Oxford. Should've gone to the Royal College, that was certain.

Not Lindbergh, then.

Who?

Where'd they keep that *Pears Cyclopaedia?* Indoors somewhere. Must be there.

Ernie props open the door of the hut with a brick, to let the spring wind blow some fresh air in there properly. The dogs, at his reappearance, are at once alert, getting stiffly to their feet – in the pens; outside the back door; and here comes Pipsqueak, down the trailer steps from his snooze on the mat. He bends to pat him, feeling the faintest warmth from the April sun on his rough little coat.

'Good boy, good boy.' He feels in his pocket, but there's only crumbs. 'Stocks are low,' he tells him, straightening up. 'They'll be back soon.' And he shuffles down to the gate, Pip at his heels, and leans on it, looking along the lane.

Blimey, it's quiet. Not a car, not a walker striding out across the fields and into the hills with a rucksack, not even a bicycle. Be good to see that Janice, wheeling along on her bike with them panniers bulging, fresh faced and cheerful, ringing that bell.

Hello, Ernie!

Got any baccy?

Might have.

Striding into the house with the bags, putting the tins out, cheering them all up.

London. What's she getting up to there, then? Still, can't be worse than here. Shut down, that's what it is. Whole blimming countryside.

He leans on the gate, hearing the restless dogs in the pens begin to bark, feeling the press of the house dogs all around him, waiting for the gate to open, and the walk begin.

'Not today,' he tells them, as he's told them all, every day for weeks, letting them out only to run about the yard, then back. Nothing for it, Mary can shout as much as she likes, he's not going to walk forty dogs across them fields and get shot at. Because they would shoot, he knows it, any farmer would, seeing his sheep all shot in the head and heaped up in a ditch, watching his herd all driven away and that filthy choking smoke, them hooves sticking up, them crumpled horns—

Finches flit into the hedgerows, buzzards wheel over the hills. At least the birds are safe.

Close your eyes, hear the fowls of the air and the bleating sheep, hear that hen on her nest, and you'd think all was just as always. But it isn't, it isn't, and leaning on the gate, his eyes wide open, smelling, on the April wind, the distant pyres, and the disinfectant on that straw, outside all the farms where Dad long ago went milking, he feels another great wave of sorrow. Them farmers will be ruined; them lovely animals, sick ones and healthy, will have lost their lives; and he and the girls, out here in the sticks, with barely a farthing in the tin, and no prospects of visitors, are, like the farmers, up against it.

His cig has gone out in the wind; he drops and crushes it beneath his leaking shoe.

Blimming dreadful. Blimming terrifying.

Still.

And as he rallies – for he, an artist and curator, has never been without ideas, and has been rallying all his life – he sees a magpie, its beak stuffed full of hay, land on the telephone wire, and cock its glossy head.

Quite right, says Ernie aloud. You get on with that nest.

One for sorrow.

Don't be so blimming morbid.

And he turns and goes into the house, on the search for a nice cup of tea, and the *Pears Cyclopaedia*, where Mother used to look up all their ailments. Not that she ever gave them anything for them, not that they ever saw the doctor, not that he can remember. Only with the measles. And the mumps, come to think of it, he'd had a bad time with them mumps. Still – lived to tell the tale. Rallied.

All is not lost, he tells Pip and the rest of them, putting the kettle on, looking along the shelf. There's an exhibition, after all; them pictures will save us all.

It's half past one, and he's out in the trailer, door propped open, nice boiled egg for his lunch inside him, couple of bits of toast, nice strong cup, and he's sitting at the table leafing through the *Pears*. It's so old it's coming to bits, the pages mildewed, but still – heroes are heroes, and they're still in here. Douglas Bader. There was a fellow. Just to hear the words Hurricane and Spitfire makes Ernie go all goosey. Dogfights – ha. Battle of Britain. Up in the cloudy skies facing old Jerry, Biggles jacket and goggles and hand on the joystick, ready to die. Dad said when Bader woke up, after they'd taken his legs off, he could still feel his toes at the end of the bed, waggling away through all that pain.

Like the hens – chop their heads off, as Dad did, wring their necks, like Mother used to, and they'd get up and run across the yard. One flew over the fence, once, squawking demented, like. When he was little, he used to think it was funny. Now – wring a hen's neck? Wring Martha's? One-eyed old Jemima? Kill them? Doesn't even bear thinking about, though Mary does it, and he – a blush creeps up his neck – will eat it. Nice bird on the table, nothing like it. Gravy and roast potatoes and he'll have a leg, ta very much. Once they're dead, it's different: can't explain, just is. So long as he's had nothing to do with it, so long as he doesn't know who it is.

Now then. Churchill. His Finest Hour. *We shall fight on the beaches* . . . He'd have had a dog, bound to. Give him a bulldog? No – bit too obvious, bit too in your face. Probably had Labradors, down at Chartwell, flopping down beside him while he and Clemmie had tea on the lawn. He can see it now, the shadows of great trees lengthening as the sun goes down—

Right, then, who else?

Thing about encyclopaedias is you get distracted, looking through; you go off at a tangent. Ernie finds himself running his finger down columns and stopping. Crustacean. Damocles. Kuala Lumpur – you'd never know that was a city. And he pictures a great Antipodean mammal, swinging slowly in the heat from tree to tree.

His cig has gone out in the saucer. He picks it up, lights up with the last of the matches, hears sounds at the gate and looks up. They're back. Wait till he tells them. And how much have they made to date? How many red dots? How many commissions?

This is it, he tells Pipsqueak, snoozing at his feet, and he pushes his chair back and goes to greet them, completely rallied now, until they turn from closing the gate behind them, and pick up their bags, and he sees their faces.

Easter. Wild April skies, rain sweeping over the hills and then a flood of sunlight. Church bells: up in her bedroom, Sophie sits and sobs. Then the broody hen in her coop beneath the back kitchen window hatches two chicks on Easter Monday and Ernie yells up to her to come and take a look. Mary comes out beside her, face like thunder, but as they all bend to the battered old box, the chicken wire and hay, and hear the tiny peep beneath the wings, everything else is forgotten.

'Could be worse,' says Ernie, straightening up, looking at the vast light sky, the oak in bud and the lambs, racing around the field. 'Could be worse.' He goes to let the dogs out and they pour through the yard to the gate. 'Back here!' he yells at them. 'Get back here, you hounds!'

In early evening, taking Nellie and Pip and Benjy out just for a little run, on leads, for a mile or so down the lane, he meets old John Dickson, in the Land Rover, pulling up at the straw-strewn gateway to Broxwood Hall, where Dad, all his life, went milking. Ernie nods, touches his hat, tugs the dogs on to the verge. Dickson is looking grim. He winds down the window, leans out.

'Evening,' says Ernie.

'There's four new cases been found,' Dickson tells him. 'Up at Llanrhos. That's it, now. We're in for it now.'

Ernie feels something inside him move and turn over, in some dark, terrible place.

'That's bad,' he says at last. 'That's very bad.'

Dickson nods. He slowly gets down, and slowly walks in his

gumboots through the heaps of wet straw, and opens his gate. Then he gets back in the Land Rover, and slams the door.

'I'll do the gate, behind you,' says Ernie, but Dickson shakes his head.

'Best get on home with those dogs. Best stay there.' And he turns and bumps in, and brakes and gets out and walks slowly back again, and heaves the gate on to its latch. He gestures at the straw all round it. 'This was a precaution,' he says grimly.

And he walks back, gets in, bumps away up the track to the farmhouse, between fields where young lambs are racing to the calling ewes, as the last of the sun slips down, and night approaches.

They're there at dawn. Ernie wakes, and hears them: the shouts, the panting dogs, the bleating. Beside him, Pip is at once alert. He sits up in his sleeping bag and pulls the curtain. There they are: striding over the field in ghostly white clothing, masked, and carrying guns. The sheep stream away through the gates held open: into the next field, and the next. The first rays of sun break the rolling clouds; the gates, one by one, swing to; and then the first shots are fired.

Ernie slumps down on his lumpy pillow, and wraps his arms round Pip, and howls.

21

'Well, now, Miss Henderson,' says the consultant, and pulls Buffy's file towards him. 'Let's have a look.'

The consulting room is small and unadorned. Buffy is sick with fear. She sits on the edge of her chair and clasps her handbag so tightly that the little gold fastening digs into her palm. The pain is almost a relief.

The consultant is turning pages. He pulls out an envelope, slips out a print-out, slips it back again. He is about forty-five, she supposes, grey beginning to show here and there, designer glasses on a rather clever-looking nose. Well – to be a consultant at forty-five, you'd have to be brilliant. That's something: at least she is in the best possible hands.

'You've had a scan,' he murmurs. 'Two scans. And blood tests. Mmm.' He closes the file and looks at her. 'And how are you feeling? Generally?'

'Really quite well.' Buffy feels sweat seep into her leather bag. 'Rather tired, of course, but when you get to my age—' She utters a little laugh, gives up, and meets his gaze. 'Tell me,' she says, summoning every last drop of courage from every last cell. 'Tell me the worst.'

'Your blood count is very low,' he says gently. 'We're going to have to get lots of iron into you as soon as possible. And the scans – the truth is, we don't quite know. It could be just a horrid old lump that needs to come out, and that's the end of it.'

'Like fibroids,' says Buffy, her breath very shallow and fast. 'That sort of thing?'

'Exactly. Exactly that sort of thing.' He rubs his chin for a moment, and smiles at her – a smile she will remember later as being almost as lovely as William's, but not quite. Nothing could ever be quite like his.

'Or it could be something else,' he says carefully, and the words she has known she will have to hear come to her now as if spoken in an echo chamber, sounding over and over again: something else, something else, something else—

He reaches across the desk, and takes her hand.

'And how did you get on?' asks William, phoning next morning. 'The results of that little test – everything all right?'

It's spring – proper spring: the daffodils bright in her window boxes, the scent of the pheasant's-eye narcissi drifting in where the window is open at the top. Buffy, even at the height of her campaigning, has never been aware of the natural world with more intensity. She takes a long deep breath.

'I've got to have an op,' she tells William. 'Rather a big one.'

The phone is ringing: Janice, running down the stairs and late for work, picks it up in the hall. Through the open door to the drawing room she sees William, sitting in his chair by the phone in there, with Danny on his lap, stroking him, over and over again.

'Hello?'

'Good morning, Janice, it's Claire.'

'Oh, hi.' She gives William a little wave, and he raises his hand. Not looking quite himself today, she notices.

'Just ringing to check about tomorrow.'

Tomorrow. Oh, God. She looks at the calendar on the wall, inked in here and there in William's distinctive hand. Buffy's concert. Dentist. Phillips sale. What's happening tomorrow?

'Remember you said you would baby-sit,' says Claire. 'The Thursday after Easter, remember?'

'Oh, yeah. Sure. What time did you want me?'

'Could you be here by six-thirty? Jeremy's in court, unfortunately, so I'm going to have to pick him up. We're having dinner with friends in Blackheath – we'll try not to be back too late. I know you're working the next day.'

'OK, fine, thanks.' Janice looks at her watch. She must go. 'See you then.'

'Look forward to it,' says Claire, and hangs up, without asking for William, or how he might be, but then she never does.

So she asks him herself, from the door – 'You OK?'

He nods, turns to look at her. God, he's gone pale.

'What is it? What's up?' Matthew, she thinks suddenly, and crosses the room in a couple of strides. 'Tell me.'

'Poor old Buffy's not too good.'

How papery and pale is the liver-spotted skin on the hand, stroking Danny's chestnut coat, on and on and on.

'Why? What's happened?'

'Got to have an op,' says William, quietly. 'Poor old thing.'

'An op?' No one she knows ever uses this term – it makes the business of going into hospital sound like nothing, really. Which she supposes is the point.

'Exploratory. Probably nothing to worry about. Still – these things are never nice.' Then William gives himself a little shake, and visibly rallies. 'Go on, Danny, down you get.' And he slips him to the floor, and gets to his feet, and smiles, looking more like William. 'You must go. And I must get on – things to organise. You're here for supper?'

'No, I'm working, remember,' says Janice, bending to give Danny a pat. 'And I'm out tomorrow, as well,' she adds, straightening up. 'That was Claire on the phone. I'm baby-sitting.'

'Are you, now?' He gives her a little kiss. 'You're very honoured, I must say.'

When she has gone, racing off down the steps and clanging the gate, he takes himself slowly down to the kitchen, lets Danny out to the garden, and makes a very good pot of coffee. A spring breeze is stirring the willow tree, where he and Eve used to sit and have tea, on distant summer days. There is now, as so often, rain in the air. He watches Danny nosing about among the daffodils; hears Edith Horsley, three doors down, open her back door and call her cat. Another old thing on her own. He pours his good strong coffee into his good Portmeirion Botanical mug, carries it back up the stairs, and sets it on his open desk. Then, from the drinks cupboard, he takes his father's hip flask, sniffing the leather case, unscrewing the silver top, sniffing again. Nothing like it. And he crosses the room and pours into his Botanical mug a good big nip. And another. He screws the silver top back on.

Do not, he hears Buffy say wildly, waving the paper, with its dreadful headlines, *do not, at a time like this, talk to me about little nips.*

Dear Buffy, how she felt things. He must stand by her now, though the thought of hospitals—

He sits at his overflowing desk, his father's desk, letting coffee and brandy reach just the right spot, and pull him back together for the tasks that lie ahead, seeing Eve's darling thin face on the pillow, feeling her weightless hand in his, Eve barely Eve, her voice a thread.

It's dark, it's raining; Janice runs down the street, and up the soaking steps to Claire's front door. She knocks and waits.

Rain splashes on to the bay tree in its tub; the door is opened; Piers observes her wetness coolly.

'Come in.' He steps aside, and Janice wipes her boots about a hundred times on the fitted coconut matting.

'Thanks.' She pulls her hat off, pulls off her gloves. They need wringing out. So does she.

'Janice! Oh, you poor thing. Why is it always raining when you come to see us?' Claire takes the wet things at once. 'I'll put these on the Rayburn rail – do you want to bring your jacket in there, too? We can hang it on the airer.'

Piers slips away and Janice follows her, into the shining warm kitchen, with its halogen lighting and floor fit to eat off and glass-fronted cupboards painted in matt Shaker green. Claire is unhooking the rope on the airing rack, letting it down gently. 'There we are. Now, if you give me your jacket—'

'I feel like a drowned rat.'

All Janice really wants is to strip off and get into a hot bath, with clouds of steam wafting through William's comfortable bathroom and the radio on and the prospect of supper by the fire. Instead, she's got to flipping baby-sit. She runs her hands through her wet hair.

'Come and warm up by the Rayburn.' And Claire moves the wet gloves and tea towels along the rail. Janice stands with her back to it. God, that's better. For a second she closes her eyes. All she needs now is about twenty-five dogs snoozing away at her feet, and a mug of Mary's stand-your-spoon-up tea. She gives a little smile.

'What are you thinking about?'

'Your cousins, to tell you the truth.' And Janice opens her eyes in time to see Claire's quick little frown.

'I haven't seen them since I was small,' she says. 'I can't really remember them at all. Anyway—' She looks at her watch. 'I must be off. Now then – the children are all fed and watered, and once they're in bed you must make yourself at home. I've left our friends' number by the phone. The boys are doing their homework, I hope, and Geraldine has had her bath. She'll want a story. Light out for her after that, and lights out for the boys by half past eight. Oh, hello, darling.'

'I don't want you to go out,' says Geraldine, in cream pyjamas and soft blue dressing gown.

'I like those pyjamas,' says Janice, wheeling into action. 'I wish I had a pair like that.'

'We got them in a sale,' says Geraldine, brightening reluctantly.

'Did you? That was clever. I don't suppose you'd like to show me your room, would you? I bet it's really nice.'

Flashes of gratitude across the kitchen. The baby-sitting evening has begun.

By nine, the house is quiet.

It's dark, it's raining, a key turns in the lock. Janice half asleep in front of *Question Time*, come to with a start: they're back. She looks at her digital watch, pulsing away: not quite eleven, not too bad. God, how the rain's pelting down – will they run her home?

Footsteps in the hall. She turns to do her baby-sitting stuff: Hi, had a good time? They've been really good—

The door swings open.

Janice looks round, sees a tall, half-drowned man walking slowly into the room, like a sleepwalker, his skin white, his soaking hair plastered to his head, his eyes like stones.

For a moment she is so shocked she cannot speak or move.

Then—

'Matthew—'

She finds she is on her feet; he turns and sees her.

'Hello, Matthew. God, you gave me a fright, I didn't know you had a key—'

As if he's just popped in from next door or something, not walked out of a ward, out of a hospital, in and out of the traffic on a dark wet night, mile after drowning mile till he comes to his sister's house. Looking around for her now, in this perfect family sitting room.

Jesus.

'They're out,' she says. 'I thought you were them. I'm baby-sitting—'

Matthew is staring at her, those fathomless dark eyes like depthless mountain pools, wherein you might fall, and plunge, and never be seen again.

'It's me,' she says, and knows for the first time what it means to hear your own voice shake. 'It's Janice, you remember me—' She takes a step towards him, holding out her hand, keeping her voice as low and as calm as she can, as if she were talking to a frightened animal. 'It's OK, darling.'

Has she ever used this word to anyone?

'I'm here.' She says it again. 'Darling Matthew, I'm here, I'm here, everything's OK.'

Matthew looks down at her blankly. Once more, she can feel how utterly enclosed he is: shut away, miles away, in some far distant place; a ship far out at sea, where sky and water meet and dissolve, where a ship might slip silently over the rim of the world, and disappear.

'You remember me,' she says gently, stroking the long musician's fingers, over and over again. 'I've been to visit you in hospital, we went to a concert together, you and me and your dad—'

And at last, like the movement of water, like the first incoming wave of the returning tide, a smile breaks his frozen gaze, and he begins to quicken – she can feel it, the coming to life again.

'I think I remember,' he says slowly, smiling down at her. 'I think I remember that.'

Rainwater from his soaking clothes is in patches at his feet; she leads him over to the leaping pale flames of the coal-gas fire, and they stand before it.

'This is Claire's house,' he says, as she helps him off with his dark wet coat.

'Yes.' She lays the coat on a chair. 'I'm baby-sitting,' she says again, returning to his side. 'They'll be back soon.'

He looks around the room, at sofa and books and papers and box of toys; at the television, where farmers in the *Question Time* studio are shouting. He frowns; she switches it off, and now the only sounds are the puttering fire, and the rain, falling on and on.

'I've come to see Claire,' says Matthew slowly. 'Where is she? Where have they taken her?'

Janice holds his hand again, a little warmer now, though his face is still deathly pale.

'She's with Jeremy, no one's taken her anywhere, they're out having supper with friends.'

He shakes his head, and although he is calmer now, and warmer, and although, in his returning smile, she has seen him step back towards the world, she can sense, too, the way in which illness is coursing through him, flooding in, flooding out, draining and exhausting. He takes his hand away, rubs at his face, frowns.

'Who am I?' he asks her, from miles and miles away. 'Tell me who I am.'

'You're Matthew,' says Janice, almost in tears, as a key turns in the lock. 'You're Matthew Harriman, Eve and William's son. Claire's brother.'

And then there are voices in the hall, and Claire, all at once, is in the doorway. She sees him, goes white, and in two steps has crossed the room and taken him in her arms.

An ambulance moves down the street, its blue light flashing; curtains are pulled back at upstairs windows. Jeremy, who has called it, gets up and goes quietly out to the hall. Janice, at the window of the sitting room, watches it come to a halt, and the men jump out in the wet.

Claire is sitting by the fire, holding Matthew's hand. He is calmer now, but with every move he makes – every frown, each glance, each sudden start – Janice senses illness at the gates.

She hears the front door opened, the rushing fall of rain.

'Do you want me to go with him?' she asks, as the men climb up the steps, and speak to Jeremy in low voices.

Claire shakes her head. She looks much older.

'I'll follow in the car, I'll see him back on to the ward. If you don't mind waiting until I get back – then one of us can run you home.'

'If it stops raining, I'll walk—' But Claire is getting to her feet, saying, 'No, no, you wait here,' and anyway Janice can't think that far ahead, can't really think about anything except Matthew, white-faced, exhausted, leaning back in his chair as if he might never move again, as if he has come home.

Then the men are in the doorway, and Jeremy is saying gently: 'Matthew—' and he looks up, goes paler still, then bows his head, and lets them take him.

They've gone.

The rain is easing off. In the gleaming warm kitchen, Jeremy makes tea, and Janice lights up, watching him, her hands still shaking. She has seen him, as the ambulance doors swing to, run down the steps in the rain to where Claire is unlocking the car again. She has watched him ask: Are you sure you don't want me with you? And seen Claire shaking her head, insistent, getting in quickly, flashing the ambulance driver: All right. Let's go.

Now Jeremy is leaning against the Rayburn rail, weary, his eyes for a moment beginning to close. Smoke drifts across the kitchen, and he coughs.

'Sorry,' says Janice. 'I'll put it out.'

'No, no, it's fine.' He smiles at her, and the smile becomes a yawn. 'I'm sure you need it, after all this. At times like this, I wish I smoked myself.' He turns, and picks up the teapot. 'How do you like it?'

'Black, please. Are there often times likes this?'

'I wouldn't say often, no.' He brings a mug across, goes back to fetch his own, stirring in sugar. 'Not for a long time, in fact.'

'Do you mind me asking – how come he had a key?'

Christ, how sad that sounds. As if he must never have one, as if it's out of the question. And she thinks of him, in that ambulance, staring out of the smoked-glass window, rain streaming down it as they pick up speed. His sister is behind them: his sister, whom he has walked long, dark miles to see, is sending him back where he belongs.

Is this it, then? Is this how it has to be?

Jeremy is pulling out a chair. 'Claire gave him that key years ago,' he says, sitting down. 'Not long after we moved here. I think she wanted him to feel a part of things. I did wonder if it was wise. But he's never actually used it like this before – suddenly turning up. I'd quite forgotten he had it, to tell you the truth.' He waves away smoke, apologetically, and Janice stubs out at once.

'Sorry,' she says again.

'Please. It just makes me cough, that's all—' He drinks his tea. 'That's better. I haven't offered you anything stronger, I'm afraid. Would you—'

'No, no, I'm fine. I think I'd better just keep steady with this.' She clasps the mug; they smile at one another, two people who've just been through something quite out of the run of things, and who'll never, because of this, need to break the ice. Not that there's much ice to break with Jeremy: he's a good, kind man through and through, she can feel it. And yet—

There's something in this well-run house that absolutely isn't right.

Somewhere near by, a clock is striking midnight. Must be St Matthew's, on the common. 'I go there once in a blue moon,' William said once. 'Buffy and I went at Christmas. I suppose, come to think of it, we might have taken Matthew; he might have enjoyed the carols. But he was so ill, then, so withdrawn—'

Not like now, then, thinks Janice, and sees him again, climbing into the ambulance, as if it were something inevitable, the doors closing behind him, the blue light turning in the rain. Just as he was beginning to get better, she could feel it. And she sits there drinking her tea and thinking: of Matthew out in the hospital grounds, on windy spring days, so gentle and quiet; turning to say, with that slow, sweet smile, I do remember you. She thinks of him at the concert, lifting his finger at the sound of the piano, listening, listening, coming back to life.

And then there is tonight: Matthew unhinged, barely reachable, falling into his sister's arms.

Jeremy drinks his tea. She wants to ask him . . . oh, lots of things, but they'll have to wait.

'You go to bed,' she says, as he yawns again. 'I'll wait for Claire.'

'Are you sure? You've had such an unnerving time—'

'So have you.'

He shrugs – not dismissively, but in resignation. 'It's part of our lives. I don't mean nocturnal visits, just—' He spreads his hands. 'Just the whole thing.'

'Can you tell me—' she begins cautiously, but he's too tired to pick it up, to say more, or explain.

He just says: 'It's worse for Claire. It must be, though she never really talks—' And then he gets up, looking drawn. 'I'm so sorry, it's just that I have to be up at six.' He touches her shoulder. 'Thanks for holding the fort. You were great. Not everyone could have done that.'

'Oh, I don't know,' says Janice, but she knows it's true. Somehow, frightened though she was, she had known what to do, had felt the connection between her and Matthew run strong and straight and true. Somehow, she understands him: it's as simple as that.

'I'm off. Tell Claire she can wake me if she needs to.'

And he leaves her, climbing the stairs to the bathroom, and then to bed. After a little while, the house is quiet again.

It's half past two in the morning. A key turns in the lock. Janice has fallen asleep at the table: she wakes with a start. It's stopped raining;

it's the dead of night. For a moment she can't think why she's here. Then it all comes flooding back.

She gets to her feet as Claire comes into the kitchen. She's strained and white: a different person.

'How is he?' Janice's voice is thick with sleep; she clears her throat. 'What happened?'

Claire drops her keys on the table, sinks into a chair. God, she looks tired.

'They've sedated him: nothing too drastic. I saw him back on to the ward, I talked to the night staff. He'll be OK.'

'Will he? Did he mind being back?'

'By the time we got there I think he'd had enough. We'll see—' She rests her chin in her hands.

'You must be wiped out.'

'Sort of.' Claire gives a little smile, looks up at her. 'You too, I should think. You're still here, you're still awake. I thought Jeremy might have offered you the spare room.'

'I wanted to wait up. He's gone to bed – he says you can wake him if you want.'

Claire shakes her head. She doesn't say: He's got to be up at six, I'll let him sleep. She just says: 'What's the point?'

Comfort, perhaps? thinks Janice. The warmth of human kindness? But she says only: 'Shall I make you something? Tea? Coffee?'

'Coffee,' says Claire, with a long sigh, and her hands go over her mouth and her eyes close. She sits there, immobile, lost in thought, and Janice, putting the kettle on, spooning coffee into the cafetière, can feel how deep this is, how enclosed Claire is – like Matthew, in a way.

How strange.

'Just going to the loo,' she says quietly, and if Claire hears her she does not respond. When Janice comes back, she's still there like that: has she fallen asleep?

'Claire?' Janice sets coffee things before her. 'You all right?'

Claire's eyes open, and she gives her little smile – coming back, like Matthew, though from somewhere – yes? – closer to home.

'You're very good. Thanks.' And she gives herself a little shake, comes to, watches Janice pour strong black coffee into a deep blue mug. Out in the garden, rain drips from tree and shrub. Janice sits down on the settle. There's a silence. There is, all at once, the soft hollow hoot of an owl. Claire listens. It comes again. She shuts her eyes, her hand goes to her mouth once more, as if, as if—

'What is it?' asks Janice, watching her. 'What is it?'

'Nothing.'

Janice knows this isn't true. She waits. The owl calls again, soft and low and haunting. Claire begins soundlessly to cry.

'Hey—' Janice reaches across the table, touches her hand. Claire shakes her head. Tears spill from behind closed lids. Janice sits waiting, observing, behind those closed lids, a terrible struggle, as Claire wipes the tears away, away, over and over, with her strong, square-tipped, capable fingers which are, Janice sees now, bitten down to the quick.

At last she is calm. She opens her eyes, feels for a handkerchief tucked up her sleeve, blows her nose, tries a smile.

'We get quite a few owls round here,' she says unsteadily, tucking the handkerchief back, picking up her coffee. 'Sometimes you'd hardly know you were in London.'

'Yeah,' says Janice, remembering. 'I heard one the night I arrived. At the back of the house, I think, but I could still hear it.'

She talks on, wanting to be comforting, and normal, while Claire recovers. 'It made me think of Shropshire – you hear them all the time in the woods.'

But Claire isn't really listening to this.

'Even when Matthew and I were little,' she says slowly, her hands round the deep blue mug. 'We used to lie awake and listen to them. We used to give them names.'

'What sort of names?'

'Oh, I can't remember them all. Merlin was one, I think. And in winter once or twice we used to see them, sitting in the trees. So beautiful. So mysterious—'

Janice, turning her tobacco tin in her hands, listens to this different woman, talking of her childhood. She sees them both: brother and sister, up against the window on a frosty night, the sky a midnight blue, pricked with stars over walled town gardens, a London owl on a leafless London plane tree, silhouette just visible—

Look!

She smiles, feeling Claire's eyes upon her now.

'They came year after year,' Claire says slowly. 'The sound of them always takes me back.'

Janice is rolling up. Without thinking, she says, 'Did you share a room, then?', although she knows, of course she knows, that Matthew and Claire each had their own room, right at the top of the house, for she, after all, is living in one of them, is she not? She's living in Claire's blue-and-white room, with its white-painted shelves, and the bedside rug with the blue-and-white animals, going round and round the perfect childhood, by the bed set beneath the casement window, curtained with pandas, barred for safety, against the long, long drop.

There's a pause: she looks up.

And Claire says, very quietly and deliberately, 'No, no, we didn't. Not officially, that is.' And she holds her in a long and burning gaze, which says, unmistakably: Look at me. Look at me. Understand.

Janice can feel her heart begin to pound.

And then there is a long, long silence.

No, please no.

She cannot look at Claire. When at last she does, she feels a blush, deeper than any she has ever felt, begin to rise, and spread, until it is flooding through every part of her. She turns away, can hardly breathe, turns back. Their eyes meet again.

Claire says at last: 'There are things you can't tell anyone, ever.'

'Why are you telling me, then?' Janice asks at last.

'Because—' Claire is burning, burning. 'Because I hardly know you. Because I must tell someone.'

Her eyes drop, to the beautiful deep blue mug, with its thin gold ring, like a wedding ring, enclosing everything.

The church clock chimes the half-hour. Janice thinks: I was in one world, half an hour ago, and now I'm in another. Then the owl calls again, and she thinks: That sound will mark my life. Not in the way it's marked Claire's but it'll be there. Always.

She picks up the roll-up. Claire watches.

'Do you mind?'

Claire shakes her head. Janice lights up. Even though she's been smoking all evening, she feels the nicotine like a hit.

'And Jeremy?' she asks, wondering about his life, his kindness, his terrible fatigue. 'You've never told him. About . . . you and Matthew.'

It is terrible to say these words. Saying them fills the room, the world.

'No,' says Claire. 'I haven't. I never will.'

'Don't you think he might understand?'

Claire is silent. Then she says: 'He loves me. He loves me and the children. We're very lucky.' There is a twisted little smile. 'With three children, you can blot out a hell of a lot.'

'But not for ever.'

'No.' The mug in her hands is held so tight.

'And if you were to tell him—'

'I can't. I'm not prepared to take the risk. And anyway—' There is another silence. 'That time belongs to Matthew and me. We were everything to each other – it's precious, it's ours.' She is trembling now. 'But I had to tell you.'

'Why?' asks Janice, filled with the enormities of the night's disclosure, and deception. 'Why?'

'Because . . . because I thought you were falling in love with Matthew.' Claire waits, crimson. 'I could feel it. Is it true?'

'Yes,' says Janice, who has carried his name, his melancholy, his musicality and his extraordinary smile within her, since the first moment they met. 'Yes, I'm afraid it is.'

They sit in silence. Rain drips from the trees.

'What are you trying to tell me?' asks Janice. 'That because . . . because you and he – is that what made him ill? Is that why he broke down?' She can hear her voice rising, as if she has something to avenge. 'You said he was schizophrenic—'

Claire flinches. 'That was the diagnosis. When he went into hospital. No one has ever said anything different. And I don't know if there's any connection. I think it would have happened anyway.'

'Why? Why should it?'

She makes a gesture, huge and full of questions. 'No one knows. It happens, more often to young men. Matthew was at the classic age. You read all the literature – I used to read it. Is it genetic? Is it reactive? Do you treat it with drugs, with therapy? What brings it on, when it strikes? All my life I've blamed my parents – so wrapped up in one another, so in love, that they never saw what was coming. And it's true that they didn't notice much. They certainly had no idea—' She stops.

237

'But perhaps I was just thrashing about, casting all the blame on them, when really . . . Perhaps when Matthew left home, all the guilt caught up with him, perhaps it did trigger something that was lying in wait—' She covers her face, rocking. 'It nearly killed me when he broke down. And now – I don't know, I don't know, I don't know.'

'And what are you saying?' asks Janice again, as the milk float hums down the street, and tyres swish in the wet. It stops: there is the chink of bottles. Such blessed, ordinary sounds: things to remind you, after a long, terrible night of illness, that you are still alive.

'You're warning me off,' she says slowly. 'Why? Because he's so ill? Because he can never recover? Or—' She cannot meet Claire's eyes. 'Because you still love him yourself?'

There is another silence. It goes on and on.

'I can't answer that,' says Claire, her voice breaking, and upstairs, deep within the bedroom of her married life, an alarm begins to ring.

It's almost dawn: out in the street, where water is gurgling along the gutters, the faintest light breaks the darkness, and the stars in the rained-out sky are pale. Puddles are everywhere, shining in the light from the sodium lamps, and from one or two porch lights, left on all night.

Janice stands in the middle of the wet pavement. It feels as if she will never move again. She hears Claire's revelations; sees Matthew's beloved, haunted face.

Where is she? Where have they taken her? Tell me who I am . . .

She starts to cry, and then she starts to run, sobbing aloud, racing along the wet pavements, past curtained houses with who knows what dreams and desires and suffering within, through the silent, shut-up Village, and down the well-kept streets to William's street, and William's beautiful, cherished, roomy family house. She leans against the wet railings, gasping.

Dawn is breaking; the birds are starting up. She hears the whistle of an early train and then, as it dies away, the blackbird's liquid, glorious, full-throated stream of song.

She takes out her keys, and climbs the steps to the porch, where trailing wisteria is just in leaf, and the milk bottles have been rinsed and set out. She unlocks the door, very quietly, closes it behind her, quieter still, but Danny, down in the bowels of the earth, is at once awake, and gives a sudden bark behind the closed kitchen door.

Sssh, she whispers to the empty hall. Sssh, go back to sleep.

And slowly, carefully, to avoid the creaking treads, she climbs up the staircase, right to the top of the house.

22

William drives Buffy to hospital. Her little case is packed, and rests on the back seat; she sits beside him, clasping her handbag, dreadfully still. For once, it's a beautiful day.

'As soon as you're better,' says William, slowing down at a zebra crossing, 'we'll go to the sales. I've got the catalogue, I've had a look. There's a lovely old place in Gloucestershire, sounds a dream: everything must go before they sell up. I'll pack up a hamper—' He changes gear, drives on. 'You'll love it.'

'And when is this?' asks Buffy, as they swish past shops, and shoppers, and normal life.

'Middle of June. After the election. Just right.'

'The countryside is closed,' she says, envisioning an avenue, rustling trees, peaceful parkland, safely grazing sheep. Not any more. 'Remember? Just because it's not on the front page every day doesn't mean it's stopped happening. There were twelve new cases yesterday, didn't you hear? And anyway—' She tightens her grip on the handbag. 'I don't know if I'll be quite up to sales by the middle of June.'

'We'll see.' He turns to glance at her. God, what a white little Buffy. He gives her a pat, drives on. 'We'll see how we go.'

And Buffy, filled with fear and apprehension as she is; facing facts, as she has made herself do; is, with the prospect of a sale, and tea in a tent, infinitesimally comforted.

Then they come to the hospital gates, and William starts talking about parking, and she shuts her eyes, and braces herself for it all.

He settles her into the ward, carrying her case in, looking for Sister.

'Not Sister,' murmurs Buffy. 'Admissions clerk.'

'Ah.' He's forgotten all this, or perhaps it's changed. He strides down the ward, and heads turn.

'We'll soon have her right again,' says the student nurse who finally, finally, shows her to her bed.

'Of course you will,' says William, and pats Buffy's arm.

'Almost worse for relatives, I think,' the girl goes on wisely, all of eighteen, with a stud in her nose. 'Especially husbands.' She gives them both a special smile.

'Well, we're not actually—' William begins, and sees Buffy's sudden, quite unexpected blush, and gallantly, automatically, courtesy and kindness in his every cell, adds sweetly, 'Would that it were so.'

'Don't be foolish, William,' Buffy says briskly, through her blush, and the student nurse looks from one to the other and says, 'Oh, dear. Trust me.'

'Now then,' says Buffy, when she has gone, and looks about her.

She's in a bay of four beds. Two are occupied, one has curtains round it. I'm going, she thinks, in a sudden access of dread. I shall leave, now, I'm not going to have this op, I'll just have to die at home.

'Dear Buffy,' says William, watching her. 'How brave you are.'

She shakes her head. 'Not really.'

'Yes, really. Now – is there anything else I can do? Shall I leave you to unpack, and then come back to say goodbye? Would that be the thing?'

'Yes,' says Buffy. 'I think it would.'

'I'll have a little wander, bring back some tea.'

'Before there's that ghastly Nil by Mouth sign up,' says Buffy, and he frowns, and then remembers, and takes himself down to the Friends Shop, and Flowers, where he buys a huge bunch of dreamy pink-and-white lisianthus, realising, as he pays for them, that they are just what Eve would have loved. In fact, they're probably just what he bought her, when he took her in to Barts. Or perhaps it was roses. Yes, perhaps it was.

Someone is talking to him.

'I beg your pardon?'

'I said here's your change,' says the girl, and he comes to with a start, and takes it, and goes back up to the ward with two teas and the flowers in Cellophane.

Buffy has unpacked, but not undressed. She's sitting in the bedside chair, Ackroyd's *London* on the locker, dressing gown on the end of the bed. Her eyes are closed and she looks drawn and old – for a moment he sees her as a stranger would, and everything that makes her Buffy vanishes.

'Here we are,' he says cheerfully, and she opens her eyes, sees the pink-and-white flowers, is Buffy again.

'Heavenly. Heavenly. Thank you.'

'Is there a vase?' He goes to look for one, is sent to the sluice, finds something made of weightless tin, which he assumes is not a urinal. How strange it is, he thinks, taking it back, to be in a mainstream hospital. He's so used to visiting Matthew, week after week, year after year, but that's different, at least on Matthew's ward. He's accustomed to being patient, to thinking about the life of the mind, trying to guess at the life of Matthew's mind, talking to consultants about drugs and occupational therapy. All this – the curtained beds, the Nil by Mouth, the prospect of dreadful operations – it feels more real, more frightening, now. He's frightened for Buffy, suddenly: truly afraid.

'Here we are,' he says again, and takes out his pocket knife, to slice through the tape on the Cellophane.

'I've forgotten something,' says Buffy, watching. She gets to her feet, with difficulty. 'While you were gone, I realised.'

'What's that?' He crumples the Cellophane, starts to arrange the flowers. That vase. He shakes his head.

'Just some little things of Mother's,' says Buffy, helping with the flowers. 'It sounds so silly, but suddenly I want them with me. I put them out, on my desk – her scent bottle, and her little bell, that might be useful. How could I have forgotten them?'

'I'm sure there's a bell here,' says William, and finds it, a buzzer encased in cream plastic, at the end of a long, cream, medical-looking tube. Horrid.

'I'd rather have Mother's,' says Buffy, eyeing it.

'Of course you would. Don't worry, I'll go and get it. And the scent bottle – anything else?'

'No, I don't think so. There's no rush. Just . . . when you can.'

'I'll bring them in after the op. Give me the keys, and I'll pop in, as soon as they say I can visit. Or would you like me to go back there now?'

'No, no. I can look forward to having them. When I wake up. If I do.'

'Of course you will,' William says quickly. 'Don't be silly.' And he takes her hand.

'Oh, William,' says Buffy, on the verge of crumpling. 'I'm so sorry.'

'Sorry? What do you have to be sorry for?'

'It's just—' She hesitates. 'You're being so good and kind. And I know it must be awful for you, I know it must bring it all back.' Her lips are trembling. 'Poor Eve.'

'Nonsense.' He grips her hand. 'You mustn't think about it, don't give it a thought. It's you we're concentrating on now.' He leans forward, kisses the top of her head. Her hair comb is put in all wonky, he notices. 'Now then.' He straightens up again, and taps his pocket. 'What would you say to a little nip?'

It's late: the afternoon sun is streaming through the gap in the blue-and-white curtains, with their pandas, contentedly chewing bamboo. Janice stretches, turns over, sees the clock, remembers.

Should she be at work? She shuts her eyes. It's . . . Friday? Yes. She lies there for a while, coming to, feeling the darkness of those night-time hours, that conversation, lying within her like a stain, a shadow, something she'll have to live with.

After a while, she gets up, goes downstairs, not looking at Matthew's old room, phones Sandra. She's ill, she says, she's sorry. And she won't be coming back. Yeah, she'll work out her notice if she has to, but she's leaving London. Soon.

She puts down the phone, feels the quietness all around her. Where's William? Where's Danny?

Down in the kitchen, she finds William's note, and Danny in his basket, tail beginning to thump at once. She fondles his ears, lets him out, reads the note.

Taking Buffy to hospital – the West London. Back for supper. You were late last night—? Lots of love, Wm PS If you would give Danny just a little run . . .

Janice makes a mug of milkless tea, and carries it up to the bathroom. She runs the deepest bath of her life, pouring in the very last of Eve's bath oil. 'Sorry,' she says aloud, as the room is filled with the scent of roses.

She peels off her nightshirt, she sinks beneath the waves.

Emerges, gasping, hair dripping into her eyes; wipes her face; lies back, drinking tea, and thinking, thinking.

☆

William, emerging from the hospital, swings the car round to go home. It's just after four: he'll miss the rush hour. He turns on Radio 3, hears something that sounds like Harrison Birtwhistle, and turns it off again. Right, off we go.

This time tomorrow, Buffy will be coming round. God Willing. What a long wait.

'I'll have visitors afterwards,' she told him, as they said goodbye. 'Over-Sixties bods, Dorothy and so on. When I'm feeling up to it. I don't want anyone now. Just you.'

He squeezes her hand. 'Chin up.'

She lifts it bravely, like Little Grey Rabbit, captured by the stoats. Or was it weasels? Weasels, he thinks, and thinking of Buffy, all alone in a long, long frightening night, he pulls up at the traffic lights and turns left. He'll go to the flat now, get Mother's things, something to comfort her, while she waits. And he drives back to her street, parks in a Residents Parking Only bay, leaving a note: Doctor on call. Well – it's worth a try.

Inside, he presses the time switch, climbs up the stairs. God, you need to be pretty fit for this. Poor old Buffy – how will she manage, when she comes out? He unlocks her door, through which, over the years, he has carted in many a box of china, and carted it out again. Now then. Where did she say?

Inside her windowless little hall, he puts the lamp on; he opens the sitting-room door. The afternoons are getting longer, but still, it's not Summer Time yet, and dusk is falling. And it's cold in here. The sitting room is full of shadow, and she has half drawn the curtains, so the room has a strangely suspended atmosphere – between night and day, light and dark, here and there.

Not nice, being in someone else's empty place: he doesn't like it – especially at this dusk-filled hour, especially with Buffy ill. He makes his way to the desk, sees the soft gleam of the glass-and-silver scent bottle, the little silver bell. And something else: the whiteness of a letter, propped up against the walnut letter rack. Something she's forgotten to post – well, he can do that. Is there a stamp? He puts on his glasses, has a look, sees his own name, his own address. He picks it up.

Darkness is gathering quickly now. He puts on the desk lamp, picks up her paper-knife, remembers buying it for her, years and years ago. He hesitates. Should he read this now? Is that what she intended? Or was it meant for—

He slits it open, unfolds it – rather good paper – and sits at the desk, the heart of her campaigning: all those leaflets and posters, all those envelopes.

> *Dearest William,*
> *This letter is for you to read in case I don't come back. I hope I will: there seems, all at once, to be so much to live for, but – you never know. I want to tell you something I have never been able to tell you, all these years. I hope you won't think me too foolish, or carried away . . .*

The clock on the mantelpiece is ticking softly into the empty room. He turns the page.

> *It's this: that I have always loved you – I know that now. Even when darling Eve was alive, even though I was so terribly fond of her – such a good friend, and didn't we all have such lovely times together? All those outings, all those happy years on the stall.*
> *Anyway – that's all such a long time ago. I'm really talking about now, about how much you mean to me.*
> *I've never written such words to anyone.*

William leans back in Buffy's chair: an old swivel, upholstered in bottle-green moquette – a man's chair, he realises, probably her father's. He's never sat in it before. He looks around the room, observing with enormous tenderness its antique rose paper, and shelves of china, the worn old sofa and ancient television – so many things just like his things, going back decades, impossible to part with.

There's another page.

> *You have been an endless strength to me. You have made me laugh, you've been wonderful company, always – and didn't we have a heavenly Christmas? You're generous and clever and kind, and, well – I just have to say it, even if it's from the other side:*
> *I love you.*
> *Buffy*

Darkness has fallen. Between the half-drawn curtains the window-box daffodils are ghostly against the pane.

William puts down the letter, with its declaration. How has he not seen, not known?

'Oh, Buffy,' he says aloud, into her empty flat, so filled with her presence, her absence.

And does he love her? Does he feel the same?

Well. He cannot imagine life without her.

And he gathers up the empty scent bottle, the little silver bell, the letter, brushing it with his lips, and prepares to go to her.

The room is cleared; her things are packed away. Janice tugs up the zipper on her bag and drops it on the floor; she takes a long look round. That's it. That's done, then. Good. And she stands looking out of the open window, on to the garden far below, where the magnolia, amidst the mossy flags, still damp from the long night of rain, is in full white waxy bud, ready to burst open, any day now. Beyond, the long street stretches, filled with spring, the fresh, sharp limes, the bulbs in bed and window box, the distant tops of plane and chestnut in the park. A train is approaching the station, slowing down; it brakes, doors slam, and the whistle blows; then it is moving off again, up the track to the London she has hardly got to know; up to the mainline stations, the Intercity trains.

She'll be on one, soon.

She goes to the desk, sits down with the notebook and pen from her shoulder bag.

Dear William—

What can she possibly say?

She thinks of the last time she wrote to him – not the domestic little notes they've got used to leaving for one another, but the letter she struggled to write, months ago, up in her bedroom in Curlew Gardens, snow and silence everywhere in the winter fields, the telly blaring away downstairs. *Dear Mr Harriman—*

She was a different person, then.

She reaches for her tobacco tin, rolls up, sits smoking, thinking, picks up her pen and tries again.

Dear William—

She pictures him, coming into the empty house, calling her name, seeing the envelope on the hall table, picking it up, frowning, taking it through to the drawing room, reading it by the unlit fire. She sees his face. She sees herself, hunched up in the corner of an Intercity carriage, speeding up to Shrewsbury between the lifeless fields, away,

away, leaving him, leaving Matthew—

She thinks: I can't do this.

In the silence of the house she hears all at once a sound on the stairs, and turns, quickly, towards the bedroom door. It's not quite closed: there's a scrabbling, then it's pushed open, and a chestnut nose pokes through.

'Danny—'

He trots in, looks up at her, beats his tail.

'Oh, Danny—' She bends down, scoops him up against her pounding heart, buries her face in his coat, carries him round and round the room, weeping and holding him close.

Dusk approaches. Danny is on her bed, curled up on the blue-and-white bedspread like a cat, but keeping a half-open eye upon her, as dogs do.

The letter is abandoned.

For the hundredth time Janice goes over the previous night: sees Claire's burning gaze, and Matthew's deathly pallor. He's taken himself out of the hospital; an ambulance has taken him back. Is this to be the pattern of his life for ever?

Oh, Matthew—

Matthew is far out at sea and drifting, drowning. She has glimpsed his desperate efforts to return, old drugs ebbing out of him, new drugs streaming in; she has watched him struggle to remember what day it is, where he is, who he might be; lifting his head at the first great chords on the piano; walking through the soaking night; – and is she to abandon him now?

Janice gets up. She's suddenly very hungry – she's spent hours up here, sleeping, writing, thinking, wondering what to do.

'Come on,' she says to Danny, and he's off the bed in a trice, nosing through the door, off down the stairs. He stops at the turn, to look back up at her. But Janice, on the dusky landing, is suddenly still.

Here, a few paces away, is Matthew's room, which she has never entered.

She enters it now. Quietly she turns the handle, and steps inside.

The bed is covered with an Indian cotton spread; the rug beside it is an old cotton durrie, striped in blue and green. There's a desk, a chair, an armchair. Everything's very plain.

Some of the things which furnish the room of Claire's childhood, and of her adolescence, are in here, too: more things, in fact, for Matthew, after all, has no new home. There's nowhere he can take the books, or school photographs – everyone lined up in blazers, squinting; the cricket team, with him – she looks, and finds him, yes, that's him, down in the deep, miles away in the long summer grass, waiting for the catch. Where can he put the heaps of music, except in the piano stool downstairs, or up here, where they lie on the bookshelves, gathering dust?

There's his violin.

It rests in its case on top of a long, low bookshelf: she crosses the room, sees the thick film of dust all over it, reaches out a finger, draws it back. This is his. He's the one who must clean it up, open it up one day.

The whole room smells of dust; the air is musty, shut up and still. She goes to the window, opens up the casement to the fading light, feels the fresh, rained-through evening spring air on her face, lets it enter the room. She leans out, and looks down on the walled back garden, where the willow is stirring, just a little, in the breeze. She looks beyond – to garden upon garden, set here and there with tall trees, chestnut and sycamore, plane and mountain ash. One or two people are out, snipping things in the dusk; she sees a cat leaping softly up on to an ivy-covered wall, she hears the birds of London gardens, settling for the night; she hears, all at once, in the distance, the low, breathy hoot of an owl, as dusk descends, very suddenly now, and then it's dark.

Buffy's bed is empty when he gets back. Must be in the loo, unless they're doing some ghastly test. Surely not, not at this time of day. She won't be having supper – just as well, to judge by what he saw on the trolleys. He sets her little things on the locker, beneath the pink-and-white lisianthus, just opening now in the central heating, and paces about, nods to one or two other patients, goes over to the plate-glass window of the bay and looks out.

West London spread beneath him, fourteen floors below. Darkness and fairytale strings of lights, tiny lines of traffic, moon coming up. If they weren't in here, with the prospect of tomorrow, it could look rather romantic. He feels the letter in his inside pocket, next to his heart. Well. Here's a thing.

Where has she got to? Better have another look.

And he leaves the glittering panorama of the city at evening, and goes back into the main ward, looking up and down.

Someone is coming along from the bathroom, in a pale blue woolly dressing gown, and mules; a towel is draped over her arm, she's clutching a flowery sponge bag. Her grey hair is up in a knot, and she's pale, but walking determinedly, giving a faint little smile to one of the nurses, looking about her, trying, he can tell, to get her bearings: which bay was it? And his heart turns over: how brave and strong she is, how independent, after all these years alone.

'Here we are,' he says, walking down the ward towards her. 'Here we are.'

'William!' Her face alight with happiness. 'What are you doing here?'

'Thought I'd pop back,' he says, his hand beneath her elbow, guiding her back to her bed. 'Thought it might be nice for you to have your things tonight.'

'Oh, it would.' She sees them, on the locker, beneath those lovely flowers: the glass-and-silver bottle of scent, the little silver bell. She has had them beside her for years and years. She puts down her towel and sponge bag.

'Is that from the National Trust?' asks William.

'It is, as it happens. I couldn't resist. Oh, thank you so much, I can't tell you how much better it makes me feel to have these things in here.'

And then she suddenly stops, and remembers. She'd left the bell and the bottle on her desk because she was preoccupied – with writing that letter, trying to get it right, sealing it at last, and leaving it for him, just in case—

She doesn't know where to look.

'William?' she says, because she has to know, she'll never ever sleep tonight if she has to worry about all this, as well as whatever hell lies in store tomorrow.

'Yes?' He's picked up the little bell, and he shakes it, gently: what a sweet, old-fashioned sound. Perhaps they could start collecting these. He shakes it again.

'I wrote you a letter,' says Buffy, feeling herself go pink. 'I wrote you a letter, but I didn't mean you to read it, not yet. I must have been terribly flustered when I left the flat—' She's terribly flustered now; this is dreadful. She looks up at him, sees that smile, feels weak. 'Did you get it?' she whispers.

249

He puts down the bell; taps his pocket.

Then he draws her close to him, folding her in his arms.

She's not going to leave. She can't. Not yet, not until she's seen him again, tried again, found out what hope there might be. She realises, unpacking her stuff, putting it back in the drawers, that this is how William must have felt for years: going on and on, hoping and hoping, against all the odds. Well. Well – if you don't have hope, you'll die. And down in the kitchen she eats two bowls of cereal, whistles up Danny, clips on his lead. 'Come on. Let's have a run before supper.'

It's cold again, it threatens rain again, but she doesn't care: she must get out, go walking. Danny is thrilled. He trots along the pavement, sniffing and lifting his leg at every third railing. She tugs at his lead. 'Come on!' God, but it's different from walking the Shropshire lot.

And how are they? she wonders, turning her collar up, turning the corner of the street. How are they coping with the crisis, poor old bats? God, it must be hard; she had better write.

She walks briskly on, tugging at Danny – get a move on, get some proper exercise. The wind is beginning to blow: she feels it, cutting across the park. There's a moon, rinsed clear as glass after all that rain, rising, rising, high above the trees.

'Hello? Anyone at home?' He closes the door behind him, smells something delicious, feels a great wave of contentment. He hangs up his coat, looks in the mirror, gives a little wink. 'Hello?' he calls again, making his creaking descent to the bowels of the earth. 'I'm back.'

'So it seems,' says Janice, stirring at the stove. 'Hi. How's Buffy?'

'Bearing up well.'

He gives her a little kiss, looks for the corkscrew, finds it.

'Yes?' He waves it at her.

'Yes, please,' says Janice, taking the pan off the heat.

'And what is that?' he asks her, peering.

'Mushroom and courgette sauce, to go with spaghetti. Is that OK?'

'Very OK.' He has a look in the wine rack, uncorks a bottle of red. What a very satisfactory sound it makes: never fails to cheer one, after all these years.

They sit drinking together, while Danny snoozes.

'Manage to take him out? Well done. Well, well—' He raises his glass. 'Cheers. Quite a day. What with one thing and another.'

She looks at him: he's much less strained and anxious. 'How do you mean?'

'Oh—' He gives a little wave. 'We'll talk about it later – all in the fullness of time.'

'Is she going to be OK?'

And then a shadow does cross his face again.

'Let us hope. One can only hope and pray.'

'What time is the op?'

'Half past ten – they said I could phone in the evening.' He lifts his glass again. 'God, that's good.' He looks at her, looks again: rather pale, rather drawn about the gills. 'And what about you?' he asks her. 'You were *very* late.'

'Yeah,' says Janice. She reaches for her tobacco tin – he's got used to it now, he doesn't mind. 'We stayed up talking,' she says, and feels a blush begin to rise.

He raises an eyebrow. 'Did you, now? What about?'

'Oh—' She gazes down, teasing the strands of tobacco.

This isn't right – she knows it. Matthew is his son, he walked out of hospital, all that way through the rain and traffic. He might have been killed. How can she keep this from him?

She takes a breath. She'll say it, she'll keep it as cool as she can. There was a bit of a do last night, to tell you the truth. With Matthew—

And then she thinks: But he's safe, he's safe now. William's got Buffy to worry about, with everything else. I'll tell him – I will, if Claire doesn't. But not now. Not yet.

And she rolls up, runs her tongue along the Rizla paper, reaches for her lighter, saying: 'Oh, this and that. But you're right, it was too late. I'm having an early night.'

'Very wise,' says William, waving smoke away. 'I think I'll do the same.'

It's morning. William wakes early, as is his habit. He lies for a moment, coming to, listening to the birds, as is his wont. It's spring, but it's still dark: how they go on, in spite of this. Something's happening today: for a moment he can't remember what. Then he does. He looks at his clock; half past seven, three hours to go. She's probably been awake for hours; they wake you at the crack of dawn in hospital, it's brutal. He can remember Eve, who rarely complained, saying how hard it was,

251

when you'd hardly slept all night—

He shuts his eyes. 'Oh, darling.'

Then he gets up. He pulls on his dressing gown, has a look in the mirror, picks up Eve's photograph, which has stood there in its leather frame on the chest of drawers for years and years. Taken . . . when? He can't remember – probably when the children were still at home, growing up, but still here: there's only the hint of white in her hair, she still looks young – but then she always did, almost to the end. He picks it up. What a sweet smile – you could tell Eve anything. No wonder Claire went to pieces when Piers was born. You need your mother then, of course you do.

He holds the photograph out before him, brings it close again, kisses the glass. 'You don't mind, do you?' And then he puts it back, goes to the window, draws the curtain, sees the daylight begin to break through, and the last star fade.

It's morning: Janice sleeps on and on.

When she wakes at last, she lies there, looking at the sun behind the panda curtains, thinking: something is happening today.

What's that?

Buffy.

Yes, but something else.

Matthew. She's going to see him again.

It's almost nine: breakfast over, the paper looked at, Danny getting hopeful. Bang of the letterbox: ah. And what do we have today?

William climbs up the stairs to the hall and peers along it. Bills. And a square of white. He walks along the polished tiles – God, one day Mrs T. will have them all in hospital – and bends to the mat.

A Shropshire postmark, but the writing isn't the wild hand in which he remembers Mary addressing him last autumn. It's a good hand, a clear, artistic hand. Well, now. He takes it to his desk, picks up his paper-knife. Outside the window, he notices the blue tits flitting back and forth across the garden, beaks stuffed with bits of moss. Lovely, must be the ones he fed all winter. Now then. And he takes the letter out.

Dear Cousin William,

This is your cousin Ernest writing. I am truly sorry to trouble you after all these years, but we is on the brink of ruin . . .

252

☆

He's asleep. They've put him in a side room, on his own, near the nurses' desk. His door is half open, and the curtains on the window into the ward are half drawn back: they can keep an eye; he won't walk out again.

'I'm a friend,' she says to Eileen, on duty again. 'Remember?'

Eileen nods. 'That's good. He needs a friend.'

She tiptoes in, she blinks. It's the middle of the morning, and the sun is bright outside, but in here it's all dim and quiet. Not in a soothing way – in an institutional way. Coarse grey curtains, pale vinyl floor, pale bedspread – everything colourless, lifeless, in this poky little room.

He's breathing heavily, lying on his side, facing the door. He's so long limbed and tall – his feet beneath the bedspread are right up against the end rail. She takes off her jacket, and sits down in the plastic bedside chair.

'Matthew?'

No answer. God, how pale he is. She leans forward, strokes the dry hair which once was springy, strokes his sunken face, takes his hand, and lifts it to her lips. Then she sits there, holding his hand in hers, watching the slow rise and fall of his chest, saying his name now and then, waiting.

Another nurse comes in, and checks his pulse.

'How long will he sleep?' asks Janice.

'He should wake up soon. It should be wearing off.'

A houseman looks in. 'Are you a relative?'

'No,' says Janice. 'No, I'm a friend.'

He nods, like Eileen.

'Talk to me,' says Janice, looking at him straight. 'Tell me the score.'

He smiles. He's young. The white coat suits him. She feels he will tell her the truth.

'He's been very ill for a very long time,' he says, not sitting down.

'And?'

'Until last night we were getting hopeful. I think they were going to call his father in, make plans. The new medication – it does seem to be waking him up.'

'And now – after last night?'

'He'll be OK. I think he was having a bit of a bad reaction – all

253

those substances, swirling about—' He's nice, she thinks; he's human. Probably taken a substance or two himself, in his time. 'If we get the dose right now, he'll be happier, I hope. And he's musical, isn't he? That might pull him through.' He looks at her, sitting there, holding Matthew's hand. 'And are you . . . how shall I put this? Are you intending to stick around?'

Janice looks back. 'How shall I put this?' she says. 'Give it to me straight. What are the chances?'

'Of—' But he knows, he knows what she means. He sits on the chair by the basin. 'Of normal life.'

'Yes.'

'How long have you known him?'

'Not that long.'

'But . . . you care for him.'

'Yeah.' Her grip on Matthew's hand tightens; she turns to look at his sleeping face, all the night's trauma smoothed away. How beautiful his eyebrows are. 'Yes,' she says. 'I do.'

'In that case,' says the houseman, 'I should think his own chances are somewhat better than those of a hell of a lot of other people in here. And as for the two of you – no one could pretend it would be easy. But you're pretty young, aren't you? If that doesn't sound too personal.'

'We're talking personal,' says Janice. 'That's exactly what we're talking.'

He smiles, then his pager goes off. 'Excuse me.'

Janice sits there, stroking Matthew's hand, listening as the houseman talks to another ward. Yes, he's on his way. Hang on a tick. And he switches it off, gets up from the plastic chair.

'I don't know,' he says, looking at the two of them. 'You can only give it a go, can't you? If that's what you both want – give it a try. Why not? If it doesn't work – well, as I say. You're young.' He smiles again, slipping the pager back in his pocket. 'A doctor speaks, for what that's worth.' He goes to the door. 'I think he's pretty lucky,' he says. 'If that's not too personal.'

They smile at one another. Out in the ward, the coffee is coming round.

'Can I ask you something?' Janice says, as he pulls the door wide, and the sun comes in. 'How much do you know—' She swallows. 'About his background. His family.'

He turns back to look at her. 'Not a great deal. I'm new. Whatever Fisher knows will be on file. Why? Is it important?'

'I don't know.'

The sun comes through the open door. There's a patch of it on the grey vinyl floor, and on Matthew's pillow. Janice drinks her coffee, and goes on sitting there. Matthew stirs, gives a long, sleepy sigh.

'I'm here,' she says, and puts down her polystyrene cup and gets up, leans over him, kisses him gently, on the forehead. Then on his lips. 'Here I am.'

He opens his eyes, he sees her: she can feel him swimming up to the surface, breaking through.

William writes back by return.

> *Dear Ernest,*
> *How good to hear from you. We have been thinking of you all so much: what a dreadful business this all is, and of course you must be feeling the pinch. Janice Harper, the nice young woman whom Mary recommended, has told me so much about the Museum, and all your good work. I hope you will accept this small enclosure, just – as it were – to keep the wolf from the door. Soon, I hope to come up for a visit. I have a dear friend who's rather under the weather – in hospital, in fact. As soon as she's right, I might bring her up for a little spring break—*

You fool, William, he hears Buffy say, at her briskest. There's no such thing as a little spring break any more, that's the point. The country-side is closed, can't you understand?

But didn't they open the fells, at Easter? No, perhaps not. Everyone wanted them to, but—

He crosses that out, with a long, elegant sweep of the pen.

> *As soon as everything has settled down, and you're back in business, we'll be up. I might bring my son, who's making great progress, I'm pleased to say. A family reunion – wouldn't that be fun?*

It would be, it would be marvellous, after all these years. And he puts down his pen, and thinks about them all, all together again, with everyone on the mend, and getting on.

But first – first there is Buffy. It's half past eleven – she'll be in theatre now.

He sits there, watching the slender gold hands of the carriage clock on the mantelpiece creep slowly round.

It takes for ever to get him out of bed, on his feet, down to the toilet with a nurse, who takes him through. By now, the mid-morning sun is pouring in through the windows of the main ward, and the grounds are full of spring light and shade.

'How about it?' she says, when he comes back. 'Fancy a little turn?'

'Might do him good,' says the nurse. 'Give him a bit of an appetite for lunch.'

'Matthew?'

He looks down at her from his great stooping height, bends his head in polite enquiry.

'Shall we go outside for a little while? Get some fresh air?'

He nods. 'Yes. I'd like that.'

She feels a little rush of happiness.

Outside, the squirrels are everywhere, bounding over the grass, leaping among the firs. Janice puts her arm round Matthew, ushers him slowly to a bench. They sit in the sun, her arm round his shoulders, watching, letting the warmth sink in.

'You do remember me,' she says at last. She looks at him, gently turns his head towards her, so he has to meet her eyes. He does.

'Yes,' he says, with a slow half-smile.

'What's my name?' she asks him, and then there is a long, long pause.

'That I don't know,' he says at last.

'It's Janice.'

'Yes, yes, of course. I remember now. You looked after me once.'

'And when was that?' she asks him, filled with emotion.

'When I was drowning,' he says slowly. 'I do remember that.'

23

'You see?' Ernie is triumphant. 'You see? Blood is thicker than water, family is all.' He waves the cheque before them. Mary snatches it from him. 'Give that to me.'

'No fear.' He makes a grab.

'You'll tear it,' says Sophie. She puts her hand to her mouth.

'Now look,' says Ernie, banging the table, as Mary waves the cheque aloft. 'What we have here is a hundred pounds. For all of us. But made out to *me* – I'm the one what wrote.'

'*Who* wrote,' says Mary, tucking it into her pinafore pocket.

'I wrote. You know I did.'

'No, you old fool, I'm talking grammar.'

'Grammar? Grammar, when we is on the brink? Them dogs—' He gestures towards the open window, the endless barking. 'Them dogs is on emergency rations, no walks, no exercise—'

'It's out of our hands,' says Mary, slamming the kettle on. 'A crisis is a crisis, it's not just us.'

'I know that. We all know that. But we're talking grub, not walkies. Not one visitor. Not one. No income. And *you*—' He glares at her. '*You* was the one what ruined my show. That would've brought us a bob or two, that would have kept us going. More than that—' He waves his arms about, thinking of it all – the fame, the acclaim, money in the bank and a diary of appointments. 'You and your temper. You and your rages. Now give me that cheque.'

'No.'

'Oh, please,' whimpers Sophie, backed up against the door to the stairs. 'Please, please, please don't argue—'

But Ernie's blood is up. 'I had a dream,' he tells Mary. 'A proper steady life, a proper income. You've gone and ruined all that. I had

257

another. History. Heroes. Visitors in droves—' He's spluttering now, gasping for a cig, but there's no cigs now, not a penny for baccy nor papers – nothing. 'That blimming Janice,' he says all at once. 'What did you want to go and send her off to London for? Nothing's been right since she went.'

And he turns on his holey heel and makes for the door.

'Yes, go!' shouts Mary. 'Get out and stay out!'

'You menopausal old hag!'

Sophie is sobbing. Mary is beside herself. She picks up the rolling pin, and Sophie shrieks.

But Ernie has scarpered, banging the back door so it's almost off its hinges, hobbling across the yard, where hens fly up in astonishment, feathers everywhere.

'Go on!' he shouts at them. 'Out of my way! No blimming use anyway, no blimming eggs—'

It's true. Even the hens have stopped doing their stuff. They flutter up on to the fence and sit there, croaking, while the dogs go mad.

'Useless old birds. Put you in the pot, that'll learn you.'

And he stumps up the rotting steps, missing a fall by a whisker.

'I'll be back!' he yells across the yard.

'You haven't got a bank account!' shouts Mary, from deep within the house.

He slams the trailer door.

Pipsqueak is on his filthy old sleeping bag, snug in a patch of sun. He jerks up at the violent sound of the door, and begins to tremble.

'It's not you,' Ernie tells him, slumping on to the bunk. He's shaking all over. 'It's not you, old chap.' He strokes him with a shaking hand. They sit there together for a long time. Ernie's head is bowed. 'I dunno,' he says, over and over again. 'Blimming women. I dunno.'

After a while he spots something. Under the table, right in the corner. Baccy! A little bit of baccy in a screw of gold paper – what's that doing there? Must've dropped it, painting. Forget about everything when you're painting, that's half the joy. He gets up, shuffles over, bends down carefully so as not to bang his head, fumbles about. Got it! He comes out backwards, gets up, and bangs his head.

Never mind, never mind, there's hope yet. And he rubs his head, and unscrews the paper, and yes, there's enough for a couple of cigs.

He puts the kettle on, scrabbles about in the table drawer, with its filthy old stained spoons and marbles and bits of wire and useless blimming tin opener. Must be a packet of papers somewhere, must be.

The kettle begins to sing. He finds two torn papers, right at the back.

'Things is looking up,' he tells Pip, but Pip has gone back to sleep, twitching.

Ten minutes later, Ernie is sitting at the table, drinking weak sugarless tea and smoking. Ah. That's better. That's much better. The wireless is on, posh people talking about the European papers. Europe! What do they know?

'The French believe Britain is having a collective nervous breakdown...'

Ernie draws in an enormous evil breath of tobacco smoke, and looks out over the empty fields. No sheep. No lambs. Filthy, disgusting black smoke, rising from beyond the trees. Them pyres have been burning for weeks. No visitors. Mary off her rocker.

'Too blimming right,' he murmurs, drinking his horrible tea. 'Too blimming right.'

Buffy is getting better. She is sitting up and taking notice, nibbling at fruit. The Over-Sixties sent an entire *basket*. And she's had the results back from the lab. This was the moment she dreaded: the drawing of curtains round the bed, the consultant sitting down beside her, quiet and grave. But instead—

'It's benign!' she tells William, propped up against the pillows, using a mobile phone for the first time. That nice little student nurse has lent it to her.

'What's that?' God, what a line. 'Speak up.'

'I said it's benign,' says Buffy, as loud as she can without making a spectacle of herself. 'Everything's all right. They've taken it all out, and I'm clear. No chemo, no radiotherapy—'

'No tricks, no unpleasant bending,' says William, and she starts to laugh, then stops, as the stitches tear. Goodness, how sore she is. But still – who cares? What's a few painkillers, compared with—

'This is marvellous,' says William. 'Splendid. I'm coming over.' And she can hear his relief, his complete light-heartedness. She feels just the same. 'What would you like me to bring?'

'No grapes,' says Buffy, who never wants to look at a grape again. 'Nothing. Just you.'

'I'm on my way.'

☆

'And now,' he says, sitting at her bedside, holding her hand. The scent of the roses he has brought her fills the bay: two dozen, long stemmed, cream and pink – the very best he could find.

'Look at them,' says Buffy happily. 'Just a dream.'

'And look at you,' says William, stroking her hand. It's thin and white, like her now – she must have lost half a stone at least. There's a nasty little bruise from the drip. But still – she's here, she's perking up. 'Now,' he says again, leaning forward and kissing her. 'Convalescence. We must find just the right place.'

'People don't convalesce any more,' says Buffy, stroking his face. Even this is an effort, and she leans back against the pillows again. She's on the mend, but the stuffing's taken out of her, no doubt about it. Except when she thinks about William, and William and her – then she's a helium balloon, floating o'er hill and dale . . . She brings herself back down to earth. 'There's no such thing as convalescence,' she tells him. 'People don't even use the word any more. You're ill, you go into hospital, you die, or you're out in the twinkling of an eye and expected to get on with it. I'm coming out on Tuesday.'

'Tuesday? You only came in here—' He counts.

'Five days ago. I know. But they need the bed. And they say I should be up and about. They say it's good for me.'

He shakes his head. 'Well, you can't go back to the flat. Isn't there some nice little place? Tempting meals? Fluffy towels? A garden?'

Eve had died in hospital – he hadn't had time even to think of such a place. And Matthew – well, that's a different kettle of fish altogether.

'By the way, I must tell you,' he says, patting her hand, but carefully, avoiding the bruise. 'Matthew seems to be turning the corner.'

'Really? Oh, William, that's marvellous. Tell me.'

'All thanks to you,' he says. 'Well, in the beginning. You woke me up, got me going. They've taken him off those fearful horse pills, put him on something much lighter. He's coming to, talking more. Much more. Quite lucid, sometimes. I saw him yesterday. And he and Janice—'

'He and Janice what?' asks Buffy, looking at him intently,

'Well, I don't know. But she's often down there, at the hospital. And she wants to bring him home. For a visit, I mean.'

'Very nice,' says Buffy. 'You'll enjoy that.'

'I tell you what,' he says, and everything is clear to him now – of course, this is what they must do, he always knew he should hold on to the spare room, in spite of all Claire's fuss. 'You must come home to me. I'll look after you. I'd love it.'

'Are you sure?' What a heavenly thought.

'Certain. And Janice is the most marvellous cook, you know, there'll be lots of little meals on trays.'

'It does sound . . . well, William, it sounds quite perfect. If you're sure.'

'Certain,' he says again. 'Good, that's settled. And we'll have a little party, once you're up to it. Have Matthew there. And Claire and the family. A celebration.'

'How is Claire?' she asks him, exhausted by the very thought of all this. She'll have to be careful, she mustn't let him get carried away.

'Not really sure,' he replies. 'Haven't heard from her for a bit.'

'That makes a change.'

'Well – one day we'll sort it all out.'

'She's not about to announce a divorce, do you think?'

He's horrified. 'Oh, no, no, no, no, I'm sure not. Jeremy's the most marvellous chap.'

'But are they happy?' asks Buffy, and this he cannot answer.

'No,' he says at last. 'No, I don't think they are. I don't see how she could be as she is, if they were. But still – I do hope they'll stick it out.'

'Why? Why, if they're not happy?'

'Well – you know. The children. All that.' He shakes his head again. The very idea. 'We don't go in for divorce,' he says. 'We're a monogamous lot, the Harrimans. When we get married, that is,' he adds, thinking of the mad old cousins. No one could possibly marry them. And he tells her about Ernie, and the cheque. 'Might take you up there, one day. Would you like that? Once all this business is over, once everything's opened up again. Little spring break – or perhaps in the summer,' he adds quickly.

'I'd love it,' says Buffy, and she would, once everything's opened up. But, oh, those poor, poor animals – do they really have to die? 'It's not even as if foot-and-mouth kills them,' she says. 'The sheep can get better, certainly. Even the cows, sometimes. It's all about yield, and profit, it's awful.'

'That sounds like my old Buffy,' says William, leaning forward and kissing her cheek. 'You *are* on the mend.'

She holds his hand to her cheek. 'Thanks to you. *We're* happy, aren't we?'

'Very,' he says, and it's true. He wakes up in the morning and he feels – contented. Especially now they've had the results.

'Shall I tell you something?' says Buffy, as a trolley comes rattling along. Coffee? She peers. No, library books. She hasn't touched the Ackroyd. Now she can really enjoy it at last.

'What's that?' he asks her tenderly. 'Anything – you can tell me anything.'

Is that true? Will that always be true? She hesitates.

'Do you know,' she says, 'that for ages I thought . . . I thought—' She feels herself go pink again.

'Thought what? Go on, my darling, what did you think?'

'I thought you were falling in love with Janice,' she says, and is scarlet now.

'Ah.' He looks at her over his spectacles; he takes them off, releasing her hand, and wiping them on his handkerchief.

'And were you?' she asks him, fearful now.

'She made me feel young,' he says at last. 'She cheered up the house, no doubt about it. Still does. But—' He puts his spectacles back on, dissolves her with his smile. 'It would hardly have been suitable, and anyway—' He leans forward, kisses her tenderly on the mouth. 'You and I are going to have a very nice life together.'

'Kiss me again,' whispers Buffy, and he does.

'And you're really, really sure I can come and stay?' she asks him, over a hospital lunch. He's been down to the Friends Shop, brought up a shrimp salad sandwich and coffee which he has while she struggles with something in a compartmented dish. 'I'd better eat it,' she says, poking it about. 'It's vegetarian, I must have ordered it.' The prospect of tempting little meals on trays, of being looked after in that lovely house—

But all those stairs—

'You're sure it won't be too much for you?'

'Of course not.' He pokes a shrimp back into the lettuce. Rather good.

'And where—' She hesitates. 'Where will I stay?'

'In the spare room, of course.' He looks at her over the top of his specs. 'At least for now.'

It's June. Buffy is up and about again. Still having naps in the afternoons, still having breakfast in bed, brought up by William or

Janice, but so much better. Soon she'll be back on the stall, which William, all this time, has kept going. Sometimes, in the mornings, they go for a little potter about in the south London auction rooms.

'I say, William, do come and have a look at his.' She picks up an octagonal bowl, patterned in green and white, with a thin gold base. They peer at the trademark. 'Oh. For a moment I thought it was Worcester.'

'Could be,' says William, pushing his spectacles up his nose. 'Worth getting anyway, don't you think? Terribly pretty.'

He goes back that evening and bids, comes home with the bowl, and six Masonware dinner plates.

'What do you think?'

'Lovely,' says Buffy. 'How clever you are.'

It's just like the old days, but better. He kisses her. It gets better every day.

One hot Sunday, Matthew comes home. Just for the day: that's how they'll take it – one day at a time.

William goes to fetch him, taking Danny. Buffy and Janice prepare the lunch. Janice carries the garden table out of the shed and sets it up beneath the willow tree. Long strands brush her face as she goes to and fro from the house, carrying folding chairs, a green-check table-cloth, silver and glasses, white china, green linen napkins. All William's lovely old things. She's nervous and happy, cutting a spray of palest pink Albertine roses from the ramblers on the wall, pricking her finger, running water into an antique vase and setting it out on the garden table. There. Perfect.

Buffy observes all this, and keeps her counsel. They hear the slam of car doors at the front. Janice goes racing up the stairs.

In the hall, she stops, takes a deep breath, steadies herself and looks in the mirror. She runs her hands through her hair, brushes a willow leaf away. Here they are, coming up the steps. Here's William's key in the lock, here's Danny, nosing in at the first chance, here's Matthew—

She stands there, dead still, as the door swings wide, watching him walk slowly through, his father behind him, patient and unhurried, and he, so tall and so beloved, coming into the cool of the hall, patterned in emerald and violet light, seeing her, holding her in his gaze, flooding her with his smile of recognition.

She walks towards him; he takes her hand.

☆

'Well, now,' says William, under the rustling willow tree. 'Isn't this perfect?'

He uncorks a bottle of 1995 Pouilly Fuissé, glistening with cold; he unscrews a bottle of elderflower, icy to the touch. He fills their glasses, one by one. Everyone raises them, Matthew too.

'Cheers.'

'Cheers.'

'And all we want now,' he says, over chilled mint-and-cucumber soup, 'is for Claire to be here. With all the family.'

Nobody answers him.

Even under the willow, it's dreadfully hot. After lunch, they all go up to the drawing room, where the huge tall windows are open and the air is cool.

'Oh, that's better.' Buffy sinks on to the sofa, William sinks into his chair. 'I'll make the coffee,' says Janice. 'Matthew? Would you like coffee?'

Matthew is standing at the front window, looking out on to the front garden, where the magnolia is leafy and full, and the afternoon sun on the flags is dappled by its shade. He's very still.

'Matthew?' She goes up and stands beside him, slips her hand in his. 'Are you all right?'

He nods, he turns and looks down at her. 'Just thinking,' he says, in his beautiful low voice, so much steadier now, so much clearer.

'What about?'

'Different things. Many different things.' He shakes his head, he turns back and looks around the room: at his father, long legs stretched out in the old armchair; at Buffy, surrounded by cushions, watching him intently; at the piano, with its crowded family photographs, of him and his parents, him and his violin, him and Claire, him and Claire, him and Claire.

Janice can hardly breathe.

His gaze moves away; it lights upon the violin case, which she has brought down, and dusted, and polished but not opened. It's resting on the piano stool, and the leafy sunlight dances over it.

'That's mine,' he says slowly.

'Yes.'

He drops her hand, walks across to it, runs a finger over the polished wood. The stillness in the room is palpable.

'This is mine,' he repeats. 'One day I might play this again.'

'Do you want to play it now?' asks William gently, from across the room.

Matthew looks at him. It's a long, slow look whose meaning Janice can't begin to guess at. Then he bends down, and slips the brass hooks on the case. It takes him for ever to do this. Nobody offers to help. He lifts the lid, he looks down, at bow and violin, resting there, as they have rested for years.

Out in the garden, the breeze is stirring the leaves of the magnolia; blue tits flit back and forth to the nest in the wall; somebody's cat pads softly across the flags.

Summer in London. A train goes rattling past.

Matthew bends down, and slips the bow out from the lid. He runs it through his long musician's fingers. He lifts out the violin, and blows off a film of dust, takes out the duster from the bottom of the case and runs it over the body. He lets it fall to the floor.

Then he stands up straight, and tucks the violin beneath his chin, stops, readjusts himself, settles. He lifts the bow, draws it slowly across, tunes up, adjusting the keys. Everything is hesitant, everything takes for ever.

Janice walks over to the piano stool and sinks upon it, filled with such feelings as she has never known.

William's eyes fill with tears. Buffy observes this, and swallows.

Everything in the huge, airy room is concentrated into this moment, upon this man.

He begins to play.

24

Late June. The Sunday paper flops on to the mat. Buffy, in her dressing gown, goes to pick it up.

She bends down – goodness, how difficult this still is; perhaps she should be having physio.

'Or yoga,' Janice has been saying. 'Yoga would do you a power of good.'

'I'm much too old for yoga.'

''Course you're not.' Janice is radiant these days. She thinks anyone can do anything.

Buffy gets up slowly, dropping half the paper. God, what a weight, it's absurd, no one needs all these sections. At the hall table, she puts it together again, as best she can, smoothes the front page, looks at the headlines.

Needless slaughter of up to two million animals.

'I knew it,' she says aloud, trembling with fury. 'I knew it all along.'

Late June, very hot, and in London the pock of Wimbledon, back and forth, back and forth, hour after hour. In the country, some of the lanes are open again, and some of the footpaths.

Ernie and the dogs go walking, hour after hour. Sometimes Mary does it, sometimes Sophie. They're talking to one another again, things is looking up.

But still. They have barely a farthing. A hundred pounds is a hundred pounds, and in the end he let her cash it, but where does it get you nowadays? What they need is capital. Investment. Serious money.

Sitting in the trailer with the door and windows open, the breeze blowing in and the breeze blowing out again, listening to the hens,

266

scratching across the yard in the sun, seeing the dogs flat out beneath the trees, he picks up his pen, and writes another letter.

'A family reunion,' William says to Claire, holding the letter in his hand. He reads it out to her, sitting at the phone in the drawing room, having a lunchtime snifter, windows open, blue tits darting about. 'Do come, darling, it would do you so much good. A little break. Bring the children. Bring Jeremy.'

'I'll see,' says Claire.

'We haven't seen you for months.'

'We're very busy. Jeremy's always in court.'

'Yes, but still—' He's determined not to give up. So much has happened, and she's been outside it all. 'Buffy's staying here,' he tells her.

'Buffy? Whatever for?'

'She's been very ill. She's convalescing.' He takes a deep breath. 'If you would only come here, darling, I could tell you things. I don't like to give you all the news and never see you.'

'What news? What are you talking about?'

'Never mind,' he says wearily, damned if he's going to talk about wedding plans over the phone. What's wrong with the girl, what's wrong? He has one last go. 'And Matthew's much better,' he tells her. 'Or perhaps you know. They've changed his drugs, he's turned the corner.'

There is a silence.

'Hello?'

'I don't suppose Janice told you,' Claire says slowly at last.

'Told me what?'

'That he absconded from hospital. In the spring, when she was baby-sitting. He absconded and walked out all the way here. He was off his head.'

William is so shocked he cannot speak. At last he says: 'And why did nobody tell me? Why?'

'What was the point? You'd only have got in a flap. I took him back. I rang the next day and he was all right.' There's another pause. 'What do you mean when you say he's getting better?'

'He's happier,' says William. 'He's much more alert. He's started to play again. He's been home several times now. And he and Janice—' He hesitates.

'What? What about him and Janice?'

'I think they're in love,' says William slowly. 'I know it all seems . . . well, improbable. But I think they are.'

There's a huge, dark silence – even from here he can feel how huge and dark and strange it is.

'Darling? Claire, darling—'

Then the phone clicks dead.

'You didn't tell me,' he says quietly to Janice later, when Buffy is having her nap. They're clearing up in the kitchen, after lunch.

'Tell you what?' But she knows, as soon as she looks at him. 'You mean about Matthew. Leaving the hospital. Claire's been talking to you.'

'Inasmuch as she ever talks to me,' he says. 'Inasmuch as she ever says a word. She did tell me that.' He opens a cupboard, puts away the pepper and salt, turns back to her. 'Please,' he says carefully. 'Don't ever do that again. Don't hide things from me. Not about Matthew, not things like that. I'm his father, I have a right to know.'

'I know,' says Janice, feeling her cheeks begin to burn. 'I know. I'm sorry.'

She takes out her tin. He pulls out a chair, and sits down opposite her.

'Something is terribly wrong with Claire,' he says. 'I've got to face it. Do you have any idea what it is?'

'No,' says Janice, on fire all over, twisting and twisting the paper in her fingers. 'No, I don't.'

It's evening. The sun is setting over south London gardens, glancing off greenhouses and sinking into the green-gold depths of lily ponds, filtering through the trees. Buffy is soaking it up after supper, lifting her face to its warmth.

'I'm better,' she announces. 'I can feel it, through and through.'

'Marvellous. Dear Buffy.'

William, in the garden chair beside her, pats her hand. Janice is visiting Matthew; they have the place to themselves.

'I want to ask you something,' he tells her, slipping his Panama down a little, shielding his eyes.

'Ask on.'

'Janice and Matthew. What do you think?'

268

'You mean in the long term?'

'Yes.'

They sit there holding hands.

'I'm not sure,' says Buffy, 'and that's the truth. What do you think, William?'

'Oh, I don't know.' He shakes his head. If it weren't for Buffy, how old all this would make him feel. 'It's a hell of a thing,' he says. 'Let's face it. Hell of a thing for a young girl like that – young woman, rather.'

'It is.'

'On the one hand . . . well, it's wonderful. All these years of emptiness, and now, the prospect of . . . well, the prospect of some kind of future, at last. Look at how much better he is, playing again, taking part in conversations. And the way they look at one another – it makes me feel happy, I can't help it.'

'I know.'

'But am I being irresponsible?' he wonders, reaching for his glass. 'Do you know what Claire told me, this afternoon?'

'No.'

He tells her. Buffy is shocked.

'Oh, dear.'

'Of course, that's some weeks ago now,' he says, swirling the last of the ice. 'Matthew's clearly been going from strength to strength since then. But Janice didn't tell me. I had to confront her, I'm afraid, give her a little talking to.'

'Quite right.'

'And Claire—' His sigh breaks the spell of the summer evening. 'Oh dear oh dear, that poor girl. She went so quiet when I talked about Janice and Matthew. I think she hung up on me, to tell you the truth.' He drains his glass. Thank God for whisky. 'What is to be done?'

'Nothing,' says Buffy. 'I hate to see you upset by her, year after year. She's a married woman, William, let her get on with it.'

There's a silence. On this perfect golden evening, he can feel their first little rift. So can she.

'Oh, darling—' She turns to him. 'Lift up that Panama. Look at me.'

He does both these things.

'That's better. Do I sound terribly harsh? I know I can't possibly know what it's like, not really. When you have children, I'm sure you must *ache*—'

The rift begins to close. He squeezes her hand. 'I'm afraid it's true.'

'So what do you want to do?' she asks him. 'Should we invite her to supper? Invite both of them? Or do you think you should go and see her? Have it out, once and for all. It might clear the air, dear, it really might.'

'It might,' says William, but the prospect terrifies him. 'I'm afraid I've always been a bit of a dodger,' he says. 'When it comes to unpleasantness. Not very good at having things out, when it comes down to it. Oh, dear.' He lifts her hand, rests it upon his heart. 'What an old fool you must think me. How brave you were, writing me that letter.'

'I thought I was going to die.' How far away it all seems now. The way she feels tonight, she could go on for ever.

She tells William this. He lifts her hand and kisses it.

'I'd never have woken up,' he says. 'If you hadn't written to me. That's what I mean – I don't see things. That's what Claire has been saying for years.'

Buffy kisses his hand, so wrinkled and papery, but still, underneath, so strong. 'You see quite enough. You're a dear, loyal father: no one could wish for better.'

He shakes his head, but he's comforted. How good love is.

'How good love is,' he says, thinking of Buffy, thinking of darling Eve, whom he can sense there, somehow, out in their garden on a summer night, understanding everything. It's getting dusky now, but still it's warm.

'Indeed,' says Buffy, thinking of William, thinking of Janice and Matthew, so strange but, at least for the moment, so happy. 'She's a strong young thing,' she says, knowing she's understood at once. 'We'll just have to wait and see.'

'I suppose we can pick up the pieces.'

'If we need to.'

'Quite.'

The sun is slipping away, the dusk is deepening. Two soft hollow notes sound from within the trees.

'Those owls,' says William. 'They come back year after year.'

A golden summer evening. Out in the hospital grounds the long, deep shadows of the firs are splashed with light. People are out and about, walking slowly, sitting on benches outside open doors. There's a little game of croquet; someone is laughing; swallows swoop low.

Matthew holds Janice in his arms. 'You're bringing me back to life,' he tells her. 'You're making me well again.'

'Me and the pills,' she says, looking up at him. Tall as she is, she has to do so. His eyes are clearer; they hold such tenderness now that she can hardly breathe.

'Mostly you,' he says quietly. 'I think it's mostly you.'

A warm summer night. They've all been out to the park in the afternoon, and played cricket. Hugo is going to be good, no doubt about it. Jeremy tells him, and he flushes with pleasure. 'Almost as good as Piers,' says Jeremy, taking out the stumps. Piers is in the first eleven now: he's often away on Saturdays. This is the first time they've played as a family for ages. Geraldine has run like the wind, though her batting, Hugo tells her, is pretty pathetic still.

'Shut up.'

'That's enough.' Claire comes in from the deep, where she likes to be.

'You don't *have* to always be fielder,' says Piers, as she walks up, back to them all.

'I don't mind. It gives me time to think.'

'And what do you think about?' asks Jeremy lightly, dropping the ball in the bag.

'The thoughts of a mother of three.'

Now it's time to go home. Other families are doing the same, walking towards the gates, their shadows long on the grass behind them. Some of them they know.

'There's Martin,' says Piers, and raises his hand to a plumpish boy, walking between his parents.

'He's a nerd,' says Hugo.

'He's OK.'

Martin's parents are waving to Jeremy and Claire. Pleasantries are exchanged at the gates.

'Isn't it funny,' says Derek, rubbing his beard. 'That we all knew that Shropshire girl.'

'What Shropshire girl?' asks Martin, as Claire goes on ahead.

'You remember. From the Dog Museum. She fetched up at Drake's, in the Village.'

'That Dog Museum was wicked,' says Martin.

'Oh, I *wish* we had a dog,' says Geraldine.

At home, next door come over for drinks. It goes on for ever, as the sun slips down. The children get peckish, then grumpy. Crisps won't do it for ever. The air is full of the smell of barbecues. Next door go back to theirs. Sausages come over the fence; the children perk up, while Jeremy sizzles away.

'How can you put away *more?*' he asks them, turning the kebabs Claire made that morning, thick with marinade.

'Easy.' They burn their tongues on mushrooms, shrieking, and come back for more.

At last it's time for baths and bed. At last, after the tucking up of Geraldine, as the boys settle down before the bedroom computer, Jeremy and Claire are alone. They wash up, they clear up, at last they sit down. Jeremy has brought out the map of France; they sit at the garden table, tracing the route they'll take in late July. They've rented the house before, a couple of years ago; now Geraldine's older the journey won't be quite so bad. And once they're there—

Once they're there, it'll all be non-stop, just like here, though with another family they can share the load a bit.

'Time we went off on our own,' says Jeremy, leaning back, letting the last of the sun sink in. 'Time we did our own thing, don't you think?'

'Mmm.'

He lets his arm rest lightly across her shoulders. There is no answering gesture, no turn of the head. He's used to this. He's had to get used to this.

'Claire? Was that William on the phone? At lunch-time?'

'Yes.' She smoothes the map out, her hand running over the Loire, the Auvergne, the Cevennes. All those beautiful places, he thinks, watching that hand, with its bitten-down nails. She lifts it now, to gnaw; gently he pulls it back. She shakes him off.

'Stop it.'

He lets his arm fall from her shoulders; he lets his eye fall upon Paris, and Chartres. That view of Chartres from the plain; that blue. They went there before the children were born. It wasn't quite right, even then, though then he had not dared to think this.

'How was he?' he asks, as the birds settle down in the trees. 'William?'

'Oh – all right. Buffy's living there, apparently.'

'Buffy?' He's always had a soft spot for her. 'How come?'

Claire explains, and begins to fold up the map.

'Well, how nice for them both. How cheering. We should have them to supper. And is Janice still there? Or has she gone back to Shropshire?'

'She's still there,' says Claire, and now the map is folded. 'Coffee?'

'In a minute. Stay here for a moment.' What a week it's been. What a year. How long is it since they sat out here like this?

'And Matthew?' he asks her, and feels the blinds come down. 'How is he getting on?'

'Fine. Much better, apparently – but then we've been here before.'

'I don't remember you ever saying he was much better before.'

'No. Well, they've changed his medication. I'm sure I've told you that.'

'Perhaps.' And perhaps she has, and perhaps he wasn't paying attention, after the usual day. The briefs on his desk in their bedroom make two piles now: somehow he must get through things before France. He thinks of it all: the heat, the long afternoons upstairs, the shutters pulled to, the children out with the other lot, and he and Claire—

He knows what it will be like.

'Darling?' he says now, and draws her to him again. 'Do I not listen enough? When you try to tell me things? Are there things you want to tell me?'

'No,' says Claire. 'No, there aren't, everything's fine.' Briefly she rests her head on his shoulder; then she gets up. 'I'll make the coffee,' she says, and goes inside.

This is our life, thinks Jeremy, gazing out over the garden. This is how things are. He hears the coffee beans grinding fiercely; the smell of them wafts out through the open kitchen window. When it stops, he can hear the owl they've heard all summer, calling from somewhere nearby. It's almost as if he belongs here, he thinks, listening to that slow, sad cry.

It's gone very quiet in the kitchen. After a minute, he gets up, goes to the window, looks in. Claire is just standing there, very still, as the kettle begins to fill the room with a dreamy cloud of steam. He's shocked at her unutterable sadness: he can feel it, even from here.

'Darling—'

She looks at him, her dark eyes enormous in the shady room.

'I'm sorry,' she says, her eyes brimming, now. 'I'm so sorry.'

'What for?' And now he could go in, he could take her in his arms, he could take her upstairs and tell her, over and over again, that he loves her, that he will always love her—

He doesn't. He's done that before, though not for a very long time, and sometimes he's felt as if he were saying these things to himself, that nothing – nothing he can ever say or do – will truly bring her to him.

So he waits: for her to make the move.

'What are you sorry for?' he asks her quietly.

And this is a defining moment in their marriage: he can feel it – a turning point, the possibility of naked truth between them.

Then Claire turns, and takes the kettle off the hob, and says through her tears: 'Nothing. Nothing. Forget it.'

Scalding water pours into the pot. He stands there in silence, unable to move. Claire puts everything on a tray.

'But I will say this,' she says to the empty air. 'My life would be nothing without you all.'

25

A family reunion. William has booked them all into a nice little inn, outside Oswestry, for they can't, of course, stay at the Museum overnight. But they can, of course, spend the afternoon there.

The car speeds up the motorway, William and Buffy in the front, Matthew and Janice in the back. His arm is round her shoulder, she leans against him. This is the longest time he's been out of hospital for years. Danny is in his basket, tucked beside her. The smell of summer grass blows in at the window, as they turn off the motorway, off the bypass. They drive down the lanes with their towering hedges. Danny sits up, and presses his nose to the glass, his ears streaming back in the wind. They look through the gates. Most of the fields are empty.

'Dreadful,' says Buffy sadly. 'Dreadful. There should be sheep, sleeping under the trees, there should be cows, munching away—'

'I've told you,' says Janice from the back. 'If we were all vegan there'd be no need—'

She can hear herself going on; just as she did to them all in London; just as she used to do with her parents, and with Steve. Tomorrow she'll see them all again. And they'll all meet Matthew – she feels a little twist of nerves, but they'll manage, William will see them all through.

'That's enough,' he says now, slowing at a crossroads. 'If we were all vegan, the country would have not a single sheep nor cow. And how would you like that?' he asks Buffy, watching a lorry rumble past. It says Sun Valley Chickens, all over it; crates of white feathery birds are piled high within, he knows it, and hopes she hasn't seen.

'I wouldn't like it at all,' says Buffy, who's seen it perfectly clearly. 'No, of course I wouldn't. But . . . oh, dear.' And she looks out of the window, wondering what's for the best. I shall start a campaign, she thinks, as soon as I'm properly fit. I shall take out a sub to Compassion in World Farming. I shall send money to donkeys, in the Far East.

'We're almost there.' Janice is suddenly hugely excited. She turns to Matthew. 'Can you remember them at all? From when you were little?'

He shakes his head. 'Perhaps when I see them I will.'

Here's the sign: The Dog Museum, painted on wood in black and white, tied up in a hawthorn hedge. Here's the house, and there are the huts beyond it, and here, at the gate, a million dogs are waiting in the sun.

'Well, well, well,' says William, braking. And then is frankly speechless. He hoots; they wait.

Ernie and Mary and Sophie come slowly down the yard, in ancient sunhats.

'Get back, you hounds!' shouts Ernie, and tips his hat and lets the gate swing wide. In bumps the car, and a million dogs mill round it, barking madly.

They sit at the kitchen table, drinking tea. Sophie's hand is fluttering over her hair slide. It took her for ever to choose which one. In the end, she chose the bluebirds.

'Bit more normal than them cockatoos,' Ernie says in the morning, when he sees her. 'You look batty as a fruitcake in them cockatoos.'

'I don't want another penny spent in that shop,' says Mary, banging out jam tarts. 'I hope that's clear.'

Sophie says nothing. Never to go in there again – she twists her handkerchief.

'If we play our cards right,' says Ernie, 'we can buy the whole place up.'

Mary sniffs.

'I'm not talking extortion,' he tells her, dipping a filthy finger in the jam. She slaps it away. 'I'm not talking blackmail or bailiffs. Just investment. He must be rolling, old William. Treasury pension, roomy family house—'

As soon as he sees the car, he knows he's right.

And here they all are, sitting round, proper family, just as it should be. And that Janice, back again at last. He gives her a wink.

'Got any baccy?'

'I have, as it happens.' She passes the tin across, and he opens up happily. Ah, that's more like it. He looks across at Matthew. Something not quite right there, and no mistake. Still, if that's what makes her happy. And he lights up, feeling better than he has for months.

'I do like that hair slide,' says Buffy to Sophie, and she flushes with pleasure.

'Ta very much.'

Mary glares at her. Sophie takes no notice.

'I like your combs,' she says to Buffy, admiring the tortoiseshell.

'How kind of you.'

They smile at one another, in perfect understanding.

'Now then,' says William, finishing his ghastly tea, Danny on his lap and a hundred dogs at his feet. Dear, dear, dear, what a set-up. 'I'm longing to see round.'

Ernie needs no second bidding.

'Right, then.' He gets to his feet. 'Follow me.'

Inside the huts, William and Buffy and Janice and Matthew walk from booth to booth, from moth-eaten Labrador to mouse-filled St Bernard, with his panting felt tongue and little keg. Janice has seen it all before, of course, and tried to describe it, but no description could ever, ever—

'But this is magnificent,' says William. 'This is artistry.'

Buffy gazes at the shining fish, the huskies, the Northern Lights.

'This is unique. We must preserve it.' Her mind is racing. The Museum of Childhood, perhaps, in Bethnal Green. A grant? There must be a grant, for something like this.

Ernie is bursting with happiness and pride. 'What I have in mind now,' he tells William, when at last they've done the rounds, 'is a series of exhibitions. Now, if you'd like to step into my trailer—'

'Are you sure they'll want to do that, Ernie?' asks Janice, but he takes no notice. He's on a high, on a roll, the world is his oyster now.

Inside the smelly old trailer, he shows them it all, everything he's done since the Healing Arts fiasco. Portraits of Pipsqueak, and Nelly and Spot, portraits of Tilly and Ben. They're all taped up on the walls.

'Fantastic,' says William, and means it.

'It makes me long for a brush,' he tells him, and Ernie picks up his tin box of paints and flourishes them.

'No need to spend a fortune. I've managed with these. Mind you,' he adds quickly, 'sable would be nice. Can't beat a good sable.'

'Indeed,' murmurs William, as Danny comes bouncing up the steps.

'Ah,' says Ernie, picking him up. 'Now you're a nice little chap. Why don't I do your portrait?'

'There's a thought,' says William. He can see it now.

The sun is slipping down. A million dogs are eating from a million tin dishes: in the pens, in the yard, outside the back door.

'But where did they all come from?' asks William. 'How did it all begin?'

'Little by little,' says Mary, patting a greyhound. 'It's an endless task, a life's work. But worth all the sacrifice, worth all the effort.'

'I'm sure.' He's completely baffled. 'But how on earth can you feed them all? It must put you to dreadful expense.'

'Ah,' says Ernie, Pipsqueak in his arms, 'now if you'd like to come back to the house, perhaps we can have a little talk. Man to man,' he adds, and everyone melts away.

It's early evening. Everyone's happy. William, inside the house, has listened. He's looked at the business plan. Well – why not? It is, after all, unique. And as the others troop in at last, and Mary, uniquely, fetches a bottle from the snug, and some really rather good little glasses, he takes out his cheque book, takes out his beautiful old fountain pen, unscrews it, and writes an enormous cheque.

'I've made it out to you,' he says to Ernie, waving it to dry. 'Is that right?'

'It is,' says Ernie, who has opened an account with a pound, just yesterday. 'It is indeed.' And nobody says a thing. It will, after all, be to everyone's benefit.

It's dusk. They're all outside, sitting on hard chairs with their drinks in the long, long grass leading up to the field gate. Bats flit about, the hens are making their way into the hen-house – 'Before that wicked old fox comes along,' says Ernie – and the sky is streaked with gold.

Matthew and Janice are holding hands. 'I think I do remember this,' he says, looking around at it all.

'We remember you,' says Sophie. 'You and Claire. Dear little things, you was.'

The sun dissolves at the edge of the farthest field, and then is gone. More bats, and then, all at once, through the dusk, they hear an owl, calling from deep within the woods.

Janice's hand in Matthew's tightens. His expression, in the dusk, is unreadable. The owl calls again: those two hollow notes, timeless, mysterious, achingly sad.

'I wish Claire was here,' says William quietly. 'It isn't right, without her.'

He looks at Janice, and she looks back: such a long, long, searching gaze he gives her; she has to turn away.

William is no fool. He knows she's keeping something back. Does he know what it is? Does he guess?

The owl is calling, the scent of summer grass is everywhere, the darkness is almost upon them now.

Could anyone, ever, guess that?